WinterGames

Genesis Of A Dæmon

"Winter Games! Lake Placid should be so lucky!" giggled the Chief of Protocol, a most attractive foreign lady indeed. She was at an October cocktails, in one of the homes of one of the Board Members of the Lake Placid Olympic Committee.

"But Darling, The Committee wouldn't *tolerate* any defection as you foresee!" the hostess responded. She, a native, was used to speaking about The Committee as if it had been described in the verse of Homer, so sacred was the organization in her mind. Lucille McSorley had been one of the founding forces which had helped Lake Placid get the Olympics after all. "Anyhow, what do you care *how* your Deputy acts, just as long as he doesn't act like *you!*"

Lucille was a bitch, but a very suave one, as opposed to Heidi, who simply was not suave. But if two men were put side by side and asked to choose which woman they would rather have sex with, men inevitably picked Heidi, insane giggles or not. There was just something very...edible...about her.

People at the cocktails were sweating in the uncanny Indian summer air. For an evening, the temperatures were as balmy as if it were a summer day, and everybody's temper was in keeping with the weather...hot!

Patting her puffed-up brown wig, Lucille just raised a disdainful eye and let it be known: "Well, Heidi, in *your* position, you just do what you *damn* well please. Fire the bastard, if he doesn't toe the line. There're obviously millions of college kids just dying to work for The Committee, and you can have your pick. I'll never see *what* you hired him for in the first place." One more swig, then Lucille dashed away from Heidi to go spread more cheer in the ear of another Member of the Board.

Lucille McSorley, whose family had lived in Lake Placid the long, long time of three whole generations, felt that even Whiteface Mountain was a figment of her imagination. She owned hotels, she owned restaurants, she owned shops in Main Street, and she often felt she owned The Committee. When she would step to her "rustic" balcony of handhewn pine logs, and stare to her sloping lawn of moss and stones and birch trees just dizzy with gold (as it was autumn)...she would glare out across the calm black waters of Lake Placid and sometimes curse Whiteface Mountain for blocking her view. Deep in her heart she *hated* the fact that Placid had ever been granted the right to host the Olympic Games, since it was the Games, in essence, which had brought so many flashy foreigners (Americans included) into her once totalitarianly controlled domain. Where before, Lucille McSorley, widow, had been an heiress, a landowner, a social *force*, now she often felt just some tag-along Board Member, bored out of her scheming brains, just another

1

nobody to veto or approve the stupid ideas she kept hearing discussed at Executive Meetings that made less and less sense. Clutching her double neat Scotch (Glenlivet) in her flawless hand, and getting more and more aggravated by the calmness of the water of the Lake, a very wicked thought suddenly struck her. Hmmm...she didn't really *like* that Heidi after all. The only reason Heidi ever got the job as Chief of Protocol was because she was married to the *Director* of Protocol. Now, if there was one thing in this town—which was so infinitesimally small that for all its world-wide ramifications few people realised that the population of Lake Placid is only about three thousand—it was that people *talked*. But Lucille had the advantage over almost everyone, at least over all the ever increasing amount of foreigners, since Lucille was *born* into all this bitchery...and rather revelled in it. If it was anything Lucille loved, it was a good fight, with gossipy overtones, and so she began to think, there on her "rustic" balcony, that she just would have a little fun...

On The Committee was one very distinguished man whom everybody loved and respected. That's saying something for a start, since most people loved and respected no one. This man was a gentleman and a scholar, and those were hardly a dime a dozen in the Adirondacks. Chelsey Levitt, a former United States Ambassador to Tokyo, as well as a former Secretary of the Treasury under a very controversial Democratic President, had returned to his home territory in Keene, New York, in 1977 in order to work on his memoirs. He had been in the political Arena, and avoided all its worst temptations, since the New Deal, and everybody felt that his survival factor alone had warranted his being hired as Chief of Protocol, not to mention any number of other top Executive positions. Needless to say, though, given that he was not married to the Director of Protocol, the job had gone to Heidi, whereas Mister Levitt had been hired as Governmental Representative, a position which required no little amount of diplomatic training just in trying to figure out what the position was really meant to be.

For that matter, everybody at The Committee constantly was wondering just what his or her position within the organization really was. Nobody had ever received a detailed summary of one's job-duties, neither Executive nor Secretary, and it had begun to seem, as the Olympics drew near, that the more one had thought one was hired for this or that qualification had less and less to do with what one was really doing. One of the most constant games, besides talking about everybody behind everyone's back, was wondering what one's job was all about.

Ambassador Levitt was pondering such a line all the time he was amiably chatting to the wife of a prominent doctor in town, and all the time Lucille kept a slow advance on him. For one solid hour the Ambassador kept an eye peeled on her brown wig that kept circling in her large living-room ever ever closer. He could feel her coming, and almost knew what it was she was after. The two had known each other...for years.

"Chelsey," sighed the hostess as she gave her stuffed moose head over the mantle a rude look, "I think you need a bit of air. How's that *bug* you've been fighting?"

Bug? What bug, he thought, but let himself be led out through the jabbering salon. The doctor's wife was getting insufferable anyhow, complaining about the Luge run and how she thought it would never hold up come winter, even though she'd never been in or near a Luge sled in her life.

Chelsey stood on the "rustic" balcony expecting the worst. Particularly poignant, the leaves this year had been flaming crazy...as if popping their bloodvessels in dire premonition for the Games to come. Reds were just everywhere. He could barely see the gaudy golds of the birches beside them.

"Beastly weather, isn't it?" she remarked to the heat, but the Ambassador knew quite well she honestly couldn't care if it were hailing in sunshine. She quickly got to the point: "We were talking about some of the new recruits." Then she shook her head, meaning they were all dogs.

"Oh," the Ambassador said, wrinkling his white eyebrows as if the statement had weight.

"Well, the workforce is increasing by such leaps and bounds I never know if one of my shopgirls in Main Street this week will be elevated to a Department Director next week!" She hugged herself with her free hand. "Really, I've *never* seen such crazy personnel policies!"

"*Are* there any?" Levitt casually asked.

"Oh come on, the place's a zoo and you know it! You're on the Board, you see it every day."

Don't remind me, he thought. "Well," was all he uttered, and hastily took a drink.

"Well...*what?*" Lucille now was in full steam, like some raucous paddle wheel plying through an Adirondack pond. "Heidi's upset."

"What's new?" he asked while really wanting to ask nothing. Sometimes even diplomats slip.

"Nothing—but this time it's serious." A sudden gust flared up and dumped a load of golden birch leaves onto the balcony, and they chased each other about upon the floor.

Oh what's serious around here, the Ambassador heard himself asking. "How serious?" he inquired. "Middling to low?"

"*Super* serious!"

Not known for her understatement, thought the Ambassador, a short man, who stared up to Lucille's wig a moment, then let his eyes drop. Lucille really was a character!

"I'm telling you, she's out to draw blood, and she'll *draw* blood!" the lady snapt.

3

Just at that moment, the Chief of Staff, one of the local Judges, stept onto the terrace. He too was very well liked, but only in certain quarters, and was not universally loved. But...few Judges are! "How's that?" he wondered aloud, knowing quite well what the two were talking about. "Heidi spouting off again?"

Judge Ronson could call his shots, and get away with it. He could also dress the way he wanted, and get away with that, too. He usually came in to work with a shirt that was knit and short-sleeved, and with that he wore a Texas-style string-tie. Board Members who were far less imaginative hated him for this nonconformity, as they'd have to deal with him daily, either for business or for pleasure. And there was nothing they could do about him, since he *was* a Judge. So, to both the hostess and the Ambassador, the Judge said: "Heidi should know when to leave well enough alone, but never does. If she didn't expect Ivor to become just what she wanted...then she never should have gone ahead and hired him! Besides being an Olympic Gold Medallist, he's a damned hardworking boy, and I'm not afraid to say that he's been incredible in keeping that scatterbrained woman together! I wish we had *more* guys like Ivor aboard this silly ship...perhaps the organization would seem a bit more healthy!"

So there, Lucille thought with a smile inside, though she showed a miserable scowl outside, and she savoured the sound of the Olympic Athlete's name—pronounced EYE-ver—in her mind. "Well, leave it to the Judge to call a Spade a Spade!"

"That's right. And it'd be far easier if Ivor *were* a Spade! Then Heidi wouldn't be scheming right now to fire him!" the Judge stated, then relit his eternally lit pipe.

Hating pipe smoke, and feeling cantankerous, Lucille winked and declared: "Yes...you know, I have been very upset that The Committee has not hired a *single* Black to work here! We've allowed Canadians, French, Italians, Germans..."

"No, *Swiss*, remember Heidi's *Swiss*!" the Judge corrected.

"How foolish of me, of course," Lucille chuckled. "But any-how...all these damned *foreigners* come sneaking across the border to run *our* Games, and well...we could've been more lenient and hired *hundreds* of foreigners right within our own country!"

"Are you saying Blacks are foreigners?" the Judge laughed and wondered, knowing that was precisely what the lady *was* saying.

"Where're *you* going?" Lucille suddenly gasped, as the Ambassador was excusing himself and walking away.

"My wife..." and Levitt mumbled something apologetic and pointed to his wife, who indeed was standing in the doorway beckoning.

"Lucille?" Judge Ronson asked, to distract her.

"What?"

"Why don't you invite Ivor over..." and on that note the Judge let out a large, emphatic puff of smoke in Lucille's face.

4

She didn't flinch an inch, and replied: "You think it'll do any good?"

"Can it do any harm?" he responded.

Lucille didn't answer, but just gazed down upon her balcony floor. The occasional gold leaf was flitting up and down, up and down, up and down, as if palsied. Something just didn't seem right...this autumn. The Games...were only four short months away...yet Lake Placid seemed light-years away, mentally, in preparedness for whatever onslaught the world was going to let loose upon the tiny mountain town. You could feel the tension everywhere, as if some dæmon were ready to hatch from some evil and gigantic egg that had lain dormant inside one of the ancient rounded-down hills that had granted the area its fame.

The Olympic Ideal

Ruth's Diner, at the corner of Main Street and McKinley in Lake Placid, was not a very popular place with non-Adirondackers who worked for The Committee. But to the locals, and to the workers, it was a godsend. It was cheap, it was warm, and it was a place, one of the few left, where just-plain folks could go and complain about what was happening to their own turf *on* their own turf.

Ruth's was where Ivor liked to go, simply because it was so unfrequented by the people that he worked with. Given that the uncanny heat had kept up, and it was payday, the fellow in his late twenties was in a happy mood even though his boss, Heidi, had been treating him like shit. Halloween was coming up anyhow, cause for celebration, and with that thought the crazy idea to throw a costume ball hit him. No—*stupid* thought! But—why not?

As long tall Ivor sat there crumpled at the bar, chewing on a cheeseburgher, he kept thinking about other jobs he'd had, other places he'd lived in, other opportunities...

Why in Hell he'd ever left London for Athens...but no, that had indeed been a smart if not a fated move. But...why in Hell he'd ever left Athens...for anywhere...especially for Lake Placid...was a question nobody with whom he worked could figure out. Even in its grottiest moments, when the pollution over Athens got so thick it seemed potent enough to hoist the Parthenon up and plant it down in Piraeus, never had life in Athens seemed so dreary as life here in Placid. But strange events have even stranger resolutions, and Fate (that great Greek conception) had worked its six-armed way to making Ivor take the risk to voyage across the Atlantic, aboard Jimmy Laker's Skytrain, to New York, all on just a visitor's visa, then to shuttle northwards on a Greyhound bus, or was it a Trailways, to the hills called Adirondacks, like so many similar lemmings whose one purpose this year had been to *get* to Lake Placid and then to secure a job...and with any luck with the Lake Placid Olympic Committee. But luck indeed had been with Ivor, and he'd been hired by The Committee within a matter of days. And for a lucky bastard like him, he shouldn't have been so amazed...

Ivor *was* a bastard—literally. His father was some faceless Canadian from Manitoba he'd never seen, some horny soldier shipped to Belfast with a bunch of Commonwealth forces. In Northern Ireland he'd seduced a girl, then left her pregnant when his battalion deployed to Scotland. Later, due to intervention of a kind-hearted Catholic priest, Ivor was put in foster-care, then in boarding school in Somerset. Still later, as a bright pupil, he'd done well and been admitted as a Queen's Scholar to the prestigious Westminster School within the compound of Westminster Abbey. The privileged "public" education had provided no little saturation in things Greek, as anybody who knows anything about such education knows, but his strenuous athletic training (especially after he went up to Oxford) had prevented his ever getting to Greece except once, prior to his Olympic Medal run, when he competed briefly north of Athens. But Greece had been calling to the fellow all his life, and at last he gave in to the urge and simply moved there, this past May. During summer he had found a job working as a teacher of English in one of the many so-called language institutes popping up in every suburb of the Greek capital and, in one of them (Maroússi), a particularly bright and attractive young student turned out to be none other than the daughter of one of the Members of the National Olympic Committee of Greece. The girl's father became one of Ivor's ouzo-buddies, and it was he who had planted the idea in the Athlete's brain that it would be good therapy for the recently divorced Runner to cross the Atlantic and check out Lake Placid, so that's exactly what Ivor decided to do. *Therapy* truly was what Hefferon needed, since he was just then undergoing a crisis that *all* Olympic Athletes suffer. It was called: What in Hell do you *do* with your life...once the Olympics are over? And for Ivor...they'd been over four solid years!

It had been another Athenian friend, whom Ivor had known for years, Professor Aristídis Rembetikós, the Senior Member in Greece of the august International Olympic Committee, who had come to the Athlete's rescue and who had been kind enough to make the proper introduction to the Lake Placid Olympic Committee. So, whilst the Olympian was calling in on the Adirondacks late this past August, all it took was a short note from the venerable Professor to smoothe everything out beforehand. All that Ivor was lacking...was the visa. But that would be no problem, the IOC Member assured Ivor, when the Briton phoned Athens early this past September. But yes indeed...Greece...now seemed a million miles away...

In Ruth's Diner...those Athenian months just appeared fleeting recollections of some mad mad dream. Had he ever really *lived*...over there? Where life *was* lived...

Something was just so *wrong*...here in Lake Placid! Everyone's mind seemed *constipated*...not the locals' who *weren't* employed by The

Committee, but everyone else's. God, he'd never seen so many drunks in one place except along the Liffey of Dublin, up by Phoenix Park! And *this* town didn't even boast a Guiness brewery!

Cheeseburgher, great American concoction, away, Ivor just sat there on the diner barstool, when it hit him! The problem with the whole of Lake Placid, and with the Olympics, and with the whole Olympic Movement, as far as he could see it, was this: There wasn't a drop of *Spirit* in it anylonger! What was the *kagathós*, the Olympian Ideal, that superb wedding of Muscle and Mind, as epitomised by the Ancient Greeks, to a bunch of hopped-up bureaucrats? Why *was* there so much bitchery, so much in-fighting, on every level of the Lake Placid Olympic Committee? Why was Politics such a brute force within the Games themselves...where the Games supposedly were to do *away* with Politics and assert the Human Being striving for Perfection...aside from Machinations...aside from Bureaucrats...aside from Technicians? Ah but aside from the *Spirit*...nothing occurs within the human organism! *That* lesson has been one which History *has* taught! But everywhere that one could turn at Lake Placid...a Machination kept rearing like a dirty rapist, a Bureaucrat kept bogging all creative progress down, and a Technician...well...where were the *Athletes*...in rooms chock full of Texas Instrument computers, copy machines supplied by Xerox, forms ad infinitum ad nauseam, data being stored being stored...

So Ivor finished lunch with a plan: Come Hell or High Water, he'd *put* some Spirit back into the Olympic Movement...if it only meant putting a little life back *here*! He'd throw a Ball...for Halloween...knowing full well that Heidi would not like the thought of his doing it. Hadn't her husband *warned* Ivor, when he was getting hired, that people "who work for Protocol are to be seen and not heard"? And...how old was Ivor when he had last heard such rubbish?

"Seen and not heard *ay*?" Ivor mumbled as he paid his bill. The waitress thought she was being made fun of, in some strange British fashion, so she laughed. The locals are nice, Ivor said to himself. They understand...that their town would soon hatch...some monster.

On Stage On Ice

That Indian Summer weekend saw Lake Placid inundated with star-struck mamas, sequined tutus, and Apollo look-alikes all vying for camera angles interviews, acclaim. If it sounds like Hollywood or backstage at Covent Garden, that's precisely how the world of figure skating appears, and is, in essence. To the world, a Gold Medal in Figure Skating is an instant ticket to international pop superstardom, and all these kids competing here know it, whether they're from New Jersey, Java, or just plain Jersey!

"Well they all look like *queers* to me!" snarled some gruff idiot who weighed a ton and who was propping up one of the makeshift bars

7

set up in a corner of the new Olympic Field House. He was not at all impressed that the Field House was a marvel of Adirondack Architecture, that its flying buttress outer structure was reminiscent of Notre Dame (if not of the new and highly controversial Beaubourg Centre of Paris), and that *four* huge ice sheets would soon be beneath one big roof! To this Schlitz beer drinker, who himself was an electrician so he knew what he was talking about, the whole thing was a great big waste.

"But Frank, I don't care. It's done *wonders* for the region and..." his wife countered and pulled her scarf closer to her eyes to hide her rollers.

"*What* wonders! How many locals has it put to work huh?" Frank snorted. "All the contracting's been done from *outside!*"

"Well...it's nice to see something happening, anyhow."

"Oh what the Hell do *you* know! You just like looking at all them pansies' *crotches* out there spinning round like snowflakes with hardons! Is *that* why all this money's been spent...so *fruits* like *him* can whiz round on million-dollar ice?" Frank downed his plastic cup of Schlitz and ordered another.

Ethel just walked away and went to one of the shiny new and blue-painted railings which overlooked the first level of seats in the eight-thousand-capacity Arena. To Ethel, it was all glorious, Frank or no Frank. The Devil only knew when she'd get him in a good enough mood to take her anywhere...let alone to Lake Placid...and for her to see some real figure skating, live, was the thrill of a lifetime. Why in God's Name did Frank *always* have to ruin things for her? God knows she'd never get near the Olympic Primary Area during the Games...as the whole mountainous region was going to be cordoned off, like some tremendous concentration camp, to prevent sabotage, terrorism, and all those horrid realities which she only read about in the papers...

Down on the ice sheet, two of the most perfect beings she ever had been lucky enough to see were skating to some magnificent piece of orchestral music, the title of which she couldn't ever identify, nor would she want to try. The sounds of the classical harmonies, the grace of the couple all ablaze in mad skin-tight suits the hue of tangerines, the crowd so happy and so jubilant in their applause each time that the couple, from Czechoslovakia, would execute a flawless double-axle throw...it was all such an untouchable dream to Ethel...such an untouchable dream...

The huge crowd suddenly roared, as the young girl on the ice bent backwards and spun ever downwards, ever downwards, with the grace of a prima ballerina. She certainly ushered from such a totally different realm...than Ethel...that what did it matter from what country she came! *Why* did the Olympics get so hung up about people's *countries*...wondered Ethel...as she tried to see...through her tearing eyes...through the last spin of the incredible girl on the ice...whose hair now was brushing a circle as she revolved around the muscular legs of her handsome partner. The crowd now was jumping up...jumping up wildly...to the most ecstatic applause that Ethel had ever witnessed in her life. The whole thing made Ethel weak inside. This...wasn't just your rowdy roaring football mania. This...was true *appreciation* being displayed...*true* appreciation for something utterly extraordinary. Ethel couldn't take it anymore, and hurried back to find Frank, still propping up the bar.

"Frank—did you *see* it! It was *fabulous!*" Ethel felt her words weren't expressive enough, but her voice was registering her feelings.

Frank just swilled a bit more beer, then muttered: "Is it *over* now?"

Backstage

Just like an opera the public never see half of what's really going on backstage. It all looks so meticulously arranged, but the *things* that go on in the wings...well...warrant some explanation.

This Monday, the second week in October, had seen a sudden snowstorm swoop across the United States from someplace out West and the thing had done total havoc to the Skating Festival. But of course, the show must go on, and did. Given that the Field House had just been completed, Olympic Law required that the Arena's ice sheet be tested by international competition prior to the Games, so snowstorm or not the skaters and their coterie were required to assemble, to dazzle, to strive for those Bronzes, Silvers, and Golds. Too bad for the spectacular foliage, which was exactly the same colours, this wicked storm came stomping over from Buffalo, where most of these storms stomp from, and had wiped off all the foliage in one fell swoop. Everybody had become sick at heart, and especially the kitchen crew in the Field House Cafeteria, who were located in the Link Building (an actual suspended link, a true building, stretching, midair, between the old 1932 Arena and the new 1980 one). This crew had the best view in all the Adirondacks; and with the fully fledged autumnal display, which from their vantage point showed them an enormous expanse of the great sloping vale which spread outwards and downwards towards all the many mountains of the whole southern horizon...well this kitchen crew got quite upset to see these fabulous colours suddenly vanish. Now, the great rounded mountains, just yesterday garbed in cloaks of Renaissance brocade, whose variance of earth-tones would have held Lorenzo de' Medici spellbound, now looked covered by yesterday's dishrag, as if all the many kitchens of Lake Placid's horde of tourist hotels had tossed all their washing-up right out their windows. Everyone was depressed.

In this Cafeteria Ivor had just bumped into Rebecca. With no holds barred, Rebecca was one of the true *personalities* of the Eastern Seaboard. Fresh air itself, especially in an atmosphere of soggy frankfurters, Campbell's soup, sweaty athletic supporters...Ivor loved her.

9

"Have you seen Mrs Winchell?" the Deputy Chief of Protocol asked hurriedly, as if he were dashing to a fire.

"The columnist's wife? Is *she* here?" Rebecca wondered, in her very, polished Montréal-cum-Vassar accent. She was forty some said, but looked better than most girls sweet-sixteen. She was a prominent doctor's wife, but not the one at the cocktails of Lucille. Her husband was the direct descendant of the founder of the famous cancer research centre, the Harper Institute.

"No—this's serious! I'm trying to track down Mrs Winchell, mother of one of the New Zealand skaters. Her daughter's had a purse stolen or something...and I've had to notify the Consulate in New York about it to try to speed up getting her a new passport."

"A New Zealand passport?" Rebecca Harper asked, not terribly interested. "I was there once. I loathed it and I never knew why since I *love* Maoris!" Rebecca was joking, since she had never been to New Zealand and had no special affection for Maoris.

"I'm in a hurry...we think the woman's playing us for the stooge," Ivor stated, looking about the Cafeteria.

"Don't let *that* surprise you!"

Ivor frowned. It had already been a bad day, only two hours into it. Protocol wasn't nearly so fun as he had been led to believe. "Well I've rung the Consulate *six* bleeding times on that lady's behalf, and waited an hour and a half this morning for her to show up, so I could inform her ruddy arse how she can get her new passport, but the sodding *bitch* didn't even have the decency to ring me to say she wouldn't show!"

"I'm in no rush," Rebecca said provocatively.

What did that mean, Ivor wondered and looked at Rebecca's marvellous get-up. Not possible to out-do her, Rebecca was Heidi's number one complaint in town. Rebecca should have been cast as the Deputy of the Hostess Department, but because Rebecca was such a gorgeous woman and had such flair, personality, and reams of contacts as long as your arm, Heidi had taken an instant feline dislike to her, totally out of jealousy of course. For that matter, *any* pretty woman with an ounce of intelligence was seen as a threat to Heidi who, as a Swiss alien, knew that she was dispensable. How in Hell a Swiss alien ever got to *be* Chief of Protocol, in America, was something that bothered everyone who knew her. Rebecca in particular had tried to be accommodating to this tigress from Switzerland, but then Rebecca had good breeding and connections and was *used* to jealous women. Rebecca's husband, Doctor Reginald Harper, was one of the best-looking and most personable of all the MDs of the region, and attractive women *always* were attracted to him. Even Heidi was, which was the straw that broke the camel's back...

"Well...come with me then," Ivor offered and was pleased to have someone to talk to. Ivor and Rebecca had hit it off instantly. Both zany and quite aristocratic in their whole approach to life, which meant that

10

they just floated about in a realm all their own, oblivious to bourgeois values beneath them, Rebecca had warmed to Ivor due to his travels, his sick sense of humour, and his knowledge, and Ivor had warmed to Rebecca due to her knowledge, her travels, and her...more modest though hardly holy sense of humour. Ivor would talk about the Erechtheíon and erections all in one sentence, and Rebecca wouldn't bat an eyelash and would go right on to eye-shadow, shadow-puppets, and string-pulling within the Olympics!

When Ivor and Rebecca walked together...people noticed. Both very out-front in their appearance, both tall, the only thing that Ivor couldn't match...this Monday morning as the pair strutted down the rather gloomy blue corridor along the south side of the Field House, as a bevy of skaters in all hues were down on the ice sheet practising for to-night's ice-dancing competition...was Rebecca's hair.

Something must be said here about Rebecca's hair: It was a work of Art, a political statement, an impossibility, a marvel, and an affront to middle-class values all in one. Words could never capture it...but the hair was basically blonde, blonde of all shades of meaning, and it was *meant* to bother people, and did. Rebecca obviously spent absolute hours before the mirror each morning, but it always looked like she jumped in the car right out of bed. Very long and very thick, Rebecca had more straight hair that always looked curly than most women could dream for, but the way she did it up...a shank here...a swirl hung up there...a whole thick bunch stuck up on her head and seemingly balancing up there in defiance of gravity...but somehow it always worked, and worked wonderfully. Lesser women, without guts, would look like tramps, but Rebecca always looked every inch a totally eccentric and irreproachable Duchess.

"Where in God's Name are you leading me?" Rebecca wondered as Ivor led her past the far bar where Frank had been glued. Some Pinkerton Detective now was standing guard beside a locked door which led down to the innards of the Field House, the area off-limits to the public, but which was accessible to Olympic employees with the proper accreditation. At this Skating Festival the status symbol of status symbols had become the ugly pink plastic laminated ID card which everyone who was anyone had dangling on a flimsy little chain around the neck. This little thing, with one's ghastly Woolworth-style photograph, got one anywhere...and so Ivor and Rebecca reached for the bottom of their chains and hoisted up the pink thing to flash in the face of the guard, who showed not one hint of emotion as he unlocked the door and allowed the two VIPs to pass. Rebecca, one has to say here, was the Deputy Chief of Volunteers. She had been hired by Alicia Ponsonby, after Heidi had made it impossible for her to be hired by the Hostess Department.

"We've got to find Mrs Winchell. I have to know *now* what she wants me to do about this visa, I mean, passport problem! The Judge thinks she's pulled it off as an insurance caper, since she's also claiming she had traveller's cheques and other what-not nicked. It's all a crock...as far as I'm concerned!" Ivor stated and held a downstairs door open for Rebecca, which issued them into the Practice Rink at the Field House's back-end. Just there, they were greeted by a very svelte brunette, Ann Porter, coach of the US Olympic Figure Skating Pairs Team, who was watching the Johnsons, the top US couple.

Ann knew the scoop, and instantly stated: "Ivor, have you heard the latest—you'll die!"

"Oh oh," Rebecca said after a hasty introduction to Ann. "What's up?"

"Ivor, now listen to this, and I don't know if it's been verified but I've just heard that Mrs Winchell's *found* the missing passport," Ann said apologetically, trying to soften the blow and watch the Johnsons all at once. "Perfect," she declared emphatically, in appreciation of a faultless double camel.

"What!" Ivor stuttered. "But...but...but I'd been phoning the Consulate all morning! I'd got the approval of the Consul General himself to sneak her a quickee passport and now she...are you *sure* it's not missing?"

"Not sure at all," she followed then shouted: "Bravo!"

The Johnsons certainly were good!

"Well, thanks for the information," Ivor muttered and left the lady to her business.

Opening the double doors, Rebecca and Ivor immediately were in the Zamboni Vomitory as it's called. This disgusting name of vomitory is what the hugest exits leading onto the Arena floor are called. The western one was where the machine that cleaned the ice, the Zamboni, was parked when not in use. In this hallway, and straight out the vomitory, one could see the ice sheet, which's where the two now headed.

Luckily for Ivor, Mrs Winchell's daughter was just getting ready to go out for her practice with her cousin Mark, her partner. Mrs Winchell, in her exotic chinchilla coat, of course was there cheering on her little stars. Of all the skating-mamas, this New Zealander had quickly earned the reputation in the Field House as "The Fur", meaning she'd do anything, even take the hide off your back, to make her daughter and sister's son *win!*

"Do you think she's making the whole theft *up*?" Rebecca asked as the two approached her.

"Anything could happen in Lake Placid!"

"Never a truer phrase can ever be said!" concurred Rebecca, who stood there on the bottom aisle of the rink fidgeting with her coiffure and glaring at Mrs Winchell's chinchilla.

"Hello, Mrs Winchell, how are things?" Ivor benignly asked.

The Fur just answered, "Uh Cindy's just going on, I'm very busy!"

"I don't care if you *are* very busy...*I've* been busy on *your* behalf for two whole days! Why didn't you show the courtesy of phoning me this morning, to cancel our appointment?" Ivor was looking stern, and Rebecca came over to block Mrs Winchell's escape.

"Well...what do you want?" asked The Fur if she had never seen the two before.

"I want the truth," emphasised Ivor forcefully. "This is a most *serious* matter, your having us involve your country's Consulate, and I have just this morning received the verbal agreement of your Consul General that should you and your daughter go to New York on your way to California that the Consul General will be more than happy to issue your daughter a new passport."

"Oh...that's very kind," Mrs Winchell said, obviously quite distracted and trying to turn her attention to her daughter now on the ice. "How should we go about it?"

"First of all I have to be absolutely *certain* that the passport indeed *is* missing."

"What are you saying?" enquired The Fur as credibly as a liar at Confession.

"I have just heard, from a very reliable source, that your daughter's passport in fact is *not* missing...but has, this morning, been *found.*"

"*Do* you have the passport?" Rebecca interrogated, in a way that only a woman could fish for.

"Uh......well..." Mrs Winchell began to look as grey as her coat.

"Well...why don't you go *up* a few bleachers," Rebecca put in diplomatically, "and look in your bag. It's *big* enough..." and Mrs Harper scowled at Mrs Winchell's atrociously large alligator purse, "...to lose a *dozen* passports in!"

On that hearty note, The Fur did as told, and likely would have tried to crawl away were it not for Rebecca's eyeing her the whole time. Just at that instant the short practice stint of Cindy and Mark was finishing, and the two in lime green came skidding to a halt by the rail, snow flying everywhere.

"Mark," Ivor began authoritatively, "I have been told by officials that you have indeed found the missing passport. Is that correct?" Ivor was rather revelling in his rôle as cop.

"Don't say..." Cindy began, to try to cover up.

"Oh shut up! God—I don't see what all the hassle's about, but *yes* we found the thing in our luggage, last night..." Mark blurted honestly, looking quite scared.

"*Last* night?" Ivor shouted. "Well...*why* then did no one inform us? Do you realise I've involved the Consul General of New York in this charade?"

Then, turning on Cindy, Mark yelled: "Your *mother's* got it!"

"Leave her *out* of it!"

13

"*Out* of it—she certainly *is*! Don't listen to Cindy, Sir, but Mrs Winchell has the thing in her bag. I swear it!" Poor Mark, he obviously was in hot water now, at least if not with the Law with his mother's sister. Cindy just skated out and away, going again onto the ice to work off her anxiety in a few wicked spins.

Hearing all this, Mrs Winchell suddenly stood up like a popped cork and began flashing a passport like it was gold. "I *found* it," she shouted stupidly, "I found it right here, can you *believe* it?"

After going to her and telling her *precisely* what The Committee thought about her, Ivor and Rebecca walked up the Field House's aisle, as the former was muttering: "*Believe* it...I'd believe *any* old thing in this town!"

Mister Protocol, Mister Protocol

When the public weren't thinking about wasted money, about restriction of access, or about accommodation problems in Lake Placid, but when the public were thinking about the Olympic Games, the public were thinking about athletes, about the many many years of arduous training, and about the glory that surrounds each sport. But, inside The Committee, the non-public were always thinking about *Protocol*.

Even if one didn't have the opportunity to work directly *for* Protocol, Protocol had its ramifications all over The Committee, like jam on the face of every tot in kindergarten. Protocol just smeared all over, and stuck to everything. Nobody could do *this* without first getting it ok'd by *that*; nobody could sign a memo without the approval of one's whole list of superiors; one dared *not* fuck up.

But of course, on the other hand, where would the International Olympic Committee have been...*were* it not for Protocol? All those National Olympic Committees from all over the globe, all those participating Sports Federations, all those old men on the International Olympic Committee...why each and every one of the top brass of all these groups had to be pampered and made to feel that they were absolutely the cat's meow within the Movement, even if they've never participated in a single sport, other than sex, in all their life! But then again, just like in opera, these people are the Producers, if not the Patrons, and such people just must be babied.

Well it was Protocol's job just to make sure everyone's tucked in. Protocol said who's acceptable, and who's rubbish. Protocol required the President, of each and every country hosting the Games (or Head of State, or King, or whatever one's called) to hop to, to come and open the festivities, to accede to every whim and flight of fancy of the International Olympic Committee. So, Protocol started right at the very top, and therefore, of course, was a Divine Invention, of none other than the very Gods of Mount Olympos; and it likewise governed everything that ever happened at Olympia! So, you see, it just dribbled down, to all the other departments of any other organization that has ever had the least likely thing to do with anything pertaining to the Olympic Games. Protocol told you when it was time to relieve yourself, and when it was time to wipe yourself. Protocol was fun! Well...Protocol was fun at Lake Placid, and everyone loved to be in line, so Protocol made sure that everybody was. Lake Placid certainly wouldn't have been able to have coped...*without* Protocol. And Protocol itself certainly wouldn't have been able to have coped...without *Butch Barley*.

Butch, as his all-too-few friends called him, was, inexplicably, short for Donald, and however he was called he still was the *Director* of Protocol. Now, to get things straight, Butch was Heidi's husband, not vice versa. She was *Chief* of Protocol, not *Director*. The difference was vast. Butch, as a Division Director, meant that he was governor of nine whole Departments within The Committee. Therefore, already, you see that Butch and Protocol covered a colossal amount of ground, and both were extremely important, because lots of patches of ground certainly *needed* covering up.

Butch called Ivor to his office, or should one say summonsed. This was Wednesday, and the Skating Festival was almost over. Most people had seen so much bloody skating it was coming out everyone's eyes, ears, noses, and throats, and everyone was on edge. No major diplomatic incident, other than Mrs Winchell's "theft", had occurred, much to everyone's relief. Ivor, therefore, wondered what it was Butch really wanted.

One should just digress for a moment to say that the supreme command of the Lake Placid Games was centred in the quite ornate little building called Town Hall, an orange brick rather classical rectangle surmounted by a neat white wooden cupola sporting a clock and a bell to toll the hourly time. This, on the lower end of Main Street, was past most of the shops, and situated next to a petrol station. It was also across the road and a bit down from the local High School, which had a façade like the Notre-Dame end of the Louvre and which, illuminated at night, looked quite the spectacle. It was also across the road and a bit down from the famed Olympic Speed Skating Oval, which sat in a playing field squat before the High School. So, inside this building was where Ivor was working and where Protocol was lodged. Board meetings, fiscal hassles, and many other interesting corporate clashes took place here also.

Having just entered Butch's office, a rather too large one for the small size of the man behind the desk, Ivor just sat there, quite blasé, and wondered what would happen next.

Butch did not look terribly amused. Maybe the State Department had just phoned saying the President had decided that The White House didn't wish to open the festivities after all. That would certainly be enough to put *any* Director of Protocol on edge...

15

"Uh Ivor?" Butch asked and for a split second looked just like Hitler. When was the last time the man washed his hair? Right from the very beginning Ivor had been forced to live a lie, to try to pretend that he *liked* this fellow, his boss, whom he honestly did not. Butch's attitude had been so flitting...first he showered all this affection on one, just after the hiring-papers had been signed, but then as soon as one was integrated into the system he dumped one and never thereafter bothered to say hello, except once, on the uppermost floor as he whizzed past Ivor at the Xerox machine and patted the bloke's behind. Very strange...

"Ivor?" he repeated in a higher tone. "So I hear you're throwing a Halloween Party?"

The question was asked maliciously, as if the very thought were blasphemy. Ivor began to seethe inside, especially as the boss then followed this by: "I only called you down here to remind you *not* to include The Committee into it officially..."

"It's a *private* party," was all that Ivor replied.

"Then, keep it private." Sometimes Butch did not look at all like a man, as his face was quite bizarre and conjured up a mouse. Big deal if he'd worked for Chaste Manhattan Bank as a prized whiz-kid theorist; so what if he'd directed the whole of Chaste's European operations? Something was *wrong* with the man, and he was notorious for sequestering himself in his office and just scheming in there, to himself, how best he and his wife could keep on top of all the gossip, all the intrigue, all the power-plays which, rumour had it, had more than once tried to bounce him *out*.

Given that Butch Barley didn't seem to wish to pursue the conversation anylonger, Ivor simply rose and left the office. Right next door, literally to the right, was Ambassador Levitt's office, so Ivor popped his head inside and said hello, then joked for a minute with Butch's cute secretary, Sheila Gallup, an aspiring singer who was quitting soon so she could carry on through the winter not as a drone but as an artist! Ivor liked her, admired her warm Joni Mitchell type voice, and quietly without Butch's hearing wished her well on her new and obviously far more exciting endeavour.

"Sheila, what's that bloke's problem?" Ivor asked and pointed in the direction of Butch's office. "He called me all the way down here just to tell me to keep my party private!"

"He's cracked. Who knows! I've been trying *not* to figure him out for months and months!" Sheila confided and winked. Truly, Sheila *had* been with The Committee...months and months...almost from the very beginning...and she had seen so much that she just couldn't *take* it anymore.

"Oh well, not to worry I guess." Ivor said and made for the door which led upstairs to the top floor, where the ersatz quiet of his office could be found.

No Peace For The Wicked

Not one single office ever *was* quiet...at The Committee. There was always some delivery coming, some VIP's arse to kiss, some contractor with plumbing problems, some phone out of order, and much office moving. The favourite game inside The Committee headquarters was to see how many desks you could get assigned to in one month, how many new phone extensions you could get, and on how many floors you could set up your office. It was all like musical chairs, nobody knowing when the Chief of Staff would next have to get embroiled in another controversy over whose typewriter was going where, whose rolodex had been stolen, whose feelings had been hurt.

As Chief of Staff, Judge Ronson obviously had far more to do than hassle with bitchy staff members, since he dealt with far more magnanimous problems of Security and the like, but a huge amount of his time was wasted in keeping tempers toned down.

The Judge was upstairs this Friday afternoon in October when the impossible actually did happen: The ceiling fell in! The Judge was upstairs calming Sandra down, since for six solid months she had been working for the Legal Department but had just been told by Personnel that she was being moved to Office Services which, according to Legal, was about as far a plummeting as a poor Legal Secretary could go. The Legal Secretaries felt that they were on a plane with Members of the International Olympic Committee and so, to woebegone Sandra, it was the pits, her "demotion". There she was, collapsed on her IBM Selectric, sobbing her little heart out, saying she just couldn't *take* it anylonger, and making all the other girls in the Department feel like *shit*. So, as usual, the Judge was called and he came up to try to soothe the ruffled feathers. Sobbing Sandra, looking a fright, kept saying: "I'm quitting, I'm quitting, I'm quitting!"

"Well, *quit* then," said the Judge calmly, with a puff on his pipe, at which moment the ceiling fell through.

Now this didn't happen on top of Sandra, but almost on top of poor Gretchen, who worked in the Computers Department. To describe this you have to know what a Skinner Box is. A Skinner Box is a torture device devised by sick psychiatrists and/or psychologists, likely both, to take their aggressions out on *rats*. A Skinner Box traps a rat in a labyrinth, and if the poor beast can sniff his way out he can get the piece of cheese. Psychologists and psychiatrists come to orgasm in watching this, documenting this, and storing the data. So too with the uppermost floor of the Administration Centre: Designed like a Skinner Box, Science has yet to devise a more cramped office set-up; but lo and behold, at the end of the day, if an employee made it outside *alive*, he or she *might* receive the coveted piece of cheese...but there were no guarantees. Many a day went by when employees did *not* get the aforementioned morsel of cheese...

"What's happened?" shouted the Judge in midstream, as Sandra kept blubbering away. On hearing the crashing ceiling, she literally went all to pieces, and was told by her superior to "go home".

The Judge, far more intrigued now by the debris and chaos it had caused, left Sandra to her sorrows and trekked across the narrow hallway, if that's what one could call it, and stopt inside the Protocol Department, or a good sector of it that is, where everyone was walking around holding his or her head and saying: "Do you believe it? Do you believe it?"

The sky had literally fallen in. Nobody really was surprised, other than Sandra who, with her legal mind, could only cope with notarised documents, but still everyone was rather unsettled to see clouds of dust still waffling down from a great gap in the makeshift if not jerrybuilt ceiling that had only recently been hung. Truly, a whole chunk of the ceiling had given way, and had landed on Mimi Tiny's desk. Mimi, a whiz with a calculator and an even better singer than Sheila Gallup, was a long drink of water, but everyone adored her. She was damned lucky that she was calculating other than at her desk, insofar as the girl had been speaking with her boyfriend on somebody else's telephone when the mishap occurred.

"I'm not cleaning this *fucking* mess up!" Mimi kept stating to no one's amusement. "And somebody better send a cleaner *quick*, or I'm gonna call the *cops!*"

Mimi, who almost looked like Dame Edith Sitwell, was so long and elegant that most people missed the point. She had had the guts to volunteer, even though she was a calculator, to help clean up the ice during the Skating Festival. In other words every night this gorgeous woman was out there like a lackey, and loving all the attention and controversy it caused. That was when Ivor spotted her, talked to her backstage, and had found out she could sing...so he had offered her a spot at his party, to perform a torch-song drooped atop a piano.

Irate and telling people so, Mimi was not thinking about torch-songs when Judge Ronson walked in to inspect the damage. "Could you please put that pipe out...we've got *enough* dust around here now!" she snapt, much to the Judge's amusement. He liked people with spunk.

"I'm not cleaning this *junk* up!" she bellowed, her huge brown eyes bulging out, as the poor thing pointed to the detritus aflop on her desk and work-space.

"No one says you have to," Ronson replied quietly.

"What *next* around here?" she queried. "It's *nuts* here, absolutely nuts!"

"No one says it isn't," he added. "Are you doing volunteers tonight?"

"I don't know!" Mimi replied in a way that meant yes.

"How's your uniform fit?" the Judge queried ribaldly.

"How would *you* like to know!" she retorted. "I have a *job* to do... and I *do* it ! "

"That's more than the *majority* around here," the Judge laughed, and Mimi laughed along with him. It was really hysterical working for The Committee.

"I hear you're singing a torch-song for the party," he wondered, changing the subject abruptly as he was wont to do. "You should come to *my* house...I have some good old 78s you can listen to anytime. My Dobermanns don't bite."

"I bet!" she said and excused herself, to go to the lady's room, "God—I need a sedative!"

The Judge turned about to come face to face with Lucille McSorley. "What brings *you* here?" he asked, really wondering what she *was* doing here.

"Just inspecting the wreck...The Committee that is," she said and laughed. Thank the Lord to-day she was wearing one of her better wigs, the cream-coloured one, not the one with orangey highlights. There was something of the vamp about Lucille, for her fifty-odd years, that even made men *dream* about her.

"Looking good, isn't it?" chuckled the Judge.

"We can only thank our lucky stars no one's hurt. Wouldn't the Press just love that: GIRL KILLED AT TYPEWRITER BY FAULTY CEILING! We'd *never* fulfil our Solicitation Drive."

"How *is* your soliciting coming, by the way?" the Judge wondered with a leer. Lucille was Chairperson of the Solicitation Drive, which had earned her no few jokes about town.

"Oh...millions and millions...just *aren't* coming in!" she tartly responded. "I'm ready to go national television and quit screwing about with these fussy mail order forms. Nobody *reads* that crap-mail anyhow. If somebody sent *me* one, I'd chuck it out so fast..."

"But Lucille, *you* are unique!"

"Why *are* my opinions so defined?"

"Speaking of which, I bet I know why you *really* came to Town Hall to-day," the man whispered slyly.

"Of all the men in town...why in Hell is it *you* have to be the one who reads my mind?"

Lighting up his pipe again, Ronson replied: "So what did the boy *say?*"

"What boy?"

"You know what boy. Did you ask you-know-whom to come to dinner?"

"Well, Mister Justice, did it ever strike you that I'm old enough to be the boy's *mother!* "

"Did that stop Oedipos?"

"Oh be sensible!"

"So, is he *coming*...or not?"

"I'll let you....guess!" And on that note Lucille winked goodbye and walked into the Finance Office to haggle over bills.

Palpo Island

Over by Whiteface Mountain, and in the Lake called Placid, sits a fairly large pine covered isle which the natives now call Palpo. The owner of Palpo Dog Food has a camp there, you see. So do a few other privileged beings, one of whom was Lucille McSorley. Nobody had ever counted how much real estate this woman controlled, but rumour had it that her holdings stretched as far south as Atlanta, which is where her late husband, a botanist, sprang from, and lies, buried.

Lucille was in the mood to "get away". Such moods were very rare indeed, since she felt compelled to keep up with all the dirt about town, and to leave for even an hour was like risking your reputation. She also felt like "having a fling", so she had asked Ivor over for a drink and then had quickly whisked him down to her private dock, from which she had jumped into her cabin cruiser, revved up the engine, and dashed off with the young Englishman across the Lake. Again, contrary to expectations, the weather again was balmy, and all the snow had melted, but had left a dismal environment all around...no fancy shades to camouflage the otherwise lack-lustre trees. But, all in all, under a crystal clear blue sky, it was invigorating to be coasting along so quickly, shooting off towards Whiteface Mountain.

"I adore it here, honestly!" she stated grandly as she stood regally at her wheel. She, no mean eccentric herself, was wearing a very odd if not cumbersome chartreuse green chiffon "thing" that had many many folds and almost looked like something from Ancient Greece. It was long-gowned and went right down to very ugly green patent leather shoes. Ivor kept thinking that she could come as "that" anytime, to his Costume Ball, and inevitably she'd win the prize. She was even wearing a wide-brimmed greenish-blue felt halt, with a long chiffon tie-ribbon that was a good yard long by either cord, as well as being about a foot wide. Something tragicomic in her stance made Ivor think of Isidora Duncan, during her final ride in that automobile on the Riviera, when she choked to death by the scarf flying backwards and getting caught in the car's wheel. For Lucille now, standing and steering at the same time were immensely difficult, as she kept holding her hat by one hand and playing captain with the other. It was so ludicrous that Ivor didn't even offer to take the rudder, but Lucille wouldn't have let him anyhow. Obviously, in this situation, the lady wanted to stay on top.

Before Ivor knew it, the ride was over. The boat was berthing alongside a canoe, at a dock painted the most typical of all colours used in these hills: shit-brown with blood-red trim. Before the woman could hop out Ivor did, then, extend her his hand, and upon which extension he was quite surprised, upon landing, that she didn't release it.

Not far up a winding path, just a kicked-along dirt track in fact, was a nondescript shack of those same two hues, shit and blood. "I adore this place...much much more than my five hundred thousand dollar pad across the water!" she stated on unlocking a spiderwebbed door.

"When was the last time you were here?"

"Oh...just last week. I inspect the joint at least every other week."

"You mean...fortnightly?" Ivor asked devilishly.

"Why're you damned Brits always *correcting* us!"

"I was an English teacher, just this past summer in Athens, you know. I even correct Heidi, with no compunction."

"Somebody should. Sit down, take a load off your mind. Care for Scotch...Glenlivet?"

"It's bloody good *someone* knows how to drink Scotch here!"

"Darling—I've spent *more* time in Scottish castles, on all fours, than you *ever* care to know. Here. Cheers."

"Oh...where?"

"Don't ask. All of them! *McSorley*...hear the ring?"

"So much more poetic than Hefferon."

"Why couldn't your family spell it "H-E-F-R-U-N?"

"It's Welsh really. Don't ask me...I don't worry about such things. I'm half Irish."

"Well, nobody at The Committee knows how to pronounce *either* of your damned names!"

"EYE-ver," the Runner stated. "Rhymes with fiver—you know—a five-quid note. And HEF-run, well, that rhymes with *nothing!*"

"They tell me you're a *divorced* man..."

"As of last April..."

"Don't you miss *having* a woman...as often as you *need* to?" Lucille asked suggestively, and licked her lips. It was still early in the afternoon. The last of the season's birds were chirping everywhere. "No one ever comes to the island...at *this* time of day," Lucille said provocatively then stood and made for the door. "Coming?"

"No...just breathing hard," Ivor responded and bolted out the door after her.

The two walked midmost into the isle's forest of pines and to a spot where three large rocks, with not one jagged edge on them, upraised themselves in an eerie almost cabalistic stance. Inside them, one almost was lost to the world, and therein Lucille sat down, square beside her bottle of Glenlivet. For the first time, hunched before her, Ivor noticed that her body really wasn't all that old, and that her breasts were huge. He reached for them, then pulled her to him.

It was a strange, animal, rather horrid embrace that took them both quite by surprise, as they rolled on top of each other, abed on the moss and the needles of the pines. The warm wind kept rustling

21

through the grove and the birds kept singing as if nothing was happening, all the time that Ivor was stripping off the delicate chiffon but quite macabre gown and stroking the lady with his hands.

"I've got to see your *cock*! I bet it's as long as a *moose*!"

"I've never *seen* the cock of a moose! I've never seen a *moose*!" he said as she unzipped him haphazardly but got out what she wanted.

"Oh Jesus! Sweet Brother of Sin, *save* me, it's *uncut* meat!" she moaned as she began stroking his prick and pulling his trousers down at the same time. Half naked herself, breasts flopping in the crisp autumnal air, Lucille lunged downwards as some crow in a tree squawked like it was being raped, just at the moment that she swallowed half of his cock. And in a few more rolls-over Ivor was out of his knickers altogether, and Lucille was just about out of her dress.

"In my *ass*!" she whined, and got all hot thinking of him spitting down into the crack of her arse then gobbing saliva on the head of his shaft. On all fours like a beast, Lucille soon was ready...as her young lover made a few jerky thrusts then rammed his organ way up into her digestive tract.

Not without displeasure, and not at all restraining himself in his moaning like a fool, Ivor kept it up, and kept it up, squeezing the woman's large tits and pushing so hard on her that her face was all but shoved right into the muck. No matter how you look at it, Lucille got quite a rough fucking, and one that the poor thing had been craving for weeks and for weeks. After Ivor came maniacally, yelling like a pig, he collapsed onto the old woman and had to be shoved off rudely. "God— trying to *kill* me!" she panted.

"Frightfully sorry," he responded sheepishly, feeling rather unsportsmanlike for the brute display. "Can...can I help you into...your things?"

"Well—what do I *expect*...on an island that's named after *dog* meat!" and then Lucille roared uproariously till the tears came out of her eyes. "Come along...hurry into your junk and we'll go sit by the fire and have a good long juicy *gossip* session!"

Petunias

First, a little bit of geography: The Lake called Placid, where we have left our two lovebirds, was not, we repeat, *not* the same lake on which the *town* of Lake Placid was situated. That always threw people, but it's nevertheless true. Lake Placid town was located on *Mirror* Lake, and but a tiny sliver of the town of Lake Placid was fronting the Lake called Placid, and this sliver was called Holiday Harbor, spelt with an O-R not an O-U-R, do note, and to which we shall return in due course. Now, the famous "Club", and nobody who knew anything called it by any other name, was this huge rambling estate of "cottages", as they're deemed, and condominiums, and a bloody big sprawling hotel that nobody now knew how to govern, as it was examplary of how ungovernable the whole United States had become...it just carried on somehow, regardless. On this big property, on Mirror Lake, of the town of Lake Placid, and not the *township* mind you, "cottages" (though they truly were as big as mansions, some of them) all had the names of things indigenous to the Adirondacks. Hence, one of the cottages was mis-named and yet the name had stuck: Petunias.

Petunias was the pretty place where the Barleys lived. It reminded Heidi, for some strange reason, of the goose-farm near Bern where she grew up. God knows why Heidi thought this way, but if *you* had grown up on a goddamned goose-farm, *your* thought-processes would be feather-brained, too. How she ever made it off that fowl set of acres, and wormed her way into the consciousness of Lausanne's world headquarters for the International Olympic Committee, was an eternal mystery. And how Heidi and Butch ever fell in love, in Lausanne, if that's what you could call such a mating, is a whole other *volume!*

We should have mentioned earlier that Donald (Butch) Barley really wasn't quite right after all, as he officially went by the name of B. Donald Barley. Nobody on Earth knew what in Hell the "B" stood for. Rumour had it that it was Bonehead. But we heard that it could have stood for Broderick, Bela, Billy, Buzzard, or even Boozer. Yet, if nobody called him Donald anyway, but Butch, then the name became B. Butch Barley, or B.B.B., or Triple-B, like some low-grade Hollywood movie, some gay-ranchero cow-poke burger-ranch, or some pint-sized bra.

This late afternoon, Petunias had seen the Barleys at home. Mrs Barley was studying her G-List, or maybe she was playing with her G-Spot, as the question had come up whether or not to invite to attend the Games all fifty Governors of all fifty States. All your top VIPs, from Union Leaders to Ambassadors to Kings to their Chauffeurs, get "G" Accreditation at the Games. Some people have said that "G" must be short for "Goody Goody", but we have never seen that in writing. With respect, or with disrespect, to Heidi, everybody at The Committee joked that "G", in her case, stood for "goose-farm", where, everyone added, "she was hatched".

Mr Barley had been babysitting the twins, two chubby little humanoids who were just at that age to be extremely irksome. Mr Barley, while being taxed to the max by the twins, had been debating sending a telex to the Director of the International Olympic Committee, Madame Tanette Dupleix, imploring her to cable him a nanny. Reflecting on this impossibility he decided to telephone somebody *somewhere*...in order to get some decent help for the kids.

"Heidi!" he bellowed.

No response.

"Heidi, damn it!"

The Swiss wife opened the door to the den and peeked out: "What *now!*"

"These twins...we *must* get someone to watch them! How can I possibly co-ordinate my approach to the Diplomatic Corps of Washington if I have to *babysit* all the time!"

"But Butch, that was our agreement, don't you remember?"

"What to Hell are you talking about?"

"You *know* what to Hell I'm talking about," she purred and raised her voice sensuously in order to entice him. Her short blonde hair did look most attractive, having just this morning been done.

"We never set it in *writing!*" Butch countered.

"Have you forgotten? I'm *Chief* of Protocol during the day...at the office...but at home...I'm *Director* of Protocol," once again she purred, then closed the door.

Fiendishly mad, Butch stormed down the hall to his den: "What is this nonsense? Are you crazy!"

Heidi just pretended to be organizing her G-List, but she was really rocking back and forth on her G-Spot, which she did frequently. This eternal *rocking* on her part could directly be credited to her husband, who had difficulty in keeping up with his wife's omnivorous sexual appetite. A few months ago, while crying in his beer with the visiting Junior IOC Member in Japan, about the extraordinary capacity that women have for multiple orgasms, the IOC Member, an astute descendant of a proud Samurai family, pulled out a couple of metal Benwah Balls from his dinner jacket, at an Olympics benefit at Park Avenue's Waldorf-Astoria, and handed them to Butch. "Insert these...into your wife...and you'll have *one* happy camper!" assured the Oriental. But my God, Butch soon realised that his wife had quickly become *addicted* to the Japanese Balls and, moreover, she refused to part with them...ever. And...they had *not* made Heidi a "happy camper", they had made her *worse* to control than before, a "crappy camper", as Butch now phrased it. So much for Japanese Technology!

Heidi refused to look up. She was almost at the point of orgasm.

"Damn you! You've fallen for that English *bastard*, haven't you! You're starting to act like *him*...going off conducting yourself like an aloof aristocrat when you're just born on a fucking *pig*-farm!"

"*Goose*-farm!" she said and rocked.

"Well...I'll put a stop to *this*, you know! Before long...*you'll* be throwing Balls, just like *he's* throwing *his* balls all about this town!"

Heidi just looked up and smiled like a Playboy pin-up. She now *was* having her orgasm, silently, like *all* her orgasms. She even had them at work, in Town Hall, she was so damned clever.

"You know, Woman, your *looks*...those polished good Swiss *looks* of yours...have gotten you in a *helluva* mess already here. Now: I'm telling you: Tone your own self *down!*"

"Or you'll *what?*" Heidi glared at her husband defiantly. "What could you *possibly* do that could bother me?"

"You should never have been given that job!"

"How dare you!"

"Dare? Dare had *nothing* to do with it! You wouldn't have crossed the Atlantic had you not been offered a piece of the cake!"

"To Hell with *you*! *I* was offered the job, by Madame Dupleix herself, and if it *weren't* for my allegiance to *her*, and *not* to you, *you*, Butchy Boy, *never* would have crossed the Atlantic...*either*! You'd still be *ciphering*...laying waste at Chaste...at that bank-desk!"

"At least I *paid* for my job! I didn't have to *sleep* for it!"

"So—you're *sorry* now you brought me here?"

"Your working with me has given me *constant* trouble! No other Executive has his wife working so closely *with* him!"

"Well...how would it look to *you*, Mister Barley, if I just pack my bags and leave? Of course, I'd run my pretty little arse straight to Madame Dupleix, you can be quite sure, and tell her every little mean thing you've done to me, including how you got me addicted to the Japanese Benwah Balls! How would *that* look, Butchy Baby, to the *other* Executives! You wouldn't have *me*...to rely on!"

"You're such a sick *cunt*! I *could* get along!"

"With whom? With...with...Ivor?"

"It might be quite...educational."

"Oh yes, his posh accent...his casual manner...his style...his twelve inch cock..."

"You're jealous of him *and* in love with him, aren't you, Heidi?"

"Hardly as much...as *you*! I've watched your *eyes*, Butchy, caressing Ivor's *balls*, each and every time you two are in the same *room* together! Men don't think women *notice*, but we see *everything*!"

"Well, since it does come down to this, I'm telling you now, Heidi, either you tone that Limey down...or else I shall have to take him *from* you!"

"You'd only be robbing him...from *yourself*!"

On that sour note, Butch, with what masculinity he retained, was shaking like a leaf. He turned to leave, wondering how in Hell his life ever got to be in such a sorry mess. He curst Chaste for ever sending him to Lausanne on that business trip! He never should have left Geneva!

Heidi, meanwhile, just smiled to herself. Her G-List, or was it her G-Spot, still was quivering with delight. Butch was such a *pussy*, such an *easy* man to control. Just a silly little gander. One just had to *catch* him...when he wasn't ensconced behind his desk. Let Butchy Boy watch the kiddies for awhile. It'll show him what a *woman* really goes through...

The Birch Burns Quick As The Pine

The Sun had set, and Lucille's island camp was warm as toast. Pine and birch logs kept burning in the fire, and before them, on a chaise,

Ivor and Lucille reclined like newlyweds. She hadn't revealed any more of herself than he had revealed of himself, but together they had talked for hours, about all sorts of things pertaining to both of them.

"You know, you mustn't let yourself get depressed over it all here," she pleaded. "The Adirondacks is truly the most beautiful place in this whole State. It's just...well, we're *all* going through an enormous amount of changes, due to these Games, and nobody really knows *how* to cope with it! I certainly don't...and I've been living here all my life! But I've just about thrown in the sponge, and at this point rather prefer to sit back and just see what's going to happen."

"They're certainly preparing for trouble!"

"Do you blame them? With almost every damned Ambassador from Washington here, not to mention Secretaries of Departments of the Government, visiting Ministers, Parliamentarians, Kings, Queens, Crown Princes and Princesses, and the President himself if there's not a war on then...can you *blame* them sending in the Secret Service, the FBI, the CIA, the Army, the State Police, the Local Police, the Anti-Terror Troops...just...in...case...?"

"It's all rather much..."

"Rather much?" she mimicked him his accent. "It's an effing Mongolian Gang-Bang! No *wonder* the poor locals are all getting drunk out of their minds every night! This tiny place has never seen such a conflux of people...ever! *Never* have so many wackos gathered together in this small inaccessible area in such numbers...as they forecast! It wasn't *like* this, back then, during the *other* Winter Games here! To suddenly go from 3,000 to 50,000 people per day...is asking for a non-stop nervous breakdown of all the facilities, all the capabilities, all the people's resources to withstand it! I've had nightmares, for months, about it all!"

"Hasn't anybody done any studies of the psychological effect all of this will have on the *people* of the region?"

"Oh Ivor, you needn't call in a team of flunkies with PhDs to see that the place already is *totally* freaked out! There's *madness* in the air...everywhere! Can't *you* feel it! God...*I* can certainly, every shitting time I walk inside that den, Town Hall! You can *feel* the insanity...coming *at* you...in horrid *ripples!*"

"It did seem a bit...pent up...when I first got here. But then again, I've been undergoing culture shock since the moment the jet landed at JFK. This certainly was some change...from Greece..."

"Greece, shit! There's *nothing* round here that's *Greek* about all this...other than that photo of that ancient athlete's statue shown on the cover of *The Olympic Charter*, but once you turn the pages you realise how *little* of the Olympian Ideal *has* been retained nowadays!"

"Why don't you *say* something about it then, if it bothers you so?" Ivor queried.

26

"Look I've been shooting off my mouth, in this town, for fifty fucking years, and still I shoot off my mouth, but *where* I ask you...*where*...has it ever gotten me? It drove my poor husband...to the daisy patch!"

"I'm sorry..."

"*Don't* be! His croaking had nothing to do with *you!*"

"What can I say?"

"Wait a minute..." and Lucille slipt into a private thought for a few minutes...that's right...maybe she *could* use Ivor for something *other* than a dildo. Maybe he *could* become her mouth-organ, as well as her sex-organ...

"What *are* you pondering?" Ivor asked finally.

"You said you sensed that this place had no *Spirit*, right, no *Soul?*"

Ivor sat still for a longer period than he wanted, wondering what she was up to. "You know the area...far far better than I...better than I *ever* can."

"I can teach you...a *lot.*"

"Why?" he asked, then smiled slyly.

"I'll do you a favour, Ivor..."

"If I but do...what?" was his response. "Sell my Soul?" he asked and laughed. "Mephistopheles lives! *Viva!*"

"Don't be a punk! Now listen: Where're you *living?*"

"Main Street. Five doors down from Town Hall."

"Do you *like* it?"

"My room's tiny, monastic almost, but it's comfy, and the people in the house are nice."

"Well...*I* like you, too, Ivor, and your company *has* been fun. But if I ask you to move *in* here...with me...this town would have a *cow!* They'd *never* stop talking, not that I'd *mind*, since at least it would get their gossipy *Souls* fired up but...I *think* we can put your valuable services to *far* better use..."

"How do you mean?" he asked, warming to the challenge if not precisely rising.

"Well, to me, you seem the *perfect* person to publicise the Olympian Ideal! Who else could get *away* with it...but an Olympic Gold Medallist, for Pity's Sake!"

"What? You must be absolutely bananas!"

"Bananas or not...I have a scheme. And *you're* now part of it!"

"How?"

"Well you just said how little *Spirit* the place's got! So—you'll put some Spirit *into* it."

"With what?"

"With *money*, of course!"

"But I'm practically broke!"

"Darling—you're missing the point! *I* shall give you...the funds,"

27

and Lucille beamed like a debutante being presented to a queen. "I'm *loaded*...and bored stiff here...so why *not* liven the zoo *up* some? What've I got to lose? I can write it off as a tax loss."

"But—what can *I* write off?" Ivor objected, feeling rather one for the weather.

"You can write off...*poetry!*"

"But I sodding well *can't* write...a rhyming *couplet!*"

"No matter—I can dash off a few lines, and together...we'll triumph! We'll set you up as a private non-profit corporation, just like The Committee, except *your* product won't be Bullshit, it'll be Soul!"

"Oh dear Zeus—please *save* me!"

"I *am*, you Idiot! We'll call it...Pindar Produce, Incorporated! No...Pindar...Productions...*Unlimited*...that sounds a lot more classy! By the tie-in to the greatness of Ancient Olympia, then we can promulgate preservation of the Olympian Ideal! We could even save the whole Movement, if not the whole damned world!"

"You're cracked!"

"No I'm *not*...damn you! Now you *listen* to me, Ivor Hefferon! This is...an offer you *can't* refuse! Do you...do you *really* just want to sit there and be bullied by that damned bitch Heidi, and her wimpy little dictator of a spouse-mouse, with their repulsive attitudes and ways? The pair of them...and a whole host of others here...personify *precisely* just where the Olympic Games have gone! Pierre de Frédy, or de Fredi, however it's spelt, the Baron de Coubertin, reviver of the Movement in 1896, if he came to Lake Placid now, from the grave, he'd just be appalled...absolutely horrified! I mean, T-shirts with raccoons' heads on them...I never! It's all just *publicity* hype, and it gives me *hives!*"

"Well...what can we do...to stop it?"

"Just be human, for a start!"

"That's asking for a lot!"

"Well...*is* it impossible...in this day and age? Has being human ...become passé?"

"You know...last night I had a weird thought. I was reading *The Olympic Charter*," Ivor began proudly, "when it suddenly hit me that the whole Movement was about to die."

"It *is* dying! Without *Spirit*...there is *no* Life! The Olympics *can't* continue like this...like some manifestation of the Living-Dead..."

"It is...just like a zombie now," Ivor muttered and shook his head sadly. "It's very frightening...that's exactly why it struck me that if the Games are to be saved, if the idealistic Movement of de Coubertin is to walk again in full health, then I firmly believe that no longer should the Games be allowed to be shifted about every alternate four years!"

"Bravo!" shouted Lucille in concurrence.

"Furthermore...to perpetuate the perceptions of the Greeks ...I shall even go so far as to state that from now on the Games *should* once and for all be *returned*, permanently, to Greece!"

"Perfect! *Give* them back! Right where they belong! The Greeks could certainly do *no* worse than *we've* done! And moreover, anything a *Greek* touches always has more life to it than if it's touched by almost *anybody* else! Look what happened to *Jackie*, when Ari married *her*! *She* became a *book*-editor!"

"I'll drink to that! Greeks have guts—and the whole world loves them for it!"

"Aside from the Turks!"

"Well that's an Asia *Minor* inconvenience!"

Lucille laughed. "Imagine Turkey's wrath...should Greece get the Game Games again *permanently?*"

"Well—it won't work if it's *not* permanent! Look at all the time wasted, the money wasted, the manpower wasted, the creativity wasted, the bitchiness caused, the political haggling caused, the international incidents caused...each and every four stupid years that some new place has to foot the bloody enormous bill, that never stays in bounds: It's *insane!*"

"It would certainly ease a lot of international tension!"

"Sodding Hell—the only reason the Games of Eld continued for a thousand years was due to one simple cause: Permanent location!"

"Put in simple words: The bastards *knew* where to go! I mean Placid here, St Moritz there, Sapporo there, Munich here, Rome there...you've got to be a goddamned millionaire, and I *am*, to keep *up* with it all...and *I* certainly can't! Ye Gods...those good ole Grecian days...would Lucille give *anything*...to have one of *those* models...for one of *those* statues...ravish the *bajesus* out of *me!*"

"One just did...out by *those* rocks!" Ivor mimicked, pointing.

"Say for example that the International Olympic Committee wakes up and realises that this once-every-four-years nation-hopping is self-destructive...and say that they do finally give the Games to any country *other* than Greece...imagine the furor *that* would cause?"

"If Argentina got it? Or The Congo? I'd love it to be settled at Tahiti..."

"You get my point," Lucille stated and stood to put another birch log atop the last one of the pines.

Ivor responded: "Greece founded the Games...and Greece should have them *back*. It's only proper."

"I agree! And from this moment on...Pindar Productions Unlimited shall strive for *nothing* less. I'll ring my lawyer to-night, as soon as we get back ashore!"

V.D. Castle

In Lausanne, Switzerland, where Heidi Barley was groomed to conquer the globe, the International Olympic Committee has been headquartered for quite some time. The building wherein Heidi worked for this august body is called the Château de Vidy, but everyone in Lake Placid always referred to it, in their inimitable rustic way, as V.D. Castle!

If Madame Tanette Dupleix ever knew what half of Lake Placid thought at any given moment, she would immediately have withdrawn the franchise from the town and given the Games to someplace kosher, such as Grenoble. The Madame, as you recall, was the Director of the International Olympic Committee, to whom everyone always bowed. At present, Heidi Barley, one of Tanette's former slave-girls, excuse us, one of her executive secretaries, was in her office on the third floor of Town Hall, or in European terms on the second floor, but whatever it was it was the top floor, and she was sitting at her desk trying to draft a tattle-tale telex to Madame Dupleix. This was not easy, as Heidi was really rocking back and forth on her G-Spot again, while faking that she was thinking kind thoughts about the twins as well as thinking unkind thoughts about the forthcoming visit of Sheik Abu Muhamed bin Kam-El, the International Olympic Committee Member in Saudi Arabia. Kam-El not only was a big man in the Olympian world, but he also was a tour de force in Washington, as his real reason for visiting America was to discuss oil prices directly with the President. So, of course, one could imagine the diplomatic ado over his pending arrival in Lake Placid. Rumour had it...he was already on his way...on the New York State Thruway...with a fleet of nineteen pink 1959 Cadillacs. He had been a great dévoté to both the late Marilyn Monroe and the late Jayne Mansfield, both of whom he had honoured for all time by establishing The First International Mansfield And Monroe Memorial Museum in Mecca. People never knew what he would dare to do next. In the jet-set, he was otherwise known by the correct pronunciation of the word Sheik (almost like Shake), and his lady friends lovingly referred to him as Sheik Rattle-N-Roll. Needless to say, the imminent arrival of someone so dashing, no matter if you were happily rocking on your G-Spot, would boggle anybody's telex!

Heidi was having particular difficulty with her English this morning, and couldn't think of another word for "confusion". The problem was over the whereabouts of another of the IOC Members, the uncle of the Shah in fact. Even imagining a Pahlavi coming *near* Lake Placid was enough to give the whole world heart failure, and thus the Chief of Protocol was trying to pretend that the town might *not* be in trouble by trying to think of some way to suggest to His Imperial Highness...*not* to come. But, thinking of the word "come", Heidi *did* come...

Obviously, to-day she was getting not one iota of assistance from her two assistants, Jason and Medea, as she liked to think of them. In fact, Maria actually could have *been* a Medea, so lustrous, so full, so magnificently wild was her flame-orange hair. Lucky Maria was everything that Ivor certainly was not. For one, she was a woman, and a shrewd one, and a local, and the daughter of a Board Member, so

30

there was nothing that Heidi could really do to bother her. Although...Heidi bothered everybody! Anything that Ivor knew about Placid...he got straight from Maria, and Maria had been a great buffer between the two taxing personalities of the Chief and her Deputy. But whenever Heidi wanted the two...they never were around. Either in the loo, or at the Xerox, or making the rounds on official business in some other building where The Committee had installed its affairs (and these others we'll turn to in due course)...Jason and Medea were always off doing their own thing. No—that's being harsh, Heidi thought and reflected on the constant barrage of tasks she always seemed to think up. At present, the two were performing one over at The Club, inspecting rooms which would be used in February by the International Olympic Committee, by the Presidents and Secretary Generals of the Participating National Olympic Committees, and by the Presidents and Secretary Generals of the six Participating International Sporting Federations. Keeping all those people and/or their wives and/or their mistresses and/or their boyfriends (boyfriends for both sexes) *content*...in a ramshackle old musty hotel that everyone believed would go broke before the Games...also could take one's mind off the proper wording of a telex, orgasm or no orgasm on your G-Spot.

Why in Hell every major decision had to go through V.D. Castle was another silly idea some *man* must have thought up, Heidi surmised as she bit the end of her pencil. Why can't decisions just be made *here*! But oh, that was truly sacrilegious pondering, and Heidi knew it! Hadn't Heidi herself been one of the toughest upholders of the V.D. Castle Supremacy Law, when she was nothing more than a jumped-up secretary for that very Château? If Tanette could only hear her now, Madame would beat Heidi black and blue! And how Heidi would *love* it!

"Heidi?" interrupted Eileen, a very alert and cocky girl from Boston who had intercepted a call that Heidi wouldn't answer. "Uh it's some character from the State Department."

"Who?" and for no reason at all Heidi giggled, as she would.

"He won't say. You taking calls?"

"Yes please," Heidi said and released the pencil. It wasn't the State Department after all, just some nobody from the State of New Hampshire...trying to get VIP Accreditation. "No—I'm sorry, it's *not* possible," Heidi stated and giggled, then hung up.

Just at that moment a memo was delivered from the lower floor to her, from her husband. It was classified, and stated: "MME DUPLEIX JUST TELEXED, SAYS PAHLAVI IS ALIVE AS FAR AS SHE KNOWS AND HE HAS RIGHT TO COME HERE. FORGET SENDING TELEX TO THE CHATEAU. I'LL ANSWER TO-MORROW."

Hmmm—no telex to-day to V.D. Castle, thank God! That freed the Chief of Protocol of one other laborious duty, so she sat there...rocking back and forth again...thinking...when it hit her...she'd have Jason and Medea come over to her house...after lunch...

31

Sheik Rattle-N-Roll

Sheik Rattle-N-Roll did in fact arrive in Lake Placid with a fleet of nineteen pink 1959 Cadillacs, much to the whole of the Adirondacks' astonishment, and everybody wondered if this were truly a premonition of things to come? It had already been a giddy day for The Committee, since Ivor had distributed five hundred invitations, printed at Lucille's expense, advertising his Halloween Ball to be staged in fact in only nine days. So, as everybody in all the offices of The Committee had dropt their work for half an hour and pondered whatever it was they could dream up to wear, Ivor and Maria had bounded off to inspect The Club and the Sheik's wheels had rolled ever northwards towards Placid.

Lake Placid was *not* prepared! Firstly, nobody in their right mind knew what the Sheik in question actually looked like, since how could you tell one Arab from another, all wrapt up in their headgear and all in nineteen look-alike cars! For security purposes the Security Department had been advised by the State Department that His Highness would *not* be arriving in the first or the last automobile, but in one of the other seventeen. In fact, the town did try to be ready, but since nobody knew what time the entourage would arrive nobody had actually enforced the authorisation to clear enough parking space for the said fleet, and you can imagine how much space nineteen Cadillacs take up! Parking space, one of Placid's eternal thorns in the brain, never seemed more of an international headache as this morning.

So—at ten o'clock the President of the Placid Committee had stormed into the office immediately beside him, into that of Judge Ronson. The President, the Reverend Arnold C. Courtney (who was blest by Divine Providence as being directly answerable only to God, which therefore made him not only universally respected and loved but also totally above everyone's suspicion), asked the Judge kindly to phone up the Police, who also were housed in Town Hall, but down on the ground floor, and tell them to clear at least one side of Main Street from the Olympic Field House all the way down to Administration Headquarters.

"But..." gulped the Judge, and choking on his pipe, "why don't you? *You* used to be the damned Cop!"

"Since I defected to Jesus, those guys never listen to a thing I say!" Reverend Courtney bellowed in his terrifyingly authoritarian *deep* voice, which always scared the little secretaries but which didn't even faze the wise old Judge. "I'm now a man of the Cloth—you're a man of the Gavel—and no matter *what* we both are, we've got a damned *carnival* coming to town. There's already more Press outside than all the athletes who'll ever be here come February!"

Ronson just puffed. The Reverend liked to be bombastic, and his nitty-gritty sense of humour was one of the few factors of sanity in the upper echelon. Responding to the predicament, thus, Judge Ronson rose and said: "I'll do it."

But the gesture already was too late. A State Trooper, positioned as a look-out atop the 90-Metre Ski Jump, suddenly walkie-talkied into the President's bleeper which he kept on his belt to say: "Holy Jesus—they're really here!"

"How many?" the Reverend inquired, a sparkle in his eyes.

"Shhh! I'm counting! Twelve. Fourteen. Fifteen...and...seventeen ...eighteen...oh my God it it's true! Nineteen pink 1959 Cadillacs *are* now heading past The Horse Grounds and into town!"

The Trooper, just a kid, sounded absolutely hysterical. As a local, obviously he had never seen anything so absurd in all his life, and the Reverend commented as much to the quick puffing Judge.

"Well...where're they parking?" Ronson asked.

"Damned if I know! It's *their* problem now!"

"Ring Heidi!" Judge Ronson said and laughed. "Let your Chief of Protocol work it out!"

"Could you see *her* outside...directing traffic?" the Reverend snorted and guffawed.

"She'd sure as Hell do a better job at it than Butch!" chuckled the Judge.

The Man Of God just shrugged and said: "Oh Lord—I'm just going to crawl inside my office—and wait!"

Pink Cadillacs were everywhere. They came up the incline of Main Street from the one traffic-light in the whole town, down by the Bobo Filling Station. You should've seen the natives, who had been warned by the radio all morning, rushing out of their homes and shops to see this Arabian hilarity. Passing the Sports Offices in the old Grand Union on their left, passing Jack LaHart's green warehouse for vending machines on their left, passing Mister Mike's Pizza Parlour and passing The Legion, then right there on the right stood the bastion of The Committee, Town Hall, and each Arab car pulled up, one by one, and honked a raucous and musical horn, which played a different 1950s show-tune!

The whole Committee rushed to the windows for this one. It even beat the day that Elsie The Cow came all the way to Placid to shoot a real-live television commercial smack on the lawn of Town Hall, which was a diplomatic visit of such otherworldly overtones that the poor Chief of Protocol, and the whole of the Protocol Division, did not even know how to cope with it. Everybody in the world knew who Elsie was...but how did one *deal* with her? What would one do if she *shit*?

But this case was utterly different. The Sheik was *not* a Celebrity Cow, but a *Sacred* Cow, given his rank as IOC Member, and he had to be identified anyhow, so Heidi was summoned (Pronto!) to do her duty and to stand beside the President's desk, to help him if any "international incident" might occur. Not, of course, that she could translate Arabic; Hell, she couldn't even translate *English*!

As we said, pink Cadillacs were parking everywhere, and many an Arab chauffeur looked mighty cross, not used to parking just anywhere! But that was just the best of it. The Arabs, need we divulge this information, were ninety-five strong. The local Police Force felt that there had been a Saudi invasion. But no Policeman dared ask why so many people were accompanying, if that's the correct word, Sheik Abu Muhamed bin Kam-El. Given that they all were *men*, it wasn't possible that the whole troupe was the Sheik's Harem, unless the Sheik was the biggest *queen* in the whole Middle East! Rumour soon spread, though, that these were his gambling partners, although nobody could verify the idle gossip.

If a possible Halloween Party could unnerve some people, imagine what a circus like *this* could do? People just attempted to grasp it all...but none of the Olympic employees could...and every so often one or two would wander away from the windows, as they kept wondering why were the Arabs queued up single-file in a snake that stretched all the way from the President's office and into the hall and out through the door and down two runs of stairs and into the ground-floor hall and out the front door and into the street and almost down to Ruth's Diner? And where...the Olympic employees were wandering to...was into the rest-rooms...in order to swallow sedatives, Excedrin, and to smoke joints in order to be better able to cope with it all...

"Hi!" Heidi kept saying to each new Arab who kept coming into the Reverend's office alone. Always alone, each Arab looked exactly like the next...and the Chief of Protocol, as well as the President, kept hoping that things *must* get better before the Games!

"Are you the Sheik?" Reverend Courtney kept asking till he didn't even bother anymore. "Well where in Hell *is* he?" the Reverend commented like a Cop, not very reverently, to Heidi at one lull between introductions. It was too unreal for words. Nothing was said but "hello", then a hand-shake, and then another Arab would come trooping in.

"Can I *go* now?" Heidi asked, getting tired of just standing there. She had to pee.

"No—keep your place!" were her orders, upon which utterance none other than the Highness himself at last entered, with arms outstretched for none other than Heidi Barley, who backed off and let out a terrified little giggle. She almost wet her pants. Outside she was shaking, but inside...her G-Spot was throbbing to beat the Dickens!

So for the next fifteen minutes, as the other members of the entourage paraded in then out, Sheik Kam-El kept babbling about this and about that, mainly oil, nothing of which either the President or the Chief of Protocol knew a thing, and yet they both just smiled amicably and listened politely as His Highness carried on quite oblivious.

Then, right there in front of them both, the Sheik knelt down on a little prayer-rug placed down by a servant, and prostrated himself in the direction of Mecca, to give thanks for his safe arrival Upstate.

IOC Blues

Two days with the Sheik had left Lake Placid's Olympic Committee bewitched, bothered, and bewildered, not to mention just plain boozed. Arabs were everywhere, just like in London, and Ivor had felt right at home. He had also escaped a daily tongue-lashing by Heidi, since the President had placed the Arabs onto *her* lap, and "allowed" her the responsibility of caring for their manly, excuse us, many needs.

"Well...he *is* a Member of the International Olympic Committee, so what can I do?" Heidi kept saying to anyone who would listen to her problems, and there were plenty, since all the Arabs, all ninety-five of them, wanted to see everything...but each wanted to see things at different times.

"I give up..." Heidi said and did. She did not report for work on Thursday morning, but stayed home. The Arabs had departed anyways, so had the dinners and the cocktails and the special VIP trips to the Olympic Village and to Mount Van Hoevenberg's Bob and Luge Runs, all venues of which the Arabs seemed to know more about than their overworked guides.

So there sat Heidi in her den in the cottage called Petunias, not even bothering with her G-List *or* with her G-Spot, and she was feeling dreadful and was daydreaming of a holiday back at the goose-farm, when up drove Jason and Medea, whom she had requested come visit her at home.

Ringed with books in the horribly cold den, gorgeous bound books that she and Butch had brought from Lausanne, Heidi just sat there, shaking, that is until the two arrived, at which point she braced herself and put on a good act that everything was fine.

"Medea I mean Maria," she began, not on a very good note, "did you do that correspondence?"

"Yes, Heidi."

"Did you send that telex to the National Olympic Committee of Saudi Arabia, thanking them for the visit of...well...just His Highness and not all those ninety thousand others?"

"Yes, Heidi."

"What about the rooming chart for The Club?"

"What about it?" Maria asked and flicked back a great amount of lovely red hair. Her poise, under fire, was grandiloquent.

"Have you started it?"

"No. You didn't ask me to," replied Maria cool, calm, and collected. How she kept her demeanour was an eternal wonder to Ivor. Redheads weren't supposed to.

"I did too ask you to, didn't I, Ivor?" Heidi asked with a whine, which meant she was ready to blow poisoned darts.

"I don't think you did. I didn't hear anything, if that's what you're asking." Ivor sat back a bit, pulled his coat tighter about his shoulders against the cold, and wondered what was her problem to-day. Maybe she couldn't locate her damned G-Spot! She certainly should have enough experience, in *that* direction, by now!

"Maria—I notice you made a mistake in a telex to Madame Dupleix," Heidi declared triumphantly.

"Oh oh," joked Jason, who poked Medea.

"It's serious!" stated Heidi quite flustered. "It's *never* done!"

"What isn't done?" Maria asked, again with the cool of a cucumber.

"You *never* should say that an IOC Member is an IOC Member *of* Mauritius, for example, but you *always* should say that he's the IOC Member *in* Mauritius!"

"Wonder if he's from Trinidad?"

"Oh Ivor! It's a mistake, and it's inexcusable! IOC Members do *not* represent their country *to* the IOC, they represent the IOC *in* their own countries! The important preposition is *in*! Don't *ever* forget it!"

"Maria, you've been a *very* bad girl!" Ivor said and laughed, while Maria just pretended to be taking the whole thing down in notes. Maria took *great* notes...all the time...but the cagey dame always threw them away, as soon as Heidi was out of sight.

"Now—I've got all this correspondence for you to do. Can you do it?" Heidi asked in a way which meant you bloody well *better* do it! Somehow, it was hard to believe that Heidi was only what...thirty-five...since most of the time she acted a cantankerous eighty!

"Now...I guess that's all, Maria. Ivor, can you stay a minute longer?"

"Sorry—I've got a hot date waiting in the next cottage," he replied matter of factly, not cracking a smile.

Heidi flushed, then carried on. "Maria, you can go now." So on that abrupt note, Maria did go, and left Ivor all alone with the viperess.

After making double-sure that Maria *was* gone, hearing the car pull away, Heidi began her attack, which obviously had been a-brewing since the argument with her husband some days before. Plus, the Arabs had undone her; not one had tried to rape her, much to her annoyance; and she just needed some psychological target for her own release.

Ivor though, not a stupid twit, realised instantly by the snake-like cold stare in her eyes, albeit covered somewhat with a phony smile, that this summons had been quite methodically planned...and obviously wasn't thought up solely by her alone. Ivor just could tell, instinctively, that Butch had something to do with it.

Ivor had long felt that Butch had been ignoring him, not out of any lack of time but because it was more basic, more Freudian, than that. In analytical terms, Ivor was a very virile man, and a threat therefore; moreover, the Olympic Gold Athlete was the man closest to Butch's physically attractive (if not mentally pleasing) wife. Ivor's constantly working with Heidi...had not gone down well with

Butch...who, it seems, would have been far more jolly having hired some gal.

So without more ado, Heidi began: "Ivor, there has been a problem I want to talk over with you." She looked wicked. Even though he couldn't really care, Ivor still felt victimised inside for even having to suffer the audacity of this woman who now was talking to him as if he were a tiny child. "You're throwing a party..."

"So what?"

"Well it's come to my attention..."

"What has?"

"Well...it's not an *official* party..."

"Nobody ever said it was."

"But you've passed out invitations this week to everybody who works for The Committee!"

"So what?"

"Do you think that's *right*?"

"Why're *you* fretting. *You're* not invited."

Heidi could not believe her ears. Her mouth dropt open a mile.

"My *friends*...are dying for a good-time, so I'm going to *give* it to them!" he defended himself vigorously. It was futile trying to talk to this Swiss vixen about the philosophy backing the whole party venture, since she obviously never had come close to a volume of ethics in her life. Moreover, since she had hit home and gone for the meat on a personal level in all this, the Runner would have to stick to things personal, too. "My party is *none* of your business," he stated.

That said, the woman changed her tactics. "About that incident in the Field House..."

"Which one?" Ivor asked cockily.

"That's what *I* want to know...since there've been so *many*."

"What in Hell are you *talking* about?" Ivor stated and glared at the devious woman.

"*Two* incidents, for example: First, you introduced yourself to the IOC Member from Mexico..."

"Wrong. I introduced myself to the IOC Member *in* Mexico. Remember the preposition is *in!*".

"Well who in Hell said you *could* introduce yourself to him?"

"Who in Hell says I *can't*? The bloke was *standing* there, and then asked *me* a question."

"You should've just answered him, and walked away."

"Rubbish! Who in Hell do you think you're talking to? Have *you* ever competed...in an Olympic Games?"

"You know, Ivor, IOC Members don't want to know *you*! They don't want to know anybody *like* you! Even if you *are* a goddamned Olympic Gold Medallist! They just want to be *special*. They just want to be left *alone*."

"So why in God's Name did Butch ask *me*...to have them

publicly introduced...if they all, according to you, just want to remain *anonymous?*"

Stumped on that one, Heidi proceeded aimlessly anyways. "In Protocol, we're just supposed to do our *work*, and let all the *others* feel special. *You* should comprehend that...*you've* had VIP treatment...in days gone by!"

"Your insulting behaviour knows no reticence, does it, Heidi," Ivor said with cool disdain, and glared the bitch in the eyes. No, thought the Athlete, it's *you*, Heidi, who's craving a bit of limelight, with nobody else in sight. Ivor chuckled inside, but remained silent.

"Well...what *else* have you got to say for yourself?"

"Absolutely nothing," the man replied.

"What about the way you talked to poor Mrs Winchell?"

"Poor Mrs Winchell was a *crook*! She falsified a theft of Government Property, and involved another Government in the theft!"

"You should have been kinder!"

"Where were *you?* Why didn't *you* go handle it?"

"I have my *own* duties!"

The two just eyed each other, with mutual hatred.

"And...I'm your *boss*...so I'm telling you...keep a *lower* profile ...from now on."

"Thank you for your gentility," Ivor lied. "We haven't really talked...since the first day that you hired me."

"I'm terribly busy."

"I'll try...to toe the line," said Ivor rather wickedly, "but then, internationally, I'm known for being good on my toes *and* on my balls..." he added as he scratched his balls so that Heidi would watch every move he was making, "...of my feet."

Pretending not to notice, but having a spasm in her G-Spot, she began to play with her nails. "You're an *alien* here, you know."

"So are *you*."

Silence.

"I can have your papers revoked."

"I can have *your* papers revoked," was his reply.

"That will be *all!*" she snapt.

As Ivor was standing and putting on his coat he stated: "Even a blind man could see that *you*, Heidi, are *jealous!* I've made *more* friends, in the few short weeks I've been in town, than all the two years *you've* been here. In fact, every person you've *alienated*...is a friend I've *made*. Think...about *that* one...a little while." Ivor departed, with not another word said.

Rocks In The Air

The Luge Run blew up that Friday. Some worker had put the wrong stick of dynamite beneath the wrong outcropping of bedrock on Mount

Van Hoevenberg, and boulders just went flying everywhere. It was not an incident that the Press did cartwheels over, since the Press never did find out. That's to say that the Press Department of The Committee knew of course, but didn't let any other people in the media get wind of it.

Jack Sennett, the head of the Press Department, had certainly not believed his secretary, Eloise Witty, of the famous Witty Believe It Or Not Wittys, one of the most famous household names of any family in the whole of North America, a family that had been making people laugh for generations, and Jack firmly told rich Eloise so.

"Well—it did too happen!" Eloise held her ground militaristically. "I just talked to the guy that lit the fuse!"

"Was anybody killed?" Jack replied, obviously on the look-out for a good scoop.

"Oh how could you! The Luge Run is *ruined*! Isn't that bad enough...with all the things that've gone wrong!"

Eloise was no dummy. All the girls hated her, since she came from such an illustrious clan, and since she had more connections than anybody in the whole of North America, but she still was a secretary and a damned good one, too. She was notorious for being known as a good deflector of questions against any nosy Reporter snooping about the Press Department for a bit of inside dirt. Her family, in their famous column, hadn't, for ages, been talking about the *truth*...for nothing! So Eloise just sat there, totally in the right, behind her desk, and looked perky as all-get-out with her lovely strawberry blonde straight hair brushed back sternly from her forehead. She also was known for her lovely ears.

Jack, not to be outdone, decided to take her up on this one and muttered: "Look Eloise, you've *never* been wrong...but there's always a first time!"

"Well...take the van and go scout for yourself!" Eloise dared, and which is precisely just what Jack decided to do.

Hurriedly, the Press-Boss descended the one floor to the street and jumped into one of the official Olympic vans, one of those blue and white Ford ones seen everywhere running all those many official, unofficial, and unauthorised errands. Once, one wayward employee had even been spotted in one in Nome, Alaska, and when questioned by a trustworthy Trooper he meekly replied: "I only was sent to fetch some snow...since *The Farmer's Almanack* predicted none for February." It was a rather agreeable lie, if not a white one.

Now Luge...is a sport about which so few people know a thing that most folks don't even know that the lugers themselves don't even know, since the Luge Run itself occurs so suddenly that it's over even before the lugers know it's happened. But Jack Sennett knew all there was to know, and then some, about Luge. It was his all-time favourite sport, so when he heard that the Run had been blown up...well would *you* have believed it? Then he thought of espionage...maybe some Nazi goof from Innsbruck, who wanted the Games returned to Austria, set the fuse? As he drove past the Ski Jumps then headed down the rustic road towards Hoevenberg, it occurred to him that this indeed was a story that *needed* to be hushed up...and hushed up quick! Turning right off the highway towards the mountain...Jack didn't see any smoke rising which was a relief but which raised his suspicions all the more. Maybe this was all one big practical joke being played upon him by that never-erring Miss Witty!

If this weren't all he had to think about to-day...what with a visiting delegation coming at one o'clock for lunch from Tass's main headquarters in Moscow! When he thought of *that* one, as the look-out tower of the Luge Run loomed in sight, poor Jack panicked and wondered what would happen if the guys of Tass found out about *this* ...why Moscow would have a field day blowing it out of all proportion! Lake Placid, in direct competition with Moscow anyway for her hosting the Games this coming summer, had not been getting good copy by the Reds as it were. God—hadn't it been a nightmare that the public, for the opening of the new Field House, had *booed* each time that the Russian figure skaters came onto the ice...and the nasty fans shouted out loud: *Go get 'er, Igor, hey Igor!*

It seemed every single problem of The Committee always fell right on poor Jack's lap. Protocol had a piece of cake in comparison...what with all its arse kissing...and the Sports Department was on holiday till February...just waiting for the safe arrival of the teams...but Press...why Press got the shit, from everyone! Press had to tell all the little truths and all the little lies...Press...just one little department...had the whole world's *rotten* opinion to cope with! What a nightmare!

Jack never felt appreciated for all his hard work. He should've stayed with CBS in New York and never bothered moving north to Placid. His blood pressure had gone up, his temper had flared, and his diet had vanished.

Parking the van...suddenly he saw it. Oh my God it was true! Miss Witty *hadn't* been taking the mickey out of him after all. There was the poor Luge Run...in shambles!

Workers from all over the mountain, which has the combined Bob and Luge Runs almost snaking down the slope together, had convened at the damage-site like flies and everyone was in shock. Thousands and thousands of dollars of havoc had been caused...just by one bloody big rock.

"But..." Jack stammered as he fell in line with the rest, gawking at the tremendous stone, squat in the middle of a wrecked trough of cement. The thing had hit right at one of the curves. "How'd it happen?"

"Went flying through the air!" some worker said and laughed.

"It ain't funny!" Jack sighed. "Can it...can it be *fixed*...before the Games?"

It certainly didn't look it. As if a tank had blown a great gap through one whole side of the curve where the luge sled would have to come sliding...there was a lot of work to be done.

Suddenly, in the midst of all the construction workers, Sennett spotted Madonna, head of the Luge Department.

"Frank, come here!"

A husky Silver Medallist at one of the previous Winter Games, Frank Madonna was the perfect man to talk to.

"Think it can be fixed?" Jack asked.

"Nothing to it...damned shame ain't it?" Madonna replied.

"How'd the goddamned stone *get* here?" Jack wondered.

"See up there..." and Frank pointed to a spot where there was a bulldozer further up the slope, "that's the new public access route we're putting in and...well...they've been blasting for weeks without trouble ...but you know sometimes things backfire and..."

"Is there anyplace in Placid where things *haven't* backfired?" Jack asked with a grin.

"Least no one was hurt...that's the main thing," Frank offered. "A worker could've been killed."

To Jack, sequestered in the rat-trap of Town Hall, just being out here on the mountainslope was a refreshing experience, even if it was just to see the rubble. The air, the casualness of the workers, the true hard work being demonstrated, the manliness of it all...all these things were far more appealing than the wretched feline office environment at Administration Headquarters. Here...in the woods...you could almost grasp what the Olympics were all about. Jack certainly envied the heads of the various Sports Departments their closeness to the essence of the Games. The people who worked for Sports...were so very lucky, he felt, as he turned away from the destructed Luge Run in order to leave.

"Where're you off to...ain't you sticking round?" Madonna asked in a friendly way. "Amble on down to the canteen...we'll give you a cuppa...to warm yourself up."

Frank was a good guy, and Jack really liked him, but he said rather sadly: "Off to the grind again...you know. Have to hurry back and brief myself on the visit of the Russians."

"Russian *athletes*?" Frank asked interested, as he of course mainly thought of sports.

"Just some boring Reporters the fuck-sticks in The Kremlin're sending. Buncha assholes from Tass." On that politically incorrect note, Jack turned and retraced his steps to his official Ford van.

Fifty Pumpkins, Fifty Pillars, Fifty Pies

Halloween fever, that bizarre manifestation of American madness which haunts the Yankee imagination every All Souls Eve, swooped upon Lake

Placid with the vengeance of an Irish banshee. Ivor's Ball was a confirmed success, even before the doors ever opened.

With no one to compete with, given that nobody in his right mind had decided to stage a Ball at all, the thought of getting all dressed up to let loose...had captured everybody's imagination. The Committee in the dumps anyhow, such a psychotic release was just what everybody needed on the thirty-first of October. Ivor and Lucille, their combined forces under the aegis of Pindar Productions Unlimited, had decided to go all out for this one, to use the opportunity to drive home once and for all the fact that the place needed some *Spirit* injected into its tired veins.

Lucille *had* got ahold of her lawyer, a very charming man, but one who happened to be a character in town, one who was universally, how shall we put it, "wondered about". Nobody knew where Attorney Turney got his seemingly limitless funds...but was it really anybody's business? Lucille certainly didn't mind, and all her chosen friends were controversial anyhow...

Attorney Turney, besides being in private practice, was also a Member of the Board of The Committee, and Lucille decided to call on him under the pretext of needing to discuss the wisdom of dumping her embarrassingly huge block of AT&T stocks on the New York Stock Exchange...just for a wicked female Halloween whim to see what it would do to the US Economy...but she never quite got round to that one and chose instead to ask Turney about his *own* holdings...a certain warehouse in particular which he owned being a perfect site, she emphasised, for a little Ball...

Never being one to ignore one of Lucille's whimsicalities, Turney just scratched his stubble, as he hadn't felt like shaving that morning, and said: "Anything you want...you can have. Just talk it over with Mercurio...and I'm sure everything will go off fine."

That being that, Lucille immediately trotted over to see Mercurio. Now...before we get carried away, we need one more geography lesson: Holiday Harbor, aforementioned, was a world all unto itself, a grand dockside conflux of edifices that housed some of the most fun places in all of Lake Placid, the New York State Labour Office notwithstanding. It housed, beside the Labourites, Sassafras, which must be mentioned here with the full honour it warrants.

Sassafras was the watering hole of local watering holes when it came to "action". By that we mean that Sassafras was a Disco and a Bar, dockside in an old boathouse that inevitably drew scores of thirsty dancers each and every night. More things happened, for the better, each night, at Sassafras, than ever happened, for the worse, within the whole of the Lake Placid Olympic Committee. And...that's saying something!

In the same building, but right on the floor directly above the Disco, was one of the town's plusher restaurants, Holiday Harbor proper. And in the office immediately to the right of the entrance to this posh place was where Lucille found Mercurio.

"Mercurio Darling," she boasted and strode into the Dickensian room full of packing crates and what-not. "How's life been treating you...since you *quit!*" Mercurio was one of the lucky ones, who had decided that he couldn't take it anylonger at The Committee, but who was fortunate to have been offered a good enough job to quit!

"Marvellous! Everyone should get away! I feel *human* again."

"Well Darling, you've only been away a month, and it's plain to *me* you're not suffering from Cold Turkey. My...look how clear your complexion's become! But then...when *haven't* you been gorgeous!"

Mercurio was such a handsome Cuban that all the women just creamed their jeans over him. And now that he was managing the Harbor enterprises, he had plenty of opportunities to cream on and inside the ladies' jeans.

"Well Darling, I'm here to bother you a bit, you know."

"Such is my purpose on this Earth!" he said with the courtliness of his forefathers, marquesses from the very old Spanish line of Sanchez-Perpiña, who had owned vast sugar plantations southwest of Havana.

"Well it's about that boatwarehouse over there. You see, Turney's just said I can use it for a Ball for The Committee..."

"A Costume Ball?" he perked. Such an idea fit his Latin sensibility.

"Exactly. And I've got a brilliant young British boy to stage it for me...you know...that Gold Medallist in town...Ivor Hefferon...Heidi's new Deputy?"

"Poor fellow. I hear he talks *back* to her...and that she *loves* it!"

"Isn't there any gossip you *don't* know? I'll send him round..."

So that's how it began, and reams of people got involved and jumped on the bandwagon for the fun. The staff of Sassafras, under the infectiously creative direction of Miss Judith, all rallied round to the ok of Mercurio Hidalgo Sanchez-Perpiña y Mendoza-Brillo. So the Ball took shape...in a flash.

Pindar hired five professional design artists from New York to fly up and turn the sooty marine warehouse, filled with all sorts of gobbledegook, into a true place for Inspiration, Contemplation, and Orgy, not necessarily in that order. Given that the party was a Disco Ball, a DJ area combined with a stage was set up to look like the famous Athenian Portico of the Karyatídes, the Maidens on the Akropolis itself; and given that they had recently been taken down from their stance of over two millenia and stored in the Akropolis Museum, it was a political statement to recreate them, even if only in papier mâché, in Lake Placid. The rest of the warehouse was turned into Ancient Olympia, and this needs some explanation.

The Greek motif was chosen, because (Rumour was circulating) the Government of Greece had recently decided that it would, after years of debate, turn over to the IOC a sizeable bit of acreage of the country, so that a Permanent Games Site could at last be established on Greek soil. But as yet, this was only hearsay, even though a lot of tongues were wagging about it.

For the Ball, fifty Doric columns, of papier-mâché, were created and painted gleaming pentelic-marble-white and installed to form an oval, simulating the ancient athletic Arena of Olympia. Also, and rightly so, they set off the boundaries of the dance floor. In between the pillars, and set back against the walls, fifty round café tables had been positioned, each of which sported a pumpkin that had been cut into a grimacing face, like some Dionysian character of Comedy or Tragedy, of someone interesting on The Committee. After the first few faces had been cut, Lucille bitchily complained that they'd have to resort to *other* organizations...for interesting characters!

For fun, Lucille had hired a bouzouki band to come up from Astoria in the Big Apple, so that repetitive interludes of Grace Jones and Donna Summer could vie with arm-linked dancing right out of *Zorba*.

"This's *just* what we've needed!" Lucille commented jubilantly to a rather amazed Ambassador Levitt, who came wonderfully dressed as a jaded Indian Maharajah with full dangly earrings and all.

But beside the pillars and the pumpkins, the pièces de résistance, everyone agreed, were the *pies*! Now, for you who have not spent time in the U.S.A., a pie is a curious edible dish of which Americans are particularly if not inordinately fond, as they come in all shapes and sizes. Pies almost always have crusts, and many times *two* crusts, a bottom one and a top one. In this case Lucille had racked her brains trying to think up something humorous and at the same time emphatic enough to state her aims for going to all this expense. But then, one evening a week ago, it hit her as she was dining at Doctor and Mrs Harper's, when her hostess Rebecca had just mentioned the cliché "you are what you eat": It struck Lucille that *that* was precisely what she wanted to get at! She would serve her guests something... *meaningful*...to eat! And the kinkiest thing she could think of, as a satire on the All-Hallowed All-American Apple-Pie Old-Saw, would be to serve her guests...*pie*!

"Pie? At a Ball?" Mimi Tiny, dressed like Eleanor Roosevelt, gasped as she gazed down at this *thing* that had just been placed on her café table. "What the *Hell* is *this*?"

Someone, already drunk, spat: "Maybe Ivor finally *butchered* Ole Heidi...and is serving her ass up...*minced!*"

"Then I *definitely* ain't touching it!" Ms. Tiny responded. "I wouldn't eat her asshole *alive*...let alone *dead!*"

Everyone gathered around each table and peered. One per table was a pie...some cream pie, some coconut, some banana, some butterscotch, some tapioca, and all covered by this gooey white frosting into which some artist had drawn, in appropriate colours, the five intertwined Olympic Rings. Well, if *that* wasn't enough to get people talking and to clear the dance floor, there was also some unidentifiable *cipher* inscribed beneath the Rings.

Ivor, acting as Master of Ceremonies and in full evening wear, since he was impersonating the Duke of Windsor, announced into the microphone, which Mimi Tiny had just vacated (she had, in fact, done a truly stupendous rendition of "Embraceable You" on top of the piano, all alone up there with her accompanist...in eerie blue light...placed strangely on a ledge beside the papier-mâché Karyatídes), that each of the unidentifiable ciphers was a letter from the Greek Alphabet. Then Ivor finished his monologue by saying: "And when you all eat pie...you should think about what the Olympic Games are really *all* about..."

This part of his speech was greeted by cat-calls, booes, and whistles!

"Now now! You'll all be pleased to know that each pie has been injected with *steroids*...to make you all better personifications...of the Olympian Ideal!"

Cheers now, this time!

"Furthermore...the contents of these pies...taste like no Official Olympic Sponsor you'll ever eat!"

Hip Hip Hurrah! Corks flew...as drunks started guzzling the champagne. Ah...till the DJ played "Sing, Sing, Sing", the finale number from the famous Benny Goodman concert recorded live at Carnegie Hall in 1938, the most moving Swing song ever put to tape, the Spiritual Revival Party went on...and on...and on...till all fifty pies were assimilated into everybody's system, till all fifty pumpkins somehow vanished into the hands of departing guests, till all fifty pillars toppled over onto the dance floor...in homage to the columns of Ancient Olympia...which so very long ago had been shoved down...to the dust...down...to their all too ignoble repose...

The Jump

Now that it was November, with only three full-fledged months before Opening Ceremonies, the pressure started increasing logarithmically, as if working for The Committee was a mediæval torture instrument bent only on squeezing out all its employees' brains.

To relieve the agony, and the doubts each person felt about how the whole thing was going to work, the President felt that the Executive Manager should give every department a pep talk. So, a week after the party a council was convened down on the ground floor, next to the room reserved for Judge Ronson's trials, and in this meeting room the luminaries of the Protocol Department had gathered. All of them.

Well...*not* all of them! Of the Division of Protocol's nine different Departments only four were represented, since the others had offices in other buildings and it was too much of a hassle to summons them, too.

Pep talks were certainly Burt Dubczek's forté. Burt, a very handsome middle-aged man with a lovely wife, was Czechoslovakian, though nobody could believe it. Well his father was from the Old Country anyway, so Burt had always striven to become as American as he possibly could, and he did. He was as American as Andy Warhol, also of Eastern European extraction. But of course...Andy...was a genius...whilst Burt...was just...Burt...though he *was* the quintessence of your corporate executive, neat, personable, and a very tough nut to crack. Rumour had it that he'd been hired, only a year back, by The Committee, for the unrealistic figure of half a billion dollars, just so he could come in with his monetary expertise and save the Games. Rumour also had it that he, in fact, *wasn't* going to save the Games, in other words *not* keep the whole of Upstate New York from defaulting, and that the half a billion dollar investment in him was money down the toilet. Rumour *also* had it that should the Games actually break even or (imagine) make a profit, Dubczek would get one percent of the profits which, if that's a million dollars, is not bad profits.

For all the macho-man's charisma and awesome responsibilities, and for all his reputation of having been the marketing whiz who so successfully packaged that modern necessity, *Castroturf*, he wasn't related to the Dubczek of Czechoslovakia whom the Russians knocked out of power in their illegal invasion of 1968, and neither, for all his reputed sex-appeal, was he related to Burt Reynolds. Nor was he related to Castro. But all the girls still loved him, anyway.

"I've only called you here to-day to tell you we're doing fine," he began as twenty employees glared at him incredulously. Everybody wondered what he was *on*.

"I've cancelled the Games!" he stated dryly for the comic value but, as nobody laughed, he carried on with his prepared notes.

"No...we're really on top," Burt began in a more serious vein, at which point the door was opened abruptly by someone from Press who shouted: "Burt! An employee's just committed *suicide* off the Ski Jump!"

"You're...joking," he stated and tried to carry on.

"NO! I'M SERIOUS!" the girl shouted, horrified. Then she fainted dead away.

"Dismissed," Burt declared ashen-faced.

"Well...who *was* it?" everybody tried asking the girl, as soon as she came to, but she just broke down and cried. "I don't know...they won't tell me...but I think...think I know..."

Well that broke the pep rally up to be sure. Burt, after trying to make light, told Ivor (and before his two superiors, the Barleys): "You threw a great party, and we all appreciated it." Then he turned to the Barleys, after Ivor exited beaming, and said: "Easy come, easy go. Watch that Gold Medallist. He's dangerous. You know who's in on this god-damned *Greek* nuisance with him?"

"Of course," Butch declared proudly. "We have our spies."

"Keep them. That *Lucille* whore...with an ally like *her*...our Olympian can do *nothing* but wrong..."

Having said that, Dubczek turned to leave, to return to his office in order to find out who just committed suicide. The Boss-Man's top floor of the building was in a flurry. Just off the Legal Department, all the lawyers and their secretaries were in a huddle discussing the awful news.

"Well...who *was* it?" Burt asked, hating to fish for such an answer. He was bracing himself for the worst, envisaging some poor person tormented enough by life to sneak to the top of the highest man-made concrete Ski Jump in the whole Northeast. The image made him shiver.

Chief Counsel for the Games, whose office was right next to Dubczek's, came and took the Manager aside. "It's not an employee after all...so relax! The Cops just rang and said...it was *Schroder!*"

"You're kidding!"

"I know...a *Board* Member! But just thank our lucky stars it wasn't some secretary or something...*that* would've just been the end!" Dick Docteur, the Counsel, said honestly.

"Come inside my office," Burt commanded, and the two vanished very suddenly behind a closed door.

"Now—the important thing to remember—and God knows the Press will capitalise on this one—is that such a death is *not* the fault of the The Committee!" Docteur declared.

"But what made the poor bastard *do* such a horrible thing?"

"He hadn't had the nerve to come to the meetings for weeks! You know he went bankrupt this summer!"

"But everybody rallied round him!"

Docteur shook his head. "It killed him...the man had seen his life's business fold...and with it went all his pride. The Bank tried to salvage him but couldn't. This damned *inflation* was what did him in!"

"The same inflation that's turning this town in a monster!" stated Dubczek with dismay. "Sometimes I wish this place never *bid* for the Games!"

"All the natives feel just the same! The place never will be the same...come March."

"Poor Schroder...and he was one of the ones who pushed and pushed and got the Ski Jump *built!*"

"Well...what should we do now?"

"I guess...what *can* we do? I'll tell Stephanie to order lots of flowers, a spray from the Board, some from the Staff, and...from my own office, too."

"Don't take it so personally...Burt," Dick said to try to be of consolation.

"But...it's going to get worse...before it gets better."

Wakes Are Never Easy

Lucille McSorley was hit particularly hard by Schroder's death. Mourning his loss as only one local for another can, as one person with faults sees but ignores the faults of another and loves the person in spite of his faults, so Lucille truly pined with this loss of her friend.

"Poor Schroder," Lucille lamented to Ambassador and Mrs Levitt in her home after the funeral was over. "I loved that man so much...he was such an underdog!"

"I know, poor fellow," sighed Grace Levitt. Grace, very slender, epitomised a diplomat's wife in all her statements, gestures, and decorum. But beneath all her propriety, there was the heart of a sensitive little girl there...beating and beating and suffering for everybody who had not had the chance to all the advantages in life that she had had. "I felt so badly...three years ago...when he lost his wife."

"That's what started it, wasn't it?" asked the Ambassador, who was standing before the picture window which opened onto the rustic balcony. The Lake now...truly looked forbidding. No hint of the Sun could be seen, and the whole sky was a mess of grey and turbulent storm clouds. Whiteface Mountain completely was hidden from view.

"Yes...Doris died...but I don't believe that he ever really loved her," Lucille stated and shook her head. "Before my husband passed away...the four of us used to see a lot of each other...before Lake Placid changed so. It was nice then...thinking that the Games would be so fun..."

"Oh...they still *can* be," Grace interjected.

"I hope they *will* be," her husband concurred.

"Someone was saying that it would take a top psychologist to come here and figure it all out," Lucille said sadly. "But I don't think that even dear Margaret Mead, God bless her Soul, could've successfully analysed all the tribal patterns at work here...of which Schroder's death was indicative."

"How do you mean?" the Ambassador was curious.

"Schroder..." and Lucille choked up, "...he told me something awful...he *did*...the week before he died...I mean just *last* week!"

"What...did he say?" Grace asked weakly.

"He was drunk! I certainly didn't believe him! He came barging in here, what was it...seven nights ago, and thank God I had no guests. He started to cry. Such a big man, you know, it just just broke my heart..."

Grace reached for her friend's hand...and held it kindly.

"The poor man...he started talking about our childhood...you know...we all grew up together here...of course there was the same snobbery...it's always been a *private* place, Lake Placid...but you know back then, times were different and...and the locals *knew* each other better. His..."

Lucille could not go on. Grace tried to ask her to stop.

"No! He...he said...his mother, may the Lord keep her, I loved Anne Baxter so much!"

"Lucille," said Grace softly.

"Anne...as you know...used to run the same shop Schroder ...inherited and...when inflation hit him so bad...the dry goods shop...it wasn't a flashy restaurant like mine and...oh dear God I feel so much the blame!"

"*Stop* this now, Lucille. Quit torturing yourself. You did what you could! And far more than so many others!" the Ambassador stated sternly.

"I could've *saved* him...but didn't!"

"You bailed him out more than once! You even offered to buy the shop from him, didn't you?" Grace volunteered.

"He refused—and yes I did help him financially, many times! But in the end, when the shop just couldn't be supported any longer, and instead of facing up to the reality of another proprietor having his family business in Main Street...well...he got rid of it!"

"He was a Board Member already by then..." mused the Ambassador who was considering another side of the situation.

"That's probably what did him in!"

"But...but how?" Grace wondered, truly bewildered.

"Oh don't you see, Dear?" her husband asked. "It was just because he *was* on The Committee...with everybody else who appeared so successful and able to cope with it..."

"That he just *couldn't* cope!" Lucille declared. "What *other* Member had gone bankrupt...*gambling?*"

"Such a shame. Everyone tried to help him..." Levitt stated gravely.

"But nobody actually could!" Lucille responded. "The nest-egg he had from the sale of the shop should've stood him in good stead for years...but just last week when he came here....he told me how he really felt. He said...he said he was going...he was going to teach us *all*...a lesson!"

"Oh dear Lord!" Grace sighed and patted Lucille's hand.

"But do you think anybody will *listen?*" Lucille ended the conversation with the truly disturbing epic question.

One Man's Lesson Is Another Man's Lie

The death at the Ski Jump seemed to cast an irremovable pall over everybody in Placid. Poor Schroder...he had been a gambler...but he had gambled with Life and had lost. Something was so indicative of his demise...for the whole Adirondack region.

On the other hand, the death spurred the majority of the townspeople on. When Death travails...temptation either gives in to it or does fight it, and in this case many people firmly decided to fight it, to work ever harder, to prepare themselves and their town ever better, to raise the opinion which the horrid US press had painted to the country about the town. It certainly was no easy fight, but likewise was one truly worth fighting.

"Well what the Hell are we *supposed* to do now...sit back and *croak*?" Lucille lamented to Reverend Courtney in his big Town Hall office. If there was anybody in the whole of New York State that Lucille really loved and respected it was the good Reverend, whom she had counselled so often when he was un-ordained. Few knew that it had been she, in fact, who had urged him into the priesthood, since she felt that his empathy for humanity, as a Policeman which he was, would be better served saving people's Souls instead of their Bodies.

"Well—Schroder's going like he did didn't help our publicity!" the Reverend boomed so that all the people outside his office could hear him.

"I just want to say, Arnie, that you gave a very touching... oration...for poor..."

"Well...it came from the heart!" the Reverend said sadly. "And let *me* tell *you* this, Lucy...you just *keep* up what you're doing. Your weird Pindar kick has raised lots of hackles, but as I always said as a Cop: *Piss* on the dog with the hackles: Act like a *cat*! So don't you *dare* give up. Ivor's a good kid...a little bit too exotic, maybe, for this crazy place, as a *Summer* Olympic Gold Medallist, for this crazy place, but he too does fill a need, so we've *got* to keep him aboard..."

"If *Heidi* doesn't shit-can him."

"Oh leave Heidi to me! You just do what you think best here...and I'm telling you now, Lucy, you've got *my* full support!"

"Really, Arnie?" and Lucille flew to the President and gave him a great big sloppy kiss.

"Of course...you gotta admit your *Greek* infatuation *is* a little queer..." he joked. "But—queerness balances everything out."

"You really *think* so?"

"I *know* so. It's my job, at the top here, to be *objective* about all this goofy stuff I see going on below..."

"I don't even *dream* of envying you your job at all..."

"Don't give it a thought. Somehow—God gets us through. The *Lord* won't ignore the prayers...of Lake Placid."

"But how many people...are *praying*?" Lucille asked honestly.

"There's a lot more *good* people out there, hoping and praying with all their hearts, that everything will go just fine, than the damned Press ever will let us admit!" he stated with conviction.

50

"Too much love and labour have gone into this...right?" Lucille queried as a new idea sprang fully armed into her head.

The Reverend just stared at her...and laughed. He saw that cagey twinkle in her eye. *"Now* what're you cooking up?" he couldn't help asking.

"How much money *does* this wretched thing need...from now till February...to keep it all alive?" she wondered, deep in thought.

"Haven't the wildest notion!" the President stated proudly. "Not one single person has *any* idea!"

"The stupid figures *change* every week, don't they?"

"Well damn it—prices go *up* every week!"

"But Arnie...why don't we just leave it to *Lucille*...for a few days..."

"How do you mean?"

She smiled mischievously. "Because...I've just thought up a way...to raise the Committee's prestige...as well as to put some moola back in her pockets..."

And on *that* arcane note...Lucille exited from the President's office, feeling like she had the world on a string.

The Gala At Carnegie Hall

Besides her many friends, Lucille had many more enemies, a large percentage of whom worked for The Committee. So Ivor was delegated by her to do the legwork...in this one.

"Ivor Darling..." the fastidious lady declared as she came upstairs in Headquarters to visit him. She sat on a rather cold metal folding chair that sat beside his desk for visitors.

Looking about to see if Heidi were there, which she was but inside her own office around the corner, as opposed to out in the middle of the warren where her Deputy's desk was stuck, Lucille then crooked her finger provocatively in order to have Ivor bend towards her to hear her Confession.

"Now...this is *absolutely* confidential, my Boy," she dictated with the pomposity of a Cardinal. "But I have just been down in the President's office, discussing situations beyond our control, and yet this new idea came to me." She had fires in each of her eyes. Ivor had never seen her so childishly animated.

"Now what's going on inside that devious mind?" he asked wickedly.

"We're going to do a *Gala!"* She emphasised the last word as if it were gold.

"Oh...well...everyone's been badgering me since Halloween: So what're you scheming now, they're all wondering. What *is* it, then, that I should tell them?"

"*This* one will knock their socks off! We're going to rent Carnegie hall, and do a Grand Olympic Ideal Gala, right there on its famous stage!"

Ivor could not believe his ears. "We're *what?*"

"You heard me right. I said Carnegie Hall," and she whispered the venue's name. "It must be kept a total secret!"

"But...why *there?*"

"Why the Hell *not* there? It's the best damned stage in the whole of this Empire State! That's why..."

"But..."

"None of your...buts! Just promise me *one* thing."

"What's that?"

"That after I leave here you'll ring the Booking Office of Carnegie and find out what dates are available. Then talk to the House Manager and find out the rates we can charge for the different tiers of seats, and what surcharges there are for staging a production."

"But...what *kind* of a production, God!"

"Oh...an *easy* one. You can be the MC..."

"What!" Ivor shouted out loud, causing secretaries in all directions to fire him dirty looks.

"Shhh...you'll get us *both* fired! Listen...what with your plummy accent, you're a *natural* for the stage!"

"Bugger off!"

"Bugger yourself!" she laughed. "No, I'm *telling* you, it's easy. It'll be a Gala Literary Evening, with Orchestral Interludes! It'll be in two Acts, the first emphasising the contribution to the World's Consciousness by Ancient Greece, and the second emphasising the contribution to us by *modern* writings, all of which can be enacted as *theatre* pieces, you know. There's *plenty* of material to draw from for *both* Acts!"

Lucille was hot now. Her mind was racing like a comet. Ivor looked purely dubious. "How can this *possibly* be done?"

"Where's your goddamned Limey imagination!" she snapt. "God, it's so easy it's dumb: We get Helen Hayes to come on and read Homer; we follow her with a modern writer, Norman Mailer reciting Plato; that *alone* would draw the curious in New York! Then we put Colleen Dewhurst together with Angela Lansbury, doing a scene from O'Neill's *Mourning Becomes Electra*....and we play 'The Olympic Hymn' and composed 'Fanfares' and all sorts of rousing music between Stars! It would be fabulous. People would talk about it for months! And you...*you're* a draw...you're a damned Gold Medallist yourself!"

"So...*that's* my homework?"

"You always complain how *bored* to tears you are here! So this will give you something to do when you're not logging in what stupid ambassador wants to come to town for a freebie."

On that note Lucille stood up. Her atrocious prune mink looked wonderful on her. It was cut very boxy, in the new Paris fashion. She was wearing a very vulgar canary yellow shot-silk cap on her head, and had its tasteless yellow net pulled firmly to her lips. What a vision! She whispered on departing: "Now remember...not one word of this to anyone or we'll *both* get screwed blue."

"That could be fun!"

"Leave the dirty work to me. Certain people in The Committee will have to be broken into the scheme of things...little by little. And the less they know *now*...the better we are *later*. Especially not...you know who..." and she pointed over the wall to Heidi's office.

"Don't worry!"

"See what Carnegie says...and I'll ring up a girlfriend of mine on the Social Register and ask her to chair a Society Committee. Adelle just *loves...getting involved!*"

Lucille vanished and Ivor immediately set to phoning Carnegie Hall, and was absolutely flabbergasted when he heard the Booking Office reply: "But yes! We've been *dying* to do a benefit for the Olympics, but nobody's dared approach us!"

"But..." Ivor could not believe it. "But...you *will*? Truly?"

"Where're you from?"

"London."

"Sounds it! Who's speaking?"

"My name is Ivor..."

"Not...Ivor *Hefferon*...the Gold Medallist? God—I'm a Marathoner—but not of Olympic calibre, of course."

"Yes, I'm the Runner," the Athlete admitted. He always felt embarrassed when confronted by his own fame, especially when, as now, the other party lapsed into stupefied silence.

"Well...we've got a couple of dates free...in December...and some in January. What'll it be?"

"January," Ivor chose off the top of his head.

"You know...they're doing this big benefit at Radio City, too?"

"Are they?"

"That's the middle of the month, so if you take the thirty-first of January you'll have no competition."

"Super. Can we reserve that?"

"I've got three other bidders on hold, but I think, one runner to another, and for the *Games* of course, we can bump them aside. Ring me in three days' time, so I can firm it."

So, Ivor had three days' reprieve, time enough to plan in more detail with Lucille, who was so hopped up about the project that she could hardly eat that night. She celebrated the success of the idea by taking Ivor to the Alpine Cellar restaurant, where they both had delicious Wiener Schnitzel and Mexican beer. The restaurant, cozy with crisp German efficiency, was at the edge of town. Wouldn't you know it, that evening, the Barleys also arrived after the pair were seated. And since the waitress placed them side by side, conversation was in code.

"Well Adelle's *gonna*...and reams of people she knows..."

"Stars?"

"Darling...she *owns* Stars!"

"Her idea though?"

"A director?"

"A problem?"

"Hollywood. She's ringing there to-night."

"Who?"

"Some young up-and-comer."

"Stage?"

"Stage *and* Screen."

"Expensive?"

"She'll get him down."

"Put him up."

"In *her* house she'd *lose* him."

"Park Avenue?"

"Where else."

Heidi and Butch, all ears, couldn't make heads nor tails of it. Every now and then Lucille would turn and smile queerly at them. Ivor's back was to them, so that was all right.

"Adelle sees *Gloria* all the time."

"Swanson?"

"None other."

"Gloria wants to help out."

"Super."

"That's a draw if *anybody* is!"

"I want Raquel."

"Beatty for me!"

"What a Green Room!"

"Just the Parquet alone..."

"A thousand and twenty seats..."

"Hundred bucks a head..."

"That's ten thousand..."

"And two hundred right there!"

"Not bad. With a full house..."

"A gross of roughly..."

"One three oh, oh oh oh!"

"Oh my!"

"Minus say forty G's..."

On hearing the word "G", Heidi squirmed in her seat.

"Production costs."

"Leaves ninety profit!"

Heidi and Butch looked up but still couldn't figure it out. They did *not* like the sound of things, though.

"Who could sneer at that?" emphasised Lucille, as she smiled once more across the way.

"So then the Initial Deposit..."

"Two thow...that's peanuts."

"Think they'll front it?"

"The Devil only knows!"

Hearing "Devil", Butch turned to Lucille and winked, which just about made Mrs McSorley gag on her Schnitzel.

Truly in a snit, two days later, Lucille picked Ivor up in her Jeep after work and drove straight to the Hilton for drinks. She didn't say a word till the martini was in her hand, when she blurted: "The bastards *have* screwed us!"

"How?"

Just then, into the lounge waltzed Heidi and Butch, who seemed to have a knack, lately, for appearing wherever Lucille and Ivor were together. Just like two nights before, the Director of Protocol and his scheming wife were placed only feet away, at a nearby table and, just like two nights before, the pair were all ears. This time, Lucille didn't flinch and spoke as loudly and as boldly as she usually did. When Lucille opened up her big mouth, people's mental tape-recorders usually went into over-drive. "First," she asked and grimaced at Heidi, "did you ask Carnegie to send up the contract?"

"It's on its way, as they've booked us for the thirty-first."

"Well—I had a long long long session, with you know whom today!"

"No—who?"

"With Clark Gable!"

"Burbank, you mean?"

"Yes, damn it, Burbank!" she spat extra audibly.

Lester Burbank was head of the Olympic Marketing Division, and a great pal of the Executive Manager who was not a great dévoté of Lucille.

"What happened to Dubczek?" Ivor wondered. Lucille had arranged this morning to see Dubczek in order to ask him if he would ok fronting the two thousand dollars needed to secure the date for Carnegie Hall.

"Dubczek floored me! He did the unbelievable this time..."

"How's that?"

"Well if you're staging a *barbecue*, you talk to a chef. If you need *money*, you talk to a money-man, so I went to Dubczek! But he just sat there, in his plush chair, and said it was *not* a decision he could make, that he was passing the responsibility to say yes or no to a Carnegie Hall Gala, which's *not* some Roni The Raccoon publicity stunt I might add, onto his Marketing Director! I absolutely, for once, could *not* believe my ears!"

"But what does *Burbank* know about...Galas?"

"Not a goddamned thing. So—I stormed over to the Convention

Building and barged in on him. He received me, I might say, with no little apprehension."

"Do you know him well?"

"Know him...why," and Lucille paused melodramatically to gaze right into Heidi's left ear, which was cocked, "it was *I* who introduced more corporations to *him*, many of which *have* become corporate sponsors and *have* contributed millions of dollars just to keep this fucking place afloat...why *all* I had to do was ring up my New York broker for a few *names*..."

"So, at least Burbank *saw* you?"

"He sure did...*see* me! He saw me at my *best*! He cowered and cooed: 'Lucille, I'm leaving to-night for New York, and I'll look *into* it'."

"Look into what?"

"Why, into the economic viability, of course!" Lucille snapt, so immensely perturbed that even B. Donald Barley winced, whereas Heidi just rocked contentedly on her insatiable G-Spot. "I mean, how *dare* him! *My* contacts in New York are solid *gold*, and don't need *any* nosing about by whiz-kids from Puke City Of The Poconos!"

"Well why don't *we* front the two thousand?"

Lucille flared like a bonfire: "Absolutely not! It's the *principle* of the thing. They're all *gaga* over the thought of having a grand high-class *do* at Carnegie Hall, but they only want to cash in on all *our* hard work and not put a single *penny* into the proposition! It's disgraceful! They want a *do* do they...well...I'll give them *doo-doo*, that's what *I'll* do!" And she scowled viciously the Barleys' way, so that both of them turned their awful faces.

"From *their* view, is it a *risky* investment?"

"What's two *G's!*" shouted Lucille loud enough to deaden all gossip in the whole place.

Hearing *that*, Heidi gushed right through her panties and set her skirt sticky with female jism. She'd worn her Benwah Balls to the Hilton, since Butch had been forced to return them to her.

"Nothing," answered Ivor with a leer, as he gestured his head in Heidi's direction so that Lucille would notice that the Chief of Protocol had a great big wet spot on the rump-end of her skirt. Heidi was rushing off to the lady's room, embarrassed to tears. Her Benwah addiction was totally out of hand. She was now ready for Rehab!

Unseen to Butch, Lucille gave the fleeing adversary the finger, adding: "Precisely. *Nothing's* what they'll get! Ivor, you wouldn't *believe* how much money I've poured into this organization already!"

"And got nothing for it?"

"That's right! Just insults! And I'm goddamned fucking *sick* and *tired* of it!"

At that moment, some lout accidentally spilt a whole vodka gimlet onto Butch Barley's lap, causing him too to rush to the rest-room.

Lucille went on the warpath. Two days later, she was out for blood! Burbank returned from his foray in New York and reported: "It's too much of a risk. The production costs are too high, even with a full house. We simply cannot risk it."

"Not even for a possible ninety thousand dollars? Not even to promulgate the positive factors of the Olympian Ideal?" Lucille could not tolerate such thoughtlessness.

"That's right, Lucille. Not even for the good ole Olympian Ideal..."

So, nothing is *exactly* what the Lake Placid Olympic Committee got. A glorious event, which had been organized in the matter of a week, went down the drain like a piece of shit. But Ivor at least had a choice souvenir, a contract from Carnegie Hall, a sad memento of what a spectacular evening it could have been...

Sour Grapes Become Sweet Vino

It was the last week in November and still there was no snow. With only two full months to go, nerves were jangling all over the place, and many people just couldn't take it. Everyone in town by now had heard that Lucille and Ivor had almost got Carnegie Hall, but instead of harassing everyone about it, both just clammed up and forgot it. What...was the use? With a barrage of other things to tax her, Lucille in particular received great consolation from her friends. To be sure, Lucille had fallen in love.

"But that's *insane!*" a girlfriend snapt, this best mate in particular being Tricia Wymms, who worked at the Olympic Village in Ray Brook a few miles out of town. Lucille had driven there to pick Tricia up for lunch at the Belvedere restaurant in Saranac Lake, but the two had ended up in Tricia's office for hours, talking. Tricia was Lucille's late mother's goddaughter, so the two had always been like sisters. Lucille was only one year older, fifty-four.

"But...you're robbing the cradle, Lucille!"

"I could care less! He *fucks* like a stallion, and what *more* do I need at my age? And it makes me feel good, in *all* my orifices, not to mention in all this business bullshit with The Committee. So...if I can spend my money on some goodlooking young *thang*, I'm *gonna* spend it! Wouldn't *you* like having sex with an Olympic Gold Medallist...*again!*"

"But you two're a full-fledged *scandal* now!"

"Where?" asked Lucille, with the disdain of a Princess Royal.

"You've *always* had a weakness for Limeys!"

"The British have the biggest, juiciest cocks in *all* the world."

"How do *you* know?"

"Tricia...take it from me...I've sucked every single one!"

The girls laughed uproariously, and slapped hands.

"Well...since your mind's on DICK...I guess you won't care to see how our Olympic Disco's shaping up..."

57

"Not unless you've got something well-hung there waiting!"

"God you're awful to-day!"

"*You* should take a young lover...*again*! How can you *stand* it, cooped up here, surrounded by all these *studs* doing construction work all day long, and not getting a *little* on the side now and then?"

"Listen, Honey, you know I *ain't* no Virgin Mary. I get my *bit* on the side...*on* my side...now and then...don't you worry!"

"Well *I've* never felt healthier. It's all that juicy young sperm...keeps an old hag like me nice and oiled!"

"You're making me all hot to trot—you're *rotten!*"

"No—I'm just being goddamned *honest* with myself. So there!"

"Well...just in case you're wondering...everybody's *talking!*"

"*Let* them. They can *all* kiss my ass!"

"Doesn't it *bother* you?"

"In *my* rebellious phase of life, menopause, I *ain't* pausing on men, my paws're all *on* men! I wouldn't mind if the whole son-of-a-bitching Board of goddamned Directors for the whole *fucking* Committee *came* into my bedroom and taped me shooting a *blue* film!"

"You're shocking!"

"Oh don't give me that horseshit!"

Both ladies laughed. There was nothing, absolutely nothing, they couldn't talk about.

"How do you like working here?" Lucille wondered, meaning the Olympic Village.

"It's really *getting* to me...being behind two rows of prison fences all day long. Minimum security clink this's supposed to become... later...why it's fortified better than Fort Knox *now!*"

"Let's break outta this joint then, and go get some fresh air!" volunteered Lucille.

Tricia chuckled: "Only if you take me straight to some massage-parlour, where I can get myself oiled to oblivion!"

So the two gals left Tricia's office in the Administration Building of the site, and couldn't help but look about at the austere beige brick walls, the barren lot in the middle of an Adirondack forest that had been cleared of pines to house a couple thousand athletes for a fortnight. The place, with a freezing cold November gale whistling macabrely through the forest at the other side of the double ring of security fences, seemed as forbidding as a looney-bin on the Moon.

"Oh well," Lucille sighed. "At least no terrorists could ever get inside *this* slammer!"

"Yeah," replied Tricia as she was sliding inside Lucille's Jeep, "but that's just what they all said, about Munich, too..."

Lucille crossed herself and started the engine. "Let's pray to God...everything just goes faultlessly...according to schedule." And on that note, the two "dirty broads" left the isolated Olympic Village behind.

Fart For Fart's Sake

It was now the first week in December. Needless to say, the Carnegie Hall fiasco had not died down with the turn of the month, and Sophie Loeb-Lowenstein in particular took a sudden violent dislike to both Lucille McSorley and Ivor Hefferon.

Sophie, straight (but not sexually straight) from the cultist, anal, oral, immoral, insufferably bitchy, venal, and just-plain cock-eyed, not to mention just-plain cunt-eyed, Art World of New York City, had been hired by The Committee, two years before, to co-ordinate its Arts Festival, about which something now must be said. Sophie, therefore, had relocated straight from the West Breast Artists Co-Operative over near the Hudson's gay whoring and/or cruising district, which doubled during daytime as Manhattan's meat-packing district (same thing!). Given that Sophie had been born in the West Village, inside a yellow-cab no less, since her mother always was rushing from gallery opening to gallery opening via taxi, Sophie had grown up with a thoroughbred "artistic" *attitude* that brooked no nonsense and that was on the go, if not on the make, all the time. She fit right in, here in Lake Placid, with all the other monsters.

In the Village, Sophie was on first-name basis with all the trend setters of Gotham, bar none, and with those who wished to be trendy, so it was rather anti-climactic for her to reside in such an out of the way *boîte* as Lake Placid in the first place. About forty, Sophie was also on first-name basis with all the intellectuals and prime-movers of Tokyo, London, and Paris, so moving to the Adirondacks had been like going to live in Hoboken, New Jersey. Anyhow, Sophie thought it all would look good on her résumé, after the Olympics were over, which she was praying would be soon, plus, when she left New York, she was still under the influence of the aforementioned Olympian Ideal, so she said, and to which she, as a Photographer in her own right, had said she'd tried to emulate. Nobody ever believed a word she said!

Sophie did have balls, there was no doubt about them, castiron mothers, but she also had shown that she had less of the Olympian Ideal than she had of the crooked ways of Greenwich Village imbedded in the reticules of her testicules. Such back alleys, when it came to Art, were pretty basic. So as not to lose face with her international artistic constituency, and so as to seem eternally *avant* enough to them in her aspirations and endeavours for her Arts Festival for Lake Placid, Sophie felt compelled, every step of the way, to choose only those artists and their creations considered *worthy* enough by New York and by its fickle if not totally incomprehensible proclivities. So, aside from her own very dedicated and biased staff, Sophie had made very few true friends in town, since she had alienated just about everybody in her albeit righteous crusade to embellish Lake Placid with only the most *worthy* works of Art.

This book does not have time to air all the views about this one, nor to explain the well-worked-out philosophy of Ms. Loeb-Lowenstein, nor to diagram for the Reader the very controversial pieces of Art in question, but one in particular must not be overlooked, as it was impossible *to* overlook it. The work in question was a sculpture, and sat on the left lawn before the Old Olympic Arena which had been built for the 1932 Games. It was on this site that Sophie ran into Ivor, one rather warm Wednesday morning, or should we say Ivor ran into Sophie?

The Deputy Chief of Protocol was on his way with a pile of rolled blueprints under his arm, heading towards the Convention Building Annex to the Arena which had been built some years ago along the Arena's right flank. This wing was where the aforementioned Marketing and Volunteers Offices were housed, and it was to the latter that our subject was aiming. But—Sophie, on the upper sod-level where the said sculpture was being installed, shouted down to the fellow as he was passing.

"Ivor? Can I have a word with you?" she hollered, trying to be audible above the traffic in the street and above the jack-hammers noisily plodding away on the façade of the Old Arena, which currently was undergoing a huge and very time-consuming restoration, one hoped *finished* before the commencement of the Games.

With some ado Ivor climbed the twenty foot incline to the statue's site, and asked what it was Sophie wanted. The statue, by the way, looked like it was made out of tinfoil, and was basically this: A bent metal structural frame of one welded piece (the piece was huge, what, forty foot long?) and to this bent piece five metal-ribbed lobes had been stuck.

"Like it?" Sophie asked curiously.

"What in sodding Hell *is* it?" Ivor wondered.

Sophie looked at him as if he were an utter philistine. "It," she began, "is a sculpture."

"What's it called?" he asked."

"*Homage To Sonja Henie,*" she stated proudly.

"Looks like *Sonja's Balls*, to me," Ivor commented dryly. "All five of them!"

Sophie, turning away, did not deign to laugh. Turning back, she muttered: "You know—you have a most *impudent* attitude! You sound just like these foolish *locals!*"

"Well..." he returned, "...*Sonja's Balls* look a bit better than some of the *other* rubbish you've strewn around town!"

"You, an Olympic Gold Medallist, do not know *what* you're talking about," she snapt.

"I know wot I like. And this rot ain't it!" he volleyed, in a particularly cruel Cockney accent.

"You people in the United Kingdom...it's too bad you're living in the artistic backwater now."

"Are you attempting to exercise some *wit?*" he answered.

"This's serious, Runner!" Sophie was on her soapbox now. "And...and who do you damned well think you *are*...anyway!"

"Wot's it to ya," again he replied with a Dockside tone. "'N who d'ya bloody well think *you* are!"

"Look you...I took a *flogging* due to you!"

"Show me your *welts*, or...is *this* one?" Ivor asked and pointed up at the sculpture. "Or maybe that's one of your *whelps?*"

"Why—this will be *gorgeous* when they turn it on!"

"Yeah?"

"Yeah! It's going to shoot water and throw flames!"

"My my. Sounds like someone I'm talking to!"

"You bastard! I'll *get* you for that! You know—you had absolutely *no* right to go contacting Carnegie Hall like that—and you know it!"

"Say what?"

"Who *authorised* you, huh! That slut *Lucille* you're dipping?"

"Temper temper."

"Forget it, Medallist! Anything at all having to do with the *Arts* here in Placid is *my* bag, you hear!"

"Wouldn't touch your *Farts*...with a gas-mask on!"

"Stay *off* my turf!" My—was Sophie hot.

Ivor just laughed aloud and turned away from both Sophie and her looming sculpture, leaving her to cogitate on the freedom of expression and on the ingrained attitudes people have against things that they don't consider...Beauty.

Pindar Reborn

At the end of the first week of December, that weekend, both Lucille and Ivor sat down to map out strategy. Seated in her huge house's huge living-room, and before the inquisitive eyes of the enormous stuffed moose, Lucille decided to pull out all stops, since to her, *war* had already been declared.

"They're out to *get* us, and that's that!" she stated in mock paranoia.

"Well...what should we do, set a few traps?"

"God—I've got a few *bear* traps in the cellar that could kill a tank! I'd *love* to leave a few about town..."

"First...give me a nice big..."

The moose didn't flinch a love-muscle as the two spent the next hour doing rude things upon the couch. Anybody could have peeked in, since not a shade was shut.

"Now...where were we?" gasped Lucille, pulling her silk Korean peignoir back about her.

"I haven't the foggiest..." Ivor sighed weakly.

"Did I ever mention...my newest idea?"

"Oh no..."

"Don't you oh-no me! This one, I believe, we discussed *weeks* ago!"

"Weeks ago, I was in better health," again Ivor uttered weakly.

"Your balls, too."

"That's the problem!"

"Now listen. We've got to write an *ode*, and write it to-night."

Ivor only groaned and rolled over on his side.

"Listen! Pindar Productions has to keep the Spirit *up*! If we sag."

"We can't remain erect all bleeding day!"

"We don't expect you to! Just...most of it! Now listen: I'm going to wage a campaign...to wake these old hills up!"

"How now, Brown Cow?"

"Money, of course! Have you forgotten? So...we *have* to write an ode...and then I'm going to pay for full-page ads in all the area's newspapers, but that's not all, the *succès de scandale* won't be here locally ...but will be New York!"

"Not another bloody Carnegie, I hope!"

"Save me—where's your *Spirit*?"

"Between me legs...and hanging down past me knees!"

"Men! Absolutely *useless*!"

Grunt.

"I'm going to pay for one of those letter-to-the-editor-type things they often publish in *The New York Times*, you know, which they run if enough people sign and if it's for a controversial enough cause."

"Such as?"

"Such as the *Olympics*, you Goof!"

"Oh."

"Do you or don't you want to save the Olympic Movement?"

"Of course I do," Ivor pledged with his hand over his heart.

"Then get your balls in gear and start transferring that macho energy of yours down there *upstairs* into your brain!"

"Only if you help me."

"When *haven't* I helped you?"

Next thing, Lucille sprang off the couch to her wall opposite the moose, which was one big bookshelf. She looked through her collection of Loeb Classics and found Pindar, which she quickly ran to the couch. "Now...we'll just look and see what he said about the Games...in the old days."

"I know my Pindar," Ivor objected, thinking back to Westminster School and the fights he used to have in Little Dean's Yard.

"I don't give a damn if you can recite him in Sanskrit backwards and blindfolded!"

So the two protagonists sat themselves down before the moose and took a good long look back into the Pagan Past, at the words of the

immortal Poet who died the same year the Parthenon was completed.
"What year was that?" Lucille wondered.
"Four thirty-eight BC," Ivor replied.

Finding a legal-pad in the bathroom, and knowing neither why nor when she left it there, Lucille took pen to hand, as did Ivor, and together they tugged verbally for the rest of the evening, in order to produce some ode that was not only meaningful to the Present but which also could be seen to have drawn its inspiration from the Past. No mean task, this wasn't just going to go into the school gazette, but would be published as an advert in the prestigious *New York Times*, for a price of course, so the thing had better be extraordinary.

Near midnight, or was it well past, the two finally had grimaced and bit their pens enough, and dropt the legal-pad for the last time. Halfways intelligent, the first draft was quite a combined effort but not a totally dismal one. It was about two athletes, one from Russia, one from America, both Speed Skaters, who met and wanted to become friends but who found this impossible in the end...because of the political problems that such friendship would provoke. It was a sad story ....how the Russian had been turned into a machine by his State, had been made sick by an overdose of steroids before having left Moscow for Lake Placid, and how the American had had just the opposite experience, never enough money with which to compete or train properly, although he hailed from the richest country on Earth, and how his family had sacrificed what little they did have so that he could qualify to become that sacred word...Olympian.

Having spent the night there, and rousing at a civilised hour next morning, the poem didn't look bad at all, so the two revised it again, then Lucille typed it up. It was long, sixty-three lines, nine stanzas of seven lines each, but that would look good in a whole-page advert in the *Times*. The poem was really quite forceful, and ended on the note that the Olympics *are* for the Athletes...and that the Games *must* be given back to Greece...

Even if everybody hated the thought, at least the statement and publication of it would get an enormous amount of people talking. And no matter what came out of that...it couldn't be all for the bad.

So, next Monday morning, Lucille drove round to all the local newspapers, with Xeroxes of the text, then the next day took a flight to LaGuardia, to buy space for that succeeding Sunday's *New York Times*.

D-47

Well if shit didn't hit the fan! God, you would've thought somebody published a dirty novel and not an ode, so much commotion erupted over a few scraps of verse.

In the local weeklies, the *Lake Placid News* and the *Lake Placid Reporter*, the public saw the results that Thursday and Friday, respectively. For the larger *Adirondack Daily Enterprise* published in Saranac Lake, a daily, the ode appeared that Saturday. In the *Plattsburgh Press-Republican*, an even larger daily, it appeared likewise that Saturday, as it did in the even larger daily, the *Watertown Daily Times*. So, the whole of Upstate New York got the message that weekend.

Of course, the penultimate publication in America being *The New York Times*...well...anything published there takes on an æthereal quality all its own...and when the locals Upstate heard that what they'd just read was also in a full-page advertisement in New York City...people started making for their phones!

"People who never even heard of Pindar..." stated a rapaciously angry Director of Protocol, Butch, to his being-chastised Deputy, Ivor, "...now are saying the most outrageous things about that crazy organization you've got going with that Lucille McSorley!"

My, but Butch was mad!

That Monday afternoon at four o'clock, Ivor had been requested to come into the boss's office "for a moment". Well, the moment turned out to be a bloody hour of a harangue you would've had to have *been* there to believe! Vituperative was hardly the word!

Butch, looking a bit under the weather, as usual, had a shit-eating grin on his face that said: *Hi, I'm Napoléon!* Well, the only resemblance was in the height factor, of course, which didn't look any higher by Butch's slumping lazily down into his plush chair, obviously a gesture which could only mean: *Hi, I'm Napoléon!*

"I shall first tell you what's on my mind," declared the omnipotent one. "If I had wanted you, an Olympic Gold Medallist, to have thrown parties...I would have *hired* you to do so. Do you get my point?"

"No."

"Two: Had I wanted a Deputy to throw *galas*...in New York City...I would have *hired* one to do so. Do you get my point?"

"No. For that matter, for a measly two thousand, The Committee *might've* had the chance to make almost a hundred!" Ivor retorted, wanting to belt the bloke one.

"That's *not* the point."

"Terribly sorry."

"I don't think you are, or you wouldn't keep acting like you do."

"Frightfully apologetic."

"Then there was your introducing yourself to the IOC Member from Mexico."

"No, that was the IOC Member *in* Mexico," Hefferon corrected. "The important preposition, in these instances, is *in*."

"You know, in Protocol we're supposed to be seen and not heard."

"So why're *you* talking *now*?" Ivor replied and stared the man in the eye.

"You know, Hefferon," he began then paused, "I'd like to tack your shoes to the floor."

Appalled at the vulgarity of such a remark, Ivor just stared at the man who obviously was having some trouble focusing on reality.

"That's right...the way you go about The Committee...bothering people who have an enormous amount of work to be done!"

"People *like* me, you know. I can't help it if I'm socially acceptable to an echelon of this town to which you aspire."

"Such as Lucille McSorley?" Butch asked wickedly.

Ivor said nothing.

"Your private life..."

"Is my *own!*" the Olympian manfully stated. "It's none of your *fucking* business."

The two just stared at each other. And more and more nonsense of this was repeated, Butch dipping into the past like a retired naval officer fishing in a polluted river and only bringing up used condoms. The whole thing...was just very low-class.

Thus, at the end of such a stupid tirade, Butch decided to go for broke and announced proudly, with a puerile smirk on his mousy face: "I have no other alternative...no...wait a second..."

"I've got all day." Ivor said and yawned.

"Yes—that's what I wanted to say," and Butch reached for the previous day's edition of *The New York Times*. "Did you write and publish this garbage?"

"Do you know how long it would take me to write *all* the material you're holding up," Hefferon remarked to the whole copy of the newspaper, "let alone *publish* it, too?"

"Your British sense of humour is simply fiendish! How *dare* you work for The Committee and even *think* that the Games should permanently go to *Greece!* Why—that two-bit country just had a *Junta* a few years ago! Why—this damned ad's now a major international diplomatic *incident!* I've had *dozens* of calls about it just this afternoon!"

"Pro or con?"

"You know...this has almost got you fired! But on the other hand...I've never seen such a capable person for *detail* as you are."

"Many thanks."

"Lucille, obviously, *she* must've paid for this...this Pindar nonsense!"

"The Olympic Movement...is *dying*, Butch."

"Due to people like *you!*"

"*Don't* you ever—I say don't you *ever*—count *me* in your *own* bunch! *I*...have *won* my Olympic Gold...fairly and squarely. But what've *you* ever won...fairly...*or* squarely?" the Athlete said powerfully and glared the Director right back into his chair. The elder turned away.

"You listen to nothing! I'm forced to tell you that I'm *demoting* you...from Deputy Chief of Protocol to Administrative Assistant..."

Ivor was burning inside and was aching to jump over the desk and squeeze the son of a bitch's neck. "Hmm, Administrative Assistant. That's the position Maria is applying for."

"No she's not...she's just a Bilingual Secretary!"

"Sorry, Old Chap, she *has* applied for Administrative Assistant," Ivor objected cooly.

On the phone instantly, Butch rang Personnel and asked that Maria's file be pulled immediately. Barley looked green when Personnel's Tom Carley concurred with Ivor and reported that Maria's advancement was in process of being effected. "That changes *nothing*," Butch snapt after hanging up. "*Two* Administrative Assistants...what's the goddamned difference?"

No reply.

"Furthermore," Butch continued, "I'm docking your salary five hundred dollars, token, per annum. The effect will be negligible."

Infuriated at this asinine outrage, Ivor hardly knew what to say now. The whole affair...was Gestapo tactics. Somebody was *cuckoo*... somewhere...

"From thirteen thousand down to twelve thousand five hundred...you'll never notice a thing."

And the boss handed Ivor the employment form called "D-47" used in instances of "change of status". It was almost all blank except for a low line called "Remarks". For "Remarks" about this whole ugly appraisal, there were only three words typed: "Change In Responsibility".

How sick, Ivor thought, and handed the form back to a rather jubilant Butch. Then, he strode out of the office.

Zig-Zag Wipe-Out

Still with nary a flake of snow, the Adirondack region had gone for broke and decided to hold its Bobsled Try-Outs anyhow. All the big fellows from all over the States, as well as a few teams from overseas, were here to tackle one of the toughest Bob Runs in the world.

Ambassador Levitt's daughter, Asiana, twenty-three, charming, and a knock-out on Renaissance guitar, had gone out to the Run that Saturday afternoon with Mimi Tiny, whom she had met at the Costume Ball on Halloween. Together, the two girls were wonderfully paired, one so tall she was a skyscraper and the other so short she...no, that's not true about either. Mimi was just plain-tall, and Asiana was just somewhat shorter.

Asiana had been Ivor's Guest of Honour at his Ball, though very few even realised it, since she didn't even vaguely resemble the Duchess of Windsor, thank God (Ivor, remember, had personified the exiled Edward VIII). That evening Asiana had dressed as a Flapper, but of course to-day she was dressed as an Eskimo for the cold. Neither she nor Ivor publicised their friendship, the extent to which this ranged not even Lucille hazarded to wonder.

Insufferably cold, the pair of girls had been standing at the deadly twin-turn called Zig-Zag for an hour, and had already seen fifty-four wipe-outs. No, that's an exaggeration. They already had seen *one* wipe-out...and that had sickened both of them. Mimi, literally, had fainted to the ground. And people rushed from everywhere.

"Help!" Asiana shouted and dropt to her knees to revive her girlfriend. "Good God, Mimi, at least it wasn't *you!*" Asiana stated as Mimi's eyes opened.

"What in Hell do you *mean*...it wasn't *me?* Who *else* just passed out...*you?*" a rather dizzy computer expert snickered as she attempted to sit up.

"Lie down!" and Asiana pushed her backwards. "No—of course I didn't faint...I never do!"

"You will if I can stand up and *belt* you one!" Mimi could be humorous in certain situations, which was why she and Asiana, an eternal laugher, got along so well. "How many boys're killed?"

"All of 'em," Asiana joked. "No—really it was none of 'em, aren't you glad?"

"No—I'm nauseous!" Mimi extended her arm, and some big soldier in full uniform and wearing a walkie-talkie outfit on his back yanked her up with such animal energy that she all but fainted away again.

"Need more arm?" he asked lewdly in a toothy Southern drawl. "I *like* helpin' ladies..."

"Over and out," was all Mimi replied and turned away.

"I think we're evacuating," Asiana concurred and took Mimi's arm and led her downslope towards neutral territory.

"Snobs!" the soldier whined and spat.

Screaming upslope came the ambulance, great siren blaring and light flashing, and in its haste and in everyone's chaos to jump the road quickly it skidded into a poor VW from Vermont.

"Imagine being saved by *them?*" Mimi moaned and fell on top of a large wet rock, then broke into tears, totally unnerved by Mount Van Hoevenberg. Just then, the VW's driver came screeching like a stuck pig from inside the now huge group down the Bob Run a bit, where the four injured sledders were being given first-aid. From California, the sleighers were so beaten up they hadn't even noticed their sled continuing all the way down the course upside down.

"Oh my God—my God! My car's totaled!" the running owner shouted practically in tears. "You motherfuckers'll *pay*...through the goddamned *nose*...for this, you *cocksuckers!* You'll *pay!*" The man was in a silvery ski-suit and looked tough enough to lift the ambulance off its wheels and throw it. Troopers seemed to be arriving from everywhere.

Thank God for Troopers, as the ski-suited furious man toned

down his tongue on seeing them and decided he wouldn't beat the ambulance crew's heads in after all. On closer inspection of his vehicle anyways, there really wasn't that much damage, even with such a loud crash. The little bug had only been pushed about twenty feet uphill. Its back-end was bent out of shape, but nothing more. The sturdy ole ambulance wasn't even scratched, aside from a broken head-light.

"You're *lucky*...you know!" the owner screamed as the crew were hastening out to yank their stretchers to go get the team.

"Let me take care of this here!" yelled a very bellicose Trooper with his gun out, who looked even tougher than the VW owner.

"Ugh it's Wild West time," Mimi whimpered and covered her face with her blue mittens.

"If they shoot each other, I'll let you know!" Asiana laughed, loving every minute of the chaos.

"No, don't...please! I think I'm gonna puke..."

"If you dare...you're *walking* back to Placid!" Asiana snapt, since she had driven.

"Being Pepto-Bismol again, aren't you?" Mimi stated and tried to watch the fun.

Arguing now with the Trooper, but not getting anywhere, the VW man realised this was an emergency situation of more urgency than his little car, so he just shouted: "Well...they *better* give me their names after they rush these guys to the hospital!"

"I'll get them for you, just cool yourself down," the Trooper said calmly as he played with a bullet.

Within a minute the efficient ambulance crew were on the march upslope with their wounded. One boy had had his teeth knocked out, well it looked like all of them, so bloody was his head, but it turned out later just five went...and nobody ever saw them again. Another lad broke his right arm in three places. The third had simply been knocked out cold, and was in a coma for twenty-four hours. Whereas the last...he had got away with only a broken pelvic girdle. Clean sport...Bobsled!

People were shouting, moaning, complaining fighting everywhere! As the four injured were stored inside the ambulance which was backing down a ways to turn around, a flurry of controversy over the wicked curve Zig-Zag broke out. Suddenly people appeared from downslope, from upslope, from every slope on the whole huge mountain.

"Uh...time to leave!" Mimi said wisely, having regained her equilibrium.

"Not on your life!" Asiana deferred. "This's great!"

"Oh yeah! You're the type that likes watching Roller Derby too— seeing the Frisco Bay Bombers tearing into another team of bulls and beating the guts out of the man-sized wenches!"

"You said it!" Asiana said, yanking her girlfriend along. "How many's *this* make?"

"Many what?"

"Wipe-outs at this one curve in the last week?"

"How should *I* know?"

"But you store such data in the computers, don't you?"

"You'd be surprised what goes into those machines!"

"I think it's scary...all that recorded information."

"It ain't any more scary than *this* damned place!"

"Five I think..."

"Five what?"

"Wipe-outs."

"What's that make...they've now slaughtered off the whole American try-out team?"

"That's the point!" Asiana laughed.

"Well...they won't have any sledders for the Olympics, at this rate!"

Over the PA system installed in the trees some guy was announcing that the Run had been closed for the rest of the day due to "bad conditions".

"My buns, too! Bad conditions, do you hear that junk? Why doesn't he just say...*impossible* conditions!"

"Well, it's not like your tracks in Europe," Asiana admitted with great dignity.

"How in Hell would *you* know? Thought you were hatched in Japan or someplace Asiatic!"

"On *European* Runs...the sleds just go down the course by themselves..."

"Oh shut up!"

"They hardly *need* a driver!"

"Oh you don't know shit!"

"But here in Placid...it takes expertise. A driver just can't sit back here...and coast down for the joy of it. It's treacherous, and the sled must be *driven*..."

"What *are* you talking about!"

"An inch or so difference on a difficult turn...the sled tips over."

"Well why'd they *design* it so tough then?"

"Why're you asking *me*! You're the damned computer expert!"

Both girls laughed, but promised themselves that on the way back to town they'd stop first at Placid Memorial Hospital...to check up on the battered boys.

A Childe Is Born

For every injury, there is a recovery. For every death, there is a life. For every disaster, there is an exultation await around the corner. So everybody's Spirit raised when the hockey teams pucked into town.

One of the all-time great spectator sports, ice hockey is to figure skating as tin soldiers are to war. Need one say that all of Northern New

York couldn't wait to see such great teams as Sweden, Czechoslovakia, Canada and Russia...no, sorry...we can't call it Russia, since officially it was called by its abbreviation, USSR...competing against the USA. Everybody was all excited, but then the ticket sales were announced: Dismal!

Was it prices or was it timing? Staged the week immediately preceding Christmas, and the last game actually scheduled on Christmas Day, the timing admittedly was off. But...ticket sales shouldn't have been. They *wouldn't* have been if somebody in the Olympic Hierarchy hadn't *priced* the bloody things so damned high!

For a Hockey Festival occurring on five solid nights and days, packing eight thousand people at a shot into the Field House shouldn't have been such a problem. For one, given that it was the Holiday Season, most locals who would've gladly entered the House for a couple of dollars simply couldn't...for ten. Local people, over-taxed, over-charged at the petrol pumps, over-thrown by their kids all clambering for the space-age toys being advertised on TV, why, the locals who wanted to go for each and every game and who were your built-in market for filling the Field House just couldn't afford it! And everybody was grumbling, since everybody wanted to go for each and every game.

"I don't care...I *hate* hockey!" Ethel said. You remember Ethel...from On Stage On Ice?

Frank, contrary to Ethel's prognostication, indeed did return to Lake Placid before the Olympics, and had dragged Ethel out from beneath her beautician's hair-dryer in order to shuttle her, on Christmas Eve, to Placid to watch the USSR battle the CSSR, otherwise known as Czechoslovakia. Poor Frank had dreamt about a real Olympic hockey game as long as Ethel had her figure skating, so she had given in and let Frank splurge, even though this was only *pre*-Olympic hockey, on six tickets, the cheapest ones mind you, since it was Frank's "Christmas present to the family", all four kids included.

The kids, three big boys and one tiny little girl, were beside themselves with adrenalin build-up if not testosterone, and even their pouting mother began to catch the fever as the crowd kept coming into the House.

"Small showing, ain't it?" Frank grumbled, beside the bar he was propping up for a "quick one".

"Different crowd..." Ethel remarked, wondering where the kids had vanished, hoping they *had* vanished.

"Well *well!*" suddenly boomed the big man. "Why look who's here!"

"Wendy!" screeched Ethel in obvious giddy delight to see some face she knew.

Wendy, bright-eyed, bushy-tailed, in her early twenties, had long straight brown hair, and was a maniac for ice hockey! She also was a secretary for the IOC-Session Department of the Protocol Division.

"Why little Wendy Dion! We haven't seen you for five whole years!"

"Before college..." Wendy smiled, embarrassed, as she stood aside to present a very very pregnant girlfriend of hers and the girlfriend's husband. "Meet Veronica and Miles Ross, friends of mine from school..."

"From Albany," Veronica said kindly and took Frank and Ethel's hands.

"Miles is a direct descendant of Betsy Ross!" Wendy said, "They *think*, anyhow. It's on Betsy's brother's side. Betsy and her brother had a baby...together..."

Receiving a friendly poke from Wendy, Miles would have just as well remained out of the conversation, so he ended it (he thought) by announcing: "I'm a construction worker."

"You don't say?" smiled Frank. "So am I. Here I'll buy you a beer!"

Ethel and the girls carried on. "How many months?" Ethel couldn't help asking Veronica, whose long straight blonde hair went all the way down to her bulging belly.

"Two more weeks!"

"You're joking! And he brought you *here?*" Ethel couldn't believe her ears.

Just then her children ambled up. Each of the three boys looked a smaller version of the other, and each resembled their father.

"Where're you sitting?" Wendy wondered. When told she couldn't get over it: "Why—so're we!" They were in the balcony, above the VIP Section which was number 21. "I've been ushering every night, since I love it so much, but to-night I bought tickets for Roni and Miles."

"Isn't she a Saint?" Ethel laughed and poked Roni. Ethel could not help recollecting that Wendy damn well didn't *used* to be a Saint, since she once spray-painted a big red "MC" on the back of her loud-mouthed beagle Barky. The "MC" had stood for "Montréal Canadiens"...since even at the tender age of twelve Wendy was a hockey freak of no little reputation in Ticonderoga, New York.

Thinking this herself, Wendy led all eight people back to Section 21 then upstairs. Veronica, looking a bit green about the gills, did not seem particularly conscious, let alone in the mood for the uproar as soon as Russia, that is, the USSR, started getting the you know what beat out of them by the Czechs.

Wendy knew all the plays and could call all the penalties. It was a scream. Every time something was exciting, Wendy would shout out the correct tactic, so correct in fact that the whole bleacher section was aware of her verbal and sportswomanlike prowess. Even Frank, who could call the shots too, was most impressed at each new and never-wrong outburst. And even *Ethel*...was impressed, though not really sure at all what was going on. She just knew that she was getting all wet

71

inside, rooting for the lovely Czech boys and urging Death down upon the Russians, neither of which nationalities she ever had had a chance to meet. But Ethel just knew it wouldn't be right to root for the Reds...

The only one who wasn't really with it was poor Veronica, who couldn't really get involved with the puck and its passion. Other more pressing things were on her mind. She kept her hands on her swollen abdomen the whole time.

But halfway through the third period Veronica strangely began to seem better. She even cheered as the Czechs got one more goal, which caused pandemonium in the House. After applauding quietly, Veronica just sat there with a weird Madonna-like grin on her face. Then, as the game was just over, and people began to rise in order to leave, what everybody feared actually began to happen!

That's right...right there, inside the new Olympic Field House, Veronica Ross, whose husband was a living descendant of the famous Betsy Ross and her incestuous brother, broke her water, and a *baby* started labour to be born. And the awful thing about it was that Veronica refused, adamantly, to budge from her spot in the balcony bleachers.

"But you're *not* having it here!" her husband hollered and carried on madly, totally out of his wits with embarrassment and paternal concern for his parturating wife.

"Frank's just freaking out *totally*," Ethel said as no help. "Look at him!"

Frank indeed had gone grey, but revived under the smelling salts of two Nurses who suddenly ushered from somewhere inside the huge House.

"You sure you don't want the hospital, Honey?" the Nurses kept pleading to no avail.

"She's nuts!" Miles kept saying.

"It's all a big publicity stunt," one crappy Nurse declared, as she stormed off to call the only Doctor she could think of who would dream of coming to deliver a baby in the Olympic Field House on Christmas Eve! Rightly so, she felt that the Official Olympic Medicine Man, Dr Ansel Oberlin, would *have* to come, in his revered position as head of the Placid Olympic Medical Commission. How could he ever face his patients, if he sat *this* momentous one out?

This Nurse knew her Doctor! Without a blink the good man nodded at the news and announced it proudly to his whole huge clan gathered together for a delicious turkey feast that Christmas Eve inside his impressive mansion atop the prestigious neighbourhood of Lake Placid called Signal Hill. With a smile on his face, having hung up and returned to the festive table with a glass of champagne in his hand, the kind man announced: "A Childe Is Born!"

Well everybody so gathered was certain that he was talking about The Baby Jesus, but they were wrong. Nobody could believe

it...when he announced to them *where* the said Childe *was* being born...
"But you're *not* going to participate in *that?*" his wife incredulously asked. She had already had about enough commotion tonight...what with her case of near-laryngitis.

"Honestly..." everyone just gasped, as Dr Ansel Oberlin rushed away to attend to the birth. And...was it ever a *long* one.

Not really...given the circumstances, which were a bit bathetic, but it was somewhat of a quick birth after all. Six hours later, well into Christmas Day, the proud Doctor held up a healthy seven pound baby boy and prayed to God that the ambulance was still waiting outside. Quickly cutting and tying the cord, then having the baby washed in a tub brought especially from the hospital (there had been time, after all), the Physician simply said to the gathered crowd of Reporters, whose cheers were echoing all throughout the deserted and gigantic building, that the boy had better be swaddled STAT...to prevent him from contracting pneumonia. Even though electric-coil heaters had been produced, like miracles, from the innards of the cold building, and arc lights had been set up in a makeshift operating room, poor Father Miles was just about delirious by the time the experience was over. All the time that Betsy Ross's descendant was following his stretcher-laden wife down the stairs leading out to the ambulance, following on the arm of Doctor Oberlin who was old enough to be his grandfather, he kept mumbling: "I'll never go to a hockey match again...I'll never go to a hockey match again...I'll never go to a hockey match again..."

But as usual, the *woman* had the final word in such matters. Veronica kept muttering over and over: "But I really was praying for a *midwife!*"

Chinese Hockey

This Christmas in Lake Placid was made even merrier by the presence in town of the Red Chinese, or we should say by two Attachés representing The People's Republic Of China. For those of you who do not know, each country which participates in an Olympics gets the right to send not only a Team but to delegate an Attaché...who deals with his or her nation's problems and those of his or her Team Members, along with problems that the Protocol Division always manages to stir up. Attachés, therefore, are middle-men.

After the International Olympic Committee Session in Japan earlier in the autumn, when it was agreed upon by the IOC to allow The People's Republic Of China to participate in the Olympics, both Summer and Winter, you should have seen the fluster *this* caused at Town Hall. "Taiwan", which already was participating, had not been called "Taiwan" at all; therefore, when the Japan meeting came out with its now famous dictum that "China" *could* participate...well...that certainly, raised some hackles back in the island-country which prefers to label itself as "The

Republic Of China". Note here, that nowhere in that labelling does the said Republic refer to itself as "Taiwan". But never mind, that's what the IOC decided to call the place and, furthermore, the IOC said that if the said island didn't toe the line and change not only her flag and national anthem...at once...then the said island could pick up its toys and go home. On top of all this Alice In Wonderlanding...the IOC also decided, then and there, in Japan, which never liked *either* Chinas, that the National Olympic Committee of "Taiwan" had to be called *this*: The Chinese "Taipei" Olympic Committee (quotation marks are ours). It all made very little sense, and truly was all too Oriental for Lake Placid to begin to comprehend.

Ivor, therefore, had been caught right in the thick of all this international balderdash...since he kept files...hear hear...and none of his files had been labelled "Taiwan", but all had been labelled "Republic Of China" or "ROC" as its official Olympic abbreviation *had* been. Also, the odd telex kept creeping upstairs from the Director of Protocol's office...pithy little sentences originally emanating from V.D. Castle...which stated that The People's Republic Of China actually was coming...and that the official Chinese Attaché was coming too, in advance, along with his official Translator...both from the Far East.

Well...nobody in his or her right mind had ever seen a Chinaman set foot in the whole of the Adirondacks, let alone Lake Placid, since way before the Revolution of Mao and the legendary Long March! So, the imminent arrival of *two* Chinamen...was setting the whole of Upstate New York a-tingling.

Good at working with omens, the two Chinese indeed had arrived, in secret, that Christmas Eve, aboard some bus, from God knows where. Nobody had a clue where they were staying, but they had been sighted that evening in the Steak-And-Burgher fast-food restaurant by someone who worked there and who lived in Ivor's rooming-house. This was Jackson, who had a well-peeled eye for weirdos, both domestic and foreign.

So, Ivor knew the Chinamen's whereabouts even before his bosses, who weren't scheduled to meet the two until Christmas morning, also in the Steak-And-Burgher, since Town Hall was closed for the holiday. For some reason, the Chinese had zeroed in on Steak-And-Burgher...and decided to eat all their meals there. Rumour had it they were *sleeping* there, right inside the restaurant.

Heidi, arriving fashionably late, and arriving alone, was not at all amused even to *be* inside a place so obviously working-class, especially not on Christmas! But the two Orientals, who never celebrated Christmas anyway, looked quite jolly, so Heidi relaxed and decided to join them.

Sitting down to be waited upon, Attaché Dong did not feel compelled at first to tell Heidi that she had better go and wait on herself, since this place was proletarian and self-service. Heidi had never been in an American "self" in her life, so upon being told she got all giggly and decided to try it once just for fun. Anything would be fun, to-day, she said to herself, since Butch, in another mean streak, had taken away her Benwah Balls for Christmas. What a horrid Christmas present, having to sit facing a pair of Orientals, which just reminded her all the more of her craving for her Benwah Balls, which ushered from *their* part of the world, or at least from *near* it!

Christmas without Benwah Balls emphatically was *not* fun! But being forced to carry one's *own* tray of...was it *really* coffee...on The Lord's Birthday...was just the pits! Oh—she'd cream Butch good, when she got home! She'd deep-fat-fry his anus in lard!

"I brought your *tickets*..." Heidi said, stirring the grotty liquid and groping for words to say. God, this was a worse experience than trying to identify one Sheik out of ninety-five Arabs! Then, just like a woman, she started dipping about in her bag, but could not find the tickets she was looking for.

"Our tickets?" asked Attaché Dong. Long Dong, his translator, really was asking all the questions...or was it vice versa? Pretending to be confused, which wasn't difficult for her, Heidi really did begin to wonder which Dong was which. Was Long Dong Attaché Dong's cousin...or were they really brothers? They looked alike.

Absolutely flustered, Heidi then got all red in the face and asked *both* Dongs if she could excuse herself. "I just can't find the hockey tickets!" she mumbled and stood, really wishing she could crawl away for years. Imagine how *you* would feel, slipping up so in the presence of such honoured guests? Heavens—if she only had her Benwah Balls right now, to get her through this!

Heidi, who really did have the tickets someplace on her person or in her purse, had do something quick, so she hastily called the two men over to the farthest corner of the restaurant, which gave the best view out the plate-glass windows towards the Field House just across the street. "See that nasty little bar there, the one they refused to tear down?"

The bar in question was a favourite local pub called the Arena Grill. Square before the Field House, and matching it in a whitish grey, the nice bar looked a right shack, at least to Heidi's mind.

"Well above that you see that entrance way?"

The Chinamen were looking every which way.

"There?" Long Dong asked and pointed, lost in space.

"Not *there*...the main entrance right *there*! Right beneath the Link Building!"

"Oh...*Rink* Building..." Attaché Dong stated gleefully.

"At two o'clock...I'll meet you both *there*, right at that entrance. Ok? Not later, not before. Right at two o'clock."

The two from Peking (excuse us—*Beijing!*) were scrutinising the woman, but bowed a bit as she hastily departed. Needless to say the two didn't have any other appointments Christmas Day, so they simply sat and waited for three whole hours inside Steak-And-Burgher. Fearing that somebody might think they were spies, the Attaché didn't once unzip his attaché case...and neither did Long Dong unzip his.

At two o'clock everything got better. Precisely on schedule, fearing to cause a major diplomatic incident, the Chief of Protocol was ready and standing with the two admittance tickets in her hands. Her whole composure was a lot more relaxed. She had really gone all the way back to Petunias to force Butch to give her back her Benwah Balls, which she now was contentedly wearing once again.

"It's the USSR versus the USA," she stated exuberantly, wondering how the Chinese would react to *this* melodramatic treat! But neither showed a hint of preference either way...

For once, the size of a crowd to fill the House was on hand. Heidi was very excited, and very proud to escort the first Chinese ever to set foot within the Olympic Building. Everybody she knew kept coming up, as they walked from the vestibule in the upper floor of the Link Building, then leftwards round the concourse of the House itself. Even Lucille McSorley couldn't resist a quick poke Heidi's way: "Well, who are *these?*" she asked, knowing all too well who they must be. "*Boyfriends* of yours?*"

Long Dong just couldn't resist either and, with gestures and all, translated that remark to Attaché Dong, who laughed uproariously. Heidi, shocked to her wits over this display of vulgar humanism, tried to whisk the two along but Lucille wouldn't give an inch. "I'm on the Board," she stated, just to let the Chinese know what was what. Then, Lucille strutted away, very pleased with herself.

Fuming, Heidi led the two along and bumped right into Jack Sennett of the Press Department, then Mercurio Hidalgo Sanchez-Perpiña y Mendoza-Brillo who didn't warrant introduction as he was only a *former* employee, then the Executive Manager, Burt Dubczek along with Lester Burbank the head of Marketing, and then Judge Ronson, all of whom were most interested to be presented to the two distinguished visitors.

As soon as Heidi led the men down into Section 21 for VIPs, the Attaché and Long Dong were quite convinced that they were Movie Stars, so much attention had been lavished upon them. So, when everybody in the section started cheering, they ate it up and threw their arms high to milk the people's applause.

"Strange business, ain't it?" Wendy Dion asked Ivor, since both were standing in one of the aisles, pretending they were ushering. But on seeing Heidi, they actually began to take their ushering seriously. Then, shortly thereafter, Butch appeared, which made them usher double-time.

After ushering, Ivor returned to his seat and was pleasantly surprised to find two Chinese sitting next to him. Never really having had the chance to talk to any, Ivor suddenly felt that this was his golden opportunity. He'd always wanted to go to China anyways...

"Enjoying the game?" he asked no Chinaman in particular. Then he introduced himself and told them with whom he was working.

"Oh...Protocol?" Long Dong asked.

"That's right," Ivor replied regrettably. "Where're you from?"

"Peking—excuse us—Beijing!"

"I've always wanted to visit *Tibet*," he replied, to tantalise them, since Tibet supposedly still was taboo to foreigners. "Could I...*visit* Tibet ...with proper clearance?" He was hoping to get Butch and Heidi into trouble, by sparking a diplomatic incident.

The crowd suddenly roared as the Russians, excuse us, the Soviets, just let a puck slip into their goaly's goal. The Chinese were smiling, obviously liking to see their Communist brothers get the shit beat out of them. So Ivor asked: "Why don't *you* bid for the next Games?" He didn't really want *anyone* to bid anymore, since the Olympics should be put in one place, but just for the sake of argument he asked anyway.

The Orientals wisely not answering, Ivor ignored his own query and asked another: "In Peking...you could have the *Summer* Games... wouldn't *that* be fun?"

"Ooh," said Attaché Dong suddenly, as a big American boy just belted a Russian almost through the protective glass shield.

"It's fun seeing the crowd get so anti-Russian! They really *hate* them here!" said Ivor provocatively.

The Chinese just loved it, and flashed big brown defiant eyes. My, but how much more human these two seemed, as opposed to the stone cold Russians with whom he had tried to speak so often. All the time that Ivor kept jabbering pleasantly to the amiable Orientals, Heidi he noticed kept glancing backwards then upwards to where he was seated. Obviously, she didn't trust him a split-second with her distinguished guests.

Then suddenly, Heidi bolted. Up and out of her seat she dashed, coat in hand, as if The Devil himself were after her. Maybe her Benwah Balls, all umpteen dozen of them (the whole Pin Ball Alley full of them) had just *bitten* her snatch, Ivor thought and laughed. God, he'd better not let *that* secret slip out, to the visiting Dong Brothers or Dong Cousins, whatever in Hell they were. But he chuckled to himself, as he wondered if there was a good translation for the word "snatch" in the Mandarin, that all Lake Placid, due to the Japanese IOC Member's big mouth, now knew about Heidi's incurable habit.

The first period wasn't even finished, and it seemed sacrilegious to exit in the midst of such a fierce contest on the ice. Oh well, Wendy Dion was enjoying herself whole-heartedly, as Ivor could hear her sixteen seats away.

The game kept proceeding badly for the boys from Moscow. By

the end of the second period the score was 3 to 1, with the US obviously Kings Of Defence. So Ivor took a break from the fun Chinese, and went to the snacks area in one of the corners and ordered a hot cider and an obscenely large frankfurter that would've set the Marquis de Sade a-slobbering. Never a quick eater, Ivor seemed to take forever in gulping the ghastly thing down.

On his way back to Section 21, Ivor suddenly was accosted by a very unnerved and quite flabbergasted Chief of the Ceremonies and Awards Department, Balthazar Wesley Breighbourne, who was married to Dr Ansel Oberlin's daughter, Cecille. He considered himself quite the young author about town, having penned a nonfiction book on Lake Placid, and he was undeniably proud of the fact that he was the youngest member of the whole Lake Placid Olympic Board.

"Haven't you *seen* her?" Breighbourne shouted, practically in hysterics, as if he and Ivor had been gossiping for hours, their wont.

Taken much aback, Ivor just flinched and said: "Seen whom? What to bloody Hell you waffling on about now?"

"Heidi, of course!"

"Sod her..." Ivor stammered, not really wanting to think about his boss at all. "Why *should* I have seen her?"

"She's *missing!*"

"Her Benwah Balls again?" Ivor declared, rather delighted. "Fancy that."

"She's nowhere in sight..."

"Oh wait a minute...midway during the first..."

"She left! But—she's due on the ice—in ten minutes!" Balthazar screeched in high register, getting more and more flustered by the second. Indeed the clock over the ice was ticking.

"Why *her?*" Ivor wondered. "She running the Zamboni again?"

"Why! She's to take part in my Awards Ceremony, that's why!"

Breighbourne always referred to any Olympic Ceremony as "my Ceremony". Ivor just muttered: "Well, it's her own bleeding fault if she's not here. You know how she is..."

"Well...*do* something!" Balthazar commanded.

"What?"

"*Find* her!"

"How can I possibly *find* someone...who's not here?"

"I'll leave that one to you," the Awards Chief grumbled. "Ring Butch...*he's* not here, either! He'll jack *both* our asses if this Ceremony fucks up!"

So...Ivor rang Butch, much against his mettle, but he was forced to. Indeed, Heidi was not there, either, so Ivor surmised that the husband was frightfully upset and heard him say: "She suddenly remembered she had two *more* Chinese arriving at the Plattsburgh Air Force Base this evening...and sped off to pick them up."

"Why two more?"

"Can't say... official business, Ivor. Official business..."

"May I... then... as Deputy Chief of Protocol... go out on the ice... in her stead?" Ivor wondered. That would be a coup, Hefferon thought, but was surprised that Butch (who had only recently, remember, demoted him to Administrative Assistant) now simply gave him his blessing. Something obviously was up...

Something *was* up! When he made his way, down to the side vomitory where the red carpet was being unrolled, it did certainly seem so strange that soon Ivor Hefferon would be walking out onto the ice sheet with the President of the Lake Placid Olympic Committee and with the President of the International Ice Hockey Federation. It all was bringing back, in a flash, his *own* Medal Ceremony, four summers ago, and it was making him catch his breath. Life certainly did have bizarre twists...

Then, when the announcer over the loudspeaker was introducing him as "our own famed Olympic Gold Medallist, Ivor Hefferon, Lake Placid's Chief of Protocol..." well, it was too damned late to turn back now... thus out onto the red carpet the Athlete strolled, wondering what miserable Heidi *and* Butch would say when they both got wind of *this* one, that a mere scum-bag Administrative Assistant had suddenly usurped the Swiss Miss's hallowed Executive Position! Then it struck him, as he stood there properly like the Duke of Edinburgh, with his hands linked behind his back, but not by putting his heart in his hand (sorry, we mean his hand over his heart) in the proper American way of saluting the flag, while "The Star-Spangled Banner" was being played, that maybe the whole thing was one big plot? Probably some twit would rat to Heidi and say that Ivor had distinctly *asked* to be introduced as Chief of Protocol and not as the lowly Assistant he now was... just to get himself fired!

This thought haunted him all the way back to his seat, when the show was over. He hardly had been able to see the hockey players skating up and clomping atop the three-levelled dais, as he stood before it on the fresh red carpet. Too many jumbled thoughts were storming through his brain... too many tangled Olympic memories...

But there, still beside his coat, were the Chinese. "We were guarding it..." Long Dong boldly said. The Chinamen obviously had been conditioned by the rapacious things in America shown by films set in New York.

"Many thanks..."

"No. Many congratulations to *you*... Mister *Chief* of Protocol!" both Dongs stated together, then bowed low in the oldfashioned pre-Mao manner of the Subtle and Noble Orient.

Almost Killed

It was Boxing Day evening. Nobody could have been prouder of Ivor's coup than Lucille McSorley. She decided to celebrate the occasion by taking him to a very chic party way off in the sticks of the Adirondacks, at some private and colossal estate not known to any but the most privileged people in the whole wide world, since the family that owned it *was* one of the top families in the whole wide world.

Of course, none of this Lucille mentioned in advance, as she sped off towards some unknown destination in her baby-blue Lotus. Ivor didn't want to pry, but once past the town of Saranac Lake he couldn't refuse any longer.

"Where *are* we going...by the way?"

"Oh...to the Ampersands', that's all," Lucille said matter of factly and put on her dims, since a car was coming.

"NO!" stated Ivor, who had heard, for years, even way across the Atlantic, of this illustrious clan that was known in all the banking, social, and philanthropic circles of contemporary Western Civilisation.

"If it weren't for the Ampersands...New York would not *be* the Empire State she is!" Lucille lauded adulatorily. For Lucille to laud anyone, or anything, was saying something.

Soon the Lotus was shooting down a very private road, in a forest, fog all about, since again the weather had altered and it now was unseasonably warm. Before long this great huge mansion off to the right could be seen illumined.

"This it?" wondered the Brit.

"Don't be stupid," Lucille snickered and stopt by an iron pole blocking the road. "This's just the gate-house."

Harking back to country weekends he could recall whilst at Oxford, Ivor slipt into a reverie at the thought of being entertained lavishly once again. A gate-house...in America...he murmured softly to himself...

"The Ampersands need to be protected!" Lucille allowed, as the Gatekeeper came rushing out of his own private mansion in order to unlock the gatepost and hoist it up for safe passage. "Wouldn't *you*...if *your* family had donated museums, universities, institutes, and other magnanimous charities...all to the Planet Earth's Public Good?"

"People in this country must be jealous *crazy* of them?"

"They are!"

Suddenly, three other mansions spread out before one's view, and to the right of the middle one was a large wooden tower tall enough to be a skyscraper and looking just like a light-house.

"That's the Bell Tower, to call summer guests to table," Lucille admitted.

"And winter guests?"

Pulling up to a screeching halt, Lucille replied: "Speaking of icicles…the last time I was here…our friends the Barleys were too!"

"Joy to the world!"

"Even if they do come…it'll be good for them to see *you* here!" Lucille coached maternally and led the way to the door.

Then there was Priscilla, legendary figure in her own right and daughter of the late Governor Ampersand's late brother Charles. Priscilla, the hostess, was middle-aged and a very dearly belovèd friend of Lucille. The two embraced warmly, and Ivor was presented in due course.

Instantly made to feel at home, as only one can be in an aristocratic setting which simply accepts one's *presence* (that is, once one is allowed to *be* there), Ivor liked the relaxed atmosphere immediately. The only thing that the house didn't seem visibly to have…was servants, although they were probably cachéd somewhere.

Once in the salon, the inlaid birch ceiling, very upsloping and with rather wild art-déco effects about the windows, took his attention immediately. The woodwork in the house was just amazing, and Ivor would have been more content just looking about instead of making stabs at small-talk.

But Ambassader and Mrs Levitt were there, as were the Executive Manager and his lovely wife, all of whom Ivor admired, not to mention some lovely young lassies he'd never seen, so the perusal of *things* had to be turned aside in favour of *talking* of things.

Just at the moment when some ravishing beauty began telling Ivor about her love for a "good hard ride", which made the lad feel all sticky inside, in walked the you-know-whats! That's right, ruin a good evening, but there they were, the Barleys!

The look both Butch and Heidi gave Ivor, shocked out of their social sensibilities at seeing the Olympic Gold Medallist there, was one of true and unbridled horror! But…like good civilised beings, it was all gone in a flash, and the two monsters pretended to carry on, quite blasé.

"At least on the outside…" Hefferon said aloud to the ravishing beauty, "I mean…on the outside of the horse!"

"*What*…on the outside of the horse?" the girl asked, quite perplexed, but willing to suffer any solipsism from the posh accent of this stranger. She was a high-class gal, but nevertheless one with one helluva man-sized hardon…for Olympic Gold Medallists.

"Oh…*spots*, you now," he replied absently.

"But why spots…*how*?" To her, it was like talking to Lewis Carroll every time she *met* an Englishman.

"They just come and go…" Ivor muttered as up stalked a rather ravishing Heidi herself. She had obviously spent quite the time before the mirror before leaving the house. Blood red did suit her.

"Well, Heidi," Ivor began, hoping the other ravishing beauty wouldn't budge. "We heard you had two more Chinese to pick up last night?"

Answering by a giggle, she just shrugged her shoulders yes, then extended her hand and introduced herself to the ravishing beauty, eyeing her up and down as swift as light.

"And I'm...Veruscka *Lee*," the beauty responded, her nose a mile in the air.

"I was almost *killed* last night," Heidi instantly replied to that one.

Not to be outdone, Veruscka stated: "A rapist?"

Where on this Earth did all American girls, no matter what their social status, get such *balls*, Ivor wondered.

Showing inimicable Swiss élan, Heidi commented: "No, it was a traffic pile-up on the *autobahn* coming out of Plattsburgh."

"I've never gone *near* the place," declared the girl, from Virginia or some such snobbish place.

"I was on a diplomatic mission," Heidi announced casually.

"Shopping?" Veruscka wondered.

Ivor, amazed at this repartee, wouldn't touch it with a grotty barge pole smeared in swamp-scuz. Why were women *like* this?

"Getting two Chinese from the Washington Embassy," Heidi matter of factly said.

"Oh, so you're a *chauffeur*?" replied Veruscka, who seemed to understand everything now.

"I almost was in a *car* crash!" Heidi snapt, losing her patience with this snotty American.

"How exciting," responded the other, who really had wanted to say how nice.

"Thirty cars were piled up...didn't you *hear* it on the *news*?"

"I never deign to watch television..."

"Well it was horrible!"

"I'm sure it was..."

"Cars were burning on the roadside and bodies kept running out before my eyes...I almost hit somebody dying...*twice*!"

"Well, it *all* was for the good of the Olympics, wasn't it, Dear?" Veruscka stated, then walked away. Ivor then noticed that the ravishing beauty was winking at him, so he too left Heidi there to her horrid memories of the night before, and walked away.

Suddenly feeling very lonely, Heidi heard herself saying aloud: "But...I was almost *killed*!"

Then her husband walked up, having caught her talking to herself, and muttered: "You're going *crazy*!"

The Fun House

"You don't know of a taxidermist on the way to Saranac Lake, do you?" Jackson asked. He, the aforementioned worker from the Steak-And-Burgher, also was a resident in Ivor's boarding-house. "No. Why? Want to stuff Buffy?" Ivor responded and laughed. Life in The Fun House, alias 333 Main Street, Lake Placid, certainly was a hoot.

Jackson laughed, since Buffy was the puppy Samoyed, or however it's spelt, who also was a resident. Buffy had just that morning gobbled up one of Jackson's prize hats. The little fluffy white dog looked just like a docile lamb, but her always-growing appetite and teething jaws made her as notorious in the establishment as a full-grown lion. Buffy was the property of Penelope Jay-Stones, otherwise known as Head Teller of The Bank. Penelope ran the boarding-house, when she wanted to, when she wasn't trying to hustle a little cash on the side by working nights at the Bobo Petrol Station down the road. Everybody in the whole Olympic Primary Area was doing a little something on the side, even if he or she worked for The Committee, even if he or she worked for The Bank, just to keep up with inflation...which The Committee obviously was causing.

Ivor was the only person in the house who worked *for* the Committee, per se, although *everyone* in the region could be said to work *for* The Committee in one way or another, just as everyone was tied to Kafka's *Castle* in some inalterable manner.

"The Fun House truly *is* fun," stated another resident that late-in-December morning. Alexandra Heinz, as in the Heinz cake-mix fame, from Saratoga originally, was just responding to the query of a Reporter from, *Rolling Stone* magazine. The Reporter, very bushy beard and very bushy Afro, since he was Black and from Oakland, California was a recent friend of Ivor who had cajoled him into coming to The Fun House to interview the "inmates"...so that he could publish a report on what it was really like to be poor and working-class...in Lake Placid. Ivor also was to set the Reporter up with a White Trash Family that lived in a shanty on the edge of town, whose opinions were known to be rather different...

"We're doing a Gala New Year's Party," admitted another resident this grey Saturday morning, the last Saturday morning of the rather forgettable year of 1979. This resident was Mary Pills-Berry, whose name must not be accented on the Pills but on the Berry, a point about which Ms. Mary was quite contrary.

Oh—before we go on we must apologise for a very glaring error. Ivor was *not* the sole worker for The Committee, but Mary Pills-Berry also was a lucky employee. Mary had not been an employee for same when she swang into town, but had been hired first by Howard Johnson's, and Ivor had felt sorry for her, so presented her to Personnel in Town Hall, but should've left well enough alone. One never learns. "I was making more on tips, my hours were better, and the customers *liked* me!" contrary Mary stated with aplomb, watching the tape recorder beside the microphone-holding Reporter the whole time. She was the only person in The Fun House with an advanced degree in economics.

"Well...what do you *do* for the Olympic Movement?" he asked.

"I'm a Scissors Technologist. I clip articles all the live-long day!" Miss Pills-Berry wasn't pulling any punches.

"She also does a mean jitter-bug," Strider Galt admitted for her. "She's the *hit*...of Sassafras!" Strider was *awfully* witty.

"What's Sassafras?" the Reporter asked, obviously not in the know.

That was a remark that Kookie (pronounced Cookie) Schuss just couldn't keep quiet on: "Why...it's the Official Olympic Disco!" Kookie's voice was five octaves above the mean.

"Do they have the right to use the Official Olympic Logo?" queried the Reporter blandly.

"Don't ask me!" Kookie twittered. She was only in high school, but was living in such a rowdy house, first because she liked it, and second because her brother wouldn't let her live with him. She was up in Lake Placid from down near New York, to be able to go to school surrounded by plenty of ski slopes.

"Been skiing a lot?" wondered the Reporter.

"Does it look it?" she squeaked. "Show me a *flake* of snow!" Charming Kookie's sarcasm fit right into the scheme of things at The Fun House.

"Are you planning to try out for the US Ski Team?"

"Uh uh," Kookie retorted. "Just Pro. I'm in it solely for the money. If I got a Gold Medal, I'd hock it. And look at Ivor—what the Hell good has Gold done *him*? *He's* here—with *us*—in this working-class bordello!"

The big Reporter scratched "bright kid" in his pad, so Kookie read it and replied an octave off the piano: "I'm *always* on the honour roll!"

"She lies..." smiled Penelope wanly, as she lit up another cigarette. Penelope knew her inmates. "Let's get off this Olympics bullshit, and talk about Pindar Productions Unlimited and the next party..."

All members of The Fun House had become honorary members of Pindar Productions long ago, and so the only one who hadn't said anything so far, Hortense Malone, who also worked at Steak-And-Burgher, declared for the Reporter: "We might not work for The Committee...well some of us anyway...but that doesn't mean we haven't got *opinions*! Gossip's the *name* of this town, and we know what we *hear*!"

84

"What's that?" perked up the man from Oakland.

"Well...just from my own profession..." Hortense began.

"He ain't *got* one...don't let him shit you!" Strider Galt, ever quick on the draw, since he hailed from Out West, remarked. Strider was a professional hitchhiker, and knew a profession when he saw one.

"And you *do*?" retorted Penelope, acting out her rôle as Big Mama. Strider had been doing the odd job for the landlord lately, helping him load and unload vending machines.

"Jackson," wondered the Reporter, "how did an Italian-American *White* Boy like you ever get the *Black* name Jackson?".

"My ancestors were *slaves!*" Jackson said in a deadpan voice. His humour was like a banana peel, it always tripped you up. He was forever asking nonsensical questions and beaming cutely with his tweaky black moustaches. He shacked up with Alexandra, in room number four, right across from Ivor's room, number five. They had sex so loud it felt like they were doing it on your face. It was hard not to get a hardon while they were fucking, and they were *always* fucking. Even female Buffy had a perpetual hardon in *this* house! *All* the women did!

So, downstairs in The Fun House kitchen, where this Mother Of All Interviews was taking place, in this old white farmhouse shaped like a barn, and with its homespun white picket fence, jocular Jackson just was laughing and staring back and forth from Alexandra, then to Ivor, then to Alexandra.

Alexandra, who used to work at Steak-And-Burgher but who now was a waitress at The Wood Shed, a step in the right direction, then condescended to say: "His *mother's* Italian...but his father's a direct descendant of President Andrew Jackson...*and* some slave girl-friend...get the connection?"

Even if it wasn't true, it made good copy.

Buffy suddenly began wetting on the mat beside the back door, not bothering to bark to be let outside. Puppies will be puppies...

"Buffy!" her mistress, Penelope, let out a scream heard all the way to Montréal.

The Reporter, angered, shut off his recorder. "Well," he shrugged to nobody in particular, "I'm not getting much help here."

"Well *excuse* us," Penelope remarked caustically as she began wiping up the mess with a paper towel.

"Buffy!" screeched Strider. "God, what a garbage-slut she is. Just like a woman—look at her!"

Kookie giggled: "*All* female dogs're disgusting. They *all* eat their pussy in public!"

Mary inserted: "But *this* cheese-hound's so gross, she comes up to your face right afterwards, and *burps!*"

You could tell the Reporter was wishing he never entered The Fun House, by the grimace on his lips.

"I can spill *all* sorts of beans...about The Bank," Penelope

85

volunteered, to raise the level of conversation somewhat above the pre-pubescent.

"Can you?" replied the Reporter with such eagerness that Buffy stopt licking her genitals and barked so bloody loud that the West Coast man broke the press-button off his recording machine. "Damn! Why this mother of a machine—it don't *never* work right!" Then—embarrassed to have so unabashedly lapsed into Street Lingo—the Reporter had a coughing fit.

"Neither does *anything*...in The Fun House," lamented Penelope, to the agreement of everyone around.

"Just like Lake Placid?" Hortense asked.

"Just like Lake Placid," concurred Penelope sadly. She *was* a local after all...and she *knew* what it was that her town had recently become.

The VIPs Finally Get Invited

Given that everybody gets possessed by The Holiday Spirit, as opposed to The *Holy* Spirit, at the end of any given year, so too here in the Adirondacks life got giddy as preparations went underway to leave the 1970s behind. Everybody thought that if the 70s were bad then the 80s couldn't be worse, and so a sudden albeit timid optimism crept into town and rubbed shoulders with all the folks.

Over at Town Hall, on the very last day of the 1970s, a Monday, very few people showed for work anyhow, but Heidi Barley certainly did, and was very punctual, for once. This was because Butch had stolen her Benwah Balls, *again*, the night before, and she was trying not to slip into Cold Turkey, which in her case could likely be called Cold Goose.

Right there at 8.30 AM Mrs Barley had made a pair of New Year's Resolutions: (1) Never again to rock on her G-Spot, and (2) Never again to be tardy. She had begun to practise these two a day in advance. Ivor, not showing, due to needing the day to set up for his New Year's Party, scheduled at the Whiteface Inn Convention Hall, therefore was no help at all to poor Heidi, who got it in her mind to get out *all* the Invitations to *all* the VIPs on her G-List that very day.

"I want a 1979 postmark on these letters!" she ordered, and set Maria and Wendy Dion and Eileen Kaminski to folding hundreds of Mag-Card form letters, stuffing them with 1980 Olympic Games Schedules and with blank ID Forms to be filled out, and making sure that the right letters got into the right envelopes then down to the Mail Room in time to get postmarked that day. It was just awful!

Mag-Card form letters, by the way, were the saving grace of the business end of the entire Olympic Movement. Heidi simply couldn't, nor could anybody, get along without them, during the atrociously nerve-wracking pre-Games buildup. Whoever Mag was, who invented the IBM typewriter which had a computer card slotted into it and which automatically typed the same letter over and over and which made each one look like it was done to order...was a genius...and should be canonised...Heidi had thought many times. And despite not being Catholic, she had honestly thought about writing the Cardinal in Switzerland to implore him to begin The Devil's Advocate Procedure.

But to the stuffing secretaries, Mag was nothing but a Scag! "He should be fist-fucked...sideways!" Eileen snarled at Maria who laughed. The former was known in the office for her forthright All-American Dirty Mind.

Maria, red hair falling in her eyes the whole time, had never been so harried in all her life. Her tongue was ready to fall off, so glopped-up was it with envelope glue. She suddenly rushed off to the ladies, to gargle with Listerine.

"Where's Ivor to-day?" Heidi queried to the quickly vanishing redhead.

"Sore throat! Just what those envelopes are giving *me!*"

Hmmm...why's everyone on edge? Heidi was feeling fine, but no one else seemed to be.

"Heard you were almost killed?" Eileen casually remarked. "Lot of cars?"

"And I had two VIPs with me, too!" giggled Heidi back.

"I'm sick to death of VIPs anyway!" Eileen admitted, and got a poke from a not less diplomatic Wendy Dion. "Ambassadors, Princes, Counts, Ministers, Secretaries of Departments of Governments, Governments in Exile, Excretions in Exlax from Washington, Movie Stars...they *all* suck the bone!" Eileen spat. "I'm just sick to death of *all* of them!"

Heidi, shocked out of her gourd, did not admit to hearing such blasphemy. Wendy was cackling her fool head off.

What in Hell was in the air? Laughing gas? Nobody seemed in the proper frame of mind...no one was on the proper tilt, Heidi surmised, stuffing away gleefully a letter being sent to the Ambassador of Finland. She was proud to be so Swiss; but why couldn't the whole world be Swiss like her; why couldn't all Earth function like the cuckoo-clocks her homeland was infamous for? Even when Heidi rocked upon her G-Spot, she did it to a non-stop beat, like a metronome, the Swiss way! All life should be so synchronised.

"Have the Chinese said if Washington's sending us their Ambassador?" Wendy wondered aloud.

"Maybe," Heidi said but gave nothing away. She was beginning to sweat. She was craving a good rock upon her G-Spot.

"All the *others* are coming! God, it'll be just like a mini-Washington DC..." Eileen stated.

Wendy's mind couldn't really conceive of such a flurry of diplomatising in "these here" hills.

But Eileen, being from Boston, hailed from territory where

diplomatising had been occurring since The Very First Turkey Day, so she knew what she was talking about.

Fresh from the loo, with a tongue no less glopped for malice, Maria couldn't help asking aloud: "You know...isn't it too *late* for these damned invitations anyway?"

Heidi turned white with wrath, but said nothing.

Maria carried on oblivious: "Well...we should've got all this crap over and done with in September!" Maria, usually the most docile redhead you'd ever want to meet, was not to be shut up when something really was bugging her, although few things ever did harass her...visibly.

"I know...pretty *stupid*, ain't it," Wendy asked, as if she had never spoken good school-book English before. She really could speak properly, when she wanted.

"What's the sense?" Elleen concurred. "I mean...VIPs or no VIPs...the Games don't exist *just* for VIPs!"

"What's *that* you're saying?" Heidi now couldn't resist.

"Nice day if it don't rain..." Eileen began to whistle.

"VIPs shouldn't be allowed *near* an Olympics!" Wendy declared...as Heidi cut her tongue on an envelope.

Jabbering girls or not, Heidi now was bleeding, so rushed off to the ladies, much to the girls' relief.

"*Bleed*, Bitch!" they all chorused, then fell upon each other's shoulders in stitches of laughter.

"Honestly...the whole shit and shebang would be far better off...if all these stuffed shirts stayed home!" Wendy growled and slumped on a desk for a breather.

"I agree totally," Eileen remarked. "Just as Ivor's been saying: The Olympics exist for *athletes, not* for officials!"

"*Used* to exist..." Maria stated grandly, with a theatrical pause, "...for athletes! But...be honest...doesn't it make it a *little* more exciting knowing that some great big, rich, handsome, and of course well-hung *Prince*...just *might* show up?"

"I'll take the well-hung one...you others can take the rich and the handsome!" snickered Wendy.

"Oh come on, you don't think he'd deign to be seen showing *us* anything?" Eileen disagreed.

"Don't put yourself down so..." Wendy contradicted. "He could just show me the first *inch*...and *I'd* fall straight down to my knees!"

Eileen gave both girls a rotten look. "Well, I still stick to my *same* point. I think one of the biggest wastes about this whole thing is all this bull about the minority that's *proper* versus the majority that really wants to *see* these sporting events but is so discouraged that they haven't even bothered buying tickets."

"That's right...ticket sales are piss-poor!" Wendy wasted no words in saying.

"Everyone's scared crazy about sabotage and all that. All this security, though, it's only been set up to protect VIPs, and not even the *athletes!*" Maria added. "Really, the Olympics should just tell all the VIPs to go *home!*"

"To go...sit on it and *rotate!*" Eileen put in, with a grin.

"Maybe Ivor *is* right," Maria said at last. "He's always going on about how there's no *Spirit* left in the Olympics."

"He's absolutely right," Wendy asserted. "There's only *Money!*"

"*Big* Money!" both Maria and Eileen shouted together.

On that note in walked Heidi again, her forked tongue once more ready to do business.

A New Decade – Or – Who Stole The Cold-Tap?

Well, it was the last evening of the 1970s, and The Fun House crew had been corralled into helping out with the Gala New Year's Party staged by Pindar Productions Unlimited. Pindar had been laying low...since the media blitz a few weeks back. And for some reason, though, Ivor's heart just wasn't into this extravaganza, which had taken far too much energy and time than he would have wished to have donated.

Lucille had been feeling funny, too, but with actual physical laments which the night before had landed her on a privately hired jet bound for her New York gynæcologist, since out of pure snobbery she never let any *local* doctor spread *her* legs to administer to her female needs.

The poor woman, it turned out, had been admitted to Flower Fifth immediately and had had a hysterectomy about midnight the night before. Fine way to welcome in the new decade...

Having succeeded so well with the Halloween affair, even more time and effort had gone into this one, not in decorations but in trying to drum up a public to voyage way out to the boondocks along the opposite shore of the actual Lake called Placid, to the *other* famous fantastical "club"...The Whiteface Inn.

So much money had been pumped into The Inn lately (a complex with its own golf courses, rambling old lodge buildings, cottages, and condominiums, just like its competitor, The Club, on Mirror Lake) that Ivor and Lucille had thought that the locals would love to have a nostalgic old party once again at The Inn...but it seemed that the locals had made other plans.

Penelope Jay-Stones, seated at a ticket booth by the front door of the huge auditorium of The Whiteface Inn Convention Hall, kept saying: "Well...they'll all be coming just after midnight."

Ivor, worrying about Lucille and about life in general, simply surmised that everyone had stayed in town to go pub-crawling, or bar-hopping as it's called Stateside. Poor Lucille had sunk a wad of money into this one, all a loss, and only a hundred or so people had showed

"Pindar did what he could!" Penelope stated, counting the dismal till of door-money at a quarter to midnight.

"Pindar advertised his damndest...but he *still* lost money!" Ivor stated, at a point when he felt like returning home to England. "Ye Gods, what a *wrong* place to pass New Year's Eve—in some wooden Victorian Adirondack vaulted-roofed white-elephant that only last week was a storehouse for insulating material, old beds, old dressers, and castoffs that this Inn couldn't cope with in its restoration!"

"Happy New Year, Ivor," Penelope stated sadly.

"My, though, Mister Hefferon...it looks so nice here! It's a marvellous party," stated Kirstin von Waffensberg who hailed from Munich. She, a gorgeous and quite lively blonde, was a part-time fashion model in Germany and a part-time employee for Olympic Games. She already had worked at Innsbruck, Munich, and Montréal. "How'd you hang those streamers on the Casablanca fans?"

"My Head Bartender, Strider Galt, did that. He's nimble on a ladder," Ivor replied, really wanting to leave. Depressed with the turnout, and with the turnout of his whole experience with the administrative aspect of the Olympics, Ivor more and more retreated into his own private world as the clock progressed ever closer towards midnight.

"You don't want to dance?" Maria asked, as she came up to wonder about the champagne. But even as midnight *was* in fact happening...as noisemakers, horns, and blowouts were doing what they were supposed to do, and as the champagne was being poured and offered all around...Ivor hardly saw any of it at all...

Was there even the same group that played for Halloween onstage? Was the bouzouki music appreciated by the crowd? What did harking back to dead distant Greece have to *do* with anything living and now? Where were the fifty columns...those fifty columns of papier mâché?

A Hall this size could've been turned into the Parthenon...but wasn't. A gargantuan Broadway or a West End production on the theme of something we have lost...could have been presented on that stage ...but wasn't.

"Something's just not *right* this New Year's Eve!" Penelope snapt, as she left the boxoffice and decided to forget it all and dance.

Ivor just stood there, gaping. Had all his months here...just been a waste? Who *cared*...about returning to smarmy old values? Wasn't it just *daft*...trying to make people change their ways?

The party ended...and everyone left before three. Cars were piled in, and most of The Fun House crew piled into Penelope's beat-up...was it a Dodge? Penelope had got so shit-faced drunk, as she called it, simply to antidote Ivor's infectious and imbecilic depression, that she could hardly steer on the way home, but it didn't matter, as few cars were braving the elements.

Next morning, after having worried all night about leaving empty untouched kegs of Miller beer inside the Hall, since it was impossible to lock the old building, just what Ivor had predicted did occur. Somehow somebody had come into the building before Ivor and Jackson had arrived to clean it up...and had walked off with two full kegs and one of the two cold-taps used to draw up the beer.

What a sodding great way to kick off the new Olympic Year...with a bout of depression and then with an alcoholic burglary!

Termination!

Never having had much to do with Tom Carley, head of the Olympic Personnel Office, Ivor had not been *hired* by Personnel but he was obviously being *fired* by Personnel. Well, Personnel, usually more content to do the grunt-work, now had a ready-made scandal on their hands, and it looked as if they had been set up for it. It was the first day after the New Year break.

"Butch's home in bed with a terrible lung ailment," Tom began as he escorted the Olympic Gold Medallist into Butch's big office and shut the door.

"Fancy that," was all that Hefferon replied.

"And...he's requested your termination," Carley stated bluntly without warning.

"Just like that?"

"You know the reasons."

"I don't believe I do."

"I believe he reiterated them to you, in person, a few weeks back."

"We had a talk."

"About what?"

"About *The Facts Of Life*...his latest creative-writing project."

"Life never *is*...easy."

"Tell me about it."

Neither Ivor nor Tom really wanted to deal with the issue at hand, which were the *facts* which warranted one's termination.

"It must have been a personality clash from the very start," Carley stated slowly and wisely.

"It must have been," Hefferon answered.

"There are certain careful things you have done, of which we all are proud," he added. "And, of course, you *are* a world-class Olympic Gold Medallist."

"How very kind. It's always nice to be thanked for a job well done."

"You keep very good charts. You write superb letters. You are one of the best proofreaders we have..."

"And so you're firing me, how thankful."

"No...*I'm* not personally. *Heidi* has asked for your termination, and Butch then signed it, and then the Executive Manager signed it after them. Termination takes *three* signatures."

"Isn't that interesting?" Ivor wondered aloud.

"No, it's unfortunate. It's Pindar Productions Unlimited...you know."

"No, I don't know. Tell me all about it," Ivor coached.

Fighting to keep his cool, the Personnel Director said: "You had no right to involve yourself with a Member of the Board..."

"Oh? I'm guilty of...what...Moral Turpitude?"

"You are *scandalous!*"

"Really?"

"Why...did you do those stupid things...like...like putting those huge advertisements in...well...in *The New York Times!*"

"Why don't you get rid of Lucille, too?"

"She's too deeply entrenched!"

"And I...an Olympic Gold Medallist, as you phrase it...am ...dispensable?"

"Heidi has had a *terrible* time with you...these past few weeks."

"Heidi is a low-life *Cunt*, with an Uppercase C in italics, and you bloody well *know* she is!" Hefferon stated forcefully, and glared Carley in the eye. "Furthermore, putting *Spirit* back into the Olympic Movement is worth each and every *sprain*...suffered on the road to success..."

"What in Hell do *you* know...about *Spirit?* You speak about the Olympic Movement...just because you've *competed* in Olympics and *won*...as if it gives *you*, and *only* you, the unassailable right to state that *your* opinions, and your opinions *alone*, are worthy of consideration! You're really *contemptible—*as if you're the *sole* person who works for this whole *huge* organization who's *ever* gone to church!"

"Church, all too sadly, has *nothing* to do with it!"

"Can you see a bunch of *priests*...running the Olympic Games?"

"They did...for one thousand years!"

"Where?"

"Don't you know the *History*...of the organization for which you work?"

Staring at each other in a Western-style showdown, Tom quickly changed tactics. "You are free to transfer into another department...but I've checked with a few...and nobody seems to want you."

"How interesting."

"I don't think we have anything more to discuss."

"I think we could sit and talk about this...for hours."

"Ivor, I honestly do *not* have the time."

"Nobody does...that's the *answer*...in a nutshell!"

"I'll hold your termination papers," which he then brandished as he stood, "through to-morrow. Should someone wish to hire you, within The Committee, we can discuss this again at that time."

It was near five o'clock. Feeling like a lorry-load of soggy newspapers some delivery boy left in the rain, the Olympian returned upstairs to his paper-crammed desk and began telling the secretaries that he was finished.

Lucille's Revenge

Never having worried about money, Lucille, on hearing poor Ivor over the telephone, revived considerably from her ills and told him not to worry, that she would be leaving New York the very next day.

"But...how? Aren't you feeling badly?" Hefferon wondered, amazed. He was truly feeling guilty for the rough way that he had been fucking her, and assumed that her hysterectomy had been triggered by his over-aggressive sex. But then...she had been pretty aggressive herself.

"Don't *worry* about me. Just use my keys...you know where I keep them...and set yourself up in *comfort*...at *my* place. You've *earned* it. And everybody *knows* we've been screwing each other's brains out anyways, so what in Hell's the *difference* at this point, because it's *obvious* that your hanging around with *me* has been the cause of what got you into such hot water! I'll simply charter a broomstick and be *flown* up...medical bed and all!"

"You will?"

"Of course I will! Damn it—I *don't* like the sounds of this one, at all! You see...I leave home *one* single minute...and what happens? In the meantime...speak to the Judge about this! But for God's Sakes *don't* ring the New York State Labour Board, to be sure...since just like *Heidi* you're an *alien*, and aliens have absolutely *no* rights. Cripes Almighty—I wish to Hell you *were* a New York State Resident...*then* we'd show those *cocksuckers*...since I know the Commissioner of Appeals in Albany!"

"Who *don't* you know! But you're absolutely sure you're well enough to travel?"

"Darling...I'll bring my bed *with* me! I won't move a love-muscle!"

And she didn't! Lucille McSorley in fact did arrive that next day and Town Hall of Lake Placid will definitely never be the same for it again. Not a great growth of a woman anyhow, Lucille had planned her entrance into Olympic Headquarters with audacity and aplomb, as if she were some operatic diva making some ceremonial stage-visit as an Empress on Progress Royal. She was *borne*...

Having bought a used child's hospital bed on wheels, and one narrow enough and short enough to fit through doors and into freight lifts, Lucille could just about go anywhere, anytime, anyhow...and did...

Nobody had been warned, since enough people had been paid off in advance, so Lucille McSorley's now historic entrance into Town Hall took the place completely "unawares". She had been flown secretly into Adirondack Airport at Saranac Lake, then had been transported

93

under armed guard by an Army ambulance loaned by the Commanding General of Fort Drum, whom she had known for years. So this controversial woman arrived in style, accompanied by two amazingly handsome young uniformed Black Privates and a knock-out of a blonde-bombshell Army Nurse. On the way in, though, certain key people of the Press, whom she knew, had been advised of her imminent arrival, so the proper amount of Reporters and Photographers were on hand outside Town Hall's doors. That had been handled by Miss Witty, whose Middle Name was Subterfuge.

"There's the Army ambulance!" shouted someone in the crowd that had grown to over a hundred. Everyone was standing on the lawn beneath the four flags. To-day's display of a foreign country, besides the flags of the United States and New York State and the International Olympic Committee, was the flag of Spain, due to the visit of a Habsburg cousin of King Juan Carlos.

But in America, no Royal Duke ever could engender the type of hysteria that a bedridden Olympics Board Member could engender, especially a bedridden Olympics Board Member who'd just had a hysterectomy, not to mention who'd just suffered the termination of her young Olympic Gold Medallist gigolo. Town Hall's lawn became total pandemonium. The scene even out-did the by-now-legendary appearance of Elsie The Cow.

In her tiny bed, with her knees up, but covered with an ultra-exorbitantly-expensive coverlet of Russian sable, especially ordered as a prop from B. Altman's, and with an ermine muff, and with Persian lamb mittens, and with a gorgeous orange silk scarf about her neck by Dior, and with emerald pendants a yard long from Harry Winston's, and with an Inca rainbow-hued skicap purposely given to her as a good-luck charm at La Guardia Airport by the Consul General of Peru, and with makeup by Helena Rubenstein, Lucille was ready for anything...even *Interview* magazine...even Lake Placid, New York!

So, right there in the open air, which again had become queerly balmy, Lucille staged her press conference to beat all press conferences, one so Hollywood that it would have brought Hedda Hopper to climax, in the old Studio Days, when La Hopper's caustic column could cause an actor's suicide.

"First, let me say that I *adore* being back...in the North Country," she began sarcastically, "...where everyone's *always* so goddamned warm!". Reporters were recording every word she said. Video cameras were scrambling for best angles. Everyone in Town Hall, by now, was craned out the upper windows, trying to catch each nuance.

That line got applause, from the windows-crowd.

"Second...I honestly must admit coming back here...for a *purpose*..."

"For *Ivor?*" a Reporter, from *Interview* no less, had been baited to ask. *He* was decked out almost as sartorially as was Lucille, wearing a matching sable, but one purchased in an East Village flea-market. But *his* emerald earrings were definitely *paste.*

"That's right, Darling. For Ivor Hefferon, the Olympic Gold Medallist, the *late* Deputy Chief of Protocol..."

"*Late?* Has he committed *suicide?* Is he *dead?*" Pressmen of all shapes and sizes asked at once.

Gasps could be heard from the upper gallery. Maria even screamed out: "Oh God *no!* He's not *dead,* is he!" as she started crying.

"Wouldn't *you* be, Darling, if *you* were fired...*unjustly...*from *your* comfy office at TIME magazine?" she said to one particularly handsome fellow whom she knew.

"Is *that* why you returned from New York...for Hefferon's *funeral?*"

"Ivor..." and she brushed a mock-tear from her eye, "...was just a part of something *much* larger, Darlings. I mean if I, a *sick* woman (and I admit that, to you all, I've *always* just appeared some unusual *sicko*), a *sick* woman I say who's just lost her most *private* and most *vital* organs..." and she coughed melodramatically, "...feel the *compunction* ...the *need*...to release myself from one of New York City's *nicest* hospitals...and Darlings, you should've seen the *view* I had of *Central Park,* not to mention of *Harlem,* from my corner suite at Flower Fifth ...and the *constant* stream of VIPs visiting my room each and every morning, noon, and night...including the *Mayor* himself no less...and the Borough President of Manhattan...well...it was a *very* comfortable stay...but I left it *all* behind...and for *what?* I left it all behind...risking my *goddamned* health in the process...for a *cause,* I tell you...and I do mean for a *cause célèbre!* Do you see what I *mean!*"

"What's that?" asked another bit of bait.

"Besides...being my *escort*...Ivor Hefferon *has,* and you *all* know that he *truly* has, performed *other*...more *valuable*...duties...for me!"

The scandalous dame was getting to the good part. Reporters by the dozen were hollering: "Such as?"

"Such as...well...I think it's time I give Confession...right here and now..." and she paused for the effect and glanced all about, even up to the windows of Town Hall, "...I...am...The Mother Of *All* Scarlet Letters...do you understand?"

"Not hardly!" a *couple* of hundred voices now were hollering, since the crowd kept growing by the minute. Others kept shouting: "Is Ivor really *dead?*"

"Clarify yourself," one Reporter after another kept shouting.

"Evil...*begets* Evil...and I...truly...*tainted* this young and quite idealistic British Athlete!"

"YAY! HOW!" everyone yelled. God, this was a Media Exultational Experience as close to Nirvana as any Reporter ever would get. "Tell us HOW!"

"By Sex...by Money...by Ideas...by Attitudes...that everybody thought originated within Ivor's *foreign* brain...but which really were the cesspool outslimes of my very own *local* noggin!"

"Long Live *Upstate* New York!" shouted the windows of Town Hall in unison.

"Pindar Productions Unlimited...was *my* idea...right from the very start."

"Why *Pindar?*" a few pressmen wondered.

"Go look him up in the *fucking* encyclopædia!" Lucille spat, then smiled wickedly.

"But now that Pindar has helped get Ivor *fired*...what's the *next* step?" one rather intelligent Reporter asked.

"Should anybody *have* been terminated...it should have been *me*...but, of course, I was off to Fun City...having my *uterus* yanked!"

"But they'd never dare fire *you!*" someone else remarked.

"Of course not. Stupid as they *are*...they didn't *realise* that I'd come *back* here...and do *just* what I'm going to do...*right* now!"

Silence.

Just then, from beneath her lowest pillow, Mrs McSorley reached and retrieved a round black ball with a...with a *fuse* on it?

"*Holy Christ!*" Reporters screeched and scattered to all the cardinal directions, and then to a few that even Cardinals never blest. Everyone thought she was totally *crazy!* But she sure gave great *copy!*

"Dare me?" the Board Member shouted to all the people on the street, then glanced up to see what chaos was occurring inside the place called Town Hall. Not a person was staring out the windows; mass evacuation was occurring out the building's back door.

"You're all *wicked!*" she bellowed. Then, she pulled a gold Tiffany's lighter from one of her pockets within the ermine muff. But, just as she was holding the bomb over her bed, in order to light it, she played the goof on everyone and used a cord to bounce the black rubber ball up and down on the pavement. "Hah hah hah—you're *all* fools!"

The Reporters loved it, and the whole of the Administrative Staff, peeking round the corners of the building, suddenly surged forward, in a camel-charge, applauding the outrageous woman the whole while. Her bed soon was being ringed with fans, who were shouting: *"Bravissima! Brava, Diva! Bravissima!"* as if she were a grand coloratura soprano onstage at The Met. It was a performance that definitely merited a symphonic orchestral accompaniment—brass instruments at the very least!

On that grandiloquent note, as the kudos continued, Lucille's two handsome Fort Drum Army Privates and her spectacular blonde-bombshell of a Fort Drum Army Nurse reappeared. They'd been cued to disappear...with the Reporters.

Everyone now was laughing, thinking that even though Lucille may have failed to have re-installed Spirit into the Olympics before...she sure as Hell had succeeded in doing so *this* time! Hysterectomy or no hysterectomy!

"Now, Soldiers, lead me *in!*" she commanded, and into Town Hall, to the continuing *bravas*, a very content Lady Board Member was wheeled, followed by the whistles of all the Reporters, who couldn't help ogling the curvaceous derrière of the Army Nurse, which was swiveling to beat the band.

Needless to say, no more work got done *this* January day! Nobody could get over it...which was precisely Lucille's point. She had planned this one as only a scheming and an older woman can...as she knew precisely what it was she was after!

She looked so fit in fact, all made up and gowned, and chipper in her kiddy's bed, with her knees up, that all the office girls began wondering if she really *had* had an operation after all?

"It's all a *gimmick!*" Heidi said, though she was marvelling at the woman's ability to carry it off. Right then and there, the devious Chief of Protocol decided that to-night, come Hell or High Water, she'd *force* Butch to give her back those Benwah Balls, which he'd stolen on her *again*, or she'd hop on the next flight for Basel! There was *no* way that she could make it through all this ever-worsening strain...*without* them!

Lucille, meanwhile, began her now legendary social-calls, with a chit-chat with The Committee President, the Reverend Arnold C. Courtney, then Personnel's Tom Carley, then Judge Ronson, then over to Ambassador Levitt, then upstairs to Manager Burt Dubczek, then last but not least Heidi Barley herself, whom Lucille was particularly keen on hassling. Of course, once inside Town Hall, every single employee was praying she'd stop at *their* office next, just to be able to say, once she'd gone, that he or she was included on *Mrs McSorley's G-List!*

Lucille let herself be wheeled about, in exactly that planned order. She would just let everybody know what was on her mind...and she would save the best...for last...

It Snows For The First Time All Season

After *that* number...it was The Weather's turn. Never to be outdone in the Adirondacks, The Sky decided to follow Lucille's example and to drop a bomb in Lake Placid's lap, so the wind it blew and the stuff it flew...for hours, and hours, and hours. One *could* go on for hours, here, just explaining what it was like to live through it, but we shall let the Reader use the brain for this one.

It was about bloody time it snowed, anyhow, everyone kept saying over and over till it got boring. People had already tired of Lucille's stunt, so it was high time that The Sky did something dramatic to take people's minds off thinking about how much Olympic Spirit they did or did not have.

For that matter, talk about show...given that Ivor had all but moved in with Lucille, in thanks for her handling of the depressing situation he was undergoing, and in order to minister to her recovery needs, Lucille was certain that her ultra-deluxe house was being spied upon, so every so often Lucille, just to be scandalous, would strip Ivor's trousers down to his knees and do rude things to his manly parts...all right in the living-room...so that anybody could see what her tendencies were. Ivor, oblivious to public opinion, didn't seem to mind, and most of the times would read a good book, of which Lucille had plenty, all the while that his lady-friend was exercising things other than her feisty vocabulary.

"Aside from going out and playing in it, Ivor, don't you think *sex* is the best exercise whenever it snows?"

"I honestly wouldn't know," he replied while being fellated as he tried to read an old issue of *Adirondack Life*.

"Well maybe to-morrow or so they can start up the Ski Jump... they've got the snow-making equipment...but lots of good it does... since it keeps raining."

Looking outside, with a furious blizzard, Ivor could hardly imagine it stopping, let alone turning to rain. No matter what had happened to him, being inside a warm house while it was storming outside certainly was nice...

"I love cross-country, too, but what're they going to do with no snow?"

"Good God, Woman, will you stop *talking* about the bleeding weather, and continue on with what you're doing!" Ivor moaned and rammed the still abed and recovering woman down onto his thickened shaft. The article on moose mating wasn't very much fun anyhow...

Saying nary a peep till Ivor had at last come...Lucille then commanded him to bring her a sedative. "I'm *supposed* to be supine, but *inactive*, you Bastard! I should've stayed in Flower Fifth!"

"Why? Did you meet many well-hung Male-Nurses?"

"*Sick*, the humour, if that's what you *can* call it, of the British, is *sick*! Yet the answer to your question is *yes*...of *course* I met all the well-hung Male-Nurses!"

"You *love* penises, don't you, Dear," Ivor joked. "Now, open wide..." and he gave her the sedative to calm her down.

"I've got *more* phone calls from people, who work in *all* the other parts of The Committee, saying they *loved* what I did to Headquarters...so I'm convinced that pulling such a stunt was worth every penny!"

"Well...it certainly got *me* back on the payroll for a laugh!"

"Grin and bear it, Darling. If you can take Heidi a few more weeks..."

"Oh my God—stop—I've never *once* considered *taking* her! She's got the Benwah Balls to service herself, remember?"

"You just continue *doing* what you've been doing, Ivor, and

that's that. I *settled* it...with a few threats *here*, a little dirty work *there*...
Darling, I *know* these errant personalities, inside and out! And...I play
best, with maniacs, when I draw *blood!*"
"Such poppy-cock anyhow...trying to *fire* somebody just weeks
before it all begins..."
"You *live*...and *sometimes* learn...at least if you stick around
Lucille!"
Meanwhile, one week of January was just about over, and the
hard-hit tourist industry of the Adirondack region, which had suffered
so badly by lack of snow, began to say novenas for Lucille
McSorley...whom God had obviously blest...and who, Rumour had it,
was The Force that had caused so much commotion to the Olympics
that The Sky had laughed so hard that the poor bruiser just snowed
tears of crystal joy...

Biathlon Backlash

Snow doesn't last forever. That pertains to the kind you snort and the
kind upon which you ski. Matter of fact, the six-inch base and the two
inches of powder, making a combination of eight big inches, disappeared as dramatically as it had come...overnight.
Well, not really *that* quickly. Powder and base had remained
intact three full days, and word had sped round the world like wildfire
that at last it was ok to send your Biathlon Team to the Adirondacks.
But you should have seen the Biathlon Team from Italy. Now that was
one pack of angry *ragazzi*!
If there's anybody *not* to cross at a Winter Olympics, it's a
Biathlonist. The reasoning behind this is simple: Biathlonists carry
loaded *guns*!
For you who don't know about this Nordic sport, Biathlon is a
cross between Cross-Country Skiing and Pugilism. Easy on the Cross-
Country Skiing...
Many skiers in the world would like to go out and shoot their
neighbours, and this sport was invented as a sublimation factor for this
need. Sigmund Freud once tried to do a dream analysis of a Viennese
who was fond of this activity, but gave up, since the sport's thought-
processes were much too complex even for Freud's nimble mind to
grapple with.
"No damn you...we *don't* have speedy tempers!" snarled the
favourite Biathlonist of the Italian Team. He looked just like the boy
who posed for Michelangelo's *David* and was causing the lady
interviewer from *Pecs'N'Pricks* magazine palpitations of the clitoris,
which is somewhere around the neighbourhood of the G-Spot. (Science
still, as of this publication, is trying to hone in on the precise locale of
said Spot.)
"But here...just *look* at our magazine. It's for *men*..." she

tantalised, "...*real* men...like *you!*" and she handed him the latest four issues.

Seeing the whopper-erections on the covers, he threw them high in the air and shot them full of holes, just to get the woman's dander up. Pretending it all wasn't happening, she simply said: "Well, in case you want to take a *crack* at something other than flying pin-ups, here's my number in town!" She handed him her card.

All the other chaps were laughing their sunburnt faces off, and the *Pecs'N'Pricks* girl couldn't help picturing them all in bikini-briefs, standing on some lonesome promontory of Capri, which she had fantasised seeing her whole life. Why was she so *nuts* about Italians! Why were *most* women...with healthy libidos!

The David replied: "Look—if I pose for your *porno magazino* ...you give me lots of *dollars*, no?"

"Of course..."

"Well—contact me as soon as I win the Gold Medal—then I sell you anything you like!"

She was melting inside as fast as the snow outside. That was the problem you see, since the other boys were getting angrier and angrier all the while. They didn't fly all the way from Milano, where they doubled as fashion models, to wade through woods-muck. It wasn't possible to keep a *bella figura* in all this slop. And if there's anything an Italian male has got to preserve, it's spotless clothes and a *bella figura.*

"Missing the homeland immensely?" the girl continued. "I'll cook you a *mean* carbonara! Even in my hotel room at the Hilton! Even if I have to go out and *steal* the hotplate!"

"*Il Maestro* always gets the girls!" snapt a jealous teammate, pointing his rifle at the challenger.

"Whatta we gonna do?" another queried, a short one but tough as an ox. "Let's leave Mastroianni here!"

"But whatta we gonna *do* now?" another wondered. There were *five* others in all.

Gazing over the soggy expanse of the Biathlon Shooting Range, which by now should have been well covered with white stuff, and wondering why the targets had been set up down at the end of the field anyway, if nobody could practise his sport, the *Pecs'N'Pricks* girl decided to invite all *six* to come call on her. Or *call come* on her, she hoped. At least it would beat standing in the rain.

"Why this weather in America so damn crazy?" the David asked. He obviously had not wanted to hear his "girl" invite all the other blokes, too.

"We're *coming!*" they all were shouting now and brandishing their firearms with evident macho delight. "We *come*...in *your* house!"

"Hotel room!" the woman insisted, getting nervous.

"Now now now now now!" the David objected. *"Ma sono tanti!"*

They all broke into a furious argument in Italian, which excited the girl no end. It was one of her oldest fantasies, to have a whole pack of randy Italians fighting over her...in Italian! She loved it whenever Italians spoke *any* word...*spaghetti...lasagna...ravioli...*

"No...is *finito*! She go with *me*...you go *home*!" the David decided.

"*Ma tua madre! Sempr' eguale! Basta così!*"

Well the David did leave with the *Pecs'N'Pricks* girl under his arm, and departed to the vicious invectives of his teammates. "*Tua MADRE!*" they all shouted as he jumped into the girl's fancy Jaguar.

Also along the roadside, waiting out the drizzle, was a much more cool-headed American, about twenty, who had recently begun working for The Committee as a Driver. Having been allotted the Latin Lovers, this was Attorney Turney's son, Francis, whom all his friends called Flip, because he already was a conditioned airplane pilot known for his dare-devil flips in the clouds above the Adirondack Region. In more ways than one, Flip was a local Star, but never showed it. He spent the whole summer driving his father's boat, the *Taurus II*, the most famous plier of the Lake called Placid, the number one tourist boat which gave the best spin for your money about the gigantic pond. Flip was a big boy, barrel-chested, curly-haired, and he knew *all* the dirt and local legends, but never let on, only to friends, one of whom, early in September, had become Ivor.

"Where do you want to go now?" Flip asked kindly. He had the fun job of transporting the Italians wherever their hearts wanted to go. Right now, they wanted to be driven back to Milano!

"*Non lo so!*" they all answered as one, looking glum.

"Sports Building, Town Hall, Olympic Village, Shopping..." Flip began asking. The last of the litany always was everybody's favourite.

"Town Hall?" one asked curiously. Suddenly they all were talking about Town Hall...in such speedy Italian it sounded like a 45 played on 78, at least so it sounded to Flip, who began driving down the road leading away from Mount Van Hoevenberg.

Getting more and more loud all the time, Flip finally had to tell them all to *shut to fuck up*, since he couldn't drive! But even though the fellows *did* shut up, since if there's anything an Italian responds to it's brute force, Flip's remark made the still furious *ragazzi* steel their resolve even more...in order to stage a mock take-over of Town Hall...in defiance of the ever-melting snow!

Obviously Flip never knew what in God's Name they were up to, since he didn't speak Italian, or else he never would have participated so innocently in their whimsical caper. But all being D'Annunzian "men of action", these boys never were ones to let rotten weather spoil *their* fun.

So, asking to be let off at Town Hall, the five teammates hoisted their rifles high and made sure that they were unloaded before entering the building of their spoof, then in they walked single file, up the first flight of stairs and into Headquarters itself.

Quite sexy in their red, white, and green nationalistic ski-suits,

101

designed by Armani of Milano of course, and fitting so tight about their cocks and balls that every secretary in the place just started typing *do it do it do it* across the letters they were working on...well these Italian boys could have walked in with bazookas and nobody would have cared, security being negligible downstairs anyhow.

"Ok," one asked the receptionist, "where we find the Press Office?"

Jezzibel, so dumbstruck by these handsome foreigners, just kept staring at their bulging crotches and couldn't say a word.

Woken up rudely by a rifle butt tapped on her shoulder, lightly of course, but which still sent shock waves straight down to her sweet derrière, Jezzibel at last was able to stutter: "Uh...it's uh...uh...just uh... through that...uh..." All the poor thing could do was point, her switchboard lights flashing like the place was on fire.

So...into the Press Office strode the five, causing an equally gutsy reaction there. Eloise Witty, who had seen lots of characters come and go in her stint, had been praying to Jesus for something like this to walk through her door ever since Lucille McSorley's melodramatic "take-over" of Town Hall. Given that it now was Thursday, the tenth of January, something like these Italians definitely was needed.

"Hi!" Eloise perkily said, and began playing with a strand of her lovely strawberry-blonde hair.

"Ciao, Bella!" the boys said in return.

"What can I *do* with you...I mean...do *for* you?" she asked, all fantasies in her mind on "go".

"We uh wanna take *over* this place!" they all said, and pointed their rifles at her.

"Super," she replied and smiled, "I'll just ring my boss! He'll love it."

"It's raining outside," one of the gun-holders said to her as she was dialling.

"Awful day," she responded. "We've all been waiting for something like this to happen. What took you guys so long?"

It was fun being held hostage after all, she surmised, and wondered what all the fuss in Iran was all about. "Uh...Jack? Hi, it's me," she began. "I'm, outside your office, where in Hell do you *think* I am?"

"What do you want *me* for?" he bellowed plain and loud above the metal partition.

"Just wanted to say I'm being held hostage..."

"You're *what*!" he screamed.

"Oh it's marvellous, really. They're all very kind. All *hunks*. Shall I *call* anybody?"

"Ring TIME, this's right up their alley. But can I *go* now—I've got a copy deadline to meet!" The Press-Boss hung up, not believing a damned word of the previous conversation.

Jack Sennett never believed Eloise anyway, so Eloise did ring her contact at TIME anyhow. This was the most fun she had had in weeks.

"Hello, Angela? Put me right through to Dirksen, I've got the *hottest* story you'll ever hear coming out of Lake Placid!" Eloise winked at the boys, and gave them all the V-sign.

One of the fellows was standing against the door, so nobody was being allowed in.

"Hi, Dirky? It's Eloise oh...not too bad. Yourself? Well, listen. You'll love this. What? No—not too serious—but I'm just ringing to say that the Italian Biathlon Team is holding us all *hostage!*"

The boys beamed.

Pandemonium suddenly hit the TIME-LIFE Building of Sixth Avenue in Manhattan. "You...let me ask you to repeat that one *more* time?"

"No, you heard me the *first* time, don't play footsie." Eloise was a marvel, and could pull the wool over anybody's eyes and make them like it. So for the next fifteen minutes Eloise wove a yarn that would curl the page-plates off the printing-press of *The Bible*. "No," she fibbed at the last, "they're absolutely *not* doing it for publicity, don't be silly. It's just... they *don't* like the fact that there's no *snow!*"

"*Bravissima!*" they stood and cheered her, just as they'd done many times for their favourites at La Scala. "*Tanti saluti!*"

"Anytime, Boys." And Eloise stood and shook their hands. They all trooped out of the Press Office as quietly as they came, and not before handing Eloise a giant Italian National Olympic Committee pin, a rare one, from the Games held at Cortina-d'Ampezzo in 1956.

"Thanks a million," she sighed. "It was *great* fun!"

"*Non c'è niente...*" they all said and bowed, in a manner of exquisite European courtesy, then exited the stage.

Faulty Contracts

With the second week of January now in full swing, and not to mention the furor caused by Eloise's funny stunt which had "snuck" into *The New York Times* in a press-leak from TIME, though the truth of the matter had come out in the wash way before TIME could set the scandalous joke to ink, tidings now got a bit tedious. And the warm weather wasn't lending an iota of First Aid.

But stories started busting out all over...about this or that thing *not* going according to schedule, much to everybody's chagrin. No, that's not true, since nobody had expected things to flow smoothly anyways.

The most pressing thing that occurred was seen by many to be a minor technicality, although it affected everybody in the Olympic Primary Area. The said technological hang-up involved the afore-mentioned Club. With its three hundred rooms (plus? minus? no one knew exactly)...it was where the vast majority of VIPs of all persuasions would be lodged...or...where they were *supposed* to be lodged.

"But I can't *exist*...without The Club!" stated an incredulous Chief of Protocol who had made one of her rare visits to another Olympic Building other than Town Hall. She was calling on the Reservations Department, housed in the aforementioned Sports Building.

"In the Sports Building...nobody shouts," calmly stated the head of Reservations, a handsome curly-haired fellow, Kirk Divine, whom all the girls *believed* Divine, since he was young and always dressed in dapper suits. In reality, Kirk wasn't Divine at all, but quite a man to stand up against pressure groups, one of whom was standing before him now.

"Heidi—The Club has *defaulted*—and that's that!" he stated strongly.

Backing him up was his Deputy, a genius of a pretty girl with her computations, and *this* tour de force, named Nancy Evans, started rattling off all sorts of figures...since it was Reservations' job to know the facts about room assignments, billing customers, and who owed what. "Nobody in the Northeast *likes* us...since we have our figures down pat!" Nancy stated, alas.

Kirk fired back: "Furthermore—neither does *V.D.Castle* like us," he said belligerently, knowing that the Lausanne Château was where Heidi learnt all about which way the wind blowed. "We've been getting telexes from Madame Dupleix up the *wahzoo!*"

That infuriated Heidi, who knew she was beat: "You're *not*, I repeat, not *ever* supposed to speak to Madame Dupleix *directly*! It's *Protocol's* job to deal with the Château!"

"Well that's *tough shit*, Honey!" Nancy shot back, loving a good row. "The Club's gone belly up—bust—bankrupt! And there's not a single powerful *money-organ* in all of the whole wide world that wants to bail her out one *more* time!"

"But..." Heidi was about to cry, picturing all her Princes, Generals, Grand-Dukes, and Plenipotentiaries all tossed out into the...well there wasn't any snow...into the *glop!* "But...we signed a *contract* with them!"

"We never *did* sign that stupid contract," Nancy said with pride and with the greatest pleasure in informing Heidi of something about which Heidi was not au courant!

"Why...why wasn't I *informed* properly..." Heidi muttered sadly.

Nancy rose to her full height and said imperiously: "Because, Woman, *nobody* in The Committee really cares whether you shit *or* rot!"

"But...how can the Games go *on*...without...without...my VIPs won't have...neither will the IOC Session...which opens before the Games...*nobody* will have anyplace to *go!*"

It was all too unreal, a true nightmare.

Just then the telephone rang. Laurie, a British subject but one who'd lost her accent ages ago, answered, then calmly repeated aloud all of what she was being told, as questions. "The following contracts now are...*void*? We have no more insurance coverage...for the whole fleet of *all* our Ford vehicles? We have been told by the High School that the proposed International Press Centre, which the High School is supposed to turn into for the whole month of February, now is...*unfeasible*? We have been informed that every small and foreign sports club that was planning on coming to Lake Placid has *cancelled* reservations in all the region's small motels? And...going against their agreement at last, the workers of the 1932 Arena, which is being restored, have *just* walked off the job...too pressured to complete the renovation before the thirteenth of February? Anything *else* happening to-day?"

"Else!" everybody shouted at once.

Heidi, looking like she'd faint dead away, had to sit on Laurie's desk. She broke down and blubbered like a baby. Everyone was *glad*.

"If only it would *snow*..." Kirk declared to lift the gloom, "...so bad we'd have to *dig* ourselves out!"

"Why won't one of the filthy rich IOC Members *buy* the damned Club?" Nancy wished aloud. "*That* would save it all...or at least *one* of our problems..."

Like a phoenix, Heidi suddenly raised her head, as if from the ashes of her runny mascara, and stated almost in a rapture of euphoria: "Brilliant!" She actually jumped up from the desk that she'd collapsed upon, like a pop-up stick-doll. It was horrific. "That's the *answer!*" Head spinning, and not feeling the need to verbalise her newest answer, Heidi raced out of the Sports Building in a flash.

"Oh well," Nancy sighed. "At least *we* were the ones who finally got the bitch to shed tears."

Everybody was relieved that the monster had gone.

Laurie remarked: "She *never* likes setting foot down here anyway!"

"That's because the Sports Building is too damn *close* to what the Olympics are all about," Kirk said with great dignity. He was a man who knew what he was talking about.

Nancy gazed up to his deep blue eyes with puppy-love, as if she were glimpsing the Incarnation of nothing less than one of the Olympian Gods.

The Bank Is Robbed

For months Penelope Jay-Stones had been ragging about the truth: The Bank in Main Street had so little security that somebody was sure to rob it. Well, one day, somebody did.

It was the beginning of the third week of January, and the weather had got a bit colder, but not enough of a change to bring about snow. The town, if not the whole of the Eastern Seaboard of America, was in a foul mood about the weather and about the prospects for the Olympics and the Olympic Movement in general...what with the weird world situation and all. Margaret Thatcher and Jimmy Carter had already been mutually goosing each other into overdrive, about their stupid Moscow Olympics Games Boycott scheme, whose only result was to spread wads of ill-will all across the whole of the sporting globe.

So, to punctuate the intrusion of Politics into Sport, two masked marauders had decided to take the situation into their *own* hands. Therefore, given that everybody who was anybody knew that there never was a guard outside or inside The Bank...somebody who knew that this was the Official Olympic Bank decided to blow the whole place wide open by robbing it.

Bank robbing in America being the national sport that it always has been...this stick-up was absolutely inevitable. The Bank had even asked for it...not keeping the place posted.

"Well...I stood right here...as I usually do," Penelope stated, her eyes wild with the shock she had just undergone. The Committee's official Medicine Man, Doctor Oberlin, had just injected something into her to calm her down. Need one say, that at this moment, noon, that The Bank had shut itself up tight. The good Doctor's syringes were getting a heavy-duty workout, this crazy day. He was making the rounds throughout the staff.

Only one Reporter, from UPI, was allowed inside to ask all the questions. The robbers, we forgot to say, had got away.

"I..." Penelope began but couldn't go on.

"Take your time!"

A teller who worked with Penelope was crouched beside her, as the Head Teller was slumped on a rug on the floor. People were in a daze everywhere.

"No one was *shot* anyhow!" the other teller said soothingly.

"Thanks for small favours!" Penelope whimpered. "Well...why *me*...always they come to *me* first!"

"How'd it happen?"

"I...was counting the day's returns...from the Solicitation Fund...money asked for by mail, you know...from little old ladies from Pasadena or wherever...who contribute their last dollar to the good ole Olympic cause..."

"I know..." stated the UPI man, all choked up.

"And...and there was this pile of cheques this thick," and Penelope measured out a good eight-inch length with her hands. "Cheques from anywhere from a dollar...to a hundred...from all over the country...people who care enough to *save* the Games!"

"You were counting *that*?" he wondered.

"What do you think I *do* all day...play tiddly-winks? Sure—I count *money*!"

106

"Now now..." apologised the other teller, who herself wanted to tell the Reporter to *sod* off, which in American would be *fuck* off!

"Penelope's had a very *trying* morning..." another teller came over and stated. She too plunked herself down upon the rug.

"How much of yours, then, did they take?"

"*All* of it!" Penelope snapt. "God you ask *dumb* questions!"

"How much was it worth...your Solicitation Fund pile?"

"I'd just counted thirty-seven thousand two hundred dollars ...and I had fourteen or so more cheques to go..."

"My my..." lamented the Reporter, "...couldn't the Olympics *use* that right now?"

"No shit, Sherlock!" Refusing to answer any more stupid queries, Penelope stood up and walked towards the back, towards Mirror Lake. But that had just been the tip of the iceberg. All the other tellers, too, had been robbed of cash and cheques, many being Olympic related, but the true loss had happened from the desk of the Manager. Hunter Whippet, Manager of The Bank, was very tall and very slow in his movements, but of course he made up for it by his ultra-quickee mind. Located beyond the locked gate, the Manager had tried to stash away what it was he was working on when in walked the two you-know-whats. But given that crooks know that Managers usually don't deal with *little* amounts of cashflow...the crook doing the dirty-work had shouted out: "All right...who's the boss round here?"

"Me," announced Mister Whippet chivalrously, since he didn't want any of his tellers murdered. So, basically out of a fear of bloodshed, the Manager offered to let the robber take whatever it was that struck his fancy. And fancy be struck...the robber took the whole contents of his desk.

"It was a disaster!" Whippet stated dolorously to the UPI man. "Wouldn't you know...I'd be working on the Olympic *Private* Accounts..."

"The *what*?" gasped the UPI Reporter, unable to contain himself any longer. "*Escrow* funds?"

"Well...you don't think that such a huge organization keeps all its money in one *single* account?" The Manager could not believe the Reporter was so naïve.

"How many accounts...does the Olympic Committee have?"

"I can't say," Whippet stated in a tone which meant that he either knew and wouldn't say or that he himself did not know.

"My God," the Reporter wondered, "well...how much then did the robbers get from *you*?"

"Don't ask...don't ask...I honestly have *no* idea," the Manager declared with an air not unlike pride.

"Do you know who it was...the robbers?"

"Never saw them...but again...they were behind masks. Maybe they were locals, maybe they weren't, nobody here can say, nobody recognised their voices."

"These...*Private* Accounts stolen...are there records of the files?"

"I'd asked for everything...the files from The Committee...just this morning...so perhaps some were copied elsewhere...perhaps others were not..."

"My God!"

"I was reviewing all the accounts at once...to determine a few things..."

"What things?"

"I'm not free to say."

"But..." the UPI man was dumbfounded. "But...what're you going to tell The Committee...that more than a *million* was lost?"

"I'd have to say...a bit more." This Manager was certainly no easy chap to deal with, but under the conditions who could blame him?

"Uh...well..." the reporter apologised, "I'd better leave you to your...work. I hope the losses aren't all that large, and you can get the majority of it back...if it was covered by insurance..."

The UPI man left as a bevy of other officials began arriving, investigators, the FBI, the President and Executive Manager of The Committee, and later throughout the day a whole host of others...who all asked the very same questions...but who all interpreted the answers each in his or her way.

The Games Default

The bank robbery caused chaos with everyone and everything. The investigation of losses took one whole week, one horrible week of aggravation for the community, for the tellers and staff, and for the Lake Placid Olympic Committee. It just didn't seem fair...everyone said biliously and got roaring drunk.

Given that it was so late in the preparation for the Games, and all the corporate sponsors had already been hit up for the maximum amount of donations, it was impossible to rely upon donations to recoup what losses had been sustained. But...the figure at the end of the week, Friday the eighteenth, had come to almost six million dollars that had to be accounted for...a lot of money! Nevertheless, in the middle of the week The Club had been saved by a private loan...and everyone breathed a bit easier...so now people were praying for a similar miracle for The Bank, but none as yet had materialised.

Because so many people and corporations and nations had invested so very much in the hope of seeing the Winter Olympics take place in the Adirondacks, nobody had wanted the President of The Committee to go ahead and make a speech...a speech which he had been dreading, but writing, all week.

"But..." he began at a very sad press conference held on the dais of the ice sheet inside the newly built Field House. He was staring moodily at the spotless red carpet that led away from his chair and microphone and that went up to the southern flank of seats, where the whole crew of the Lake Placid Olympic Committee was gathered to hear the Reverend's words, and where reporters as well, from all over the world, were assembled. "But..." he continued, "...I just don't see how we can continue on...like this."

Great murmurs rippled throughout the bleachers.

"We simply cannot make the next payroll," he added with remorse. He shook his wizened head.

People were crying. It all had been such a dream...but then people were shouting out: "We'll work for *nothing!*"

Microphones had been placed in the Press Stand as well as where the employees were seated. At this point, there were over one thousand employees.

"It would *kill* me to see all of you...laid off..." the Reverend's voice was breaking. "You've been good...you've all withstood an awful lot!"

"We'll work!" people from everywhere were shouting.

"You know," the President carried on, "God in His Way brings Grace to the most trying situation..."

"Have the Games defaulted?" a cocky reporter asked.

"We have suffered...one immense loss..." he replied. "But maybe The Lord, in His Wisdom, will give us The Power to see our way out..."

"What can *we* do?" a few people were shouting. "We'll do *anything* to help!"

The Reverend stood from his chair and stated vigorously: "Money...is...*not*...every...thing!"

Dazed by this one blasphemous sentence, the whole Committee rose to its feet to give the Reverend their adulation! Many people now were weeping.

"Amateur athletes...don't win *money!*" he continued.

Hysterical cheers greeted that remark, even if it *was* a lie!

"All our facilities are built...and ready...and waiting!" He was really socking it to them this time! "And what is *money*...to the *Spirit*...that's *willing*? Tell me, Lord God!"

Bravo! Placid had been dying to hear such phrases for years!

"We'll carry *on* somehow...Bank or *no* Bank...Club or *no* Club... VIPs or *no* VIPs...at least the *Athletes*, whose Games these really *are*, will have *their* contest! Even if they're *all* pumped up with steriods!"

Just at that moment, up to a microphone stept a now fully recovered Lucille McSorley. It was her first public appearance since her bomb-scare. Known to one and all, this Board Member commanded a sudden silence that was eerie, as she stood there dressed like the widow she really was. All in black, with black gloves, black hat, and a sheer black veil drawn over her whole face, she was quite the spectral image.

"Give 'em Hell, Lucille!"

"Stick it to 'em!"

"Jack their asses, Lucy!" the crowd roared, obviously delighted to see someone so controversial there amongst them.

"I...only...want..." she began very slowly, like Gloria Swanson, "...to tell you...all...one thing..."

Her pauses were operatic, but worked magnificently.

"I have...a cheque-book..." and she opened a small black purse and retrieved a pen and a book, "...right here. Now...I'm writing...a cheque...for... *six*...million...dollars..."

The crowd went absolutely berserk!

The Reverend couldn't restrain himself, and raced the length of the whole red carpet, tears streaming down his cheeks, to scramble up and over the railing and through the hysterical crowd, in order to embrace the woman. People close by saw that there were great tears streaming down *both* their faces, as they clung to each other like little lost kids...

It Snows Once More

If you noticed a change of attitude in the last chapter, you noticed correctly. Indeed, the whole atmosphere of Lake Placid changed overnight, as if by magic. And if you don't think that such a thing *can* happen...well...you must admit that sometimes, even to-day, things somehow turn out for the right. There is a thing that can alter people's Spirits, when nothing else on Earth will succeed. The thing that can bring all this about, of course, is *money*. All too often, money can act like magic itself.

Lucille McSorley had suddenly been raised from a Camp Heroine, an utterly scandalous one at that, to a Resident Deity. Even her enemies, legion as they were, were quiet about her for once, and said that she had done something *altruistic* for a change...and those Society hostesses who before wouldn't *dream* of including her on their G-Lists now were clambering for the "kind widow's" attention.

But the greatest accolade came right out of the blue itself. Just as before, when Lucille pulled her previous stunt and when The Sky showed his approval by dumping a tremendous amount of snow on Lake Placid in a mere eight hours, so now The Sky began to thicken with heavy grey clouds that tussled and tossed like kids in a room full of puppies. Brouhaha of brouhahas...this amassing of snow-clouds kept up and up, kept collecting over the region, till so preponderant were they that nobody could see a single mountain. The whole Olympic Primary Area vanished into a swirl of dancing grey.

Rather terrified at this control over The Weather, the United States Meteorological Service dispatched a pair of *crack* investigators from Washington. They had to be sent up on the twenty-first of January, Monday, since the snow had done havoc to all roads leading north from Albany and had also debilitated the local airports.

In the quiet of Jimmy's Restaurant in Main Street, where Lucille had agreed to meet the two for lunch, a now-famous coming-together took place.

"Lovely view, isn't it?" stated the lady, this time all in burgundy and staring bemusedly out the lakeside windows to what truly *was* a lovely view.

On iced-over Mirror Lake, snowmobiles and dog-sleds were plying, and more importantly to the meteorologists, across on the other shore, the line of pines and birches was totally heaped over with *snow*!

"But," asked one of the fellows, the younger one, "how...did you *do* it?"

"Do what?" pretended Lucille.

"Cause the snow!" urgently asked the younger, looking all but afraid that she would vanish into thin air.

"Well, let's see. I had a hysterectomy..." she began, much to the delight of all the eavesdroppers in the restaurant.

"No *seriously*!" the older one objected.

"It *was* serious! Do you want to see my *scars*?"

That shut the meteorologists up.

"And then I almost lit a bomb," she remarked casually.

"But...but *other* women have toyed with explosives!" the younger declared.

"But not so soon after having a hysterectomy! It's the *combination* that's vital!" she stated, then took a bite of her Swiss cheese omelette.

"So...*that's* your secret?" the older thought he had her pinned.

"Not at all. Then...The Bank was robbed..."

"We know," they both shouted.

"Then...the Games defaulted."

"We know that, too!"

"Then...I simply opened up my purse..."

"Aha..." the younger surmised.

"Money?" asked the older slyly. "Is *money*...your secret?"

Remaining mum, Lucille just stared outside, evidently concentrating on something quite intense. Her brows were knit, her lips were pursed, and her pupils were dilated. Then, she said: "If it suddenly begins to snow *now*...the answer to your last question is *yes*."

Remaining as mute as her omelette, which she finished eating, indeed The Sky suddenly began releasing a new flurry onto Lake Placid's frozen Mirror Lake...and the two meteorologists quietly excused themselves from Jimmy's Restaurant...leaving the lady all to herself and to whatever *Power* it was that resided deep within her eldritch Soul.

Presidential Interference

The whole world was jubilant that Lucille McSorley had saved the day!

111

Having heard all the previous gossip of course, Madame Tanette Dupleix, over in V.D. Castle, was having a Mass ascribed to Lucille's restorative puissance, and even had sent the widow her own personal telex, as if no greater honour could be bestowed upon a mere mortal.

Then, not to be outdone, the President of the International Olympic Committee sent a box of chocolates, especially made and expressly boxed solely and lovingly for the weather-wiz...and the taste of the creamy delights, from His Lordship, was so scrumptious that Lucille burst into tears. "God save The Peerage," she crowed.

But that was just the start of it. With recourse to more expletive grapevines than ever those listened to by Homer, Virgil, and Petronius combined, the contemporary Olympic Family (i.e., all those old men of the IOC, all those National Olympic Committees and Sporting Federations, and all those Committees which organize the Games themselves) vied like tots to see who could give the most appropriate thank-you to the "lady who spread wide her bounty".

"Now, Darling, look at it in *pragmatic* terms," Lucille stated to an incredulous Ivor, as the two of them gazed over the heaps and heaps of strange gifts which had been dumped willy-nilly in her living-room, "if all these donors of all this *stuff* had given a *cheque* for that amount...to The Committee...I *never* would have needed to have done what I had to do!"

"Well...you did do it, so it's now over and done with!"

"I may have jabbed some *life* back into this joint...but I still don't feel that I've accomplished my *most* important task," she stated vehemently.

"Which is?"

"*How* can you sit there surveying my booty...and ask me such an *asinine* question?"

"Frightfully apologetic..."

"So am I, Darling. I shouldn't get my blood-pressure up."

"So what's this *task* of yours?"

"We still have to get the Games stabilised, in one and *only* one spot!" Melodramatically she paused, then added: "You...have *got* to go back to *Greece*, Ivor...and as soon as Lake Placid is over. You've got to *infiltrate* the Organizing Committee for the new Olympic Nation that is being created in Athens."

"What Olympic Nation?"

"Go to Athens..."

Ivor asked stunned: "How do you *know* this? To whom have you been *talking*?"

Lucille smiled enigmatically, like Mona Lisa. "I don't mean that the Permanent Olympic Nation will *be* in Athens...but its *Organizing* Committee is now set up there."

"Says who?"

"Your friend, Lord Dalbeattie, the Senior IOC Member in Britain."

"*You* spoke with Dalbeattie? When?"

"Last night...he rang for *you*...with your best friend, Alexander Pella, that author, his nephew."

"*Alexander* rang, too? Why didn't you *tell* me?" Ivor was angry. Lucille smirked: "Now now. Don't blow a gasket. They *both* had a nice long chat with yours truly...and told me to give you the message to-day...which's what I'm doing...I'm acting on *orders*...since they said that as soon as you're done, here in the Adirondacks, that your services are required...in the Balkans..."

The Olympic Gold Medallist's eyes were wide as saucers.

"...and..." the rich lady continued, "...they told me to tell you that you're to fly from New York to London...and that you need to finalise arrangements with them at home. Of course...both Dalbeattie and Alexander will be *here*, for the Games soon anyhow, so at that time they can clue you in on what your duties for them will be over in Greece. Meanwhile, just be patient. Have some more Glenlivet."

After knocking back a hefty round of Scotch in silence, Ivor said: "God knows...fixing the Olympics *permanently*...in Greece...*won't* come easy..."

"Darling, it would be easier making it snow *within* the Sahara!"

At that moment the telephone rang and rang and rang. It was hidden beneath something, since the room was cluttered with too many gifts. After hunting madly, Lucille finally located the contraption, and thanked God for doing so, since she could hardly believe who was speaking on the other line.

"You don't really want to talk to *me*, Mister President?"

Ivor only uttered: "Not...The White House?"

"Uh...I'm in *perfect* form, how're *you*? Not too well, huh? Figures...you've got *lots* on your mind. Well take it from Lucille, if *these* Games up *here* can be saved...*anything* can be! But now...let me give *you* a piece of *my* mind: Your and Maggie's *Boycott*, against Moscow's Games, is absolutely *scandalous*! How *dare* you even *consider* wrecking the Olympics with your totally *insensitive* political *interference*!" The lady covered the speaker and said: "He's laughing!"

Ivor could not believe how Lucille was now speaking to the President of the United States!

"Did you ring me for something *special*?" she wondered, not meaning to sound half so harried as she did. "Me...no...just waiting for a pot-roast to come out of the oven. Huh?"

"You won't believe what he wants!" she quickly repeated to Hefferon.

"Say *what*?" she asked, stupefied. "Well...Mister President...I just don't *know*...I mean...how in Hell *can* I accommodate you...when *you're* doing *nothing* to accommodate Lake Placid's many *many* years of

113

sacrifice—and you're *certainly* not doing *shit* to foster the Olympian Ideal—with that goddamned *Boycott* you and Thatcher got going!"

Ivor's eyes were bugging out a mile, at her *balls*, but he just whispered: "What's *he* saying?"

"Shhh! Sorry, *not* you, Mister President, but some *noisy* friend of mind...say *what*? Why...that's *too* kind, but no I'm *not* nearly the quote Miracle Worker unquote that *The Washington Post* said I was this morning!"

What a discussion, the Olympic Athlete muttered to himself.

"Of course...I'll *try*...I mean I don't want to blacken my lily-white *reputation* now, do I? Look...but I'm *not* going to do a *goddamn* thing for *you*...unless *you* do something for *me*...hardball's hardball, right?...and that's that *you* CANCEL your *stupid* Boycott of the Moscow Games...and quit *interfering* in athletes' *lives*!"

Hearing that, Ivor just about fell off his chair. God, did this woman have castiron *cujones* or what! Too mad for words...

"Thank you very much...see you in February. *Maybe.* If you *dare* show your Georgia mug *up* here in the Adirondacks, after all this miserable *trouble* you've caused the Olympics and *us*! *Ciao!*"

"You just said *ciao*...to the President?"

"Why not? It's a *good* American word!"

"Well...what's he *want* from you?"

"I," she stated, with the greatest of deference, "have been re-quested...by my President...to do the *impossible*."

"What's that...take all the peanuts out of Georgia?"

"Hah hah," she stated harshly. "Don't be an idiot! I...have just been asked..." and she cleared her voice, "...to get the Presidential *Box* for Opening Ceremonies built."

Rather stunned, Ivor said: "What in Hell's it to *him*! *He's* not even expected—his damned *Vice* President's now supposed to be sitting in for his half-rate burlesque-act!"

"Anyone who *boycotts* an Olympic Games, for political chess-plays of personal and/or nationalistic kind, is a king-sized *asshole*!" snorted Lucille.

"So what's the President *doing*, sending you a bleeding *hammer*, along with a symbolic *sickle*, from his Oval Office, to construct his fucking *Box* with? And a Box he ain't even going to park his *butt-hole* in! Makes me sick! *Fuck* his Boycott! And *fuck* the Prime Minister's, too!"

"No—he said he's schlepping me a goddamned *gavel—stolen* from the Chief Justice of the American Supreme Court!"

The *Vice* Presidential Box

Standing in a blistery wind, on the bleachers imported from The Rose Bowl of Pasadena, California, which had been assembled at the edge of Lake Placid near the Ski Jump, on a site called The Horse Grounds,

114

certain people were *not* amused, but that did not bother Lucille McSorley.

Balthazar Wesley Breighbourne was one of those *not* amused, not *hardly*, and he told the Lady Board Member so: "I don't care if The Horse-Loving Queen Of *England* rang you...certain *things* have got to be done in certain *stages!* Anyway—the damned President of the United States is going to be a stinking *no-show!*" Balthazar, for those of you who skipped his chapter, was, and we repeat, Chief of the Ceremonies and Awards Department.

"Look, can I *help* it if I got a fucking Mafioso Offer-I-Can't-Refuse...from The *White* House!" Lucille retorted.

"I don't care if you got special marching orders from the *Crab Nebula!* Why *should* we kiss this President's ass...when The White House is doing *everything* in its power to give everybody in the whole *fucking* Adirondack Region giant-sized *ulcers* while *he's* down there, inside that *rancid* Oval Office, dropping his trow and *shitting* on the whole Olympic Movement's *head!*"

This was a mock stand-off, obviously. Both Lucille and Balthazar were only trying to keep warm, as workers kept shovelling and shovelling and shovelling snow...away from the area of the central configuration of seats which was where the Presidential Box was supposed to be placed. The stand-off was *faux*, because both Balthazar and Lucille adored each other, and both of them hated the very mention of the too-much-touted word "Boycott", which the whole world lately was spouting.

"Look...everything else's in order...so the quicker this crappy *Vice* Presidential Box gets built...the better for all concerned," she stated.

"That so?" Breighbourne responded. He did not like to be rushed into anything, not even something *Vice* Presidential.

Just then a load of carpenters did arrive, in some lorry which they drove all around the Parade Oval (where the athletes soon would be marching for Opening Ceremonies), three times round and round, before pulling to a halt in the centre of the central pier of seats. Lucille and Balthazar stayed fifteen rows up where they were, so the workers had to climb the stairs to reach them.

"Sorry we're late!" the foreman said and tipped his wooly skicap Lucille's way.

"Lucille McSorley," Balthazar stated as introduction to the five men. Two had been hiding in the box of the lorry, inside with their gear.

"Oh we know Lucy already," they beamed proudly.

"They used to work for me," she said. Lucille had been the one to contact them yesterday, anyhow.

"Closest *we'll* ever get to being the Runner with the Olympic Torch," the foreman said, "so that's why the boys wanted to spin wheels around the track three times!"

Mrs McSorley laughed. They were all reliable fellows. Without more ado, Breighbourne unrolled the blueprints for the Box, as the last of the snow, which had been covering the rows, was being brushed away by somebody from the Maintenance Department.

"So, this's where the *Vice* President's gonna be!" the foreman stated with honest disbelief. To him, the Olympics *were* something that you built...with your hands! "But all of us workers we *still* don't see why the damned *President* himself couldn't get his *tired* Georgia ass up here! Nevertheless...my boys and me we're mighty proud to be doing this for our country!" the man said with such emotion that Lucille's eyes teared up. How nice it must be, she exclaimed to herself, to be so *sane!*

So, the stand from which the *Vice* President of the United States of America would be pronouncing the XIII Olympic Winter Games open...did begin to take shape under a Sky which had suddenly cleared itself of all precipitation. Even Balthazar had to admit...that something extraordinary was under Lucille's control.

It was already the twenty-sixth of January, a Saturday. In only eighteen days...so short a time...all of the pomp and all of the competition would begin. There wasn't a Soul in Northern New York who didn't feel the pressure, and the honour, of being a part of whatever it was that God would soon be allowing to happen...even if the interfering President of the United States *was* only sending his *Vice* to act in his *sorry* stead!

Air Force One

Given that the *Vice* President's Box indeed had been built in record time, thanks to Lucille, the American Head of State had allowed the Lake Placid Olympic Committee use of his plane for a few days. Not just any aircraft, this was none other than Air Force One.

Of course, many Air Force Ones have come and gone, but the name always does remain the same. Designs change with changing technologies, and even a design can change within one Air Force One...as the official entourage from Lake Placid now was surprised to see.

"Oh look," Ambassador Levitt said on entering the famous jet which had been waiting an hour away from the Olympic Primary Area in the town called Plattsburgh, New York, at its Air Force Base. It was Sunday, a horribly cold Sunday in fact, the twenty-seventh day of January. "They've taken all the *beds* out...from when *Kennedy* was President! And they *all* had black satin sheets...from Frederick's of Hollywood...in case a starlet or two was aboard!" The former Ambassador to Tokyo had been aboard Air Force One once, in Yokahama, but never while the machine was in the air.

Besides the Ambassador and his wife, the Olympic contingent

116

consisted of the President of The Committee and his wife, as well as the Barleys and a few others, all of whom entered the big-bird with glee.

Balthazar Wesley Breighbourne and Cecille Oberlin Breighbourne, the Archivist, were entering the jet, too. To Balthazar, it was all an impossible dream-come-true...since it was he who had conjured up most of what now was going on.

"Well..." corrected someone from the State Department in Washington, given that the DC group had already climbed aboard, two hours earlier, and for them the trip to Athens was going to be a very long and tiring one, "well..." the State Department chap said again, forgetting what he was attempting to say. "Oh, I remember...yes, that *Balthazar* guy who just walked past," he confided to his aide, a rather foxy looking brunette, "it wasn't *really* him, though he's head of Ceremonies and Awards, who cooked up this idea to get Air Force One."

"No?" his aide asked. "I thought it was."

"Everybody does, but it wasn't..." and the fellow turned around to see if Breighbourne were listening, "...since *I* know who *really* thought it up!"

"Who's that?" she wondered. "Is he on the plane?"

"Don't be silly...most of the intelligent people who work for the Games *aren't* on this plane!" he declared.

"You're wicked!" his aide cooed and fluffed her hair. "Where're we going, anyway?"

"Athens this time," he replied, very blasé.

"Oh...not *again*! We were just there last week! If I hear one more *bouzouki* song, I'm gonna retch! Why don't we tell the pilot to send her to the South Seas?"

"Because the Olympic Torch doesn't *come*...from the South Seas! God, sometimes I wonder how in Hell you ever passed your Selective Service Test."

"I *didn't*! My father's a Governor...remember?"

Secret Service people just were boarding and snubbing the pair from the State Department, though they knew them.

"Working for Uncle Sam's fun, isn't it?" the State Department nerd sneered.

"So what're we off to Greece for *this* time?" his dippy aide foolishly asked.

"I just *told* you...don't you listen to anything!"

"No."

"To pick up the Olympic Flame!"

"Who's she?"

"Well...just keep your *pretty* little eyes open, and you'll see!" He had to talk to her like a nursery school toddler, then she understood everything.

"By the way...who got Air Force One? Is he cute?"

"You met him already! You thought he *was* cute!"

"Where? Who?" the brunette warmed, as the Captain announced that everybody should fasten their seatbelts.

"I don't know his name, but remember...he was the middling-tall guy who was working in the Protocol Department," pontificated the chap from State.

"Protocol of what...The White House?"

"No...of the Olympic Committee! He was with the IOC Session Department or something...brownish black curly hair, sarcastic, a moustache..."

"Oh *Fabian!*" she shouted so loud it embarrassed her partner immensely. God, was she a dippy broad!

"No *not* Fabian...he was in Sports!"

The engines for the great elite jet began to rev up, and the thirty-five or so aboard hushed their bitchy banter for an instant.

"Is this really going to Greece?" the brunette at last couldn't help asking. "For a...for a *Flame?*"

"Uh huh..." the fellow responded rather dreamily, as the huge apparatus began to shuttle down the runway, and as he was picturing himself fucking the girl's brains out...again. That's all she was good for. At least she was efficient between the sheets...and everywhere else he took her. He was getting a raging hardon. She began stroking his thigh with one great long painted fingernail, then started running it cruelly along the tip of his cock.

"And...will we get to see the Flame...*lit?*" she wondered, as she seized the whole swollen glans of his penis between two hot little fingers.

"Uh huh..." he replied hardly audibly. His breathing was now laboured. He too, as a younger man, had read his textbooks. Ancient History had been his hobby...when he once was a little boy...and the Hellenic Civilisation had always intrigued him far more than had any other that had been much more exotic. But such thoughts were fast fading, as the brunette now was rubbing his cock to abandon. She did it so well. Even if she *was* mentally deficient, she sure could work a guy up. He glanced about, to see if any other passengers were looking. None were. They were seats away, doing their own thing. His sports jacket had already been placed upon his lap, to camouflage any sexual activity. Given that the flight-crew were otherwise engaged, he felt that it was now the best time to unzip himself. He nodded to the girl, and she carefully, slowly, let his zipper down, then brought out his dick. Then right there in Air Force One...she began to give him a blow-job. "We'll see...the Flame lit...at Olympia..." he growled to himself, as the girl did what she knew best, as he faced the porthole window and watched New York State vanish behind him, as the President of the United States's aircraft aimed over Canada, then over the wide Atlantic, bound for the homeland of the Culture which we have altered so very very much, but which we must live with...since it *is* our very own...

118

Boys Will Beat Boys

The President's jet got off the ground just in time. Buffalo was sending another one of her ferocious blizzards, and so was Ottawa, both of which seemed to hit the Adirondacks at precisely the same time.

"Nobody's *ever* seen anything like this!" the same younger weather-man from the United States Meteorological Service screeched to the same older one. Both were standing guard against such climactic inevitabilities at the best lookout site in the whole region, inside the cosy warmth of the lounge atop the 90-Metre Ski Jump. From there, you could just about see to China!

Everybody in the lounge was in quite the panic, not knowing where to look first.

"But...but it's *two* fucking blizzards! One with Lake Effect Snow, from the Great Lakes Region, and one with an Arctic Air Mass from Hudson Bay! And *both're* aiming for Placid at the very *same* time!" the senior weather-man gasped, in a tizzy, biting his lips and sucking on a plastic cup of coffee like it was the last cuppa he'd ever drink on Earth.

"Well...whadda we gonna *do?*" the younger hollered.

"Don't need to seed clouds for snow, at least," laughed a maintenance-man, who thought the whole thing the best fun he'd ever had. "Just a couple storms a-coming, that's all! No cause for a Kotex!" He kept laughing, hysterically, as he continued sweeping the floor. In truth, he was scared shitless.

Neither of the US boys knew what to say. They had studied some Weird Weather in their lives...but nothing, not one single textbook, had prepared the two for *this.*

"Why...they're aiming straight as *vectors!*" the junior one remarked loudly, amazed at the mathematics of it all.

"Mother Nature sure can be precise...when she hankers to!" the older stated, giving away his fetching up in the Ozarks of Missouri.

"But just look at that!" screamed the younger. "Aiming *at* each other..."

"Not *at* each other, you Fool, at *us!*" the maintenance-man volunteered, now quite alarmed at the sight.

"Aiming anyhow at a *perfect* ninety degrees!"

"Those're called *right* angles!" the man with the broom declared and beamed.

So it was. Coming from the wilds of Ontario, and coming from the north-north-west, the *black* storm was aiming south-south-east, in direct conflict with the *grey* storm that was coming from Niagara Falls, which was from the south-west-west and aiming north-east-east.

But...by the time the poor meteorologists had time to figure out this tricky computation, the black storm from Canada and the grey storm from Western New York were getting closer, and closer, and closer, then...all of a sudden Lake Placid vanished from sight...for two whole weeks!

It snowed and it snowed, and it snowed and it snowed, and it snowed and it snowed some more. Neither storm could move, not the black one nor the grey one, as both kept trying to make a getaway out a whitened valley, but each time that this was attempted disagreeing winds just wouldn't let the other storm budge.

"We'll just have to ride this one out..." said the man with the broom, who had made the place as clean as it ever could be. "No cause for a Kotex."

"Oh will you shut up about your fucking *Kotex*!" the senior weather-man ranted.

"God...what're *you*...on the *rag* or something!" snapt the maintenance-guy back.

"So...what're we supposed to *eat*...snowed in up here?" the junior official inquired, to change the subject.

"Junk food," yapped the maintenance-man. "Plenty of munchies ...in these here boxes..."

So, everybody gorged on munchies, drank instant coffee, and wondered when in Hell the Furies would wear themselves out. Only able to see a couple of feet out the observation deck's windows, the men who were stranded up there, atop the concrete marvel of the whole Eastern Seaboard, had no idea what was going on ninety metres below. But the snow...just kept climbing and climbing and climbing...

All radio and television and what-not communication had been severed the moment the two blizzards collided. Power lines and special frequency cables had been snapt like poor-quality cotton thread. The President of the United States—despite his antipathy to the Olympics in general—had been goosed into action by the conditions and had been forced to declare the whole Olympic Primary Area "a national disaster region", which, many of the locals said (after the fact, when they were able to hear that the President had done *anything*) it should've been declared *years* ago!

For almost everybody concerned...it was quite a lot of fun... regardless of the countless inconveniences. "If it ever stops, at least there'll be plenty of snow for this and any other Olympics ever staged!" Truly, that man with the broom was a stand-up comedian par excellence.

Then, suddenly, and very eerily too, the entranced and spooky snowflakes simply vanished into thin air. The turmoil was over...but certainly not as quickly as it had come.

Well...to *some* people, and not many at that, the turmoil was over. Matter of fact, to *most* people the turmoil was just commencing.

"Do you realise what *day* it is?" the younger weather-man said in a daze.

"Day Hell! Do you realise what's outside these very windows?" the older screeched back. After being incarcerated so long with this upstart, not to mention with the loony maintenance-man, he was ready to murder them *both!*

"Why..." said the younger perkily, not believing his eyes, and only trying to avoid discussing what *was* before his eyes, "...we've been snowed in here for *months!*"

"It's just two damned *weeks*, Idiot!" his superior said.

"But we got here in *January*...and now it's already *February*," mumbled the junior, who then laughed like a hyena.

"*Tenth* of February, to be precise!" cackled the maintenance-guy. "I've been cutting notches in this here table, *see!*"

"When've you been doing *that*?" wondered the junior.

"Why...when you two've been *sleeping*, which's been just about *all* the time!"

"But..." now the sight before his eyes was starting to register, "but...look at all that *snow!*"

"Good equation, Einstein!" the man with the broom said saucily. "And it'll be *me*...who's gotta clean the mother *up!*"

"No...you can't possibly..." remarked the younger weather-man so stupidly that the maintenance-man hit him on the bum with his broom.

"Serves you right!" the older laughed. "Here, give *me* a good whack, too!" and he bent over and offered up his butt to be beaten. *That's* how crazy it had got inside the Ski Jump's lounge...after a full fortnight of snow.

"But...I was just looking at all the *precipitation!*" the younger whined, and offered up his backside again. He really enjoyed getting his hide tanned. It beat the blood back into his buttocks, which got pretty tired just sitting on a chair for two full weeks!

Whack!

Precipitation...was putting it mildly. The furious days of nonstop snowing had covered every single tree and building in sight. The Olympic Area now looked just like a photograph of Antarctica from *National Geographic* magazine. White...white...and white some more ...everywhere...and it all was absolutely blinding. The Sun had just now come out...to illuminate the whole ghostly scene...

Whack!

"But look down there!" the younger squeaked.

Whack!

"Oh shut up, we've got eyes!" the broom-man muttered. It was apparent who, in the snowstorm, had become King Of The Mountain in *this* lounge-act! But even he...couldn't help staring straight down the shaft of the Ski Jump...but the shaft was no longer anywhere in sight...

Whack!

121

"Why...it's drifted up ninety whole metres..." the older lamented, unable to grasp the fact with his mind.

Whack!

"How many damned feet's *that*?" the maintenance-chap wondered.

Whack!

"Why...almost...almost...almost..." the younger couldn't even put the truth in words. He was enjoying his brooming too much to think straight.

"Fool, why it's all shy of a good three hundred!" the older declared, but hardly could grasp the fact, either.

Whack!

"You mean...if we try stepping out of here...we'd sink clear out of sight...and they'd never find us..." queried the maintenance-man, who handed the broom to the young one. "Golly...beat my ass on *that* one!" And he dropt trow, right there in the lounge, and presented his hairy bare buttocks to the weather-men. "*Hit* me...hit me *hard*!"

"That's right!" said the junior US official, as he gave the worker a sound tanning. "You step out this door...you'd never *ever* be seen again...in a *million* years!"

Whack!

Then, all three began to shake all over. Not once, in all of their dedicated and distinguished careers, had one of them *ever* come close to being involved in such a true Freak Of Mother Nature as *this* killer-storm, which laid Lake Placid low just before Opening Ceremonies of the Winter Olympic Games...

The Snow Must Go On

Well if Rome can stage a colossal *Aïda* every year inside the improbable and Olympian ruins of the ancient Baths of Caracalla, notwithstanding the cast of thousands, the horse-drawn chariots, the elephants, the big-cats, the dogs, and the cantankerous and excitable Romans themselves, victims of perpetual *paparazzi*, governmental shake-ups, and scandals, then certainly Lake Placid, once every fifty years, could dig out from under a little bit of snow in order to stage an Olympics. And believe it or not, she did.

Everybody who ever worked for, or now did work for, or who was scheduled to work for the said Games was marshalled into snow-duty, and everybody was given some kind of shovel.

It was not fun, but then again it was a hoot! The tons of snow turned out to be the Games' saving grace, putting everybody on equal footing, and making the oddest sorts of people, who'd never *dream* of associating with each other, suddenly finding themselves rubbing shoulders with each other, as every single street and pavement and path was shovelled out.

"I've met more *interesting* people...than I'd ever want to meet!" confided a very well-dressed Rebecca Harper, as gorgeous as ever. She had not seen her husband the Doctor in two full weeks, having been snowed into her office in the Convention Building.

"So have I..."

"So have I..."

"So have I..." everybody said quite honestly, to a reporter from *Der Spiegel* magazine of Germany, who of course was shovelling, too.

Most amused were the Chinese Dongs, Attaché Dong and Long Dong, who were seen shovelling out from Steak-And-Burgher. They were quoted as saying: "Nothing like this has happened to us since the Cultural Revolution! It's so refreshing...to see American people...all shovelling their difficulties away...together!"

Never a truer statement, in America, had ever been uttered.

"Work...I used to think it was too too pedestrian," Wendy Dion, outside of Town Hall, remarked playfully. She then made a snowball and chucked it into her playmate's face...that of none other than Burt Dubczek, the Executive Manager, who didn't mind a little bit of snow at all.

Everyone was there, out in the bright sunny elements, working away, busy as bees, happy as larks, healthy as newborn babes, and sober as nuns on a picnic...well, not *totally* sober perhaps, since the only way that the populace had kept its head these past flurried two weeks was with *lots* of liquor, wine, beer, cocaine, marijuana, pep pills, valiums, and sedatives, not necessarily in that order, and not all at once, of course. So, everybody was out there really rather tipsy in fact, and in truth everybody was out there with a goddamned gargantuan hangover, but it was the best snow-party anybody ever had imagined.

"Well...it won't all happen if we don't all shovel her out," Judge Ronson joked to Mimi Tiny, who had eaten far too many munchies and who felt rather less Tiny than she'd wish, rather worse for the weather, *literally* worse for *The Weather!*

"Come on, Mimi Gal, sing us 'Embraceable You'!" everybody chorused. "Give us your *torch*-song, an *Olympic* Torch torch-song!"

"Up yours!" the tall singer joked, and gave them all the finger. Evidently, *her* two weeks of hibernation hadn't altered her vibrant personality. "I'll *torch* your song!"

"Well..." declared the Judge, puffing on his pipe: "The only thing *worth* torching...was the Session of the IOC!"

"I know but..." Mimi stopt shovelling, exhausted, "well...what do all those old men *do* in those Sessions which the public never get to see?"

"Who knows?" the Judge replied. "Who knows..."

"God...can you *believe* that there're only *three* more days till the Games officially open...so if they're all going to *get* here in time to *hold* their crazy Session, then they better be on their planes right now!"

And the Judge replied to Mimi: "They are!"

"I know you've got top security *clearance*...but how in Hell'd you get top security *clairvoyance*?" she wondered.

"Are you deaf?"

Mimi was shocked. "Of course I'm not..."

"Well *prick* up your ears!" the Judge said and laughed.

"Well steer off your *prick*!" Mimi Tiny retorted.

Just as she was chuckling, planes from all directions began to break over the horizon and to roar their way towards the little Adirondack Airport at Saranac Lake. Others kept on going, aiming for Montréal, Plattsburgh, Burlington, and Albany, and all points north, south, east, and west.

"My God...it's *happening*!" Mimi exclaimed, then the whole of Lake Placid resounded in a robust echo.

"IT'S HAPPENING!" everybody began to shout!

"THE GAMES ARE GOING TO *BE*!"

Everybody began to dig dig dig frenetically, realising that this was really it...within three short days...the whole wide world would be watching Lake Placid...so the place had better be...READY!

All The Way From Olympia

The thirteenth of February...1980...it was the day that everyone had been waiting for, that everyone had been working for, that everyone had sacrificed for over and over and over again. It was Lake Placid's Day Of Glory...and now it's all retreated backwards into History...

So much...*for*...so much...

Many many tears were shed that day indeed. Snow'd been cleared, Tempers smoothed, Spirits uplifted, Hearts raised, and even those poor Souls who had not lived to see this day come true...*they* were there...content in their more peaceful seating for a few days' release from The Incommunicable Great Realm Beyond...

The radiance of Kate Smith was there...in Spirit...though she was confined to a local nursing home...Kate Smith...whose voice and whose warmth had permeated the whole of the Adirondacks for so many decades gone by...

Yes...many many were the tears that were shed...

The Olympic Stadium...at The Horse Grounds...was so very jubilant, to be sure. In the three banks of bleachers, of the rectangular seating plan, the twenty thousand lucky lucky members of the public were just ecstatic to be witnessing these Opening Ceremonies. They had gone utterly rapturous when the President's march for their *Vice* President had been played...as the second most powerful man in the whole Western World began walking into the Stadium to the strains of "Hail To The Chief"...

Somehow, like magic, even the entrance of the *Vice* President of the United States of America seemed to give the occasion the blessing that it certainly did need, but the absence of the President himself only underscored all of the dissension that had occurred until this very day. And nobody on Earth *ever* could brush *that* one beneath any rug, no matter how small nor how large!

"I hereby declare the XIII Olympic Winter Games *open!*" the *Vice* President stated clearly.

And it was all magic, from that very moment...

The Athletes then came in...from forty different countries...in groups which marched to each country's national anthem...behind flags which then amassed together...before The Tri-Pylon which would soon be supporting The Sacred Olympic Flame...

It was all so colourful, so festive, so moving...

The hundreds of voices and hundreds of musicians from The Crane School Of Music had sung and had played...so melodically...as if to melt the very mountains ringing the Stadium round...

Then...an instinctive tension gripped the mass of people so powerfully that everyone seemed to realise at once what next must occur...and a great whoop of excitation, from the bank of bleachers closest to the Ski Jump and which had its back to it, suddenly burst forth from the thousands in the crowd, as the top row of spectators suddenly jumped up and announced: "THE RUNNER IS COMING! THE RUNNER'S COMING...BRINGING THE OLYMPIC FLAME..."

The crowd couldn't contain itself any longer!

Everyone stood up, looking all about at once, but those in the central section of seats *knew* where the Runner would first appear...

Then...after a minute of racing behind the great mound of Earth upraised...and where the Athletes were amassed...and in the middle of which stood The Tri-Pylon soon to be ablaze...high upon the leftmost side of this great mount...suddenly stood one lone human being...the luckiest person in the world...he who would have the ultimate honour...of igniting The Sacred Olympic Flame...carried all the way from Greece...and that lone human being...was the Olympic Gold Medallist...the winner of the previous Summer Games' 1500 Metre Race...Ivor Hefferon...

People now did know what the Olympics had truly gone through...seeing this world-famous Athlete...

People now were standing...motionless...as if suspended in Space...

The whole of the Stadium...was hushing...

One solitary human being...was standing there...silent...alone...

What really was it...that he was bearing...

The Flame...had been kindled...by the very Sun Itself...

The days of Apollo...still could be amongst us...

Such a small, yet vital thing...this captured Fire...

125

All the way...from Olympia...from Greece...

Where the Chief Priestess...of the Goddess Hera...charmed The Sun...

Where Sun-Ray on Metal-Disc sparked Torch-Beam...

Where fallen pillars of Thunderer Zeus looked upon...

Myths of Man Before could likewise live...

As now...the luckiest man...began to run...

To the cheers of so many thousands...witnessing this experience of a lifetime...

The lone man was running...

Down the ramp which was sloping...

Sloping from the mound...

And he was beginning to race...the Stadium round...

On this crystal-clear Adirondack Wednesday afternoon...

It wasn't memories of home itself that were bringing tears to the Athlete's eyes...

It was the fact that he was once again inside an Olympic Arena...

Once again he was hearing the thousands cheering for all their worth...

Once again the memories began to overwhelm him...

As he kept on running...fiercely...fighting to stay the first...

And as that last lap raced nearer...the huge Stadium's crowd was going berserk...as in Ivor's mind he was re-enacting his Olympic Victory Race...as that man holding second place was falling behind...as that man holding second place was giving way to the speeding third...

Then...what did he hear in his mind...but "The Olympic Hymn" being sung aloud...

From whom? From fans? From his own inner mind?

The symphony orchestra and the chorus now were playing and singing so beautifully...as tears were continuing to fall towards snow...

Racing...

Faster...

Lungs burnt alive...

And the animalistic roar of Mankind...

Everyone standing...

Jumping...

Waving...

Closer...

Closer...

The end is nearing...is nearing...is almost there...

Keep on running...

Linked indubitably with The Past...The Present was vanishing in these instants...

Ancient Greece was *living*...once again...

The Tri-Pylon now was standing there...waiting...as the Runner kept receiving the cheers from all around...

He heard the Master of Ceremonies announcing his name...

But his inner mind was hearing *other* callings to Acclaim...

What, inside, was he thinking?

Soon, the Athletic Contests would be beginning...

Many people with heightened sensitivity...now were crying...

Yet many also were thinking...as they were weeping...that the Games *couldn't* continue on much longer...*as* they had been doing ...since 1896...since the world was such a *strange* place now in which to be living...

As the Runner now was reaching his ultimate destination...an intranslatable silence once again was possessing the huge crowd...and the Olympic Athlete kept standing there, in eldritch stillness, but then...

He bent on one knee and took a minute for private prayer, a gesture that touched the whole immense gathering profoundly...

Then slowly...he rose his muscular body upwards...

And slower still...he began to lift...aloft...The Torch...to salute The Sky...

Had this urge...this urge to strive towards Perfection...been a calling to Mankind...sent down from On High?

The upraised Torch seemed to be kissing whatever it was that had helped Mankind persist towards The Supra-Human Ideal...

And now...it was almost...Night...

Flickering more brightly in the dimming of the daylight...the crowd now was holding its breath...as the Runner kept making his way...to the base of the towering Tri-Pylon...whose Bowl for The Flame was standing dozens of feet above the frozen ground...

The Tri-Pylon looked like an ancient and Olympian-sized Tripod...such as may have been used by the very Fates themselves upon the snowy heights of Thessalian Mount Olympos...

The Tripod kept waiting...

The Gathered kept waiting...

The Runner could wait no longer...

Into the Bowl...on the chains which were waiting to hoist The Fire *up*...the Olympic Gold Medallist now was placing his Torch...as the crowd was now letting out great yells of joy!

Then up...

Up...

Up...

Up...

Up...

Up...

Up...

Up...

More and more high...the Bowl kept raising and raising...as if drawn by The Power of the Olympian Gods themselves...

And then the Cauldron was exploding...into an Ecstasy of orange Light...that began to radiate through the Hearts and the Souls of all of those who had gathered to greet the Night...

But to where...where...*where*...were the Games *themselves* rising?

How many *more* Games...ever...would there *be*?

SummerGames

PROLOGUE

26th April – Wednesday – 4.10 PM

Once upon a time...

I was climbing bloody Mount Olympos, late in the afternoon. I shouldn't have been where I was—I'd been lost for over an hour. Exhausted and anxious, there was nothing to do but plod on, ever downwards, towards the great central Vale of the mountain, in hopes to locate the Refuge Hut, at an elevation of 6,000 feet. I must have been totally cracked in the skull to have thought that the Refuge could be found on my own. I should have gone back the way that I came—should have stuck with our plan to meet at Skála* Peak, at three that afternoon. But like a sodding fool, I set out on my own. Now—here I was—totally lost on a sideslope of Olympos—where it seemed neither Man nor God had ever set foot.

There was a Mount...

Back in Athens were two women I made love to. One was a real case; the other just may be my salvation? Dora Cain all but had me convinced that she was virtuous. She had the widest shoulders, the smallest hips, the littlest breasts, and the longest neck that I ever had seen, but the combination had made her look taller than her five-foot-five-inch chassis. And she was always wearing those ghastly high heels. Dora could only have been American, from her false eyelashes to her tarted-up toenails. Ada though—now she was a Greek—as Hellenic as they come. She had pitch-black wavy hair cascading way down her back. Elegant features, long fingers, a five-foot-nine-inch frame, and was she buxom. And a perfectly lovely heart-shaped bum. Ada was soft-spoken. Dora was lewd and bold. Ada had blue eyes and light skin—odd for a Greek—but her family was from northern Greece, from Macedonia, from the countryside by the ancient capital where Aristotle taught the future boy-conqueror of the world. Dora's red ringlets were close-cropt, and made her best features (those pouty-sucky lips) all the more puckered and pronounced. And Dora really knew how to hook a man—with those fat green eyes—but she had horsy hands and feet, an itsy-bitsy nose, and wads of freckles. In bed, Dora was strong as a musk-ox, but overall she rounded out to what some blokes might call "cute". But Ada...now there was one *gorgeous* woman.

* Pronounced: SKAH-lah. Meaning: Stairs. *(Throughout this segment of the novel accent marks appear above the syllable of Greek words that must be stressed for correct pronunciation. Pronunciation of Greek words and names that recur or require explanation will be flagged; when known, meanings will be explained. For further help with Greek words and names, refer the Glossary at the back of this book.)*

133

Lying leagues beneath the young Aegean Sea.

I was really lost! Why in Hell was I even thinking about "dizzy dames" when it was worrying about them in the first place that put me here! Damn—women will be the ruin of men yet.

"Remind yourself," I said, "before you do this now—before you begin this slide down this glacier or whatever the flaming Hell it's called, this gigantic pile of snow angling down the hillside at sixty or more degrees—remind yourself—you're *mortal!* You don't want to go down *that.* You're an Olympic Gold Medal Athlete."

And there it sat, mute, one piece of rock...

"Bleeding Hell—down, just get *down* it," some voice inside me kept ordering.

"Down *this* sheet of ice?"

"But you've *got* to get down it—it's getting dark—they're expecting you back at the Refuge Hut."

"But I might be killed if I can't stop!"

"You might die *anyway*, if you stay here very much longer. You've *got* to move!"

"Bollocks."

"You *have* to!"

"There's an island down there."

"That's it. There's an island. A piece of land. In the middle of this glacier. An asylum."

"With little pine trees?"

"That's right. Just slide to the little pine trees."

"This's impossible."

"Do it! You have no more options. You're stuck here. The Sun's going to set. You can't go back uphill. Get going. You're lost."

"I'm not!"

"You are. Just put your bum on the snow—and *slide.*"

Until its limestone bulk was stirred to be...

Would I be sliding now, if I hadn't tried to save the Olympics in the first place? Save the Olympics—can you imagine? What a farce. Well—I saved something or other in the past few weeks here in Greece. The papers even said that I alone defeated a subversive plot to do in the Olympic Games. Lots of good *that's* doing for me now...that I'm accelerating...

"But it'll be a *good* slide down," the voice kept saying. "*Won't* it be a good slide down?"

"Accelerating too fast."

"Jesus—we're sliding—like a dunce down a runaway roller coaster's tallest bend—oh Heaven Hell *save* me!"

Whence, Time Itself roused the saline stone,

"On my arse. It's sopping wet. My ungloved hands...sore with frost. Down sliding...to Death?"
    "Olympics be damned as well!"
    "Can't keep my balance..."
    "Can't brake a stop..."
    "Can't break..."
    "Can't brake..."
    "Can't stop..."

And towards the Stars,

"Oh Hail Mary help me! I can't..."
    "I'm going to crash!"
    "That little island in the snow..."
    "Rushing at me!"

Upwards from the brine,

"On rock!"
    "Oh please save me!"

Olympos – slowly woke and left

"Jesus!"
    "I'm crashing!"

Its womb within the Deep,

"Crashing!"

For greater things, for purposes divine...

"Crashing!"
    "Crashing!"
    "Crashing!"
    BLACKOUT!

PART
I

Si quelques siècles venaient par miracle
s'ajouter au peu de jours qui me restent,
je referais les mêmes choses,
et jusqu'aux mêmes erreurs,
je fréquenterais les mêmes Olympes
et les mêmes Enfers.

—Emperor Hadrian

(from *Mémoires d'Hadrien,* by Marguerite Yourcenar,
Gallimard, Paris, 1974, page 303)

29th February – Tuesday – Midnight

Ivor Hefferon, Olympic Gold Medallist, winner of the Men's 1500 Metre Race at the last Olympic Games, arrived in Athens from London earlier in the day. A British subject, and a PhD candidate in Classics at Christ Church, Oxford, he had previously been to Greece two times. The first time was to the European 1500 Metre Championships held in the northern city of Thessaloníki, five years ago. Ivor had won. Even though he was older than most of the others competing, that win had convinced him to keep on with his training, and even to attempt to qualify for the Olympics, to which he did go the very next summer and which, to his amazement, offered the greatest triumph of his life. But to the Balkan Peninsula Ivor had not returned a second time till early last summer, some months before he had decided, on a dare, to go see what Lake Placid was like. Those crazy Winter Olympics in the Adirondacks...but days behind him...now seemed an eternity away...since Ivor was aching in his heart to be returning home...at last...to Greece...to the place he loved most upon this Earth.

Since his Olympic victory, four summers ago, Ivor hadn't had a single moment of peace. Everybody wanted something. And nobody seemed to understand that the man was serious when he admitted to the Press: "For me...the *act* of winning the race was the best award anyone could give. I don't want anything else now. I don't want to be known as a Star. I don't want to endorse any products. I refuse to cash in on the Olympic Gold for more than the memories of the crowds that applauded that wonderful day. I don't even want to *compete* again. How much vainglory can one individual greet, before it sours the naïve thrill inside that urges a man to *run*, as a free creature, in the first place? To have taken part in an Olympics, and to have *won*, is enough for me...for a lifetime."

In the forty-three months till this day, Ivor had made good his pledge. He had stood his ground, as enticements from dozens of corporate executives kept muscling and flexing his way. Nobody believed he was honestly holding out for a principle. Everyone believed he'd sell himself sooner or later. The pressures of society innevitably were out to turn one into a high-class whore, as quickly and as effortlessly as possible, flat on the back, lubricated, painlessly in, painlessly out, with bank statements giving it all meaning. And every month the pressures got more intense. Until...*this* day.

Ivor had kissed Britain a final goodbye at Heathrow, and flew with Olympic Airlines back to the capital of Greece. But little did Hefferon himself realise that The Fates were sending him off to the Balkans for a much more noble purpose than any commercial huckster could ever have had the brains or the balls to conceive.

At Athens Airport, a scandal-reporter based there specially to catch personalities caught the famous Runner at baggage claim. The

141

six-foot-two height of the fellow and the curly blond hair were unmistakable. Needless to say, the worldwide publicity that he got as the Torch Runner for the lighting of the Sacred Flame at Opening Ceremonies at Lake Placid had done nothing to reduce his Star Appeal. Before Hefferon could stop him, the gruff character was taking his photograph, then barraging him with banal questions. Since the previous Summer Games, Ivor's reticence to cash in on his Medal had done the reverse of his expectation, and had only caused the Athlete to remain the talk of gossip columns all across Europe and the States. His employment and escapades in the Adirondacks only augmented this publicity. His good looks and boyish altruism assured that he wasn't about to fade from the public eye as hastily as Hefferon would have prayed.

To every question the reporter kept asking, Ivor simply kept saying: "No comment." Finally, just to spice things up, the reporter was demanding to know why Hefferon was arriving in Athens at all. To this, Ivor's sense of humour couldn't resist answering totally off the cuff: "My purpose is to fight against the bastardisation the Olympian Ideal." Little did he realise how truthful those words would soon become.

"Like you tried to do at Lake Placid?"

"Moreso!"

Well—*that* certainly threw the reporter. But he took the quote verbatim, and it appeared splashed all over the Greek papers that evening, as a plug beneath the surprised picture of Ivor's mug. The Athlete had seen the photograph in the lobby of the Hotel Grande Bretagne only an hour ago, and had shaken his head as an obviously wealthy Greek lady had dropt her paper and her jaw at his virile approach. Ivar was in running gear, with hairy muscular thighs and protruding crotch aiming right at the woman, in the lobby of Athens's most prominent hotel. But Hefferon just winked at her, ran outside to the orange-blossom aroma of Sýntagma* Square, then on in the night towards the capital's central Stadium.

It was Leap Night, the last day of February that only comes once every four years. Inside the white stone encasing of the majestic Panathenian Stadium, the Runner was making his way round the track, by the light of a gleaming Half Moon. It was midnight.

Metre after metre, stride after stride, the legs felt good and the mind was vibrantly alive. The huge rock Stadium, inset in the grip of a hillside, had been designed for the revival of the Modern Olympics in 1896. Paid for by the wealthy Alexandrian patron, George Averoff, it had cost a million drachmas back then. It radiated coolly, like a phosphorescent fish, in the bluish spicy air of the night.

*Pronounced: SIN-tahg-mah. Meaning: Constitution.

Back in Lake Placid they're all still shivering with cold, Ivor thought as he turned the curve at the deepest end of the edifice and began to run back towards the avenue which fronted onto the luxurious Botanic Garden of Greece. Good God, this city is Beauty personified, he said aloud.

Up above, and unseen, three forms behind the upraised marble barrier beyond the forty-eighth row of seats looked at each other, pointed at the Runner, and laughed. Then two of them touched the third and nudged the third that was dressed in green towards the stairs leading down to the track. The two that nudged then proceeded in silence along the path at the top of the Stadium, then vanished amid the shadows and the hoots of invisible owls.

Ivor kept running, exhilarated by the change of climate and the thought of finally being back in Greece. He *was* at home here, as if he had returned to his very own house after an impossible quest for a never-appearing Golden Fleece. And what a Fleece Lake Placid had been!

No, in this warm Aegean evening, it wasn't memories of the just-completed Winter Games that were bringing the tears to the Athlete's eyes, as he ran. For the first time since last August, Ivor was in a *Summer* Olympic arena, on a *Summer* Olympic track, and his mind was running backwards, four Julys, to his Gold Medal race. The Runner now was hearing the thousands cheering for all their worth, as he kept on running that day, fiercely, fighting to stay the first. And as that last lap had raced ever nearer, that huge Stadium's crowd kept going berserk, as the man holding second place was falling behind and giving way to the speeding third. And what did he hear in his mind then...but "The Olympic Hymn" sung loud. From whom? Fans? His own inner mind? Racing. Faster. Lungs burnt alive. And the animalistic roar of Mankind. Everyone standing. Jumping. Waving. Closer. Closer. The end is nearing, is near, is almost there! Keep running! Out front! First place! Just a bit more! VICTORY!

On the other side of the Panathenian Stadium, almost exactly opposite where the three forms had been, one lone boy, about nineteen, was combing his hair with a hand, and was quietly gazing on the scene. He was Greek. His long curls had been dyed henna-red, and into them he had stuck mirrored Hollywood-style specs. He wasn't paying a bit of attention to the owls.

Ivor still was running, but was slowing down. The acclaim of that Gold Medal Summer again was fading into the folds of his agile brain. And Athens again was making her presence felt.

A pretty young woman now was in the front row of the Stadium's seats. She was wearing very little, running shorts, track shoes, halter-top, all in green.

Jogging slowly by her, Ivor was blinded with his own thoughts as he aimed towards the Botanic Garden one more time. The thousands of that glorious summer day had now become shadows of blueness on marble white as bone. He now was jogging in a state of exultant inebriation, alone.

Aiming ponderously for the avenue, Hefferon slowed even more and noticed that the thousands of chalky seats supported a summit sheltered with trees, a dark-coloured wood of cypress and pine. Feeling queer inside, Ivor dropt his gaze and began to stare straight ahead.

There, directly before him, as if in some dream, and along the track on which he was running, way down at the Stadium's end, but coming closer, some rickety contraption was moving. Then, it stopt. The contraption that stopt was now beginning to make music. On either side of it was a form, one black, one white.

Unable to halt, now only barely jogging along, Ivor got nearer then began a laboured walk. It was good to tone down anyways, since his thoughts had begun to get the better of him. All three, now having come to rest, stared blankly at each other, Ivor couldn't stop panting.

In the eerie azure atmosphere of the Half-Full Moon, Hefferon felt a trifle dizzy, and reached-out to steady himself on the gurgly contraption that was making sounds as odd as some cantankerous baby.

The Athlete stifled a laugh, half a belch. The two before him certainly were different. There, on the right, stood an ancient lady, all in black, and beside her, on the left, stood a tiny boy, all in white. The two ...kept staring straight at the Runner, who deftly removed his hand from their thing.

The agèd one was cranking some handle, methodically, as if she had been churning the same butter for years. The handle kept turning, making music, jarring music, a tinkly raspy music, a noise a bit too Oriental for Ivor's ears. Every few beats the tune was broken, brashly, by a very brittle and unrhythmically timed bell, which sounded like an obnoxious one a kid would stick on a tricycle. Easily...could it have been music of the Infernal Spheres.

Neither the kid nor the crone said a word, as the cranking of the organ grinding continued, as the bell's dissonance made Hefferon cover his ears. He just stood there, glaring at the two and at their odd dark-wood contraption, that could never have been ebony, at their music box.

What long spindly legs you've got, Ivor heard the voice in his mind saying. Like some runners I've known. But this thing's got wheels...just what I'd like to have stuck up some competitors' you-know-whats.

The big boxy part of the contraption sported a large roundel, a window that seemed to have fallen prey to some naïve-painter one bubbly Christmas Eve. Inside its circle was a pastoral scene, some nude shepherd, some dozy sheep, some pasture, and looming behind it some mountain. Seeing the mountain, the Athlete felt the pimples perk up out of his unclothed arms, and he shivered. He had *seen* that mountain before...he had *climbed* it...via some distant ancestor's *life?*

Then suddenly a voice behind him said: "Friends of yours?" Ivor spun round.

"Hi—I'm Dora Cain," said the young woman who had walked from the front-row seat the whole length of the Stadium. "Spare a light?"

"Sorry. I'm an Athlete. I don't smoke," he replied, curious by what he was seeing.

"What's this?" Dora asked and pointed an unlit Marlboro and its pack at the music box. "Your fans?"

"Do they look it?" Ivor returned.

"Oh don't be annoyed, Mister Hefferon," and she paused and touched the back of his right hand tenderly, "I saw your picture in the paper this evening, and," she paused again, removing her hand slowly from his, "I used my female intuition, and guessed you'd be in this Stadium to-night. I've read in your interviews you prefer your training ...at midnight."

"Smart as a whip, aren't you?" the Runner wondered, finding the woman more attractive by the minute.

"I run, too. Not like you, of course, but I do enjoy exercise. I like to keep my body...fit."

"Then give up smoking."

"I might....be talked into it...by you..."

On that note the musical contraption once again began playing in earnest.

"Don't you just love a good *lattérna?*" Dora asked. "That's what the locals call these things..."

"You seem rather knowledgeable about Athens." Hefferon stated.

"Excuse me?" the girl said, covering her ears for the notes. "Come along—up here," and she grabbed the Athlete's hand, led him to the opposite side of the Stadium, and began to ascend the steps leading past the forty-eight rows of cold seats.

Ivor pursued, obediantly, staring all the time at the girl's small backside which, by the time he got to the top, he was itching to penetrate right then and there. She turned and wetted her lips with her tongue, so Ivor grabbed her, as their lungs were heaving for the climb. The embrace was exactly what Dora was after, as she clutched the Runner tightly to her chest. He locked his lips about her mouth and received no resistance to a lengthy kiss with a penetrating tongue.

"I want you—whoever the Devil you are!" the fellow moaned and they both let themselves fall downwards onto the path behind the white marble wall.

"People are always *fucking* up here at night," Dora gasped. "I've never done it—but God Almighty I'll be damned if I'm not going to do it for all it's worth right now!"

145

"But I don't even *know* you!" Hefferon laughed and kissed her all the harder, then undid the snap on her bra with his right hand, as the fingers of his left hand pushed inside her vagina, which already was moist and inviting, nice and hot.

"*Screw* me!" Dora said. "Just *take* me! Don't worry—there's all the time in the world to get to know each other—later."

She got on her knees and pulled the Athlete's shorts down, and immediately sank her mouth about his throbbing cock. As the man kept her red head clutched within his hands, she sucked and sucked for five full minutes, then he shoved her backwards, pulled off her shorts and knickers, and mounted her, both of them now totally naked.

Not far distant, that same henna-haired teenage boy was tossing himself off in the shadows of the cypress and the pine. Everywhere, and well out of sight, owls were hooting to mates in other treetops. The night air of Athens was overtaking everyone in sight. People all over the nocturnal Arena were engaged in various postures of love and frenzy, and lubrication held the whole scene in the clenchèd grip of delight. To this rampant erotic abandon, as pagan as anything Ivor Hefferon ever dreamed, the Olympic Gold Athlete surrendered himself Body and Soul, and was only feeling the pulsing heat of the wantonness beneath his sweating torso, enjoying each and every thrust into this pot of sensuousness more and more with each heart-beat. He'd just arrived in Greece from his own private Hell—and this was the closest to Heaven he'd been in many a week. Thoughts of Lucille were far far behind him...

He kept pushing his manhood well within the woman who was crying out loud, and felt that the blood in his groin would just have to explode all over her whimpering face, but his buttocks only kept squeezing themselves together, tighter each time, and she obviously hadn't bargained on such a riotous, such a physically fit lover. But he didn't care what the woman was thinking at all—she'd *asked* for it—and now she was *getting* it! Lock, stock, barrel, and *fire!*

And then—that itchy inevitable build-up could be felt deep inside his clenching balls—and Hefferon now was moaning aloud himself, like a bull in a rutting field of lowing heifers—and he was squashing the very air out from Dora Cain's brazen lungs, coming down upon her pelvis hard as iron—and she was struggling for gasps of air—almost shedding tears—when the sperm inside his scrotum shot out, and out, and out! And owl hoots seemed to treble in intensity of desire.

6th April – Thursday – Pre-Dawn

We were on our way to Olympos, Ada and I. We left Olympia and the southwestern Peloponnesian Peninsula in the helicopter provided by the Government of Greece. To avoid the Press, who had been angry enough by being denied access to the village of Olympia after the twenty-fifth of March, it had been arranged for Ada and me that we would go secretly

146

to the north of Greece. Our mission accomplished, we now could get some rest. We certainly deserved it, both of us. A lot had happened since that first reckless night in the Panathenian Stadium. If it hadn't been for this actress, whose name was Ada, I don't know if I'd have made it through such crazy times, *far* crazier than any experienced in Upstate New York, and that's saying something.

As we flew above her fatherland, Ada translated the pilot's constant stream of information about what was to be found below. The chopper had flown as a tipsy crow would fly, quick as a wink, but weaving ever so slightly.

"Oh—there's Tropéa, Váhlia, Aroánia, and Kalávrita," Ada said and kissed me. "There's the Gulf of Korinth, and Galaxídi, Itéa, the Vale of Delphi, and now we're going right over Delphi itself."

Our copter then swooped over all of Mount Parnassos.

"Oh—look—the lights of Brálos and Thermopýlae and Lamía."

And as Ada was providing the litany, all the way north to Lárissa, our contraption curved north-eastwards towards the sea, and followed the winding course of the River Piniós in the fabled Vale of Témpe. By then, I didn't know up from down.

Mount Ossa was off to our right when suddenly Ada let out a whoop: "The Thermaic Gulf !"

A wide tar-black Aegean was spreading itself out for our sight.

"You haven't seen anything yet," Ada stated, as flecks of light from the still distant sunrise were beginning to colour the eastern horizon red. "Delay no longer, Mister Hefferon—for here we are—look!"'

Ada pointed leftwards, back to land. And there...stood the snow-topped peaks of the tallest mountain in Greece. The massive splendour of the sight, even in the dark, took my breath away.

"Isn't it gigantic?" she was asking.

I couldn't even respond. Below us was a sandy beach, at the edge of a spread of pines, trailers, caravans, tents, cafés, but as yet no bathers in the pre-dawn sea.

"There's my cottage," Ada squealed and pointed like a child.

By a small river, more like an alpine stream, our helicopter veered suddenly left, and aimed westerly towards the bulky peaks.

"The Enippéos* River," the girl declared. "And here's Litóchoron,† the village where I hope we'll soon set foot...on solid ground. Many of my relatives live there."

We were hovering above the Army base at the foot of Mount Olympos. "Litóchoron boasts one of the Aegean's main troop centres, where many Greek youths come to train," Ada translated for the pilot, who now was managing our descent.

* Pronounced: eh-nip-PAY-os; last syllable rhymes with *gross*.
† Pronounced: lee-TOE-hoe-rone; last syllable rhymes with *bone*.

147

It wasn't until we actually were landing that it hit me how ridiculous I looked. My running gear still was on, if that's what you could call it.

"Oh forget it, Ivor. After what you've done—do you think the General will want to see you any other way? You're an Olympic Runner, and a *Hero* now to the Greeks. Stay exactly as you are—you look perfect."

Hardly. I was only wearing a makeshift loincloth, a piece of fabric that Ada had torn off her gown to cover up my nudity. Ada herself was dressed in no usual manner, either. She wasn't in a jogging outfit but garbed splendidly in clothing necessary for her to wear as Chief Priestess of the Goddess Hera. In a white silken gown, an exact replica from an ancient vase from Argos, Ada in fact was the sole woman in the world whose duty and privilege it was to light the Sacred Flame, before the ruins of the Doric Temple of Hera at Olympia, for the very Torch used to light the Olympic Cauldron at every Olympic Games. But her dress, to-night, like the scrap about my waist, was soiled with black and red paint. We both were a sorry sight for eyes!

We had just been participating in a Deed Ceremony in the Ancient Stadium of Olympia, during which Greece was supposed to have turned over a sizeable amount of acreage to the International Olympic Committee in order to see created a Permanent Site for both the Winter and Summer Games. This new nation was to be at a location not far from the spot where we just were landing. After this Deed Ceremony, and in order to flee the Press, it had been our honour to be transported by the Greek Army north along the Aegean Sea to Mount Olympos itself.

Flash bulbs were popping in our faces as we were stepping down onto a red carpet specially placed for our feet. The Press would not be receiving prints depicting our arrival, as they were not to know our whereabouts. The photographers were military. The Government had promised us anonymity.

We had both just gone through a harrowing amount of shock, since the Deed Ceremony had been interrupted by conspirators out to topple the Athenian Government, the majority of which had assembled at Olympia for the Ceremony. But the plot had been foiled, both at Olympia and at Athens, and Ada and I now just wanted to get away from it all, to *recover*.

We were being saluted by a very obsequious General, on behalf of the President of the Republic of Greece. Then we were in a receiving line of enthusiastic soldiers whose hands all needed to be shaken.

Realising how drained we were, and it still was not even dawn, the General escorted us to a waiting military limousine, whence we were allowed inside and promptly driven away.

"We're going just the few miles back to the sea," Ada said, "to my cottage." She yawned, then so did I, and we both fell fast asleep.

1st March – Wednesday – 1.00 AM

Dora Cain was standing naked, framed by the window of the seventh storey room that Ivor had been let in the Hotel Grande Bretagne. From behind, she looked like a pesky little Dryad from some Hyperborean clime. One elbow was crooked outwards, and her hand was balanced on a tiny hip. She was biting the nails of her left hand, pondering what the Athlete had just said.

"But—I thought you were *English*," she whined, obviously disappointed. She kept her svelte back to him.

"By nurturing—without a doubt," Hefferon replied. He was spread-eagled on the bedspread, fondling his private parts with both hands.

"But you're not really English, then, after all," Dora stated and turned about to glare without a smile.

"What difference does it make?"

'It explains *loads* about your kooky temperament—that's what!"

"Temperament! Come on over here, and I'll take your *temperature*! Just squat down on *this*."

"Tell me about her."

"Me mum?"

"I bet she'd love to see you now—waving that purple *dick* in my face."

"Isn't that exactly what you like?"

"Tell me...about your *Irish* mother."

"Don't know much about her."

"Why?"

"Just know what I've heard."

"Why?"

"*Nosy* bitch, aren't you?"

"I like to know a *little* about a man who wants me."

"What makes you think I *want* you?"

"Look what's in your hand."

"Get on this bed this minute."

"No."

"Well—I'll just have to come and get the crumpet," the Runner muttered and bounded off the bed and was wrapping his arms about the girl before she could move a step. He was hoisting her small body into his arms and then tossing her down on the sheets, then pouncing like a panther between her legs. He began gnawing on her pussy.

"Are all you Olympians so damned *horny*?"

"Running churns the *juice* that's in our balls."

"Into butter," Dora added, as the fellow shoved himself back inside her. "No—just leave it in there—and *talk* to me. You *can* talk—can't you? You do know how?"

"What do you want to hear?"

149

"Just about... *you*."

"Look—I'm still trying to get over my divorce. It's only been—what?—ten months ago? Why'd you think I left Athens last August, to cross the Atlantic for Lake Placid? I still was having nightmares about the breakup—this past summer when I last was living here in Athens."

Dora asked: "So why'd you come *back* here then?"

"Oh..." the Gold Medallist laughed, "to fight against the bastardisation of the Olympic Ideal!"

"I know—it was in all the papers," moaned the woman, matching all his thrusts with her own. "You can't be *serious!*"

"That's the bleeding pain in the bum as well. I can't do a sodding thing without five thousand periodicals worldwide publishing every stupid thing I say."

"That's the price, Kiddo, for having gone for the Gold in the first place. Haven't you ever gotten *used* to it? You better, 'cause there'll be *another* Olympic champ this coming July!"

"Sooner the better!"

"Don't you *like* being a Gold Medallist?"

"It wasn't *Gold* I was after."

"You really expect me to *believe* that utopian crap? Maybe your teeny-bopper *fans* believe it, but I've been around the *block* too many times to take in even an *ounce* of your stupid potion."

"I'll give you an ounce."

"Don't shove so hard."

"Who *are* you, anyways? Who *is* this Dora Cain I'm inside?"

"Just some Texan. Been living abroad a lot longer than I've been in the Lone Star State."

"Where... in Texas?

"Galveston. Ever been there?"

"Only ran once in the States. Boston."

"Marathon?"

"Never do long hauls. Strictly middle-distance."

"You're doing all right in *my* middle, Champ. *God*, do you do all right!"

The pair made love in silence a few more minutes, before Dora queried again: "Where *is* your mother?"

Something in the tender tone of the girl's voice registered empathetically with the loneliness that the man was feeling inside. He held her head between his hands and stopt the movements of his pride. He scanned her face for some sort of positive feeling—and in her eyes seemed to find a haven that appeared to be kind.

"Dora," he began, "didn't you *hear* me? It's not a year... since I got divorced."

There was silence, before Dora replied. "I'm sorry."

"My wife...she just put up...with the Olympics...with my absorption in my own aims...as long as any woman *could* take.

She...never even asked about my mother. And I never volunteered the information. But I'm sure she knew. I think deep inside she really despised me...felt herself better than me...because I was illegitimate. You know how weird the British are...if something strikes them as uncomfortable...they clam up and just don't talk about it. Thus it was with my dirty-birth. Her family just pretended they knew a fat *nothing!*"

"The English *can* be bizarre!"

"Outright miserable..." the fellow responded sadly.

"Maybe...that's another reason it was ok you two broke up? Maybe you *should*...talk about it now..."

A long pause was followed by a sigh from the young man. "I've always bottled things up inside," he began. "That, too, is my British polish. And, my *own* opinion is that the less the public knows about a celebrity's life...the more the Self remains intact within. The more one gives away, the less one has to hold onto that's *real*. And in *my* case...I've had so very *little* that's real...that I've had to hold on all the harder..."

"Then you're free of excess *burden*—look at it *that* way."

"Perhaps."

"Everybody changes. Change is the only Constant in the Universe. Hell—I've been living on the Continent so long that when I see a *cowboy* hat coming at me, I cross the street. And I'm from *Texas!*"

"Don't you fancy a good heifer-hauler?"

"I don't fancy *lots* of things anymore. I don't really know *what* to fuck I'm doing with my whole life—wasting it sucking off gorgeous Greek men, I guess—hoping I'll snag me a rich one. At least I'm *honest* about it. But let me give you a tip, Ivor, if you're going to stay here any time at all: Beware Greeks! You can *never* really trust one you're not married to...and you sure as Hell can't ever trust the one you're *married* to at all."

"Why do *you* stay here then?"

"Greeks suit my moods. They're basically very *selfish* people— they've *had* to be, to *survive* all these years—conquered from within and without since the time of Perikles. They're *very* selfish—just like *I* am— just like *you* are! Greeks just crave *pleasure* out of life. They're hooked on sex, with no matter what hole, and when they *love* it's basically only for their greed for attention, for lust, and for comfort, in that order, larded with jealousy. You know, there's really no place for Idealism in Modern Greece—especially not *your* sort of *Olympic* Idealism—because there never was a place for Idealism in *Ancient* Greece, either! Greeks have been the intellectual if not the spiritual elite of this world since their appearance on this planet. It's sad but true but there have never been any Idealism or Idealists in the elite of the world. The truth is— Idealism and Idealists have only and always crawled up from the bottom—like hot air—which inevitably rises upwards to the top."

Hefferon's eyes were wide—wondering what on Earth he said to provoke such a diatribe. To lighten the mood, he asked: "Doesn't sound like you don't *really* want to hear about *my* past!"

Dora squeezed him and kissed his eyes then said: "Of course."

"Well...my mother's name...was Deirdre Cromlin...from Northern Ireland...from a tiny farm...outside some hamlet of County Down... named Attica...about six miles from the Irish Sea...against the Mourne Mountains...forty miles south of Belfast..."

"Seen the place?"

"Just once...when I was eighteen."

"What about your *kin*?"

"Everyone's dead...some even killed in The Troubles..."

"I'm...so sorry..."

"No need to be," Ivor stated then paused. "Deirdre...she was a schoolteacher in a Belfast girls school—so they say—she taught English literature. And my father..."

"Teacher too?"

"Hardly. Here's where the wildness comes from. He was Canadian."

"You're joking!"

"Ivor Hefferon was *his* name as well, from somewhere in Manitoba. He was some big-cocked soldier...who managed to hump my mother...while serving with Her Majesty's forces in the UK."

Dora didn't know *what* to ask next. The story of Ivor's life was turning into an account that she was not at all expecting to hear. Nothing about this had ever made it into the Press. "What...was your *dad* like?"

"Big romantic bloke...lots of hot Welsh blood."

"Welsh?"

"I heard he could recite the poetry of Dylan Thomas...as well as a few snippets of his own."

"A *poet*?"

"Perhaps. He met Deirdre in some derelict Belfast pub. They fell in love—at first sight—I guess. Who knows? Maybe they just wanted to fuck each other. I know what *that's* all about. It's my middle name. That's the *only* thing from the both of them I inherited...their *fucking* sex drive...the worst trait of the *both* of them! After they screwed each other...then he was posted over to Glasgow! Like an idiot, she pursued him, pregnant with his son."

Dora didn't know what to say, so remained silent.

"I've often wished to God she'd had an *abortion*...so I'd never been born!"

The young man was now lying on his back, staring straight up. "My father...I think he was transferred to Somerset. The stupid bitch followed him there—to Bath—where she had the ill fortune to befriend this kind Catholic priest, originally from Dublin—Father O'Hanrahan. By then...my father refused to see her...telling her he was a married man. Maybe he really was...who knows? Deirdre...had a breakdown. This priest pretended to take her under his wing...but he really just made her his mistress. *That* I know...because he actually *confessed* it to me...imagine! So—is it any wonder Deirdre was *hospitalised*! I guess I'm lucky to have been born *alive*. Yeah...*real* lucky! The baby was named after his father, baptised Catholic, then...given up...for adoption..."

"But...but what about...whatever happened to your *mother*?"

"Chronic depression...couple years later...she drowned herself... Bristol Channel...nothing more O'Hanrahan could do...he did manage to keep a roof over her head...though not with him ...until the end..."

"Is *he* still alive?"

"Passed away...now five years and a month..."

Dora shook her head. "Who brought you up then?"

"Father O'Hanrahan had the baby sent to London...where he was taken in by a middle-aged Irish couple. All the time...the foster parents...they were named Devlin...told the boy the truth...that he was adopted...that his parents weren't around. The foster mother died ...when the lad was eight. The foster father realised...it was best the boy go to some boarding school. So Father O'Hanrahan arranged he be sent to Somerset again, to Taunton, where he knew of this good Anglican school."

"But aren't you Catholic?"

"Don't make a bloody coddy-moddy of difference, does it? Father realised that if the child were to grow up in England, he should get a proper *English* education, thus the Anglican Church was chosen, for what it was worth."

"Didn't your wife ever ask about *any* of this?"

"Guess she didn't care."

Dora was biting her nails again: "God—what was she—comatose?"

"Met her at Oxford. She fancied herself some big scholar. She only lived for books."

"I might be *sex*-starved, but at least I've got *curiosity*! What happened next, at this school?"

"My life changed almost over-night."

"How?"

"I met a friend."

"All kids have friends. What was he, your *lover*?"

"He's an Earl. His family's ducal. They literally made me a part of themselves."

"Ducal?"

"At school my best-mate was this lad named Alexander Pella. He's now Earl of Luxborough—the author. We became inseparable, and his grandmother especially took me to heart."

"And she's..."

"Dowager Duchess of Brendon. She's the one who sent me from

Taunton, along with Alexander, to Westminster School in London, then up to Oxford. It was *she* who graciously enabled me to receive the athletic training I've been so fortunate to receive."

"Is *she* dead too?"

"No thank God. Nor is Alexander. I couldn't live without them. They're the only family I've got."

"Well, if you've got to have a family, it might as well be a Duchess's! You're still friends?"

Ivor shook his head yes. "All my wife cared about, I guess, were my so-called snob-links to the Peerage. That's the only thing about me that turned her on. She was one of those County Dames, from an old Gloucestershire clan of landed Knights. Her father's an insufferable prick, a right-pompous Baronet, twenty-third of the line. I really haven't the foggiest why his wretched daughter married me—or why I proposed to *her!*" Ivor finally let his eyes meet Dora's, then he asked: "What do *you* do with yourself, here in Athens?"

"I'm just a junior Archaeologist...for the American School of Archaeology. Working on the Agora dig."

"Then you're a Classics student as well?"

"I try. There's an awful lot to sift through, when it comes to The Past." She paused, thought a minute, then inquired: "Ivor—you weren't serious, were you, when you told that reporter that you were here to fight against bastardisation of the Olympian Ideal?"

"We each have our own causes."

"But—*you* should realise, better than anybody, just coming from Lake Placid, that the Olympics to-day are a *joke*. Look what's just busted out in the news—about this MOON group?"

"What's that?" Ivor asked, although he was abreast of the situation.

"You mean you haven't heard?" she asked and searched his face for a lie.

"Tell me."

"Over in Upstate New York you must have heard *something* about the MOON—which is short for the Mount Olympos Olympic Nation? It's the current scandal of Athens."

"The Adirondacks can be quite the isolated place. I'm sure I wasn't kept properly informed."

"The Agora, where I work, is only a few blocks from MOON headquarters. The whole neighbourhood's been buzzing with it for months. We got wind of it from our Greek maintenance staff. You know, you can't keep a scandal from a *maid!*"

"What exactly *have* you heard?" Ivor inquired. He was now propping himself up in bed. His curiosity had been aroused.

Dora placed her legs in lotus position and began to relate what she had knew: "The MOON is purporting to get established as a Free Nation, recognised as autonomous by the United Nations, and founded in the name of the Olympic Games. They want their own Permanent Site, so they say, to rid the world of all the political and economic problems caused every four years by rotating the Games to an ever-new location. But the MOON is nothing but a *front*."

"You must be kidding. For whom?"

"I knew *that* would wake you up." The girl took a deep breath, "The MOON is a front, for an insidious Greek plot being hatched right here in Athens, to undermine the whole Olympic Movement."

"By whom?"

"The Ouranós* clan."

"*Ouranós?* You don't mean *General* Ouranós? Not one of the two Greek Members of the International Olympic Committee?"

"Yes—*General* Ouranós—Junior Member of the IOC in Greece. And his whole family's right in the thick of it!"

"How do you *know* these things?" Ivor stared at the young woman piercingly.

"It's public knowledge that last week the MOON people announced that a special Deed Ceremony's being organized for Greek National Day, the 25th of March, to be held in the Ancient Stadium of Olympia, you know, where the Olympic Games were born almost two thousand years ago. You *have* heard about *that?*"

"I saw a few contradictory stories in *The New York Times.*"

"Well—it seems the Greek Government *will* turn over land for a Permanent Games Site, but not at Olympia, or anywhere near the Pelopponesian ruins of the temple-city to Zeus, but at a special site on the foothills of Mount Olympos. Thank God they got the brains not to tamper with Olympia, which would be trampled back into the mud if tens of thousands of sports fans invaded the place. But no matter *where* they stick their damned Olympic Nation, the stupid politicians here don't know what in Hell they're letting themselves in for! By establishing an Olympic Nation here...they're just opening up Pandora's proverbial *Box!*"

Ivor looked at her steadily, then repeated his query: "How do you *know* these things?"

She did not flinch. "I told you. I heard it through the grapevine."

"But Greeks have been gossiping since Homer."

"You don't have to believe a word I say, but..." and she paused, "the cleaning lady at MOON headquarters is the cousin of one of our guards. Her name's Lydia. I'll *introduce* her to you, if you don't believe what *I* say."

There was a lengthy silence, during which Ivor's mind was racing. He decided to listen to all that the woman could tell. "What *else* have you heard?" he asked.

Pronounced: oo-rah-NOS; last syllable rhymes with *gross*.
Meaning: Sky, Heaven, Canopy.

"General Ouranós...known as Affedikó, which is Greek for Boss, has two older brothers. Captain Fourtoúnas, a Greek nickname for anybody crazy for the sea; he's the shipowner of the family. And then there's Kokkálas, Greek for Bones, who deals in little things, like olive oil, wine, and oranges. The General himself runs the family-show, as President of the Board of Ouranós Ltd, the prominent Athenian construction company."

"Grow up! *Everybody* in the International Olympic Committee is monied, powerful, and firmly established in his country. That's how to bloody Hell they get to *be* IOC Members!"

"Granted—I'm not as dim-witted as you'd believe. But—the Ouranós clan's now up to absolutely *no* good. They're *Evil!* The General, you'll remember, was one of the most prominent members of the recent dictatorship—that's when he wormed his way into the IOC in the first place, during the Junta—and he himself is President of the Mount Olympos Olympic Nation Organizing Committee, MOON-OC for short. That wouldn't be so suspicious, but his *own* construction firm is contracted to build the Permanent Games Site planned to lay waste to Olympos. Think of what he'll make on *that* deal? Think of what the Sacred Mountain will *look* like...once he gets done *ruining* it."

"Doesn't sound as if anything *unethical* to the Olympic Movement's about to take place!"

"Oh no?" Dora was beaming—dying to speak her mind.

"What is it?" Ivor couldn't resist asking.

"Ivor," she said and took his hand, "of course I can't *prove* this, but...it's being whispered that the supposèd Olympic Nation on Mount Olympos is *only* being planned as a front for the right-wing element of the Greek *military* establishment!"

"I'd hate to believe you."

"I'm serious. Lydia has overheard conversations. She says that the Games Site, envisioned for the two huge foothills of the mountain—Gólna* and Stávros—is just going to be a cover-up—for what's to be constructed *beneath* them—*inside* the mountain itself."

"And that is..." Ivor didn't want to admit the possibility of what he now was hearing, but in light of events in the Mediterranean, it didn't take an Einstein to know that the arms race had not gone away.

Dora released the Athlete's hand, and wiped her brow. "Inside Mount Olympos itself...General Ouranós is scheming to build a nuclear weapons silo, totally unknown to almost everyone who would be functioning in the Olympic Nation above. It will be constructed, in secret, by his family's firm, with NATO consent, from the Army base already existing at the foot of the mountain, at Litóchoron."

* Pronounced: GOAL-nah.

156

6th April – Thursday – Pre-Dawn

From the Army base at Litóchoron, Ada and I were driven towards the Aegean, at most just five miles away, due east. We both fell instantly asleep, as soon as we settled into the back seat of the plush limousine. Too quickly thereafter, we were being woken by the driver, a young handsome soldier who had to shake me to make me stir. "You get out now," he said in passable English.

Our doors were opened and it was only on stepping out that I noticed that we were on some misty beach. Gentle waves of the Aegean looked as calm as an inland lake.

Ada, meanwhile, was already at the water's edge, with her shoes in her hands. She was doing a spontaneous dance for the water. I knew she'd been longing to return here, so went to the seafoam to be with her. She ran along, ahead of me, playfully, making fancy steps with her lovely feet. She looked so beautiful, in that archaic white gown, even though it was streaked with black and red paint, with her silken black hair loose about her shoulders. With red tints in the dawning sky, beyond the misty horizon of the sea, it all was looking like a mythical dream. She said something to the driver in Greek.

He turned to me and said: "You two go to house. I bring the luggage."

Being led along the water's edge by the woman with whom I had fallen so deeply in love, I felt tears rise up in my eyes at the notion that at last we two would be in peace. Only five weeks back in Greece...but they already seemed an eternity.

Tied to posts, a few yards from our feet, a pair of fishing boats painted turquoise blue and white were being examined by an old brown man and a younger fellow about thirty. Both men wore caps and both tipped them reverently as they saw Ada pass. She greeted them kindly in Greek. Because she was with me, not to mention with the soldier with our bags, they stifled curiosity and did not say another word, as we stept atop shells and seaweed the few dozen yards along the beach.

In foggy crimson light, still an hour from sunrise, I could see ahead a concrete wall along the sand, and atop it a tiny bungalow of stucco, painted white. Looking pink, it seemed inviting, and Ada turned to me with pride and said: "There it is—it's mine—and now—it's yours." She reached out and took my hand, then kissed the ends of my fingers.

Small cement steps, broken from years of saltwater abuse, beckoned us up to the porch of the house. A few stript tree-limbs had been sawn off to hold up the red-tiled roof, and these had been whitewashed so frequently that chunks of paint hung off like bark. I turned, as Ada was showing the driver where to leave the bags on the porch, and gazed in utter contentment at the view of the imperturbable sea.

As soon as the driver was gone, evaporating in the humid cloud that was clinging to the beach, I felt a soft hand upon my hair, and the tender words: "I love you."

Out at sea, somewhere, a fishing vessel sounded a deep-voiced horn, just once, which echoed over all the coastline.

"That's Olympos—sending the greeting back," Ada admitted then added, "you'll soon understand...Greece is *only* Mountain and Sea." She kissed my cheek, then led me inside the two-roomed cottage, and proceeded to brew a local herbal tea.

1st March – Wednesday – 12.30 PM

Ivor Hefferon telephoned England from his hotel room as soon as Dora Cain left. The call was placed to Shrove Tor, estate of the Dukes of Brendon near the tiny hamlet of Luxborough by Exmoor, in County Somerset. It had been prearranged that Ivor telephone there around noon, Athens Time, and that he speak with the Senior Member in Britain of the International Olympic Committee, Lord Dalbeattie, a Baron of ancient lineage, and brother-in-law of the Dowager Duchess of Brendon. In addition to his Olympic responsibilities, the Peer also served on The Queen's Privy Council. His Lordship was spending a few days in the West Country, and was pacing in the library when the call came. Alexander, Earl of Luxborough, stood from a comfortable chair to answer the telephone. The Earl was five months elder than Hefferon, and the two were often mistaken for brothers, both being tall and having blond hair. Ivor's was curly, whereas Alexander's fell in waves.

"Ivor," Alexander shouted and winked at his uncle, "of course it is I, you big Twit. We're *both* here—wondering if you've been bagged."

"Tell him I shall be going to the next room," Lord Dalbeattie said then opened the door to an adjoining salon, whence he picked up a receiver to join the discussion.

"Ivor," His Lordship inquired, "how are you doing?"

"I fear they've already *planted* somebody," the Athlete responded. "I met this suspicious *American* bird—who introduced herself to me when I was training last night—inside the Panathenian Stadium."

"Every loafer who reads about running knows of your *idiotic* proclivity for the midnight jog," Alexander declared.

"Who *is* she?" asked the Baron. "I'll do a security check on her, with Interpol, then leave word with Professor Rembetikós*."

"She says her name is Dora Cain, from Galveston, Texas. She claims she's an Archaeologist, with the American School of Archaeology, on the Agora dig."

"Is she good in the hay?" Alexander couldn't help wondering. He knew his friend, "I bet you poked her."

* Pronounced: rem-beh-tee-KOS; last syllable rhymes with *gross*.

158

"Not bad. Tiny bum, though, but kept me at it all night," Ivor said and laughed.

"Well done," Alexander responded.

"Don't leave yourself open for a sodding *infection*," Dalbeattie warned. "We need you. Now listen, did this Cain woman have anything to say about the MOON people?"

"Couldn't keep her *off* the bloody subject," Hefferon replied.

"For God's Sakes, then," Lord Dalbeattie shouted, "keep her humoured. Say nothing at all against the MOON lot. And should they hire you, be *doubly* careful."

"It was eerie, but she seemed to be warning me *away* from them, without even knowing that I *was* going to be calling on them as soon as possible."

"Well you know what we've discussed. You must co-ordinate everything, from this moment on, with my associate in Athens. In fact, this morning Rembetikós telephoned me and wondered why in Hell you hadn't contacted him," His Lordship proclaimed sternly.

Alexander laughed: "Poor Sod—I can picture you—huffing and puffing above that Cain gal—no wonder Rembetikós got worried."

"You must have lunch with him *this* afternoon," Dalbeattie declared. "Without fail. He's awaiting you at home. Take a taxi. He lives near the Pyníka Hill, just on the other side of the Akropolis from you. You still have his address I gave you?"

"I was at his place last summer, remember?"

"Splendid," the IOC Member said confidently. "I'm sure you'll do justice to your ability. Now—I shall let your insane *brother* conclude this conversation. I shall simply repeat...that you are to take instructions from Professor Rembetikós from now on. Unless something extraordinary turns up, you shall expect to hear from me through him."

"Yes, Your Lordship. Oh—wait a minute—are you still there? Good. I almost forgot to mention the most important thing that Dora Cain said. She mentioned that she'd heard that the MOON was simply going to be a front for the right-wing of the Greek military establishment and that NATO was behind the idea that the Games Site on Olympos be a cover for a subterranean *nuclear* silo!"

"Aimed at Turkey, in all likelihood," Lord Dalbeattie added. "Bodes ill—truly bodes ill."

"She didn't say against whom—and I didn't ask. But it just struck me as peculiar that she wouldn't be mentioning such things if she weren't trying to deflect me from the whole operation."

"Don't worry, Ivor," His Lordship declared, "I shall be discussing this to-morrow with the IOC President in Lausanne. Now, I must run. Good-bye."

"Ivor," Alexander added, "now don't you get a disease, Old Ponce. Zeus alone knows what creepy-crawly you might be mounting down there in the Balkans."

159

"Quite—the same sort *you're* mounting back home," Ivor replied. "Look—have you anything *intelligent* to add?"

"I wish I did have something ghastly to spur you on, Old Boot, like what I told you before that race of yours at the Games—but don't take Uncle Dalby too seriously now. You've got to allow yourself a *little* fun."

"Alexander," Hefferon replied gravely, "you don't know how seriously I *shall* pursue this. Coming here, after all the craziness at Lake Placid, and doing what I'm doing for your uncle, has given my life a new start."

"Pecker up...and do ring us if you need a nasty bit of encouragement. We'll be thinking of you. Cheerio." And the Earl of Luxborough was gone.

Ivor was still holding the receiver and mulling over what had just been said. The reminder that it was Alexander Pella who had spurred on Hefferon's Olympic win brought back the whole of the present plot to do in the Olympic Games. But four Julys ago, at the Olympics, the spur that his friend had given him had been purely *personal*, since Alexander had then told Ivor that the Athlete's wife was cheating on him. Ivor had become so furious, on learning the news, that he won his Olympic Gold the very next day. And, forever more, the horrid juxtaposition of Adultery and Gold, for Hefferon, had been synonymous. Thus, it was no wonder that the Runner hadn't felt any enduring satisfaction with himself, since he'd won his 1500 Metre Race more out of ire than out of desire!

Two years previously, in July, General Ouranós was in Rome attending an emergency NATO conference that had been convened to discuss the continuance of terrorism in Europe, as witnessed in Italy by the Red Brigade's kidnapping of Cardinal Arcadio Monsignani and the Archbishop of Canterbury's Representative to the Pope, the Reverend Marquess Rupert Broxbourne, a young school friend of both the Earl of Luxborough and Ivor Hefferon. It was during a break from those NATO meetings, while wandering along the via di San Teodoro side of the Palatine Hill, amid the Roman ruins where Caesars schemed and murdered, that General Ouranós conceived his Neronian idea for the Mount Olympos Olympic Nation.

Since the Junta, Ouranós had been the Junior Member in Greece of the International Olympic Committee. For some dozen years previous to that, Ouranós had been a shining light of the Greek Olympic Committee. A career-soldier, he had never learnt to respect the Senior Member of the IOC in Greece, Professor Aristídis Rembetikós, because the latter was a noted academic as well as a diligent scholar. For many decades, the amiable Doctor of Philosophy of the University of Athens had quietly and steadfastly been instilling the idea back into the world's consciousness that Greece, and only Greece, should be home to the

Olympic Games. This was his life's dream, to see this become eventuality. Rembetikós had conceived the idea, and had researched its feasibility, and had concluded that indeed it was not only possible but also inevitable that the Games should someday reside once again near their birthplace, in the southwestern Pelopónnesos of Greece.

Noble ideas always stir the basest ignobility. There always is one person who will resist what must surely be for the public good. And the Greek who took it upon his shoulders, ever since he had forced his way into membership of the IOC, to resist all attempts by his Co-Member to do some honest good for the Olympic Games, was General Ouranós. But his mind was not the sharpest of Hellenic instruments, and it took him years to whittle his bulky resentment of Rembetikós into a counteroffensive weapon.

The honing was actually done by Ouranós's son, a Major in the Army, and a superior commander of the Evzónes, the Elite Guard of Greek troops, at whom tourists love to gawk. Part of the duties of the Evzónes is ceremonial. The tallest, handsomest, and best-hung of the lads can be seen stationed outside Parliament, wearing romantic native uniforms with clogs, high white stockings, and even higher kilts, that do reveal the manliness of the bearer. Ouranós's son, about whom Ivor had heard just before winning his 1500 Metre Race, was nicknamed Movóros*, or Blood Drinker. Son and father had created, by the end of two Augusts ago, a Feasibility Study for the MOON, a document now legendary in military circles. To date, Hefferon had not seen a copy. Nor had anyone in the IOC. One of the Olympic Athlete's jobs in Athens was to locate one.

Two Septembers ago, the International Olympic Committee convened its Session for that year in the capital of the Punjab, in Chandigarh, the modern city designed by Maxwell Fry, Jane Drew, and Le Corbusier at Prime Minister Nehru's request. At this Congress in India, behind closed doors, the divisiveness between Ouranós and Rembetikós was made quite evident, when Ouranós proposed that the IOC establish a committee to investigate the possibility that Greece get the Olympics back permanently. This would have been fine had Ouranós not have propounded then and there his "novel idea" that the Games Site be Mount Olympos and not some spot nearer its birthplace at Olympia. To this suggestion, Professor Rembetikós had urged the IOC against such folly, whence Ouranós dared Rembetikós to stop him and vowed to show Rembetikós, and the whole of the IOC, "that a Free Olympic Nation on Olympos could damn well be done".

At Chandigarh, the Sub-Committee to investigate the option that Greece get the Games back was created, and both IOC Members in Greece were nominated. Lord Dalbeattie also was asked to sit, as were three other IOC Members. This was when Dalbeattie and Rembetikós,

---

* Pronounced: mo-VO-ros; last syllable rhymes with *gross*.

161

who had been close friends for over forty years, united to combat what they saw as antithetical behaviour on the part of the Greek General.

In the weeks immediately following the Punjab Session, Ouranós, back in Greece, began in earnest to lobby the Members of the National Olympic Committee of his country, the aforementioned Greek Olympic Committee. He discussed, cajoled, bribed, and did whatever was necessary to gain support amongst his so-called peers, and then commenced to turn his attention to high-ranking officials in the Greek Government. To all these individuals, Ouranós of course did not reveal his true intentions, which were militaristic and hardly befitting the upper echelon of the world of sport. Nevertheless, the General's aims seemed to be gaining silent support, two Octobers ago.

"Leak 1", as it came to be known at the Château de Vidy in Lausanne, headquarters for the IOC, occurred a few weeks later, in November. Professor Rembetikós, who was in Bonn attending an Executive Meeting of the National Olympic Committee of the Federal Republic of Germany, was invited to dine at the French Embassy with his long-time associate, François Malouette, the Ambassador. In strictest confidence, His Excellency informed Rembetikós that the Military Attaché of his Embassy had been at a NATO meeting at the American Army Base at Karlsrühe, a strategic command centre for Europe, just that previous week. Attending that meeting was the German Defence Minister as well. To both the Attaché and the Minister, Ouranós, who felt that both were allies, had mentioned that beneath the MOON site and inside Olympos itself a perfectly placed nuclear NATO base could be built. The idea, to the military men, was not all that far-fetched His Excellency said, given the ever-volatile Middle East situation. What *was* hare-brained about the proposal was Ouranós's notion that the CIA had already pledged support to him for the project.

The international scenario of the plot expanded inevitably to Washington. "Leak 2" occurred along the River Potomac, a few days before Christmas of that same year. A top American Brigadier's wife was a bit worse for drink at a Christmas party, which was being held at the British Embassy. The Brigadier's wife was in gala form, laughing at every innocuous remark being uttered by her hostess, the British Ambassadress, whom the former considered her "girlfriend". Off in a corner the Brigadier's wife whispered about how wonderful she thought it was that Greece was going to be getting nuclear weapon capability "after all this time, Darling, I mean Demokritos, who invented the atom, is no spring chicken". Furthermore, the Brigadier's wife saw that her "girlfriend" didn't even bat an eyelash, so she added: "Well it's no skin off America's nose, *what* they build beneath their proposed Olympic Nation. Just because Greece signed the Nuclear Non-Proliferation Treaty doesn't mean she can't quietly develop atom bombs inside Olympos. *We've* got them in *our* silos, inside the Rockies. Just look at Cheyenne Mountain—by Colorado Springs—close to both the U.S. Air Force

Academy and the U.S. Olympic Committee's base. Why—Cheyenne Mountain's acres of hollowed-out granite—just as tall as Mount Olympos of Greece—and inside Cheyenne Mountain the U.S. Government has its headquarters for NORAD—the North American Aerospace Defense Command—as well as SPADOC—the Space Command Defense Operations Center. So—don't you dare tell me that whole mountains can't be scooped out for belligerent purposes! I've been there—my husband did *time* inside Cheyenne Mountain! And so did I! So—I'm telling you—for NATO to gouge out the guts of Mount Olympos, which is made only of limestone, is a piece of cake!"

This conversation was related that night by the British Ambassador's wife to her husband, who was dumbfounded. He immediately informed Downing Street. The issue was then discussed in private between the First Minister and the Head of State of the United Kingdom, Her Majesty The Queen, whence a way to deal with the situation was arranged.

Downing Street, two New Year's ago informed the Foreign Minister of the matter in the Balkans. Before a New Year's Ball held in a stately home in Gloucestershire, near Ivor's former in-laws, the Foreign Minister sat in a private chamber with Lord Dalbeattie, and quietly conversed on the subject. What Dalbeattie knew was pieced together with what Downing Street knew. The following week, His Lordship spoke about the ramifications of the proposed Mount Olympos Olympic Nation with Her Majesty in Buckingham Palace. Due to the sensitivity of the issue, Lord Dalbeattie was of the opinion that it be best not to inform the UK Embassy in Athens, but that Dalbeattie discuss the situation first, and as soon as possible, with Professor Rembetikós.

That meeting transpired a fortnight later, at IOC headquarters in Lausanne. Instead of making a possibly dangerous scandal public knowledge, it was then decided that Dalbeattie and Rembetikós wage a quiet counter-offensive against the machinations of the Greek General. This plan received the endorsement of the President of the International Olympic Committee, the only other individual allowed all the information. The plan would be to utilise an Olympic Athlete, whose dedication to the Olympian Ideal was proven, and whose tenacity to said Ideal could withstand inimical odds.

Lord Dalbeattie's most trusted confidant was his aforementioned great-nephew, Alexander Pella. His Lordship, therefore, decided to wait until the Winter Games, which were less than a month away, and then bring the Earl of Luxborough into his confidence. Luxborough, thus, was asked to attend the Lake Placid Olympics as personal guest of Dalbeattie. At each Games, an IOC Member may bring one guest to be accommodated as a VIP.

So it was only two weeks ago that Lord Luxborough had been briefed on all aspects of the plot, and during the Pairs Figure Skating Finals—as a marvellous triple throw was being demonstrated by the

163

winning team from the Soviet Union—Alexander suddenly thought of his best friend Ivor, who was then no longer strapped to Lake Placid's venal Protocol Department, but who had been transferred to Human Services. Hefferon was now holed up in some old lacklustre frame house directly across from Town Hall, working with cases of nervous-breakdowns, crowd-stress, and alcoholism. Heidi had finally managed to send Ivor packing, with Maria elevated to Deputy, so during the Winter Games Ivor was relegated to a far less glamorous Olympics job. That was her reward to him for acting as Torch Bearer for Opening Ceremonies. That very evening...she sacked him! And not even the most outrageous protestations by Lucille McSorley, to anyone and everyone who would listen, made one dent in the situation. After the fabulous experience of bringing the Sacred Flame into the crowded Winter Stadium, Ivor really didn't care *what* happened to him during the actual course of the Games themselves. In fact, he was purely glad finally to be done with the horrible Barley couple. Even when the duo yanked Hefferon's Infinity Pass, which had given him carte-blanche access everywhere in the whole of the Adirondack Olympic Primary Area, it didn't matter; Ivor still managed to get access wherever he went, because, by the time of the Winter Games themselves, he was such a celebrity in the region that he could just walk in anywhere and nobody at all would prevent him. In fact, he was *welcomed*, wherever he went, because everyone felt to badly that the Barleys had treated him like a piece of shit.

Alexander was contemplating all of these nasty things that had happened to Ivor when the young Earl turned to his uncle, because the deafening applause of the full Arena would obviously blot out his words to anyone but His Lordship, and said: "For God's Sakes why don't we use *Ivor*! It would certainly cheer him up!" Lord Dalbeattie, who had a sheepish grin on his old face, nodded his head yes, and muttered: "I was *hoping* you'd come round and see sense! I've been pondering Hefferon for months myself. I just didn't want a hasty decision. But now that *you* concur—that's exactly how we'll proceed. Ivor does need a pick-me-up, to say the least. This Protocol Mess, here at Placid, has been enough to discourage even The Devil Himself!"

As the taxi bearing the Olympic Athlete whizzed past the Pláka district and the Akropolis, Ivor's gaze was fixed out the left window, on the stone remains of the two-tiered memorial gateway that the Emperor Hadrian had built. This had been the finishing touch to the Hellenophile's restoration, after an eight hundred year lapse, of the awesomely grandiose Temple of Olympian Zeus. Now, but a few Corinthian columns still were standing erect where Hadrian had them placed. Once, they had honoured the very same deity whose glory had inspired the Olympic Games. This very Temple, in Hadrian's day, had been bigger than the Parthenon high above on its dust-swept plâteau, and even bigger than most Gothic cathedrals. Now...just a few rock pillars remained...

164

Continuing to consider all that he knew about the Olympics plot, Hefferon was barely concentrating on the view out the left window. He wasn't even aware that the taxi was skirting the base of the Akropolis and had already passed the most sacred amphitheatre to actors of the Stage, that of Dionysos, God of Drama and Wine.

The taxi was turning left, into the neighbourhood bordering the Pyníka Hill, then right again, whence it stopt. The corner building was modern and expensive, and Professor Rembetikós owned the top two floors, as well as the penthouse situated on the roof. The edifice had wrap-around black glass balconies, and sparkling black marble floors. Hefferon entered the freshly mopped foyer and pressed button number 5. The housekeeper answered and allowed the door to be buzzed open upon hearing Hefferon's name. She was waiting with the door wide as Ivor got out of the lift. An honest looking woman of middle age, she wasn't wearing a uniform but an old black dress.

Behind her the visitor followed and entered a hall. The fellow expected to be told to walk, but this was not the case. She simply stept aside, opened a door to reveal a long and luxurious sitting room, and said: "Ivor Hefferon."

"My Lad! How good it is you're back here," the Member of the International Olympic Committee said in greeting. Hefferon's eyes scanned the room, the yellow marble floor, the ebony bookcases, the ancient vases and sculptures. Nothing had changed.

They shook hands. From their very first meeting at Shrove Tor, fifteen years ago, Hefferon had liked the man immensely. He was so grandfatherly, so learnèd, so concerned. He was a short fellow, seventy-four years old, but had the agility of a fifty-year-old man. He was totally bald except for two white tufts of hair above his large ears. He had a jolly white moustache that drooped and turned inward towards his cleft chin. His eyes were a golden brown. He was quite handsome, and must have been dashing in his youth.

"Come up to the penthouse," he said and Ivor followed the man up the yellow marble staircase, past a row of priceless bronze helmets.

"Welcome home...to Greece," the Professor of Philosophy declared, as he opened a sliding glass panel and as his guest stept onto the patio, which directly faced the grandeur of the Parthenon.

The look in the lad's eye was one of quiet rapture, as he stared once again at the ancient bastion.

"The Citadel of the Goddess Athena," the old man admitted as he offered the youth a chair. "*This*...is my daily inspiration," he added and gestured towards the panoramic splendour, "and now, after too many months absence, once more it's *yours*."

The punctilious housekeeper was soon at their umbrella-covered table with drinks.

"Frappés," she said then disappeared.

Ivor sipped the ice-cold coffee and milk with a silver straw.

"So, my young Hero," Rembetikós began, "you survived Lake Placid?"

"Barely."

"And...you've spoken with Lord Dalbeattie?"

"Just forty-five minutes ago, Sir. I am instructed to defer to your advice. As usual."

The Professor laughed quietly. "Dalby told me that he thought your return to Greece was propitious, because, since you last were here, we've had parliamentary elections. Of course, General Ouranós never let a mere democratic vote sway his schemes. But the chance was there that, should the opposition party win, the MOON plot might disappear. Of course, it's done nothing of the kind. On the contrary, the new party in power has only augmented Ouranós's spiritual dissatisfaction. His vow is now to install his damned Olympic Nation on Mount Olympos at *any* cost." Rembetikós paused. "His thunder and lightning have been causing havoc left, right, and centre...politically speaking, and...my sources assure me that his schemes *have* crossed the Atlantic. The latest is he's bargaining with the Pentagon for *neutron* bomb capability!"

As the Athlete gazed towards the Parthenon, he could feel his eyes welling with tears. What absolute madness possessed this feeble Earth!

"Ouranós says...that if NATO wants Greece to remain a partner, they'll *have* to give this country the know-how to construct the neutron bomb. Blackmail, or whatever, call it what you will."

Ivor fought for words. "I'm glad I wasn't told anything about all this...over at Lake Placid. It was hard enough concentrating...carrying what knowledge I *did* have."

"Now you know what the IOC have been dreading."

"But why didn't you make me *stay* here, in Greece, last summer? I could've been assisting you for months!"

"You *were* assisting me..."

"How do you mean?"

The Professor had a cagey glint in his eye. "Well, now that you're away from the crazy Adirondacks, I can tell you this: Who do you think pushed, behind the scenes, to have you, the most controversial person in Lake Placid, designated as the Torch Runner for Opening Ceremonies?"

"I thought you told me it was Reverend Courtney!" Ivor said and then laughed out loud. "Why—you son of a bitch—so it *was* you all along who was working behind the scenes! I should've known—I thought it was Uncle Dalby!"

"Well...he, too, was your big booster...but it was I...personally...who put the screws to the Barleys...and how I *did* it will forever remain my secret!"

Ivor read his mind: "You didn't..."

"Uh huh...I did..."

"So...you forced Madame *Dupleix*...to make the Barleys toe the line?"

"Uh huh..." said the Professor, who then burst into laughter, as Ivor joined him till they both had tears in their eyes. "But Dalby and I felt that it was best for you only to re-appear in Athens *after* the existence of the MOON-OC became public knowledge, and *after* they notified the Press that their Deed Ceremony at Olympia would be staged."

"Shall *I* be going to Olympia? I can't believe that...after all these years with the Olympics...I haven't yet made my proper pilgrimage to their birthplace. I'm so ashamed," the Athlete admitted honestly and paused. "Sir—I've got *so* many questions!"

"First you must penetrate the MOON offices. You must gain the confidence of the whole Ouranós clan."

Hefferon then related what had happened last night, and mentioned that Lord Dalbeattie was contacting Interpol about Dora Cain. "I shouldn't trouble myself over her. She's likely just one of the clan's stooges," the Professor said. "They have so many."

"But should I *see* her again?"

"Definitely. If she wants sex...it might give you the necessary release from your daily tensions."

Both men laughed. Ivor was always glad to find that Rembetikós was a philosopher in spirit as well as in title.

"I also wish to make a private apology to you, Ivor, about last year's collapse of your marriage. I understand how upsetting it was for you, yet we felt you needed to deal with *personal* matters first, so that's another reason that no mention of all of this was made to you when you showed up here, last May, after your divorce. And that's why I felt that your packing up and going off to Lake Placid might be quite the therapeutic experience..."

Hefferon snickered: "*Some* therapy...*that* place was!"

"So—you are *over* your divorce now?"

"It was for the best," Hefferon admitted. "I couldn't *talk* to my wife anyways...she's far better off getting screwed by that horsy son of a bitch she took up with, that Captain of The Queen's Life Guards...so it's just as well she wasn't allowed to be taken into my confidence on *any* of these matters."

"But that's precisely why I'm ashamed, my Lad. You sacrificed your own marriage...for an Ideal that few even believe exists anymore. Your wife *wanted* you to cash in on your Olympic Gold, didn't she?"

"True. She became quite obnoxious about my reticence."

"It must have been very difficult for you," sighed the Professor. "And my *own* situation here hasn't been easy. Imagine how *you'd* cope having to deal so continually, so closely, with a madman like General Ouranós? He's stirred up *so* much trouble for Greece that, if this becomes public knowledge, to his benefit, it could set this country back ten whole years. And *nobody* wants to return to the days of the Junta."

The Professor paused and sipped his drink. "I've had to pretend for months...that I am amenable to his insane idea that the Olympic Nation be constructed on Olympos. But everyone at IOC headquarters knows my true intent, as I have testified for the record, behind closed doors, that my loyalty to the IOC remains intact. However, once we decided on the course that would publicly shame the General, we decided on the course that would *save* the Games. *You'll* soon see that our decision was the *wisest*. If you go along, all will develop for the good, with rapidity."

Ivor smiled. "Speed has never scared me. It's been my luck to have been clocked as the fastest 1500-Metre Runner in the world."

The Professor extended his hand. The two shook, and Rembetikós said: "Ivor, you're a damned good sport!"

Lunch was served on the terrace by the dutiful housekeeper. She brought a delicious pastítsio*, freshly baked bread, olives, and a stewed vegetable of artichoke hearts and celery and carrots prepared in a creamy lemon sauce. They drank a light white wine from Cyprus.

On toasting, the Professor declaimed: "Where there's *one* Greek —there's an argument. Where there're *two* Greeks—there's a party."

"Serious levity," Ivor added and laughed. It would be so educational, he told himself, to resume having the Professor's counsel, whilst he stay in Greece.

"It's a classic case of Greek jealousy," Rembetikós remarked. "I'm of the senior generation of my homeland, whereas Ouranós is young enough to be my son. Therein lies the trouble. He's itching like a Titan to lacerate my balls. Patricide is a term my country invented. It's at the base of most Greek Tragedy, which was born just up the road here," and the Professor waved a fork in the direction of the ancient Amphitheatre of Dionysos.

It wasn't every day that Ivor had the chance to hear such sophistry emphasised by such a casual gesture. He promised himself to go visit the Amphitheatre as soon as possible.

"And it's even more blunt than that. In our case, what it really comes down to is the old dichotomy between Brain and Brawn. Needless to say, I'm *not* the latter. I favour Olympia. Ouranós favours Olympos. Athens versus Sparta. The Peloponnesian War."

"And both sides lost over that."

"Wait till you meet the General's *wife*, if you think *he's* bad," Rembetikós chuckled and downed his wine. "Everybody calls her Thýella†—that's Greek for Storm. That's when she's being a good little

* Pronounced: pah-STEET-see-oh; a pasta and meat dish.
† Pronounced: THEE-el-lah; first syllable sounds like the first syllable of the word *theatre*.

168

girl. Otherwise, she's referred to as Gestapo, which, I'll let you in on a secret, all Greek men call their wives!"

"Is she visible?"

"Is the Sun? She's visible all right. She's the Chief of Protocol!"

"Oh Gods! Not another vicious Lady Chief of Protocol to battle!"

"I thought you'd like that!" Rembetikós said and chuckled.

"Sorry. Thýella makes Heidi look like Tinker Bell..."

"Well...the way that Heidi liked tinkering with that *bell* of hers... with those Benwah Balls at full throttle keeping her at constant climax ...maybe I *ought* to slip a pair or two up Thýella some night!"

"*Her* pussy would bite your hand right off at the *wrist!*" joked the Professor, laughing heartily. "It's she who actually runs the MOON Organizing Committee. With an *iron* fist. It's your job...to pander to her."

"I hope I can succeed."

"You'll succeed, if you heed *this* advice: Beware her. Thýella's as cunning as Aesop's Fox. You've already been provided with a stipend. Under *no* circumstances is she to know from whence it came."

"But I have Pounds Sterling." Then Ivor thought quickly: "I'll say it's from the Dowager Duchess of Brendon, who paid for my Olympic training."

"You're also staying at one of the most expensive hotels in this part of the Mediterranean. Say you'll be looking for a cheaper flat soon— that you only wanted a bit of luxury to celebrate surviving Lake Placid."

"Ain't that the truth!"

"As well—you're *not* to be seen courting Rembetikós, but you must *avoid* him—is that clear? Take this number," and the Professor handed Ivor a blank card onto which a telephone number was written. "You and I shall next meet the same evening of the day you begin working for the MOON-OC. A secretary will answer. She'll be instructed to give you the place where we're to get together."

"Yes, Sir."

"As for the Ouranós clan, and for Thýella in particular, keep restraint in mind. Only posit your Idealism, which is well known and which, I'm sure, will be your calling-card for getting on well with *all* of them. Remember—Thýella and Affedikó Ouranós represent all that's corrupt within the Olympics—all the hypocrisy, all the hucksterism, all the self-gain, all the scandal. They'll stop at *nothing* to get the Games for their *own* glory—all to the tune of boosting the MOON site 'for the good of the Olympic Ideal' firstly, 'for the good of The World' secondly, and 'for the good of Greece' thirdly. But honestly, their talk is nothing but rhetoric, pure bullshit."

Professor Rembetikós then reached to a small stand beside his chair and placed a portable telephone on the table. The housekeeper was removing the plates and laying for the sweet.

"Here," the man said as he was dialling a number, "It's Thýella's office, which from now on we'll call by the code-name 'Tyre Temple'.

169

You'll see why I call it that when you go there. Get an appointment to see her as soon as you can."

Hefferon took the receiver and waited. Soon, a woman's voice was answering. "May I speak with Madame Ouranoú*, please?"

"She not here," the woman replied.

"When will she be in?"

"To-morrow...afternoon."

"At three?"

"No—*afternoon!*"

"Four?"

"*Afternoon!*"

Rembetikós began to laugh as Ivor covered the receiver. "Afternoon in Athens means seven—have you forgotten!"

"Seven?" Ivor asked, incredulous. He *had* forgotten...that Time is on a totally different schedule here in Greece...

"Yes—yes—*seven*. Who are you?"

"I'm Ivor Hefferon—an Olympic Athlete. I'd like to pay Madame Ouranoú my respects. Will she receive me?"

"Don't know."

"I have a letter of introduction for her...from Lord Dalbeattie. Do you know who *he* is?"

"No."

"He's the British IOC Member."

"Oh—Madame Ouranoú *must* be here."

"With whom am I speaking?"

"Maid."

"And your name is..."

"Lydia."

Shortly thereafter, Ivor was back in the lobby of the Hotel Grande Bretagne. His head was filled with all of the things that he'd have to deal with. He was standing by an armchair, rather absently staring at the bar and hearing the two horrid words "neutron bomb" in his mind, when suddenly he was tapped on the shoulder by a tall Greek teenager with long curls dyed henna-red. The fellow was wearing jeans, a purple jersey, and mirrored Hollywood specs. Beside him was an effeminate six-footer who looked as pale as Death. His hair was in a crew cut, and both of his ears were pierced. From his lips dangled an unlit cigarette.

"Hi," the henna-haired chap said. "You're Ivor Hefferon, aren't you? I saw your picture in the paper."

Ivor was tired, and just wanted to go to his room.

"I'm a big fan of yours. Can I take you for a spin? I've got a Harley."

"Excuse me?" Hefferon replied, startled.

* Pronounced: oo-rah-NOO. Meaning: Belonging to Ouranós.

170

"Oh don't worry—I'm a Rock Singer and Lyricist here in Athens—Heavy Metal—and this's my Bass Guitarist. Our group Bacchae are giving a concert for the students of the University of Athens next Tuesday night, outdoors in the Odíon, by the Akropolis, and I just thought you might like to come free. We sing in English, not Greek."

The Athlete was handed a pass for free admittance to the concert. "It will get you backstage. Sure you don't want to tour the city?" the Singer asked again.

"Ta—but maybe another day."

"Well—see you later," said the henna-haired bloke, who left the lobby as soon as his skinny Guitarist had struck a match to ignite the dangling cigarette.

6th April – Thursday – Pre-Dawn

Ada was lighting a candle before her ikon of the Archangel Michael. We still hadn't got to sleep. She felt it best first to propitiate the Good Spirits of her seaside cottage. Prone to paranormal experiences at the best of times, her psychic powers I had come to believe in profoundly. She was widely known to be able to hypnotise. "The Archangel Michael, along with Gabriel, is portrayed along every altar wall of every Orthodox Church of Greece," she said, then closed her eyes to say a personal prayer of thanksgiving for our safe journey north. Then she opened her eyes and kissed the ikon three times.

The sound of the waves had now become more pronounced to me, as if with each passing moment their rhythm was washing its way throughout my very Soul. Dawn was nearing, stealthily, pursuing the elusive hours of the day, ever closer and closer across the sanguine liquid of the bay. The potency of the Aegean could literally be *felt* within my very marrow, and I could not fall asleep now if commanded so by every earthly deity.

"You and I were meant to meet," Ada whispered, then snuggled up beside me. "And Saint Michael will protect us against Evil. No one will even know we're here. All those reporters think we've returned to Athens."

She led me through the kitchen to the only other room of the house, a tiny bedroom hardly big enough for the over-sized bed. It was draped with a beautiful red and black crochéd coverlet, and Ada sat me down upon it. She began to laugh.

"What's the matter?" I couldn't help asking.

She turned and placed a soft hand upon my cheek. Then she laughed again.

I searched her beautiful blue eyes for a reason for her mirth.

She ceased laughing, "I was just thinking of the horrid job you had to do...to the MOON lot."

"I guess I took them all a bit by surprise."

171

"Well—they certainly won't be hexing anybody *now*."

"Do you think that what I did will help, or hurt, Greece in the long run? Do you think your country will *really* get the Olympics back?"

"We've done all we could. It's now not up to us, but the Gods."

Seagulls suddenly swooped onto the porch outside and dropt fish that they had captured from the deep. The birds began to fight, noisily, for the meat.

2ⁿᵈ March – Thursday – 7.00 PM

Ivor made sure that he would not be late for his appointment at the headquarters for the Organizing Committee for the Mount Olympos Olympic Nation. Since it was already dark, he had left the hotel half an hour early, and had walked slowly through the Pláka district, stopping briefly in the National Cathedral of Greece. It was not the first time in his life that he had ever set foot in an Orthodox shrine, but the overpowering perfume of the Orient did strike him with intensity. Women in black were everywhere, kissing ikons, and crossing themselves repeatedly. Some were moaning aloud. The stranger could not help staring. Neither could a bearded Orthodox Priest, a young one, who kept himself shrouded by a column until the Athlete departed.

Hefferon then found his way to Odós* Adrianoú, the Street of Hadrian, the High Street of the Old Town. The fellow followed its narrow winding route, delighted with the low Byzantine buildings and many shops. He passed a small open square, filled to brimming with café tables and young couples enjoying themselves uproariously. Greeks certainly *do* know how to live, he said to himself, thinking how much more dour were the sullen English.

Thousands of cats, it seemed, were making riotous love that eve, in the colossal pit of the ruins of Hadrian's Library, just beyond the square. Ivor couldn't resist peeking, but only saw the odd flash of fur on floodlit shadowy stone, then pitiful squalling of two beasts tangled in fleshy heat.

Following the jagged wall of the immense archaeological site, Ivor was struck by how much higher above the ancient level of the street—a dozen or more feet—he was walking. Time had added tons of torpid soil.

Trying to locate "Tyre Temple", as Rembetikós had labelled it, was no easy trick. A newcomer can wander for days in Pláka and Monastiráki, and still not see all the archaic alleys. He knew it was somewhere off to the left, so wandered a bit further along Adrianoú then turned, guessing where it might be. The old house appropriated by the MOON-OC was on the corner of Odós Taxiárchon, Street of the Arch-

Pronounced: oh-THOS; second syllable sounds like *those*
    minus the "e" and rhymes with *gross*.

172

angels, and Odós Epaminónda, Street of an Ancient Athenian General named Epaminóndas. In this part of the world, Christian and Pagan still lived side by side. Names never changed for millennia.

Suddenly—Ivor had to halt. Looming upwards in the night, with no false illumination, but sternly standing against a white-cloud sky, straight ahead were five of the most primitively elegant shafts of stone that Hefferon had ever seen. Eerily blanched in the night, like bones, four out of five were thirty-foot-tall Doric pillars, all that was left of some temple façade. The short stature of their rock barrels harked back to an age far antecedent to the Doric. All Ivor could think of was Stonehenge.

Just then, Hefferon noticed a strange Oriental oboe, or some such instrument, being played nearby. The odd harmonies were faint, sounding as if they were being strained through the upraised shafts themselves.

Hefferon peered round the corner of the small two-storey house just off to his left, and suddenly said aloud: "Tyres!" Then he realised that this was right where he was supposed to be. Against the orange stucco wall of the house, a heaping display of fifty rotting tyres stubbornly disgraced the magnificent ruined temple but a few yards away. Only in Athens, Ivor heard himself saying. They take their heritage too casually.

Perpendicular to the house and the filthy rubber, a low concrete wall came from an adjoining stucco building at the far corner. The shawm now seemed to be emanating from beyond the fifty-foot wall.

Some ragged old man was seated before a nasty rusty doorway midway along the wall. This must be it, Ivor muttered and approached. Three sooty iron panels, side by side, each sported an upright-diamond design upon its face. "You Mister Hefferon?" the ragged moustachioed man asked unprovoked.

"Uh....yes. How did you know?"

No reply. The fellow just took a mallet and swang it crassly against the gate. The oboe stopt abruptly. A crack in the panels opened slightly. Greek language came through the gap in a torrent, just as a horrendously loud motorcycle careered into the quiet lane. Zooming past and soon out of sight was that same henna-haired kid on his Harley, who all but ran Hefferon down, but who waved this time.

"Come in—come in," ordered the inside guard, now swearing worse than ever in Greek. He seemed to want to close the gate quickly, like a housewife shutting the kitchen door against flies. Ivor ducked in, then the gate was slammed tight.

"You wait," and the guard, as ragged and bushy-lipped as his partner outdoors, pointed to a beaten wooden chair. So Ivor sat, as the bloke took to blowing his reedy instrument in the meantime. Some kind of waiting room, the Runner thought.

Whilst the guard amused himself with his peasant music, the visitor looked about the surroundings. He was surprised to be in a rather lovely garden. Off to the left, against the neighbouring house, orange trees were in blossom and were filling the enclosure with scent. Hedges were everywhere, little ones, violently pruned to a level of twelve or less inches. An elevated covered balcony hugged all the garden walls, save that of the orange trees. The doorway in which the guard and Ivor were seated was covered as well, and was in effect a blank space in the run of the balcony on this side.

At the small end of the garden, to Hefferon's right, and opposite the orange trees, was the house. A set of double doors gave off its balcony into the building. Ivor kept his eyes in that direction, but couldn't help noticing that the marble columns that supported the enclave's C-shaped balcony were decent reproductions of the Karyatídes, from the Erechthíon atop the Akrópolis. The whole seemed to have been constructed sometime in the nineteenth century, during the neo-classical revival.

Terracotta oil lamps were placed on the balcony rail, two lamps between every two Karyatídes. No electric illumination disturbed the scene. The garden was absolutely enchanting. If he were not careful, Ivor felt that he might even become hypnotised by the shawm's melody.

Honey-hued light from the lamps radiated towards the garden's epicentre, towards the fountain for which all hedges led. Watery reflections of golden rays continually caressed the statue that stood above the fountain pool. The stone sculpture, of some primitive multi-breasted female Goddess, stared benignly, as if she could give suck to all Athens and more besides.

Suddenly, a young wren of a woman in a white uniform, like a nurse, pushed open double doors and stept aside, as a matronly middle-aged blonde lady was allowed to pass. Audibly, to all the garden, the lady said: "That will be all, Lydia."

Lydia shut the double doors behind her, without a peep. And for a minute, the lady, of stunningly handsome carriage, at least five foot ten inches tall, remained motionless, gazing intently at Ivor. Finally, the guard poked the Athlete with his oboe, and waved it towards the proprietress. Ivor rose, and advanced through the hedges towards her.

"*Yiá soú**," the lady said and held her hand to him cere-moniously. Hefferon took her fingertips and placed the obligatory kiss upon the back of her hand. "Madame Ouranoú," she stated, then took the letter of introduction that Ivor was extending. She read it, then shoved it into her bosom. The faintest enigmatic smile came upon her lips. She seemed to be amused by this Olympian, and surveyed his three-piece suit of beige cloth, and what it might conceal beneath the fabric. Hefferon guessed that her hair was dyed, but nevertheless it was attractively rolled into a bun behind her ears. She almost looked the perfect Nazi warden. On the pale blue blouse of an expensive designer's

---

* Pronounced: YAH-soo. Meaning: To your [health].

suit, one could not help noticing the massive turquoise pendant and the ostentatious gold chain.

"It's by Lalaoúnis, who does all our things. The beautiful boy...is Ganymede," she stated and ran her tongue slightly over her lower lip. She almost smiled, as Ivor looked closely at the cameo that was hanging between her ample breasts.

"How becoming," the visitor added.

"Mister Hefferon, it was a pleasure seeing you win...at the last Olympic Games."

The way that she said that precluded any reply. Then she turned to the guard and commanded: "Iamídas! That will be enough!"

The shawm playing ceased abruptly.

"We have a migraine," Madame Ouranoú said in appeasement to her guest. "Come—step inside."

Doors were opened from within.

"We thought we told you to *vanish!*" the lady blurted at her cleaning lady.

Lydia did as told this time, departed in haste through the garden.

"We shall be firing that *pest* before long," Madame Ouranoú said, then smiled. Obviously, she adored telling people off. Her headache had seemed to go away. They turned right and proceeded upstairs, where they entered a room that faced the steps. Its walls were of Persian-blue shot-silk. "Have a seat," she ordered and pointed to an armchair. "Smoke?"

Hefferon refused a cigarette.

"Good—neither do we. She sat behind an antique French desk. All it had on it were a crystal vase and a few peacock plumes. "So Lord Dalbeattie has been gracious enough to send you from England. How *is* the old Dear?"

"Getting along."

"We're sure he's doing just fine. Now—you are aware of who we are. You are speaking to the Chief of Protocol of the Mount Olympos Olympic Nation. What can we *do* for you?"

That took Ivor by surprise, but he was quick in giving reply: "I'd like to volunteer my services to your cause."

"How can you be sure...that our cause *isn't* to bastardise the Olympian Ideal? We saw your quote, in the papers."

"His Lordship wouldn't have bothered to have written, had he doubted your organization's intent."

That seemed to mollify Madame Ouranoú. "Well—he's not known as the effusive letter writer," she said and grinned. "But tell us about yourself."

"I've been quite dissatisfied with my life of late," the Athlete began, "insofar as I've already attained more goals for my age than most people do in their whole lifetime. But...personally...I've not been

175

satisfied, not even with winning the Gold at the Olympic Games. As you likely know, I've just returned to Europe from six months with the Lake Placid Olympic Committee."

"Yes," the lady stated without a smile, "and if *we* had had to be placed in such close proximity to the likes of that vapid little Heidi Barley, *that* Chief of Protocol would have ended up as *fertilizer* for the whole of the Adirondack Mountains. We *squash* such bugs!"

Ivor's eyes widened, and he dared not laugh. "Well—Lake Placid's behind us all—thank God. I now want to do something positive, for *Greece*, to give back to Greece a bit of what *she* has given me, and in so doing, to give something to sports worldwide. So far, I've only been existing for myself. I've been an Idealist, yes, but just in theory; in practice, I've been a Hedonist from the start. I guess it's caught up with me, at last, and I just can't continue on as I have. I can no longer continue playing such a stupid rôle."

"So...you're looking for something...*creative*?"

"Something that I can do for *others*—so that others can benefit from my experience. Academically...I haven't really shined. At the rate I'm going...I might get my PhD when I turn ninety! I suppose the only *real* gift I have...is in sports."

"Well, there's plenty of *that* going round," Thýella remarked, as if sports were a social-disease. She stood from her desk, frowned for a moment, then turned her back. Hefferon felt the blood dropping to his feet. What had he said that was *wrong*? Madame Ouranoú spun round. "We wonder just how far...*you* can be *trusted*?" Her wicked Hitlerian eyes bore through those of the Runner. "You're so *sweet*, but you may *not* be so *naïve*. Maybe...you could just be...what we *need*?"

Hefferon said nothing. He was sweating. This woman was an A-Class Barracuda.

"Follow us," she commanded and marched round her desk to the hall. From a pocket she extracted a set of keys. She went to the far end of the hallway and unlocked two locks on a metal door of a darkened windowless room. "Stand here," she stated.

Something white was in the centre of the room. Suddenly Thýella flicked on the first switch of a theatre lightboard that sent a shaft of yellowish light from above the doorway directly onto the centre of the room. Ivor gasped aloud. It was a model of the Olympic Nation Games Site. "Mount Olympos," the lady declared coldly.

Hefferon did not know what to say. The snow-white plaster model was awesome.

"Do you, or don't you, want to be a part...of *this*?"

She was glaring at Ivor, and he heard himself saying: "Yes..." Then, she proceeded to use the lightboard to describe what he was seeing. A pinspot of golden light landed upon each venue that the lady was mentioning, one beam at a time.

"This is Litóchoron, the village at the base of Mount Olympos, on the left bank of the River Enippéos. And this is the Greek Army compound, on the right bank. The thousand-metre foothill, behind the village, is called Gólna, and the identical one, behind the Army, is called Stávros. Atop Gólna will be the site of the Summer Olympic Games. Highest on Gólna is the Olympic Village, with the buildings for the International Olympic Committee, the National Olympic Committees, the International Sporting Federations, and the MOON-OC, as well as housing for Athletes and Officials. Below is the Arts Complex, with Opera House and Amphitheatre. Below that is the Stadium, visible on the plâteau from the sea. Beside the Stadium is the Summer Sports Hall to the south and the Administration-And-Press Tower to the north, on the edge of the ravine. Spanning the thousand-metre gap of the gorge, between the two foothills, we shall be constructing a plexiglass Passenger Tube, suspended one thousand metres above the Enippéos. Alongside the Tube, cable-cars will shuttle back and forth. On the north plâteau, of Stávros Foothill, will be built the site for the Winter Games. And if you don't believe it snows in Greece, you should stay on Olympos in February."

"How high is the mountain?" Ivor asked.

"Almost ten thousand feet," was the reply. "The Stávros Site will have an identical Administration-And-Press Tower, on *its* edge of the gorge, to which cable-cars from Gólna will run. North of this, will be the Winter Stadium, for Opening Ceremonies, Speed Skating, et cetera, and down into this will issue finalists from the Bobsleigh, Luge, and even the Alpine events. All competitions will be directed to one point, for the benefit of spectators. North of this is the Winter Hall, for Figure Skating and Ice Hockey. And north of this, the Ceremonial Avenue will be built from the Principal Gate of the Olympic Nation. All spectators to both Winter and Summer Sites will arrive from the flatland below Stávros Foothill. A subterranean parking lot and rapid transit system will be constructed beside the Army camp, and the environment won't be altered one little bit. Trains will come by underground through Stávros Foothill, at the top of which a Station will function for capacity crowds to point people to the Principal Gate. Highspeed rail links between Athens and Thessaloníki, the two main cities of Greece, are to be expanded and modernised—long overdue anyways—and the Thessaloníki terminus will connect the Olympic Nation with all of Europe by rail, whereas the Athens Airport link will connect us by jet to the world. The Mount Olympos Olympic Nation will be the most modern new Free State on the face of this Earth. The latest technology will be utilised in construction and design. The Nation will be larger than The Vatican, The United Nations, and Monaco combined. And, its existence will, once and for all, end the *wasteful* loss of money, manpower, and time spent each four years to move the Games about from clime to clime."

The golden pinspot suddenly became a bath of cerulean blue, over all the Olympic Nation's white plaster arcades, turrets, and domes.

"Mount Olympos, once just a myth, now becomes concrete reality," Madame Ouranoú stated with pride, as she caused celestial illumination to fall upon the fabled high peaks. She let her words sink in, then flicked off all the light.

Ivor felt like applauding, or at least shouting *brava*, but managed to keep his composure. This steely dame was consummate, an actress of superlative degree.

Without more ado about the audio-visual display, Thýella trooped along the hall and cut leftwards into another plush room. She switched on the lights.

"The General's office," she declared. "The husband couldn't make it here this afternoon, but we wonder if you might join us for coffee in two days' time?"

"Saturday? Yes—when?"

"Noon. We'll be waiting for you in the Café Ellenikón. You can't miss it—it's the best café in Kolonáki Square."

She scribbled the appointment down on a card, and handed it to the Athlete. A cuckoo clock sounded half past seven. The dizzy bird shot out and made but a single squeak. "We bought *that*...for Affedikó one day, in Lausanne. We leave it here, to remind him that the IOC can't forget that General Ouranós does exist."

"Are the IOC known ever to forget *any* of their Members?"

"Sometimes, we have prayed that they *could* forget Professor Rembetikós—our country's *other* Member of the International Olympic Committee." But having said that, Thýella held her venomous tongue and quickly switched the subject. "As you can gather, our plans for the MOON are still on the drawing boards. We are a private corporation. Things are run tightly here, in a military sort of way. There are the Colonels, and there are the Privates."

"Is there a rank for me?" Ivor asked boldly. "You may rest assured that my experience with the Olympic Movement should only be used to advantage."

"We shall see. Perhaps you're too...idealistic...even for us," she said pleasantly. But then, an embarrassing thing happened. She began hiccuping. The lady tried to stop it, by swallowing and holding her breath, to no avail. So, she pretended it wasn't happening, and offered a hint of her enigmatic smile. She switched off the lights and escorted the Athlete down the stairs, hiccuping all the while. On the balcony, again the young man was struck by how beautiful was the nocturnal garden, all save the guard, who was loudly snoring in his wooden chair.

"Iamídas," Thýella snapt then hiccuped again. "Look alert."

The man bolted in fright, and literally stood at attention. Pleasant little lady, Ivor said to himself. A real joy to work for. Maybe she'd been hitting the bottle this evening?

"We shall see..." she repeated, then paused to hiccup, "you at the Ellenikón, on Saturday." Instead of offering him her hand, the fellow was surprised that the lady wanted to accompany him to the gate. But she halted, midway, at the fountain. She stared for a moment at the Goddess's many teats, then hiccuped. "We may be hiring a Deputy Chief of Protocol. The Organizing Committee, you may have heard, intend to participate in a special Deed Ceremony at Olympia, at which time the Government of Greece shall be granting us our autonomy. Perhaps ...due to your Protocol background at Lake Placid...you *may* be suited to assist us? We shall have to ask Evrynomía."

"Evrynomía?"

"Our statue here," the lady hiccuped and gestured towards the pool. "The Mother Of All Things...has not yet failed to provide us with the answer."

Ivor watched one more time, as reflections from the splashing water waved golden light upon the many sculpted breasts. Madame Ouranoú extended her hand, and the young man gave it the obligatory kiss. The guard pushed open a rusty panel of the gate, and Ivor was freed from this den of iniquity...at least for awhile. The haunting oboe pursued him up the lane.

6th April – Thursday – Near Dawn

We were making love, slowly, to the rhapsodic melody of the Larghetto of the *First Piano Concerto* of Frédéric Chopin. Ada had introduced me to her favourite composition before we had left the capital for Olympia. Each time that I heard it I had felt more and more that it was a composition that I had heard before. This time, as it was playing on her tape recorder, I recollected that indeed I had heard it at Shrove Tor.

Lying in the arms of warmth, of the woman whom I loved, I could not get out of my mind the sad image that the Chopin revived. The dulcet airs had been compatible allies to a stately home in the midst of mourning. Shrove Tor had seen many deaths in its time, but the most recent, that of the young Lord's belovèd, was almost too melancholy to bear. My friend Alexander had been as deeply in love as I now am, likely moreso, as his temperament was thus inclined and much more refined. His romance with the late ballerina, Marina Novikova, the prima assoluta from the Kirov, had been social news for quite some time. But her murder at Heathrow, as she foolishly was attempting to return to her homeland that she had earlier denied, was her fatal undoing—and likely Alexander's besides. When we saw her body placed aboard that jet, then took her back to the United States, and not to the Soviet Union, all Alexander could do was cry...for weeks...desperately lonely inside. His sole consolation was in Chopin. When I stayed with him and cared for him after Marina's death, it was Chopin, not I, who brought him back to life. His sister was there with us, and for hours on end she would have to play *this* very music...the Larghetto of the *First Piano Concerto*...over and over...as it was the only thing that Alexander could bear to listen to...till I thought that *she* should die. I had heard that piece performed so often, during that dreadful period of sadness, but a pair of years ago, that I had truly blocked it out since that time. But now...hearing the music anew...and as a composition revered by Ada...fresh meanings to the notation kept registering in my mind...even while poignant memories of Marina's incomparable stage-artistry kept coming back to beguile my mental sight...

The love-making of Ada and me...this time...was as if we were afraid that each might break if we held one another too closely. We were barely clinging to each other's bodies with our arms, with the tips of our fingers, but the sensation was so deliciously rapturous as to be almost divine.

Sometimes a couple can reach the most tremendous heights, simply by lying by each other's side. No word need be said. No sound need be uttered. No force need be shown. But the Souls of either do join, unprovoked, and the two become one ally, that soars ever more further upwards, towards the purest sky, then beyond this earthly atmosphere, to regions removed from the mortal mind. Such was our bliss this time—we needn't ask for a single thing but this—such love being absolutely boundless.

I barely do remember having stood with her at all. We still were being held in sway, transported outside the house by some call, by love's own vibrant kiss. Our hands were linked, and somewhere, on the beach, I noticed that the scarlet mist was as red as our own blood, that kept pounding, as if with hammers of steel, any bæstial thought away, and that kept giving us untold happiness! Life itself, innately good, should ever be peaceful...as this...

3rd March – Friday – Before Dusk

"Nobody can ever know another person completely—so why should we even try?" Dora Cain stated maliciously, as she walked by Ivor's side.

"That's insanity," Hefferon retorted. "You might as well be dead, if you truly profess *that*."

They were walking at dusk, through crowd-brimming Athenian streets. It seemed as if every housewife in the capital had roused from the day's heat. The weather had been insufferably hot and sticky. In the morning it had rained. The Athlete went silent, debating with himself *why* had he ever given in and taken this walk with this arrogant woman, whom he was fighting not to hate.

Dora shouted back: "Look—I only dropt by your *fucking* hotel to pass a little time. I thought you'd bring me out of my mood. I'm having my period, I'm sorry. I've been out of town, on an *impossible* dig, at the oracle of Dodóna, where the ancient Greeks used to go to talk to the *dead*! I guess the spooks *got* to me Plus—it's been raining up north—all week. So right now—if I *say* I believe in nothing—I do *mean* it!"

"You and I..." Ivor attempted, "...are polar opposites."

"They say that they attract," Dora snapt.

Trying to push their way through Sýntagma Square's thousands of café tables, opposite Parliament, was no joy, either. The whole city seemed in a foul mood, likely due to the air. More tourists than usual were cramming the paths and blocking the vitriolic waiters, and Ivor had never seen so many cumbersome backpacks in one place.

"It's the goddamned American Express," Dora blurted as they turned down the street past its doors. "Every Yankee bozo with a buck to cash just pushes us all aside."

Modern Greece...Ivor thought. More multi-coloured neon signs than Piccadilly Circus. A far cry from Aristotle. But soon...the modernity was passing, as the two progressed down the incline of the Street of Hermes. So terribly un-British, all this pushing and shoving and grabbing for wares...didn't these housewives have any fetching up?

"This city must have been what London was like in the Middle Ages," Ivor said.

"A king-sized open-air market...gone ape-shit," Dora snarled.

The Athenian kaleidoscope of hues kept changing in every alley that they passed. "To the stranger, it's all just a jumble of impressions..." Ivor said.

"Too many copper pots, too many native costumes, too many racks with postcards, too many shops' sparkling silver and gold, too many phony antique vases, too many ersatz bronze statuettes, and too many beige ceramic Pans with absolutely stupendously erect penises," Dora bellowed without regard for passerby, as she stopt before a shop window and pointed directly at a seven-inch satyr with a huge nobby dick.

Ivor laughed. "Go on—such tasty things didn't seem to faze you Tuesday night."

Dora retorted: "You wish."

Ivor continued: "You know—I still can't seem to get the *feel* of Athens—whether or not it's all just a hustle on the make, or if it truly *is* the modern incarnation of the city once so unique, once philosophic."

"Oh—the *signs* are here," Dora inserted as they carried on walking. "The Pagan Connection, between The Past and Now, is everywhere to be seen, but to me there's not one single link between *modern* Greeks and the signs. The signs, from The Past, just shimmy about in the welter of it all, screaming: 'Buy me—Buy me—Buy me!' Well for *your* information—the commerciality of Athens is *vulgar*—and long ago turned me *off*."

"Where're you leading me?" Ivor wondered, fearing they'd stumble on the MOON headquarters any minute, or catch Thýella's evil eye.

They were passing an octagonal marble tower set inside a field of ruins going leftwards up the hill. Dora said: "That's the Tower of the

181

Winds. Hellenistic period. I always like to imagine that Alexander the Great had it built, but he likely didn't."

Ivor now knew that indeed they weren't far from "Tyre Temple", as it could be seen off to the right, beyond the forest of felled grey granite columns. He pretended he was lost. Thank God Dora wanted to go in another direction. Hefferon wiped his brow as he noted the frieze of flying angels, or whatever antique creatures they were, that had been hovering for ages beneath the Tower's conical roof.

"Julius Caesar built this one," and Dora waved away the whole column-forest. "It's the *Roman* Agora. The *Athenian* Agora, where I work, is beyond—see—off to the right."

Creeping round countless angles of orange stucco homes, this vestigial organ of Old Athens, that festers away on the Akropolis slopes, caused Dora to say: "You know...the Akropolis is the *sole* factor that keeps this city sane."

"Shall we *go* up there?" Ivor asked. The grey-white and fir-green mount looked so inviting in the viscous light of dusk.

"Verboten,"' she said. "Closed at night."

"No sense rushing things," Hefferon admitted, wishing to see the Parthenon when time was right. Last summer, for the whole period that he'd resided in Athens, he'd avoided the Mount of Athena, for some inexplicable reason. In fact, he'd avoided *all* ruins, choosing obstinately to immerse himself only in the *modern* Athens. He'd not even let himself rent a flat anywhere *near* the Old City, but found some newly built concrete and glass structure in the northern suburb of Maroússi, close to the "language institute" where he busied himself teaching English. Such avoidance of the *heart* of the capital had, of course, been ridiculous, but given that his divorce had only just been finalised, in London, he rationalised his choice of "the modern" over "things ancient" as a way of making a clean break with his relationship with his wife, and it worked...at least for awhile...until he began to feel a true queasiness within his very Soul, which occurred late last summer, when he had to lead a coach-load of language-institute children on a daytrip to Mycenae, the rock bastion of Helen of Troy, Agamemnon, and the contrary Elektra. *That's* when it hit him that he'd been *cheating* himself out of what Greece truly did have to offer, and he felt so ashamed that the very next day he quit his teaching job, booked a flight from Athens to New York, and flew away, like an eagle that was off to seize new prey. And from JFK Airport he went straight to Manhattan's Port Authority, bought a ticket for the Adirondacks, and headed north to Lake Placid.

Soon Dora was leading the way down the ochre and rusty road of Polýgnotos, that suddenly aimed leftwards to an open iron gate. "The ancient Panathenian Way," she muttered nonchalantly.

Suddenly—it hit Ivor. Here—after all his avoidance, after all his sacrifice, after all his spent physical energy, after all his agony, after all his years of daydreams, after all his years of medals and study and books...here he was...at last...in the heartland...of *Greece*! The Olympic Athlete felt an uncanny rush of emotion. He felt afraid...he felt at home...

"Finding you...in the Panathenian Stadium...I thought you'd like to see where its name came from," the girl said, quiet-voiced at last. "Didn't you say to the Press...you never set foot in *any* of Athenian ruin? God—what were you *on*? Well...here's the Panathenian Way..."

Perhaps she *wasn't* involved in the Olympics plot after all, Ivor thought. He began to feel guilty. Perhaps he'd been wrong and had falsely implicated her. At this moment, he just didn't know. Everything was so confusing, save the sight before his eyes.

The Runner just gazed about in wonder. Right here—arching leftwards up to the rock of Athena herself—were the remaining worn boulders of the original market of Athens, over the which the daily throngs of the hapless pagan metropolis would go into their stalls, into their temples, into their halls dedicated to their incomparable Music and Debate—pursued by the relentless unshod Sokrates. This—the very nerve-centre of the town of the Greatest Inquisitor of any age—now was spread before Hefferon's bleary eyes. Ivor couldn't help wondering what it must have been like to have *spoken*, just once, with a mind as sublime as Sokrates?

Thank the Gods, Dora was astute enough to appreciate the young man's need for silent contemplation of all this Beauty. Never before, until that moment, had Hefferon ever read in any book how utterly *verdant* was Athens. He often had heard of a temple of marble called the Thission, said to be the best preserved in the world from Doric times, and yes, there on the horizon it sat, splendid, utterly flawless in its intactness. But *never* had he pictured it, in its proper perspective, *never* had anybody ever remarked how gorgeous it was, not because it was Doric but because it was surrounded by vegetation, dark green. It was isolated...pure in natural lushness of plant-life...in a veritable forest that swept all along the horizon leftwards, and upwards, along the hillslope that led to the ridge containing both the Hill of Mars, the white-rock Áreos Págos, then more leftwards up to the very Akropolis itself.

Ivor knew that both Mounts, Ares and Athena, were chronicled for their Beauty, but never had he put the two together as they rightfully must be, nor had he ever seen a photograph that showed the sweep of grace, from the high-looming wan cut-stone Erechthion down rightwards all the way to the Temple of the Smith of the Gods. And here and there—blanchèd pentelic slabs showed through the green—and here and there an upright wall could be seen...

The Athlete had to sit. Mute, the two sat atop the primitive fortification wall that crawled towards the Akropolis. Beneath their dangling feet were the well-rutted cobbles, cyclopean ones, over which horsemen, chariots, citizens of Athens, elders, musicians, and bearers would have marched, in the Panathenian Procession, held for the city's Patroness Athena, every four years, in spring.

Hefferon couldn't help but think about his Oxford years, about those months and months spent inside the British Museum, researching, pondering, writing, then inevitably falling asleep. Being an Athlete and a Scholar both...in this day and age...was an impossible undertaking. Yet almost always he would seize the opportunity to go to the room containing the so-called Elgin Marbles, which he always felt *should* be returned to Greece. He would survey the frieze sculptures that once were part of the Parthenon, that portrayed so gracefully the Procession now going past in his mind.

Dora seemed to read the fellow's thoughts, and began aloud a litany for the dead: "Sacred sacrificial oxen, cleansed, and gleaming like snow, hooves and horns gilded, and garlands hanging round their brutal necks...are clomping upwards. Exotic young maidens of Athens are following next, lithe limbs, oiled and scented, beneath gowns of freshest linen...young girls pursued...by leering marshals...chosen to represent the Gods...to keep the mass in motion. The lucky few ...precede the Chief Priest of Poseidon and Chief Priestess of Athena...to whose shrine the assembly keeps aiming...bearing the Sacred Péplos ...the Goddess's holy garment...ceremoniously held by a dévotée...who considers herself blest above all girls...since the Péplos will clothe the Goddess...as sculpted by Phidias...for a period of four more years..."

Never before had Ivor felt such affinity with Dora Cain. Never again would she allow her poetic Soul to surface. Even as her litany was reaching its conclusion, each word was uttered with such poignant care that Ivor could sense that never again would they come to be so close. In a sense, it was the epitaph to their already-brief affair. Something going on inside her, that Ivor could not fathom, had her in its grip, and that something was exuding Evil. He wanted to put his arms about her, but that something told him it was best not to dare. Only in the Ancient Past could they unite as one—it now seemed clear. Perchance, once upon a time, their two Souls had been star-crossed together, along this very Way. Ivor just could not say, and sighed deeply as he breathed in the perfumèd air.

"They say that it's the *atmosphere*...the atmosphere of all things...that makes this place as *pensive* as it is," Dora said finally, and breathed in deeply as well.

"What it *was?*" Ivor replied cryptically, and glanced to the Temple of the Smith of the Gods. The sunset, now fully blazing in the west, and just behind the long-lying mountain named Párnis, seemed a veritable blacksmith's furnace for the God whose own shrine now was basking in fiery light. "Hephaistos...was said to have built the palaces for the Gods...on Olympos," Ivor heard himself saying.

"Who knows?" Dora replied, sounding a million miles away.

The whole concrete-filled valley beyond the Agora's green edge now seemed alight with blood-red, and rooftops for miles and miles kept sparkling, a-fire in rash vermilion and orange reflections from the Sun's symphonic extravagance, before it would have to settle down to bed. Apollo, this eve, seemed wanton indeed, and whomever he was taking past the hills, to his divan, was in for an orgy of sex. The whole Vale of Attika, from the sea to Euboea, was now blazing crimson, and was making Ivor dread. This sunset seemed to be issuing a most *personal* warning...that pain can be caused by a *friend*...

Whatever battle within Dora, that she herself was waging, certainly could be felt within Ivor. She was *not* hiding her anxiety very well. But within himself, despite her, something indeed was churning for the good. Gazing at all this evidence from The Past, all these facts that Man once lived for something higher than himself, caused the Athlete to rejoice inside his heart, that his decision *not* to cash in on his Olympic Gold Medal had been the right one, no matter if the stakes were so very high. Many, if not all, had thought and still think him utterly mad. But the folly would be *theirs* to shake. Something...some positive honourable *thing*...yet was here...in Greece...waiting...though ever Present...as only The Past *can* wait...for someone to apprehend what it *is* that the land still will offer. *Whatever* it is, Hefferon was certain that apprehension of such arcane wisdom never could be traded...for any sum of mortal kind. Again, Ivor felt eerie. This sunset *was* a certain sign.

The inevitable soon occurred. Dora, who had been waiting for the right moment, as soon as the top-most arc of the white-hot Sun did set, turned on Ivor and said: "Now that you're *here*—what are you going to do with your *life*?"

A chilling wind suddenly descended the Panathenian Way, from some shaded spot upon the Akropolis. The Runner pondered what he should say. Should he *tell* her, now, that he was considering working for the Olympic Nation? How much could he *trust* this girl to know? He chose to test her. All that he said was: "Climb Mount Olympos, I suppose."

6ᵗʰ April – Thursday – Sunrise

We were in a boat. The Sun was just about to surge forth from the depths of the Aegean Sea. Not one ripple was disrupting the placid plate of the water. We were drifting, lazily.

I was manning the oars. A fish leapt out and gasped nearby, as if taking a gulp of the scarlet air. Ada looked at me, with love in her eyes.

An hundred yards or so from the beach, we could see Ada's cottage on the edge of the sand, looking like a pearl at the centre of a mirage, wavering unsteadily in anticipation of the morn, seeming pink, then white, then beige.

Above the house a small cliff rose, a dozen or so feet. Beyond that, the alluvial plain, of farmland and orchards and fallow, aimed a few miles inland from the coast. The elevation increased at Litóchoron, sometimes visible, sometimes not, as the atmosphere continued to change.

Beyond, and dominating every single glance, was the immensity of Mount Olympos. It was far lengthier a work of geology than I had ever conceived in my brain. The size of it sprawled as one entity, due north-south, fifty kilometres long, more like a mountain range than one single unit of rock. But Ada assured me that it had been born as one piece.

The most intriguing fact about it was the central peaks. They were shrouded by clouds, miles inland, straight ahead, and at the far end of a gigantic gash in the rocky length, a cut running due east-west. This was the Vale of Olympos, formed by æons of alpine creeks, dribbling by gravitational pull into one icy stream, the River Enippéos.

Suddenly—Ada touched my arm and told me: "Look." She was pointing due east, to the just-emerging cusp of the ball of orange flame.

Never in my days had I witnessed a more moving sight. Directly out of the serenity of the waves a tremendous eruption was now taking place. The heat of the upwardly arcing globe of fire immediately was sensed on the face.

But then, as if it were an organic being, like a titanic aggressive snake, the Sun rose out of the water enough to cause its ball to elongate. And thus it extended and extended, at an ever increasing rate, its plasmic warmth in a gold-orange skate, across the sea that one could feel was heaving with the elemental embrace.

Our boat began to rock, as the force of the Sun was felt, as ever closer, *ever* closer, towards us raced the light. And watching this natural phenomenon, I was mesmerised. Then, the brilliance of the accelerating rays reached our tiny vessel, and dashed past us, towards the coast of the bay.

And out at sea, higher by degree, the sphere of our globe's own Star stood more and more potently, up, up, up, as upon the beach the light did reach, then leapt upon the cliff, then over the whole Greek landscape, in a transformation of the region that was quite daunting to see, as my eyes now were aimed only at the midmost peaks.

Then, as if with a daub of paint, on a brush the size of a country, the sunlight swabbed upwards with a stroke, and illumined a thousand-metre height, hence all of the many miles of foothills of Olympos stood starkly in plain sight.

My eyes were straining to look due west, at the two most prominent foothills, between which the Enippéos slaked its seaward course. The two virgin three-thousand-foot mounds were the precise locales that the Organizing Committee for the Olympic Nation had been scheming to rape. Beyond them, hidden well beyond the Vale, I still couldn't make out the highest peaks.

"Just watch," Ada said. She seemed to intuit this Holy Mountain's innermost mood.

I continued to stare up the miles-long gorge, that was now turning gold at an alarming rate, when I saw that the clouds on the summit were black as the Gates of Hades. Lightning from them began to quake the heights.

"*Listen,*" Ada remarked.

Ever so faint, rolling from more than twenty miles away, echoing sounds of thunder came from on high, like battle-din from a distant state. But the Sun had risen far enough from the sea even to hazard an inland melee of thunderheads jousting with lightning. Then, there was one last vigorous combat above, when even *that* did abate.

I only heard a few more echoes, rustling across the waves. Ada was reaching to hold my hand in hers, when she did say: "This sunrise tells me...that your stay on Olympos *will* give you what you need..."

The majestic Mount of the Gods seemed possessed, of far more planetary mystery than even this levée of the Sun had chosen to display. I could not remove my eyes from the cloud-covered peaks, then heard myself say: "How profane Man can be. To consider an act of impiety so dastardly...as to bastardise such an intact colossus of this Earth's Nobility...is simply beyond me. How could *anybody* want to construct anything at *all* up there? Only someone out of his *mind* would dare!"

Ada's hand squeezed mine tightly. To ease my despair, she said: "Yet you *triumphed*, Ivor. The mountain now is your *friend*. Please have patience. You *will* witness what Good it must send."

3rd March – Friday – 10.00 PM

After dining at an outdoor café in the square near Hadrian's Library, Dora and Ivor walked to Sýntagma Square. The Athlete had decided to invite her upstairs. But at the desk, when he was getting his key, he was handed a note and requested to read it privately.

"It's confidential, Sir. It came at nine this evening," stated the employee.

"Excuse me," Ivor said to the American girl, as he stept a ways off to read in privacy. On notepaper of the British Embassy, the item was embossed with the name of His Excellency Sir Cecil Gambling.

"Don't know him," Hefferon said to himself. The Ambassador was urgently summoning the Runner to call on him that very night. "Bugger!" Hefferon snarled. "This ruins *everything!*"

He began to think fast. What could he possibly tell Dora? If she knew he was visiting the Embassy, she might track him there, stealthily. He could not trust her, even though her poetic side had been revealed to-night.

He retraced his steps to the woman. "Bad news," he declared, "my mate Alexander, the one back home I told you about, he telephoned to-night."

"About what?" she asked eagerly.

"Friend of ours, whom I hadn't realised was that badly off..."

"Died?"

"Yes—I'm sorry to say. To-day."

"Do you have to leave Greece?"

"No...it's not that...there's somebody I have to notify...to-night."

"My God, in Athens?"

"I'm afraid so. Someone in Kolonáki...that the family hasn't been able to get ahold of."

"Who?"

"The lad's mother. She's at a colleague's, whose telephone's out of order."

"Oh Lord!" Dora Cain obviously had swallowed the story hook, line, and sinker. "Well—*that* must alter our plans..."

"I'm sorry. I'm not looking forward to it at all..."

"I wouldn't either. Were you close?"

"Very. He had leukemia. Brilliant scholar."

"Then...why'd his mother *leave* him?"

"She...had to be here...for some physics conference. She's a scientist...at the Cavendish Laboratory."

"Gosh...well...guess I won't see you till *next* week?"

"Why? Are you going on another dig?"

"Back to Dodóna. Hope it's not raining."

"Chin up—at least you have a job—that's more than I."

"You better get ready. Better dress up."

"I'm sorry...but I don't think you'd enjoy being round...when I have to break the news about her boy. They expected him to live at least six more months. He's the woman's *only* son."

"Oh how horrible..." Dora forced a smile and kissed Hefferon on the cheek. "I'll phone...soon as I'm back in town."

"Please," Ivor said as he watched her leave the elegant lobby. "Thank God! She *took* the bait!" he said to himself, went to his room, changed into running gear instead of a suit, checked his map to see where the Embassy was located, then left the hotel in a flash.

Embassy Row in Athens is Avenue Queen Sophia, one of the capital's arteries, the dividing line between the sumptuous quarter of high-class blocks of flats known as Kolonáki, and the western flank of the grandiose greco-revival Palace now known as Parliament, built for the Nordic Kings in the nineteenth century whom the European Powers forced upon Greece after the Revolution with the Ottoman Turks. Magnificent marble villas still stood within proud parks, with palm trees wagging in the breeze, and past these clunkers from the previous imperial age the Athlete jogged, praying that Dora Cain had honestly gone back to where she came. Funny, he thought, she never had given him her address. He had no idea at all where the woman might live.

Carrying on along the boulevard, Hefferon turned a sharp left when he got to the museum that kept planes from World War II out front in the open air. He ran uphill another block then turned right, and found what he was looking for. His instructions being to show the note at the door, Hefferon did this and a brutal young security guard admitted him to the consular offices, put him in a lift, then led him through hallways to a locked gate, which admitted to the Embassy proper.

Standing in a formal hall, Ivor was watched every second by the guard, who was not at all concealing his disapprobation of the guest's attire. The Olympic Gold Medallist decided to scratch his balls, as if he had a flea, glaring like a mental case at the guard, who at last had to turn his head. "Got it," Hefferon said, and flicked an imaginary mite towards the surly bloke.

The guard grimaced and rapped on a set of double doors. The Cultural Attaché was within, and popped out his balding pate: "What *is* it?" He didn't even acknowledge the Olympian's existence, but frowned as he looked at his watch.

"The Runner, Sir," the guard said, with a Cockney accent.

"We shall see," snapt the Attaché, who slammed the door.

Five minutes passed. Every time that the guard began to stare at the Athlete, Ivor began to scratch his groin, making more comical remarks about his "jock-itch" each time. At last, the guard had to turn his body away completely, fearing that he'd lose his cool and burst into laughter. At least this caller wasn't stuffy or boring.

"His Excellency will *see* you now," the Cultural Attaché stated with disdain, opening the door and taking his leave. Ivor scratched himself *extra* hard for *this* obnoxious chap, then entered the Ambassador's office. He saw him seated in a comfortable chair, and hated him on sight.

Mean as a snake, Ivor heard himself saying, as he recoiled in disgust at how green was the diplomat's face. His jowls were fat as hams. He was puffing some cheap, smelly cigar. Dyed black hair hung down to his eyes, parted in the middle, and strands drooped over his black wire-rim spectacles, that were much too small for his mien. Sir Cecil soon got to the point: "I say...we hear you're living in *Athens* now."

"Sorry, Guv. Just passing through," Ivor replied, not caring for another invitation.

"Now don't you be *smart* with me," His Excellency barked. "You—an orphan—were brought up by the Brendons—whom I know bloody well."

"Well, if you know them so *bloody* well...why haven't I ever seen your face at *home* with us at Shrove Tor?"

The diplomat coughed nastily but paid the remark no mind: "Plus, I'm quite good friends with Dalbeattie, so you're *not* pulling any wool over *these* eyes!"

My, how very friendly, Hefferon heard himself saying. Outwardly, he said nothing. He decided to scratch himself *here*, too, and spread his thighs apart wide.

"You *sports* all think you're God's Salt Of The Earth," Sir Cecil said in disgust, blowing rancid smoke Ivor's way. "Listen—we're both Christ Church men—so why don't we at least *try* to be civil?"

Hefferon remained silent. He simply smiled.

"Quite," the Ambassador replied, somewhat appeased. Just then a rap on a side door was heard.

An elderly lady entered unexpectedly. She looked, and sounded, just like a plucked chicken. "What, may I ask, are you doing? It's going on eleven PM."

"Leave me *be*, Louella!" The woman did not vanish. "Her Ladyship," the husband stated rancorously.

Ivor stood, then sat again. Just then, on the wall against which Lady Louella Gambling had just been, Ivor recognised that the painting in oils of some Turkish pasha was really the famed portrait of Lord Byron, from 1814, that had been rendered by Thomas Phillips. It showed the great poet posing theatrically as a Souliote warrior, in a maroon velvet jacket embroidered with gold, his handsome head wrapt in a magnificent multi-hued silk turban. His bearing and facial features reminded Ivor of his best friend, the Earl of Luxborough.

"Did you tell Mister Hefferon who telephoned me?" the Ambassadress began as she fidgeted with a string of pearls. She was dextrous, and loved to show that she knew how to tie knots with one hand.

"*You* tell him!"' Sir Cecil commanded. He stood and lit another paltry cigar.

"Do tell us, Dear, what precisely is your *purpose* here in Athens?" Her Ladyship asked acidly.

"Oh—thought I might do a bit of mountain-climbing," Ivor replied.

"Mount...Olympos...perchance?" the woman said and smiled. It was obvious that she had dentures, as she adjusted her plate.

"Perchance," the Athlete repeated.

"It's no easy hike," said Her Ladyship, as if she would know. "You might be safer staying on the foothills...where the Olympic Nation soon is to be built."

There was silence.

"This evening, my young man, my dear friend Madame Ouranoú telephoned me."

Ivor said nothing, as the diplomats peered.

"Perhaps you may have noticed a certain *individual* the other night, outside MOON headquarters?" asked the Ambassador dryly. Ivor suddenly pictured the ragged guard, but responded: "Who do you mean?"

"Did you not notice somebody exceptionally...how shall we put it...*punk* whizzing by?"

Suddenly—for all his trying not to—Ivor burst out laughing and simply could not stop. The whole interrogation was too British, too ludicrous for words.

"It's not *one* bit funny, Young Man!" the Ambassadress said tartly. "We are trying to *help* you."

Hefferon forced himself to pucker his face into rigidity, though every muscle still continued to twitch. He hoped that this would be his *last* evening with British officialdom in Greece. He wondered what the iconoclast Byron would have thought, and done, high above them all in narcissistic splendour. Away from such toads the poet, too, had fled.

"You may realise, Mister Hefferon," His Excellency continued, "that our offices are privy to Intelligence...not to be found in the street."

"I daresay," the Athlete at last concurred, after wiping his eyes. "It does sound as if some *twit* of yours...was snooping...*in* the street."

Obviously, both Sir Cecil and Lady Louella were of the opinion that sportsmen were no more than co-ordinated pieces of meat.

"That punk chap, that one on that hellish Harley-Davidson, that one with that hair like your proverbial Parisian whore," blurted Her Ladyship, "we are almost *certain* is an agent for the KGB. He is the leader of the Anti-Nuclear Campaign, here in Athens, among *other* vulgar things."

"Oh," Ivor said.

"He's a student at the University of Athens, and a Rock-N-Roll Singer besides," Sir Cecil said with contempt.

"He's always stirring this city *up* with demonstrations," Lady Louella added. "For God's Sakes, you *must* promise to stay *away* from him."

"He's staging a Rock Concert next week...in the Amphitheatre of Heródes Attikós...right beneath the Parthenon...but the performance is just a front...for expounding his *radical* political beliefs. He also organized, before your arrival, a huge demonstration *against* Greece's getting the Olympic Games back—*against* the Mount Olympos Olympic Nation—and he's on record as saying that the Soviets are *not* behind the idea that Greece get the Games back, and that he prefers this *not* to be the case," the Ambassador declaimed, and blew smoke his wife's way.

Ivor didn't know how to reply.

"Whoever he is," the Ambassadress added, "we do know, for certain, that there *is* a plot brewing, right here in Athens, to do the Olympic Games *in*. And you, My Young Fellow, who have demonstrated your dedication to the Olympian Ideal, now can demonstrate this Ideal to the ultimate."

Clearing his throat, the Athlete asked: "Me?" He looked at Byron, who was withholding all advice.

"You said...when you won your Gold Medal..." the Ambassador began.

"No, let *me* finish," Her Ladyship intervened. "You said...you won that *Medal* of yours...solely for *sport*."

"But..." Sir Cecil tried.

"Let *me!*" Lady Louella vied. "If you feel *so* strongly...about the future of the Olympics...then just *don't* get yourself involved in these dangerous schemes *here* in Greece."

"How do you mean?"' Ivor asked, not giving a thing away. He still could not figure out from what source, or sources, the Embassy's information was being supplied.

"About that punk chap," His Excellency said, "we should like you to get to *know* him...for us."

"We're offering you diplomatic immunity," Lady Louella inserted with pride, as she twisted her pearls into a knot as complex as a sheepshank.

"I'm sorry," Hefferon stated, "to decline. I'm what's known, in the sporting world, as a free-agent."

At long last, the Ambassador laid his cards on the table: "I should like to make you an offer. You can't refuse, if you have even the *slightest* patriotic bone in your muscular body. You *do* revere Her Majesty, we trust?"

"What does..." Ivor began but was interrupted. He rose to beg his leave.

Lady Louella stood as well: "If you *don't* co-operate, we can have you *deported!*"

"Louella!" snarled her husband, who stood. "Mister Hefferon, we're *not* asking you to make a decision *this* evening."

"But time *is* of the essence," the Ambassadress added, "that is, if you do choose to work for Madame Ouranoú. Give her my regards, to-morrow, at noon."

So—the cat was out of the bag, Ivor said to himself. He took a deep breath and made to leave. By the double doors he turned, looked once more at Byron, and said pleasantly: "We shall be in touch. I trust your *goons* will make doubly sure of *that.*"

The diplomats waited a good three minutes, before Lady Louella almost sneezed: "Damn him! *Everybody's* tentacles are out!"

"Now now," Sir Cecil replied.

But the Ambassadress had ambitious plans. She went to the telephone and dialled a long-distance number.

"Who're you ringing?" her husband asked, although he knew. He was handed the receiver.

"Tell the Foreign Office to rush us their *best* boy," she ordered. "Hefferon *must* be followed—from midday of to-morrow."

9th April – Sunday – Midday

We were having the midday meal, on the porch of Ada's cottage. Three days had passed since our arrival, and I was finally beginning to settle into complacency. In little over a month I had delved deeper into the psyche of this tragic landscape called Hellas than most people, who think themselves Grecophiles, ever plumb in a lifetime. For the first two days, the infernal machinations of all things concerned with the Olympics plot, pro and con, had plagued my every attempt to get them fully behind me. The ineluctable beauty of the seaside was more a distraction than a solace.

But Ada's love and sensitivity kept on with their caress. She knew just the right thing to do. She was a woman of superior perception.

"You know, Ada," I said as it finally hit me that the previous few weeks now were *over*, "I just want to tell you how much I appreciate your consoling attention...and...how very much I do love you."

She smiled sweetly, and lowered her eyes. She then closed them as she took a bite of the succulent octopus dish that she had spent the morning preparing. The meat had been cut into bits, and sautéed in butter and garlic, then simmered in a cream sauce with aubergines.

"Your cooking is as good an your feminine grace," I said.

Again she smiled. "Greek men often fail to notice, and when they *do* notice...they fail to pay me compliments." She laughed like a little girl.

"How long have you been an actress?" I asked, embarrassed at never having inquired until now.

"Didn't I ever tell you?" she responded. "My mother was an actress, in Thessaloníki. I guess I followed in her footsteps."

"As a child?"

"Yes. I always responded to the Stage. When I was accepted at Athens Polytechnic—my mother was so very pleased. She thought I could have been an architect—but I was only designing *sets*. Poor Mama —I quit—after only one year. The National Theatre...was kind enough to take me on. I starred at age nineteen as Iphigenia."

"Was that the year you were asked by the Greek Olympic Committee to be the new Chief Priestess of Hera?"

"That was two years later. I was then playing Juliet..." she said very softly.

"For the National?"

"No—a private production. We ran a full year. Athens is *mad* for Shakespeare—and rightly so."

"How was the translation?"

"Translation? Silly—we did it in the original. Oh my—and was it a chore. But it did teach me to revere your beautiful language."

"You do speak it marvellously."

She smiled, pleased by the compliment. "Since playing that rôle, I've been doing quite a bit of reading on the Shakespeare Authorship Question, which is the concern of a great many scholars worldwide. I'm now *thoroughly* convinced that the Bard *was* Queen Elizabeth I's Lord High Chamberlain, Edward de Vere, the 17th Earl of Oxford. Nobody not so elevated at court could possibly have penned such intrigues, especially not some bumpkin from the Avon, as the Stratfordians claim!"

"You'd love to meet my best friend, the poet Alexander Pella. He's de Vere's descendant, and it shows, both in his looks and in his writings."

"You *must* introduce us," she said with joy. "I'd love to meet him. I heard many things about him, since our director was from The Old Vic and landed a bit-part in Pella's movie *Moctezuma* shot in Rome. Jonathan always was talking to us about the personalities of London. It's one of my secret dreams...one day...to *act* there..."

"Your career, here in Greece, though, certainly keeps you busy, doesn't it? Since Juliet, you and only you have been the Priestess who lights the Sacred Flame?"

"I've ignited the Torch for two full Olympiads, and this season is now my third. Thus, I've ignited the Torch for *five* Olympic Games— three Winters and two Summers."

Ivor smiled, as tears were welling in his eyes: "Then...you lit the Torch...for *me*...for the last Summer Games...when I won my Olympic Gold..."

Ada, also deeply moved to hear him say this, simply shook her head yes.

"It must be profoundly moving...to be the one to light the Sacred Flame..."

"The fire...is a *part* of me."

"Having recently performed the most humbling privilege of my *own* life, which was participation in Lake Placid's Opening Ceremonies as the final Torch Runner...the lucky one designated to cause the Cauldron to blaze...mere mortal words do not even approximate the truth when I say that seeing the Flame ignited, in that Stadium, is always the most emotional moment of an Olympic Games! *Everybody* knows that it is! I still get all choked up...just thinking about being the Torch Runner that day...and now...knowing that the Sacred Fire came to me from *you*...and came to you from *God*...with His Own Light of the Sun...so I can begin to sense the emotions that must course within *your* Soul...to be the one chosen to perform this Holy Rite..."

"*No* greater honour have I known. And none...shall I *ever* know..."

"Nor have I...since that first day we met..."

"I *love* you so much, Ivor! You've given me something to live for!"

"Me?"

"Yes, you. Men...here in Greece...oh they can be fine in bed...sometimes...but I have never been satisfied with their lack of concern for me as a *woman*. They think they're *Europeans* now, and therefore advanced, but they're still too deeply rooted in their Oriental past. The Turks...and the slavemasters over our race...have made our men into *men*, yes, but...sensitivity to a *woman's* needs have sadly been neglected."

"I believe in growth," I stated. "I do *not* believe in *equality* between the sexes."

"Nor do I," Ada replied. "Either sex has its faults and virtues."

"Tell me—why is it that you've never been to one Olympic Games?"

"Money."

"No Organizing Committee ever invited you?"

"Two Winter Games ago...but...I guess that I was superstitious."

"Why?"

"I thought...if I...who have lit the Flame...from the rays of the Sun...who have caused that very Flame to *be*...go to the venue where *it* has gone...it might *return* to me..."

"I don't understand."

"The Sacred Flame might go *out*."

"That's impossible."

"Is it? Perhaps my very Soul...could be scorched...forever..."

Ada took a deep sip of her retsina wine. She remained silent, still holding the rim of her glass. Our legs were interlocking, the pressure making my genitals come alive. We both were in swim-wear, hardly concealing much of our bodies.

"I think I understand," I said at last, as a large fish jumped out of the sea, close to the beach. Gulls on the sand leapt up and down energetically.

"To think, Ivor, you wanted to go straight up the Holy Mountain."

"I'm glad you made me see the stupidity of that."

"This atmosphere is bad."

"How do you mean?"

"Too much salt in the air. This morn I found a paper clip in my luggage, totally rusted."

"Already?"

"Think of what it's doing to your *lungs*—if the air is strong enough to rust *iron*?"

"I don't care. It's peaceful here. And we're together. That's what counts."

"You still haven't shaken off what you've just been put through."

"I'll admit to that."

"The one way to clear your mind...is literally to rise *above* your pain."

"Olympos?"

Ada shook her head yes, then said: "We'll leave the beach to-day."

I grabbed her hand beneath the table and pulled her towards a kiss. We stood and passionately embraced, our nearly nude bodies like branding irons from the midday heat. In her ear I whispered: "You be the guide...I'm ready!"

4th March – Saturday –Noon

"And you'll follow *our* orders," Thýella stated providentially. "You'll start to-morrow—at eight." She then brusquely removed her bracelet and plunked it by her husband's cup of espresso coffee. The clunky piece of jewelry was a stunningly valuable combination of pink coral cameos cut with the likeness of Olympias, mother of Alexander the Great, bordered by bands of rubies. "It's defective, Darling. Take it back to Lalaoúnis. Make him fix our clasp!"

Seated precisely in the centre of the art-déco black glass and gleaming brass Café Ellenikón, the whole of the chic clientele watched this peroration with curious mock-ennui. But evidently, it was Theatre, and passed the time rather effortlessly. Madame Ouranoú was every-body's archtypical Nazi. To-day, she was embellished by a smart black suit. Matching rubies were drooping off her ears and weighing down her neck.

Taking the splendid jewels and placing them on a passing waiter's tray, General Ouranós said: "Your tip."

Madame Ouranoú looked the other way, saying loudly: "Nikos—you wouldn't dare."

Nikos did not, and replaced the tray beneath the General's nose.

"Ivor's never seen anything like *this* pair of Greeks," the General laughed crudely. "Aren't we more amusing than the Barleys? Honestly Hefferon—this café considers itself the *most* chic watering-hole in the *most* chic district of Athens."

"That's not saying much!" snorted Thýella, to the chagrin of many nearby.

"Kolonáki, a state of being more than a mere neighbourhood of the capital, is considered *most* chic by everybody," Ouranós kept on.

"It has the most *Embassies*," his wife inserted, purely for Ivor's benefit. Hefferon chose not to say a word about meeting the Gamblings the other night. Then Thýella added: "Kolonáki has only *one* thing going for it...elevation."

"Mount Lykavitós," the General continued. "The higher upslope you go, the more expensive it gets."

"Which brings us back to *our* slopes," said the lady, gloating in her rôle as Chief of Protocol. "As our Deputy, your job, of course, must not taken lightly. You will not confide, whatever little you might learn, to anyone on the outside. You also understand that we, as your employers, have the right to check into your past, to make sure that you're *not* a security risk."

"Mere formality—as in the military," the General said politely.

"Since most of your adult life you've been in direct touch with the sporting world's VIPs, Members of the IOC," Thýella announced loudly and touched her husband's long thumb with a glossy fingernail, "it would be hard to imagine that you could make *too* many faux pas in that regard, regardless of whatever you may have involved yourself in...in Lake Placid. In fact, here in the Balkans...we can use to advantage *all* your past mistakes...from the Adirondacks. But if any fool is stupid enough to ask you what you might be doing for the MOON-OC, you are to be kind, but say sternly: 'Sorry, the job is classified.' Is that clear?"

The woman had been speaking so succinctly that even to the kitchen crew, unseen, her orders were perfectly *clear*.

"Absolutely," Ivor replied. Then he glanced at the General, who was certainly not in combat gear. He was as spic'n'span as he would have been for a National Day Parade. Ivor had been very surprised that the man sported a jet black, very neat, very curly beard. He was quite handsome, and six foot tall. His full head of hair was wavy, black, but greying slightly.

"Damned exciting race you ran," he had said on meeting the Olympic Athlete. The General's voice had boomed. "My sincerest congratulations." His handshake had been like a vise. If this military man weren't so crooked, Ivor had felt, then he might have even proven agreeable drinking-company.

"Yes—Olympos," Ouranós now stated. "As Deputy Chief of Protocol, you'll be assisting my wife. She runs the shop. We're now engaged in co-ordinating everything prior to the Deed Ceremony, three Saturdays from to-day. I'm handling liaison with the Government of Greece, as well as matters concerning the IOC."

If there had been dozens of conversations previous to the General's loudmouthed speech, there wasn't a single one now. Ivor glanced sideways in both directions. Never had he watched so many people stirring so repeatedly so many packages of Nescafé into so many porcelain cups. It seemed an Athenian pastime to pre-mix one's own drink, a little bit of milk, or water, stir, a little bit of sugar, stir, pounding the poor instant crystals like apprentice apothecaries. The café now was as quiet as a alchemist's laboratory.

"Speaking of the International Olympic Committee," Thýella said quite audibly, "did you get what we requested...from Lausanne?"

"Does one *ever* get what one requests...from Lausanne?" Ouranós parroted.

"Tell Ivor the latest," the lady ordered.

"My architect, a brilliant young discovery from Crete, has just

197

completed designs for the top-security belt for the Olympic Nation. Ivor's seen the model?" the man asked his wife.

She nodded yes. She looked bored stiff, and was flirting by her eyes with a lithe hairy-chested fellow, young enough to be her son, who wasn't anything if he wasn't a gigolo, and a high-priced gigolo at that.

"Administration Headquarters," said the General regardless, "will truly be the heart of it all. It has to be—as this Nation will have autonomy."

"*Somebody* has to rule it," Thýella added, suddenly interested again.

"Precisely," Ouranós concurred. "Utterly futuristic for Greece, the architecture will be like something from a science-fiction fantasy."

"It will be a pyramid," said Madame Ouranoú coldly.

"Of six-sides," her husband corrected. "A step pyramid—of twelve hexagonal solids—each inset just enough so that the whole seems a triangle when seen from the distance."

"The genius of the design is the open atrium," Thýella interrupted.

Ivor snorted: "But that's been done before."

"From the groundfloor's epicentre, looking straight up, a dozen separate balconies of hexagrams each will encircle the atrium, each one smaller than the one below it, and each pointed inwards and upwards to the one above it," Ouranós stated confidently.

"The whole effect will be to draw everything *up*," said Thýella, "as things *should* be."

"It will be like seeing inside a six-sided cone. All the balconies will be colour-graded. Pure black on the bottom..." Ouranós was interrupted.

"Pure white on top...where *our* offices will be located," Thýella announced proudly. Then she suddenly grew tired of draftsmanship and declared: "The IOC may own an Olympic Games from the moment that the Cauldron is set ablaze...but...*we* are going to control the Mount Olympos Olympic Nation...unto *perpetuity*."

"We...meaning Greece," the General defied. "You see, in our research, we've found conclusively that the running of the Ancient Games, at Olympia, was controlled by dynastic *families*, for centuries. They were entrusted by the Priests of Zeus to magistrate the sacred site. And look how long the Games continued with such a system...one thousand years. People have accused my family of monopolising the Olympic Nation but, in truth, my clan will be doing a noble *service* to the Games...my clan will be giving the Olympics *continuity* in this scatter-brained age. *Somebody* has to do the job...for Greece. And, if you've seen *anything* here, in the last few days, you've seen that *nothing* succeeds here if it's *not* done by whole families. In a way—we are sacrificing *all* that we have—for Greece."

"And—we shall *make* this damned country *appreciate* it!" Thýella added bluntly.

"But," Ivor asked, "the Olympic Nation won't be part of Greece, will it, once the Deed is given to the MOON?"

"In charter—no—the Olympic Nation will belong to the whole world. In practice—though—it will be even *more* Greek than Athens," Ouranós said confusingly, trying to make himself clear. "We are presently discussing exactly *what* the relationship between the MOON and the IOC will continue to be. Obviously, the situation, as it exists now, with the Games moving about, every four years, has to change. It's my personal belief that the number one reason that no Permanent Games Site has ever been allowed by the IOC is due to their fear of losing authority to whatever nation provides the Deed to see the Olympic Nation created. Greek politics, this century, have not been the most exemplary...to the likes of the conservative IOC Members...so that's why Greece hasn't been given the nod, by the IOC, until now, to go ahead and transfer land to their hands. They're afraid that such a land-transfer will put the IOC out of business. The IOC, having been based in the Alps, in Switzerland of all ghastly places, may at long last soon be returning home, to the motherland that sired the Membership, but whether or not the IOC's full *agglomerate* will appreciate the Games' return here...is the epic question." The General now was speaking so bombastically that the new Deputy feared the whole café would burst into applause, or at least into the Greek National Anthem. "When the Olympic Nation finally *is* recognised," he concluded, "as a legitimately established sovereign entity, then that is going to cause some *serious* problems for the IOC."

"Such as?" Thýella asked deviously. Once again she was flirting with the gigolo, who was fondling his crotch in that lacklustre stroke-the-penis manner so prevalent among Athenian males, and who, with his free hand, was alternately fingering then twirling a set of car-keys.

"Such as—why in Hell the IOC *should* stay in Switzerland, for one!" shouted Ouranós loudly. "Why *can't* they come and settle here?"

Obviously onto his pet peeve, his wife began to look in her bag for her compact, to do her face, "We'll send Lausanne a memo, Ivor, to that very effect." She found what she was looking for, and gazed fondly in the mirror. "*You* wouldn't want the IOC here, any more than *we* would," she said to her reflected image. "Why in Hell can't you let them stay *put*—in the Château de Vidy!"

"Women!" the General snapt.

His wife started painting her lips, aiming her face in the direction of the gigolo, who was getting a hardon, so the young hustler crossed his long muscular legs.

"Well," broadcast the General, "my colleagues of the International Olympic Committee *are* going to have to move here to Greece, whether they *like* the thought or not. Otherwise, the IOC might as well *dissolve!*"

"We shall see, Dear," she said, applying one last lick of scarlet to match her rubies. "Drink your coffee, it's getting cold."

Just then, a fan noticed Ivor Hefferon from a corner of the café. The Olympian was almost relieved to see somebody so obviously English aiming towards their table, and bearing a copy of *The Times* from yesterday.

"Excuse me, aren't you Ivor Hefferon?" the brown-haired chap asked out of curiosity. He looked about twenty-three.

"Well—we must be running," Thýella said and stood, not acknowledging the lad's presence, nor shaking Ivor's hand.

"And I must be off again…to Switzerland," the General complained, but gripped the Athlete's hand until it hurt.

The couple then made a grand theatrical exit. No one dared applaud them, but everybody wanted to. The whole café stared as they departed, then sighed with relief.

The brown-haired lad's eyes were wide. "Fans of yours?" he asked, as Ivor laughed. "My name's Colin," the fellow offered. "Mind if I sit?"

"Please. If you'll let me glance at *The Times*…"

12th April – Wednesday – 3.00 PM

We had spent the morning preparing our packs for the hike up Mount Olympos. For the past three nights, we had been guests of Ada's aunt, her father's sister, who had married a soldier from the village of Litóchoron. We had not listened to the radio, watched the television, nor read a single newspaper since we had left Olympia.

Ada had many relatives in town, and we had passed Monday and Tuesday making the rounds. Her whole family worshipped her, and the conviviality and food that we were given to eat was beyond description.

I liked the little town immensely. Nestling on the toe of Foothill Gólna, its twisty-turny streets and quaint specialty shops and marts reminded me of some of the West Country's ancient settlements that my friend Alexander and I used to enjoy exploring near Exmoor.

In the warmth of the reunions with Ada's kin, I began to get an idea of what exactly Mount Olympos meant to the modern Greek people. Of course, folk knew of its pre-Christian associations, but the dominant thing about the peaks was more immediate.

"Olympos helped in the Liberation of Greece," her Uncle Kóstas had said. I was to hear that phrase again and again, until I was hearing it in my own mind, as Ada and I were spending our last day before setting out for the heights.

Kóstas, a butcher, was taking a stroll with us after the midday meal and before we all retired for siesta. His shop was closed at this hour, and he couldn't resist having one of the loveliest actresses of Greece walking on his arm.

We were slowly promenading, as the whole of Litóchoron was wont to do, along the central avenue, a modern street that ran straight from the Police Station down the alluvial plain towards the sea. People would descend beneath pruned trees on one side, cross by the gate to the Army base, then ascend along the other side. And the problems of the world would seem a million miles away.

Kóstas had led us to an elderly cousin of his grandmother, a shut-in named Aunt Georgia, whom all of the family still made the effort to see. She was the venerable one, the eldest of the clan. Kóstas was bringing her some chopped lamb. A neighbour lady cooked for the nonagenarian, and kept an eye on her needs. Her little stone home was covered in gorgeous pink roses. It was in a sidestreet, to the left as one faced the sea.

Aunt Georgia was in her front garden, cutting aubergines as she sat in the sunshine. Ada loved her dearly, and the two women kissed and embraced. Ada went in and began to tidy the place, with a broom, and the two argued like old lovers because the matriarch had not talked with her for so long, and wanted to see her face. She had to hear all of the gossip from Athens.

As Kóstas sat with me, he rocked in a wicker chair and smoked. He was a bull of a man, with arms like a gladiator. He looked out of the corner of his eye, pulled on his moustache, and played with porcelain worry-beads. "Are you going to *marry* my niece?"

I said yes.

"Good. Then you'll be part of my family."

I felt suddenly very strange. Here I was, in an alien land, and taken so readily into these people's homes and hearts. Something deep within my blood told me that many, many of my ancestors had been Greeks. But how much *could* the present generation accept me, a foreigner, even *with* the spirits of my forefathers and foremothers providing such undeniable assistance? My command of their difficult language was still so weak. All my years of study of the *ancient* tongue had just skimmed the surface of *modern* usage, so it seemed.

The heat of the marvellous spring day was bearing down. From the garden chairs we could see the foothills of Olympos perfectly. From this vantage point, the alpine landscape looked more like northern Europe than that of the Aegean Sea.

"When we Greeks were revolting against the Turks," Kóstas declaimed, "whole platoons of soldiers hid out in Olympos's central Vale," and he pointed his cigarette into the mountain. "The Turks were superstitious."

"The Turks were *afraid!*" Aunt Georgia butted in, eavesdropping suddenly on our discussion. "They *knew* that the mountain didn't want them around!"

"*You* ought to know," Kóstas laughed and poked me. "*You* led the troops, so they say."

"And don't you *ever* forget it!" the woman said proudly. "I want that carved on my grave: 'Here lies Georgia, who helped rid Greece of the Turks!'"

Everybody laughed "How many *did* you kill?" Kóstas joked.

"None of your *damned* business," said the old maid. She went back to gossiping with Ada.

"More recently," Kóstas said gravely, "when World War II was over, and our homeland was being torn apart by Civil War, this Holy Mountain saved our children."

"It's a *horrible* story," Georgia shouted. "*Tell* it!"

"Family was fighting family—in various parts of Greece. It was Leftist brother fighting Rightist kin," Kóstas recalled sadly. "When the Leftists saw that they were losing, they began their big-push north. They arrived at Litóchoron, and many families sent their children into the Olympian forests to safety."

"Let *me* finish!" the matriarch out him off. "I'll tell you *exactly* what next occurred. The Leftists came in a horde. They kidnapped three thousand children! *Count* them! Three *thousand*! They absconded with them north. They illegally *took* our children, out from Greece, and fled to the Communist countries of Eastern Europe, to Czechoslovakia, many of them, and others walked as far away as Poland. Imagine—*Poland*—*Greeks* forced to grow up in *alien* lands!" The story revolted Aunt Georgia so much that she spat.

After a disturbing silence, the elderly woman finished what she began: "And those who ran off with the kids, some were proud, some were ashamed. Way in the cold north of Europe...our youngsters found it an *impossible* change. Most are still up there—they've given *up* the idea they'll *ever* be able to come back. But others...who are brave...have kept Greece *alive*...inside their hearts. They've now begun returning... somehow. Finally...a few of our Greeks *are* coming back...against *impossible* odds...back to this mountain...this *Holy* Mountain...that they can't help but remember from their youth...back to the Olympos of their childhood dreams..."

Ivor saw that Ada, broom in hand, was brushing away tears.

"This Olympian village, this Litóchoron," Kóstas continued, "justly and proudly calls itself Gateway To The Gods. Even here, at this eastern edge of town, and miles below the alpine glory above," and again he pointed reverently to the distant peaks, "one can feel the aura of things eternal...fervently."

I gazed in adoration, from the butcher to the stoic old maid, and tried to recall when two people in England *ever* spoken to me with such passionate sensitivity. Both now were looking at the Holy Mountain that they had known and venerated all their lives.

"The mind, before such immensity, diminishes to nothing..." Kóstas said.

"Mine did that years ago," I laughed, but immediately felt ashamed for the jocularity.

Kóstas kept on seriously: "...annihilated willingly by the magnitude before it. Wait till you *stand* up there."

Looking at the two foothills, each as tall as the other, and separated by a gap equal to their height, I heard myself responding stupidly: "It really *is* a Gateway."

But no matter how hard my insecurity was trying to reduce it all to a commonplace, it was hardly a *common* place at all. Even here, in this rose garden, strange forces seemed to be at work. Nothing could prevent one from meditating on the view.

"A *fantastic* geologic creation, isn't it?" Ada volunteered, as Aunt Georgia remained wrapt in eldritch silence.

Everyone was looking straight ahead, quietly, at the two gargantuan gateposts, both a thousand metres tall. Between them, the Vale of Olympos kept stretching a good twenty kilometres inland.

"It looks as if some giant took a sword, and sliced the gorge straight down through a cake of butter," I heard myself saying.

Kóstas added: "Olympos is nothing...if not the realm of *something* supramundane."

"The Ancient Ones," Aunt Georgia stated, "did *not* elect this site...haphazardly..."

Just then, the matriarch noticed, to the right and thus to our north, that the forces of Nature were getting into the act. "Look," she ordered and pointed.

From the northeast was coming an eerie file of black clouds, like a column of smoke on its flank, being blown by some fiend towards the southwest, now charging vilely in a rampage towards the Gate, along the ridge of the north plâteau, of Stávros.

"Look at that," Ada shouted. "God—I forgot how *quick* weather changes up here."

"It's fourteen kilometres long," Kóstas remarked accurately.

Indeed, just as he said that, the whole length of Stávros was now being pinned beneath the fourteen-kilometre black snake that was presently slinking faster than a train. Already, the insensitive storm was beginning to blow nearby pines along Aunt Georgia's lane.

"Macabre," I said, as Kóstas was shooing us in, and as Ada was taking the matriarch's arm.

"Go upstairs to the balcony." Kóstas commanded. "Watch the storm."

I did as he ordered. I had never seen anything like it before in my life, and stood in the doorway of the balcony, watching eagerly. The

203

ghostly advancing tumble of gory grey, now at the leftmost edge of Stávros Hill, just at that moment made a human-style leap, like an Olympic Broad-Jumper, over the huge abyss, over the Gateway itself. But yet—twenty kilometres behind this pitch-black leaping mass—still stood blue and white, in pristine unblemished illumination, the highest peaks themselves, that seemed to be watching this natural show with detached amusement.

Tumble, turn, twist, and try tossed the ebony storm's jump for the far bolster of the Gate. And soon, it had all but completed its bottomless leap, like some kid merely hopping across a stream. And of course the storm did continue...along the mountain's spine, southerly, towards that dusty clime called Attika, towards Athens, towards the capital of Greece.

Ada came to stand by me. "Ready to climb up *that*?"

But I was shaking. "Even before my Olympic Race...I've never known such fear."

"That is as it should be. You now *are* ready," Ada whispered, then she kissed me on the ear.

4th March – Saturday – 1.00 PM

Colin Duckworth and Ivor Hefferon seemed to hit it off on the spot. After the Runner had flipped through yesterday's *Times*, he suggested that the two grab a bite to eat. They found a sort-of takeaway nearby, in Kolonáki Square, where they munched on souvláki, freshly baked bread, and chips.

"Tell me about yourself," Ivor asked, glad for diversion.

"I'm just a student, at the L.S.E.," the chap stated. He was quite short and skinny, and had tortoise-shell glasses, gaunt cheeks, big nose, big teeth. But all in all he was presentable. He was also toting a sack, carting things about the city, and wearing corduroy jeans.

"Then you're a Londoner?"

"Nottingham. Been three years at university. Am taking this year off. I'm reading international macro-economic theory."

"What'd you come to Athens for?"

"Extended holiday. Only got here last night. I'm in a pension, in the Pláka district. Took a bleeding coach all the way from home. Through *all* of Yugoslavia. Good Heavens—what a God-forsaken place!"

"Bloody Hell—bet you're completely knackered."

"This morn I just couldn't sleep. Couples having it off, at all hours, all about me."

"Pretty seedy place?"

"Paper-thin walls."

"Yeah...that's all they do here...is *fuck*...and fuck *loud*!" Ivor said. "But then again...*I* should bloody well talk! I'm a real *moaner*!"

Both fellows laughed.

"How'd you end up in *this* square?"

"British Council's just over there," and Colin pointed diagonally to the opposite corner.

"I've never bothered visiting."

"I popped round to see if they were advertising any cheap digs."

"Anything promising?"

"Not yet."

"I'm in the sodding dearest hotel in Greece. Place's getting to me...gobbling up my budget."

"Where?"

"Sýntagma Square."

"Blimey—why don't we see about finding something cheap this afternoon? Could we share expenses?"

"I only know I'm going broke at the Grand Bretagne."

"There's got to be something reasonable in Pláka."

"Well—let's take a tour and see."

So the two Englishmen walked the few blocks to Avenue Queen Sophia, then entered the Botanic Garden of Greece, a short-cut behind Parliament to Pláka. By a pool of ducks, surrounded by excited children, Colin asked: "Who were those two at your table in the café? I was afraid to go up to you. I thought you looked terribly busy."

"Glad someone did, though. You got rid of them," Ivor laughed and they carried on beneath the shade of exotic trees. "Prospective bosses. I got a new job, starting to-morrow."

"Sunday?" the student asked.

"Will it be?" Ivor said aloud. "Hmm—guess they have queer hours."

"What is it—something military? That gentleman looked every inch the Colonel."

"General. It's for the Olympics."

"That should be easy for you."

"Hope so. It's the only thing I'm good at, anymore!"

They exited from the Botanic Garden by an avenue of stately palms, that placed them on the corner of Sýntagma Square. Throngs were milling about on the pavements, vying for trams and buses. Children were screaming in fits and starts for balloons or sweets or attention. Kiosks and vendors ran the whole length of the enclosure that bordered the formal garden. After pointing out his hotel...Ivor aimed the two across the road and turned into the quieter confines of Pláka. All was still until they entered Kithathineíon Street and descended to a tiny Byzantine plaza. Colin was looking at everything, absolutely entranced.

"You're just as pie-eyed as I was when *I* got here!" Ivor laughed. already feeling the big-brother.

"I just can't believe I'm here!" the student replied. "Certainly beats the flipping School of Economics."

From a public subterranean urinal suddenly emerged a huge Black dude, American obviously. He was decked out in Soul finery, with a beaded nylon suit of chartreuse green, and a wide-brimmed snakeskin sombrero. He came up to the pair and began a smooth speech: "Hey Man—got any *blood* you can leave?"

"What?" Colin asked, astounded.

The Afro-American flashed a grin and continued: "*Blood*—Man—*blood!* You well it—we sell it. Gets you *lotsa* spare cash."

A scraggly-haired hippie-type girl suddenly appeared from nowhere, and shoved the dude: "Don't mind Frank—he's a vampire." Then to her partner she snarled: "Hey—Dope—those're *English* tourists. You won't get *blood* outta *them!*" And the two headed off up the street.

"Heavens—this part of Athens has more freaks than England and Scotland combined," Colin announced wide-eyed. "Did he really want my...*blood?*"

"It was *you* who wanted to live here."

"Maybe not."

They left the colourful square and turned right at the next corner, into Hadrian Street.

"Now I recognise where I am," Hefferon said and led the way. "I wouldn't mind living a bit further down—at the bottom of *this* lane."

They scurried along the toe-hold of the flank of the street that passed for pavement. Vintage cars and motorcycles added even more danger to the narrow road. Ivor lost count of the jewelry boutiques. He had never seen a city with so much crafted gold.

Suddenly, a Harley-Davidson stopt abruptly at kerbside. It was that same singer with the henna-hair, whom the Gamblings had found such a fright. He winked at the Olympic Athlete, and smirked at Ivor's boy in tow. "What's happening?" he joked to Hefferon. "Picking up some *loose* change?"

Ivor's mind raced. For a moment, back in the Botanic Garden, he almost had concluded that Colin must be an agent, but the lad honestly seemed much too naïve for anything but a university. But now, here was this so-called Rock Star, and Ivor felt intuitively that the singer just might prove a valuable key in this conspiracy. So Ivor decided then and there to get to know the person, but on his own, without the British Embassy's complicity. He answered him: "Scouting for cheaper digs. My hotel's too dear."

"Forget *that* dump," the Singer said. "By the way—call me Theatrínos—my stage-name."

The trio shook hands.

"This's Colin—he's a Student—with an Uppercase S."

"Here—have a pass," Theatrínos offered, and handed Duckworth a ticket. "Free entrance Tuesday night. My concert, at the Odíon. Show the bouncers this, and come backstage."

"Thank you," accepted the Student, gratified.

"Now—about a place to stay—put up with Evtychía*," Theatrínos stated.

"Evtychía?" Hefferon wondered.

"Just around the corner. Number twelve, Mniskléos," the Singer volunteered. "Mention my name—you'll get a place."

"What was that address?" inquired the Olympian.

"Street of Mniskles. The architect, four hundred some BC. He designed the Propýlea, the Akropolis's principal gate."

"And there's *still* a street named after him?" Colin asked, as if he couldn't believe his ears.

"After all this time," Theatrínos agreed proudly, then revved his engine one time. "I'm late—we're rehearsing our new set."

The Harley took off and the Britons found the address. They were in a lane wide enough for a wheel barrow, looking up at the yellow stone greco-revival townhouse from the last century. There was a rock doorway, an unlocked set of green-painted double doors, and above that a little wrought-iron balcony. The sound of a piano being played was filtering from upstairs into the street.

"Maybe she's practising...if that's Evtychía on the eighty-eights," Hefferon volunteered and pushed one of the doors.

"The place looks five centuries old," Colin said. "No light bulb seems to be working."

Suddenly, out of the building pushed a young wren of a woman, like a nurse, all in white. The Athlete's eyes grew wide as saucers, as he recognised that this was no doctor's aide, but Thyélla's aforeseen cleaning lady.

Lydia, as well, looked alarmed at bumping into Hefferon here, but she caught herself when she saw that Ivor was with somebody. Her eyes, though, registered that there was something that she wished to say. For a split second, the two communicated silently. Ivor, mindful of ears everywhere, said nothing more about it, as he continued into the hallway and as Lydia continued into the street.

Marble stairs, too well worn, led upwards to a landing where more stairs led to the first storey. Off to the left of this landing, a rise of six wooden steps gave way to a thin balance-beam of a walk, that was over an outdoor courtyard lorded by the umbrella of a great green tree.

"I've a feeling *that's* where we'll be living," Colin whispered, as he peered in disbelief at the catwalk of a walkway.

Ivor gulped. The two mounted the marble stairs up to the first floor. They waited and took a breath, as the piano playing continued. Hefferon knocked.

"Rap again," Colin said almost inaudibly.

* Pronounced: ev-tee-KEY-yah (the KEY is really pronounced halfway between KEY and a guttural HEE).
  Meaning: Happiness.

Ivor was getting nowhere, so banged on the door until the knuckles pained. Presently, footsteps were heard and a little sliding window in the door was showing a female face. She liked what she saw, and swang the portal wide.

Evtychía, in her mid-sixties, was a true *personnage*. She was matron of what she termed a "guest house". Although all Athens knew her, nobody ever knew from where she came. To look at her, she almost appeared as if she could have come from Paris. There was something French, something *fin-de-siècle* about her stance, as if she embodied the totality of the Athens that had been obliterated by World War II, that had been bulldozed by the welter of modern high-rises and tree-less thoroughfares, as if she were the very last of the old generation who preferred to speak French over English. Even the way that she pushed back a lock of her orange-dyed hair seemed a Gallic gesture, that said that though she had to *work* for a living she was as proud as any woman anywhere. There was great *nobilité* to her. Both fellows liked her immediately.

Evtychía soon was speaking a surprisingly good French with Colin. She hurriedly led us back down the stairs to the catwalk, on which two cats, literally, now were sprawling.

"Didn't I tell you?" the student jeered.

"These are the *garçonieras*," Evtychía said. The cats meowed, as if *they* were the *garçonieras*, and not at all amused at being disturbed. To the pussies she purred: "Not you, *mes Petites*," then to the boys added, "it's the *rooms* that are called *garçonieras*. I never understood that, a *Spanish* word, made from a *French* word, here in *Greece*, for *bachelor* quarters!" The *garçoniera* she led to, at the end of the first run of the walk, turned out to be a mere room, stuck to the side of the neighbouring building like a wasp-nest of mud to a cliff. Handing Hefferon the key, Evtychía stept back gingerly, awaiting reaction.

Ivor was appalled. The condition of the room was a disgrace, but for some weird reason all that he could say was: "It's...quaint..."

Next door, Colin's reaction was not dissimilar. He could only ask the room's price.

The two young men met again on the catwalk and looked at the horror on each other's face. But when you're young and foolish, you'll try anything.

"I'll take mine...if you'll take yours," Duckworth could at last communicate.

"Right," jibed the Olympian, "I'll show you mine, if you'll show me yours!"

"*D'accord*," Evtychía said agreeably, pretending not to get the dirty joke. "Come back with your bags, and I shall hold them both till eight."

On that note, the matron returned upstairs. The piano practising again was heard.

"A Nocturne?" Colin wondered.

Ducking his head to enter his doorway, Ivor left the open air and retreated to his newly-let room. Duckworth, on his heels, could not stand the curiosity.

"Is yours as bad as mine?"

They both started laughing uproariously.

"It does reek of mildew," the Gold Medallist said and opened the one small window that gave off to the street, as uncountable cats of the quarter began to wraowl agonisingly.

"They mustn't fancy Chopin," Colin laughed.

"To have gone from the *best* hotel in the city...to *this* tatty bit of Old Athens..." Ivor groaned and grabbed his head and sat on the single-bed. "This sodding mattress is *lumpy* as fruitcake!"

Colin was peeping in the loo. "How can we *live* in rooms with no heat, no hot water, no flipping toilet seats on the bogs?"

Quickly, Ivor's mind was racing. Strange, he thought, bumping into Lydia like that...especially after being led here by that Singer. Stranger still, Colin inquired about Ouranós and his wife, but hadn't asked a thing about Theatrínos. Duckworth...is *he* part of some trap? *Couldn't* be—he's too bloody naïve. But I shall have to have him traced—when I call on Rembetikós again. "Some *strange* reason made me take this place!" Hefferon admitted, "Christ—the older I get the stranger my fucking *reasons*—if that's what they can even be called! Don't know why—but I almost feel as if this's precisely where I now *belong*."

13th April – Thursday – 8.00 AM

"Now you're *really* home," Ada said and gazed about with glee. We were putting down our packs on a rock by the icy creek. The Enippéos was crystal clear. "Go ahead—drink," she urged and bent down to cup the rushing liquid.

I squatted and let my fingertips feel how cool the water was. It had been years since I had let everything in my life come to such a halt. The peace I felt, the novelty, was sincere, and the alpine stream a virile caress. "Just being able to hold *water*, like this, naturally, and to be able to *drink*, without fear of pollution, is something our generation hardly knows anything about..."

"Imagine how many sad people, born on this globe, never once in their lifetime get a single chance to drink fresh water out of their own two hands? It's a tragedy."

My pack was carrying the pup tent. We undid it and began setting up camp. We had been hiking from Litóchoron only an hour and a half, having set out before the Sun had come up. "We'll be taking the scenic route," Ada said, "going first up the Vale, via the River."

Every so often, after the Sun arose, I would stop dead in my tracks, captivated by something as ordinary as a shrub, a flower, a rock. *These* were the jewels of Nature, I thought. What a joy...just to be back amongst them!

The rocks in particular were of extraordinary beauty. There were oval-shaped pebbles that seemed to be poured from the purest of marble—with swirls of snow-white and tar-black designs. And then there were soapy stones, that were blue, or were green, soft to the touch, not crystalline.

Ada found my boyish delight in such things a healthy sign. "Just play...to your heart's content," she said. "We're in no rush at all. This's the best medicine you can possibly have."

She was particularly fond of butterflies. "I've never killed a single one. I used to cry if anybody would harm them," she said as we were finishing with the tent.

A pair of bright orange butterflies were tumbling upon each other in the air about her head. "See how the tiny creatures like me?"

"Such loveliness as yours has turned them on!" I said and grabbed her and gave her a violently erotic kiss.

"Make love to me," she sighed, "in the tent."

"No—right here—outside! There's nobody around for miles."

"And if there is...who cares?" she responded as we stept a ways along the bank, to a ten-foot boulder upon which she lay. I could feel my heart beating rapidly, as I stood on the ground and reached across her body to unbutton the snaps of her blouse. We both were wearing track shorts and khaki shirts. I undid her bra, then buried my face between her breasts. Her nipples were what she liked best for me to place my mouth around.

We had not slept together since leaving the beach house. Ada's aunt was of the Orthodox school. We had to have separate rooms. We had been dying for each other, for over three days.

Neither of us was quiet in the act, and here we had sex with no restraint. We let our moans pierce the air of the mountain enclave. The woman whom I loved was powerful when she moved, and by now our amorous motions were beginning to be as synchronised as if we had been mating many years.

In the morning Sun, with dew still glistening on the grass around, as birds were chirping lewdly and hopping branch to branch, a Cyclops could have trundled down the frigid brook—and what would it have mattered? We now were prisoners of The Blood, captive to pulsations old as Time, knowing bliss on this green Earth, together Man and Woman joined in Rhyme, Shaft to Pit, Bone to Skin, Mouth to Tongue, squeezing to the maddened Breathing, fleshly Push to Shove. My God—my cock felt strong, felt like it was her *own*! She seemed to suck it up inside so deep, I felt I'd burst inside my very *Being*!

And up I'd come and she'd be right there with me. A human pair, in love, as animals mate, missing nothing of the exquisite feeling that no other joy can compensate.

It seemed an eternity unity kept us linked. I don't know how many times that Ada was swept away, by her glorious female excitement that mounted a steed, and rode her off through wilderness indeed, past her own private orchards of embrace, where she withdrew from the horrors of humankind, to ecstasies solely in her noble mind. She *was* a woman...any man would hunger for! I lay panting, spent, within her, yelping, praising, try to desist. But making love to such a woman always made me crave to have her *more!* To bury my Soul inside her ambergris...

5th March – Sunday – 8.00 AM

Thýella was trying to stick a fancy alexandrite pin over her right tit, when Ivor Hefferon arrived at the headquarters for the MOON-OC to begin his new responsibilities. He knocked, and stuck his head in her office.

"How's our Deputy?" she asked the mirror into which she was staring. "Come here. Let *this* be your first duty." She handed him the pin.

The bitch turned and puffed out her chest. "Right here," and she pointed five inches above her nipple.

Without a flinch, Ivor did as he was told, however extra-curricular. He glared at her after it was securely pinned. Her purple silk dress was an elegant print.

"Like it?" she inquired about the jewelry.

"Not bad," he responded.

"It's Pythón chasing Letó."

"As a classics scholar, I would never have guessed."

"Zeus was lolling in infidelity again," the lady said, "having sex with Letó. They were coupling as quails," and she pointed a magenta-painted nail towards two tiny mating birds. "In a jealous rage, Zeus's wife had Pythón chase Letó all around the world. Do you blame her?" Thýella asked coyly.

"But Letó gave birth to Artemis and Apollo *anyway*," Hefferon said and smiled, tactful in his erudition.

"Come this way," was the boss's sole response. "Take off your coat. You can leave it there." She opened a door off her room that was on the corner of the two small streets, and led the Athlete to a much smaller chamber. "This will be where we'll stick *you*."

There were the obligatory desk, filing cabinet, telephone, and chairs.

"You'll have to answer the telephone."

"I did in Lake Placid."

"We heard."

"Don't you have a secretary?"

"Only at home. We're not officially *deeded* yet, so we've been striving, against odds, to keep ourselves invisible."

Must be tedious for *her*, Ivor thought, just as she saw the white-uniformed cleaning lady pass the other door that led into the hall.

"Lydia—you're late!" Madame Ouranoú exploded.

"Please excuse me!"

Thýella snapt her tongue and said to Ivor: "Wait. We must go down to the basement—where there's a special briefcase the General left outside the safe." Then before she descended she bellowed: "Lydia—our office—before anything!"

The sound of the boss's footsteps soon diminished. Through Hefferon's doorway off Thýella's room, he could see that the cleaning lady suddenly began gesturing, motioning him to come her way. Hastily she started whispering: "Yesterday—I couldn't speak—but I've *got* to talk to you. Urgently! Say nothing about what I'm doing here—I'm on *your* side!"

The telephone suddenly rang. Ivor broke out in a sweat, not knowing what he should do. He figured that he'd better answer it, no matter what.

"Hello—Mount Olympos Olympic Nation Organizing Committee," he said, thinking that that was one Hell of a mouthful.

"No—for the Devil's Sake—don't *ever* say that!" a woman's voice screamed. It was Thýella, testing him.

Ivor was already beginning to feel nervous as a mongoose with a cobra. He sat at his desk and looked to the Chief of Protocol's room, startled to see that Lydia was taking a key from Thýella's desk, going to a filing cabinet, and opening it. But he had no means of knowing whether or not this was something she always did. Whatever the case, he now had to deal with his employer on the telephone: "We'll get on fine," she continued, "when you learn to play by *our* rules. Remember—this is *not* yet a chartered Olympic organization, at least not to Greece, and we're *still* trying to work out the precise relationship we'll be having with the IOC."

"Yes, I understand."

"Call me Madame."

"Yes, Madame. So what *do* I say on the telephone?"

"Say nothing. Never give your own name—not even if they ask. Say...say you're the answering service. Just hello will do. Ask them who they are, what they want, what's their number. If *we* are here, and if they're on our *list*, which we'll give you when we come back upstairs, then we *may* speak with them. Emphasise *may*. You must *never* let our office be contacted, unless we say so in advance."

"But how will I *know* that?"

"You'll learn. We usually don't speak with *anybody*."

"How do you conduct business?"

"When we *want* something, then we ring *out* for it...like high-

212

class room-service. And Ivor, what we *want*...we always *get*." She hung up.

Hefferon thought that he knew enough about the MOON's bureaucratic ways already not to interfere with whatever it was Lydia still was doing. Flipping furiously through the files, she obviously was looking for something. A couple of minutes passed. When she seemed to find what she needed, then kept standing there, saying something aloud over and over and over, then closing the cabinet, looking it, trying to beat the approaching sound of footsteps, then beginning to return the key to Thýella's desk when the Chief of Protocol herself walked in.

Aghast, Madame Ouranoú pounced towards the poor wren of a woman in white, and began screeching like a banshee. "Lydia—you little *burglar*—we honestly don't *believe* this! What on *Earth* are you *doing* with our *key?*" She snatched it from the cleaning lady's hand.

"Nothing. Nothing. I was putting it back. I just found it on the floor."

"Is that the truth?" Thýella shouted at Hefferon.

"Excuse me?" he asked, recalling the look that he and Lydia had exchanged last night. He decided to play dumb. "Sorry—I was busy speaking with you just now and I didn't even..."

"Useless! Like *all* men!" Thýella snapt then turned her anger back on Lydia. "*Where* on the floor?"

"Beneath your desk—*honestly!*"

"We don't *believe* you. This's the *last* straw. We're not going to *tolerate* your snooping about another *day!* You—you nosy piece of *shit*—are *fired!*"

"But I *need* this job," the girl pleaded. She looked about thirty, and desperation took over her face. "My *mother!*"

"*Fuck* that old bag! Perhaps you should've considered your *behaviour*—awhile *before.* You *disgust* us—low-class scum like *you*—always *scrounging*—*never* to be trusted with a thing! Four months ago we never should have *hired* your scrawny frame! *Remember* how we made you hold out your ugly *hands?* Remember what we *saw?* Dirt! Dirty *knocked-off* fingernails. The *crud* beneath your cuticles should have *warned* us *then!*"

Lydia now was bawling, begging the lady to stop, to reconsider.

"Never! You're *fired.* Those filthy *fingers* warned us...that we never should have *trusted* you a minute...since you've been digging for *secrets* since you've been *employed!*"

"Madame—please!" the girl sobbed.

"*Out* of our sight! You and your *cunt* of a mother can take the first train to *Hell!*" Madame Ouranoú hollered. She began to wave a thousand drachma note that she extracted from her bag. "Add *this*...to what you've *already* stolen," she snarled and flung the note on the floor.

Lydia bent over for it, whimpered, then headed out the door.

"Quite the introduction...to Athenian Society...*isn't* it, Mister

213

Hefferon?" Thýella said after a minute of catching her breath. She stalked to Ivor's desk, bearing a briefcase brought from downstairs. "It has *instructions*—in English. Read them *carefully*." Then she went into her office for her telephone list. "And study *this*. The first page are Members of the Organizing Committee. Even with *them* we often need not speak. The General, on the other hand, *always* must get through. The same goes for his two brothers, Kokkálas and Captain Fourtoúnas. Our son, Movóros, a Major, gets through, as does his brother, Sitherás*. Psychopompós† is here when *we're* not here; he's our son as well. *Others* of the family can *fiddle*, till *we* are in the mood, exactly like all *outsiders* on the list."

She went into her office again, and returned with a little white book. "Coming from Lake Placid, you needn't be told about *this*," Thýella said with the hint of a gruesome smile. "*The IOC Directory*, otherwise known as our *Bible*." She handed it to the Olympic Runner. "Members of the IOC might telephone at any time. If we're here, we're to stop whatever we're doing and speak. When the IOC *barks*, we *piss* up a tree."

"Yes, Madame," Ivor replied dutifully.

"All except for Professor Rembetikós. When *he* telephones, we *never* give him the time of day. We always ring him back, a few days later. But then, that's *Greek* Protocol!"

She retreated to her room, soon to return. She was bearing a calling card. "This is your ID. It's the official MOON-OC employee card. It also will double as your Accreditation for the Deed Ceremony at Olympia, if your services should be required. Do you see this infinity-symbol at the top? Just as in the Adirondacks, it means you're allowed access to *all* Olympic venues. One never knows where one's services *might* be needed and—with the infinity-symbol—nobody will *dare* stop you—*anywhere*! First—we must go to the basement again, where we can stamp it."

The telephone rang.

"Ignore it," Thýella ordered and led the way downstairs. From the main hall she came to a locked door which she opened. "Iamídas is having you made a set of keys. Perhaps this afternoon, if he can organize himself that far."

They descended a stone flight of stairs to the house's bottom-most level. Like a bunker, a single concrete hall gave access to numerous metal doors. The concrete had not been painted once.

"We've an immense amount to do before National Day. You can

* Prounounced: see-theh-RAHSS; second syllable's *th* said as in *this*.
  Meaning: Iron Man.
† Pronounced: pihSEE-ko pome-POS; last syllable rhymes with *gross*.
  Meaning: Soul Conductor.

214

be a *very* big help," she said, unlocking the furthest door as she passed the one beside it, which she said was the walk-in safe.

"I hope I *can* help."

She switched on a light. The room was for supplies.

"Protocol *is* our salvation! It often gives us a migraine, but without it, honestly, we'd go madder than we already are, in less than a day. We realise only too well that *you* have come to us...as an *Athlete* with a *Capital A!* But you've also now come to us as a *man*, broken in, like a stallion at stud, to the rigours of *Olympic* Protocol, due to your rather untoward experiences with Ms. Heidi and Ms. Butch. But never *mind* the Athlete in you, it's the *Protocol* experience that counts! That you've even *competed* as an Athlete, well, that's *your* problem, granted, but in the world of Olympic Games, you've got to admit how *little* an Athlete *counts.*"

"I accepted *that* since I *started* to compete."

"So—you see what we mean! Not that sport is dispensable but, when compared to the huge amount of *organizational* work involved in staging a Games in the first place," she said and found the MOON-OC stamp and snatched Ivor's card back, "the Athlete *pales* in comparison to all the *other* work that's been and continues to be done. The Athlete is *just* the flashy bit in the pinball-game called Olympic Organization. But in that *one* machine...lies all the technology of the ages."

On that note, Thýella smashed down on the stump of the stamp and pressed into the small white card the MOON's official seal. She then signed the back, and asked Ivor to sign the front, then flicked a switch on another machine that looked like a miniature conveyor belt.

"The Athlete," she continued, "is only the part that *shows*. But *all* the Officials, *all* the VIPs, *all* the Support Personnel, and *all* the Many Others...*we* are the ones who make the Games *be!*"

She slipt the card onto the moving belt, and it vanished inside a box containing steaming plastic, soon to usher out complete. Then she put the laminated card in a punch and slammed her open palm down on the handle of that. A little hole was now drilled in the upper corner, near the infinity-symbol, and the hole was metal-ringed. She removed a ball-and-socket chain, shoved one end through the hole, and put the two ends of the chain together. She then draped it round the Olympian's neck.

"Now—you're *accredited*. Why can't *everything* for the Olympics be so easy? We just hope that *all* our accreditation equipment arrives before National Day." She switched off the light and locked the door, then rabbited on, all the way upstairs. "For weeks, this Deed Ceremony has been *killing* us! When it was conceived that the MOON *would* gain autonomy, we hadn't any idea what we'd let ourselves *in* for. More VIPs have got to be invited than we imagined *existed* in the whole world of sports. And *everybody* has to be given special attention, Members of the IOC most importantly, as some are Heads of State, thereby getting

215

the *ultimate* degree. And Ambassadors, they can be a *real* pain in the arse, but their *wives* are inevitably *worse*. Hell forbid that *they* feel slighted. But thank whatever that we worked in Washington—and even once in Warsaw—so we were somewhat prepared for *Olympic* sized snobbery, not to mention *Olympic* sized niggly detail."

The Chief of Protocol sat her Deputy in her office.

"Then, there are the limousines. Do you realise that Greece doesn't even *own* as many limos as are needed three weeks from to-day? We're going *crazy* dealing with that!"

"How can I help?" Ivor asked.

"Listening—simply by listening! *That* will be a miracle unto itself. This job is *Living Hell!*"

Was she playing? Obviously not. She stood. She had a long work-table in the corner, covered with all sorts of papers and charts.

"Here it is." She unrolled what looked like a map. "Hold this end. It's Olympia—all of it."

"Shall I be going there?"

"Yes. Now—*this* is what we're up against. Complying with IOC Protocol will be our *death*. Both the President of the IOC and the Head of State of Greece are coming. I could *cope* with that, if that were *all!* But as you know from Lake Placid, that's barely the hors d'oeuvres! You're now all too aware that the IOC have official categories for who goes where—A through G. So—*we* decided to put the IOC and our Head of State, and wives, in Category A, and have them wait for entrance into the Ancient Stadium from the Temple of Zeus, even though we should have put the Ambassadors in Zeus since there're going to be *twice* as many of *them*, but then we thought that *this* would cause a major diplomatic incident if the *Ambassadors* got the biggest and most prestigious temple over and above the IOC—who *own* the Games— would that they did *not*—so we decided to put the Ambassadors in the Temple of *Hera* and were relieved that we can make them appeased— because we can tell them that *that's* where the *Sacred Flame* is ignited. Well—this was a cinch compared to Category B, the *National* Olympic Committees, only the Presidents and Secretary Generals and their wives, mind you, but *they* take precedence over *any* Ambassador, so we had to put the Bs in Hera anyways, but this *still* left us with the horror of having some members of the IOC, mainly from Third World countries, simultaneously being Presidents of their NOCs! So where would *you* stick them?"

"Category A—in Zeus."

"Exactly," and for the very first time he saw Thýella smile. He did not like the sight. Eva Braun must have smiled the same. "One *last* thing, before you can take *everything* off that table and memorise it. Let us say a word about dealing with us *Greeks*. Your being from a more *civilised* clime," she jested, "must realise, as to-day, that *no* Greek will ever tell you *exactly* what's going on in his or her mind. They know that

216

such an attempt would be certain folly. We've *all* studied Sokrates. But seriously—we have tried, in the last few minutes, to mention a bit of what the MOON must deal with, but you're an astute enough young man to realise that such matters are merely the tip of the iceberg. Greeks love the serious jest. Bear in mind, *we* are the people who *invented* Comedy...*and* Tragedy. And it's quite safe to say that your recent adventures in Lake Placid, about which we've been *thoroughly* briefed, and from *both* sides of the fence, will soon be understood by you to have been *Comedy Personified*...compared to what *Greece* is going to be shoving down your throat these next few days...which is *Tragedy*...in *all* its myriad guises. And *that's* a prophecy! Indeed...you can only get to know us Greeks...gradually. We may *like* you...we may include a little *part* of you in our *own* dismal lives...and we may *even* let you in on a little *scandal* or two. But—we're really *nasty* little kids with *knives*. We *wait*—oh we wait *forever*—curiously—like kids watching for our playmate to *falter*—to make an *ass* of himself. We love to watch your *ignorance* of our ways. We're really *quite* sadistic little people, in that kind of *evil* delight. It's a holdover from some *Oriental* trait. We're *throwbacks*...in that regard! Even the *best* Greek...won't let you in on *all* his thoughts. Remember that, Ivor. You'll be *miles* ahead. You certainly *can* run—*that* we've already seen—four summers back—but *now* you must prove whether or not you can *walk*. So—take these things away— and go to your room!"

"Yes, Madame. One mortal question, though. Where's the *loo?*"

14th April – Friday – Morn

I awoke to find Ada bathing naked in the River Enippéos. The shallow pond, a bit upstream, had been our delight all Thursday. We hadn't moved further than there. The vision of the lovely body of the woman, with her long black hair, was something out of a dream. There was nothing to do but join her, so I stept into the water, as naked as we'd gone to sleep, and hopped across dry stones towards where she now was beckoning. Then I steeled my nerves and dove in. The water was freezing.

"You'll get used to it. Feel how hot it is already," Ada laughed.

It must have been eighty in the shade, but still I was shivering.

Ada joked: "Don't make me ashamed. I thought that yesterday you were turning into a *Greek!*"

I charged for her, tackled her, then we rolled in the pool at play.

"No—seriously," she said sternly. "I've been thinking...there's something I must now say."

I gulped. "What've I done *now?*"

"It's not you. It's something you need to know."

We both climbed onto a looming rock, and lay down in the Sun.

"About what?"

217

"About *whom*," Ada corrected and kissed me.

I joked: "Who?"

"Thýella."

"What could be said about her that I *wouldn't* believe?"

"Do you remember Wednesday, at Aunt Georgia's, and we were talking about the Civil War?"

"Such fratricide is so impossible to comprehend."

"Needless to say, Thýella has a very disreputable past. She had managed of late to put on quite an impressively sinister act. You told me last night that she told you, that first day you went to her office to work, that no Greek will tell you all about himself...ever..."

"That's correct."

"She's right. We Greeks *are* a secretive people. Aunt Georgia and Kóstas...they, too, could have told you a *lot* more about Madame Ouranoú."

"You don't mean...no...you're not related to *her?*"

"God forbid! I've got enough problems! But Thýella—she *sprang* from here—and she did so in the true sense—fully armed."

"She's from Litóchoron?"

"Yes."

"So *that* explains her fixation with Olympos!"

"Precisely. Yet I've only been waiting to tell you this—not to keep it from you—but to give your wearied Spirit time to recuperate. If you had known the whole story sooner...well I only kept it until now to *protect* you."

"Carry on."

"*Curses* be upon her, but Thýella *was* born here, at the base of Mount Olympos, sometime after the end of the First World War. She hails from a poor local family, small farmers. By World War II, she had wed Ouranós, yes...who was only a Private then. But Ouranós's family has a *past* as well—and how! The Ouranós were an almost *noble* Athenian family, supporters of the Monarchy planted here by Germany. In fact, the previous Madame Ouranoú was Queen Friederike's Lady-in-Waiting."

"I see."

"Young Private Ouranós was as randy then as he is to-day. Thýella caught his eye from the Litóchoron Army Base, and set his trap, getting herself with child by him. Her father made sure that it was a shotgun wedding. Ouranós's family was scandalised that he had married somebody so low, but the Private was the youngest of the three brothers, and the other two had married in their class. The first son, thus, that Thýella had was Sitherás, the nickname for Iron Man, the son who was to become Director of Constructions for the MOON. He was born just before Hitler invaded the Sudetenland. By the time the Nazis overran Greece—and of course Ouranós was conscripted into the Nazi Army, due to his familial connection with Royal Germany—Thýella had borne him another son, in the midst of the War, named Movóros, or Blood Drinker, the MOON's Director of Sports." Ada shook her head. The tale was making her sad.

"Do you want to carry on?"

"You must hear this," she remarked and took my hand. "Greece was a living nightmare then. We have truly come light-years away. Every family has skeletons in closets—but Thýella and Ouranós have more than their share. Ouranós, colluding with the Nazis, supposedly for the good of Greece, made Thýella stay put at Litóchoron. She had never been near Athens once in her life. She was a wild-girl, with a skull bulging with schemes as big as this mountain here. He was embarrassed that he had to marry her. She, though, was never to give him up, even though she let herself fall madly in love with a different soldier, one who came from the other side."

"How do you mean?"

"She fell in love with a certain Theódoros, from southern Crete they say. He was as Left as they get, as Left as Ouranós was Right. Theódoros was a man on the run, whom she harboured and with whom she slept. They had a child, the son Thýella nicknamed Psychopompós, or Soul Conductor, who later became the Orthodox Priest and then the MOON's Director of Communications. Theódoros, the father, was Thýella's match. His radical politics filled the huge vacuum in her head. He promised her better things than her Nazi husband ever could extend. He was *Greek*—with absolutely *no* love for Germans—or for *any* sort of Monarchy."

"What happened?"

"Ouranós got wind of it somehow. He bounded back from Athens, after World War II, but then the Civil War began. Theódoros escaped with a bullet in his side, but then Ouranós was recalled to the south. Feeling it was safer, no matter what, in Litóchoron, Ouranós sent his own mother to the north, to keep an eye on Thýella. He rented the village's largest house, and thought that the new-found luxury would stop Thýella from thinking of Theódoros at all. The presence of old Madame Ouranoú did nothing but fire the daughter-in-law's vivid imagination. For hours on end she would listen entranced to tall tales of the Athenian Royal Court. She especially loved to hear about Prince Andreas and Princess Alice, and their dashing son Prince Philipp, then deeply in love with the Princess who would someday inherit your English Throne. However, late in 1948, Theódoros showed up, exhausted and once again wounded from military scrapes."

"Thýella put him up?"

"Against vitriolic protestations, on the part of the Lady-in-Waiting! Yes—Theódoros not only was nursed, he was given Thýella on her own plate. Old Madame Ouranoú continually was catching the vulgar pair *in flagrante delicto*. One day, after it had been getting to be too much for the old aristocratic dame, she saw them at it one last time, and Ouranós's mother was driven insane. The two half-brothers, Sitherás and Psyohopompós, were outside playing. But Movóros saw it all, at the age of five. Madame Ouranoú took the pistol that Theódoros had left by the gate, and in the kitchen she shot herself, in the brain. Imagine...the poor little boy..."

"What a nightmare...for everybody."

"People believe that the boy was so traumatised that he blocked out the whole of his childhood to that point. He became bellicose...only interested in things of Hate. He went on to become a noteworthy boxer, recall, an Olympic boxer, Middle-Weight Champion of Europe, at age nineteen."

"So...*that* explains Movóros," I said and sighed.

"But he never threw Thýella's clutches. He tried and tried to escape her...but he couldn't."

"What a story."

"I have *yet* to get to the good part. Do you remember hearing Aunt Georgia saying that the Leftists kidnapped three thousand children?"

"You don't mean..."

"Thýella fled Litóchoron in '49..."

"With her children?"

"No. With all the *others*."

"Dear Lord!"

"The suicide of Madame Ouranoú severed whatever shred of humanity that Thýella possessed. She had learnt *all* that the Lady-in-Waiting could express, then, when she was no longer needed, she drove her mother-in-law to her death. It was ghastly. But villagers say she even took on all the dead woman's archaic courtly mannerisms, which she has retained to this day. Her speech, her glances, her disdain...all came from the General's mother."

"Where was *he*?"

"Somewhere in the Ionian Sea."

"So he didn't have a chance to intervene?"

"He didn't have to. As the Leftists were heading north, brave neighbours one day snatched her three sons from her home, and hid them, here in this valley. By then—the Civil War was in its gory finale. It was eye for an eye, tooth for a tooth. Everybody correctly assumed that Thýella would run away—and children were being kidnapped all along the route the Leftists took. So, to pay Thýella back, for the matricide of her lawful husband's mother, the local people kidnapped her *own* boys, and thereby saved their lives. I can still hear the innocent children's cries...whenever I'm in this very location...which is why I wanted to tell you these things *here*. Whenever I'm in this great Vale, all I can think of is the unfortunate children and their untold heartache."

There was a lengthy silence between us. I kissed Ada's cheek, then quietly asked: "So Thýella fled?"

"With Theódoros. They massed with the Leftist forces that were on the Long March from this homeland, and yes, she *walked* to Northern Europe."

"Where did she end up?"

"Poland."

"In fact—she did tell me that she'd worked in diplomacy there."

"In Warsaw. She was shrewd, as always. Like hot air, she rose to the top. In Poland she totally left her past behind her. She used an alias, a pun upon her maiden name, and fabricated a whole biography. Somehow, she became Chief Translator for the Greek Embassy, directly responsible to the Ambassador. In Athens, in 1951, Ouranós had become a Major, and had access to certain papers of State. He came across a Polish dossier, that described a Translator who sounded something like his wife. He never had divorced her, and being mad himself, had never lost the manic wish to reclaim her. The typical Greek *man* in him reared its ugly head. He couldn't be satisfied till he knew for sure if she were alive or dead."

"What happened?"

"He managed to get himself transferred to Warsaw, as Military Attaché. The Greek Monarchy still was on the Athenian Throne, and his background lent itself readily. He found her there, in '51, taking her completely by surprise."

"And she came back?"

"Imagine post-war Poland—under Stalin's influence. Post-war England or Greece were bad enough, but conditions in Warsaw were beyond belief. Thýella was fed up. Having had first-hand experience with Communist policies, the woman had long been disillusioned with Leftist dreams."

"So she went with him?"

"No. She still refused to return to Greece. She now had her scopes set on bigger things."

"What?"

"America—it was all that post-war Europe talked about. Ouranós, meanwhile, begged her to come home. He even bribed her with diplomatic immunity, and secured her safe passage from behind the Iron Curtain. She now was a Polish citizen, remember. He told her of his family's thriving business back in Athens—how the three brothers were rebuilding the ravaged capital. He told her of plans to expand all over Greece. But she said, stubbornly, that she needed a year of freedom, at the very least."

"In the States?"

"He gave in—and managed to get her to America."

"How?"

"Through the Greek diplomatic corps. It was a risk, but it was one he was willing to take. He had a secretary flown to Poland, a woman with whom he worked in Athens; he had her come in as his wife. She

221

and Thýella did look somewhat similar in the face, and were the same height. She was heavily made up and wearing a blonde wig. She brought Thýella's papers with her from Greece, those that Ouranós never destroyed from before the War, plus others he doctored recently. Inside the Embassy, the two women did their quick-change act. Thýella emerged from the lavatory looking exactly like the other woman. The other stayed on as secretary for awhile, then went back to Greece. You *see* now—how Ouranós and Thýella were *made* for each other?"

"Does Thýella still wear a wig to-day?"

"Nobody knows. Some people swear that her hair is dyed—that it's for real."

"Whatever happened to Theódoros?"

"They say she killed him."

"I'm not surprised."

"Late in '51 the Greek Government named her Cultural Attaché to the Embassy in Washington, D.C."

"Inevitable. So much slime ends up along the Potomac."

"Ouranós pulled strings. She told him that she *would* come back to Greece, if he'd give her that year of grace."

"Which meant?"

"He *not* follow her to the States. Only then would she take his name again, and renew her citizenship of Greece. So he smuggled the blonde *poseuse* out of Poland, in a military plane that was bound for Vienna. From Austria she went with him to London, where she boarded a flight for New York."

"And he stayed behind?"

"For over two whole years."

5ᵗʰ March – Sunday – Eve

As soon as Ivor's first day on the job was completed, he walked along Odós Adrianoú to the small square by Hadrian's Library, the one with all the cafés, and immediately telephoned the number that Professor Rembetikós had provided. A woman answered, and requested that Hefferon dine with the IOC member that eve. She said they should meet in the distant neighbourhood of Ághia Paraskeví, which lay at the foot of the long-lying mountain Imitós, northeast of the city.

To get there, the Athlete was told to take a bus from alongside one of the back buildings of the University. She gave him the number and told him to tell the driver to stop at a certain street. The Professor would be waiting there, in a black Mercedes.

After a forty-five minute ride, Ivor found himself being told to get off in the middle-class residential district as requested. It was all new dusty streets, many yet unpaved, with spanking fresh condominiums and pastel concrete blocks of flats with sparkling glass balconies.

"I thought you'd welcome the change," Aristídis Rembetikós said in greeting.

Ivor replied: "Indeed. There's nothing old out *here*."

"Except me. After central Athens, a little bourgeoisie can be a real treat," the man said and drove through an unlit street. He soon was pulling alongside an outdoor taverna. It was on the corner of two roads covered by arching pine trees. A few strings of bare bulbs were swinging in the breeze.

"How'd you ever find *this* place?" the Medallist inquired as they got out. Bouzouki music was playing over speakers, into the open air.

"My sister's daughter recently moved nearby."

The men sat themselves at the outermost table, away from the others, to be able to speak in private. The place could not have been more modest. All that it had was a dozen wood tables and a man and wife for staff. But the couple seemed to welcome the gentlemen, especially the elder, whom they assumed correctly was someone quite distinguished, although they had never been indiscreet with nosy questions.

"Pommes frites, tzatzíki, tomato and cucumber salad, aubergine salad, beef steaks, and rosé wine," Rembetikós ordered, then broke apart a long pretzel stick. "I could eat a horse to-night. The fare's good and wholesome. Nothing gourmet. So—how have you been?"

"I don't know where to begin. So much has happened since last Wednesday. She's made me her Deputy. I almost feel like I'm having sodding *flashbacks* of Lake Placid, but all the flashes are *far* more sinister!"

Wine was brought in a glass carafe. The Member of the IOC poured. "Maybe *this* will refresh your memory. What stood out in your interview?"

They hoisted their glasses and clinked.

"Thýella, of course. She started hiccuping."

The Professor laughed uproariously. "Very good sign."

"Excuse me?"

"That silly woman—all Athens has tolerated her incontrollable nervous system for years. Thýella *always* hiccups, when something absolutely Evil comes to mind. You see—from the very start—she began to scheme how to *debase* you."

"She *can* be quite convincing. I was given the audio-visual display. They have a room that has nothing in it but a plaster architectural model of the MOON. I noticed nothing extraordinary. It could have been the venues of *any* Olympic Games. Of course, they do have it planned that both Summer *and* Winter Games be staged there. Mexico City, however, is at a higher elevation, so I suppose that athletes *could* perform without strain."

"Did anything at all hint of a link between the Army base and the Games Site?"

"Not that I could see. This morning, I was told to commit to memory all the material that she'd stacked on a table in her office, and I carefully went through that."

"Any leads?"

"Not one thing. All matters I was entrusted with were absolutely legitimate."

"Gestapo's crafty. You watch—she *won't* slip up if she can prevent it."

"I had charts and maps pertaining to the Deed Ceremony. Who could have drawn *them* up?"

"Her son Psychopompós, likely. Did you see *him* yet?"

"The Priest? No—I've met *none* of the family, other than the General."

"How'd that go?"

"He was off on a pipe-dream. We met in the Café Ellenikón. He kept nattering on about architecture of the Administration Headquarters he's planning."

"One has to excuse him. He does own one of the country's biggest construction companies."

"As for the Army Base, Thýella only said they'd be building a subterranean parking garage and a train station, and that the commuter line would be cut inside Stávros Foothill, to emerge outside the Site's Principal Gate."

The Professor tugged on his moustache and winked. "When I mentioned the neutron-bomb facility Ouranós is scheming to put beneath Stávros, I should've told you more about how this's supposed to be done. But I had a feeling Thýella would try and entice you with her plaster model."

"You've seen it?"

"I had to...once," Rembetikós admitted, now all but whispering. "They invited me there, about five months ago. As I told you Wednesday, the IOC's plan is to *shame* the MOON-OC—publicly—so that the Ideal of Olympism remains inviolable. Of course, fur *is* going to fly. Thýella's tufts, more than anyone else's. I had *no* choice but give their organization my tactful nod, under orders from the President of the International Olympic Committee, but all the while retaining my allegiance to Lausanne. Anyways—I should have told you that this subterranean commuter train, from Litóchoron proper, up and inside Stávros, is going to be the means by which Ouranós and his clan are master-minding their whole satanic prank."

"How?"

"Ouranós Ltd., their construction firm, has plans to build a triple-tiered underground train line, that will only appear on the drawing boards as double-tiered. The *top* two tiers will function as a normal commuter system, bringing passengers to and fro. But *beneath* this will be the *third* level, that will side-wind directly to the Army base.

It will utilise rubber wheels, like the above two tracks, and no one will hear a thing. But this tunnel will *not* go up to the Station by the MOON's Principal Gate. It will carry on, deep inside, aiming straight into the mountain, which will be bored out, hollowed, then manned as a nuclear base."

"But—if the Army is so keen on putting something like this inside Olympos—why don't they just *do* so? Why go to all the immense amount of trouble that building a bogus Olympic Nation will take?"

"It's simple. Litóchoron's military installation is being monitored constantly. By all of NATO's forces. By the Russians. By the Yanks. By the Turks. It's under surveillance by the whole Eastern Mediterranean. If any abnormal troop or vehicular movements are noted, anywhere in the region, signals sound everywhere. Can you conceive how many special machines it would take to construct a missile base inside Mount Olympos? This is Greece! We are still a *poor* country, compared to Britain or the United States. If foreign powers were to note that such aberrant activity was going on at Litóchoron, all Hell would break loose. Greece tries to remain independent—of course—but everything this country does is dependent on foreign politics, whether or not the populace agree with that at all. It's just a fact of life. Therefore, the excuse that a huge amount of legitimised construction should take place at Olympos is the perfect foil for *other* endeavours being fostered underground. With thousands of workers and tons of the latest equipment drilling about for years, in the name of Amateur Sport, who would dream that a more nefarious ulterior motive was dealing a death-blow to Sport as a vehicle for worldwide Peace?"

"What a nightmare situation this has put you in," Hefferon stated, in attempt to be consoling.

"There is *no* way they can win! And *you* will help us triumph!" The Professor poured more wine. "The public have the IOC maligned. We honestly *have* tried to keep Politics and Sport apart. But—Politics *is* mankind's *greatest* Evil—and there is *no* way that Evil *can* be denied, when a group as powerful as the IOC must meet. Opposites do attract— it's basic physics—and when an organization exists, whose purpose is an Ideal, then instantly attracted to this, with razor-sharp talons outstretched, will hie every single force that wishes to see this Ideal victimised, stomped on, dead, rotting."

"I think you're very brave to be waging this fight against the General."

"Do you *know* what he's been saying? He's been wooing the gullible members of the Greek Olympic Committee, not to mention the idiots in Parliament, by boasting that the MOON will *impress* the world, as a tourist draw for Greece, plus, that it will cause the Government, finally, to construct a national rapid transit system, so that everybody can come to his merry little fair. But—he *only* has his scopes set on his ever-invincible Army. He wants a middle point, for a quick invasion route. From Olympos, it's readily apparent that his new speedy trains could march simultaneously south, on Athens, and north, on Thessaloníki." The Professor paused, then sighed gravely. He shook his head.

The Runner then felt that it was time to mention the *other* new development. "Two nights ago I was summoned by Sir Cecil."

"To the British Embassy?"

"Lady Louella's office—it would seem!"

"Quite—that Ambassadress *should* be called His Excellency."

"They tried to force me to become their spy."

"Really?" The Professor laughed.

"I didn't think it funny. How much does my Embassy *know*?"

"As far as I have been assured by Lord Dalbeattie, Downing Street and the Foreign Office have *not* brought Sir Cecil into the picture."

"Then—why is the Embassy suddenly concerned with *me*?"

"What'd they ask you to do?"

"Snoop on that Rock Star...Theatrínos."

"I see," the Member of the IOC said and nodded. "Well then the explanation's simple."

"Tell me."

"Thýella and Louella often have tea."

"Then this's *Thýella's* doing?"

"It can't be anybody else's."

"Should I play along?"

"Absolutely not. You would contravene our course established with the approval of your country's Queen and First Minister, as well as that of the President of the IOC."

"They want an *answer* from me. They're offering me diplomatic immunity."

"Let the Embassy get *back* to you. And when they do, tell them you simply can't agree."

"But do you think they *know* I'm the MOON's employee?"

"Evidently. Just keep your nose clean."

We finished our meal, and were now letting the proprietress clear the table for the sweet. The Professor ordered a delicious nut cake to go with our Greek coffee.

"Have you found any information on Dora Cain?" Ivor wondered.

"Not a thing. Interpol has her under surveillance."

"She says she's on an archaeological dig, at Dodóna."

"She is. In fact, everything you told me has proven to be the truth. But we're still checking."

"I have a *new* one," the Athlete said with a laugh.

"No doubt. Aren't agents like *flies*?"

"A Briton, a young chap named Colin Duckworth," then Hefferon told the man about the "coincidence" of being invited to the

Café Ellenikón and meeting the supposèd Student the very next day after being with the Gamblings in the Embassy.

The Professor took some notes. "So you say you've moved? And this Duckworth chap's next door?"

"He seems to be all right—I only thought you should know."

"I'll have Interpol do another check. For the time being, don't tell Thýella where you're living."

"Why?"

"Just don't. Take my word for it. I shall let you in on more when next we meet. You already have enough to deal with—keeping Thýella amused."

"That's the truth. Why does she always speak in the Royal We?"

"Oh my God—we'd have to take a whole *day* off for you to hear *that* one! But to-night, I've got too many things to attend to at the house. Let me drive you back."

The black-windowed Mercedes returned to the centre of the capital by a route hugging close to Mount Imitós. The IOC man and the Olympian talked about other things. Ivor was getting quite fond of the old philosopher, and hoped he would have the pleasure of his company again before too long. "When may we next meet?" Ivor wondered.

"From to-night onwards, you must telephone that number every day."

"When?"

"Are you still training at midnight?"

"Yes."

"Then that's the legitimate time."

"Isn't it too late?"

"For *Greeks*? We're just on our first *course* by then. To-night was *way* too early to dine!"

"It's only nine o'clock."

"That's what I mean. Now listen—I'm letting you out by the Odíon. You just walk over the Akropolis, straight up the pavement, and you'll be at the top of the Agora. Then you can find your way easily to the Street of Mnískles." The car pulled up to the kerb and came to rest. "Remember," the Professor warned and pulled on his moustache, "the woman who answers the telephone at that number I gave you is trustworthy. Give her a daily report. If anything is urgent, tell her and she'll contact me. If she wants you to speak with me, she'll give you a number. Do not, I repeat, do not *ever* telephone that number from the MOON-OC. Nor use the telephone from where you're now residing."

The two men shook hands. Ivor thanked him for the meal.

"I believe in you, Lad. You know what we're up against. Lastly— I only want to say that, to the IOC, the most important thing is for you to try to get hold of those sensitive dossiers—the Feasibility Study and biannual Progress Reports. And do keep Thýella humoured."

"I shall try."

Hefferon got out. His head was aching. There was just too much to think about. He looked above to the Akropolis and sighed with relief. Perhaps, by climbing and breathing its potent air, he might clear his mind.

Even though he was wearing a two-piece suit, the Olympic Gold Medallist felt the need to run. It was that time of the night when his body was conditioned. So, he picked up speed and started running, leaving his worries behind, and soon was bolting up the marble walk that led to the Odíon itself.

The waning Moon did not assist his run, and the night air was fiercely sharp. Owls were hooting to herald his passage through their wild pine domain. Suddenly, Ivor couldn't logically believe what he was doing. Was he expecting to get onto the Akropolis at night? Weren't police there—twenty-four hours a day—alone—with the shadows—alone —with the muffled noise of merriment masquerading in the metropolis below?

As during that first night in Athens, so again the Olympian was drawn, hand unseen, but this time it was upwards—*upwards*—away from all the contradictions below. Ivor had never been this way before— not once—but up the marble steps he kept running—tingling with the feeling of doing something mad—revelling in the sensation of being human—just one person attempting a little Good amidst so very much Bad.

Then—there—it stood stark before him—there stark and glowing —grey in the night—the marble of the gate Propýlaea. The gate was locked—the gate was iron—the gate was bars. But one could see through them—but one could not crawl through them.

The Olympian gript the freezing metal with both bare hands. No one was around as he peered—up—peered up to the Doric shrine before him, through which so many millions of Souls had meandered in the passage of slow, slow Time.

Then, way at the top, through the rectangle door, the last door one penetrated before seeing the Parthenon's inimical and total splendour, there at the top suddenly appeared three black forms. Three forms—silhouettes or police or ghosts, who could say—but three forms, in file, marched from the plâteau dark beyond, and walked through this wan portal, walked like soldiers for the dead, down the stone steps towards the fellow. And...he fled...

15th March – Saturday – Morn

We were on the road to Stávros. We hadn't been that very far from Litóchoron after all. Our two days together, alone, had made it seem that we were a million miles from anybody.

"I knew that was the one thing that you needed—total isolation," Ada said. "From all the world but me."

I was following behind her. We were starting to ascend. "The Army built this road," she added.

"It's not bad," I answered and adjusted my pack. "You're built better though."

"It's a fairly decent job of engineering," she joked. The road was nothing special. "It's just a road," I said. We became silent. Nobody was using the road. Ada had promised us a lift. Not a lorry nor a car were in sight.

"Birds," Ada said. "I could walk all day and never tire of listening to the birds."

"My sentiments precisely," I answered. "It's amazing how prosaic one gets..."

"Surrounded by living poetry..." Ada interrupted. We walked more. And then we walked even more. We both were getting tired already. "This is it," Ada announced after awhile.

"What?"

"Uphill—from here on out," she said and yawned with exhaustion. I just nodded. We were surrounded by pines. "Crows," Ada said. There was a bend up ahead. The road now was making hair-pin turns to ascend. Something in me was beginning to doubt the wisdom of climbing the colossal mountain. Suddenly Ada said: "Listen."

"What?"

"Someone's coming. Bells."

"I don't hear anything."

"Maybe it was my imagination," Ada apologised. We kept walking higher, nearing the bend. "There it is again. Didn't you hear *that*?"

"Think so." Suddenly—we were turning the bend and heading back towards the Vale itself.

"Look," said Ada. She was pointing. About three hundred feet away, coming at us, we watched as three women in black, on donkeys, were riding side by side. "They never do that," Ada announced, sounding worried.

"What?"

"Ride like that. One always follows the other."

"You know them?" I asked.

"No—I mean—*anybody* who rides a donkey," she stated, looking more nervous the closer they got. "*I moira sou*."

"What was that?"

"Nothing," the girl said, trying to smile. She then crossed herself three times, and halted dead in her tracks. "Don't move."

I didn't. Ada's anxiety was contagious.

The three women now were close enough for us to see that they were ancient crones. The one on the donkey on the left was holding something with her left hand. The middle woman was ringing a little bell. The one on the right was poking her hand into a rough sack. Crows in the pines loudly began to caw.

"Say nothing," Ada ordered.

The three were coming towards us. We now could see that the first old woman was gripping a small hand-spindle. The middle woman ceased ringing her bell, when they were a few yards from us. The one on the right suddenly found what she was looking for, let out a cackling yell, then held aloft a ball of wool. The thread was passed to the woman with the bell. The three donkeys suddenly stopt. They were right beside us. Crows left their roosts and flapt.

The bell was passed to the one on the right, who dropt it in her sack. The middle crone was pulling a length of thread from the ball, as far as her arms were wide. The one nearest us pulled from her dress a very long carving knife. Its handle was made of bone. She passed it beyond the middle crone's reach and the handle was seized by the one on the right. In a wild slash she cut off the thread, with a laugh, just missing the middle crone's hand. One of the donkeys brayed. Crows began flying everywhere, making a fearful din.

Then the middle one reached in the third one's sack and got the bell again. She began ringing it, furiously, as the third whipt the string up in the air. Just then, a crow nearby swooped from a pine. It glided directly towards us, then braked its coal-black wings enough to slow its flight, so that its little claws could grab the string. Then the bird flew off, straight down the road, and onwards, past the sunlit bend. Light from the east was falling in majestic shafts through the glen, and kept crossing the three women's backs, as they continued their progress down the mountain.

We watched them, until they turned at the curve, then they vanished from sight. Ada had tears in her eyes.

6th March – Monday – 7.30 PM

It had been a very long day. Hefferon had managed to process all the invitations to the Deed Ceremony, to be held on the twenty-fifth of March at Olympia. These had to be posted to every Member of the IOC in the world, plus to every President and Secretary General of all the National Olympic Committees and Sporting Federations. Special invitations had already been delivered by messenger to the Ambassadorial Corps and to officials of the Government of Greece.

"To-morrow, you'll have to attend to the Press," ordered the Director of Communications for the MOON Organizing Committee, a rather frightening looking black-bearded, black-hatted head, that was biblical, beady-eyed. But though the General's step-son Psychopompós had pupils the size of peas, huge white eyeballs had kept looking the Athlete up and down all day. The monkish holy-man had been his boss this Monday, as Thýella was otherwise engaged.

Psychopompós had explained earlier that he was thirty-five years old, one year younger than the as-yet-unseen brother, Movóros, and one year elder than the other brother, Sitherás. All these statements were lies, Hefferon realised, as he had already been briefed on the family's chronology by Professor Rembetikós.

Just by observing him, Hefferon had quickly deduced that the Orthodox Priest had grown up with a tremendous inferiority complex. "I hated my two brothers," the mock ascetic had even said. Perhaps he did—but why tell Thýella's Deputy such problems, when the two hardly had met? Ivor had already been told by the Professor, the night before, that the Orthodox Priest was born a bastard. So, at least the Priest and the Athlete had one thing in common, illegitimacy, if nothing else! "I'm Affedikó's son," Psychopompós also lied, speaking authoritatively like a messiah.

"I know," the Deputy Chief of Protocol replied, going along with the fib, and got on with signing letters for Thýella. He was getting to be very good at forgery. Anything to keep the nasty Priest shut up.

"I handle all the MOON's print," the bearded-one said.

"Where do you get it done?" Ivor wondered, but then realised that that had been the wrong question, as the Priest did not deign to reply. The two were on the ground floor, in the Communications Office, so to speak. Behind Psychopompós's desk was a large coloured print of some man, with a rounded crown.

"The Patriarch of Constantinople," the Priest had said, taking note that Ivor had been gazing at it.

Atop the religious man's desk was a glass bowl filled with rocks. Whilst stuffing envelopes, the Priest had told the Runner: "All these come from Mount Áthos—one pebble from each of its monasteries. I keep them there to remind me of my vows." No comment. Under no circumstances did Hefferon wish to hear about those.

"My two brothers used to beat me," the Priest carried on. "I learnt to compensate for their exclusion by turning my thoughts to Jesus."

I bet, Ivor heard himself silently saying.

"I developed on a truly different plane than the two other boys," he added, "who became a Major and a Mechanic respectively." The Priest sighed.

What is this? Confession? The Deputy just continued stuffing letters into plain envelopes.

"Only the women of the family understand me, given that I've always felt myself ever more aiming unstintingly towards Things Divine."

Bullshit—absolute, outright bullshit! But Ivor looked up and gave the Priest a great big, omniscient smile.

"As a Priest, though," he continued, "I also have a crafty mortal streak..."

No doubt.

"...that my father long ago tended. The General considered it a wise diplomatic gesture, to the Orthodox Church, that I be given the title, Director of Communications."

Well, you certainly aren't lacking in gift of gab. Now all the envelopes needed to be sealed. At one point, the Priest removed his odd tassel-less fez-type hat. Without it, the man was somewhat handsome. His face was virile, an exemplary Greek countenance in its prime. Unlike older priests. this fellow's beard wasn't grizzly, nor grey, nor greasy, but fresh, and sable, and trimmed. His hair was cut, too, unlike many in the Church, and could even be called stylish, with well-attended little crow-hued curly locks. His hands were in the pockets of his voluminous robe. He removed the left one. In his palm he showed Ivor an antique Cross of gold, not unimpressive, on a lovely heavy chain.

"I want *you* to wear this," Psychopompós stated and offered it to the Athlete, like a small boy handing a playmate a chocolate.

Ivor felt suspicious. "*Why?* What's *this* for?" He examined the Cross.

"I saw you some days ago," he began, and paused, "inside the Orthodox Cathedral. I saw you...had doubt on your face."

Oh God, here comes the sermon.

"The bastardisation of the Olympics, which you seem so keen on resisting, *isn't* the fault of the times, as everyone would have us believe."

"What *are* you saying?" Hefferon asked.

"For all its goodness, *Christianity* has done the Modern Games in," this Priest of Christ stated vigorously.

Hardly believing his ears, Ivor retorted to the Cleric: "How *do* you mean?"

"Come on, Athlete. You're *not* as naïve as you'd have us believe. We all *know* you were committing *adultery*, in Lake Placid, with an Olympic Organizing Committee Board Member, the wife of a dead-man!"

"Mind your *own* fucking business, *Priest!*" shouted the Olympian, handing the creature back his Cross.

Both men stared each other in the eye. So here comes what Ivor had been dreading: Every misfit of the whole Ouranós clan knows exactly why Hefferon was sent to them! But Psychopompós side-stept: "Tell me—*what* were the Ancient Games for?"

"Honest competition," Hefferon replied.

"Wrong—and you know it. The Ancient Games were for *Zeus*— not for competition at all. They were for religious *worship*—of a Pagan *Deity*—as expressed through *Sport.*"

"So what're you saying—we build a Temple to *Zeus*—on the Olympic Nation site?"

"Maybe that *would* work! *Anything* would be better than the Spiritless Games, as you've publicly been quoted as calling them!"

"Well, listen, Psycho, I'm going to tell you something—as an Olympic Gold Athlete who's *competed* in those Games you would malign!

There is *plenty* of Spirit—in certain quarters—and that *Spirit* is between Athletes with an Upper Case A, who are few and far between! It's just the overabundance of goddamned *officials* and *VIPs*—like yourself—who never fail to muck the Spirit *up*! Anyways—*you're* supposed to be a *Christian*—at least when you wear those *robes*. Isn't it *blasphemy* to proselytise for *Zeus*—in this day and age? What would your sodding *Bishop* say?"

"The Modern Games exist as a *Pagan* Fest revived in a *Non*-Pagan Age, *that* is the Games' basic problem," Psychopompós argued hotly. "The spiritual base for holding them in the first place doesn't *exist* now. The Glories of Greece and the Olympian Ideal *you* keep prosyletising...why...they're *nothing* but a front! All this attempting to enliven an Ideal, that once was worshipped as Spirit into Flesh, now just misses the mark, since to any idiot to-day it's *plain* that Spirit *left* Flesh...centuries ago! The Olympic Games were a *religious* festival, for the worship of Olympian Zeus, so how on Earth could they *possibly* be the same to-day, lacking *worship* of Olympian Zeus?"

"You, as Director of Communications for the new Olympic State, how can you possibly communicate *that*, being a *Christian* Priest? Does that not put your *priesthood* into total contradiction?"

The so-called Holy-Man stood. "This Cross I was offering you...perhaps could provide you the answer. Christ's Immaculate Birth resolved the contradictions of *all* mankind...forever and ever!"

"You're saying *Jesus* can save the Olympic Games?" Hefferon asked.

"Perhaps. Through Christ...*anything* is possible," the Priest replied. "Now—throw those letters in this box—and follow me to the postal machine." In silence the robed one led Ivor to the basement, to the first door at the bottom of the stairs. He opened it with a key and showed the Athlete how to use the franking machine that stamped pre-paid postage on envelopes. "I'll be back at seven thirty," Psychopompós had said and tried to leave, but Hefferon cut him off.

"Do please be punctual. I'm meeting my friend Colin at that time."

When the Priest returned, on the dot, Hefferon was sitting in a chair, waiting, feeling like a pasha's lackey. He did not rise when the faux Holy-Man entered the room. "To-morrow—you won't be needed here," the Priest said and smiled snottily.

"I'm fired?" the Runner asked, wondering what Rembetikós would say. The nasty taste of Lake Placid returned to his mouth, and made it go dry.

"No—don't be silly. I just spoke with Madame, and she said that the Press invitations can *wait* a day. She hates reporters as it is. You two at least have *that* in common."

"I never said I hated anybody."

233

"That's right—you *give* your publicity away."

"I don't indulge...in publicity."

"Maybe you can learn. Are the envelopes *done*? All the European ones in a pile? All the ones to the other Continents separated? Good. Now—we'll be lucky if they *get* where they're *going*. We can only give them till Wednesday week. Have you ever used a telex machine?"

"Why?"

"If those we've written to-day don't contact us by the fifteenth, we'll have to telex them all individually. What a bore. Can you type?"

"No," Ivor lied.

"*Panaghía mou!*" the Priest said. "Well we'll deal with that later. The first thing is getting these people to reply. They can telephone, telex, or cable."

"So what am *I* supposed to do to-morrow?"

The Priest gave Ivor the cardboard box of invitations and motioned him into the hall. He locked the door. "Were there any calls?"

"None."

"To-morrow then," Psychopompós said as they mounted the stairs from the basement, "Madame wants you to meet her when she gets back in town. You are to be at the Propýlaea Gate of the Akropolis at 5.45 PM. The guards there have already been advised, and they will let you onto the Akropolis for a 6.00 PM rendezvous with Madame. You are to go to the far right-hand corner of the Parthenon, alone, at the back end of the Temple, the side closest to Mount Imitós." The Priest then locked the doors of the Organizing Committee headquarters itself.

Ivor followed with the box, as the two passed through the lamp-lit garden. The pungent aroma of the orange blossoms was almost strong enough to knock a prizefighter out. Hefferon glanced briefly at the fountain. Iamídas was playing his peasant shawm by the gate, but promptly stopt and rose. In a jiffy he unlatched the principal gate then shut it behind the two.

"Under *no* circumstance are you to go into the Parthenon unless Madame is there," the Priest was emphatic to relate.

"I have to turn here. I told my mate to be around the corner in Archangels Square."

"Where're you two going?"

"We thought we'd wander towards Omónoia, for a bite to eat."

"I'll direct you then, if you accompany me to the Old Cathedral of the city. It's on your way. Then, you can carry the box," the Priest said cagily.

Just round the corner from the Organizing Committee, in Archangels Street, a small Orthodox Church was in the middle of the tiny block, on the other side of the lane. It was filled with old women in black, lighting candles, day and night. The Priest crossed himself the whole length of the façade, then stopt in the little square that was formed by the Church's flank. There were a couple of craft shops open for business, with reed mats and other goods outside, and in the centre was a single deciduous tree, against which Colin was leaning. His back was to them as they approached and Ivor made him start with fright, especially when he saw the Priest. "This's Colin. He's a Student of the London School of Economics," Hefferon bragged and let the two of them speak, as the three now began following the wall of the archaeological dig of Hadrian's Library.

In Mitropoléos Street, Colin inquired where were they going. The Priest said he would bid them adieu a couple blocks away, and would direct them to Omónoia Square. They turned left for a few yards then right again one block, to come upon a midget-sized Byzantine Church of Ághia Kapnikaréas, that looked as if it was sinking into quicksand, so low was it beneath the round-about that came right up alongside its toffee-coloured stone walls. Buildings all about hemmed in the dinky shrine that was too large for the mite-sized square wherein it sat.

"All the buildings here seem fighting for space," Colin said, but the Priest did not look amused.

They turned left in Hermes Street, and soon found themselves being led through a marvellous neo-classical arcade. Colin pointed at the Karyatid pilasters, but Psychopompós said: "It's *more* famous for textile shops." Then out the other end, a large squat and lengthy pink stucco structure was looming ahead. "Saint Irene's," the Priest said matter of factly. "It used to be the Cathedral, in the 1800s, before the new one was built."

At the front corner, Ivor was relieved to give the Priest his box.

"I'll take these to the Post Office—once I'm through in here," Psychopompós said and begged his leave.

Once he was gone, Colin couldn't resist saying: "Gave me the *creeps*! You don't work with *him*, do you?"

"Sorry to say I do. He just showed up to-day. He's a right pain in the arse! I really just think he's in drag. I don't believe for a minute he's a fucking Priest at all!"

"Are they *all* like that...where you work?"

"Just about."

"God...was the Olympics like that...over in Lake Placid?"

"Uh huh. Just different costumes. Different accents. They were *Comedians* over there, though. But here in Greece...they're all *Tragic Actors*!"

"Do you know where we are?"

"Well—let's look around here. We have to get to Omónoia Square by ten."

"Why's that?"

"A woman I met wants to meet me at some café there."

"Guess you won't be needing *me* then!"

"Oh yes I will. I need you to *protect* me! She's a weirdo. From the

235

States. Where *all* weirdos, *true* ones that is, hail from, right? She won't mind. Come along. Maybe she's got a girlfriend you can ride," Hefferon said as the two walked around the Old Cathedral's base, towards the apse, when suddenly they were in one of Athens's most charming outdoor markets.

"Good Lord—a potted-plants and live-tree mart!" Colin exclaimed. "You know—this city's amazing. I've fallen in love with it already. I'm never going back to London. I got a *tutor* this afternoon."

Now devoid of buyers, the plants in their pots were relaxing in the warm evening air, an air suffused with the soporific perfume of roses.

"Didn't I tell you—I'm going to learn Greek!"

"Good luck," Hefferon said.

"She's a pretty student at the University. I saw her name advertised this morning at the British Council."

"You still hanging out *there*?" Ivor responded, but he wasn't really listening. "Sniffing round for pussy, ain't you?" He was gazing up at every building that they passed. "Wonderfully well-preserved, isn't it?"

"What?"

"This quarter of the city. It looks like the only greco-revival one they haven't managed to tear down."

Instinct led them on towards Omónoia Square. Tiny crowd-filled romantic streets followed one after another, a wealth of edifices from the previous century, beautiful little buildings, usually of cut yellow stone, inspired by the ancient days of Greece, laden with incomparable ironwork ledges for sculpted windows and balconies defended by gryphons and other mythological beasts.

15th April – Saturday – 10.35 AM

The strange old women on the donkeys had made us both go silent. I had my own ideas about who the three had been, and Ada seemed to be thinking likewise. But before we could discuss it, along came our first ride. "Thank God!" Ada said and stuck out her thumb.

An Army jeep was sending dirt flying, and a dust cloud was billowing in the rear. Before too long the vehicle was coming to a screeching halt.

As ugly as the previous callers had been, this one was as good looking. Some young officer, with a sexy moustache and dimpled cheeks and dark as an Egyptian, was telling us both to get in. Ada and he commenced speaking Greek. She did not give away our identities. And soon we were flying over the road, round bend after bend, then suddenly were onto a plâteau.

"Look—the whole plain," Ada shouted for joy. "You can almost see all the way north to Thessaloníki."

Indeed, we now could see behind us all the alluvial plain drifting from the base of the mountain to the Aegean Sea. The waters were visible for dozens of miles out from the beach. And our range of vision north-south was uncanny.

"We're already at an elevation of three thousand feet," announced the girl in a burst of happiness.

I was just as happy with the staggering view, as the driver gunned the pedal to the floor and charged like it was a grand-prix race. Then, just as hastily, he stopt. Another screeching halt.

"Thanks," I said a bit dizzy.

Ada said the same and stood shakily by my side, as we waved at the young officer heading further up the road. "God—that was quick!"

"I'll say!"

We turned. Upon a rise, on this plâteau of Stávros, what looked like a Swiss châlet of sorts greeted our eyes. The rise was of unmown grass, and the rustic beauty of the timbers used to make the building contrasted well against the green.

"This is the First Refuge," Ada said. "Looks like the Alps, doesn't it?"

"Looks like the backlot for *Sound Of Music!*"

"I wonder if Óphion still runs it?"

"Who's that?"

"Wait till you see *him*. If you think those three on the *donkeys* were weird, wait till you see *this* man, of an even *more* obtuse pedigree."

"Who *were* those women, anyways?" I asked finally.

But Ada wouldn't respond to my query, and was making her way along the dirt path leading to the cabin-style building. The Refuge was two-storeyed, and had a wooden porch facing the Aegean Sea. Down before the porch tumbled the grassy hillock, at the bottom of which began the interminable trees. We went round to the porch, and looked for signs of life. Not a Soul seemed to stir inside.

"They said it was open," Ada complained. "Knock and see."

I replied, "What else can we do?"

"I'm starving. They're supposed to be serving something at midday."

"I could have eaten those *donkeys*," I joked.

"No—that would have *killed* you!" Ada said seriously. "They're Spirits Reborn...of people who were *bad*."

"Are you *serious?*" I asked with alarm in my voice, but since she didn't respond, I decided to made a quick circuit round the Refuge, but all that I could report was that I had seen a pair of tired burros tied to a hitching post.

"At least that means he's *here* someplace," Ada answered.

"Let me rap," I said and began pounding on the door for all my worth. "Damned inefficient way to run a sodding Refuge!"

"He's very old," Ada consoled and put her arms about me.

"Looks like three quarters of the population are, here in Greece," I said and stopt pounding.

We both sat on the edge of the porch, not really looking at the lovely view. My stomach was growling. Ada tried stalling my hunger by announcing: "Imagine—right where we're sitting—Ouranós and his dæmonic crew were scheming to construct their marble Nation."

"*This* is the very place?"

"For the Winter Games Site—yes."

"Therefore," I asked, "directly beneath our bums we'd be sitting on the powder keg?"

Ada shook her head. "A neutron bomb mill—think of it—right below our feet." Suddenly, a rattling was heard by the door, and it sounded like keys. "That's him—you just sit," Ada ordered.

"Gladly," I said, too hungry to get up anyways.

Presently, on the girl's arm was an old bugger who looked too dilapidated to speak. I shivered when into the light they stept and saw that the codger's skin was cheese-green. He looked scaly as a snake. How could Ada touch him? She was a Saint! The geriatric case had tiny green eyes that had long ago seen way too much. He had been bald for centuries, and he *never* had had any teeth. "This's Óphion," Ada introduced, then she joked, "the oldest man alive."

I stood, relieved that the fellow did not offer his hand.

Ada told her friend that I was an Olympic Gold Medallist. All that the old man could say, with great effort, at last, was: "You two getting married?"

6th March – Monday – 10.00 PM

The ultimate tawdry café, in all of the whole wide world, is the Kapheneíon Néon, in Omónoia Square, Athens, Greece. That's like saying that it's in Soho, Pigalle, or Times Square. Ivor and Colin fell into it as if slipping down a chute, and collapsed onto century-old wrought-iron chairs. They braced their elbows on a wooden-legged dirty-marble-topt table.

"That chicken dinner was just great!" Duckworth said.

"Hit the spot," Hefferon agreed and patted his tummy. "So—you think you *like* Athens after all? Well—get a load of this!"

"Looks the local emporium for your wayward Hun," the Student said and laughed. "You can feel the place churning up your guts!"

"Especially when it's painted mustard-yellow."

"It's all these scabby pillars."

Hefferon counted five central columns in the smoky place, standing erect amid two hundred or so small tables set about in the haphazardest fashion. "It's gigantic. Dora could be here right now. And through this smoke we'd never even see her."

"Let her come to *us*," Ivor said and hiccuped. He and Colin had been washing down Rabelaisian quantities of retsina wine. "Two ouzos," he said to a truly fat waiter. "Just look around..."

"My soggy head can't take it all in at one time," Duckworth admitted. "Guess it's that flaming pine-sap wine."

"Not bad grog, is it?"

"Why'd this Dora Bird pick *this* godforsaken place?"

"Ain't got any class. She's American. I *still* can't get over this hole's colour—mustard-yellow!"

"No it's not. Look closely. The first six-foot of the walls are stew-brown. You're blind as a bat. It's the *rest*, the twenty foot above, that's *tumeric*-yellow!"

"Long past its prime in spiciness."

Two ouzos were set upon the table with a clink, followed by two glasses of water.

"Ever drink this stuff?" Hefferon asked. "You mix it in your water."

They mixed the brew and toasted each other's ill health. Just then, a woman in a bright red plastic raincoat and red plastic-framed sunglasses came in. She was wearing a polka-dotted turban that did not match in colour.

Colin saw her first. "Look what's coming. *She* certainly compliments the seedy décor."

"Good grief—that's Dora. Told you she's a sight," Ivor laughed.

"For some rabid dog in heat," Duckworth added. He had already decided that he didn't like her one least bit.

The feeling was mutual. Dora Cain approached with the obvious air of a woman who felt that three *is* a crowd, and that she was nothing if not the number *one* cut of beef.

"Howdy, Hefferon," she snarled. "Who's your boyfriend?"

"Colin Duckworth—Dora Cain," the Athlete introduced and helped her with her chair.

"Is this a favourite *haunt* of yours?" the Student began for starters.

Dora ignored this, and said: "I didn't know we wouldn't be alone."

"*Can't* be alone in here—with four hundred old Greek geezers," Hefferon replied. "Want some ouzo?"

Seated about were men, singly, in twos, threes, fours, and fives, mainly playing or watching backgammon. A few literary types were reading cheap tabloids. Others were gone, staring light-years into Outer Space. The most erudite were talking to themselves. The sole sounds that ever drowned out the noisy traffic of Omónoia Square, the city's busiest, were male voices at game—endless political arguments and tired dirty jokes—and the rattling of dice thrown upon boards or the snap of chips from one pile to another.

239

"I'll have ouzo, *yepper*," she replied after she thought. She removed her raincoat. Beneath was an outmoded second-hand puce cocktail dress.

"Spring outside?" Colin wondered and looked at her feet. She was wearing ugly blue shoes.

"Look—what's *with* this creep?" Dora asked Ivor bluntly.

Colin only laughed. "What happened to *her* to-night, get run down by the grouchmobile?"

"Children—children!" the Olympian intervened. "What's wrong, Dora Darling?"

"Don't *bug* me! You said you'd *ring* me!"

"You never gave me your number," Hefferon responded.

"You lie. Didn't I? Maybe I didn't. So, where in town're *you* holed up now? Find some wealthy *floozy*?"

Her ouzo was brought and she mixed it in her water quick as a pro, downing a great big shot. Ivor ordered another round. "Don't worry, Kiddies. Dora knows how to guzzle," she said. "I'm a *Texan* remember. So—what're *you*?" She glared at Colin.

"Student at L.S.E."

"What's that short for? Losers Stand Excused?"

"Isn't she a bundle of laughs?" Duckworth asked his mate.

"London School of Elastics," Ivor corrected.

"When'd *you* boys meet—last night at the Pláka *gay*-bar?"

"That's right," Colin answered. "We left when we saw *you* walking in...with that transvestite."

"Buy me another shot and I'll claw your fucking *eyes* out," Dora spat.

"Have a bad dig?" Ivor wondered.

Colin couldn't resist: "You a *clam*-digger?"

"Soaked me to the bone. All it does is rain up north! Plus, I've got to go *back* to-morrow, which's why I thought it'd be fun to see *you*. But seeing how you've already found yourself a *pussy*..." She cut herself off. She bored easily with her own conversation. "Hemingway would've felt *right* at home in *this* joint. Good place to shoot yourself."

"So would Humpty Bogart," Colin ventured.

Dora shot an evil glance Ivor's way but winked and said: "Maybe the little dink's humour's all right *after* all?" She turned to Colin: "When're you going to start to *shave*?" Then she said to the Athlete: "How was I even going to be sure you'd end *up* here to-night?" Then to Colin she added: "The bastard moved *out* on me—so I don't even know where to *find* him anymore."

"Oh—Ivor and I have found a nice *cosy* place," Colin said with a smile and winked at Hefferon.

"Figures! How *stupid* of this dumb broad not to have guessed. Well, let me *tell* you, Collie, Ivor's a *stallion* between the sheets."

"I know," Colin joked, as Dora got furious.

240

The whole gargantuan room of the Néon Café was done in pre-cast iron from the Victorian Period, that is if one could say that Victoriana ever reached such a low. About twenty bare bulbs hung fifteen feet down into the chamber. Perhaps five unused four-propeller swivel fans were not moving an inch. The floor was old dirty-white dirty-black patterned tiles. Dora looked at all these things, and decided to change her tactic. She became nice. "Hefferon Honey—I brought you a *present,*" she said extra sweet.

"Tablet of cyanide?" Colin asked.

"No, Collie," she replied and shoved a hand down into a floppy green leather bag, "a book. That's 'cause our Athlete's so very bright!" The book was more like a booklet, and was called *Mount Olympos.* "Did you tell your *bosom* buddy that you and I are going to be *climbing* this thing?" Dora asked Ivor and pointed to the cover's peak.

Suddenly, the Athlete was honestly intrigued. He started flipping through the pages of the book, examining the black and white photographs with intense curiosity.

"Oh let him be a little boy and gawk," the girl said and adjusted her turban. "I picked it up to-day, at the office of the Greek Alpine Club. They publish it."

There was silence while Hefferon held a double page open and stared transfixed at a terrifying panorama of the two top peaks of Olympos, Mýtikas and Throne of Zeus, looming impossibly high above a Grand Canyon sized valley. Absolutely no vegetation at all was growing from it. Ivor's stomach began clenching.

"Never before have I ever seen a photograph of Mount Olympos," Hefferon said and passed the book to Duckworth.

"It's awesome," the Student said in all honesty.

"It's just...big..." Dora concluded, staring down at Hefferon's penis, whose size she knew all about. "*Any* real mountain is!"

"Maybe I'm deluding myself...that I *could* climb to the top of such a rock?" Ivor wondered aloud. "Seeing it in this book...it just doesn't seem possible..."

"I've never climbed a mountain in my life," Colin admitted, "and I *ain't* going to start, either!"

"Well—Good Ole 'Lympic Gold's *gonna* climb it, ain't you, Sweety Pie? You ain't chickening *out* on me now, are you?"

Hefferon took the book back and stared at a picture of Skála Peak.

Suddenly, Dora made the attack: "Okay Ivor Conniver—just *what's* this bullshit I'm hearing about you working for the MOON? I suppose your lover-boy here doesn't even *know* yet?"

Ivor's mouth dropt open to his knees. "What?"

"You *heard* me! Lydia, remember her, the cleaning lady? Well the poor thing came crying on her cousin's shoulder, like a baby, saying how that *bitch* at the Organizing Committee kicked her out on her ass, and *you* just sat there, with your thumb up *yours*, doing *nothing*! Fine Olympic gentleman *you* are!"

Hefferon had to think fast. Caught in a trap, between two people who were being checked by Interpol, neither of whom he could trust, his tactic all night had been to let the two go at each other. But this move on Dora's part certainly let the pussycats out of the douchebag!

"What exactly *are* you working for?" Colin asked Ivor, but innocently. He only sounded curious.

"Don't you *know?*" Dora answered. "He went against *all* my advice! I told him *not* to get his ass involved with those vipers at the Mount Olympos Olympic Nation! But—did the Dip-Shit listen—no—he went ahead—and he did the opposite—Mister Spry Thighs—naturally!"

"I thought you were doing something for the *Greek* Olympic Committee," Colin confessed.

"No—the Organizing Committee I'm now with *isn't* connected in any way with that."

"So what *are* you doing with them?" Dora burst loudly.

"I'm sorry, Dora, the job is classified."

Both the girl's and the boy's eyes bugged out. Dora couldn't restrain herself. "You *know* what I told you about those people! I thought you were really *worried* about your goddamned Olympian Ideal and your so-called reputation! This will *ruin* you, Ivor!"

"There's a *need* for the Games to have a permanent abode, Dora," Hefferon said vehemently, in an attempt to explain himself.

"But who says you must *shit* on your own hands, with such a sorry bunch of criminals...who are cheering you with your pants down?"

"Who *are* these people?" Colin asked,

"I'll tell you later!" the girl snapt. "Ivor—you're *nuts*! You've gone off your fucking rocker, Kid! I don't believe it. I said to Lydia—no—it *can't* be the same guy! But—she assured me that *you* were the Olympic Athlete. And—*you* said you came to Greece to fight the *bastardisation* of the Games? Honey—you've just joined *forces* with the Bastard League! Good luck—Champ! Hope you get out of it as much as you shove into it!" Dora then finished her drink and ordered another round. "Doubles!"

"Let me explain," Ivor began.

"How? You've sold *out*! I don't even want to *talk* to you anymore." She turned to Colin: "What's new along the Thames, Childe Hair Rogue?"

A double round of ouzo was brought.

"Dora," Hefferon pleaded, "you don't *understand*!"

"No—I don't!" she shouted. Even the dozy old men at distant tables now were peering.

"Then *listen* for a second. Yes—of course I stand by all of my past, my support for the Olympian Ideal. *That* cannot be changed. But in any Olympic Organizing Committee there always have been workers who are *good*, and workers who are *bad*. Christ Almighty—on that note I can sing an *opera*—having been so embroiled in the goofiness of the goodies and the baddies of Lake Placid! But there has to be *one* good person in an Organizing Committee...one who believes...or else the Games are just a load of rubbishy hype, and it's *all* a sham! I feel I'm *able* to contribute some sense of the Good—by lending my presence to the people of the MOON. Maybe I can even quietly work to *change* their ways."

"What're you—a goddamned *martyr?* Do you *honestly* believe your own stupid words? Don't you know yet—from just one single day in that serpents' den—that not the *least* diddly-shit thing you do will *ever* change *those* people's rotten ways? Oh—you're so *fucked-up* it smells, Hefferon! It really and truly does stink!" She stood to leave.

"Where're you going?" Ivor asked dumbfounded. "Hey—don't leave like that."

She took a few steps then turned, "Well—how will I contact you, if I *ever* want to see how you've survived? I'm certainly not going to call *that* crappy place!"

"Uh...when are you coming back from your dig?"

"Friday night, I guess. Why?"

"Well—meet me at the outdoor café in Epaminónda Street—just round the bend from my office—at ten. It's only a few blocks from the Agora."

"I know where it damn well is! I'll *think* about it," she snapt and took a few steps more, before she turned. "But—you do as you're *told* now, and you *read* that pissing book. I never should have wasted my hard-earned cash...on *trash!*"

"Thank you. I *shall* read it."

"Money down the drain, with *you!* Take it to *heart*, Athlete. When you read that book, think about what the *drek* you're working for are hoping to *wreck*. It's not just *any* ole hill they want to destroy, Mister Gold Medal, it's Mount Olympos! And now *you're* part and parcel of their evil schemes. Hope you're *proud* of yourself. Take a good *long* look—in a *king*-sized mirror."

Dora Cain pointed across the smoky café to the best thing in the place, the gigantic mirrors. Then, she left. In one of them, Hefferon could see a blurry facsimile of himself. The mirrors ran all along the mustard walls towards Omónoia Square. Above each one loomed two huge tumeric-hued sphinxes. The sphinxes were carved as bas-reliefs. They really were frames that held up phony windows.

Hefferon paid the bill then belched. He looked at Duckworth for consolation, but ouzo had got to *him*, too.

"Better get going," Ivor announced. "I gotta run...go jogging," and he attempted to stand, but only could weave. He left the gift-book behind. Colin grabbed the book then charged through the café and got ahold of Hefferon's sleeve, then flung his arm over his shoulder as he guided the besotted Olympic Gold Medallist out.

16th April – Palm Sunday – Eve

Óphion proved a good old egg. He was of a kindly heart. He had to be—to survive on such a tempestuous ridge—when he could have easily hopped on his ass and descended to the warmer more agreeable plain. But, he had explained to us, in a story the previous eve: "I'd grown sick of humanity's ways. Up here, nobody bothers me. Only the best sort have the guts to forsake Evil long enough to put their plots behind them, in order to brave Mount Olympos."

When Ada explained to the geezer that we had managed to prevent desecration of the mountain that he loved, the fellow had spent the rest of yesterday cooking us a delicious evening meal. "The mule trains bring my supplies up. And the Greek Alpine Club lets me live here for free."

He had cooked us a lamb stew. Ada had helped him in the kitchen. The two were very fond of each other. He was an old friend of Aunt Georgia. But to-day, the weather had turned on us. All we could do was wait out the inclemency. "Some Palm Sunday," Óphion kept saying. "For sure, the storm will be gone by morning."

"I think he knows what he's talking about," ventured Ada.

"He should—he's lived here as long as Zeus!" I responded.

After polishing off the same lamb stew this evening, by the light of a kerosene lamp, we three were now hovering over a large relief map of the Olympian Vale and the central peaks. "Now—here you are," he stated and pointed a bony digit to a spot marked X. "Damned electricity —always knocking out!" He moved the lamp a bit closer. Every time lightning struck, our shadows danced throughout the hikers' dining-room. We had a log fire burning in the fireplace, so at least the room was warm. "Well—think nothing of it," he snorted and carried on. "You next go here, to Prióni, the end of the Army road."

"No—I want Ivor to see the monastery," Ada objected. "It's Holy Week."

"Nah! What's the sense of gawking at ruins of stone? You can do that, to your heart's content, down below!" Óphion retorted with such passion I feared that he'd have a heart attack. He coughed, then spat into the fire. Lightning struck nearby again, and our shadows danced a jig.

"There's someplace you *must* see," Ada countered quietly and winked at me.

Óphion caught all this and simply said: "Women! And their superstitious religion!"

Ada rubbed his tired old back and had him point out the path leading to the main Refuge Hut, at twice this elevation above the sea. "There's snow up there," the old codger warned and glared at me. "But—it's melting."

"That's why we're not in any rush," replied Ada pleasantly.

"This is one Hell of an intelligent girl," said the testy fellow. He started off towards the stairs, then turned at the balustrade. "Now be good, you two Lovebirds. And blow out that lamp when you go to sleep." Then he remembered as an afterthought: "Let the candle in the kitchen keep the ikon lit. Maybe it'll help clear the storm."

"Good night," we both said simultaneously.

It took old Óphion an eternity to struggle up the wooden stairs. Watching him made us melancholy. The two of us embraced by the fire, grateful for our strength, our youth. A log snapt, then hissed. Lightning hit one more time. Our shadows raced round the walls like uncouth mountain sprites, returning to our sides to watch us kiss.

7ᵗʰ March – Tuesday – 5.45 PM

Hefferon stood waiting at the barred Propýlaea Gate. Over the rise chords of electric guitars were being strummed onstage, at the Odíon, the reconstructed ancient amphitheatre that graced the Akropolis's flank. No guard had yet showed up to let him inside, so the Athlete was passing time by listening to the Heavy-Metal number being rehearsed; but then, just as quickly as it had begun, the intensely amplified Rock Song died. Ivor figured that the large crowd, that he had to wade through, along the marble path that led from the Agora to the outdoor theatre, was at last being admitted. Hefferon hoped that Theatrínos would pull a full-house.

"Testing, one, two," said a man's voice over the sound system. "Testing, one, two."

No problem hearing this show, Ivor said to himself and laughed. What a juxtaposition—Rock-N-Roll and the Akropolis!

"Testing, one, two."

Just then an angry-looking uniformed guard was peering from the other side of the gate of iron. He didn't like what he saw—too many weird-looking young people hanging around the rocks and lounging under the olive trees. Ivor wished that he were there with them, going to the concert and not having a so-called rendezvous with a venomous snake.

"You...Athlete?" the guard asked gruffly.

"Me...Athlete," Hefferon mimicked and gave his name.

"Just you—no more," the guard stated and hastily shooed a few stragglers away, then slammed shut the gate. Ivor looked at the man, short and unshaven, and tried to see if he had eyes beneath that cap. The guard didn't want to be messed with, and just waved his hardened hand, upwards, through the Propýlaea compound. Glad to be alone, Hefferon continued solitarily to mount the zig-zagging series of steps that led up to the plâteau of the Akropolis.

Testing, one, two," the announcer repeated many times.

The crowd in the amphitheatre began clapping in unison, stomping feet two times, then putting hands together once, again and again, just as in the live concert LP by the Rock-Group, Queen.

It had just rained. The Sun had just about set. There was still enough light to see the colours of the marble mountain top, further up the steps, upon which the grandest temple of the Greek world did sit. Between the graceful Temple of Wingless Victory, on the right, and the ancient painting gallery, the Pinakotéka, on the left, the last of the stairs were made of wood, and rose like a grandstand of a sports stadium.

For his whole lifetime, Ivor Hefferon had dreamt about this very moment, when he would ascend these very steps, and would walk upon the Akropolis, towards the Parthenon. Never did he dare to think that he would have this fantastic opportunity...alone. The place was always under siege...by tourists.

Then, the last of the steps was behind him. The Olympian at first would only glance down. He could hardly believe that the plâteau was really of marble. He kept staring at the pinks, the crimsons, the tans, the golds, the streaks of white, that usually go ignored by the tens of thousands of eyes that visit the Akropolis solely to see mortal might. But the beauty of Nature, bathed and heightened by Rain, truly was an awe-inspiring sight.

It *was* spectacular, this vast marble floor, polished by millennia of feet. Rarely glimpsed beneath its hot coat of dust, the stone now glistened, as if freshly waxed, for oncoming Night, like a superlative gem, most fit for the Goddess of the Mind, for the eternal Patroness of Athens herself.

Then...there...all alone...directly ahead...with not one single tourist in sight...stood the Parthenon...freshly washed...waiting...in the fading light...

There was no sound now from the Odíon below:.

It must not ever be an *easy* walk, Ivor said. The mount is so very steep. Think of *who*, likewise, has walked up here...far greater intellects than mine...

The mental effort to strive, so far backwards in Time, to a period that could point to this very sanctuary with such pure pride, is all but impossible to-day. Each and every person must approach the Parthenon ...with his or her own notions or dreams. And some...approach with footsteps of wonder...

What supernatural schemes the ancients were capable to perceive, to design, to execute with such finesse! And even though so little does remain...what does...does still seem invincible...able to awe the most jaded, the most erudite viewer...able simply and honestly to *impress*. What a powerful and pleasing pantheon of Gods could cause such an edifice as the Parthenon to exist!

The Olympic Gold Medallist could not possibly *rush* up to Athena's Temple. There, to the left, the marble Erechtheíon was in process of total restoration. Iron-pipe scaffolding was set where workers would sweat over each and every piece of white stone. The building's most famous component, the Karyatídes Maidens, already had been taken down, to be lodged inside the Akropolis Museum forever, relieved of their job, retired from supporting the portico, reduced to being helpless victims of urban air pollution. It was almost too much to bear. Their absence brought tears to the Athlete's eyes.

After so many ages of foreign domination, the Greeks themselves now were being victimised, by exigencies of their own colossal city, that they themselves had lately inflicted on their own renowned Valley called Attika. The Karyatídes had literally rotted away—female faces once immortal stone—the Karyatídes had decayed—like mere mortality...

For centuries, minds have praised the *atmosphere* of Athens. Merely *breathing* its aromatic air was said to make the dullard philosophic. But now the city's atmosphere is sooty, sulphuric, sad.

Right at this moment, a storm was flashing lightning on the other side of the capital. Black tumulus clouds were hovering above Mount Párnis. From where Hefferon stood, at the plâteau's edge, the whole of Attika still could be seen, now just one bumpy mass, polluted concrete. Strange, the fellow said aloud, this birthplace...of the so-little-understood word *democracy*...had allowed her own contractors to run amok, to build helter-skelter, without city-planning, recklessly, wild, free. People like Ouranós certainly were to blame. Now, Ivor was about to go and treat with the wife of the Construction King. Ivor turned, to face the Parthenon's long majestic flank.

Upwards, over the marble height, the roar of a young human crowd was rippling sound across the fallen stones. But the masonry was embracing itself tight, was staying mute as bones.

Alone, angry, cold, and visibly depressed, the Athlete slowly made his steps for the Seat of Wisdom. Night was taking its good old time, too, not bothering to blacken the dead-lead sky. But there stood the Parthenon, all right, with nary a person to contend with in sight. Ivor felt a sudden chill of dread, to be going, finally, up beside it.

Where was Thýella? In it? Behind it?

With not one Soul to relate to, with no sound of the city now noiseless below, on this high Plane of Thought, Hefferon felt the blood dropping to his feet. Loss of oxygen from the mind suddenly made him dizzy...as he kept advancing, slowly, as he kept approaching those huge marble columns...when it hit him: What was he *doing*, with his Life?

He went on, up to the awesome building's base.

There, for a split-second, eerie recollection of having once stood, on this very site, shook him with fright. His spinal column twinged.

Ancestors had been *Greek*! Anyone who thought that a flash of déjà-vu was anything more than ancestral-memory percolating towards consciousness was a fool!

He shivered. Hastily...the speaking-voice from the bloodlines fled, like a stone dropping down some pitch-black bottomless well...leaving nothing more than a haunting echo...

Again, the crowd-roar assaulted him from behind. Ivor looked. There was nobody. Then, the same two-stomps one-clap cheer resumed. On the third beat, the throng shouted *Bacchae*, name of the Rock-N-Roll group.

The sky was bluish-black now. It heightened all the more the marble of the shrine. Without a doubt...it was one of the most moving moments of the Runner's life...deciding to do what he'd been told *not* do...as he was waiting beneath the uplooming pillars...as he was taking in a very deep breath...then...as he was forcing his weight...up...up...up the hallowed rock steps!

The crowd in the Odíon was going wild, but was continuing unabated the stomping: *"Bacchae! Bacchae! Bacchae!"*

Carefully, carefully, the Olympic Gold Medallist was walking ever so slowly, atop the second level of the stylobate, to the Temple's Piraeus front...then...he was aiming up again...up...up...into the very midst of the Goddess's sanctuary itself.

"Presenting: *Bacchae!"* the MC was finally announcing like a scream. Music was suddenly blaring for all its worth. The Rock Group was launching into its opening song, their instrumental introduction, Blues, that would lead their Singer on.

Those minutes there, in Pallas Athena's gloried abode, were ones that the Olympian never would forget. Such naked grace...such architectural excellence...made all his pretensions fall upon the floor, like humbled slaves. Just being inside this residence of Wisdom ...brought Ivor Hefferon to tears...as he could feel the weight of his whole life...weight like stonework...weight a compound of paltry lies. It struck him that *nothing* he ever could do, nothing he ever could say, would come close to the profound yet simple eloquence of this very spot, where his feet, that had run so far, that had carried him to what little greatness he had experienced on this Earth, were now standing, as if rooted forever, to this Temple's stone floor. He had to take time...to sit...to get *used* to the idea of *being* in this place, where, once again, he suddenly experienced a shivering sensation that *ancestors* had been here *before*. Yet *that* flash, too, like the other one, vanished again into thin air, assaulted by Rock-N-Roll...

Seated upon the petrine base, in the Temple's very centre, where Phidias's famed sculpture of the Goddess once loomed, the Athlete just let the tears fall.

Columns, all about, seemed suspended from the sky, that now was the colour of ink.

Atop pillars, white stone blocks, set end to end, from capital to Doric capital, so high above, seemed a virtual albino ring, hovering in mid-air, from which cyclopean shafts of rock just were dangling down, like mere wax candles, from some common dripping-frame. Ivor shuddered. Then...the gloved hand of a woman reached out to touch him. "Where's your briefcase?" she snapt. Of course, the woman was Thýella.

Hefferon wiped his face. He turned. For a split-second, the fellow saw her staring at his tears, saw her framed between two huge Doric columns, just yards away, saw her laughing. She was wearing black gloves, clutching her right hand to the collar of a lush woolly coat, some odd fur, a curly long-haired sheep, dyed a brilliant orangey-gold. It looked like Jason's Fleece. Her laughing head was bound by a spectacular black turban, embellished with jangly loose jewels of jet. Then suddenly, the whole Parthenon was washed in a bath of light, blood-red.

The General's wife cackled even more, then she stopt. At that moment a cheer arose from the Odíon. Theatrínos was making his entrance. Ivor stood, and Thýella said mock maternally: "Don't worry." She gestured to the whole Temple. It's just the technicians. They're testing this season's Sound and Light. Red will be used a month from now, when the influx of tourists begins."

Then a silence from Thýella mated with a beautiful young masculine voice, that was rising up and over the Akropolis's edge. Theatrínos now was singing out his heart, a potent lament of some pure love desecrated. The Parthenon was breathing, as mortal flesh. Neither Ivor nor Thýella made the smallest move. Finally, when the song below was finished, Thýella inquired: "From where is the word *hero* derived?"

"It's Greek."

"How wise you think you are," the lady jested. "Hero comes from Hera."

"Queen of the Gods."

"The Hero...was the Sacred King...sacrificed...annually...to the Great Goddess..."

"And...you want *me* to be...*your* Sacred King?"

"Now you really *are* wise. Being in this philosophers' asylum has had *some* positive effect."

From Bacchae's concert below, the muscular sexy voice of Theatrínos could be heard beginning to say something unaccompanied: "Friends—now you know we *never* care to meet without a *little* welcoming speech!"

"Damn that boy!" Thýella snapt. "*Another* example of his *insane* rabble-rousing gimmickry!"

"Who?" Ivor pretended he didn't know.

"That *bum* they call Theatrínos!"

"We just wanted to say," the Singer's amplified voice continued, "that in less than *three* weeks' time, our country's generous fathers are going to be giving away a little piece of *land*...a little piece of our *homeland*...our homeland *Greece!*"

"He wouldn't *dare!*" Thýella was enraged. She looked mean enough to stomp right off the Temple and literally fly in wrath down to the stage below. "He organised a demonstration against the MOON— before *you* arrived on the scene!"

"Don't let him bother you so," Ivor intervened.

"But this is *no* ordinary plot of dirt, it seems," Theatrínos continued, then he blared out loud for the whole Attika Valley to hear: "Tell me *what* the rats are planning to give away!"

"Bastard!" Thýella shouted and waved her fist.

"MOUNT OLYMPOS!" the whole Odíon screamed.

"Again?" the singer taunted. "Tell me again!"

"MOUNT OLYMPOS!" the thousands hollered and leapt from their seats.

Thýella was in a raging fit of vitriolic antipathy, charging between the columns bathed in crimson as if she owned them. "*Bacchae! Maniacs!*"

"*This* song's for the *Government,*" Theatrínos announced, "and it's called 'Let Them Break Our Heart'."

The Chief of Protocol now was at the corner of the Parthenon that looked down into the amphitheatre below. She screeched: "Stupid little fools! Look at all those *thousands* of mindless idiots! *Rock* music! And that hopped-up dyed-haired *kid*—who thinks he's got all *Athens* by the balls! Well—we'll SHOW that punk who's in power here! We'll make his asinine guitars *wail*...for something *other* than puerile dreams! *Government!* And wrecking *our* noble schemes! What does that falsetto mock-troubadour *know* about the truth of such things?"

She turned and glared at Ivor, who had never seen such an emotional soliloquy, even on the London stage. "Well—*what* do you say—Deputy?"

Ivor was dumbfounded, but had to say something. "I...can't understand, Madame...*why* you're allowing this concert to upset you so!"

"Oh *can't* you? Well—then you've got *more* to learn than we at first believed. What in Hell *did* you soak up...over there in the Adirondacks...other than Lucille McSorley's post-menopausal *drippings!* *Are* you as stupid as you look right *now?*"

If he hadn't been charged with a mission, he would have slapt the silly bitch's turban off her face. Ivor said nothing.

"We *do* have powerful contacts in this town," she bragged. "How do you think *you* got here to-night? My son Movóros's commanding officer's *brother* is Director of the Akrópolis—*that's* why! We've got *ears*, we've got *hands*, all *over* Greece, and in *all* her vital walks of life. And— we *shall* have our way! *No* little runny-nose *chanteuse* like him," and the horrid woman pointed towards the music, "is ever going to take *that* away! Our Olympic Nation *will* be built—and all our plans *will* be realised. And Ivor, to-night, we brought *you* here to *insist* that you volunteer us your *help.*"

"That's why I came to you and offered you my services in the first place."

"We *have* to trust you—explicitly."

"You have my *pledge*, upon the Parthenon's stones, that I shall act according to the best of my ability," Ivor said, but meant for purposes to do *in* the likes of her.

"Good," she stated, visibly relieved. "We've *needed* someone strong like you for weeks."

"I'm here."

Thýella took and squeezed her Deputy's steady arm. The two stood silent in scarlet light. "Do you know what we shall do?" she asked.

"We shall do even better for you than *you* may have conceived. You, Ivor Hefferon, are too *noble* a Soul to waste time as our mere *Deputy.*"

She paused. What was she getting at?

"No—due to your announced diligence—for the best of the tradition of Olympic Sport—we shall create a *special* Post for you."

"What...may I ask...is that?"

"We shall, from now on, designate you our Keeper of the Olympian Ideal."

She's mad, Ivor said to himself. She's completely, indubitably mad!

Thýella now had been transported into whatever sick realm of horrible fantasy over which her last bit of humanity sometimes did preside. She even had a grin on her face, like that on reptiles after they had just devoured some gristly prey. She was fingering a brooch that she had pinned above her dark-painted eyes, some antique cameo of black coral, that had been fished from waters off Indonesia. It portrayed the Three Muses, fathered by Zeus upon Mnemosyne.

"My *Hero*," Thýella said, then motioned the Olympic Athlete away. "We shall descend presently. You, though, now may leave."

A roar went up from the concert below. Hefferon did not turn to see the Temple, that was the hue of fresh-butchered meat, and left the Parthenon behind. The Rock Group began to play a song that sounded like bells in the nocturnal sky.

18th April – Tuesday – 8.03 AM

The storm didn't cease till dawn on Tuesday. We awoke and the weather was dandy. In fact, there wasn't a cloud in the heavens. Even old Óphion had a leer on his unshaven face, as he waved us good-bye.

Hoofbeats and bells had roused us just after dawn. Ada had sprung out of bed and said: "Mules! Shhh—listen!"

"Mules?" I thought I must still be dreaming.

"It's about time."

"You mean—we don't have to walk?" I asked, quite relieved, as I rubbed the sleep from my eyes.

"We'll see," she responded then charged downstairs to waylay the beasts before they could flee.

When I struggled outside the Refuge, there was Ada petting the nose of a surly black mule. Two other creatures, one brown and one grey, were nuzzling her way, seeking similar attention.

"Room for two," Ada shouted. "He says it's allowed."

"Super," I nodded, still asleep. "Book us and hold them till breakfast." I returned inside.

Óphion was setting out fresh bread and herbal tea. I fetched the butter and fig preserves, as a very dark-complected, rather rubbery-looking bloke, obese as a grease-ball, somewhere near forty, with the hairiest eyeballs you've ever seen, began glaring at me. Ada came to stand by my side.

The fellow began a very rough Greek which, it was plain, intended solely to abscond away with Ada, alone, and to leave me high and dry. Ada ignored the fat crude chap and sat to eat. The fellow began stuffing his ugly face. He never had seen such a pretty girl in his life.

After the disagreeable repast, we got our packs and lugged them to the mules. Ada pointed to the packs, then to the mules, then spoke as gruffly as the man. Then she ordered me to throw the packs round the two wooden humps that were sticking from the wooden "howdah" of sorts on the black mule's back.

"It's not far," she assured. "He's a guide."

"To where?" I wondered. "Hell?"

"Where we're going," she replied and suddenly was on the black brute's back. Its bell was jangling from its hairy neck.

"What about me?" I shouted, as the crude man weighing down the poor grey beast already was beating the lead and dashing off.

"He's got to pick up some sand up above," Ada shouted and waved. "I'll meet you there!"

"Meet me where?" I shouted for all my worth, as the three bell-bonging mules, the nasty man, and the infidel with the name of Ada were vanishing up the road, then round the bend. My anger suddenly boiled over and I pitched a fit right there—as Óphion beside the house was coughing with laughter—as I pounded my fists in the ground. "Up your bleeding guide's pock-marked backside!"

But the only person who responded was an echo.

Now what was I supposed to do...just gallantly carry on, walking a bit, seeing the sights?

Appalled—I wished that I could accept what had just happened with better sportsmanship. But those blasted bells kept reverberating through the titanic pines. At least the mules were buckled with the baggage—why complain? Don't press your luck with Greeks...

I began to round the bend. But then I heard laughter, a woman's and a man's, and realised that I had been swindled. "Why you!" I shouted and ran towards the two, who were splitting a gut on their mules. "Big joke! Funny! Oh you two are a *real* pair! Damn you—let me on!"

It wasn't a cinch, but somehow I got in the saddle. It was the first time I'd ever ridden a bloody mule, and certainly hadn't expected to on Olympos. We began to move. Gradually, my anger cooled, and I just let my mind flow free. There was really nothing else to do, what with the omnipresent pine trees for "scenery".

"Bless his hairy heart," I said one time, meaning the guide. "These beasts' saddles don't look the sort to throw on a Viennese Lipizzan."

"Hardly," Ada replied.

"Matter of fact, one of these mediaeval torture instruments would likely maim any *decent* horse...grotty old things...look at these harsh wooden frames!"

Suddenly—my mule reared upon its haunches and only sheer will kept me on its back. The animal all but caused a mule stampede, since the three beasts were linked by leather chains.

"A serpent!" Ada screamed.

The guide began cursing in a Greek not heard since Homer's day, and jumped off his saddle in a flash. He was simultaneously trying to steady my mule with one hand whilst aiming at the snake with a pistol he'd pulled from his belt. The reptile was curled in a ball, ready to strike, beside the road. The guide opened fire and shot, sending the little beast flying.

We dismounted, both Ada and I. My nerves felt as if *I* were the one who just got the bullet, it had all happened so fast. I grabbed Ada's waist to steady myself. "Tell him...tell him to go on ahead," I said. "It's probably not that far anyhow, is it?"

"To Prióni? It's not—I'll walk with you," Ada said. Then she informed the guide that we would carry on alone. I unhitched our packs.

The fat fellow laughed, didn't even look twice at the serpent, and again mounted his mule. He shot in the air, in final salute, then clomped away with the beasts of burden. We listened as the bells faded round another bend. Before continuing our route, the both of us peered at the two-foot snake. It was light brown, fat, and had a diamond-shaped head the size of a fist.

"A viper," Ada observed. "Its tail's still twitching."

"Wonderful. 'Spose it will till sunset?"

"Maybe...forever?" she laughed, then resumed her seriousness. "It's a sign."

"Of what?"

"Already the Gods have begun to test you."

"'Why?"

"You're now stepping foot in their abode."

10th March – Friday – 10.00 PM

Café Kéa, at the Monastiráki edge of Pláka, sprawled its rickety oil-cloth-covered tables on both sides of Epaminónda Street, just a block away and round the corner from the headquarters of the MOON.

Hefferon and Duckworth had been dining on moussaká and Greek salad for the previous hour, and now were on their third pair of Amstel beers.

They were silently enjoying the sideshow atmosphere of the outdoor café, watching innumerable young people from foreign lands performing variety acts for a few drachmas of change.

Right beside them an untrimmed floppy hedge of white-flowering jasmine was orgiastically scenting the night. The bushes managed to hide quite well an old Turkish mosque that nobody now was ever allowed inside.

"Phew—this bleeding jasmine's gone straight to the gob in my head," Colin snorted then sneezed.

"It's the beer, Mate."

"Here we go—getting sloshed again!" Colin said and tossed a few coins in an anæmic Nordic girl's black felt hat.

Ivor, who was facing the corner leading to his office, was staring at something.

"What're *you* gawking at?" Colin wondered. "Dora? How's the silly bird making a fool of herself now?"

Sashaying like a sylvan tigress, slowly, slowly, moving with the ololu wailing of some dog-ear-piercing flute that was accompanying an out-of-tune bouzouki song the management were broadcasting for customers from a lopsided speaker over the main door, one mangy skinny-dick alley cat, once white, but now mottled with grime, was making her way directly for Ivor Hefferon.

"You certainly do attract them," Colin joked.

The pussy was an obvious case of sensitisation to Oriental "harmony". Each pad she placed on the road perfectly matched the ill-timed pace of the freakily high flute. Ivor was mesmerised. Then someone tapped him on the shoulder.

The Athlete jumped and spun round: "Dora!"

The cat wraowled and vanished into the jasmine.

Colin had been hushed by the girl. *She* certainly looked bizarre-enough to scare away *any* wild pussy. Dora Cain was wearing sienna-coloured body-hose and black-leather highheel ankle-boots, which were ok. Over her torso, though, was a leopard-spotted leotard. And over her right arm was a sleeveless silver-fox cape.

"Where're *you* going?" Ivor asked, aghast.

Colin all but started to laugh.

"Not where I'm *going*—where I've *been*," she said.

"Like *that*?" both Hefferon and Duckworth exclaimed together. Every man in the neighbourhood now was straining his eyes, to see the leopard-spotted derrière being pointed his way. All the waiters had halted whatever they were doing. They were whistling. "I've been breathing heavy," she said. "I have aerobics on Friday." Then she added: "Be right back. Package up the hill I have to get—it's pay-day—they're holding my little dress."

"Anything you say," Ivor offered and raised his glass, then watched her butt wiggling all the way around the corner.

Colin wiped his brow: "Blimey!"

"She's a Yankee! What can I say?" Hefferon stated, but now it was Colin who was staring at something strange. The dark form came round the end of the jasmine, then suddenly got on all fours. At first Colin thought that it was just another goofy American, wrapt in a full-length mink, crawling on the ground to find her earring. But on closer scrutiny the Student let out a shrill laugh and said: "My God—do you see what I see? I don't believe it! It's a real-live honest-to-God...*bear*!"

"No," Ivor mocked and turned to glare. "Oh my Lord—you're right."

It *was* a fabled dancing bear at that, muzzled, and not a small bear, either. The poor animal didn't seem a bit conscientious about being on a gypsy's led. Nor did being the sudden focus of an astonished taverna bother him. No—his gruesome metal muzzle didn't deter him from putting on airs—pantomimic ones—at the harmonic instigation of his owner, whom everyone was appalled to note soon was followed by a gaggle of gaily-garbed gypsy women bounding round the corner, and each and every one was holding a three-year-old child who had been trained to pretend to be terminally ill. Obviously, their bear was only the bait.

For once, since this band of gypsies had a bear, and a rather entertaining one at that, everybody at the taverna dug *deep* into his pocket or her bag for drachmas and gave plenty.

The gypsy with the bear almost looked middle-class. The two resembled each other in more ways than one. The owner started up creature-pleasing music, playing a very deep-voiced tambourine that sounded like an Indian drum, and with whose banging he sang. His voice was the human equivalent to a bassoon. His beast was sporting a studded-leather collar, to which the gypsy had tied two yellow and one blue balloons.

This bear was extremely conscious of his star-status. As the gypsy women joined in the act, with a bit of wailing, straight from the hollows of the nose, the bear began flip-flopping, to and fro, from both front feet to both back feet, from both front feet to both back feet, repetitiously, as if to annoy those watching. He did so, since he irked the people all the more by incessantly wanking his fuzzy skull up and down, snout yanked spinewards then snapt bellywards, snout yanked spinewards then snapt bellywards, all the while eyeing those gawking.

"I thought such entertainment died out with the Industrial Revolution," Ivor could only say, awed.

"Don't forget...Greece never *had* one of *those* revolutions," the Economics Student added, equally dumbfounded. The bear was now a couple feet away. It was so uncanny. This whole quarter of the capital of Greece had come to an abrupt halt...all for a bear. But then...so halted the performer, who suddenly ceased his rocking.

By a puddle, in a pothole by the kerb, the bear began to lap. At that instant...he turned from an attraction back into a poor captivated animal. The begging and the music ceased altogether.

There was an uncomfortable silence in the whole of the street. Everybody froze, and just peered at the sad and thirsty chained bear, who was drinking, just like a dog.

At that moment, round the corner of Epaminónda Street, came Dora Cain, walking backwards. She was talking, and walking, at the same time, to some older man, some Greek. She wasn't looking where she was going, but carrying on towards the two lads' table all the time. She was wearing that silver-fox cape. And wouldn't you know it, the dizzy girl bumped right into the drinking bear!

Well—our poor sad creature suddenly became a pugilist prizefighter! *Anyone* would have died of fright right there, to have been growled at and shown those huge yellow teeth, as the animal stood, on hind legs like a man, and held up his claws to attack. It was evident he didn't approve of Dora's furry fox cape. One woman nearby fainted dead away.

The gypsy women dropt their suddenly-normal babies and rushed to the bear's defence, spitting and shouting anathemas at Dora, the poor unsuspecting Soul who, as Ivor and Colin guessed, wasn't about to take anybody's bull...or bear!

Dora had almost had a heart-attack from fear, and looked as if she'd lost ten pounds right there. The Archaeologist broke out in a cold sweat but, tough little American cookie that she was, she sure could shovel out the language as well as any gypsy bride on Earth, with plenty to spare. It looked like a huge cat-fight was about to burst forth.

All the waiters suddenly came running from the four cardinal directions, to ward off the gypsy women, to shout at the music maker, to gawk at the still growling bear. It was a Greek free-for-all. Everybody began cursing everybody else. Hefferon and Duckworth were doubling over with laughter. Dora was screaming bloody murder at everyone. The whole café was crying, because everyone was splitting a gut.

The head-waiter, whose back was as wide as a billboard, and who every so often could be coerced into dancing in the street with a pretty tourist, suddenly saw the humanity in it all, and rose to the occasion. He literally swept Dora off her feet, and began waltzing her all around the road. Grinning like fools, the uncanny pair now looked like some giant trying to mount some dwarf.

The bear now was beginning to gyrate again, still on two legs like a man, and the gypsy again was making music with his voice and his tambourine. And once more the gypsy women were wailing, now doing a swirling dervish dance, pounds of petticoats of all hues imaginable elevating towards the sky. By now, every single Soul in the whole Athenian neighbourhood had come running. A huge throng was standing in the street, groups were hanging out of windows, and the whole lot began clapping along with the beat. Dora, still dancing, was the *heroine* now, and was suddenly shedding her fur on a rich gentleman's seat. The delighted crowd, seeing the waltzing leopard-spots, was going absolutely wild! The whole place began bursting into applause and loud cheering. Colin's and Ivor's eyes were welling with tears of delight. And they didn't even mind when the head-waiter was placing Dora down beside them in her seat, nor when the wealthy gentleman was bringing her back her cape, then paying for a huge feast for the three.

When the girl regained her breath, when the applause was fading in the night, and when the gypsy and his women and his babies and his bear were vanishing round the corner of the street, much richer for the wear and tear, Ivor thought that he had seen it all, but he was mistaken. Dora wanted more than a twirl in the fast-lane, to-night.

"What's new with *you*, Collie?" she asked.

"He got himself a job," Ivor said.

"Oh—you too? Where? By Sweet-Knees' side?"

"In a new discothèque that's opening," Duckworth announced proudly.

"Blow me down. Knowing you, it's probably The Bitchy Bacchante," the girl said snidely.

"How do *you* know?" Colin gasped.

"Am I right?" she beamed. "I just *figured* that's where *you* might belong. Everyone knows it's going to be Athens's biggest *queer*-bar!"

"No it's not," defended Colin. "It's going to be a much-needed nightspot for *young* people."

"How'd you worm your way into *that* then?" she wondered. "Or should I use my imagination?"

"The owner hired me."

"Theatrínos?" Dora blurted. "That radical instigator?"

"How do you know about *him*?" Ivor inquired.

"Don't you read? Everybody in town knows every time that kid takes a piss. The papers and magazines are fruitcake over him! But he's a *real* weirdo. Have you *seen* that Rock Group of his?"

"I was at their concert Tuesday night."

"And he picked you *up*, I suppose?" Dora needled.

"We were allowed backstage," retorted Colin.

"Yeah, he saw you both *coming*...a mile away," the girl stated.

257

"*You* should talk," Colin at last couldn't refrain from saying. "Look how *you're* dressed. Very becoming...for a *Junior* Archaeologist."

"So what're you *doing* at The Bacchante? Rubdowns? In the Green Room?"

"Helping to get the place ready for Opening," Colin confessed. "I'm pretty handy with a hammer."

"Yeah—a *ball*-peen one, no doubt." Dora then turned on Ivor: "And what've *you* been up to, Jock? Still working for The Destroyers Of The Games?"

"Sorry—classified."

"You two really are a pair of *sorry* cases."

"Then why don't you just *sod* off, and leave us two alone?" Colin said snottily.

"No dice, Darling. I'm still hooked on what Hefferon's got between his knobby legs," she cooed naughtily and ran a hand up above one of Ivor's knees. "And I don't think even *you* can give a blowjob good enough to compete with *me*." Then again to Ivor she said: "Come on, Big Boy, why don't you drag Dora *home*?"

"I have to run," Ivor answered. "You know I do that every night."

She was feeling up his balls beneath the table. The man began to get hot, so he said: "Meet me in the Stadium, you know where."

"What time?" she asked.

"One o'clock," Hefferon replied then ordered: "Now go home, wherever that is, and change."

"Thanks. I'm *dying* to suck your *cock*," she whispered loud enough for the Student to hear. Then she left without saying another word to either of them. Colin, now horny as Hell, remained silent till Hefferon asked: "What do *you* think?"

"She's fishy," Duckworth decided. "How on Earth could she have known I was working for The Bitchy Bacchante?"

18ᵗʰ April – Tuesday – Midnight

We were stand in the moonlight. Palpably blue, illumination from a lustrous Full Moon was falling down into the Olympian Vale, like rain. We were in the roofless ruined shell of the Orthodox Monastery of Ághios Diónysos. Two angled walls of solid black pines curved for what seemed like miles above us, in a gigantic V.

We hadn't gone that far with the mules after all. Having left the viper behind, Ada soon found a path that led to the bottom of the gorge. For the rest of the day we hunted for the ancient monastery. But all that we found were walls.

Though most of the sky was blocked from our vision by the mountain, more stars than we had seen in many a night were out in dazzling array.

"I've always dreamt of spending the night here, during Holy Week...with someone I love," Ada confessed as she held me closely, "and now that dream has come true."

"That's why dreams persist," I said and kissed her forehead.

"I wonder where the shades of those who lived and worshipped within these walls are now?"

"Even if they're watching us," I answered, "would they bother you?"

"Now that I've found *you*, Ivor, I'm not afraid of anything."

We both looked upwards at that moment. A shooting-star was falling, in the direction of upstream, towards the highest peaks.

"Thank you," she said, in silent adoration of her own God or Goddess. She pulled away, and sat on a tumbled capital from the monastery's nave. She breathed deeply of the night air verdant with moisture.

"What are you thinking?" I wondered, after she was silent awhile.

"Do you remember telling me about what the General was most proud?"

"His Wall."

"With an Uppercase W."

"Futile man. Scheming to build the biggest restrainer since the Great Wall of China."

"Round his entire Olympic Nation."

"Then dividing the Nation into stone-fenced sectors, too."

Ada sighed. "Poor Athletes—segregated—no, *imprisoned*—inside a Village that they'd never be able to leave."

"Ouranós wanted to brag of creating the most impregnable Olympic Village ever conceived."

"But look at this monastery."

"Rubble."

"And previously a stone *bastion*...for the Christian God."

"Maybe the forces above, on Mount Olympos, didn't *want* this *non*-Pagan edifice to survive."

"Exactly."

Ada resumed her contemplation. After a while, she quietly said: "Sometimes Greece must seem like such a contradictory land to you."

"How do you mean?"

"My country has not, to this very day, resolved the differences between the Christian and Pagan mentalities. Sometimes—the things the Church does to Greece make me so furious I could scream!"

"Then do!"

"They'd arrest me."

"So?"

"People just would laugh and say: I told you so. I can get away with a lot more than most—but only because of my official status as

Kindler Of The Olympic Flame. I can be as *Pagan* as I need. Do you realise the horror the Church in Greece has for the naked human body? Their views are absolutely *un*-Greek! Especially when one knows a thing about The Past. But if anybody had caught us bathing nude, earlier this week, we would have made headlines everyplace! The whole *country* would have been scandalised—and not that we were making love, which is Pagan, too—but simply because the Church has a hate-campaign against the normalcy of human flesh!"

"Against that...what can anybody do?"

"We *pure* Greeks, those of us who *dare* to relate to our Pagan roots, have a love-hate relationship with our Orthodox Church. Nobody of us would ever dare to deny the immense contribution that the Church has provided, over long centuries of alien domination, and especially under the Turks. If it were not for the Church, our Greek language and culture would be dead. And to this saving of our ways, often under extreme duress, we owe our Church an eternal debt. But— to-day—when the unity of Modern Greece has been achieved, there need not be such paranoia by those who are guardians of our Faith."

"Such as?"

"By paranoia I mean that Orthodoxy is terrified of letting our Greek youths gain knowledge about the wonders of our Pagan Past."

"You're joking!"

"I most certainly am not! You should *go* to an Orthodox school! You should see *what* the Church does to inquiring minds! You should see how our young are *hungering* to know, to be *allowed* to relate to the majestic legacy of our own dynamic civilisation. Why is it that, to foreigners, so many of us Greeks *don't* seem to appreciate our own Past? Why do foreigners always know *more* about this Past than we Greeks? Do you think we'd be so ignorant if we weren't *encouraged* to be? No—we've been filled by fear to learn *anything* about pre-Christian Greece—for years. That, in a nutshell, is why even we Greeks ourselves are debating the good of having the Olympic Games back! The Olympics are the world's *greatest* Pagan Festival Of Youth, and the Orthodox Church is scared to death of the Games and their undeniably *un*-Christian influence. It didn't surprise me in the least that all this scandalous controversy came to a head, over the Olympic Games, in my own country, here on the soil that spawned them. God forbid that the Games would simply be allowed to exist, let alone to flourish. Not in *this* country! No—that would be too much to ask for from Orthodox Greece!"

I went to Ada to console her and said: "In this setting, where you obviously feel so upset, perhaps you'd feel better if you'd say a prayer for concord, to whatever deity or deities you'd choose to address."

"Yes—please let me be—for a bit."

"I'll be in the tent," I said softly and walked through the moonlit ruins of the sanctuary that had been dedicated in the name of The God Of All Gods. And I couldn't help wondering...just what puissant factor

260

of existence could create one human being, let alone one mountain as overpowering as Olympos. What did it all *mean?* Just then, one more shooting-star sparkled across the sable heavens, then the host of twinkling diamond brights above did doubly gleam.

11ᵗʰ March – Saturday – 4.30 PM

Everybody in Athens began to crave meat. Officially, the pre-Lenten weeks of Carnevale had begun the week before, but, Psychopompós explained in his sermonic tone of voice: "To-night is Meat-Eating Week Eve. That explains lots of things, including the bear," the Orthodox Priest intoned. "Silliness is in the air."

The Deputy and the Director of Communications had just finished devouring a saddle of mutton, in the Organizing Committee's garden. The Holy-Man had called it "a day of rest, in the ancient Palestinian manner". All of the invitations for the Deed Ceremony to Officials and the world's Press had gone out earlier in the week. The pair were now awaiting next week's deluge of replies.

"To-morrow," Psychopompós bragged, "from nine o'clock onwards I shall be at the National Cathedral, helping to officiate at a celebratory Mass presided over by the Patriarch of Constantinople, then attending a banquet in his honour. Therefore, you must be here till three, whence I shall return for my siesta. Is that clear?"

"Quite," Hefferon replied, obediantly.

"By the way," the bearded-one said, as he wiped the grease from his hairy lips, "it has come to our attention of late that you were recently calling on His Excellency."

"Of whom are you speaking?"

"Sir Cecil Gambling."

"He's my country's representative of Her Majesty."

"And an admirable Ambassador at that. Madame and he often exchange pleasantries," the Priest said pleasantly, then tapped his wrath. "Come on, Mister Hefferon. Do tell us *why* you refused to offer your Ambassador your idealistic anonymity?"

Funny choice of words, Ivor thought. Was he in quicksand? He'd have to say something. "I...never *refused* Sir Cecil at all. I told him that I would *consider* what he and the Ambassadress had been saying."

"That you *do* become friendly with Theatrínos? Haven't you decided that this *is* necessary?"

"To whom?"

"To your Embassy?"

"And...to *this* Organizing Committee?"

"That punk has made matters somewhat *controversial* for us, with his ceaseless negative publicity," Psychopompós stated and stood. "Let us continue this discussion with a little walk. The ancients used to promenade, after serious dialogues with Sokrates."

261

I shouldn't compare myself, Ivor heard himself saying.

Glad for a change of scenery, Ivor and his Overseer left the garden and faced "Tyre Temple". Sunset was approaching. The Orthodox Priest silently led the way through the Byzantine streets, up towards the Akropolis.

The two had just scaled the trodden stone stairs that led to the top-most road above Pláka, the one hugging the ramparts of Athena's shrine, Theorías Street, when Psychopompós paused: "This past Tuesday, Madame gave you new responsibilities, didn't she?"

"Madame invented a new *title*...for my job," Ivor said mockingly.

"Madame never merely *invents*...a thing. What we have in mind, in light of the fact that this Theatrínos character is continuing unabated his public campaign against everything that our Organizing Committee is attempting, is a valuable contribution that only the likes of *you* can provide."

"How do you mean?" Ivor asked, expecting the worst. But nothing in his wildest mind could have prepared him for what he was about to hear.

The Priest led the Olympic Gold Medallist a few yards to the right, towards the tiny Byzantine Chapel of Holy Sotiría and Paraskeví, just over the low metal fence to the left. Suddenly, atop a phallus-shaped votive post of stone perched a snow-white cat, with scary blue-white eyes. As the two approached, the beast hissed like a lizard trying to frighten a foe.

Psychopompós put his hand to his eyes, belly, right then left breasts, three times, then opened his right palm and pushed it at the animal. The gesture, one of the rudest in Greece, meant that shit was being shoved in the cat's face. He followed this with: *"Kallikántzeros!"*

"What in Hell's *that* mean?" Ivor asked, feeling strange, but thankful for the appearance of the cat, which now had vanished round the shed-sized white church.

"An *Evil* Spirit," the robed man said, with evident anxiety. "It was giving us The Evil Eye."

Giving *you*, likely, Ivor said to himself. Then his curiosity to hear what the Priest was just saying goaded him to inquire: "Do come along, then, and forget the bloody cat! What was it you were just going to say ...that I can provide?"

The Priest tried to regain his composure, but was not having an easy time. Evil, and nothing else, had turned on him now, and he was struggling for control. He aimed along the Promenade, passing the Agora's ruins below, on the right. He halted at the base of the Áreos Págos, Hill of the God of War, and said loudly: "Saint Paul preached here."

The Athlete made no reply, and waited for the Priest to say more. The Holy-Man looked as if he were wrestling with some dæmon beneath his robe. Ivor feared that the fellow might even be

262

masturbating. "The *Areopagiticus*, of your poet Milton, was named after this very spot."

"Of that I'm *quite* aware," Ivor said confidently, trying not to stare at whatever the Greek was doing inside his robes. "Now tell me...what *was* it you were just saying?"

The internal fight, in the Priest's wretched body, did not cease. All his satanic lips could say was: "I was...was just going to say...that...that you...we can offer you the chance...you can show your loyalty to our Organizing Committee...very easily."

"How?"

"By posing for us—by doing photographic publicity!"

Ivor was dumbstruck. Never had he done that to date, for anybody. Never had he yet given in to the temptation, though back home in Britain, opportunities had been legion. Psychopompós recognised quickly that again he had the upper hand, so he struck, like a venomous snake: "Don't be *shocked*, Young Idealistic Friend. Isn't this *why* you left your oh-so-civilised England? Didn't Lord Dalbeattie *send* you here, to *us*, so that you *could* demonstrate, to the whole world, that you publicly *were* taking a stand against bastardisation of your belovèd Olympic Games? Well...you should know, by now, that *our* intentions *are* as equally noble as yours. You should know; by now, that *our* interests *are* the same. Then—by lending your superb athletic frame for *our* use, by letting us print your photographic image, as the world's most speedy man—don't you see how you *will* be doing yourself, as well as us, the biggest favour you could possibly lend? Answer me! Don't you agree? Don't you *want* to demonstrate, now, once and for all, your *loyalty* to your constantly bruited Olympian Ideal?"

The Athlete's head was swimming. He was leaning on the low metal fence below the fortress of the Akropolis. How often, on this very spot, had tempters, throughout millenia, striven to desecrate a righteous Soul?

"What's your response, Olympian? Is it yes—or is it no?"

Never had the literature of the ages involved his whole intellect as much as now. Had not Faust been posed with such a question? Did not Sokrates himself, only footsteps away, battle such a query and seal his Fate with Death, else he compromise his Inner Voice?

Prom this thought, Hefferon made his mind concentrate for an instant on Professor Rembetikós. What would *he* now say? Whatever decision Ivor must now make, it would end up being the IOC Member's responsibility. The Gold Medallist turned his gaze from staring passerby, and fixed it on the Priest's face. The Professor would never condone that any of his protégés should consort with The Devil.

"You are *fully* aware of my history," Hefferon began. "I do *not* have to stand here, informing you of how my *principles* have made certain difficult decisions *necessary* for my life. You are also aware, I'm sure, that I even lost my *wife*, of late, because she, like you, wanted me to give in and do exactly what *you* now wish me to do. Can you imagine that I would be so invidiously *low*, that if I would *not* do for my very own wife just this, that now I gladly would embrace *your* Organization's base desires?"

The Priest took out a leather wallet from his vesture. "How much do you need?"

"Are you *bribing* me? You? An Orthodox *Priest*?"

"Certainly not. All models are always paid for such photography."

"I do *not* accept such duties. And you may *tell* your superiors *precisely* that!"

Hefferon and the Priest locked eyes. The bearded-one at last looked away and said: "Do you remember that Cross I tried to give you?"

"What about it?"

"I'm keeping it close to my balls," the Orthodox fellow said. "It's apotropaic."

"Whatever turns you on..." Ivor said and shook his head.

The Priest fumbled in his robes, near his crotch, and brought forth the Cross and shook it at the Athlete. "It's *Evil*-warding! Now let the *Forces* go at *you*! You don't *deserve* protection from Jesus Christ! *Now* you'll have to answer to The Arch Fallen Angel...and *soon!*"

On those nasty words, Ivor wisely held his tongue. The tormented Priest had already turned, and was making his way in haste, down the rough-bouldered path that led from the base of the Áreos Págos towards the Panathenian Way.

Curious to follow where the possessed Religious was going, Hefferon climbed the steps that had been cut from the living pink boulder of Ares' Mount, and was startled out of his wits to see none other than Dora Cain, sitting cross-legged and looking glum upon the rock. She was watching the tail-end of the sunset, facing Mount Párnis to the west. Hefferon couldn't help thinking that the whole evening had been a set-up. It was probably previously arranged that she be there after Psychopompós's offer to buy Ivor's self-respect. He almost returned whence he came, but she suddenly spun round and spotted him.

"Well, well, fancy meeting the likes of *you* here," she called vulgarly, and disrupted the whole hilltop.

"Shut up!" two Germans shouted at her.

She flipped them her middle finger, but silently sat till Hefferon was by her side. He did not sit. She rose.

"It wasn't bad last night," the female admitted.

"To-night—you're not dressed for All Hallows Eve," Ivor said as she kissed him on the cheek. She was only wearing baggy cotton trousers, in pedantic brown, a plain white blouse, with a rose-printed shawl. She looked as middle-class as she ever got.

264

"Are you horny?" she asked.

"Don't you *ever* get enough sex?" the Runner wondered, then laughed.

"Same to you! Got your briefcase, I see," and she pointed. "Top secret dossiers?"

"Nothing inside at all. They've given me nothing for homework."

"Come with Dora—*she'll* give you some."

The pair made their way back down the rock and immediately aimed rightwards into the low pine forest. It was that funny hour after dusk when it was difficult to see.

"Follow me," the American said as they were stumbling downhill. She produced a torch from her pocketbook, and switched it on. The overgrowth made visibility tricky. "Don't want to fall in any booby-traps."

"I've been *wanting* to walk through these woods," Ivor said as he dodged stumps and odd bits of stone from eras before. They were walking quite close to the twenty-foot cliff formed by the eastern edge of the Áreos Págos rise, when suddenly Dora shone her light into the mouth of a great dark cave.

"Do you want to do it here?" the fellow asked.

Dora said: "No—wait!" They turned left. Again they were in the woods, still going downhill. There was a trench to be crossed. "From an archaeological excavation," Dora announced.

"One of yours?"

"Before my time," she confessed.

It was long overgrown by weeds, in the midst of which they scared a young Greek couple, stark naked, actively performing *soixante-neuf* in the violet light. The young man grunted and continued with what he was doing to the supine girl, who never released his penis from deep within her clamp-like mouth.

"*Philotimó,*" Dora said.

"What's that?"

"Greek for 'saving face'! It also means you always should preserve your natural dignity. Especially when fucking. Especially when fucking with people *watching*! Greeks love playing games with such concepts."

"I'll say," Hefferon admitted and pushed away a sudden image of the Orthodox Priest's bearded face.

Off to the left, before the two, now was an unspoilt, untouristed, lonely field curving southeastwards, of ruins in a pasture of tall grass, of mere foundations and floors of what once stood before.

"The ancient workers' quarter," the young Archaeologist said. "Now a run for dogs. A place to walk in. To think. A basin. A toppled column. A place for lovers. Room to be lost in. Holes where prospectors have dug for gold coin. A few rough mosaics. Pines. Time."

"In another poetic mood to-night?" Ivor wondered. It was a welcomed change.

She wrapt her arms around him. "Your *body* does it to me! It makes me feel on *fire*! It makes me feel *alive*!" She held her head back and opened her mouth to be kissed. But then playing hard to get, she dashed through the grass and disrupted a flock of quail that fled towards the east. A dozen yards away she stopt by a block of stone. When Ivor caught up to her she aimed the torch on it and announced: "An ancient votive altar."

Just sitting in the open air, the carved piece of white marble never had been put in a museum, though any in the world would covet it as a cherished exhibit. Dora promptly sat upon it, in lotus position, and handed Hefferon the torch. "Walk round it," she commanded. "Look at the bas-reliefs."

The first side faced west and showed the slaughter of a goat. The animal was held by the horn, by a handsome naked youth with a lion's pelt slung over his left shoulder. The lad was gazing upwards, into the eyes of the Goddess Artemis, who was bearing aloft in her left hand a sacred bowl. Her right hand was gripping a flaming torch. Seeing it...Ivor felt shivers go up and down his whole body.

The Goddess's right breast was exposed, and when the Athlete flashed the torchlight on Dora, her right breast, too, was exposed, and she was fondling her nipple, making it erect. Hefferon grinned, then aimed the light back upon the Goddess. She was standing between two vines, each boasting gigantic grapes. To her left a second youth, semi-garbed, was holding the tail of the goat with his left hand and was brandishing aloft a great club with his right. It was just the moment before the beast would be struck dead in sacrifice.

The second side faced south, and showed a great bull. The creature was tied to an altar, awaiting slaughter. Below this was a prostrate calf. A half-clothed youth had its muzzle gripped with his left hand. The right hand was jabbing a dagger towards the poor calf's neck.

The third side faced east, and was never completed. But the sculptor had cut outlines that were plain nevertheless. It was showing a scene of eroticism, two beautiful boys, both nude, one arm of each around the other, one arm over a shoulder, one arm round a waist. It all seemed in motion, as if the lads were dancing for the third figure to their left, a satyr gaily playing the pipes and putting his left hand atop his head in sensuous musical abandon.

And lastly, the fourth side faced north. It contained three lines of classic Greek letters, badly worn and never completed. Only the last word was legible: APTEMIN.

"To Artemis, " Ivor said aloud.

"Goddess of the Hunt and of the Moon," Dora answered.

"*Pótnia Thirón,*" Hefferon said softly.

"Mistress of Beasts," the girl replied. "I, too, have read my Homer."

"And now," Ivor said and switched off the artificial light, "do your *beastly* mistressing...and let me savage your insides!" The man grabbed the woman and spread her legs akimbo, then nudged his groin up against her private parts. Even though they both were clothed, the altar was exactly the height to make love be a perfect fit. In a mad rush the Athlete yanked down the woman's trousers then his own and let his sex-organ swell with pounding blood, then into her warmth of moistened skin sacrificed the knob of his swollen manly pole.

By the Monastiráki Station, of the single mass transit line beneath Athens, Dora was saying: "It was great bumping into you like this—but I have to get some work done to-night."

"At home? Where *is* that?"

"Didn't I ever tell you? I live on the other side of Victoria Square. I'll have to have you round sometime. You know," she said but paused, "when you were deep inside me...I got to thinking about my girlfriend, Ada."

"Who's she—*another* one of your sex-partners?" Hefferon asked. It was the first time that he had heard mention of Ada's name.

"Oh—you'd *love* her. She's the girl who lights the Olympic Flame."

"The *actress* Ada? The one who's been Chief Priestess of Hera for some time? You and *she* are friends?" Ivor could hardly believe his ears.

"I *do* know a *few* interesting people! Now listen—I'm off again to Dodóna to-morrow. I'll try to catch her and arrange something for next Friday night, when I'll be back. Phone me at the Agora, at seven o'clock Friday." She gave the Gold Medallist the number. "Bye. I have to run."

When she vanished into the Station, Hefferon walked the few blocks up the open-air market of Odós Pandróssou, in a daze, recalling the day's events. He turned right at Mnisikléos, then entered the old townhouse of number twelve. Upstairs, Evtychía was practising her Chopin, the same Larghetto as always, as Ivor was crossing the catwalk. Before opening his door he banged on Colin's, but the Student was out so he started unlocking his own. Two notes were pinned upon it.

He entered his tiny musty bedroom, aghast as always that he had chosen to live there, and opened the fancier envelope. It was from Sir Cecil Gambling, and read: "We would love to have you for dinner some evening. Do ring some morning."

"I *bet* they'd have me for dinner...boiled then deep-fat fried!" the chap fumed aloud, and ripped the note to bits. He put the bits in a pocket to do away with when next he ventured out. "How'd they find out where I'm living?" Hefferon suddenly started. "Could Duckworth have told them? Maybe *Thýella*? Does the Organizing Committee even know?

Theatrinos—who sent me here?" I've got to stop *talking* to myself, the fellow said silently, opening the other envelope.

"Urgent" was its first word. "Come upstairs immediately! Evtychía."

So up he went.

The peep-hole slid open. Evtychía's *visage française* became visible. "Are you alone?" she asked.

"Yes."

"Come in." She opened the door and as usual her entrance-room was full of artistic clutter, old books, prints, strange magazines, paintings that boarders had long ago left. She was famous all over Athens for the most "interesting" collection of original "art" by unknown "artists" this side of Montmartre. She gestured for "Mister Hefferon" to enter her "salon", the next chamber to the immediate left. On doing so— Ivor did see a sight!

"Lydia!"

"Yes—*ssshhh*—it is I—I'm Evtychía's daughter."

"You're joking! Really?"

Ivor had to sit down on *that* one! Evtychía returned to her place, the piano bench. Even in her printed dress she was lost within the sixteen-foot-high by twenty-foot-long wall completed covered, every square inch, by original "art", of all shapes, sizes, and hues. And that was just *one* wall. The three others were as equally covered, and as equally colourful, too.

Evtychía's daughter was in a somewhat comfy gold-damask armchair, long past its prime. "Good God—I was just thinking about you to-night," Ivor ventured, fearing that this was another set-up. "Dora Cain told me that she had seen you lately."

"That rat—don't believe anything that liar says!" Lydia snarled as quietly as she could. "I haven't been out of this house since I was fired last Sunday."

"Then—Dora's really on *their* side? I should've known. Are you *really* a cousin to somebody who works in the Agora?"

"I was posing as such—yes. It was necessary for me, occasionally, to 'gossip' a bit in front of Dora Cain."

"Who *is* she?"

"We still don't know. That's why *you're* here—to find out."

Ivor swallowed.

Lydia continued: "Dora is the mistress of Thýella's son, Movóros."

"The Major?"

"That's right. Have you met him yet?"

"No."

"Wait till you do. He's Greece's number one Macho King. He could be a Film Star with those looks. I caught them *innumerable* times

268

—having sex—all over that building! That Cain slut thinks of nothing else."

Again Ivor swallowed.

"That's why Dora thought it was à propos for her to become my friend, so to speak, in order to try to keep 'the cleaning lady' on her side. So I pretended to go along, and made as if I *were* her gossipy buddy, whenever I happened to be in the Agora."

"Why did Thýella say you had *dirty* hands?" Ivor wondered and stared at her fingers.

Lydia laughed. "Because it's my *business* to! Up north, my husband and I own a plant nursery. I *love* gardening."

"In fact, she's a widely respected Botanist," her mother said proudly. Evtychía rose to shut the salon door, as well as that giving off to the balcony above the street.

"Listen—I am on *your* side. I've been told to tell you this to-night—in light of recent events that have befallen you."

"Told—by whom?"

"Why—by Professor Rembetikós," Lydia said.

Ivor breathed a loud sigh of relief.

"And—if you don't believe *me*—let me tell you the number that he requested I telephone," and she rattled off the very same one that Ivor used, then dialled it. When the woman on the other end answered, Lydia said: "It's Lydia. He's here. Tell him it's all right."

The telephone was passed to Hefferon, and confirmation was made. Ivor related to the woman, as well as for the benefit of Lydia and Evtychía, the whole story of to-night's development by Psychopompós, and how Ivor had flatly refused to be bribed. The woman on the other end said that she would relay this information to the Professor, and that she would try to arrange a meeting with him for to-morrow evening. Ivor was told to ring the number in the morning, before he reported to work. She told him lastly to be in a certain café in Odós Adrianoú to-morrow at four o'clock.

After hanging up, Ivor's face was glowing, as he looked upon the two women in the room. "I can't tell you what a *relief* it is—knowing at last there's somebody I can speak to about this!"

"How do you think *we* feel!" Lydia exclaimed.

"My poor daughter's sacrificed the last four months of her *life* to this Olympics cause—and, as her mother, I'll only be able to sleep at night when it's over!"

Even Lydia's "little wren" look was now different. Her face had the perspicacity of a falcon. She was well-dressed, in a smart beige suit, and better made up.

"Tell me—who *are* you then?" Ivor asked.

Lydia began her story. "I am the daughter of Evtychía and Andréas Theristákis. My father, a composer, now dead, was a distant cousin of Professor Rembetikós."

"I see."

"Andréas and I met in Paris, where I was studying," Evtychía said with pride.

"Does the Ouranós clan know you and the Professor are related?" Ivor asked Lydia.

"Even Thýella, for all her resources, wouldn't be able to find the relationship in the books."

"It goes too far back, and the Turks destroyed the records," Evtychía sadly reported, "to Antioch...before the expulsion of the Greeks in the 1920s."

"I'm sorry."

"That's history. Many things were burnt," Evtychía added, then nodded to her daughter.

Lydia continued: "From the middle of this past November, I agreed to do the Professor this favour. I gave up my previous identity, my own husband and family included, who live in Thessaloníki, and have been staying with my mother here. That's why you saw me that day. I wanted to speak with you then, but that *boy* you were with, I couldn't be sure if I could trust him."

"I have my doubts, too. The Professor's still having him checked."

"Be careful what you say," Lydia warned. "My alibi with Thýella was that I was just back from working in America, in New York's Greek neighbourhood of Astoria, as a single waitress, where I'd gone to earn money for my poor mother. I told Thýella I'd worked like a slave and saved. She loved that, and hired me as her cleaning-lady. She had me followed—for days on end—it was a living nightmare. I'm glad she fired me finally—it was torture working for her that long—I even came close to thinking I could easily *murder* her!" The little wren in the uniform had disappeared without a trace. Here was a fighter, who, Hefferon believed, *could* do whatever she said.

"But," Lydia continued, "I got exactly what I was searching for!"

"That last day I saw you—when you were in her office?" Ivor asked.

"I have here the combination number to the walk-in safe. The Professor is sure that the MOON-OC have stored enough documents in that basement to incriminate them all forever."

"I certainly hope so," Hefferon said gravely, as he accepted the combination written on a small piece of paper. "So...that's what you were doing as you were leaving?"

"Trying not to forget the damned code, yes."

"Tell me—does Iamídas ever go inside the house?"

"Her guard's instructed *never* to leave his place in the garden."

"Then—if nobody's in the building—it's possible for me to open the safe?"

"You *have* to!"

"Are there any hidden video cameras filming the interior of the house?"

"None I've ever detected."

"Have you yourself ever been in the walk-in safe?"

"I only know which door it is."

"So do I. She pointed it out to me."

Lydia snorted. "She *loves* doing that."

"How will I get beyond the first door? It looks exactly like the rest...and I *don't* have a key."

"I had one made," and Lydia handed an ordinary-looking key to the Athlete.

"How'd you manage to get *this*?"

"Thýella is scatter-brained. She's a monster, but she doesn't have all her oars in the water. Once, she stupidly had me go get a set of basement keys duplicated for Psychopompós. I went to a locksmith Mother knows. Psychopompós was standing right in the shop with me, but he's off on some evil cloud, and of course the smith had his back turned to us. I used sign language to have him make two keys at once, then I paid him for the extra set later. Whenever I cleaned in the basement hall I tried a key, and that one I gave you is the one that works."

"Did you open the door?"

"Yes—and the safe is only a yard away," Lydia said and rose. She declaimed: "Well—Mother—*my* work is done!"

"Thank God! Now—I guess you're in a hurry to get back to Lavréndi and the children," Evtychía said sadly.

"I think I should get some sleep now," Ivor volunteered, because it was evident that the mother and daughter wanted to say good-bye to each other in private. "Thank you, Lydia, so very much...for all that you've done. Your sacrifice to save the Games is nothing less than noble."

"I'll be glad to return to my family."

"Can I help you with your bags?"

"Thank you—but my husband fetched them last weekend. I just have one last case, and that I can carry myself."

"How're you getting there?"

"My husband—I'm meeting him at Kiffissiá. From here—I'm taking a taxi to Omónoia. I'm used to subterfuge by now. I just pray for *your* sake that you complete your mission *quickly*. Here—before I forget—if you need someone to talk to—dial me in Thessaloníki collect." Lydia handed the Runner one last series of numbers and shook his hand. "Give my love to the Professor, when next you see him."

"I shall."

Hefferon then descended the stairs and crossed the catwalk over the courtyard to his room. As he passed Colin's *garçoniera* he heard the rampant moaning of a young man in the throes of sexual

271

heat. The whole building was shaking, and the Athlete feared that it would tumble off its frame and collapse into the courtyard. The woman engaged with the Student was equally loud and kept saying "don't—don't stop—don't" after every breath she'd take. For a moment, Ivor was certain that the woman was Dora, but he entered his own bedroom anyway, and promptly fell sound asleep.

19ᵗʰ April – Wednesday – Noon

We had hiked three hours, from the monastery back to the road, taking our good old time. It had been beastly cold last night, but we had zipped our sleeping bags together and bundled snug as a bug in a rug.

Up ahead, a widening of the Vale was coming into sight, just as the last of the Army road was nearing. The Enippéos was like a riverlet here, dashing over a space thirty-yards wide, but most of the bed was dry. Rounded rocks and boulders from æons of spring thaws spread everywhere, as if this were a beach.

"This is Prióni," Ada announced. "It means Hand Saws."

"Funny name," I said and chuckled to myself.

"I think we should set camp here."

"But it's only noon. Don't you want to go the whole route to-day?"

"It's best not to."

"Why?"

"Because I'm tired," Ada laughed. "From here on out it's nothing but straight up. It's hard to tell, because the trees are blocking the sight."

"I've been noticing deciduous trees."

"Beech, I believe," she responded.

We came upon a mound of sand that a bulldozer had scooped from the side of the valley, at the road's dead-end. "This's where that fat guide with the mules was headed."

"What in Hell are they using *sand* for...up here?"

"I think old Óphion said that the Refuge, up there," and she pointed on high, "is adding a new wing."

"Sounds like some stately home."

"Just wait—it is!"

"Rubbish."

"I'm not joking. Leftéris has run it for years. He's turned it from a place that bedded thirty to one that soon will bed two hundred."

"What's he operating—a bloody Hilton?"

"No little enterprise. He charges admission, and the climbers buy food. Then those he takes to the top have to pay."

"Olympian capitalism—ey?"

"At its best. I've never once heard a complaint."

Ada led us across the stream to the leanto, constructed of fresh

272

timber. It was on the left side of the Enippéos. She set down her pack, and sighed with relief. "I'm much more at home by the seaside," she exclaimed.

"You're doing alright," I said comfortingly. "This height isn't exactly conducive to people's breathing."

"I bet we'll see the mules coming back. Remember they went downhill yesterday?"

"Do those poor beasts *never* rest?"

"They've got dozens they use."

"I guess supplies are constantly needed—if two hundred hungry mountain-goats have to be fed."

"Don't get nervous, Ivor."

"It's just that I'm enjoying so much...being *alone* with you."

"There won't be nearly that many in April. That's only for the peak July-August period."

"I don't think I could cope with two hundred *others* yet. Must be a flipping zoo—so many up here at once."

"They say it's quite fun."

"Any deaths—you know—falls?"

"Of course. Olympos claims quite a few. The Army sends up a helicopter, to bring the bodies back. Some people who make it to this elevation are under tremendous strain, and when they get here...they snap. There have been cases of suicide."

"And murder?"

"I guess. Even a place as eternally beautiful as *this* cannot remain at peace as long as *mankind* is around. No matter where people go, they lug their troubles with them, some beneath the sea, some up into the sky."

"Admirably said."

We held each other tightly, and listened to the warbling water's melody. Then Ada said: "But sometimes Olympos *saves* those...for whom it reserves special blessing."

12th March – Sunday – 4.00 PM

The Athlete had found the address that Rembetikós's woman had given him, number 110 Adrianoú. It had turned out to be the Kapheneíon Pholéganthros. On the way from work he had picked up from a street-vendor, along the wall above the ruins of Hadrian's Library, a second-hand book, to lose himself in, the French original of Marguerite Yourcenar's *Mémoires d'Hadrien*. He was flipping through its leaves when he stopt on page 143:

> *Je retrouvais dans ce mythe placé aux confins du monde*
> *les théories des philosophes que j'avais faites miennes:*
> *chaque homme a éternellement à choisir, au cour de sa*

273

vie brève, entre l'espoir infatigable et la sage absence
d'espérance, entre les délices de chaos et celles de la
stabilité, entre le Titan et l'Olympien. A choisir entre eux,
ou à reussir à les accorder un jour l'un à l'autre.

Ivor was reading this aloud, savouring the words of the wise Emperor. At this corner of Phléssa and the lane named after the grecophile, the reader suddenly began to be lulled by the strangest voice of any woman he had ever heard, by some music even more Oriental than the bouzoukía heard all over town. This music, coming from a speaker above the little bar, sounded as if it were from India. Out of curiosity Hefferon smiled at the young proprietor and asked him what it was.

"**Oom** Kol-**thoom**," the chap said. "She was the greatest singer of Modern Egypt."

"She's dead?"

"Sad to say—yes," the fellow responded and brought Ivor the Greek coffee he had been making.

"Sit down, would you please?"

"Thank you. My name is Tólis. My father owns this place," announced the young man pleasantly. They shook hands. "Your friend will be here shortly."

"Good," Ivor responded, but wondered *which* friend? "I'm really enjoying that music."

"Its secret is the hypnotic drum beat. No music on Earth is comparable to that of Egypt," Tólis said. He had deep black hair, a quick erotic smile, and excused himself to bring them both an ouzo. He poured the shots into their glasses of water, and they clinked. "Are you married?" he asked.

"Used to be—just got divorced," Hefferon replied. "My wife's Egyptian. She and I met in Alexandria."

"Don't you miss it?"

"I miss the music especially. I consider myself blest to have seen **Oom** Kol-**thoom** once. This music is from one of her concerts. All Egypt used to shut down, when she was known to be singing."

Just then, the incredibly gorgeous wailing of the woman, who was chanting a haunting lament of love-lost, was rising to a riotous crescendo. Men in the audience suddenly began moaning in an ever growing wave of sensual abandon. At the moment when the audience erupted into sing-song applause, Hefferon felt himself being caressed on the top of his head. "It's me. Sorry I'm late."

The Medallist spun round and was astounded to see the Singer Theatrínos. He and Tólis then embraced like long-lost brothers, kissing each other on the cheek. As quietly as possible, Ivor asked: "Okay, would somebody tell *me*—what's going on?"

"The Professor sent me," Theatrínos said pleasantly and brushed a hand through his henna hair. "Here—I'll telephone his number—it's the same one *you've* been using. He repeated the seven digits and went behind the bar. "It's Theatrínos—yes, he's here—and so is Tólis." Then to Ivor he said: "She wants to have a word with you."

The woman on the other end assured Ivor: "Yes—Theatrínos and Tólis—*both* are trustworthy. Enjoy your afternoon. When your meeting there is done, you and the Singer are to meet the Professor at six."

"Where?" Hefferon wondered.

"In Piraeus," she replied. "Take the train and wait across from the Station. Theatrínos will drive by with his motorcycle and will meet you."

"Fine. Thank you." He hung up, then smiled at the two Greek lads.

Theatrínos was leaning on Tólis's shoulder and said: "This is one of the best Folk Singers of Greece."

"Thanks, Theatrínos. That's quite a compliment—coming from none other than the best Poet-Lyricist we have to-day in this country. As for myself—I only have a select following," Tólis replied.

"He hasn't cut a record yet, but we're working on it," Theatrínos announced with pride and playfully slapt his face. "By the way...there's nobody who sings the Blues as beautifully as **Oom** Kol-**thoom**."

"I used to be one of the Professor's students," Tólis confessed and told the two to sit at the small café table, one of the dozen or so in the little bistrot. The tape had just shut itself off. Tólis then turned off all but one light, locked the doors, then put out the *Kleistón* sign.

"Well," Hefferon said with sudden pride. "Since everyone's full of surprises, so am I."

"What's up?" Theatrínos asked, as Tólis poured ouzo three times.

"This morning," Ivor stated proudly, "I got the material, from the MOON-OC's walk-in safe, that can put them all behind bars for life!"

"Smashing!" the Singer said.

"I have the Feasibility Study, the semi-annual Progress Reports, and other documents in my briefcase. Do you want to see them?"

Tólis cringed. "Not me! I know too much for my own neck already. Wait till you meet with the Professor—later this evening. He'll know what's best to do."

"I agree—keep them locked up in this," Theatrínos said and drummed a little rhythm on Ivor's briefcase.

Tólis queried: "How'd you get them?"

"Last night I spoke with Lydia, who gave me the key to the door and the combination to unlock the safe."

"I've been dying to tell you about her—why do you think Rembetikós thought I should get you a room at her mother's place?" said Theatrínos nonchalantly.

"You Greeks work in labyrinthine ways."

"But the Labyrinth was a Greek invention," Tólis stated, then raised his glass, "To the Labyrinth."

275

"To seeing the way *out!*" Hefferon replied. "So this morning there was nobody at the shop."

"They were all at the big State service at the Cathedral," Theatrínos correctly surmised.

"When Church and Government and Army align," Tólis nodded, "that's a triumvirate custom-built in Hell."

"Sad but true, for *this* hapless country," said the Rock Star.

"I was downstairs at ten," Ivor continued. "The key Lydia slipt me opened the hall-door easily. I locked it behind me and only a few feet away was the huge metal door of the safe."

"And the combination *worked?*" Tólis asked.

"Lydia never fails," Theatrínos replied. "That's *one* smart dame. She figured out the instructions, in a file in Thýella's own office—instructions were written in German!" He whistled. "It was a Swiss *bank* safe!"

"So *that's* how she did it!" Ivor gasped. "I was wondering."

"It took her *weeks* to find the instructions—then weeks more to translate it. She could only read it during the short while each day she was allowed in Thýella's office, and then only when Madame was away." Theatrínos paused. "Speaking of which—I have something to announce." And to Tólis he smirked and said: "You're going to die when you hear *this!*"

"Let it fire," Tólis commanded. "*Nothing* would surprise me anymore."

"Remember how I've always been telling everybody that I grew up on Cyprus? Well," and the Singer paused, "till now I haven't been confessing the whole story."

"You mean—you're *not* from Nikosía after all?" Tólis shouted. "You dirty bastard!"

"That's it—right on the head!"

"What?" asked Tólis, dumbfounded.

"Bastard," Theatrínos calmly said, "that's precisely what I am."

"So?" Ivor retorted. "Some of the most entertaining, and enterprising, people of history have been."

"Stop trying to butter me up," the Greek responded angrily.

"I'm not," Hefferon retorted firmly. "I, too, am a bastard son."

"No! *You?* Go on—you're an Olympic Medallist!"

"What in Hell does *that* have to do with anything?" Ivor said and paused. "My mother simply fell head over heels in love with some horny bloke who couldn't love her equally, some soldier who fucked her then forgot her. I'll tell you all about it, sometime, when I've had more to drink. Now—what about *you?*"

Theatrínos sighed. "Now I can understand perfectly...why you're fighting against bastardisation of the Olympian Ideal." The Singer shook his head sadly. "As for me, I did grow up on Aphrodite's isle. And I did grow up an orphan, that's still true. Yet I also grew up—contrary to what I've always told people and hiding what I've known—knowing *exactly* who my father is."

"He's alive?" Ivor queried.

"Too much so," the lad replied.

"Well—who in God's name *is* he then?" Tólis demanded to know.

"Hold onto your seats."

"Who?" both friends insisted.

"General Ouranós!" the chap confessed.

Ivor's mouth dropt open. Tólis began a tirade of abuse in Greek, then started dancing about his café, flailing his arms.

Theatrínos laughed at the thespian display and shrugged: "Typical Greek."

Tólis collapsed against his bar and snapt: "I *don't* believe this."

"Get used to it—it's the truth!"

"But—he's a madman!" the proprietor's son replied.

"I know! *I'm* mad, too!"

"But—you're a Singer—you sing The Truth! The Greeks *love* you! My God, if they find out whose son you are—they'll *ruin* you!"

"*Now* do you get it? *Now* do you see why I've been so publicly *against* this man, this satanic General, this *father* of mine, these past months?"

"He's *going* to get you!" Tólis screamed. "He's going to *get* you good—for your insurrection against his family name! He could easily have you murdered!"

Theatrínos laughed. "He *loves* me."

"Oh come on! That's the sickest thing I've heard to date! He *loves* you? What...he's *queer*? But wait a minute—he and that wretched bitch of a wife of his, they love *nobody*, those two! I suppose you're going to declare next that Thýella's your *mother*?" Tólis was fuming.

"No, thank God," the Singer stated and burst into a fit of laughter. "I *knew* you'd react this way."

"Well who's your *mother* then?" Ivor asked quietly.

"Some woman he raped, from Páphos."

"Is she alive?" Tólis wondered. He was just calming down.

"She died in a fire, shortly after my birth," Theatrínos said softly. "Listen—I never agreed to be legitimised by that man. The General's repeatedly tried. I ran away from Páphos many times, as a child. I ran off, finally, to a village outside of Nikosía, and went underground. I was kept in a monastery."

"So *that's* why you like the Church so much?" Tólis queried. "What'd they do, screw you to the bed at night?"

"Funny—ha ha," the Singer answered. "That's all behind me. It was quite an education, though. That's when I started singing—with the monks."

"Was this under the auspices of Psychopompós?" Ivor asked.

"No—by then the General forgot all about me. I was free, from all

277

of them, thank God. I grew up quickly, and my voice changed at age thirteen. I started at a different school, in central Nikosía this time. I was getting rebellious, and wasn't the best influence on the crotchety monks. I was also an excellent swimmer. I wanted to compete in the Olympics. I thought, there's no way in Hell I ever could do it under my *own* steam, except by surfacing, and getting General Ouranós to help me. So I borrowed some money and took the boat to Piraeus. I was just sixteen."

"Three and a half years ago? When you staggered in here? When we met?" Tólis asked.

"That's right. You put me up—remember? And you introduced me to the guys in my band," Theatrínos said affectionately and laid his arm around his friend's shoulder.

"But—*why*—why didn't you have the guts to tell me *then*?" Tólis insisted. He looked very hurt.

"Because—I was scared. I knew my old man was one of the most powerful characters in Greece—but I also wasn't sure if he'd accept me. I was a refugee—from Cyprus—you see!"

Tólis and Theatrínos gazed at each other intently. The former had tears of rejection in his eyes. "So what was going on behind the scenes?" Tólis queried but said: "As your older brother, Kid, you *could* have confided in me!"

"I *wanted* to—honestly I *did*! But it all got too sticky! I wanted to tell you it *all*—like I am right now—but the General put the screws on me! He hurt me badly! If he'd been more of a *father* and less of a *military* man...I *could* have told you everything!" Theatrínos now was almost crying. "You've been so good to me...I feel so rotten..."

"Don't," Tólis said and the two embraced. Tólis kissed him for a long time on the cheek, as Theatrínos hugged him tight. Then the two pals pulled away. "So what did he do? I hate to think..."

"Three years ago—I was hot! You remember! Bacchae rocketed to the top of the Athens pop-scene in a matter of six short months. I was giddy with excitement. It happened so quick and was beyond my wildest dreams. I guess the kids just were ready for a Heavy-Metal sound from a group of their own nationality—but who sang in English like the world's Top Stars. Remember how you told me: '*Do* it—don't stop now!' So we didn't—Bacchae became number one—and here we are—still the biggest draw in all of Greece! You *saw* what we can do—just last Tuesday!"

"It was phenomenal," said his friend. "That last number especially...what was it called...'Love's Worth Living For'? It was super—you had them dancing in the aisles and rushing the stage. I'm so very proud of you!"

"But was my *father*? Was that maniac of a *General*? No—he couldn't cope with the thought that he, a top brass in the military hierarchy, a top schemer against his own country's natural progress, had sired a Rock-N-Roll Singer—someone who struts his stuff onstage!"

"But you're successful!" Tólis interrupted. "You're making more money than you can count!"

"My goddamned manager's working out the itinerary for our first European tour—to end in London itself—imagine!"

"Surely *that* impresses even the sorry likes of him?"

"It does—it infuriates him. And he's almost had a nervous breakdown over my opening The Bitchy Bacchante, *without* his help."

"He's jealous, probably," Hefferon inserted.

"Damned right he's jealous! I've decided to invite the whole clan anyhow, to my grand-opening. Just to *flaunt* the place in their conniving faces!"

"Good for you," Tólis said.

"Did you *really* hire Colin?" Ivor couldn't resist asking.

"Who's he?" Tólis wondered.

"I'll explain him later—let me finish this first. Now—what exactly the General did to me was this: He knew I still was eager to become an Olympic swimmer. And I knew that, because of his being a Member of the IOC, I could get this country's very best training."

"But you didn't," Tólis countered. "Why?"

"The General said I could get whatever I dreamt, when it pertained to the Games, only if I played *his* game first."

"And that was..." Ivor asked.

"I get up onstage and publicly renounce my love for Rock Music, confess it's sinful, and vow to give it up forever!"

"You're joking!" Tólis said, enraged.

"He damn well did!" Theatrínos said and stood angrily. "He went further. He said he'd gladly give me his *holy* family name afterwards—as if I'd take it!—he said: 'What's the problem—choosing between the Elevated Spirit embodied in Sport, or the Denigraded Spirit embodied in Pop Music!' I almost spat in his bearded face!"

"Well—you certainly didn't go *along* with him, did you?" Ivor queried.

"I most certainly did not! I vowed, then and there, before him, out loud, that I'd show this country, some day, just what an Olympic hypocrite he really is! Now—by the Fates—I'm fortunate—since *now* I'm having my way!"

"You'll triumph," Tólis said comfortingly, "you always do."

"Is Thýella aware of this?" Ivor asked.

"Not that I know of," Theatrínos responded. "The General was too ashamed to tell her that he was my father. Why do you ask?"

"Because...the night of your concert...I was late. I'd been summoned by Thýella...to the Parthenon..."

"Her favourite place, for the dramatic encounter."

"It was. She saw you performing. I thought she'd have a nervous breakdown right between the columns."

"Wouldn't have been the first time. She treads a very fine line. Insanity is no stranger—to her. What a diabolic pair they make. The crazy arsehole Ouranós says, though, that he *loves* me!" Theatrínos blurted out and smashed his fist atop the tiny table.

"Can you blame him? In a way, you're more like the General than all his other kids combined," Tólis announced bravely.

"Now I've heard everything."

"Who *else* in the family is so goddamned reckless as you? Who *else* does the crazy things most people just daydream about? Who *else* dares to defy the General? Nobody but you! Deep inside the bloody flexors of his devilled heart, I bet he really *does* adore you!"

Ivor laughed. "Yeah, you probably give him a hardon, every time he thinks about you!"

"At least a nocturnal emission or two!" Tólis joked.

"Hardon or not...we shall see what becomes of him...after the twenty-fifth of March..."

19ᵗʰ April – Wednesday – 8.30 PM

For the first time since leaving the village we made a campfire. We'd spent a good part of the late afternoon gathering wood. And together we brought the rocks to contain the fire. The activity certainly brought back memories. Seated on the soil of this Earth, beside someone whom you loved, and staring contentedly into the glowing embers...who could ask for more?

"To-day was a truly *good* day, Ivor," Ada said and snuggled up close.

"I'm so glad you made us stay here. I think I'll be able to deal with people, up above, with a more positive attitude."

"Everybody needs to get away from it all, every once in a while."

"Indeed," I responded and kissed her cheek. "I never could just call a halt to it all...with my former wife. There never was time with her...just to relax. I was forever in training. I had to be on the road, in foreign lands, or even on foreign continents, for all those competitions."

"For your sake—it's probably better, Ivor, that you and she never had children."

"Ada..." I said softly.

"What?"

"I love you. I love you more and more each day. You're the perfect sort of woman I've been looking for. Your mere presence takes my breath away."

"You're too complimentary to me."

"It's the truth! I never could be *too* complimentary! That's a contradiction in terminology. I couldn't be any more incapable of expressing to you...how I feel. It's always been far easier for me just to take to my feet...and *run*...to run from anything and everything that ever

280

troubled me. I've never been the best...when it comes to expressing my own emotions..."

"You're doing fine."

"Only lately—because of you."

"Love is a powerful entity...that needs to grow at its very own pace."

"Then mine sprang to full flower the very instant I first set eyes upon you! Don't you think that I *have* truly tried—so very often—till my heart would break—to conjure up a love as good as this—which, pledge to me, Ada, *isn't* going to break!"

"I pledge...upon my very Soul!"

"It has *not* been my gift...from those on high...to be able to elevate, with words, my gravel-bound thoughts...towards what is reality and not just towards some vaporous dream..."

"Go on..."

"I only have been granted power...to run...a quickness that has helped me towards some of life's goals. Perhaps, after all is said and done, it has only proven that I may have a bit of worth...because, here I am...seated next to you."

"Oh Ivor..."

"And now...that Fate has led our lives to this...momentary pleasure I pray it's not. For...I don't think I can persist...without you now...you're too precious to me...I'd rather die than leave you here alone. So...in this feeble manner that I speak...I'm begging you to take me home within your heart. You *are* all my life, now, Ada...*you* have made my dreams come doubly true. Won't you...be my *wife* now? I can't *live* without you!"

She was crying.

"Oh God—don't! You mustn't!" I pled and kissed away her tears.

She tried to smile and then began to say: "To-day...this afternoon...we saw our very first eagle...flying low..."

"Yes!"

"And...secretly...last night...I prayed for this..."

"When I left you alone...inside the monastery?"

She shook her head yes. "I apologise...if my ways are often strange. I cannot alter my consciousness at this stage—which often baffles me. But I prayed hard...last night...I prayed for the Earth...for the Olympics...for Greece...for you...for me...and I prayed for a life *with* you...by my side..."

"Did you?" I said, touched to the core of my being. I began to weep. "Nobody...ever...did say...such a thing...to me..."

"That's very sad. You're such a *good* man, Ivor. You've *not* had an easy life. You've lived for an Ideal that most of mankind think dead. You've sacrificed. You've been hurt. Yet you *have* known extraordinary triumphs, in the end. There *is* a place...for the likes of you...on this Earth...yes...even in this mechanised age. And may The Forces Of The

Universe strike me down, if I *don't* choose to stand on that lofty plâteau *beside* you!"

"Then—you'll marry me?"

"Yes—yes—yes—Ivor! I'll marry you right now—right here—if you like!"

"Oh God—I don't believe it! I don't believe it!"

We both stood and embraced and let the tears flow a long, long time. Then, when our hearts were gladdened, we took each other's hand, left the campfire to its crackling self, and silently stood beside the stream. It was a night to remember, years from now, one that nobody ever could forget, one that nobody ever could take away. Indigo were the skies above, and diamond brights were pulsing now with time-travelled Light.

11ᵗʰ March – Saturday – 6.00 PM

Theatrínos was the first to leave the Kapheneíon Pholéganthros. He roared off through Pláka, on his Harley-Davidson, en route to the principal harbour of Greece. After another thick coffee, Ivor said good-bye to his new friend, Tólis, and slowly aimed for the Monastiráki Station. The proprietor's son had told him not to worry about being late.

The rickety old yellow trains, with wooden interiors and brass fixtures, truly were an anachronistic joy. Hefferon never tired of them. The ride was always an adventure, as the people invariably stared at foreigners. It had been a bit chilly, and he was glad to be wearing a suit. The briefcase certainly made him look official.

He was as nervous as a tomcat in a room full of rocking chairs. Carrying such dangerous material on his person was neither a cause of delight nor a usual experience for him.

I'll be damned happy when Ouranós and his cohorts go to gaol, he said to himself and clutched the briefcase as if it were laden with Schliemann's horde of Mycenean gold.

The train seemed to take forever, slowly inching its way to the final stop. The Piraeus terminus was not unlike Earl's Court in a way. He liked the old vaulted ceiling, and the little shops. But no time to dawdle, he was past his allotted hour, so hastened towards the front doors. It now was dark.

"Come on—Slow Poke!" Theatrínos kidded by the kerb. He was revving the machine and signing autographs for a gaggle of giggly girls. "Can't go anyplace anymore!" he complained, but it was plain that he adored the attention.

Ivor hopped on. Neither wore a helmet. The Athlete could only hold on with his right hand, as the left had the briefcase. "Where to?"

"Up the road a stretch," the Singer answered. It was a powerful machine, and certainly wasn't mute. People were gawking beneath street-lamps all along the waterfront. They headed west. With his

282

unmistakable henna-dyed hair, and notoriety to boot, the cycle was assured countless waves from pedestrians who wished that they could be hitching a ride, too.

A car of leering teenagers, with a tape-deck blaring one of Theatrínos's songs, whizzed up and began to tailgait, then to honk an outrageous horn that played a stupid tune. Theatrínos may have been used to it—and likely asked for it—and Ivor even found it somewhat fun. But the Olympian almost was left on the bonnet of the car, as the Harley suddenly thrust into high-gear.

Off they zoomed, flying down the coast, past the lights of numerous marinas, docks, pastel condominiums, and outdoor cafés. They must have ridden for a quarter of an hour.

Suddenly Theatrínos swerved left, to a deserted street that led down to the sea, past palm trees and garden walls. It was a private road, and they stopt at a private quay.

"It's a little inlet. The Professor's sister's boy keeps a boat here," the Performer said and led the way down a short flight of steps to a cement pier. At the end of this the Professor's nephew was waiting. "Pétros—this's Ivor. Ivor—Pétros," Theatrínos introduced. "You the skipper to-day?"

"Yes. Uncle Ari's below deck," said the chap. He was husky, about Ivor's age. He looked like he pumped iron.

"Sorry we're late," Ivor said.

"Don't worry."

They ducked and stept aboard, going down a small flight of stairs. She was a modest cruiser, only thirty-foot long and double-decked. Below were two spacious cabins, planked with oak, fore and aft, with a mid-section with bunks on both sides of a narrow hall, up from which rose a ladder that Pétros now was climbing. Above, the deck was open and Pétros was taking the wheel.

"She comes from France," the Professor said. He'd been quick to notice that Ivor was examining the vessel's wood. "Choicest oak. She's fifty years old."

"No!" Ivor retorted.

"She's at least thirty," laughed Rembetikós.

Theatrínos fixed some Metaxas brandy while Ivor and the Professor sat. He brought it to them. They all gathered round a wooden card table.

The Professor began: "I was at the harbour this afternoon—having lunch with an Admiral friend of mine, who's also a publisher, so I thought I'd see if Pétros could take us for a spin."

"To sneaky ideas," the Singer toasted.

They raised their glasses.

"Now," Rembetikós continued as the boat began to move, "he'll just guide her towards Aegina and back. Looks a quiet sea to-night. Let's hope so—given you both have news."

"Why don't *you* go first," Ivor said to Theatrínos.

"Fine. Ivor of course has been briefed on our relationship," Theatrínos admitted, "but even though I told him that I am a mere disciple to you, the master, as Plato was to Sokrates, I wanted to wait till now to tell him that we always don't agree."

The Professor laughed heartily. "I couldn't bear being around anybody who took me seriously *all* the time." Then to Ivor he confided: "This Pop Artist is really a *philosopher* at heart."

"So I've noticed," agreed Ivor.

"For example," Theatrínos continued, "my stand against the Games. Now let me explain to Ivor—I am definitely *not* for General Ouranós—nor his MOON group—but contrary to the Professor, I'm still not convinced that it's the wisest thing that this country *gets* the Olympics back permanently."

"Perhaps Ivor will change your mind," Rembetikós kindly said.

"Perhaps," Theatrínos allowed. "I do find him a rather inspiring figure. In fact, I began a poem about Olympos, for which he sparked the idea, the other night."

"Really?" Hefferon asked, quite amazed.

"Anyhow—I wanted to wait to inform Ivor that even before he arrived from England, you and I agreed that I would follow him."

"You...were *trailing* me?"

"For your own good, Ivor. We didn't know who else would," the Professor clarified.

"Oh. Then thank you."

"Well we now know that it was smart," Theatrínos explained to Ivor, "because you and I were spotted by one of Thýella's goons."

"Where?" Ivor asked. "In the hotel lobby?"

"No—in Hadrian Street—when I tipped you off about a place to stay with Evtychía."

"That's why Thýella contacted the British Embassy," the Professor deduced, "to see with whom you were in complicity."

"Which explains why His Excellency wanted me to go after *you*," Hefferon said and pointed to the Singer. "But by the time of your concert last week, Thýella seemed convinced that I was working alone."

"Precisely," Rembetikós concurred, "because you did your job well."

"Thank you. By the way—Sir Cecil had a note tacked to my door at Evtychía's."

"When?" inquired the Member of the IOC.

"Last night. He said he wanted to have me for dinner. Those were his exact words. I ripped up the note—but afterwards I wondered how he knew where I lived."

"I bet it's Colin!" Theatrínos snapt. "I fired him to-day."

"What's all this?" the Professor asked.

"This Duckworth, whom Ivor knows, came backstage at my

concert, snooping about, and sweet-talked me into being a DJ for my new disco. I said I'd give it a try."

"You're joking," Ivor laughed. "Nobody told me that."

"I wanted to tell you now. Anyway—I'm a pushover for plummy accents and felt a British one would give the disco class."

"But Colin's got a *middle* class accent! Absolutely bland!" objected Hefferon. "No colour whatsoever!"

"Well—I tried him out all week," the Singer said. "He was rather good. Till to-day, we got a telephone call at the office. And when the secretary asked who it was, they said: British Embassy. I was right beside my girl, who whispered to me, so I told her to transfer the call to the DJ's booth, but I would listen."

"Was it Sir Cecil?" Ivor wondered.

"Lady Louella," Theatrínos replied.

"What a trashy piece of work she is," the Athlete growled.

"Louella squawked that Colin was useless. She said he was giving them nothing for their money. It was hysterical!"

"Poor Colin," Hefferon laughed.

"Hire him back. Ivor, tell him to-night to return to the disco, that Theatrínos reconsidered," ordered the Professor.

"But..." the Singer countered.

"Do as I say! It's in our best interest to keep that Embassy shut up, till all this blows over. Louella can handle Duckworth. She'll likely have him recalled. Now Ivor—about that bribe by Psychopompós—that's the most serious issue."

"What happened?" Theatrínos asked.

"The Priest offered me money. He wants me to pose for publicity stills—as an Olympic Medallist—for the MOON."

"What did you tell him?" wondered the Singer, grinning widely.

"To get stuffed," Ivor stated.

Suddenly the boat slowed down, then stopt. Pétros was dropping anchor. They were in the middle of the bay.

"I don't blame you one damned bit," Rembetikós intoned. "He's a dirty sneak! He's as much an Orthodox Priest as *I* am!"

"Thank you. I've been worried about your reaction."

Theatrínos wondered: "Is he *really* ordained?"

"He's a king-sized *whore*, whom every *gay* Greek Priest *and* Layman has buggered silly!" retorted the Professor savagely. "If he's ordained, it's no credit to Christianity! As for your standing up to him, of course I side with you one hundred percent. You did the *right* thing! I know how strongly you feel about the subject!"

"I've withheld myself from such endorsements ever since the last Summer Games! And now that I've ended up back here, working for you, I didn't want to taint *your* reputation."

"And you have not," the International Olympic Committee man said.

285

"Wait till you hear *my* confession, though," Theatrínos said and laid an arm over Ivor's shoulder. "You might just cast me overboard!"

The Professor gazed admiringly at the two brave lads and was pleased with himself for bringing them together as friends. They both had The Devil in their eye, and the old man knew that something untoward was about to be announced.

"Got a firm grip on your seat?" inquired Theatrínos.

The Professor pulled upon his white moustache, and said: "Shoot."

"Who is my father?" the boy asked.

"I don't know...I thought you...didn't either..."

"General Ouranós," the lad whispered and looked like he'd die for shame.

"General...you don't...no...go on...wait a minute...let me look closely at that sexy face!" The Professor began chuckling, then snorting, then showing a wide toothy grin, then bursting apart at the seams. Theatrínos started heehawwing, too, as did Ivor. They all began to laugh like hyenas.

"*You're* that arsehole's *son?*" the Professor repeated a dozen times, each time dancing about and examining the fellow from a new vantage point. Then he ran to the hall and shouted up the ladder, "Pétros—get down here! Hurry! Theatrínos is Ouranós's son!"

Then down in a flash tumbled Pétros, who really began to carry on. Everybody laughed so hard till he cried. A new round was poured, on *that* note.

"Let me explain!" Theatrínos finally begged, as he hoisted his glass.

"Don't bother!" Pétros intervened. "This explains everything!"

"Tell me the gory details later—don't ruin my evening!" laughed Rembetikós. "God—I haven't heard such a good one in a century."

"Two centuries," Pétros chortled.

"Oh dear me—you've put the icing on the cake, my Lad," the Professor said and raised his glass: "To Theatrínos—Affedikó Ouranós's son—Rock-N-Roll Prince Of The Greeks!"

"It's a miracle," Pétros agreed.

Wiping tears from his eyes, Rembetikós went and embraced the boy and kissed him paternally on both cheeks and on his forehead. "Don't despair—we still love you!" And again they all broke into laughter.

"Oh my Lord—*my* story now will seem like prune juice after champagne," Ivor said, still giddy.

"I think a little of that *would* be perfect—we could all *shit* our worries away!" the Professor jested.

They all sat down. Everybody sighed.

"You Greeks are *crazy*—but I love you!" Ivor admitted, carried away with the mirth.

"How do you think we survived the Turks?" Pétros asked.

286

"Laughing as we cried," answered Theatrínos.

"Now Ivor—Good Sport—*what* can you possibly tell us!" the elder wanted to know. Without another word, Hefferon went to his briefcase, and made the proper combination to unlock it. Then, he placed it on the table and opened it up. The Professor's eyes bugged out.

"What're these?" Pétros asked.

Nobody touched.

"I didn't have time to read through them. There were four separate cartons on the floor of the safe, each filled with the various reports you see. I grabbed one from each, threw them in my briefcase, then locked it before I left the safe," Ivor explained calmly.

"The evidence! The evidence!" shouted the Professor, in absolute delight. "Oh dear God in Heaven—this has been a night!" And he started pulling out the contents, one by one. On the very top Hefferon had placed the most damaging document of all.

"The Feasibility Study!" He held it aloft, for all to see. It was a bound report, with a blue and white cover showing the flag of Greece, simply labelled with the words the Professor just said. He flipped it open. Its first page read: "Top Secret - Report On The Feasibility Of Constructing A Nuclear Military Base - Inside Mount Olympos - Beneath The Proposed Site For The Mount Olympos Olympic Nation."

The old man was shaking. He now had tears, but of Tragedy, welling in his weary eyes. He let the classified document drop. He began to weep, quietly at first, then he began to sob. "Oh dear God! Greece! My country! What has happened to you! Traitors! They're *traitors!*"

The three young men were touched to the very centre of their hearts.

"These monsters!" screamed the Professor. He stood. "Monsters! Not content to see our country try to thrive! Not content to purpose Life for Peace! Not content with anything save ignobility!"

Pétros rose and put his arms about the old man, and rocked him back and forth like a babe, "Don't worry, Uncle Ari, don't worry! We'll *win!* We'll triumph! You *know* we'll win!"

"I'm sorry," he said, and blew his nose loudly. "I'm so sorry...for the Games...for Sport...for..."

"Don't be," Theatrínos said and wiped his eyes. "I can't bear seeing you hurt by...by my shit-faced *father* like this! I'll *kill* him! I'll *kill* that man! Now I *know* I'll kill him!"

"No— you mustn't!" the Professor said angrily. At least the boy's insistence had snapt the old man out of his pain. "You mustn't. You *must* let him live!"

"Why!" screamed the General's tormented son.

"Theatrínos—we can *use* him—to work for *noble* benefit!"

"Don't you see?" Pétros intervened, and stared at the Singer. "You'll *have* your chance for revenge."

"When!" the bastard son hollered.

"Our plan, as agreed, *must* proceed," asserted Rembetikós. He blew his nose again, wiped his eyes, then slowly returned to his former place. Pétros poured more drinks.

"The Progress Reports," announced the Professor, now almost composed, "date to a year ago February, then last August, then this past February—just a couple weeks ago." Each Progess Report was about a hundred pages long. All were bound in red.

"The Third Report," Ivor stated, "Is what you're looking for."

"Why's that?" the IOC man wondered.

"It's a series of Xerox-reduction blueprints of the Mount Olympos site...underground."

"My God," Pétros said for everyone.

"And on the bottom of the briefcase are three pieces of correspondence that I took," Hefferon admitted.

"Why only three?" Theatrínos inquired.

"I didn't want to get caught—plus—these three say more than enough."

The Professor held aloft the letters and noticed: "They aren't addressed to anyone, except to a code."

"Which is?" Pétros asked.

"MT hyphen O," Ivor stated.

"Look here," Rembetikós read: "It's dated 3rd November, two years ago, and says that a West German NATO General expresses 'optimism' that Greece will receive NATO go-ahead to construct a nuclear defence centre and missile silo inside Stávros Hill of Mount Olympos, near Litóchoron Army Base. This is of strategic importance for European defence."

"The next one's from the CIA," Ivor announced. "I only took the top letter, from each of the NATO, CIA, and Bank files. In other words, correspondence for this whole surreptitious scheme started only two autumns ago."

Rembetikós shook his head, but read from the CIA letter: "Dated 15th November, that same year, the CIA confirms funding for 'MT-O Proposal' and requests setting up an account with the Bank of Lausanne. It's from the Director's Office!"

"Of the CIA?" Theatrínos and Pétros asked simultaneously.

"It continues...that this decision was the result of weeks of deliberation on the Feasibility Study, and mentions a meeting between Ouranós and a CIA Director's Aide in Madrid, during a Mediterranean defence meeting held on the 31st of October."

"The monsters," was all Pétros could say.

Theatrínos was speechless.

"The third letter dates to the 27th of that same November," Rembetikós said.

"Must have been a jolly time for Thýella. She likely threatened her private secretary with drawing and quartering," Theatrínos blurted.

"Carry on," Pétros begged.

"At least the rack," added the Singer.

"I'll be getting the Iron Maiden," Hefferon cut in.

"For sure," the Professor intervened. "This one's from the Bank of Lausanne, as per a visit by Madame Ouranoú..."

"I told you!" the Singer interjected.

"...setting up an External Account...opened in *her* name!" the Professor could barely contain himself. "Why that two-faced hooker of a dead rapist's slut! Imagine—in her *own* name!"

Pétros begged: "Please carry *on!*"

"It says: With facility to move monies in and out, under whatever currency she chooses, and the first deposit..."

"How much?" Theatrínos inquired for everyone.

"One million Swiss Francs," the old man said and sighed.

Everybody was silent, on the mention of the sum. Pétros felt it best to start the engine, so left the three below. He ascended the ladder. The engine turned over. The vessel began to move. Aristídis Rembetikós sighed. "I was going to wait for Interpol to ring me to-morrow, but I have a feeling I shall be ringing them to-night."

"Looks like you've got some homework to do," Theatrínos essayed.

"Ivor," the Professor said, "should I contact Interpol, I shall let you know by ringing Evtychía's. I have a feeling that these documents will send them all to the clink for many years to come."

"The international repercussions, the scandals that this will cause, are what now worry me," Ivor stated.

After sitting with his head in his hands for a few minutes, the Professor exhaled deeply and offered: "Let's all get some fresh air."

"We can use it," the Singer said, as Aristídis messed his hair.

Ivor led the way and the three climbed to the deck. The harbour lights of the great Piraean Bay, with its dozens of coves and hundreds of busy quays, sparkled magnificently in the placid black water of the sea.

"Of a clear night, next month, you'll be able to see the Parthenon...illuminated brilliantly," Pétros said sadly.

The Melancholy, of the meeting below, was now meandering through their bloodveins, migrating to their very Souls. But the Beauty before them...Mountain...Sea...Sky...Night...and more ships than a sailor ever could count...was a drug that was appeasing.

Ivor suddenly recalled that Dora Cain had said that she wanted to introduce him to the actress who lit the Sacred Flame. He took a deep breath, then told the Professor.

"Ada?" the old man asked. "Why yes—we know her well—don't we, Theatrínos?"

"What brings *her* up?" wondered the Singer.

"Dora Cain says she's her girlfriend. She told me last night she wants me to meet her."

289

"If you do—I bet you'll fall head over heels for her," the Professor smiled.

"All men do!" Pétros agreed. "She's gorgeous."

"What in Greek we call *Gómena*," added the Singer. "*And*...she's got brains."

"More than her share, Pétros said enviously. "I've tried to go out with her *hundreds* of times!"

"She knows you'd squash her!" Rembetikós joked. "Don't worry she doesn't *really* like Dora anymore than *Lydia* did."

"By the way, did Interpol get you any news on Dora or Colin?" Hefferon wondered.

"They said they'd ring me to-morrow," the man repeated.

"Oh that's right—to-day's Sunday. This screwy schedule of the MOON has really bollocksed me up!"

"Don't worry—once the Chief Priestess of Hera gets her hands on you," the Member of the IOC laughed, "she'll set you straight."

"I'll strike a bargain with you," the Athlete said to the elder. "For getting you these documents...will you put in a good word for me...to this Ada?"

"I think that can be arranged," the Professor said and chuckled.

20th April – Maundy Thursday – 7.25 AM

"I just had a powerful dream," Ada began as she bolted awake. "I just saw Dora Cain in my sleep, coming, at the both of us, with two bloody butcher knives upraised, bursting in on the church service for our wedding. This monstrous vision, this attacker, was rushing up the aisle, screaming curses at our happiness. I turned in my bridal gown, and invoked the Archangel Michael to come to our aid. Then the church split in two, by our feet, and Saint Michael was rising through the floor. He blinded the attacker with cerulean light, then sliced her apart, right down the middle, with his sword."

I held Ada close and rocked her. "Then it was a *good* dream. Evil was vanquished."

"Dreams are prophecy," Ada whispered, "to those who can perceive."

"You're a very gifted lady," I said comfortingly.

"This paranormal gift *scares* me, Ivor!"

"I know."

"I love you so very much. I don't want anything to intervene against our unity."

"It won't," I said. "The dream predicts this. You've *already* beaten Dora."

"Have I? You made love to her."

"I never made *love* to her—it was only sex."

"She doesn't know what love *is*."

"*None* of those we've fought have seemed to know."

"I was *forced* to know Dora...because the Professor thought it would serve the cause."

"It did."

"Did it?"

"Who *else* discovered Dora's identity? Nobody else but *you* would have conceived of the idea to *hypnotise* the girl."

"She was drunk."

"You were lucky."

"She wanted me to have *sex* with her!"

"That same night—after *I* had sex with her—on the altar of Artemis?"

"That same night! She told you she'd try to contact me and she did. I knew from Rembetikós that things were coming to a head. Of course, you and I hadn't had yet met."

"Thank God we did."

"I knew who you were, of course, before you ever left England for Greece. I'd watched you on television...when you won at the last Summer Games. And of course, I saw you light the Cauldron at Lake Placid, which was beamed to Europe from the States. When Rembetikós told me that you'd be coming to Athens—I knew inside that we'd *have* to meet. I kept pestering the poor Professor to arrange it—but he kept telling me not to rush things—because you had more than enough on your plate. When I heard—from Dora herself—that *she* had met you first—and of course she bragged that you two had had intercourse in the Stadium that very first night she met you—I was *insane* with jealousy! Hearing her describe your body, I wanted you all the more!"

"But you acted so cool at first."

"I was scared—scared I'd lose you, if I came on too strong, like *that* little whore!" Ada said passionately, then paused. "Then, when Rembetikós told me that you had been taunted by that hypocritical Priest, my mind started working triple-time, and I became *determined* to punish that bitch with some of her *own* medicine. She'd been playing up to me, for months, as it was public knowledge that the Professor and I were in league. She got to know me under the pretext of trying to worm her way into the young intellectual circles of the capital. She knew that I had many powerful friends. I had been pretending to her that I had this secret love. When she had me visit her flat that evening, by Victoria Square, we started talking about men, her favourite subject, and she persisted and persisted that I tell her about *my* secret man."

"You never told *me* about him!"

"He didn't exist! So—I made sure that Dora was good and drunk on Scotch, which she preferred, and told her I *would* have sex with her if she would just relax."

"Oh—here it comes."

"Exactly. She was boozy already, in an altered state of mind, so it was a cinch to hypnotise her, in fact, it couldn't have been easier. She was flat on her bed. I began to talk to her in her hypnotic trance. We both were *clothed*, thank you."

"And that's when you got it out of her about her *past*?"

"Yes. I asked her if her name was Dora Cain, and she said yes. I said, were you raised by people named Cain, and she said yes. I said, was your father's name Cain, and she said no, it was Clinton. I said, what was Clinton's christian-name, and she said Orville. I wondered if she was raised in Texas as she told us, and she said yes, in Galveston with the Cains but that Orville Clinton lived in Houston."

"But the part that knocked me flat was your *next* series of questions."

"I asked if she was related to the Cains, and she replied that she was. I wondered how, and she told me that they were her paternal grandparents, that her father's mother had remarried. I asked her why she hadn't been raised by her parents, and she said her father wished it that way. I said, what about your *mother*, and she said that her mother had left her with the Cains."

"Then you said she had to be regressed deeper into the trance?"

"Her eyelids were closed but were fluttering. I felt she'd awaken before I could finish."

"Why didn't the Professor tell me about this on the boat?"

"Because—you already had more than your share to cope with. This was a team-effort. Each of us had something to do. He also wanted to plow through all those documents you gave him that evening. I'd spoken with him that very morning, since I'd only just hypnotised Dora the previous night. I guess he wanted to align my report with your documentation, before he said anything more to you."

"So—you put Dora further into trance?"

"It wasn't easy, either. Her psyche knew it was being investigated, and recoiled. Getting her into the first stage of hypnotic trance wasn't difficult, but a deeper delve was almost beyond my means. She was a case of Pure Evil! It was almost like performing an exorcism. I had to invoke Powers Of Darkness to appease her. If I had called on *God*, she would have snapt out of it instantly. Secretly, in my mind, though, I shrouded myself by protection from Saint Michael." Ada paused. "At last the horrid creature was under control—and I worked my way, gradually, to the crucial question. I said, did your father not want you, and she answered no. I said, why was this, and she said the word *shame*. I wondered about this, and she answered that the family was very rich. I said, how did the family explain your existence, and she said that her father's sister just had been killed in an automobile accident in San Antonio, that the Cain family had adopted Dora in their daughter's memory, and that all of the people of Galveston society had thought that this was a very virtuous thing to have done. I said, Dora, you are now digging in the ruins of ancient Dodóna, and she said yes. I asked, what was Dodóna famous for, and she replied that it was an oracle that existed in order to speak with the dead. I said, is your *mother* dead, and she no. I asked, does your mother live in Galveston, and she said no. I asked, does your mother live in Houston, and she said no. I asked, does your mother live in America, and she said that she used to. I asked where, and she replied, Washington. I wondered if her father had met her mother in Washington, and she said yes. I wanted to know if her parents were married, and she replied no."

"Then did she try to break out of the trance?"

"Yes. I began speaking to her in the voice of the Oracle of Dodóna. I told her, I am Dodóna and you have come to speak with me. Do not be afraid! I also speak with the Living. What is it you wish to know? And Dora paused but said: My mother. And I said: I am the Mother of the Dead—tell me the name of the woman who bore you. And she replied: Thýella!"

"Then she woke up?"

"She sprang from bed—like a cat—and pounced on me!"

"You never told me that!"

"I didn't want to worry you!"

"Worry me—my God—she could have *killed* you!"

"I shouted: Dora—what's come over you—by The Power Of Christ Jesus—get *off* me! She looked wild-eyed—like a dæmon was in her Soul—and screamed: *Dodóna—Dodóna! You've led me to The Gateway To The Dead!* I shouted back: *You're* the one who's digging there! You've fallen asleep! You must have had a nightmare!"

"And that calmed her down?"

"She shook her head and I had to keep repeating that she'd fallen asleep and had been dreaming. At last...she did calm down...yes."

"My God. Dora...Thýella's *daughter!*"

"When I reported to the Professor what she'd told me under hypnosis, he compared that to references in the Progress Reports you'd given him."

"Architectonics, Inc., based in Houston, was documented as being the design and engineering firm to build the Olympic Nation."

"And the nuclear site," Ada said.

"As opposed to the lie of the General, that a brilliant young architect from Crete was doing the job."

"That proved, once and for all, that the intelligence was coming from America," stated Ada.

"With funds being laundered by the CIA and NATO."

"A satanic scenario."

I agreed: "Too bad it didn't succeed."

"The ultimate punch-line occurred when the daughter—whom Orville Clinton sired on Thýella, when she was working for the Greek Embassy in Washington—attempted to reunite with her mother, who long ago had returned to Greece," Ada said. "Imagine in the 1950s—a

293

Cultural Attaché, whose previous assignment had been Warsaw, getting pregnant in Washington by a professional lobbyist to Congress for the construction trade! This was the McCarthy period, remember. And Clinton was friends with people like Richard Nixon. Nevertheless, Thýella flaunted her belly as if she didn't even care, and traipsed off to Houston for 'sabbatical', chasing after Clinton to beat the band, which was when the illegitimate daughter was born."

"Years later, in Greece, Thýella got Dora in her *clutches* all right—and gave good ole Orville Clinton a run for his money."

"It's coincidental that it was so easy for Interpol to trace Architectonics, Inc.?"

"The name just existed on paper, as a tax shelter for Clinton Enterprises."

"You think that they could have been a little more devious."

"Ada—these people never *dreamt* that they had the slightest chance of getting caught."

"Their delusions went far beyond the plane of the merely psychotic."

17th March – Friday – 5.15 PM

Metamorphosis, believe it or not, is an actual neighbourhood of Athens. It is not found in a single guide book. To get there, one must board a city-bus from Monastiráki Square, and travel a few miles east, beyond Pangráti, to a slope of Mount Imitós, on the end of the mountain nearing the harbour.

Ivor and Dora rode out together. It had been pre-arranged between Ada and the American girl that they would get together with the Athlete this Friday. Ada was going to introduce Dora, at long last, to her secret lover. Unbeknownst to the woman from Galveston, Interpol had confirmed this week that pieces of the puzzle, as one assumed, did fit neatly. Interpol had informed the Member of the International Olympic Committee that Dora Cain's father, Orville Clinton, did own Architectonics, Inc., and that he had made the Cultural Attaché of Greece pregnant in Washington, D.C. Nor was Dora aware, to anyone's knowledge, that she was walking into a trap, by agreeing to go to Metamorphosis this very evening.

"Been up to your eyeballs in Olympian schemes?" she had asked Ivor en route.

"I've been so busy I haven't been able to think. How about you—has it been raining at Dodóna?"

"The weather was great for a change."

"Find any buried treasure?"

"We're still at the beginning stage. We're working on a new site. It's painstaking."

"So is what *I'm* doing. But I do think we've finally got all the invitations processed for next week's Deed Ceremony at Olympia."

"Charming. All those crazy suckers littering up the old Olympia Stadium—should be a great big bore!"

"Don't worry, Dora, *you* won't be invited," Hefferon countered, although he figured that she likely *would* be there, as Major Movóros's mistress.

The bus at last stopt at their destination.

"I daresay this is Metamorphosis," the Athlete exclaimed and stood.

Dora added as they got out: "You can say that again."

After the bus pulled away, they noticed a beautiful dark-haired woman on the opposite side of the road. She was leaning against a two-storey light-blue stucco house.

"Good Lord—my—she *is* gorgeous," the fellow said, just to annoy his so-called date.

"Yeah? Well keep your clammy mitts *off* her. She's engaged," Dora lied.

"Hello," waved the pretty Greek woman, whose lovely features lit up all the more as she witnessed the famous Runner's approach. Upon introduction, she only offered him her hand, rather coldly.

Ada had her hair up, accentuating all the more her delicate features. She was dressed in tight designer jeans, and a soft suede jacket cinnamon brown. Ivor couldn't take his eyes off her, but let the two girls talk as was their wont. Yet he did note the scorn with which Ada had appraised Dora's looks. The poor American just didn't have a clue how to dress. To-night she was wearing what looked like a 1950s-style "prom dress", right out of some *Leave It To Beaver* TV episode.

"Don't you love it?" asked Miss Cain, who obviously thought that she looked rather sexy.

Ivor smirked, embarrassed to be seen with her. The questionable apparel was sick-pink and satin of sorts. It had bows all down the front, back, and sides. Atop her little red curls she had stuck a gauche maroon pill-box hat. She affronted what dignity she had by adding cream-hued kid-gloves. Her lips were done like chocolate-covered cherries, since a dark liner ran round a bright glossy inside.

"Aren't you cold?" Ada asked her tartly.

"We won't be outdoors, I hope," the Archaeologist replied and took the Actress's arm.

Hoping to get the mission over quickly as possible, Ada scuttled the party six blocks through the working-class quarter, past endless little pastel houses in stucco, cement, or orange stone. All of them had families on the front porch, watching their blocks like hawks. All of them snickered to themselves and gossiped loudly as Dora Cain passed by.

"Where're we headed?" the American asked.

"Just keep walking," Ada replied and turned to the right.

Suddenly, great orange cliffs were looming ahead, which in the fading light looked black. Ada aimed directly towards them.

"Metamorphosis huh—well I *do* believe it!" Dora snapt. "You don't expect my heels to scale *that*?"

Ada began climbing anyhow, much to Ivor's delight. Indeed, there *was* a strangeness in the air. Ada switched on the torch that she had in her hand. It had a handle and was powerful enough for military reconnaissance. Plus, she knew how to use it. Up the rise a bit, she flashed it, on bulky black and orange cement-mixer lorries. Up another path, Hefferon suddenly noticed that the towering cliffs beyond weren't really cliffs at all, but were cut sides of a man-made quarry. It suddenly didn't look so large, but he had to admit that a quite sizeable amount of the mountain had been scooped away. Ada said nothing at all about this. Everybody felt on edge.

"Come along the ridge," at last she stated. "We'll go higher," and down into the quarry she beamed light on shells of buildings, concrete, and with great rammed-through holes, as if the whole site had been an A-Bomb test-centre no longer in use—radioactive—this once-proud foothill of Imitós.

"Higher yet."

They went higher—up the windswept footpath. No trees—just scrub and few miniature dandelions caught light. Dead butterfly. Lot of litter. Rotting jersey. Used condom—tied at the opening—retaining its yellowing sperm. Kleenex. Scraps of metal, of wood. All suddenly glimpsed in the night.

Not having fully seen the quarry's dimensions (somehow both Dora and Ivor were convinced it was small, by some petrine trick of the eye), both were startled to hear little children's voices—voices at game—way distant—now visibly distant—a kilometre removed—on the quarry's flattened floor. Way against its monstrous man-made orange cliff—tiny tiny microscopic forms—colours, teams, miniature human beings—were playing soccer—were running fro and to. Their playing field was set aglow at the four corners by colossal bonfires throwing fulsome golden light into the whole quarry's mighty bowl.

Inside some shadow down there, some man suddenly started a cement-mixer up. Somewhere, a gruesome orange-black drum was revolving wet cargo. Somewhere, the man was beating the machine with some huge stick. Deep-throated rumblings echoed throughout the titanic site—which now seemed the size of Grand Canyon to everyone's eyes. The kids—mere specks of bright dashing yellows—oranges—blues—which occasionally squealed—were smaller than ants. The valley floor they gamed upon was pure white. Tremendous piles of white boulders fell in bizarre patterns all across the canyon floor, crawled up to the children, whose four flickering bonfires cast the eeriest shadows.

Ada suddenly shone her light upwards, a hundred yards away, past a pile of black stones. Overlooking the whole quarry two wreckt cars, one black, one grey, leant precariously at the slope's edge, as if ready to jump to their death.

"Who in Hell *lives* up here!" Dora at last demanded.

Ada didn't answer, but led yet higher, towards the junk cars. Behind them, in her torchlight, rusty shells of rear-ends of old transport lorries tilted thither and hither amidst debris of motors, appliances, barrels, lumber, scrap. Ivor turned to look at what they had just left behind them—Athens—just a white bumpy electrified sprawl—two bumps more pronounced than the rest. In its epicentre, an almost unidentifiable Parthenon poked above a welter of roofs and antennas. To its right, a nipple-shaped Mount Lykavitós let most-chic Kolonáki traipse down its rocky teat. In the other direction, a beclouded three-quartered Moon groggily hung over Piraeus and the Mediterranean Sea, just some sailor, soused on too much ouzo.

"This junkyard—it's my boyfriend's," Ada said matter of factly. She pointed further upwards: "His house—just over there."

"Hurry up, I'm starving," the vulgar American said.

Fifteen yards ahead was the house. Its one-storey sky-blue modesty was hedged by a jerrybuilt wall a couple feet high, of small orange quarry stones, terracotta fragments, a great heap of sawn wood.

"You don't expect me to highjump *that*—I'll split my goddamned dress!" Dora complained.

Ada answered: "I should've told you we weren't going to some varsity sock-hop!" Then she flashed the torch downslope a few metres, to a twin-pylon electricity receiver, a two-poled perfect representation of an alpine tree.

"No *true* tree would do this place *justice!*" Dora snapt, as she was assisted by Ivor and Ada over the wall and inside a small garden. Then Ada aggravated Dora even further by pointing out a fig tree, a peach tree, a rotting wood trellis with one grapevine, and a few oil tins filled with dirt and sporting a flower or two, set upon cinder blocks.

"Charming," Dora blurted. "Now let's get our asses *in.*"

The place's complete disregard for convention, not to mention its location, amused the Athlete greatly.

The American said: "Wipe that giddy shit-eating grin off your face, before I *slap* it off!"

Ada then knocked and entered the kitchen. Clutter was everywhere. Covered pots, a loud quartet of them, were heating atop an old stove. "We're here!"

"Where's the host?" Dora wondered, suddenly thinking of a garish scene from Edward Albee's play, *Who's Afraid of Virginia Woolf?*. "Shit—I've worked me up *some* thirst—hitchhiking clear across the whole Vale of Attika!"

"Hello!" Ada yelled again.

Water was running.

"Scrubbing his armpits," Dora surmised. "Hope they're cleaner than *this* greasy-spoon."

"They are," Ada vowed and sat by the kitchen table. The main sitting-room, if that's what it could be called, was visible a few steps down. Likewise, it was a jumble of odd-bits.

Suddenly, from the bathroom on the other side of the house, came the place's owner, a young man, head in a towel, freshly showered, stark naked. Of course, the whole evening had been planned in advance all week, between Ada and Ivor and the host. He had a hairy chest, of black short curls, definitely sexy. His body was fabulous, lean, supple.

"Good grief—he doesn't have on any clothes!" Dora screeched and covered her eyes with her hands.

"Oh that's all right, Dora," Ada said nonchalantly, with perfect acting ability, as if the scene had been rehearsed. "I see him like that *all* the time. In fact, we're all going to be *eating* in the nude."

"What!" Dora uncovered her eyes and stared, evidently titillated beyond control, right to the tips of her titties: "For Cripe's Sake but— ain't that *Theatrínos*? *He's* your boyfriend? This Rock Singer?"

The owner of the house, minus the towel now, was standing beside his guests, perfectly handsome as God had made him, except for the dye-job, saying: "Pleased to make your acquaintance."

Ivor was pretending he was shocked, as he shook the Performer's hand for the "first" time.

Dora was so dumbfounded that the ruse had pulled the wool right over her eyes. She simply said: "Dora Cain."

Ada was disrobing already. "Well—what're you *chickens* waiting for—*Christmas*?" Then to Theatrínos she said: "I don't think these foreigners ever heard of this—but you know—to-day's the first day of Carnevale Weekend."

"Guess I forgot," Dora managed, as she gawked at Ada's luscious breasts, just revealed. She then kicked off her shoes and poked Ivor, saying: "Well—when in Greece, get *Greased!*"

"Thank God the office's closed till Tuesday," Ivor said, looked "aghast", and inquired: "Just what *is* this Friday supposed to be?"

"It's *Free* Friday—when *nobody* wears any clothing—an ancient Pagan custom here in Greece—when *everybody* has sex—even kids!" Theatrínos said with a very blasé expression.

Ivor almost burst out laughing. He knew what was going on, but couldn't say a word other than: "Oh—I see. Well, I'll just pretend we're in some locker-room." And he began taking off his shoes, socks, corduroy jeans.

"Bet you've seen, or experienced, *plenty* of sex, in a locker-room or two in your *heyday!*" Dora ejaculated wickedly.

"I think she's trying to say that all Athletes are *queer!*" the host remarked.

"Well, you can't stand there and tell me that, once all the rest of the team clears out of those locker-rooms, a couple of horny guys don't start feeling each other up inside those showers!" Dora replied.

"We know *you'd* start a feel-up!" Ada answered, and grinned.

"Damned straight I would!" responded the American, thinking back on a few similar situations in Texas. "Hope you guys keep the heat turned on," Dora added. "Can we wear our cigarettes?"

"Sure," Ada said, now completely naked.

Ivor was certainly aroused mentally, but had to play dumb. But, he couldn't help noticing that the Actress was a truly magnificent sight.

Dora was getting a rather trashy looking six-inch plastic lighter from her purse, and offering everyone a cigarette. Theatrínos accepted and she lit it.

"Kinky lighter," the Singer remarked, and ran a finger up and down the phallus-shaped soft purple object with LAS VEGAS spelt on it in rhinestones. "Hot flame," he said and flinched as a blowtorch of heat, hefty enough to weld an I-beam, almost scorched his baby-face.

"It's soft—but it does the trick," Dora laughed.

"*Isn't* she fun?" Ada asked her supposèd boyfriend. "Is dinner ready?"

"Ready? *She* comes equipped with dildo in hand!" Ivor chuckled.

"How *'bout* my drink? If we're gonna *screw*—you better start loosening me up," Dora announced then began laughing. "Free Friday— I never—in my whole life!"

"Sit yourself down in the den, and I'll bring you something to loosen the sphincter of a constipated nun," Theatrínos said and scratched his groin.

"Don't you have holidays like this in *Texas*?" the Actress asked candidly.

"Only in brothels!" Dora roared then hopped on a sofa crammed with pillows and pop magazines.

Theatrínos brought a bottle of Stolichnaya and poured everybody a large glass. "Neat—or *with* something?"

"Got no orange juice?" the American asked.

"Lime juice—that okay?" Theatrínos replied.

"I'd love some of that," Ivor remarked from an easy chair. He spread his legs apart wide, played with himself a little, then threw a thigh over the chair's arm. He was beginning to act less "nervous", that is, was getting into the act.

"I'll have some, too," Ada agreed.

"Hey—Singer—put on some of that *Blues* of yours," Dora ordered. She was beginning to make herself right to home. It didn't take her long, to take right over. If she had been shocked at first, to discover that she was in the house of one of the leading agitators against her mother, Thýella, she wasn't about to give a thing away.

Ivor was wondering what was going on in her devious mind. He suddenly got a chill down his spine when he realised that, in fact, Dora and Theatrínos were almost siblings, that she was his step-sister. Theatrínos was aware of this, but every indication was that Dora was not. Trying not to think about this, Ivor said: "I've heard some of your music myself. I'm very pleased to meet you."

"The pleasure's mine," the henna-haired Athenian smiled and poured Rose's Lime Juice in everybody's drink. He passed the glasses round. "To Free Friday," he said.

Everybody chanted: "To Free Friday!"

Music was put on with a tape. Powerful speakers jarred the rafters of the house. "It's my new LP—not yet released. The cuts come from Bacchae's concert last week in the Odíon."

"You recorded live?' Dora inquired, nosy as ever.

"The whole thing," Theatrínos said with pride. "The best part's the raunchy dialogue with the audience, which we're leaving in. It was videotaped, for broadcast all over Europe next month."

"I hear your group is considered *dangerous*," Dora said playfully, and poked Ada, also on the couch.

"They're very political—typical Greeks!" Ada allowed.

"I hear you really stir people *up*," Dora continued.

"So do you—when you merely walk down the street," Ivor joked.

"You beast! I mean—people really get carried *away* at Bacchae concerts, don't they?"

"Some girls even wet their frilly knickers," Theatrínos teased.

"Aren't you one of the city's big *agitators*—I mean—don't you get up and say things like...for example...*against* the idea Greece gets the Olympics back!" Dora said provocatively, then shot a glance at Ivor.

"Of course," the Singer agreed. "It's The Artist's Number One Obligation...not only to speak out about The Truth...but also to guide people away from those who would corrupt it...so that *all* traducers may be *defeated* in the end! That's my Manifesto! That's Bacchae's Manifesto! Listen to the tape."

"Well—*he's* working for the Mount Olympos Olympic Nation Organizing Committee!" Dora said defiantly and pointed at Ivor.

"Look—to-night's *Free* Friday—ok! Everybody can do *whatever* he or she likes," the host said. "Don't you know that *anything* goes... during Carnevale?"

"I just thought you'd like to know you had an *enemy* in your house," Dora remarked and sipped her drink.

"You Americans can be so *tacky!*" Ada retorted.

"Colonists," Ivor agreed.

"Oh don't start that stiff-lipped crap with me, Kiddo," Dora said hotly.

"They never *can* take a joke," the Briton added.

"You goddamned British haven't been able to take a fucking

joke since 1776," the Yank responded. Then she turned sweet, and asked the host: "What's for chow, Greek God? Ambrosia?"

"How'd you guess? You eat shrimp?"

"Does...she...eat...shrimp! Did she grow up on the *beach!*" bellowed the Texan. "Where's Galveston, facing Nebraska *wheat!*"

"I thought she was raised in a *barn*," Ivor joked.

"Even *that* wouldn't have prepared me for the animals *to-night!*" Dora retorted. "Free Friday—well—when do we get *on* with it?"

"Have you had enough to drink?" Ada asked seriously.

"Huh? You gotta be joshing. She's pulling my stump, isn't she?"

"No, Dora, it's you who pulls *my* stump!" Theatrínos kicked in with glee.

"Who says? I'm *allergic* to redheads!" Dora announced and ran her hand through her own hair. "I never *could* tolerate sleeping with myself."

"A truer line won't ever be said to-night," Ivor stated. "Let's drink to that!"

"Ain't he a pig!" Dora poked Ada to agree.

"I think he's adorable. I think I'll go *get* him!" Ada remarked and stood. She strutted right across a handmade provincial rug and sat down on Ivor's lap, which was what the Athlete had been praying for all along. Then—playfully—she waved back at Dora who was visibly irate, but trying hard to hide it.

"Well, in that case," and the American reached for her naughty lighter and began flicking its wick and shooting foot-long flames at everyone, "I'll have to burn you all up." She began crooking her index finger the host's way, enticing him to sit on the couch.

"Sorry Luv—I smell your meat burning," and Theatrínos rose from his chair and ascended to the kitchen.

Dora followed him, armed with her dildo and cigarettes, and sat by the kitchen table. "You're well hung," she observed and sent a burst of fire towards his crotch. "Ever think of dying that black pubic hair henna?"

"Your tits are too small," the Singer said rudely, and stirred the stew.

"No they're not," she replied, hurt.

"For me—they're too small."

"I suppose you go for *floppers*, like Ada's?"

"Hers don't flop."

"They could raise the *Titanic!*"

"Are you gay?"

"*I've* slept with women. Have *you* slept with men?"

"One Free Friday, I went through a whole soccer team. More goals than the team ever scored!"

"I bet your balls got kicked *bad!*"

"You're not gullible, are you?"

"Who—me? No—Americans aren't gullible—are we?"

"I think you're all crazy. I prefer the British. I don't like the way you people *talk!*"

"Aren't *you* the diplomatic host? Well—why don't you go suck Ivor's dick."

"Maybe I will! You'd *like* that—admit it—you'd *love* watching two guys get it on!"

"It'd make me sick!"

"No it wouldn't—you'd get a *bang* out of it."

"Okay—it *wouldn't* make me sick."

"It wouldn't bother you at all—would it? Wonder if I go muscle up to your boyfriend, Mister Hefferon, right now?"

"You're not *man* enough."

"Bullshit. Wonder if I get it on...with Ivor...*that* would be switch, wouldn't it? That would show you that I've got an open mind."

"Who—*you?* You rabble-rouser—you just get people going for the Hell of it—don't you? You don't really believe in a goddamned thing—admit it!"

"And you *do?* Why *should* I admit a thing to you? I'd sooner be dead," Theatrínos said and shouted to the den: "Ivor—get those rubbery hands off my woman—and let *me* sit on your lap."

"You wouldn't dare!" Dora taunted.

"Oh no?" the Singer answered. "I think it would be a peaceful gesture—Ivor and I—in each other's arms—two *enemies*, as you say. Wouldn't you *like* that a lot?"

"You don't have the *balls!*"

"Don't I?" Theatrínos said angrily and squeezed his testicles in his hands. "Just you watch."

Dora did, and stubbed out the butt of her cigarette and grabbed another one to smoke.

"Get up," the host ordered Ada.

Ada rose obediently from the Olympic Athlete's lap.

"He can't even get it up!" Dora sneered and pointed her dildo at the Runner's penis, shooting a foot-long flame.

"*I'll* get him up!" Theatrínos seductively said, then slowly sat down upon the Gold Medallist's lap.

"Damn lighter!" Dora swore. She was flicking and flicking and no flame was igniting the wick. "Fucking thing's *always* doing this to me—it's made in *Japan*—what do I expect!" She kept trying and trying to get the thing lit.

"Aw—poor Dora!" snapt Theatrínos, now with his arm around Hefferon's neck and stroking his chin. "What's the matter, Dora Bitch?"

"What'd you call me?"

"I called you—*Bitch!* What's *inside* that dildo of yours—a *camera?*" the young Greek said and pounced off Ivor's lap.

Dora's agility caused her to leap to the kitchen. She suddenly grabbed a butcher knife and screamed: "Stay back! Stay *away* from me! All of you! You're all *sick*! You're *all* crazy! And you actually thought I was *swallowing* your stupid gimmick? Free Friday! What a crock! What do you think—I know *nothing* about the goddamned Greek *calendar*! Well—I got it *memorised*—and there's never been and never going to be *any* day called Free Friday! You thought you'd get me drunk, screw me silly, then hypnotise me, like that jumped-up sorry tramp *there* did to me that other night! Well—you got another thing coming if you think Dora's gonna fall for *that* shit twice! You actually thought I *was* that dumb? Come on—give me more credit than *that*, Guys! But don't you *dare* come a step nearer! I do know how to wield this knife!"

"Stay back—both of you," Ada shouted at the men, both of whom were standing, ready to jump at the girl. "Let her go!"

"That's right, Big Tits, you just tell them what to do! Be a *nice* Goody Two-Shoes. You tell them—I'm getting myself dressed and hustling my red little snatch right back where it came!"

"And *we* know where in Hell *that* is!" Theatrínos snarled, then paused theatrically, to heighten the effect: *"From Thýella's pussy!"*

"Let her get dressed," Ada ordered and tossed her her clothes. "Get out of here, Dora Cain—and make it quick!"

"You *know*—don't you?" Dora asked. "You *know*!" she kept repeating as she dressed herself—all the while clutching the butcher knife.

"Sure—we *do* know," Ada admitted calmly, "that your mother has you brainwashed—and that you seek consolation in the arms of your own half-brother Movóros!"

Dora was dressed to leave now. "You *know*," she whined and pointed the knife at Ada, transported away into some dismal ecstasy. "And to think...you were trying to *trap* me!"

"Get her!" Theatrínos ordered.

Ada screamed and held him back: "Don't! Let the monster go! Just let the monster go!"

"Are you crazy?" the Greek exploded. "What're you—out of your mind?"

"Let the monster *go*! What can she possibly do *now*—that she hasn't already done?" Ada hollered.

"You just *wait*! My *mother* will see to *destroying* you! She'll destroy you *all*!" Dora bellowed, then was out of the house in a flash, almost in a puff of smoke, out the back door like she came. She was carrying her own torch in her bag, and illuminated her own way. Her red lips were puckered as never before. She looked as if she had just masterminded a successful satanic ambush, and now was marching for Calamity and Armageddon.

20th April – Maundy Thursday – 11.00 AM

"The slower you climb, the quicker you'll reach the top," Ada told me, over and over, as we kept aiming for the Refuge Hut.

I just shook my head, and kept tramping, losing myself deep in thought. Images from that uncanny first meeting with the Actress— naked in Theatrínos's den—kept popping into my mind's vision, and wouldn't be banished thence. And maniacal Dora...with that dildo...and that butcher knife...and that scowl...

Even though Dora *must* have run straight to her mother, to Thýella, or at least to her mother's son, her sibling, her incestuous lover, Movóros, and even though the whole Ouranós clan, without a single doubt, had heard what had happened that Friday, nobody said one word to me about anything that had transpired at that house in Metamorphosis...until sometime later. But it was the inebriated weekend of Carnevale, when any and all things go, when all Athens was acting awfully strange.

As we climbed ever higher, along a narrow path, I couldn't help remembering more recent delights, how Ada and I had just been making silent and slow, slow love, in our tent this morning, after she lad finished telling me her story. But that was two and a half hours before, and many metres below. Now we were both feeling less invigorated, and I, especially, wasn't used to *vertical* exercise.

All that we were doing now was climbing, climbing, climbing...

"Walk walk—uphill uphill—damn—I'm just not *used* to it!" I was surprised to hear myself shouting, defiantly, then stopping dead.

"I guess it's not run run—downhill downhill," Ada answered, also glad for a temporary break.

"I think your damned hobby isn't mountain-*eering*, it's mountain-*jogging*," I remarked. "You've certainly got fit legs—for an Actress who's played *Juliet*!"

"*Yours* just aren't conditioned to going in this direction," she chided kindly.

"You can say that again."

Continually we two chatted as we went ever higher, sometimes through forest, sometimes through wide open spaces with spectacular views, but always deeper and steeper into the Vale.

"Look at this panorama," Ada suddenly said and pointed to the whole vista before us. From where we were standing, we could look miles down the tremendous gorge. "Do you see the way we're now ringed by the tallest peaks?"

We admired the magnificent sight.

"I call this huge natural bowl the Amphitheatre of Comedy."

I laughed: "Yeah—that's what I called Lake Placid—except it was the *flush* kind of bowl!"

Ada snapt her tongue at my banter: "Oh you *loved* it over there in the Adirondacks and you *know* it! Come on, admit it: You *did* have a decent time... *because* of all the crazies."

"Educational... that's what it was."

"And Lucille? Didn't you enjoy knowing *her*?"

"Educational... that's what *she* was, too!"

We both laughed.

"Everything is so *green* here," Ada said seriously, "in this *eastern* Vale of Olympos. Certainly... this part of Greece must remind you of the mountains of New York State."

"It does... and I was just thinking that very thought."

"I know. I read your mind."

"You always do. I don't have a bleeding secret left!"

"I love how this valley is filled to the brim with this lush pine and beech forest that the Gods call their own."

"It truly is magnificent."

"They say the Olympian Deities recline up there... on their thrones," she stated and pointed to the west. "I always wondered if they're *amused* by this fertile drama way beneath them. But on the *other* side of the peaks, further west, they certainly must frown upon what they have to see."

"Why is that?"

"The Amphitheatre of Tragedy," Ada replied. "From the top of the mountain there's a sheer drop, three thousand feet, to a desert-like canyon without one single tree."

"Let's take the theatres one at a time," I answered. "You seem as if you've been climbing such heights all your life."

"Just about," she answered enigmatically. "I was taken to many sacred places... that I understood better when I was a little girl."

"You never went against your Will?"

"Will? What's the meaning of such a silly word?"

"Do you *believe* in Free Will?"

"Honesty is often so very brutal. So is Wisdom," she responded and paused, "which is the sense to act upon The Truth, yet to live The Life Of Faults."

I gazed all around us, trying to fathom the incomparable might of the upthrust stone above, and said: "I don't understand."

"Free Will is exercised *once*... in every Human Being's lifetime," she said and smiled.

"When is that?"

"Before conception," Ada replied. "Each Soul... has to make the choice... of what type of Life it will lead, and in which Body it will do it. This choice is *free*. But, at the instant that The Soul enters The Chosen Being, it sacrifices itself now to *Destiny*."

"Which is?"

"The path The Soul already has chosen for The Body to see."

I glanced down to the dirt upon which we were walking, and

shuddered. Nobody said another word for many minutes. The Body just relinquished itself to The Interminable Mortal Climb. All our muscles were aching. Air was not in great supply. Suddenly, almost half an hour later, I yelled: "I think I'm having a flipping heart-attack!" Exhaustion was snapping me like a bow releasing an arrow. I was hearing bells—maybe mules—maybe not? Even though we now were within sight of the Hut, we were so high up that our breathing was coming only in little clips.

Regardless, Ada was literally skipping along the path, giddy as a goat, happy that it was almost raining, ecstatic that the atmosphere was *arctic*!

"I thought you preferred the seashore!" I yelled. "Bugger—if I'd known that the contrast between Olympia and Olympos was *this* severe, I would have booked us a training-trip to Lapland, instead of landing in *this* bleeding Lap Of The Gods!"

"What's wrong?" Ada queried, as my cheeks were turning blue. "Burdened by your bags?"

"*And* the sodding journey," I growled. "Look—I *must* stop. Sorry, Luv, I just wasn't brought on the sodding Matterhorn!"

"Now now," she replied to console me. So we halted again. Suddenly, along came the mule train that had been jing-jing-alinging closer and closer for the past fifteen minutes. It now was past twelve o'clock.

"My heart's thumping so fast I can barely move aside," I gasped as the mules charged towards us. Ada, though, leapt a distance away, so gingerly, that I feared she was trying to highjump a mule coasting past her. The aforementioned fat guide, asquat sidesaddle and going by proudly, smirking like a maharani bound for her paramour's pavilion, pretended he didn't see me, but did he ever grin lecherously and exchanged a few greetings with Ada. Then...the train was on its way, traversing the last few hundred metres, and bearing the burden of washed sand, as well as terracotta tiles this time, for utilisation on high.

"Oh horrible!" Ada wailed. "Did you see that bleeding *animal*?"

"The one on the saddle?"

"No—the mule! It was *bleeding*!"

"Where?"

"From its belly."

"Oh God..."

"Poor things—they work them worse than slaves—having to haul such dreadful loads. The cinctures are rubbing them raw. I could see its poor skin—the straps aren't right!"

"I wonder if *anything's* right up here?" I said, still fighting for breath.

"Come on," she said kindly, yet firmly, and began the hike again. "The quicker we're there, the sooner we'll rest."

"*Die* is the word," I said, but grudgingly followed.

Ada ignored this manipulation of her maxim and jogged along, then pointed up to a waving Greek flag at the edge of a high abutment: "There it is—the Refuge Hut!"

After fifteen more excruciatingly painful minutes, during which the two of us actually had to cross our first field of *snow*, the first I'd seen since the Winter Olympics, at last we were being greeted by a boisterous barking Alsatian attack-dog, bigger and meaner than Cerberus.

"Blimey—he's huge enough to bite the bollocks off a Brahma bull!" I hardly had wind enough to utter.

"At last! We're here!" Ada shouted at this elevation of six thousand feet above the Aegean. She was in full-voice, miraculously, and sounded like an opera diva.

Indeed, at long last, we two *had* mounted the difficulty. Now we were walking atop the fortress-like akropolis that sat high within the Amphitheatre of Comedy, proud as an eagle's eyrie. Ada turned to me and whispered: "You won't believe the goings-on of *this* place!"

19ᵗʰ March – Sunday – 9.13 PM

By evening of the nineteenth of March, it was apparent that all Athens was being swept along in a totally insane, totally erotic, totally anti-Christian pre-Lenten madness called Carnevale, of which Theatrínos's threat to stage a huge anti-MOON demonstration on National Day was only a bit-part.

If one has never had the good fortune to witness what Carnevale induces, in such a pleasure-craving city as the capital of Pallas Athena, then it can only be stressed that one *go* there, right before Lent. Granted, other *New* World metropolises are far more famed for their Lusty Pagan Binges, Rio de Janeiro and New Orleans to cite two, but *Old* World Athens undoubtedly should be right at the top of the list. Yet it's never cited in guidebooks for giving a *great* Carnevale.

As soon as Dora Cain had left Theatrínos's "Free Friday" party the other night, the Singer had dedided to speak to his father about the worsening situation. He got the General on the telephone, and proceeded to tell him to "lay off". Theatrínos did have guts, if nothing else, and even told Ouranós that he would make good his threat to organize the largest anti-Olympics rally ever seen in Athens, for the next weekend on the twenty-fifth, if the General refused to put a damper on his wife and on her friends' dirty tricks. When Ouranós laughed in his receiver, and said to his popular son that he must be drunk, Theatrínos retorted: "Don't push me, Old Man! If you *don't* invite me to Blood Drinker's Banquet on Sunday, I shall call a press conference, to-morrow, and not only announce to the world that I *am* your son, but I'll also blow the lid off your whole fucking satanic organization!" Against *that* possibility, Affedikó Ouranós reluctantly agreed to let Theatrínos appear at Major

Movóros's penthouse for the *répas masqué*. "Plus," the Performer said, "you'll tell *everyone* at the Banquet to follow me, through the streets, in a Snake Dance, so that they'll *all* come to the Gala Opening of my discothèque, The Bitchy Bacchante."

"*That* should prove enlightening," the General replied in closing.

"That depends upon *your* complicity," answered the son.

Meanwhile, Ivor already received his invitation to the Costume Banquet a week in advance, and planned to bring Ada as his guest. Professor Rembetikós urged the Athlete to go as Ephíaltes, since the theme was Great Moments In Greek History. The Professor, of course, was not invited. Nevertheless, he suggested that Ada go as Hecate.

Hefferon found this idea highly amusing, given that he was still a Classics scholar at Christ Church, at least the paperwork at the Master's Office still showed his name as belonging. Very few at the Banquet, if any at all, would know, or care, who Ephíaltes even was.

"The joke is he's a Titan," Rembetikós laughed, "a pre-Hellenic pre-Olympian deity, and his name means He Who Leaps Upon. Thýella should enjoy *that* immensely."

"If she *gets* it," Ivor replied.

"Ephíaltes was one of the Giants, a bastard son of Iphimedéia, the daughter of Triops and the Sea God, Poseidon. He also was a grandson of Hecate—and if Ada goes as the Goddess of Witches, that means she'll be accompanying you as your grandmother. But the prank on Thýella and Ouranós is this: When Ephíaltes and his brother Otus were nine years old, the boys declared war on Olympos. Ephíaltes swore to the River Styx to outrage Hera, Queen of the Gods, and Otus swore to do the same to Artemis. First the boys bound Ares, God of War, then laid siege to Mount Olympos. Then—when the boys were both throwing javelins at Artemis, in the guise of a dove—their spears pierced each other's breast, and they perished. Nobody has to know *that*, of course," the Professor laughed, "nor that they were bound to pillars in Tartarus, and tied by cords of living vipers. But...it's an interesting sideline that they worshipped wild Muses and personified orgiastic Nightmare."

"Just like kids to-day," Ivor responded, "*not* to have around the house! Me and Hecate, we'll make one awesome pair!"

So with the help of the Actress, who knew every square inch of all the Athenian costume warehouses, they found something to wear this Sunday night. Ivor donned a knee-length skin of a long-haired goat, grubby furry sandals, and a matted tit-length black wig. Round his neck Ada drooped a necklace of lions' teeth. She painted his body, what could be seen, brown, and gave him a gnarlèd oaken club for protection. His mask was a helmet sporting five viper heads. For herself, she hid her own identity with a three-faced mask, much as the primæval Goddess would have appeared back then. Her lion face represented her magical jurisdiction over Heaven, her dog face ruled over Hell, and her mare face presided over Earth. "I can bestow on any mortal, or withhold, any gift that one should ever deserve," was her byline for the evening.

The family fête was well under way when Ephíaltes and Hecate made their entrance. Given that everyone was addressing everybody else by one's costume-name, this procedure will suffice till this evening be over. Thýella came as Helen of Troy, in order to show off her jewelry and guile. Psychopompós, as befitted an Orthodox Priest, came as An Impoverished Eremetic. And Affedikó, Thýella's husband and President of the MOON, dressed in a sartorial manner that one would expect of so august a personage, as Helen's hapless lord, Menelaos. But no matter how people dressed, it was the last night of Carnevale, a good excuse to orgy one evening more, before Clean Monday would cleanse the capital's wantonness for the month's abstemious preparation for Holy Easter.

The host and hostess were receiving on their unconventionally large penthouse terrace, high above the lower echelons of most-chic Kolonáki, overlooking, it appeared, the whole wide world. All the monsters, princesses, myths, feats, and dreams, in garbèd finery, were out on that terrace, gawking at the twinkling city-view, complimenting the party with great esteem.

The host, Major Movóros, was wearing the traditional dress uniform of the Elite Guards, the Evzónes. This was the first time that either Ephíaltes or Hecate had seen him face to face. "Rumour has it," Hecate whispered as they approached the man, "that only the most intelligent, best looking, tallest, strongest, and most well-hung lads can become an Evzone. And their Major is supposed to be the best-hung of them all." As Chief Evzone, the host of course was standing in those gorgeous white stockings, showing off all of his legs, and then some, given that his kilt was hoisted well up above the bulging pod of his potent manhood. "So that's Dora's lover," Hecate said and smiled, imagining what what a stud the Chief Evzone was nude in bed.

Every movement of the Evzone was slow, refined, graceful, in the most manly way. The gesture for which he was most notorious was when he would slowly run his right middle finger down the length of his facial scar, that extended from his right ear almost to his lips. He would then stare at a woman, and run his tongue around the end of his longest digit. It always got the woman aroused. He was charged with sex appeal. His straight black hair was greased back. He never turned his head or body quickly. He was the tallest of the Ouranós clan, six-foot four-inches of love-muscle. "The papers say he's so elegant that everybody in Greece is convinced that he's Italian! He even married a rich girl from Genoa," Hecate said quietly.

The hostess, nicknamed Sultana by the family, stood by the Evzone's side. She was dressed as a Circassian, a slave to Turks, whom the Evzone had captured from Topkapi, the decadent Istanbul Palace. She was absolutely ravishing, a tall green-eyed blonde, from the north Italian aristocracy. She was stunning to-night in a priceless ensemble of heirloom sapphires, giant ones, set in scads of diamonds. Looking like that, she didn't have to bother with *any* clothes, but had deigned to slip into multi-coloured embroidered silk pantaloons.

After obligatory greetings, Hecate and her Grandson strolled away and blended in the ever more boisterous crowd. The two wandered through the two storeys of the house, and were honestly impressed by the lavish series of glittering rooms, all decorated with a tasteful *nord-italiana* eye. Every single salon boasted a different inlaid marble floor.

Into the midst of a chamber the size of a ballroom, imported *in toto* from a demolished Genoese palazzo, Helen and Menelaos suddenly stept. A hush went through the throng, then ripples of gossip began coursing beneath the boars' heads mounted to the tooled Moroccan leather walls.

"Everybody here owes that bitch allegiance," Hecate said to Ephíaltes.

"Have you noticed how everyone's avoiding us?" the Giant replied.

"Pre-Hellenic Deities are out of style," Hecate laughed, then added: "Something *rancid* stinks. I think Dora's here."

"As what?"

"Who would guess? The Whore of Babylon? She could be anything—she's so small!"

Ephíaltes adjusted his viper helmet. "I've heard people giggling as we pass."

"I've noticed people handing round something funny," Hecate said.

"Have you seen *what* yet?"

"No."

"By your three nasty faces—look what's coming—straight ahead! Troy's Destruction herself!"

Presently, there stood Helen, fanning herself, beaming in a sunburst of diamonds. The rocks were everywhere, round her ankles, round her waist, round her neck, round her head. Her fan was certainly queer. It was some sort of postal card. "Enjoying yourself?" she asked Ephíaltes. "Good for you." She paused. "Once you recover from *this* bash, there's non-stop *labour*, till next Saturday night."

Why does she *have* to bring up work, Hecate growled to herself. She also wondered what on earth Helen was using as a fan.

"We *need* you now...more than *ever*," the horrid woman said most snidely. "*Your* services...have become *ours*." Then she paused. "You'll be leaving, early this week, for Olympia."

"Which day?" the Giant inquired.

"We shall *tell* you when," was the sarcastic reply, and Helen began to strut away, then turned to say: "Have fun, Ephíaltes...while it lasts." She fanned her face doubly hard with her postcard, then the diamonds disappeared into another chamber.

Hecate spat: "That bitch knows absolutely everything! She's even been told whom you're dressed as to-night—before she even crossed the miserable floor!"

"So what? Don't let Helen ruin your evening. At least she hasn't *fired* me yet."

"That's correct. This *isn't* Lake Placid."

"Here in Athens, they like to *hang* you by a hook, then watch you *wiggle* as you're tortured!"

"Something truly *horrendous* is up—I can smell it a mile away! She's manoeuvring—something terrifying—she's planning to *destroy* you!"

"Let's not worry about it. Please! As Helen herself said: Enjoy the Now!"

Evil *was* lording the very air this eve. Officials of the Government, Members of the Greek Olympic Committee, and their wives or husbands or lovers, along with yes-men, lackeys, and entrepreneurial "friends", all were there, having a gay old time, masquerading, gorging themselves on mounds of scrumptious food, being trotted about by hired caterers, dressed as Dæmons Unleashed From Hell.

"I think that's the British Ambassador and Ambassadress," Ephíaltes noticed, as Two Frogs, escapees from the comedy by Aristophanes, hopped by. "I could tell by their accents."

The Cow Frog croaked: "But you're certainly *not* going to speak to *him* now!"

And the Bull Frog croaked back: "But I *have* to...sometime to-night!"

"I think they mean *me*," Grandson said to Grandmother.

Suddenly making a supreme entrance—as the "untouchable" of the evening—was Theatrínos. He was masquerading as the God of Wine and Theatre, Dionysos. He had a wreath of grape leaves in his henna curls, and was holding a gold-leaf mask in either hand, Comedy in the right, Tragedy in the left. His robe draped over one shoulder, lavender linen in pleats, with a meticulous border embroidered in royal purple from Tyre. His face was painted the colour of sweet red wine.

A troupe of a dozen Server Boys, in similar cloth, danced their way to the centre of the grandiose ballroom, clacking tambourines and forming a circle for their God. Two were carrying a staff of silver, a thyrsus, twined by bronze ivy and topped by a carved wooden pine cone. This they tossed in the air, to a pagan rhythmic beat, and chanted an archaic hymn not heard in Athens for centuries.

The crowd was going wild, swept along by the retsina that was flowing like a mountain brook, strong peasant brew brought especially from the hills round Olympia itself, potent drink the hue of pinkish golden musk.

"Anthistéria," Hecate snarled.

"What's that?" Ephíaltes wondered.

"The ancient name for the original spring orgy for Dionysos," she replied.

"Who said it's *ancient*? I don't think it's ever *died!*"

"Not from the looks of *this* place!"

A live bouzouki band just was entering, and the whole environment was erupting in entwining lines of party-goers going mad with manic dancing. Before the Witch Goddess and Giant could knock back one more drink, they were being grabbed by the arms by the throng, and whipt along in the overflow of delight. The whole house seemed to start swirling, round and round, as the inebriation reached epical heights; and every single person, servant included, began to be swept into the frenzy of the primæval dance, that began revolving, un-circling, revolving, un-circling, about the figure of Dionysos, midmost on the marble floor. Thyrsus erect, then thyrsus plonked down, the rhythm kept pursuing, as the pretty little Boys kept shouting out the beat, as the band kept playing up a storm.

But still, as the mirth was persisting, the omnipresence of Evil kept resisting obliteration, kept hovering right below the sculpted ceiling. This was a charade, a sporting exercise, with musical notes, punctuated by the gyrating mob's words of general joy, of gestures, of arguments, of footloose debates, of pleasing little threats, of kind recriminations, of flattering insults, and of many good horse-laughs, in other words, of all those indispensables analogous to proper social behaviour.

Suddenly—the Chief Evzone went to the microphone by the bouzouki band—and brought a temporary hiatus to it all, which was his prerogative, as it *was* his house. In his left hand he was twirling a string of flashy worry-beads, and everyone took note, and shut up.

Dionysos, still the fulcrum of the room, now was right beside Hecate and Ephialtes when the music suddenly ceased. He winked at them both, then whispered loud enough for many to eavesdrop: "Those beads are solid twenty-two carat gold...a love-gift...from one of the Junta's Colonels."

Everybody turned askance and pretended that they had just heard nothing. Given that the Evzone *did* command presence, and given that it *was* his house, his food, his money, not to mention his country, he thought that he would do away with diplomacy, since to him it never got anybody anywhere anyway. He slowly started running his right middle finger down the length of his facial scar, then was moistening its tip with his tongue, then was saying: "Greetings, from the Ouranós family...to you all. To-night is a very special evening—since what we are celebrating is not just the final night of Carnevale, but also the weekend before National Day, the day our Republic began its honourable fight for independence. And, we are proud to say, it now is common knowledge that next Saturday, in Olympia, the Government of Greece will be giving a parcel of our very own hard-won land...away...to Planet Earth...to the

312

betterment of Global Sport. Mount Olympos...once again...is to become *more* than just a place of geographic fantasy. Mount Olympos...is to house the new Olympic Nation!"

The assembly burst forth into applause.

"*Lipón,*" the Evzone continued with the Greek word for *well,* "Greece invented the Olympics—so it's only natural that Greece *should* get them back. The first Games of the Modern Era were here, in 1896, and now, after incessant travel and incessant travail, our country has, at long last, won them again—permanently—forever!"

Another cheer arose.

"The Mount Olympos Olympic Nation is *no* small endeavour," he added. "It's no little gift for World Peace. This land, that invented democracy, now has democratically decided to give up its very own soil...and *more* of it, we might add, than the site of the United Nations."

"*Opa! Opa!*" people shouted aloud.

"*Lipón*—to-night—as you join in The Snake Dance—do keep these things in mind. This is a most *noble* venture, my Friends, one that only a fool could deny." The Evzone glared over the crowd with unflinching eyes, and let them rest on his half-brother Dionysos. The Grape God looked sideways, with a lewd grin, at his comrades Hecate and her Grandson, then winked again. "Just wait till he comes to *my* place."

Instantly, music began blaring again. While midnight had been approaching that evening, the revelling city kept glimmering in its lights. Now—Athens was literally shimmering—with all the risen body-heat from the day's dusty streets. The city looked just like Crazy Wonderland.

Down in the midst of its tangle and trysts, The Bitchy Bacchante was preparing herself for Act Two of this Pre-Lenten Party, in an old restored hotel, in the ancient Street called Sokrates.

Finally, the clock began to strike twelve. The whole insane affair began to shift gears, from the heights of Kolonáki, to the depths of this city so renowned.

Following the party's musicians, the whole penthouseful of revellers did as the boys in the band did, and began to snake-dance behind them, out the great doors, then down the four flights of stairs, to the juncture of streets named Loukianoú and Kleoménous.

Similar groups were doing the same—but not nearly so large nor colourful—all over the Attikan Plain. Building after building after building was disgorging raucous horns, rattles, and tambourines. Everybody was so delirious that nobody could ever duplicate the route. Ephíaltes and Hecate only remember having followed, having shaken crazy rattles that some maid, dressed with purplish scales and two blue tails, handed them on leaving the place.

The group did get to Sýntagma Square—that *everyone* remembered—and the five hundred café tables below the American Express building just went *wild* with excitement at this "musical" procession in the open air.

Being on the border of Pláka, Sýntagma thus was on the border of Total Lunacy. One could positively *feel* its presence, the closer to the heart, or the groin, of the action one got. The closer to Pláka they did get...the more masqueraders kept continually joining their group. Perhaps five hundred people were now in the Snake Dance, by the time it hit the down-sloping lane, Kithathineíon, the main-drag plummeting straight into the guts of Pláka, to Hadrian Street.

The bouzouki band and Dionysos, seemingly miles ahead of the Giant and his wicked Grandmother, started the inevitable descent. Everyone in the packed-tight Byzantine streets, with the tiniest buildings, was either singing, tossing confetti in someone else's face, tooting a toy trumpet, or laughing uproariously. But everyone soon discovered that the main nocturnal source of pleasure was whacking someone you didn't know on the head, with a coloured plastic club or mallet which, when it bopped you, went *whumpft!*

No cars at all dared these streets—not one was so foolish. And it seemed that all of Athens was in these tiny alleys. The poor Giant had never seen anything like it in his life. But this throbbing sea of humanity insane did part, though, as the Snake Dance made its approach, and instinctively gave the right of way.

The bold and the curious kept joining—what a maniacal mess! Hecate and her Grandson were hysterical with laughter at everything and everybody that moved. But just then, the group was suddenly veering—rightwards—turning into the High Street of Hadrian.

There, at the corner, coming out of the Kosmikón Café, in other words coming out of This World, literally, was a six-foot-tall thin-as-a-rake White Mænad, who joined Ephíaltes and the Arch Sorceress. This Mænad must have done herself some careful research, since she looked just like a ghostly resurrection of some drugged Dionysian Priestess.

For that matter, in the less than lucid state that *they* were in, Grandmother and Grandson were convinced that she *was* a Dionysian Priestess.

"I know her! I *know* I know her!" the Giant kept saying. "I met her—with Dionysos—in the Grande Bretagne! She's the Bass Guitarist!"

"A *Real* Celebrity! We won't leave her—for anything," Grandmother agreed. "Don't worry."

"She's a *he*!" Ephíaltes whispered. "Any monster touches her—gets my prong!" and he brandished his oaken club.

Hecate was using what little imagination she had left and was thinking to herself that the Mænad's ancient costume, all white and no embroidery, could easily be a Victorian garden dress. "This drag's *made* for this Snake Dance!"

Everybody from Blood Drinker's Banquet encircled the Mænad to prevent any toughs from attacking her. Indeed, there was a primitive, albeit prehistoric animosity in the air. Watching *them* surrounding *her*—all others of the Carnevale came to a dead halt, as the party continued up Hadrian's Way. The White Mænad spoke to nobody. She just strolled along, oblivious to all the commotion she was causing

Adrianoú—the street was bliss—a transformation entire! Inches deep in pastel confetti, onwards they aimed, suddenly turned right, at the site of Hadrian's Library, then onwards they aimed, towards Sokrates Street.

Pláka was thousands and thousands and thousands of partyers, streamers from everywhere dangling like vines, no cars, drunks, mates linking armpit to arm, costumes galore, native outfits, musclemen, gorillas, dancing girls, cowboys, glitter queens, punks, minks, sheiks, camel drivers, tipsy cops, sloshed singers, geishas rabbiting on, all sexes mixed, all those clubs, those mallets, those hooting hooting hooting horns!

Pláka was *bodies*—pressing each other, pressing each other, pressing, pressing—everybody laughing, enjoying the feeling of *feeling*—hot bodies—everywhere—throwing confetti, getting bopped, having long snazzle elongated roll-out snakes flying suddenly into all orifices—all to grunts, all to farts, all to hilarity—all politics long forgotten, all the scandals of Athens aside—just The City, The Polis, debauched in revelry—as The City's been doing and doing and doing—and *needs* to keep doing—since way before The Advent of Christ!

Dionysos, dressed in ancient slovenliness, hoisted his robe, entered the lane named for the teacher of Plato, then headed for his new disco-thèque. Filling the deserted road, from kerb to kerb, the raucous mob had never imagined that such fun could ever await them in this tawdry old warehouse neighbourhood. During the day, there was a different story about this place. When the Sun was up, the quarter was ebullient and alive, an aromatic open-air market that specialised in foodstuffs and spice. But at night, all one could find here were a few tired hookers, patiently awaiting some poor joker on the corner, some tired john on the skids.

So—those who knew Athens had been gossiping about this Gala for months—wondering why *this* location had been chosen over so many more "suitable" spots. The Bitchy Bacchante had certainly given more people more things to *bitch* about—and it had been written about, complained about, and threatened by closure by more than one source. Yet the nightclub was opening anyhow. And, at this moment, the sleepy street was having a Second Coming.

Dionysos, thyrsus held high, was pausing at the corner of classic corners, at Sokrates and Sophokles no less. And on the far side glared the grimey old Hotel Valkanía, where only The Furies knew who

315

flopped inside its seedy rooms in its "heyday", if it ever *had* one. It had taken half a year to ready this place for to-night—and now was the time to let it all hang.

With bouzouki band playing like monkeys, with everyone dancing in the street-wide queue, stretching backwards many a block, the whole scene was like a whirling dervish convention. So Dionysos, at the lead, suddenly put his foot down and screamed: "STOP—YOU IDIOTS!"

All the idiots stopt.

Dionysos then went a few yards ahead, and upraised his precious staff. Anybody looking as *he* was looking *would* have been able to stop traffic...in *any* capital of the world this night!

Just as the restless thousand or so began pushing and shoving and jeering in the road, up to the door of The Bitchy Bacchante, née the sleazy Valkanía, over on the right, Dionysos strode. Atop its small porch, he suddenly turned and faced the horde, and shook his pole like Aaron, causing frenzy amongst the faithful. Then, pausing melodramatically, he hoisted the staff aloft, swang it back like a bat, and sent the thing crashing for all of its worth into the wooden door. But it opened, as if on a cushion of air, to the broadcast sound of a gigantic Tibetan gong—it was all pre-rehearsed and caused music to be poured into the street like the sluice from a hydroelectric dam. This was one rousing fanfare.

Then—what music! It was the foot-stomping hand-clapping buildup to the concert Bacchae gave at the Odíon just five nights before, the group's great lead-up to their hot-licks of Blues, blared forth this night, this last night of Carnevale in Athens, as the people from the street began to pour right in!

The Bitchy Bacchante was an instant success. Once inside, the music being played on all four floors was not like anything Greece had heard in years. It wasn't Bouzouki. It wasn't Rock. It wasn't anything but Swing. Big Band sounds were bursting forth all over—the first time since the Nazi Occupation. Dionysos had spent ages, in all his friends' grandparents' houses, and in radio stations, combing private collections for the oddbit of sound to surprise the discothèque with. Athens obviously had never known an experience near it. People in crazy costumes were jitter-bugging till they dropt!

The biggest dance floor, on the top, had a stage with a red velvet grand-drape, plush as any in an opera house. The Giant went round and scrutinised it all. "Cracked," to Hecate he said, "totally and unequivocably cracked! But I *love* it!" Drunk as he was, he was lucky to get that adverb out in one piece. But if there's anything an Oxford student *can* do drunk, it's still being able to pronounce The Queen's English impeccably. Grandmother, for all her proven acting ability, didn't even venture such an adverb, she just gawked, approving the whole décor.

True-to-life vines of grapes and ivy were crawling everywhere. Virtual sprays of myrtle and laurel, that never would have to fade, were greatly in evidence. Bowls on bars were filled with pomegranates. Lions and bulls and panthers and birds and bats and dolphins and satyrs and sileni and stags and rams all were drinking and eating and mainly drinking...to oblivion...

Suddenly, Some Little Bird came up, whimpering and blubbering, into Ephialtes's arms. Hecate was not amused, and told the Bird so. "I'm sorry!" the Little Bird whined and ripped off its head. There stood Ms. Cain, red-eyed. "He's been *beating* me! Look!" the Little Bird flinched when she touched her own face. "I'm so *sorry!*"

"Sorry you certainly *are!*" snapt the Witch Goddess.

"You're pissed as a newt, Bird," the Giant said, hardly able to focus on her swollen face.

"Who hit you—you probably deserved it!" Hecate said with glee.

"She won't be so lovey-dovey with us once she sobers up!" the Grandson added.

Hecate agreed, and started yanking her Grandchild away.

"No wait!" screamed Some Little Bird. "He shouldn't have *hurt* me! He said I was causing more scandal than any family ever suffered!"

"Who—damn it—who?" Ephialtes yelled.

"Stupid—you mean Movóros, don't you?" the Witch Goddess guessed. "*He's* the one who hit you! Your *lover*—your own *half-brother!* Well—for what—or need I ask? *Incest*—with *another* family member?*"

"For *this*," she said and started feeling herself up, to locate something lost. "By The Devil—I guess I gave them all away!"

"What in sodding Hell're you *muttering* about, Bitch! Talk sense —or just shut that big fat trap!" the Sorceress shouted sternly.

"I...I gave...all...my *postcards*...away!" Some Little Bird complained bibulously, then staggered to collapse.

Suddenly, beside them stood two drunken Frogs. "You guessed it—it's *me!*" Sir Cecil said and pulled off his rubbery green head.

"I don't see any difference, do you?" the Giant asked Hecate.

"Looks better the other way," the Witch poked her Grandson and laughed.

"Listen, Mister Olympic Gold, I told you to make *friends* with that crazy Singer—Dionysos—I mean Theatrínos—but I didn't tell you to make *love* with him!" the Bull Frog croaked. "Show him that postal card, Dearest."

Suddenly, the Cow Frog was flaunting a postal card that was printed in sepia ink, and that showed two naked young men, in a compromising position, one on the other's lap. Neither's penis was erect. Some Jackal-Headed God came up and began eavesdropping. "See how you're *ruined! How* can you *dare* come here to-night—showing off that supposedly *idealistic* young face—when you've let yourself, stark naked, have *sex* with, and be *photographed* having sex with, this Rock Star, who's opening up this *den* of depravity here! I'm now definitely going to have you deported—as fast as I can get to a telephone to-night!"

317

"These filthy postal cards have been circulating throughout all Athens all evening, thanks to Some Little Bird!" the Bull Frog almost barked. "Well—we shall expect some answers from you—to-morrow at the Embassy—and by God they better be *good* ones! See you for tea—and I don't mean *after* your bloody siesta! Now I have to go chew out *Colin!*"

"Come now—away from this sick *pervert!*" the Cow Frog snorted, though she still looked just like a plucked chicken.

"Oh my God—did you see that picture!" the Giant turned to Hecate in despair. The Jackal-Headed God was still there. "She *did* take photos...after all!"

"That *dildo* of hers was certainly packing more than *flame!*"

At that instant the Jackal-Headed God walked away.

"I'm certainly glad *that's* gone!" Ephialtes sighed with relief. "Whoever it was...it looked just like the Ancient Egyptian God of the Dead, Anubis."

"It *was* Anubis," Hecate responded grimly.

"One of your primæval *enemies?*" her Grandson asked.

Suddenly—what was it, three in the morning—Dionysos was standing before his stage. He then commanded his velvet curtain to part. It did, like magic, and presented a scene to warm everybody's heart. There, on a chaise, with a classical set, reclined the White Mænad, taking grapes from a naked Boy Slave. Then, the lights went red, and she grabbed an amphora of wine, and stood, with a face to dread.

Dionysos, who'd slipt to the wings, then entered the set with a Sacral Goat, a Great-Hornèd Goat, with a long grey beard, who smelt of the need to rut. The creature was loathsome, but most thought him handsome, so weird to be seen on the stage. He strutted and pawwed, and looked to the lot, then he commenced to eat hay. The hand of the Mænad was holding the grass, to coax the beast along, and then she stopt, in the midst of the set, to glare at the gathered throng.

"This, the Goat of Sacrifice, to-night we *slay* for you," Dionysos and the Mænad declaimed, together from the stage, as a fear and a lust to see bloodshed ricochéd throughout the amazed. "Boy—you lovely one there—tender Acolyte to Mysteries—help us with our deed now—the knife and the honing stone, please!"

The Goat was tied to a votive post, and the lights became blood-red. The Boy brought both the stone and the knife, the first to the Mænad, the second to the one who led. Thus, before them all, one held as one sharpened the blade—and a tension was honed, as this nocturnal drama so skilfully was played.

Then lights went blue, like Night, as everybody stood still. No one knew what to expect; all, though, wanted thrill. And Dionysos, thus, did pause, with his dagger raised aloft...and he took his time to please The Gods...he'd sacrificed so oft. But nothing now could stop him...The

Hornèd One, tied, did wait. So his voice now gave the offering...as his words did speak of Fate:

> *Games of Sport...Games of Love...Games of Man's Endeavour;*
> *Pause to think...pause to learn...Pawns are Mortals ever.*

He went to the edge of the stage, with his sharp knife slashing outwards, as if he would put the whole group in a grave, minus benefit of casket. The White Mænad, at that moment, took a huge pair of Sacred Snakes, out of a wan wicker basket. Each one was grabbed by the neck, and each one coiled, around skinny arms. The crowd began gasping—the Slaves began wailing—the Mænad began chanting—prehistoric charms. And Dionysos continued:

> *Athletes win...Athletes lose...so do all the others;*
> *Nations rise...nations fall...Brothers must love Brothers.*

The Goat began bleating plaintively.

> *We don't know now how to play...long abandoned virtue;*
> *Rally round a temporal flag...easiest way to hurt you.*

The White Mænad now was astride the Goat, showing the scared Creature the Serpents.

> *Ancient stones know ancient lays...pretty Girls and Boys;*
> *But our Past does give To-Day...Inspiration's Toys.*

The Snakes now were crawling down the Goat's two horns.

> *We've lost touch...The Past is dead...let the dust be dust;*
> *Still it's here...still it's there...Stir it if you must.*

The Reptiles were now wrapping themselves around the Creature's neck.

> *Our Olympics are a farce...The Soul's no longer in it;*
> *Is the Medal worth it all...what's the sense to win it?*

Dionysos retraced his steps to the Goat. The White Mænad, now freed from the Serpents' grasp, got off the Animal's back. She produced a black hood to cover its head, though the Snakes, still around it, were wrapt.

> *So sacrifice...we sacrifice...to-night-we call for Blood.*
> *To the Games...Olympic Games...to raise their Glory from the mud.*

319

Thus Dionysos raised the knife, high above his hair, and above the leaves of the vine. He lifted his voice an octave more, and pled for Aid Divine. And just as he did sink the blade within the flesh of the Goat...vapours arose, and golden light wrapt the Beast in smoke. And then the anxious crowd did see that the Goat and the Mænad were gone. Only the Wine God, with Snakes held high, was left to address the throng. And so did he, with no remorse, tell it like it is: His Sacrifice would work, of course; his Magic couldn't miss.

The Games of Zeus were Festivals of Spirit sporting Flesh:
The Ancient Competition, for Zeus, tried to be best.
And here in Hellas they were sired, nowhere else on Earth:
Any Land who'd stage them, thus, can't quite make them work.
Though the Spirit powering Zeus has now become The Christ,
This Land's the same—it still is Greece—that nobody can deny!

A mighty cheer went up from all those gathered, from foreign scheming Ambassadors to Poor Lads of working-class Athens. Dionysos continued:

And somewhere in this landscape a true Revival waits—
Many don't believe it—most prefer their hates.
But it will come, will come at last, if the Land just lets it:
Then once again Greece will be great, and no one will regret it.
But this True Spirit won't return...till the Games return to Greece:
Then the Spirit...at last restored...will justly work for Peace!

Standing like a statue in the middle of the stage, with the Serpents now wrapt about his arms, great shouts in Greek were being chanted. The clapping was synchronised. But again, the vapours rose, and golden light enveloped the God in smoke. Suddenly—Dionysos was gone.

Then out of the wings came twenty-four Lads, bearing twelve roast lambs upon spits. And they set them down and began to carve, as twenty-four Girls came out with knives, forks, and plates. Then twelve Boys, and twelve Girls more, each bearing deep red wine, came to the edge of the stage, and began to pour out goodly liquid. And lastly the band was returning, was joyously starting to play.

Thus with singing and with dancing, as only the Greeks know how, the night was passed in good spirit, since all had agreed to honour Dionysos's hallowèd vow.

Or...*had* they all agreed? The young, and those still able to think, for all the food and the drink, obviously had gone along. But others, in the discothèque, were teetering on the brink, their very own abyss. For, whilst the Big Bands began to play the very final song, none other than Helen of Troy herself strode up, and scared the Giant out of his goatskin wits! She leered—she loured—she handed him a dirty *postcard*—then, laughing, she demanded too hard: "Now *what*, may we ask, is *this!* With your *paws* on each others' *tits!*"

20ᵗʰ April – Maundy Thursday – 1.30 PM

"Lefteris!" Ada yelled and ran towards a man, then jumped into his arms. The guard-dog was refraining from barking, as its owner began tossing the girl in the air like a beach-ball. I gazed on, hoping to be spared a similar salutation.

"The Hut's Manager," Ada said, now back on terra firma, as the big fellow made for me, causing the attack-bowser to charge and growl like a monster.

"Hello," he bellowed and puffed out his chest. "Meet Rosy." The brute of a dog almost out-barked her owner, and she too puffed out *her* hairy barrel-chest.

I was so tired from our climb that I now could hardly see who and/or what was approaching. I think I did extend my hand and tried to focus on man and beast, with my left eye on Lefteris's American-style black and white plaid shirt, of flannel, and his worn baggy green trousers, and with my right eye on the Alsatian's bared teeth. The man looked as if he were pushing fifty. The dog looked as if she could push fifty *men*, just with the strength of her vocal chords alone!

"Doesn't he have a great character-actor's face?" Ada beamed.

"*Everybody* in Greece does," I replied and stared at the chap's extremely high forehead framed by coal-black hair, wavy wrinkles over the brows, well-tended moustache, and a gold eye-tooth.

The tooth and its owner declared: "Ada—it's so great to *see* you way up here!" Then to me he added: "We've been close...for years."

Good, I thought. "Aren't you going to introduce us?" I inquired.

"Ivor won the Men's 1500 Metres at the last Summer Games. He beat the world record."

Lefteris did not look the least impressed, nor did Rosy, still barking at me as if I were the first intruder ever to set foot in her dog-domain. Ignoring me after we shook hands, the fellow only had eyes for Ada and began a voluble Greek conversation with her. Finally taking time-out to notice that my teeth were chattering, Lefteris interrupted himself and invited us into the stone Hut.

"Looks solid enough to be home-base for the Abominable Snowman," I noted, but got no response.

We three made for the door in order to leave behind the mules, the dog, and the pines which towered enough to put Cedars of Lebanon to shame. On *that* Biblical note, Thank God We're Going Inside, was all my frozen brain could pray; and, Thank God For Hot Kitchens; then I heard myself saying aloud: "Hot bean soup!"

"And special hot Mount Olympos *tea*," Ada added.

"And hot friends," Lefteris put in, and slapt Ada's butt playfully.

"Aren't you married?" I asked harshly, and stared the Manager in the eye. "Ada and I are engaged."

"What a different world it is up here," Ada said for diplomacy's sake.

"Ain't *that* the truth—just like the Old Wild West!" announced a new arrival, in an American-sounding accent. We turned to look.

"My new helper—Kitty," Leftéris bragged and hugged a combat-booted blonde with tits like kettle drums. In American GI fatigues, she wasn't one bit successful in camouflaging those tremendous mammary glands. They stood at attention all the more because she kept patting her silver-blonde wavy wig, then batting inch-long mink eyelashes our way in a "down-home" Yankee greeting. Her eyeshadow was liberally splashed on, in an audacious chartreuse green.

"I'm from Montana," Kitty said. "Where ya guys from?"

"She's Athenian," Leftéris said for Ada, "and in fact, she's a famous Actress. She's the one who lights the Olympic Flame."

"Golly—that's neat!" and Kitty offered her hand. She really was bubbly, and pretty, despite her outrageous false hair and tarted-up face. She had the air of a Country-N-Western singer. "And who's he?"

"Ivor Hefferon," I said for myself.

"He's the last Olympic's winner of the Men's 1500 Metres," Leftéris said, proving that he *had* heard after all.

"Cripes Almighty—ya don't say! What brings ya way up here?"

"It's a *long* story," both Ada and I said together, then collapsed laughing.

"Well, Olympian," Leftéris commanded, as if it had only just registered, "how about coming out with me...to see where you both will be staying."

I hadn't even touched the golden tea yet, and still was freezing. My stomach went clench: "But—I'm just beginning to unwind. You mean—we're not sleeping *here*?" I flashed another ten-mile jaunt uphill, to some even icier clime, to a *real* hut.

"No, my Friend," the Manager replied warmly, "you're *not* sleeping in my kitchen, that's all. Come along. Let the pretty girls get acquainted."

So, we two men exited back into the Baffin Island air and made a circuit rightwards round the Refuge Hut, ever downwards. Rosy barked and led the way.

"So—it's a split level?" I remarked but got no reply. "Nice masonry," I tried, which did engender something.

"It was begun between the World Wars. You'll be staying here," and he pointed left to a separate and lower building, past the loos that were along to our right.

"Super," I replied.

The little building to which he was pointing, also of stone, looked sturdy enough to send an avalanche back *up* the slopes.

We descended ten steps, along the building's up-Olympos right flank, and came upon a stone entrance-way, that doubled as a balcony. Straight below was a suicide's dream-drop, to a ravine with a great streak of snow looking as if it had been there since the First Ice Age. I all but said: "But how *dirty* it is." Somehow, for once, I held my tongue, wisely.

"I thought you two Superstars would need a quieter place than the main house...for your meditation," Leftéris said.

Weird choice of word, I said to myself and screwed up my face in wonder. What in blazes did the Manager mean by that? But I replied: "That's extremely kind."

Leftéris slapt me on the shoulder and said: "Rest assured—I *have* been briefed—by Professor Rembetikós, who's my friend—on what you two have done for the good of Greece, not to mention for the good of the Olympic Games. I, for one, am *deeply* honoured to make your acquaintance—especially since the Press, in Athens, have been hunting you both for fifteen solid days. Are you aware of that?"

"Ada and I have been lost to the world. We haven't really given the news media much thought."

"We have a radio up here. I've been following this story since you and Ada left Olympia. British reporters have been turning Athens upside down, trying to find you two."

"I don't even know what day of the week it is."

"It's Maundy Thursday—of Holy Week."

"Really? Good God—the President of Greece's Press Conference is to-day."

"Heaven help us—you *have* been out of touch. You missed the Press Conference by two hours. But that's as it should be, Ivor. In fact, that's what this place is *for*. Coming here...people are *supposed* to leave the agonies of so-called Civilisation...below them...on the plains. There's nothing I hate more than hearing folks...at this idyllic spot...arguing about political problems that they're *never* going to be able to solve below. My main job here is to make sure people think of *higher* things."

"Tell me, though, have there been any international repercussions yet, due to the revelation that NATO and the CIA were involved with the Organizing Committee of the MOON?" I wondered.

"We'll talk about that later," Leftéris said and flashed a golden smile with his shiny tooth. He asked me loudly: "Do you like where you'll be staying?"

"Yes—very much," I responded honestly.

Kitty and Ada arrived with our packs. They had already become bosom-friends, so to speak.

"There're only two rooms," Leftéris explained, as we followed Rosy inside, one right off the doorway, with an upraised ledge for sleeping bags, with a mattress beneath, and the other room triple the size, with boulders for walls and a fireplace in the corner.

323

Both chambers were frightfully chilly, and sticky with moisture. Rosy charged at a corner and began barking. "Mice," Leftéris said quietly.

"I think the chimney will get some sudden use," I said and tried to keep my teeth from chattering.

"Well, I hope you two like it," Leftéris said and turned to leave with Kitty and Rosy.

Then—it hit me. When one's lodging is suddenly shown, one finally *does* realise...that at long last one has *arrived.* The concern shown by so many, all along the way, from London to Olympos, at last was managing to penetrate even *my* thick skull. I hugged Ada tightly.

The gratitude I felt was real. I let out a long sigh of relief, and said to the woman whom I loved: "It *shall* be a good, and an educational, time up here..."

20th March – Monday – Tea Time

"Well—it's high time *you* showed up!" Sir Cecil Gambling snorted crudely. He didn't even bother to shake the Athlete's hand. He just pointed to a chair.

Ivor yawned. No duller day on Earth could ever exist after Carnevale. It was Clean Monday, *Kathari Theftéra*, and Hefferon would have slept straight through it had not his landlady Evtychía gone to his *garçoniera* and pounded on the door.

"So—I don't suppose an ingrate like you has any excuse for tardiness."

The guest yawned again. "What time is it?"

"Tea time! And you're bloody well late!" then His Excellency began pounding a bell atop his desk.

Ivor covered his ears. His hangover was excruciatingly painful.

"Now—I presume you didn't even get any shut-eye at all. With what were you lolling *last* night?"

"None of your sodding business," the Olympic Medallist responded.

"Listen you—it's damned well *become* my business—and if we're not careful it's going to become the business of this Parliament as well as of your own!"

"Oh come on! What to fuck are you all in a snit for?"

"Where's that flipping tea?" the Ambassador screamed, pounding his poor bell again.

Presently, double doors to Sir Cecil's office were opening, and in stept none other than Colin Duckworth, himself yawning and bearing a silver tray. "Humble apologies, Sir Cecil."

"Colin! What in blazes are *you* doing here?"

"It's a long story, Ivor," the Student admitted. He was all but unrecognisable in a dapper three-piece blue suit with white pin-stripes.

"You bet it is," His Excellency retorted and pointed to a table for tea. "Now—pour us something first—then we can concentrate on your two asininities!"

"Our two whats?" both lads said together. They looked at each other's face, much worse for last night's grog, and burst into hilarious laughter.

"I daresay—you two aren't fit for flogging!"

"He'd love to tan our backsides, wouldn't he?" Ivor said and roared with glee. "Shall I stand, and drop my trousers?"

"Look," the Ambassador stated harshly, as he fought to hold control, "whom you do, on your own free time, is your own concern. But—when you go about, comporting yourself in a revelry and, moreover, when that hedonistic activity comes to *my* attention, at this *Royal* Embassy, then I can't be blamed for finding your behaviour very *much* my concern—whether you like the fact or not!" Then, Sir Cecil handed Hefferon a sepia tinted postal card.

Ivor took it and tried to focus on what it showed. Colin came over and crouched, to examine it as well. Again, both chaps couldn't help teeheeing.

"What *is* so frightfully funny, you Two?"

Ivor held up the postal card, that depicted himself nude, seated in an easy-chair, with one leg over its arm, and in his lap was seated Theatrínos, nude as well, with one of his arms around Hefferon's neck. The Singer's head was tossed back, and he had on a very wide smile, and that was all he was wearing. Both young men's uncircumcised penises and big testicles were very much prominently displayed, though neither man's penis was erect. Ivor, likewise, had on only an ear-to-ear grin.

"Nice looking dicks," the Olympic Athlete said just to work the Ambassador into a lather, then he burst into laughter again.

To add comfort to misery, Colin added: "I'll say!"

"Do you pair of *Morons* honestly think that such scandalous trash is *funny*? Exposed *penises*—why—it's not done—it's not British!" he huffed and almost started to cough. "Do you Two know how much *sleep* I lost over this little piece of *paper* last night?"

"Salivating too much?" Ivor wondered.

"Wanking alone...in the loo," Duckworth injected.

"Oh come now!"

"*You* come now!" Hefferon retorted. "Now just what *are* you saying?"

"Saying—who in Her Majesty's Realm *needs* to say a single thing—with a picture like this one circulating round all of *Athens* to-day?"

"But perhaps...if I might say..." Colin tried and rose.

Sir Cecil brushed him away: "I'll deal with *you* later—you who were supposed to be *trailing* this Olympic Gold Medallist—so he *wouldn't* end up doing something as stupid as he's done!"

"*You*...were trailing *me?*" Ivor laughed. "*You?*"

"Sorry, Ivor Old Chap, but I *am* an employee of the Foreign Office..."

"That you are—but would it be *were!*" growled His Excellency. "If Her Ladyship weren't so bloody *batty* over you!"

"Why didn't you *tell* me," Ivor joked.

"I was going to," Colin joked in return. "But I really *am*, true to say, reading a bit of economics at the L.S.E., in spare time, which's never."

"Boys—now this's the limit!" Sir Cecil smashed his fist on his desk and rose.

"Oh—tea?" Colin said and poured nervously. He handed a cup to the Ambassador as hastily as possible.

"Thank you," His Excellency replied fervently.

"It's delicious," Ivor said to Colin. "You brew a *nasty* cup!"

"Ta," Duckworth responded and winked.

Having received his afternoon soporofic, finally, the Ambassador suddenly seemed somewhat mollified, and changed his tactic. "Now, Hefferon. We're *both* Christ Church men. I do *not* in the world wish to malign your crystalline reputation, that indeed has, God alone knows how, remained virginally intact until to-day. That, my Dear Man, is all the more cause for my empathetic alarm."

"How *did* that marvellous postal card come into your possession?" Colin wondered wickedly.

"By some trite little trollop decked out like a Bird," Sir Cecil admitted.

"Dora Cain," both young Britons said at once.

"You recognised her, too?" Ivor asked.

"Couldn't miss her a mile away," Duckworth added.

"Who on Earth is *she?*" the Ambassador inquired. He was truly starting to thaw, ever so slowly, especially since Colin had just buttered him a scone.

"Your Excellency," Ivor began, "for the sake of clarification, I do have to inform you, now, under duress, that I am *not* in any position to divulge this information..."

"What?" the elder flared again, choking on his scone.

"Please—be patient," the Athlete continued, "but—I'm pledged to secrecy, and must first consult with my superior on this."

"Listen Hefferon—you're in *heaps* of trouble! You'd better co-operate."

"Then—all you have to do is *calm* yourself—and allow me to use your telephone."

"Whom are you ringing?"

"If the person agrees to come here, the person can explain all

326

that you wish to know," Ivor said and approached the telephone. "Is the line clean?"

"What to bugger do you mean?" Sir Cecil asked.

"Is anyone *listening*?"

"Use extension 211," His Excellency ordered.

Hefferon took out a number on a card and dialled, holding his hand over the speaker. "Hello—yes—it is I. I'm in Sir Cecil's office. He summoned me. Yes. Did *you* see it? You *know* about the postal cards? You were *there*? I didn't recognise you. Yes. The Ambassador's knickers are in a purple snit. I told him *nothing* yet. I did inform him only that I had to speak with *someone*. You do give clearance to bring the Embassy up to date? You'll be right over? Smashing. *He's* there, too? You'll be bringing *him* as well? Super. Sir Cecil will *shit*! I *shall* tell him you're both on your way. We're having quite the chatty tea. Good-bye." Ivor hung up.

"Now—do you *deign* to inform us who was that?" Sir Cecil asked arrogantly, taking particular attention to crack the "A" of the word *that*, like a snobbish whip.

"That," the Athlete answered, cracking *his* "A" even harder, "was Professor Rembetikós, Greece's Senior Member of the IOC."

"I bloody well know who in Hell he is!" retorted His Excellency acidly. "Whom is he bringing?"

Ivor held up the postal card.

"Oh—honestly," squeaked the Ambassador. "I do hope the boy is clothed."

"Aw—you'd *love* to see Theatrínos in the buff," Hefferon joked.

They all laughed.

"See—you're starting to loosen up," Colin observed.

"*You* Two could loosen up a Trappist graveyard!" Sir Cecil snorted.

"We'd get the ghosts speaking in tongues!" the Runner laughed.

"Your Excellency," Colin concluded, "at least we don't have a *pregnancy* case on our hands!"

"Theatrínos wasn't *on* me long enough for that!" Ivor joked, and almost felt as if Thomas Phillips's grand portrait of Byron was smirking at the three of them. "Or should I say...wasn't *inside* me long enough!" This was just such a scene that George Gordon would have loved.

"Thank God for small favours," the old crusty diplomat chuckled. "And anyway, the boy wasn't even *hard*!"

"Quite," the Olympian stated with a grin, sipping more tea. "Nor was he wearing a condom, but then...neither was I!"

"So do tell me, Hefferon, *about* that cheesy photograph."

"It was taken by Dora Cain, an agent for the Mount Olympos Olympic Nation," Ivor began, then tried his damndest, in a small space of time, to detail the complex circumstances of his being in Athens.

"And the Foreign Office never even notified me!" exploded Sir Cecil Gambling at last, unable to bottle his hurt any longer. "But..."

"But...the decision was between Her Majesty and our First Minister," the Athlete said calmly. "And you, therefore, must bow to *superior* authority."

"Evidently," the Ambassador replied obediently. If anything, being a politician so long had taught him his place. The old man sighed. "That still doesn't excuse the fact that an international *scandal*, involving a Briton, is about to erupt in my own jurisdiction!"

"You shall be made privy to whatever facts are deemed necessary...by Professor Rembetikós."

"And to whom, may I ask, is the august Professor of the University of Athens amenable, in all this chicanery?"

Suddenly—the door was opened by a steward and Aristídis Rembetikós and the Singer Theatrínos were stepping inside. The Ambassador rose, as did the others.

"So," His Excellency said at last, making sure that he had all the facts straight, and as he poured another round of sherry, given that it now was getting rather late, "let me recapitulate exactly what transpired at that discothèque last night. *You* had a Gala Opening," and he clinked glasses with Theatrínos, "and *you* were acting as the ground-floor DJ?" he asked Colin, who nodded yes and who toasted His Excellency's health, "and *you* were dressed as a Giant," to whom the Ambassador raised a toast, "whilst *you* were observing it all, incognito, as *what*?" he wondered one more time.

"As Anubis, Sir Cecil," the Professor replied and put his sherry glass to the Ambassador's.

"I see," the diplomat answered.

"The Jackal-Headed God of the Dead, in Ancient Egypt," Colin offered.

"Oh I bloody well read Classics, too—for God's Sakes!" His Excellency wiped his face then continued. "So—Some Little Bird, as you call her, had photographed you two lads, when you were up in Metamorphosis, playing a practical joke on her, 'just mucking about', as you two put it, not really having sex at all; and, this *Bird* then went round the Gala, as well as round Blood Drinker's Banquet, telling everyone that she'd get copies of this postal card *made* for them if they'd given her their name—and *how* many people wanted one?"

"Almost a thousand, Sir," Ivor boasted unashamedly.

"I told you we were Underground Heroes," Theatrínos bragged.

"Who've burrowed out of rat-holes," the Ambassador said with a twinkle in his fat eyes. "Now, the only other person whom the Honourable Professor saw possessing the aforesaid card was the Chief of Protocol of the Olympic Nation, Madame Ouranoú, commonly referred to as Thýella. Is *that* correct, Doctor Rembetikós?"

"As far as I can ascertain—yes. By the way, Your Excellency, I only feel that it is fair at this point—for the sake of clarity, to ask you *what* is the nature of the relationship between Thýella and this Embassy? She's often seen coming here, and has kept company with Her Ladyship the Ambassadress."

"Quite," Sir Cecil replied openly, "and I am proud to say that much of what you've been telling me, these past two hours, was suspected by this Embassy. We were tipped off by the Foreign Office to keep an eye on the Mount Olympos Organizing Committee—a year ago. This seemed easy for my wife and me, because we'd already been in social contact, for some time, with the Ouranós family. In the upper circles of this city, their presence is all but impossible to avoid. They have informers everywhere. They're probably even more powerful than the more notorious *shipping* families."

"So—is it safe for me to assume, and therefore for the IOC to assume—you and your wife are *not* allied, in any way, with any of Madame Ouranoú's Intelligence activities?" the Professor asked bravely, and stared right in the Ambassador's eyes.

"You may rest assured, Honourable Member of the International Olympic Committee, that *your* aims are *our* aims, that *this* Embassy has *not* colluded, nor will it *ever* collude, with *any* Member of the Olympos Organizing Committee. Moreover, we shall, from henceforth, provide you with any and all services possible, from this Athenian post of Her Majesty's Government. To you, I shall *personally* turn over my own file that I have been keeping on the MOON, and you may do with this Intelligence what you and the IOC see fit."

"Thank you, Ambassador. Your assistance is most appreciated."

"Would you like to telephone anybody?" the diplomat asked courteously.

"Yes—Lord Dalbeattie," the Professor answered. "He *must* be briefed as soon as possible. Let me see—I believe he's in London to-day."

There was silence as the Greek gentleman looked for the proper number, and as he dialled. "May I speak with His Lordship? He's in? Tell him it's Rembetikós." There was a pause. "Dalby? It's Ari. Listen—I have your protégé, Hefferon with me, and I'm ringing from the British Embassy. We've had a tiny hitch come up, and I thought I'd bring you up to date. Yes—it was necessary to inform Sir Cecil about everything. Yes—of course—that means you *must* notify His Lordship the Foreign Secretary immediately—and advise him to tell Downing Street and The Palace that the British Embassy now is being brought up to date. Sir Cecil will be communicating with you, via Diplomatic Pouch. You may speak with him when I'm done with you. What? Who? Ivor?" Then the Professor said to Hefferon: "Lord Luxborough wishes to speak with you—when we're done. Alexander's there having sherry. Now listen, Dalby, this's serious and it has to do with..."

After the quite lengthy discussion, and after everybody had spoken, Ivor was reflecting upon his best friend's telling him that he would be arriving in Athens to-morrow, en route to *India* of all places. He was going to Calcutta, to look into the activities there of his and The Queen's common forefather, Richard, Marquess Wellesley, eldest brother of Wellington who defeated Bonaparte at Waterloo. The Marquis had been Britain's Governor General of the Subcontinent. Hefferon reflected, that even though Alexander's visit would be fleeting, it would be wonderful to sit and talk with his alter ego.

"But Ivor," the Professor interrupted the Athlete's daydream, "You never did finish telling us the finale to last night. What did *Thýella* say?"

"What all this comes down to," and the Runner held up the controversial postal card, "is that just as the Gala was concluding, Madame Ouranoú approached me and blackmailed me."

"Exactly how?" Sir Cecil was insistent.

"Thýella said that, in truth, Cain was *not* giving out these postal cards all evening, as Dora had lied, but that the lie had only been staged, in order to scare me into complicity."

"Towards what?"

"Towards doing each and every little revolting thing that the MOON people could ever want—*that's* why she was blackmailing me—*that's* why she had that infernal woman take those pictures in the first place, I gather, because I dared to tell her filthy organization that I *wasn't* going to be party to their using me for their own invidious publicity, that I wasn't about to be *bought!*"

"I see," His Excellency stated.

"But," and Ivor turned to his new pal, the Singer, "*you* became Thýella's ultimate punch-line."

"Doesn't surprise me in the least," Theatrínos said quietly.

"Thýella told me, that the General had told *her*, only last night, that Theatrínos was his bastard son..."

"He did? He finally *told* her?" Theatrínos said ecstatically. "Good for him!"

"Plus—he told her that he was *proud* of you—and that this had made her furious with jealousy."

"You're joking? Did he really? It must have been the final lines of my Sacrifice Song, when I said that Greece *should* get the Olympics back."

"That's what she said—and she looked as mad as a woman with rabies. She never had *heard* this side of the family-saga before," Ivor added.

"What else did she say?" the Performer wondered.

"She blew up—she said that Ouranós told her he *loved* you— that he loved you *more* than he ever loved *her*—that at least his *son* had enough balls to stand up against her *and* his father!"

330

"Whew!" whistled Sir Cecil, who wiped his brow.

"Did she mention anything about telling anybody *else* in the family?" Theatrínos wondered.

"Yes," Ivor replied. "She said she was so offended by the idea that *you* could possibly be her husband's bastard-son that she would never dream of soiling the family's well respected name by mentioning you as a part of it at all!"

"Whew," His Excellency sighed again and wiped his face a second time. "You Greeks are *crazy*—if you'll excuse my saying so!"

Theatrínos laughed and said: "You're excused. It's a wonder Hollywood hasn't caught on—and set more thrillers *here*—they'd make billions! Now—I've got to go about Athens in a bullet-proof vest. That angry bitch will kill me!"

"She certainly looked mean enough to *last* night," Hefferon admitted.

"I'll agree with that," the Professor added.

"When she came up to Ada and me, forcing us into a deserted corner and flashing that card in our faces, I honestly don't think it mattered one lousy hoot to her that I was on it, pictured naked, let alone on it with another young man; but the point was that the *other* young man was her *step*-son—and a step-son whom her husband was *infatuated* with—and this she only found out late last night—well, it was simply too *much* for her, one more slap in the face to that jealous woman, one more infidelity of that perpetually horny husband of hers, which she'd never be able to erase."

"So—how did it end?" Sir Cecil asked, now at the edge of his seat. "Christ—I haven't heard anything so juicy since I was posted to Buenos Aires, where all they still talk about is Evita! Lord—this's better than some of those hot-to-trot American soap-operas!"

"Quite," Colin chirped in. "For risqué...I'd class it on a level...somewhere *above* The White House's knees...but somewhere *below* Buck House's belly-button!"

All the men chortled. Even Lord Byron above, in his frame, horse-laughed over that one.

"Thýella—irate as a king-cobra in heat—screamed at me to steer clear of Theatrínos—or else she'd *personally* release this photo, of the two of us, to the World's Press next Saturday. Thereby, she was guaranteeing my complicity, at least until the forthcoming Deed Ceremony when, I have the sneaking feeling, she'll dispense with me."

"We'll think of something, also for the Press, before Saturday," Professor Rembetikós assured them all.

"I certainly hope so," Ivor replied, then looked at Theatrínos, then at Colin.

His Excellency, whom Ivor had been surprised to discover was not such a wicked old ogre after all, had a glimmer in his eye and said: "Professor, given the delicacy of this complex diplomatic situation, don't you feel that it now is à propos for Mister Hefferon to receive diplomatic immunity, as a protected diplomat himself of Her Majesty's Government?"

"Absolutely," the Member of the IOC agreed, then to the Athlete added: "It's imperative, Ivor. There's no telling what Thýella and her merry crew might try to do to you. You *must* take the Embassy's offer of immunity."

"I guess I haven't a choice," the Olympic Gold Medallist replied.

Suddenly, Professor Rembetikós looked extremely grave. He wiped his brow and addressed the British Ambassador in all earnestness: "Sir Cecil, I have been advised to inform you, by my own Head of State, that what we are discussing is just the tip of the iceberg. This morning I met with the President and the Prime Minister both. I turned over the documents that Ivor gave me yesterday. Late this afternoon the President informed me that he had summoned our Chief of Staff, Brigadier General Theotókis, and that the Brigadier had provided certain classified information of his own, in relation to the case, Theotókis is presently beginning a top-secret investigation into the military aspects of this matter. I cannot go into any more detail than this to-night, but you are to expect an invitation to meet with our Head of State soon. In other words, Sir Cecil, the situation is *much* more critical than even *I* had feared only last night. I am only saying that the MOON-OC, and certain right-wing elements of the Greek Army, have been planning the Deed Ceremony for National Day...as a bluff. Whilst all the country's attention is to be diverted towards Olympia, General Ouranós and his followers are looking ahead for something a bit more drastic to take place, here in Athens, on the twenty-fifth. Don't ask me to divulge any more. The President of my country is going to be directly in touch about this with *your* Head of State. It should prove an interesting week indeed."

"Well, Gentlemen," the Ambassador said and rose, "do let us discuss this further—with some sustenance. Won't you join Her Ladyship and me whilst we dine?"

21st April – Good Friday – Eve

It was snowing outside. The weather had been foul all day. We were grounded, stuck inside the Refuge Hut. But we didn't mind. We had each other—and that's what counted most. Ada had kept us more than busy, preparing the Good Friday procession for this evening.

In deference to the Easter preparations, it did not seem appropriate to continue discussion with Leftéris about the repercussions of the revelations announced at the Deed Ceremony at Olympia. There would be plenty of time to go into that later.

Sitting in the common-room, round a blazing fire, as wind made the pines outside bleat like lonely heifers, one lovely Israeli girl was strumming a quiet guitar. Nobody in particular was listening, but likewise, nobody in particular was *not* listening. She was as at home as the hearth's very flames, though she only had arrived this morning, though she maybe would stay but a couple of days.

Representative of so very many, she had come, to climb, for her own silent reasons, reasons needing no explanation save the notes being played on her guitar. To this clubroom, so warm, so *gemütlich* as the many Germans who came here would say, such an exciting variety of people was what Mount Olympos was all about.

The Holy Mountain did draw them, to stay for a while, to exchange age-old stories, to be with others alike, and not alike, of their kind. A pot-pourri of humanity sat at half a dozen tables made from planks, on rough-hewn benches like pews. Some were laughing. Some were meditating. Some were updating their diaries. But every single one...was pondering...far more than one ever did at lower elevations; every single one...had forgotten about the woes of the lower world...

"Here in the clubroom," Ada said softly, "no one is any better than one's neighbour." Orange light from the fire was reflecting in her eyes, and she added: "The tip-top fitness of the long-time Mountaineer, who has scaled too many hills to count, is equal, before the fire, to the Novice...who never has known a Mystic Mountain in his life."

I nodded my head in agreement.

"The True Athlete," she stated, "*can* learn from the Novice's naïveté, just as the Novice can gain Wisdom from what the Athlete displays."

We completed our meal in silence. Like last night, all that we ate was bread and wine. Ada made sure that we were fasting, observing the Passion of Christ. It had surprised me, considerably, how much to the fore came her Christianity these past two days. Her Orthodox upbringing was so intensely ingrained.

Since I had never been in Greece during Holy Week, the depth of the people's participation, with all of their Being, in Jesus's Last Supper and Crucifixion, was a revelation to me. It was as if these tragic events, of two whole millenia ago, were taking place right at this very moment. To-day, especially, being Good Friday, had spread an eerie melancholy through each and every person at the Refuge Hut.

Inside the clubroom, atop a wooden table placed midmost in the chamber, Ada and Leftéris had brought a coffin-like box painted black. It was covered with a pall of lace, and people had placed wildflowers atop it all day. The ikon from the kitchen, of Saint George, was brought inside the clubroom, and a candle had kept it illuminated since morning. Candles, not electricity, provided the lighting. The room had, for all effects, become a chapel during a wake. There were about fifteen people, including workers, at the Hut, and all were in the clubroom.

Slowly, Leftéris rose and blew out all the candles, even that of the ikon. The fire as well had been allowed to die. Nobody was looking

333

forward to going with the procession of Christ's Body, outside, especially not in the snow—but everyone rose to comply. Leftéris pointed to his mason, Vasanákis, to his carpenter, Andréas, and to the mule-runner. The three Greeks felt deeply honoured to participate, to be hoisting the coffin of their Lord.

Grabbing the handles, they struggled with the box, up the five stairs that led to the way outdoors. The rest of us followed. We all had bundled for the midnight circuit round the Refuge Hut. Somewhere, in the Heavens, was a Moon just waning past Full. Little did its camouflaging help us. We turned east.

The Greeks were singing a dirge that sounded to have come from the time of Christ Himself. The Lord truly had *died*, we all felt, and it was the saddest procession of my entire life. In fact, I couldn't help thinking how opposite was the feeling to the exaltation that I'd felt running into the Olympic Stadium, at Lake Placid, just a few short weeks ago, at Opening Ceremonies of the Winter Games, when the temperature had been as cold as it was to-night on Mount Olympos.

But *this* walk was Sadness Itself, recognition of Man's Mortal Death. And it took forever, to complete the route. Nobody had bothered carrying candles, as was usual at lower climes. Howling winds would have blown them right out.

Then, one vicious gust did sweep all the bouquets off the coffin, and they scattered and leapt off the plâteau, to perish someplace lonesome in the Vale.

21st March – Tuesday – Midday Meal

Hefferon sat still for a moment, and reflected on how he had spied the blond and handsome mop of hair that had made its way towards him. His boyhood friend, Alexander Pella, Earl of Luxborough, had suddenly noticed him, and the two had run and embraced like lost brothers. This had set the throng, in the largest café of Athens, beneath the American Express building in Sýntagma Square, gabbing more raucously than before.

But now they were dining beneath a huge tree, in the open-air restaurant named Próothos. It was at the far end of Pláka, almost next door to the Agora, and on the corner of Dioskoúron and Dioskoúron Víta, names that dated to Homer or before.

"Super choice of restaurant, Old Bean!" Alexander said with admiration. "I mean—look at *us—twins!*"

"Dioskoúron—Two Youths."

"Castor and Pollux."

"Helen of Troy's twin brothers," Ivor added.

"Good show! Now—tell us—what's eating you?" Alexander asked.

"Sorry...I just was worrying...when will we *next* be fated...to stop our stupid lives...if but for a moment...to *meet*...to *talk*..."

"You know I'd love to stay, but I've long had my sights set on India," the young Lord said with bravura. "Chin up—I shan't be in the Black Hole of Calcutta forever."

"I should like to be going," the Athlete said and paused: "I've fallen, though, into such a sticky situation here..."

The waiter was just bringing their veal sautéed in a lemon sauce, boiled potatoes, and a tomato and cucumber salad. The man seemed to be making quite a fuss at their table, not used to waiting on two blond men who looked so similar. Both were wearing dark suits. The Earl's was black and much more expensive, hand-tailored, and fit like a glove. Alexander was two inches taller than Ivor, and certainly was the more stunning of the two. His facial features were more chiselled, and his profile was as classic as that of any ancient sculpture of Apollo. Contrary to the Runner's curly hair, Alexander's was wavy, and finer. But all in all, their looks were startlingly alike. Everyone always presumed they were kin. Even their tone of voice and mannerisms were alike, due to continually having been in association since they were eight years old.

"Are you brothers?" the waiter couldn't resist asking.

"Yes," Alexander replied. "My family adopted him," he joked.

"It's true," Ivor contended.

"You're British?" the waiter wondered.

"How can you tell?" Luxborough jibed.

"You speak perfect English!" he said and walked off, highly pleased with himself.

Ivor never tired of listening to his best friend. Alexander, being a poet and novelist, added even more grace to his manner of speaking than came natural to him because of his aristocratic birth.

"Isn't *próothos* the Greek word for progress?" the Earl asked.

"Professor Rembetikós suggested it."

"So what's the Old Boot scheming to-day?"

"He's meeting with Sir Cecil and the American Ambassador about Dora Cain."

"Can the Yanks be trusted?"

"Nobody knows. What the White House says is one thing, but what the CIA does is another. Given that I found files of correspondence from both the CIA and NATO, who are backing this nuclear idea, to build inside Olympos, the protocol involving America is terribly touchy. I don't know *how* Rembetikós will be dealing with it, to be perfectly honest. He's a very cunning man. From my own experience, I know that he never lays his whole hand on the table without first seeing the other players' cards."

"So—you were telling me, on the walk here, that Dora Cain's father's name is *Clinton?*"

"He owns some construction firm, Clinton Enterprises, working with Ouranós Ltd here in Greece for many years. It appears that this is how Ouranós Ltd grew so fast in the 1950s—because Thýella blackmailed Clinton into supplying Greece with high-level U.S. technology, which was hard to get after the Greek Civil War. In other words, her only reason to go to Washington in the first place was to secure herself a 'patron', someone to back her *real* motives, which were aimed back home in Greece."

"How did Thýella blackmail him?"

"She learnt all his dirty doings when she was sleeping with him in Washington. I guess Clinton used her as his Mother Confessor. Imagine! When she succeeded in getting herself pregnant with Dora, she used his information to her advantage."

"Clever."

"Very. You should *work* with the bitch. She's now out to skin me alive."

"You'll survive her—that I prophesy," Alexander said and winked. His eye caught the washed white pebbles of the courtyard and followed them to the huge tree above their heads. "What species do you think it is?"

"Basswood?"

"Could very well be. It appears ancient enough to have been planted by Perikles."

"I prefer the palm," Ivor said and pointed to the juncture of the one-block alley Dioskoúron Vita with the longer lane Dioskoúron proper. "Speaking of trees...how's *Savaging The Amazon* doing?"

"You know, that book's done bloody well!"

"Better than *Moctezuma*?"

"How do you think I'm financing this trip to India?"

"You know—that Latin American thing you got going was the smartest move you ever made. *You* were writing about it before it became so bloody trendy."

"*Amazon* is being released in Spanish in April!"

"You see—investigating how the river and jungles are being raped by developers was worth all the hassles you went through."

"I daresay. The novel should cause quite the stir in the Portuguese."

"When will that be out?"

"In May."

"Woe to the poor Brazilians."

"Palms..." Alexander said and brought the conversation back to the Old World. "Are there palms...in India?"

"You're asking me?" Ivor replied. "In Kerala, aren't there?"

"Aren't the colours here lovely?" the Earl asked, as he glanced straight ahead past the corner. "All these buildings in sight are in different shades of yellow. Now—*that* one doesn't see in London. Just the way Athens *looks* should bring up your spirits, Old Chap! Look—you'll triumph over this MOON lot. Their day's marked on Zeus's Calendar!"

Just then, their waiter returned and posted himself nearby, in order to eavesdrop better.

"Athens does have a radiance all her own, especially at night," the Athlete answered sadly, then paused. "What do you intend to do...in India?"

"I don't know yet...check out Calcutta...that's the only fixed goal on my itinerary...you know...our Wellesley connection...sniff the spots on the sheets left by our rakish forefather, Richard The Randy Marquis..."

"Now now," Hefferon jibed, "Good Ole Dick's one of The Queen's forebears, too."

"He still was a *ponce*. Just like you!" Alexander shot back. "Who knows...I may just go on retreat. My life's moved so quickly...books, books, and more books...and films...and the House of Lords..."

"The what?" Ivor said in amazement, "you...you don't mean..."

"You haven't heard? Good God—you've been *that* out of touch? You've only been here three weeks!"

Hefferon looked shocked. He was speechless. The waiter was pretending he wasn't listening.

Alexander continued: "Ivor...I'm sorry to tell you that my uncle ...is *dead*. Thank God. You know how we *hated* each other! It happened just after you left London."

"Did you *kill* him?"

"Wish I had the guts, but no, he just kicked the bucket, all on his own. It was the very first thing he ever did...without assistance!"

"But...why didn't you say something when last we spoke?"

"He died the second of March. We spoke on the first, wasn't it?"

"I'm sure you don't miss him..."

"I danced on his grave!"

The waiter came and filled their carafe of white wine.

"Dalbeattie felt it best I should tell you myself, in person," Alexander said kindly. "He felt you had more than enough to deal with ...without worrying about me."

"This means...you're *Duke* now?"

"I suppose I am."

The waiter could hardly believe his ears.

Ivor had tears in his eyes. "Well—to His Grace, Duke of Brendon!" he declared and hoisted his glass, to honour his lifelong friend. "Dear God, your uncle was..."

"A young man," Alexander said mock-sadly. "He just turned fifty. But all *fifty* of those years were *miserable* ones. He never pleased a single Soul in his life, not even his poor mother. He had a heart attack. It was a blessing. Even his *mother's* glad he's gone!"

The waiter scurried across the washed gravel to the other

members of the staff, to tell them that a veritable aristocrat was dining in their midst.

Hefferon wondered: "But if you just assumed the title, why are you off to India?"

"That's precisely *why* I'm off to India," and he then emitted a strange laugh, half a sigh. He glanced past the tables to the doting staff, and the waiter came running, praying he was needed.

"May I help you with anything?" he asked.

"What kind of sweets have you?"

"Crème caramel..."

"Lovely. That will be fine. And you, Ivor?" There was no response, so the Duke said: "Two." He began to tap the table.

"Sorry. I'm just terribly tired," Hefferon apologised.

"I understand," Alexander said then paused. "You'll never believe in a million years whom I bumped into."

"In London?"

"No—to-day—at Athens Airport."

"Who?"

"Our old Master at Westminster."

"Which old Master? The Head?"

"The youngest old Master."

"Dempsey?"

"Wrong."

"Crowner?"

"Wrong."

"I give up."

"De Soto!"

"No!"

"Right here at the airport—Paul De Soto—guess with whom?"

"Some gorgeous Hollywood starlet, no doubt."

"Berenice Guggenheim!"

"The American *opera* diva? Since when has *he* been into classical music!"

"He *married* her!"

"Go on!"

"Even if she's not one of *the* rich Guggenheims."

"How many wives does *that* make?"

"Isn't it incredible—his boudoir career?"

"From Westminster School to Hollywood, and every woman's bedroom in between!"

"I hadn't seen him since he starred in *Moctezuma*."

"Not since two summers ago in Rome?"

"Has it been that long? He's been holed up in Bel Air."

"What's he up to now?"

"They're on honeymoon. They got married in Las Vegas, where else, then flew from the States somewhere, to Greece."

"They're staying here? I'd love to see him."

"They're sailing this evening—for Egypt."

"Why don't they just fly?"

"Can one explain newlyweds? They begged me to come along."

"On their *honeymoon?*"

"Paul always *was* kinky. Remember those jerk-off sessions he used to have us take part in, in the Abbey?"

"Biggest cock I've ever seen...was Paul's...in Westminster Abbey!"

"Oh come on, you saw *mine*...in Westminster Abbey...plenty of times!"

Both fellows roared with laughter.

"He hasn't changed a bit. Nor have you, you Whoreson!"

"Thank God all that adulation in Beverly Hills hasn't gone to his head," the Olympic Gold Medallist stated and snickered.

The waiter cleared their table, finally, having heard enough gossip for a month, and departed for the sweet. Ivor and Alexander lapsed into silence, each thinking of days gone by. Finally, the Athlete couldn't stand the lull in conversation any longer and said: "Wish they'd change the name of this restaurant."

"Why's that?"

"Progress? You know it doesn't exist!"

"This discussion reminds me of one I had with Rupert Broxbourne, in Rome when he was wrestling with something inside himself ...something I could perceive but couldn't cure..."

"Meaning?"

"I can see, quite plainly, how you're *suffering*, Ivor. It's paining me greatly."

"It's *that* visible?" the Runner allowed and hung his head. "Of all the people in the whole wide world...*you're* the one who knows me best."

"Then listen to me!" Alexander ordered. "Snap *out* of this! I *know* you're feeling trapped. I *know* you wish you'd never got involved with this mess. I *know* you don't feel it's really utilising your services to the maximum. But Ivor—I *know* you—you've *got* to see this through!"

"And then?"

"And then? Then...you relax. Come to India. I'll send you the bloody fare."

"But...don't you see what I mean?" Ivor pleaded, almost in despair. He stared at his friend's kindly eyes.

"Tell me," Alexander replied.

"I...have *nothing*...*nothing* in my life to sustain me...*nothing* from within that counts."

"What do you call trying to save the Olympic Games?"

"I wish I knew," Ivor answered, then looked away. He paused. "Alexander—you *quit* Christ Church—because you knew what you wanted in life. You are an *author*—one of the best we have in England.

You're still maligned, because you're young, because you're nobly born, but your time, for your true reputation, indubitably *will* come!"

"What're you saying?"

Ivor fought for words, since he had never heard himself voicing these thoughts to a Soul, not even to this his best friend. He breathed deeply, and finally said: "You write. You are a *creative* man. Some precious gift, from deep within your very Being, likely from some recomposite of those magnificent minds from whom you do descend, finds its way, outside, to us, to all humanity. And people do respond— and most people call it good. You, thereby, are a *privileged* individual, not by virtue of your blue-blooded birth, but by virtue the fact that you *create*, and *for* that you are given thanks and love in return."

Alexander was deeply touched, yet said nothing.

"Never...not *once* in my whole life...have I ever *done* anything for anybody...such as *you* have. Never...not *once* in my whole life... have I ever *created* anything... but *trouble!*"

"That's not true!"

"It is!"

"It's not! *You*...Ivor...have given me *untold* joy...as a friend. I couldn't even *imagine* life...without you..."

"But Alexander—my brother—I *am* trying—in my own feeble way—to tell you that I am *very* dissatisfied—with my whole life! Something *deep* within me...*needs* to come out...but can't!"

"Why not?"

"I don't know *how*...to let it!"

The two friends stared at each other.

"Then," Alexander began softly, "you must create something, too."

"But—I'll never be an *author*—like you. And I wouldn't want to, and couldn't, compete with you. Our friendship, which I value higher than all the stars in the heavens, would be destroyed in one fell swoop."

"Then—compose, paint, sculpt, dance, design edifices that exalt Mankind."

"How?" Ivor shuddered. "How?"

"The answer...is where the *urge* is...within," responded the Duke of Brendon in all due earnestness. "But come now—let us pay this chap first—then we can better discuss this, whilst we walk, as did the *ancients*, as did our *ancestors*, as did our mutual *Greek* ancestors, whose Blood Noble you know in your heart of hearts we *do* share!"

22nd April – Easter Saturday – Midday

It rained till past ten in the morning. Snow kept falling most of the night, but the majority had been washed away by the drizzle.

Ever changing were the temperatures on the Holy Mountain. A sudden breeze from the foothills began blowing up the length of the

340

Olympian Vale, about eleven in the morn. Groups of climbers had already departed from the heights, those who did not have as much time as we had on their hands. Leftéris had taken the Norwegians up to the peaks. They had left about quarter to ten.

The Refuge Hut was uncannily still. The breeze was even now taking a nap, in the towering trees behind the impregnable concrete bunkers. Even Rosy was dozing out of doors. No birds were chirping. The upper-most peaks were shrouded, veiling themselves in dour grey clouds.

Ada was with me. We had walked round the Hut's perimeter to the East Overlook, where the flowers on the coffin had vanished. This was the very edge of the escarpment atop of which the camp was located, high above the majesty of the Vale. To-day's breeze had blown away all of the clouds from the colossal crevasse, and one could see the whole length to the Aegean Sea, almost thirty kilometres away.

We leant upon the stone restraining wall, and gazed downwards appreciatively from the fortress, then mountainside to mountainside, to encompass the width of the bowl of green that Ada called the Amphitheatre of Comedy. Then we looked straight down the Valley, twenty kilometres to the two Gateposts, Stávros, now on the left, and Gólna, now on the right. For the life of us we couldn't imagine how anybody could desecrate this beauty, with anything, let alone with something as evil as the Ouranós family had been planning. We shook our heads in dismay.

The contrast was quite disturbing...between how utterly grandiose Stávros and Gólna had seemed, each looming one thousand metres tall, from the lowly vantage of Litóchoron. But now...we were one thousand metres above them both, and twenty thousand metres due west. And even *more* disturbing was the fact that more than one thousand metres above our heads loomed pure rock—pure rock gripped by snow. We took each other's hand; we both were shaking.

The seven-kilometre plain, from Stávros and Gólna to the beach of the Aegean Sea, now just seemed a finger-wide sash of fuzzy browns and greens. All that vast amount of farmland now looked less than an acre, and not one thing of the plain could be seen beyond either bolster of the Gateway, not one thing to the left nor to the right. Only the Aegean...beyond the plain...now was visible, looking as small as a lake. It was the same mélange of hues as the sky. And way out upon the whitish water, Sky and Sea were blending as one. No horizon was to be seen.

Feeling strange, we both turned one hundred and eighty degrees. Just then, now facing due west, a breeze started blowing from the east. Wind began moving in the tops of evergreens, like a dragon unloosening celestial coils, and then began stretching outwards and upwards in an eldritch sweep towards the upper realm. An eerie noise it was making.

Clouds were being pushed higher, higher, higher each moment by the breeze. Then, about eight thousand feet above the sea, the wind was being packed together by the natural geology, and funneled as if into a hole in the clouds that kept moving in one gigantic mass, upwards, upwards, level, all at the very same time, as if being jacked up by some invisible hydraulic pump. Suddenly, just when the top-most peaks of Mount Olympos were being revealed to the naked eye, Ada said breathlessly: "Mýtikas!" She had tears in her eyes.

There it was. Just then scraping the whitish pall of moisture, a grey stickle-backed row of jagged limestone teeth, like a stegasaurus's spine, was the pinnacle to this whole great height.

But wind, that had been drilling away at the clouds, in the hole caused by a drop in atmospheric pressure, punched through the layer of grey, like a fist, and a titanic gold sunray fell down, from the sky, and landed upon Mýtikas on high.

The Peak of the Balkans began to shine, like a treasure trove of Zeus Almighty, with radiantly blazing light. Then, just as quick as it became illumined, the clouds squeezed upon the Peak tight, like a sea-polyp closing in on itself, and all the clouds lowered their bulk, and concealed the summit from sight.

Ada then turned to me and said strangely: "The Mountain just answered my prayer."

I feared to inquire what it was she had asked.

"I had to know, Ivor, whether or not you are meant to go up... *with* me....or *alone*."

"And Olympos told you...what?"

"Alone."

"But...I *want* you to be with me! For the first time in my life...I'm scared."

"Up there..." and she pointed, "you will learn to deal with *fear*. Once you do that, the creativity you've been nurturing within you, all these years, will begin its inevitable journey *out*!"

21ˢᵗ March – Tuesday – Hour Of Siesta

Turning left into the block-long lane of Polýgnotos, where the path goes a few yards before halting at the wire fence and the gate to the Ancient Agora, Alexander and his ally were standing on the same worn stones of the Panathenian Way where Ivor had stood with Dora Cain shortly after his arrival in Athens.

Now—it truly was spring, that short idyllic season, when the capital's air is crisp and aromatic, and the land so green with plantlife that the ruins are all but evasive.

"It's so magnificent," Alexander said and breathed in deeply. "Let's just climb a bit."

They walked about fifty yards, upwards. To their immediate left, base stones of the archaic temple foundation of the primitive Goddess Demeter rose above their heads. They sat beneath the foundation, on a great block of marble that had tumbled æons ago into the Panathenian Way.

"Hefferon?" the Duke asked.

Ivor looked deeply into his friend's eyes. "I've missed you."

"Who?" joked the Olympian. "Don't be..."

"*Come* with me."

The Athlete's head began pounding. "But...you know how I'd love to see India...but what're you doing to me...this's one of your bleeding tricks...you know I have responsibilities here!"

"I know..." the young Lord's voice sounded too far away. "I know..." He sighed. "Plus...you've your *own* dreams...to take you to *different* places."

Ivor choked up, and had to turn away. He wanted to say that, as boys, their dreams were once the same. "Olympos?" he somehow said.

"India," his friend somehow answered. "Names...places...spots on maps...on this sphere called the Globe...why do we even travel...what do we *ever* truly learn? We see the landscape vary...then vary some more. We watch the people's faces change...then change again and again. We marvel at customs...till we have no more strength to marvel any longer...yet again we move...we keep on moving...we keep on seeking...what?...the newer horizon?...hoping for chances at Knowledge?...we keep on questioning those few with the patience to sit still...those few who remain in one place for a lifetime. We think we get closer...to Wisdom...as we wander...yet what...ever...do we learn...that's universal...about Man? Our increased intelligence...just shows us...that our steps...of which we're so vain...are only and forever...too weak..."

Ivor was weeping. He hardly heard the music that began above them both. Something was making music, jarring music, tinkly raspy music, a noise a bit too Oriental for the ear.

"The *East*...has been calling me...you know that," Alexander said.

"Yes. Since Marina?" Ivor wiped his eyes.

"Yes. Since Marina." Alexander put his arm about his friend and squeezed him tight.

"I just pray...you find...Peace...there..."

"Isn't that...risking too much?" Alexander asked, kissed Ivor on the cheek, for an eternally long time, just beside his mouth, then slapt him on the back and stood. "Let's see from where that music's coming."

The Olympian stood, glad to get up and do something. His body felt strange, as if thoughts, and no blood, coursed within it. The music had stopt. He could still smell the manly musk of Alexander...lingering upon his face.

"I've an idea," Alexander said and began scaling the huge blocks of the Demeter Temple's foundation. "Good Gods—look at that!"

Ivor hurried to stand at the top of the wall where his friend was. "Blimey—that's the pair I saw my first night in Athens. How'd they get that thing up here?"

Hefferon gawked at the same spindly music box that he had seen over three weeks ago. There was the same agèd crone, cranking that very same handle, methodically, as if she'd been churning butter for years. The handle kept turning, kept making music. Every few beats the tune was broken, brashly, by a very brittle and unrhythmically timed bell. It could have easily been the music of the Infernal Spheres.

Alexander was absolutely entranced, by the *lattérna*, by the ancient woman in black, and by the tiny boy all in white, whose head was all that was sticking up above the tall grass that had long ago overgrown the floor of the Earth Goddess's shrine. Then—he suddenly noticed his watch. "Damn— look at the time!"

"You're *not* leaving?"

"But I have to."

"When? You never even told me when your *flight* is!"

"To-night...I have to get back to the airport...soon!"

"*Must* you go to-night?"

"I'm booked. *Come* with me!"

"Stop *torturing* me—you know I *can't*! *Please*—don't *tempt* me! If I escort you to the airport, you know I'd *never* come back here!"

"You have your *own* life to lead, my Dearest Friend."

"Can you..." then Ivor couldn't continue his sentence, he was too confused by the rapidity of events of the past three weeks. More than anything in the world, the Athlete hated saying farewell. His whole life had seemed...just a constant string of good-byes.

Alexander knew this, and offered to say: "It's best...I'll leave you ...here..."

"With...*them*?" the Runner asked, and stared at the old woman and tiny lad. They were not now making music.

"Think...of what I said," Alexander confided. "Once these plots are behind you...rise above them. Climb Olympos...if you must. While you're up there, I'm sure, you'll *have* the revelation that I know your Soul desires!"

"I'll be thinking of you," Hefferon said weakly, as his friend embraced him. He clung to Alexander as if he truly had the answer to his life. The cheeks of their faces were pressed side to side, and then, ever so briefly, their lips brushed past each other, in a rapid fraternal good-bye kiss.

"I'm not *worthy* of that, Ivor! *Promise* me—you'll be thinking of your *Self*?"

"I promise. Safe journey...to India..." Ivor now was crying openly.

"Safe journey...to Olympos..." said his friend, as tears fell down to the Temple's base.

"Alexander! I *must* thank you...thank you for all..."

"Don't!" commanded Alexander, as he put his hands aside his best friend's shoulders. "Be strong. You know that I love you. You're the only brother that I have."

"But...how can I *contact* you...in *India?*"

"I'll let you know, care of Professor Rembetikós."

Having said that, the young Duke of Brendon jumped off the foundation to the Temple of Demeter, and proceeded with a wave down the Panathenian Way.

23rd April – Easter – 4.00 PM

"Lazy Bones," Leftéris shouted and shook me by the foot. "Get up! It's Easter! *Kristos onesti!** "

We were taking a nap. We'd stuffed ourselves like pigs last night, after we'd broken the fast, and had danced ourselves silly. Now we were totally knackered. Ada covered her head and hid beneath the covers.

"There's beautiful sunshine," Leftéris continued. "The blizzard's all melted. The Lord is good. Hurry up, Ivor, you're coming with me—to work. I'm sorry if it's Easter Sunday—but an emergency's just come up. Poor thing, you look as tired as if I'd fed you *margarítsa* soup last night instead of lamb!"

Maybe there was sunshine on the Hut, but not a couple hundred feet above. Creeping fog still was lurking amongst the pines, twisting round gigantic trunks like anacondas.

The Manager was leading me to the upper reach of the same snow-slick that hurtled downslope past our little cabin. At least I could shout farewell to Ada, I thought, if I slipt and fell.

We both were carrying shovels. Following Leftéris most carefully, I was shaking inside. The angle of the slope was at least sixty degrees. Fog was everywhere.

"Snow never was my favourite thing," I allowed. "Especially at Easter."

But all I could do was follow, and began plopping my mountain boots, purchased second-hand in Litóchoron, one by one, up and down, up and down, into the snow with the side of my foot, in order to secure a good enough grip to balance there till the next step could be made the same way.

"Fun, isn't it?" Leftéris asked.

---

* To say KREE-stose is wrong, but to try to coach pronunciation of the Greek letter *X* would take ages, so ask a Greek. The second word is pronounced: oh-NESS-tee. Meaning: Christ is risen!

345

My stomach was doing cartwheels. I thought: That bloke's got to be a sadist! But I answered: "I'd sooner die by *fire*—any day of the week—than by *freezing*!"

"You're English—you should *enjoy* a good jaunt in the fog."

"Thank Heavens I can't see down!" I responded. The drop was God knows how many miles. "By the way, Old Chap, might I ask what it is we're *doing* out here?"

"You're not fond of carrying round a shovel?"

Ha ha. Where did this man come from? "Following you up these ruddy slopes—I now know what Mahomet meant! Why *climb* the sodding mountain, if you can make the bugger come to *you*?"

"We're almost there."

At last, we came to a stretch along the incline where the Manager decided to stop. I was breathing so loudly, with my mouth, that it was vulgar.

"Are you consumptive?" Leftéris asked.

My—such humour! I answered: "If I wasn't yesterday, I sure as Hell am to-day! Do shoot me. Put me out of my misery."

Before I could recover my equilibrium, the fog lifted a bit upslope. And there was Leftéris already, way above. Was I just dreaming?

It looked just like a glacier to me. Not being Mary Shelley, but being in the mood to compose something as vindictive as *Frankenstein* to sic on the Manager, all I could do was keep staring at the cocky vision up ahead, a man, silhouetted, black, against a pure field of white. It looked apocryphal. But then, as I began hastening towards it, the fog returned and gobbled the vision from sight.

But that was an hour and a half ago. I was now *inside* a metre-deep hole, shoveling snow *outside*. Leftéris had told me to dig—for a covered water pipe. Snowballs kept rolling downslope, ever gaining momentum, tumbling towards the Aegean. And fog...was clouds of sodium pentathol...and had all but put me to sleep.

When was it? Last night? We were in the clubroom again. The coffin was gone. Candles were suddenly being extinguished, by Leftéris. From a glowing ember in the fireplace, he was lighting a big white taper in his hand. He was standing proudly, and saying aloud, with a voice booming forth, like a bishop's: "*Krístos onésti!*" And he was passing the flame from his candle to the next person, who was standing beside him. And this person was passing it to the next. And the next was passing it beyond...until everybody in the whole room was holding aloft a share of the radiating fire. And I saw in my mind's vision the eruption of flame that blinded me at Lake Placid, when I succeeded in lighting the Cauldron at the last Winter Games. And in the clubroom, everyone was suddenly truly joyous, because of the Risen Lord. I had never seen anything like this Greek Easter—and it made the English manner of celebration seem downright dour.

Had I been dreaming that too? But it seemed as if I'd finally succeeded in getting the *feel* of Greece...for the very first time since I'd arrived in the country. While it had stormed...those hardy Greek lads ...with their robust thighs...and those girls with their stiffened nipples... those figures right off antique vases...came to life in the Hut...last night...on Olympos. And with them...perpetual *mousikí*...

All the time I'd spent in Athens and Olympia, I couldn't recall once when I'd heard such spontaneous playing and singing as last night, Easter Eve. Christ *had* risen, for *these* folks, indeed!

Leftéris's mason, Vasanákis, had begun strumming the Israeli girl's guitar. His virtuosity was astounding, and everyone was enjoying his affability. As all the faces were singing and smiling, I couldn't help thinking that Vasanákis's harmonies almost were sounding Spanish. There was Flamenco in his Hellenic Soul!

Suddenly...three of the Greeks couldn't contain themselves any longer. Up they jumped, to the cheers of the whole boisterous clubroom. This...this very moment in Greece...was one that my heart had been yearning for. I hadn't yet found it in the country's turbulent capital. I hadn't yet found it in the place where ruins drew crowds. But here, now, way high upon Olympos...three lusty men were jumping up...to *dance!*

The spirit of joy was so very strong. No one was dancing for money. No one was dancing for show. No one was dancing for something to do. Three were dancing...for Life Itself! *Life*...which always can...and always does...*seize* one here in Greece!

Arms on each other's strong shoulders, feet backwards feet forwards, and sidesteps with grace, three moved as one, as guitar and singing and rousing harmonica hastened their gladdened hearts.

Such expression of Soul...was what had called me to Greece in the first place. Something from some past life, from the lives of my forefathers and foremothers, perhaps centuries gone by, perhaps millenia gone by, but *not* gone by far enough to be *permanently* gone by, because our Blood always hearkens to its Own! And so I joined them!

Afterwards...did we all have a banquet! Roast lamb most certainly was the *only* way to break such a fast!

But now, Easter Sunday, here I was, in this *hole*. Mind you, no *ordinary* hole. A *snow* hole. And I was *digging* it...in a *glacier*. Leftéris had simply vanished. So I leant on my shovel...and reached in a back pocket of my corduroy trousers for a handkerchief.

"What's this?" I asked myself as I pulled out a folded sheet of paper. "Good grief—Theatrínos's poem!" I wondered where I'd stuck the thing!

Once upon a time...
There was a Mount...
Lying leagues beneath the young Aegean Sea.

347

And there it sat, mute, one piece of rock...
Until its limestone bulk was stirred to be.

Suddenly I was terrified out of my skin! I thought there was an avalanche tumbling towards me!
Palsied with shakes, my nerves were all but blown apart.
Leaning on the shovel, against the uphill side of the hole, now almost
two metres deep, I was trying to pull myself together...inside the bloody
glacier. Not seeing very well for the fog, I was breaking out in a sweat,
like an overworked whore.
"Well—wouldn't *you* think it's a flaming avalanche!" I shouted
aloud, still shaking like a leaf, to the unresponsive ice, as my voice
echoed off the ravine. "Sick—sick sick *sick* joke! *Damn* that man! I'll *get*
that flipping Leftéris! He better *not* have laid a bleeding finger on Ada!"
This, too, echoed again and again.
What I thought must surely be an avalanche had only proven to
be an overpassing fighter-jet. "Sodding pilot!" I yelled. "Hope you crash!"
Flying too low, the dirty bugger *should* have smashed the flaming thing, I thought, still shaking violently. The jet was passing now.
What *noise* it had been! Happy Easter Sunday!

21ˢᵗ March – Tuesday – Dusk

Upon the cyclopean wall, by the Temple of Demeter, Ivor was sitting
where he and Alexander had stood. He was just too tired to move, and
was waiting there for sunset.
Behind him, an hour ago, the ancient lady and tiny boy had
wheeled their contraption away, uphill, towards the Akropolis. The
Olympic Athlete had not even noticed. He was lost in a daydream that
he could not control. The stones all about him were refusing to speak.
He did not even hear the approach of a woman. She had come down the
Panathenian Way.
"Meditating?" asked the woman, now directly behind him.
Ivor spun round. It was Thýella—the last person on Earth he
wished to see. Ivor stood. He looked at her. To-night she was wearing
white. She had no jewelry visible, except for a signet ring.
Ivor was expecting to be fired, but the lady was extending a
dossier, that had been fixed with sealing wax. "Where's your briefcase?"
"To-day's Clean Monday. You told me we wouldn't be working."
"Nevertheless—take this," she ordered and handed the package
to the man. "Do *not* lose this. Do *not* open this—until exactly twenty-four
hours from now."
Ivor looked at his watch, and was startled to see that it was six
o'clock.
"As you have noticed, the dossier is sealed," Thýella stated, then
extended her left hand towards his face, "by this."

348

Ivor examined the white cut gemstone set in platinum.

"It represents Lamía, the Libyan, who was so mad for Zeus that she allowed him to pluck out and replace her eyes at will. She became insane to murder—after Hera killed all her children—save Scylla. Lamía went on a rampage—butchering the children of others in revenge—then ended her days as a vampire. She sucked all the blood, at night, of the young men with whom she slept." Thýella smiled, then paused: "Her face turned into a nightmarish mask—so it's said."

Ivor held his tongue. Never in his life had he been confronted with such an icy, ghoulish stare. Thýella's mute face was screaming at him all the things he had been expecting to hear. She was saying nothing about the Olympics plot, nothing about Dora Cain, nothing about the photographs, but then she was saying: "We are convinced that you, henceforth, shall obey our orders. You are to be running, in the Panathenian Stadium, this very evening, at midnight. Do not forget to bring along your MOON-OC ID—you'll be needing it, starting Wednesday evening. And for The Devil's Sake, bring your *IOC Directory*. Leave your luggage with Evtychía. Everything will be taken care of. You'll be leaving for Olympia to-night."

Madame turned to leave, in the same direction from whence she came. Three yards away she turned and said to her hands: "We only wear our moonstone ring for occasions such as the first day of spring. And...we only use it to seal...matters of import."

The Chief of Protocol of the Organizing Committee adjusted her carriage and ascended, towards the Akropolis. Her Deputy descended, towards the dirt of the city at its feet.

23rd April – Easter Sunday – 5.00 PM

So I shoveled and shoveled and shoveled some more, in hopes of finding the bleeding pipe, Leftéris had said it was down there, someplace, that it needed to "breathe". If air didn't get to it, the glacier wouldn't melt, and there'd be no more water for the Hut. There was just a trickle to-day. Happy Easter—surprise! I dug deeper, ever deeper. And the deeper I dug, the more it smelt just like fish. And the more it smelt just like fish, the more I just thought about sex.

"Not smell—aroma," I corrected myself.

Aroma...snow?

One thought the queerest thoughts...alone...in a hole...in the snow. So I jumped out, since it was truly starting to get to me. I'd just poked through the bottom, anyhow. And lo and behold, there it was, your subglacial babbling brook. The pipe must be nearby. Somewhere.

"Good—now breathe!" I commanded, and left it alone. Penance—that's what it's been.

I was sweating. Where was Leftéris? I closed my eyes, and leant upon the shovel. I started to daydream...

349

Just four Julys ago...there had been Olympic Games...and somehow...I was in them. Fate? Funny...I gave up competition, gave up the arduous running, but still I'm running...*from* something...from my Self?

Here I come...running down this ice-sheet...lost and out of control...singlet and shorts bared to the elements...bollocks to the wind...with rocks by the wayside cheering me on...for nothing! *Nothing! That's* all I've ever accomplished with my life! *"Nothing!"* I shouted, then slumped on the shovel, my mind now drawing a complete blank. Had the Athlete inside me...just *died*?

21st March – Tuesday – Midnight

It was Clean Monday Night, the first eve of spring. And in the great city of Athens, the Olympic Gold Medallist was drunk with anticipation. Too much too soon, too much expectancy coupled with reality, too much beyond his wildest imagination had done him in, and quickly. So there he was, running like Satan himself were after him, inside the majestic Panathenian Stadium. The Runner was making his way round the track. by the luminous light of the gleaming Full Moon. It was midnight.

Metre after metre, stride after stride, the legs felt good and the Spirit felt it was flying. The Stadium was radiating coolly, like a phosphorescent fish, in the lovely bluish spicy air of Night.

As he kept running, he kept wondering what those he loved back home might be doing. If his friends could only see him now...

So Ivor still was working for the MOON. He hadn't been fired after all. Instead of racing to win in the Olympics, he now would be racing to help the Olympics win. With any luck...

This eve there were no fans, no "Olympic Hymn" being sung aloud, except in his own inner mind. His lungs, conditioned well, were now warming him. It was good to be alive.

Thank God there was no one in the Stadium, save the couples in the top rows making love. What did it matter to him if they saw him? What did it matter to *them* that he could run?

The blueness of this white-marble stone, unnaturally pulsing in the intensity of moonlight, augmented sensation of inebriation. Making the turn at the open end of the Stadium, and returning once more to the depths of the structure set into the grips of the hill, Hefferon slowed down considerably. He began looking above the chalky seats, to the summit, sheltered in trees, the dark-coloured wood, of cypress and pine. And with an eerie feeling inside his head, he bore leftwards, then leftwards again.

They...were up there, he knew. Indeed, crouched, in the dark, were three forms, Dora Cain, Thýella, and General Ouranós. *They*...were observing every step that the Runner did take. *They*...were mute.

Opposite them, and unbeknownst, above the alternate bank of seats, were Theatrínos, Sir Cecil Gambling, and Professor Rembetikós. Then, everybody began to look up.

Straight before Ivor, in a diagonal angle in the sky, a bright white helicopter, with flashing blue and red lights, slowly was descending, towards him, as if in some dream. The contraption was dropping, dropping, as if to its own inner music. On its belly were the five Olympic Rings.

Slowly, slowly, slowly it kept falling, then was coming to rest, in the very centre of the 1896 Arena. Unable to halt his running, now only jogging along, the Athlete was meeting the contraption where it was landing. The Pilot, dressed in black leather, and the Navigator, dressed in white, were seen to be jumping out.

Ivor stood, staring at the contraption, and at the two wearing leather, and the two stood staring at Ivor, who was panting. In the macabre azure light of the very Full Moon, the Olympian couldn't help wondering whether or not it was true. His luggage had already been put aboard. The two were motioning.

The Runner reached out to steady himself. Surely enough, the contraption was real. He turned one last time to look round the Stadium, then was climbing aboard.

Pilot and Navigator were buckling their seats, so Hefferon did the same. Then, the one in black was putting his hand to the stick, was adjusting the gears, and was nodding to the one in white.

Soon, the contraption was lifting off the ground, above the Arena, then above the whole gigantic white pentelic Stadium itself.

Below, human beings were staring at each other. The General was grabbing the girl and was kissing her hard on the mouth, then his wife was doing the same. Three, on the other side, were beginning to depart.

Like a graceful eagle of Olympian Zeus, the contraption now was flying, a nocturne, high above the Temple of the King of the Gods, which was completed by the Roman named Hadrian. Then, over the Akropolis it was soaring, with not a Soul thereupon to bid adieu, save the ineluctable presence of the Parthenon itself...and inside...Invisible Athena. The Runner was leaving her city so harried, for the birthplace of the Olympic Games...

351

PART
II

*The athlete is essentially a wild animal
who has brought himself under control
except for the primitive passion
unleashed in his athletic efforts.*

—Sir Roger Bannister

(from *First Four Minutes*, by Roger Bannister,
Putnams, London, 1955, page 121)

23rd April – Easter Sunday – 5.10 PM

Standing like a dunce, I figured...well, here we are...still leaning on the shovel. It didn't look as if Leftéris *ever* were coming back. The spring on the belly of the snow-slick still was a-bub-bub-bubbling away, in its hole, as if it were some cavewoman's cauldron.

I wished I'd had the bloody shovel to lean upon...when my Gold Medal was being awarded that day. Even though the Medals Ceremony didn't occur till hours after my win, I would have been content to have been *carried* to the site on a stretcher, I never was so exhausted in my life...

Probably, it *was* the apex of my Existence. Never before, and likely never to be, was the totality of my Being put into such a run. I slept for days afterwards.

Alexander had indeed made me ill the previous night. When he had described what my wife had been caught doing...I had no way to react but viscerally. In despair against *her* contravention of our marriage, I felt as if I were vomiting out all my *own* years of mortal failure...

Now I've committed myself, one hundred percent, to helping save the Games. Strange—until that evening, before the 1500 Metre Race, I hadn't given a single thought to the vitriolic debates, the politics, the dirty dealings, the wastrels' attempts to undermine the Modern Olympics. I honestly couldn't have given a damn! To me...it was all a selfish lark. Competing was my own way to prove to myself—a bastard born—that I was as good as anybody else. There wasn't the least bloody thing *noble* about my striving. There wasn't the least bloody thing *altruistic* in why I ran. There wasn't the least bloody thing, to be sure, that could be called *patriotic* about getting to be of Olympic calibre. God—that last one's such a laugh that I split my guts, even to-day, when I hear people saying: Oh I did it for my *country!* Rubbish!

Any fool who knows the barest essentials about the Ancient Games knows that individuals competed as individuals, from throughout the whole Greek race. Though the best youths of each city-state competed, though the victor took the prestige of winning back to where he lived, not for a moment did the place of origin pertain to that win. It helped, of course, one's homeland...to have an Olympian therein reside. But the principle behind the thing was that the victory wreath went to him who was *best* in the sport in which he vied. This was what always was *my* guide.

I suppose my selfishness can be blamed totally on my classical education. I was schooled to be as patriotic as the next lad, but when I ran, the word *country* never even entered my head.

People have often asked me, especially since that July, *what* was I thinking as I was running to victory? I tell you...all I could hear in my mind was: You're going to *show* them...you're going to *win!*

For so many years, I've now lost count, I was in training. Fartlek, sprints, dashes, long distance hauls. Uphill, downhill, backwards, often against my will. I still don't know if I even *like* running! How do you like *that*? But I never did give up! I *always* ran...

Unlike some boys who were blest, I never had parents to cheer me along. If that father of mine's still alive, in some forest of Manitoba, more power to the old bruiser. He certainly knows who I am, by now, since the Olympics were broadcast globe-wide. If he saw me that day, lovely, I hope he takes the video-image with him to his rotten Canadian grave. At least I hope he bought a pint and secretly raised a toast to the son he never cared to see, the son of a bitch! If he'd come to England and find me some day, I guess I'd stand him a pint. Maybe. Maybe I'd punch him in the face!

Thoughts like these kept going round and round inside my tired brain, that afternoon, when the President of the International Amateur Athletic Federation draped that weight of Gold about my neck...

Soon as that orchestra began playing "God Save The Queen" and that Union Jack was slowly upraising on that middle-most staff, and the cheering was making me cry, I then realised what a snot-nosed little twit I'd been, and I vowed, then and there, to dedicate myself to fostering the Olympian Ideal, though to-day it's so maligned. I agreed, from that moment, on the pedestal of Number One, to work, in secret, with those who *also* believed that the Games truly *were* worth preserving.

I have honestly seen, with my very own eyes, the wondrous Good and Beauty of the Games...from the inside. I have honestly seen... what love and affection they do absorb and do radiate. I have honestly seen...how youth, from all over this perturbèd planet, can and do congregate, can and do get to know one another other, can and do exchange Fun and Spirit with each other. *This* was apparent...all over our Olympic Village...as well as at every single venue of competition.

Athletes, in fact, are *the* cause supreme—but how very often, in Modern Olympic Games, have Athletes been reduced to second place. Certainly they're not treated with the protocol and the bowing and the scraping that is shoveled out to Members of the IOC. All these *officials* involved—all these formal *delegations* of overseers from Embassies—all these people from National Olympic Committees and International Sporting Federations—they *all* completely overshadow Athletes—*prior* to the Games. And then—when athletic competitions start—Athletes are lucky if any of them, especially the losers, even get a nod let alone a ta. But if it weren't for Athletes in the first place, none of this hooplah ever could take place.

Almost every single one of the world's youth, who competed with me, was honourable in his or her attempt to win. Of course, there were a few who let themselves get drugged, or used as political tools by dictatorial régimes. This was nothing new, but of course was blown too far out of proportion by the media. If reporters could have concentrated more diligently on those thousands of Athletes who simply had *trained* all their lives, for this unique moment to compete, who had sacrificed so much of their time just to *be* there, and whose families had sacrificed *with* them, then the Press would have hit the bull's eye. Each person there, from those immediately disqualified to those who won the Gold, had his or her *own* story to tell. Never have I ever read a single book about the Olympic Games, since their revival in this era, that gives *each* Athlete who is competing a small chance to put into words his or her *own* feelings about why he or she is there in the first place. Now *that* would be an Olympics book to end *all* Olympics books!

Good God—I thought as I suddenly came to, still leant upon the shovel—did *I* just think that up? Maybe *that's* what I could do?

No...think of talking to all those thousands of competitors...in a matter of a mere fortnight?

I picked up the shovel, and staggered back towards the Refuge Hut, in the failing Easter light. Maybe...I'm *not* cut out to be *anything* right now. Maybe...I *should* just resign myself...to going back to England ...to Oxford...and at long last get the sodding PhD...

22nd March – Wednesday – 1.30 AM

It was the dead of Night. Dawn was nowhere round the corner. So many stars were in the raven-black sky that Ivor Hefferon had to pinch himself to believe he hadn't died. Here he was, all alone, in the centre of the Ancient Stadium, at Olympia.

The helicopter had just vanished in the moonlight, over the pine-covered hump of Mount Krónos. The Athlete scratched his head then reamed his ears. Crickets here were loud as sleighbells.

It had been a rather different ride, to say the least. Not one word had been said until the last. The Runner had honestly thought that the Ouranós clan had quietly kidnapped him. He felt that it would be best to play along, so he had held his tongue. Then, as the contraption had been hovering, an inch above the soil where so many athletic competitions had been held for a thousand years, all that the Pilot had said was: "Get out! You'll be picked up at the Philippeíon*."

"But," the fellow had stuttered, "but...where's that?"

It was dark. The site did not seem to possess a Soul.

"Straight that way—in the ruins," the Pilot had replied, then had shooed Ivor out.

As the Athlete was hovering over his pair of bags, like a hen over sole-surviving chicks, the contraption was ascending away. Hefferon never felt more alone in his life. All he had to talk to were crickets and wind in pines.

* Pronounced: fee-leep-PEE-own

359

A chill went down his spine. Still dressed for racing, at least he could run, could warm himself up. But some pristine power held him fixed to the spot.

The Stadium was so long, both to left and to right. Only a low rise of grass curved upwards from its Arena, followed it round its sides.

It was all but impossible to picture, in this morbid burnished-silver moonlight, so different from the light of nocturnal Athens, the tens of thousands...thousands of years ago...glancing to precisely where he now was standing. All those eyes...now dead?

How could it have been, he heard himself asking, that this very place gave birth to such dreams as continue to inspire men and women to-day? How could it have been...that likewise it's caused so many heart-aches?

If it weren't for *this* ancient Track...to-day's Games wouldn't even exist, nor would the arguments of who has the right to stage them. If it weren't for *this* ancient Track...the vanity to recreate its glory, for whatever reason that misses its mark, would have likely found another cause to inspire ignobility. If it weren't for *this* ancient Track...Modern Sport would have so far less to look up to.

In the midst of the long grass bank, to the Runner's right, the sole stone seats of the Stadium sat in defiant silence. No Judge, no Official, no Honoured Guest, this night, uttered a word, but their Ghosts were peering through him, to the opposite bank, to the small white altar that looked like a throne.

Feeling strange, indeed, as if too many eyes were on him, the Athlete left his bags, and walked towards the west, to where the Pilot had been pointing. There seemed to be a tunnel ahead.

There *had* been a tunnel, centuries before, but there now was just a thirty-foot run of two parallel walls of stone, that once supported a barrel-arched vault. This had been called the Crypt, venue for triumphal entrance and departure to the Stadium for the ancient Athletes. Such routes now were called *vomitoria*, which said it all!

At the Stadium's end, a few yards inside, and across the width of the Arena, a solid starting line of twenty-one stones was set in soil. The mid-stone was half the length of the others, and Hefferon slowly stept towards it. Ten stones each spread to right and to left, where twenty Athletes used to queue up to race.

Ivor's heart was pounding. His eyes were welling with tears. He wiped them, and glanced all around. There was no one within sight. So, quickly, he stript naked, even for his shoes, and crouched down, took his mark, breathed in, then bolted.

Anybody, who has ever loved Sport, could now imagine the moment...running as God had made him...in the crystalline moonlight... in the original Stadium...where the Olympic Games were born...

Although he never had been a Short-Distance Runner, the Athlete's speed even amazed himself. He was over the finish line, at the other end, before he even had a chance to think. But that was it, there was *no* thought involved, just the *joy* of the race. But imagine...to have won...back *then?*

Regaining his breath, pacing round and shaking his naked limbs, Ivor rubbed his face then went to the line again. Once more he crouched, took the mark, breathed deeply, then bolted. Again he passed the Ghosts of Judges, and soon was at the starting end.

The naked body, now warmed, could not stop moving. Ivor felt himself being drawn upwards, rightwards, along a diagonal path traversing the grass of the spectators' mound. He continued to the top of the ridge.

Down at his feet, though, he suddenly noticed two pieces of cut olive branch, which brought back to mind the ancient victor's wreath. On looking deeper in the weeds, he saw another larger branch and decided to make a wreath himself. Yet, on picking it up from the tall corn, Ivor was totally taken aback to see that it really *was* a wreath, one already made. On touching it, Hefferon's whole frame began to shake.

The leaves, from yeaterday's Sun, had been parched to the hue of brown bronze. The Olympic Gold Medallist held the wreath gingerly, expecting it to turn to dust at any moment. It stayed intact.

He rewound a few branchlets of leaves back into the ring. Then, he placed it upon his head. He was overwhelmed by a primitive joy, but simultaneously by a sobering sadness.

Retracing his steps down the path, back to the starting line, he slowly put on his clothes again, all the while debating whether or not he should keep the wreath. Maybe it was best that he *should* leave it here, as an offering to the Gods? But Night seemed to be saying that it was meant to be *his*. All alone here, who would notice it on him, anyways?

Then, he remembered the Pilot, and the order to find the Philippeíon. The Athlete went for his baggage, then commenced lugging them towards the lane that once was arched.

It was unnaturally eerie...wind and pine and stone...and frightfully loud crickets. Shadows that looked like people turned out to be nothing at all. Columns were standing as phantasms, almost in mid-air. Dawn seemed a million miles removed.

Instinct, nothing more, or was it some ancestral memory, carried the Athlete past the Temple of Hera. He knew that it belonged to the Queen, that the wife of Olympian Zeus once had been worshipped inside. Some while ago, a friend of his had sent him a postal card of this same shrine. Right here, where he was pausing with his luggage, was the very spot that the Olympic Flame was ignited each time...

Only five evenings ago, Ivor had been introduced to Ada...to the woman who lit this very Flame. She had entranced him completely, and he had fallen in love with her, at first sight. He was aching to make love to her. That would come, of its own way, he prayed.

Hadn't the pilot said to go straight? Ivor went straight, past the length of Hera's archaic Doric shrine, and yes, there, dead ahead, was the round foundation of the building begun by Philipp, King of Macedon. So, *this* was where he must wait? At least there was a sign.

Leaving his bags outside the perimeter, the Runner stept over the two circles of cut blocks and sat on a yard-long black stone of moulding. It must have been an elegant, yet small, edifice...only about thirty feet in diameter. The building had been completed by Philipp's invincible son, by Alexander the Great. Spoils had been sent here...from the then Far East. Ivor then shook...with the epiphanic knowledge that one of his ancestors had been Macedonian, that he had accompanied the Conquering Youth to India, and that he had made it back to Greece...alive. Then, doubly hard, it also hit Hefferon that this very forebear was the *bloodlink*, between Ivor and his own best friend, the Duke of Brendon.

Off to the east, whence the Athlete just had come, phosphorescent flashes of fireflies were showing occasionally through majestic pines. Night was omnipresent and omnipotent over the Pelopónnesos of Greece.

Waiting...the Olympian began to daydream. He wondered what De Soto would be up to over in Egypt? Adultery, more likely than not, despite his fourth new bride. And his best mate Alexander...off to the Subcontinent...probably would be falling head over heels in love...with some married Maharani...

Just at that moment, off through the trees and the stones, coming through the lane, that should have been vaulted, was a bell. A bell about a hairy neck, above clomping hooves, kept bonging like a herald from the spooky stars above.

Ivor rubbed his eyes. Had he fallen asleep? He kept straining his eyes in the silvery light. Fireflies in the east weren't helping at all. He was seeing, and hearing, double?

As the bell and the hooves were approaching the Temple of Hera, the Runner saw that it might be *two* donkeys making noise. But only *one* low bell kept bonging, and that on the *second* donkey's neck, the donkey that was bearing some rider.

Ivor kept rubbing his eyes the whole time that they kept approaching. The first and riderless donkey seemed the leader. It knew precisely what to do, where to go. It knew that it was heading for the Philippeíon, obviously, Hefferon hoped, or...was somebody *else* coming to pick him up?

About five yards away, the lead donkey stopt and let out a raucous hee-haw. At that moment it seemed that owls in every direction began to hoot.

But it was the old bloke on the second donkey who put the fear of God into the Athlete. Matter of fact, he must have been the oldest man that Hefferon had ever seen. How he didn't fall off the grey beast's back, and die right there, was beyond Ivor. How he didn't fall off, anyhow, seated side-saddle like that, was beyond him, too.

The Runner stood like an idiot for a minute, waiting for the fellow to speak. He shivered when he noted that the codger's skin was cheese-green. He looked scaly as a snake, with tiny green eyes that had seen far too much. He had been bald for centuries, and never had had any teeth. He was quite menacing, in sum, especially in the aluminium light of the Moon.

The old man would not, or could not, utter one word. At last, the geezer did wave his arms a bit. That meant, Ivor guessed, that he would have to tie his own bags to the weird wooden howdah, or whatever the frame was called, on the front donkey's back. At least there was rope to do so.

Then, the codger waved his arms again. Hefferon was surprised that they didn't just drop off to the ground. That meant, he guessed, that he would have to get upon the beast's back as best he could.

"Thank God for ruins," Ivor said aloud. One of the blocks from the Philippeíon boosted him up. Then, there the Athlete was, side-saddle, on this burro, in the dim-lit ruins of Ancient Olympia.

The donkey turned to see who was on its back. It was not at all amused at what it saw, since it hee-hawwed rudely at the fellow, then took off through the long-fallen stones.

Some sodding hilarious joke from that bitch, Thýella, Ivor surmised and spat on the ground.

Again, all owls in the region hooted in jest, taking the mickey out of the Olympic Gold Medallist, their naïve new guest.

23ʳᵈ April – Easter Sunday – 5.35 PM

A woman was shouting for me. I had already begun to descend from the snow-hole when the feminine voice reached upwards through the fog. In the last five minutes it had begun to settle in thickly, so I figured it was best to try to reach the Refuge Hut before I got lost.

"Ivor?" the voice called again.

Definitely the sound wasn't Ada's—though that was my first reaction.

"Hello?" I answered.

"Where are ya?" she replied.

"Who is it?"

"This ain't Santa Claus—it's Kitty—ya deaf?" she answered happily, as I glimpsed her well-endowed form in the rolling mist. Even a blind man could have seen *those* tits. "I'm down here. Watch yar footin'. It's dang slippery."

"Nippy, too!"

"Hurry up!" She joked: "I been *waitin'* for ya all afternoon!"

I slid down the final few yards and almost landed in her lap.

363

"Hey Macho—easy doin'—golly!" she said and put her hands on her Army-fatigued hips. To-day she was wearing red eyeshadow, lots of red eyeshadow. She was even decked out in a different wig. This must have been the sixth one I'd seen on her head to date.

I couldn't resist asking this time: "Kitty Darling—now listen—I'm not trying to pry into your *person*, I mean your personal *affairs*, but do tell me how it is that a talented girl like you, with an evident taste for entertainment, could have ever landed up here...with so many *wigs*?"

She laughed uproariously. "Ivor Sweet—look—I guess ya think Kitty's kinda kooky. But I just fell in love with wigs, ya know, and they don't weigh much, so I travel light."

"I see."

"Other gals drag round tons of Gucci bags and all, but I can just toss my do's in a sack and head on down the road when times get borin'. Plus—they come in handy up here on the Arctic Circle—where it's so goddamned cold I have to be tongue-tied drunk to want to give myself a shampoo. So with my scalp *cruddy* all the time, I just hide myself under these pretty little wigs and keep my head cozy in the process. By the way—all this makeup's a defensive tactic, too. Have ya noticed what this climate does to yar *pores*? Baby—these elements are *raw* up here!"

"What were you in—the infantry?" I asked to change tactics.

"Don't ya just *love* my combat boots?"

"I'll love just getting on dry land!"

"Poor Baby—ya been in that soggy hole *all* this time? Don't ya feel better now—knowin' ya saved our lives?"

"There's enough *vino* at that Hut to fill the English Channel— twice. So I don't think you'd go thirsty without a little bit of water," I replied.

"Hey Cutey—let's sit up here and gossip. I never get an opportunity to escape too much. Lefty guards me like a chicken-hawk."

"Maybe he has a right to," I said and winked.

"Just gimme half a chance!" she responded and climbed up a steep path that led to shelter beneath gargantuan evergreens. I followed. *Any* red-blooded man would follow such a female...*any* where...at *any* time...to do *any* thing she ever could want.

"I just love it here," she admitted and sat on a fallen tree trunk.

"What's *it*?" I wondered.

"Come on over—and sit beside me." She patted the log.

I did, hoping she needed a massage or something. She did not.

"Lefteris is a workaholic!" she complained. "I just came up here to get *away* from it all, and look what I end up doin', runnin' a minin' camp. I tell ya, this place's just like the remotest parts of Montana."

"Must be gorgeous. My father was from near there."

"Ya pullin' my leg."

"No—from Manitoba."

"Stop it!"

"It's the truth."

"Ya sound as English as they get. Ya got yar Medal for *Britain.*"

"I got the Medal for *myself,* Kitty."

"Yeah—ya characters are all alike."

"What to bugger do you mean by that?"

"Ev'rybody knows the Olympics are as crooked as Patsy's Rattlesnake! Look at ya—I heard all about them hero exploits of yars back in Athens and Olympia. Word gets round ya know. Even up here."

We sat in silence a few minutes, listening to wind in the pines.

"So—ya saved the Olympics—what's yar *next* act?" Kitty inquired brashly, as only an American can.

"What's yours?"

"Shit—I might hitchhike to Cape Town, who knows. But we're talkin' 'bout *you.*"

"Are we?"

"Sure. I find ya fascinatin'. I ain't never met no Olympic Athlete before. What's it like...winnin'?"

"It's just a race."

"Don't gimme that."

"I won a *race*—so what?"

"But Ada said yar time's the fastest ever clocked."

"Things like that impress a lot of people."

"Don't it make ya proud?"

"It made me very...happy."

"So there—why'd ya quit then? Ya dumb?"

I sighed. "How many times have I been asked that very question?"

"I don't know—what's yar answer? Ya *quit*—didn't ya?"

"I did stop competing in races—yes."

"But why? If ya got the fastest legs in the world—I don't get why ya quit."

"I only wanted to compete in *an* Olympic Games, once, and win."

"So—ya did that—why not keep *at* it?"

"It's too much work, Kitty. It takes every second of your time. It's not just something that can be turned on and off like a tap."

"Why not?"

"Look," I said angrily and stood. "I succeeded in doing something that far surpassed the accomplishments of *all* the runners on this Earth! That in itself is *enough* for me! I don't *need* to keep at it and keep at it and keep at it—till I *die*—since that victory—four summers ago—was *more* than enough of a thrill for me—and it will last me for a lifetime!"

"But—yar record's gonna get *broken!* Won't *that* get ya down?" Kitty insisted, and stood as well.

"Records are *meant* to be dashed to bits. They're only mortal sightings on a clock. They don't *ever* tell what's going *on*—inside the body *or* the mind!"

"I think ya mind more than ya'll ever admit! I think a part of ya'll die, the moment some *other* runner leaves yar record behind."

"I'm very prepared for that—thank you!" I shouted, surprised at the emotion I displayed.

"I don't think ya're prepared for *that* one at all!"

"Look—we should be getting back to the Hut," I retorted and began walking downslope towards the rising chimney smoke.

"Well—I'm sorry!" Kitty said and followed me.

"About what?"

"Botherin' ya so," she tried to explain. "I always stick my big boot inside my stupid mouth."

"Don't worry your pretty self about it."

"I was...I just thought...ya looked like ya had all this canned *up* inside."

"Playing Devil's Advocate, I suppose?"

"No—just *tryin'* to be friendly. Sorry I upset ya."

"That's quite all right."

"Ya forgive me?"

"Of course."

"Good, now I'll try, extra hard, to cook somethin' special for ya to-night."

22ⁿᵈ March – Wednesday – 2.45 AM

It was a change from the helicopter. At least an ass can get to smaller places, at hard-to-reach elevations, which was exactly what the two donkeys in the ruins decided to do. Of course, the Athlete hadn't a hope in Hell of knowing where they were going. Nor did he know where in Hell they were when they got there! It was all in the animals' hands, or should one say *hooves*. They just kept clomping upwards, ever upwards, up some road partially paved with cement, but mostly made of patches of dirt, up some dusty windy road lined with cypress, with bramble. It was definitely not a comfortable ride. On top of this, or at least when they reached the top of the hill, Ivor was just about dead with need to sleep. He felt as if all those mad weeks in Athens had at last caught up with him, as if he'd been transplanted out of this world.

Whatever it was that was up here...it was spooky. The Sun was sound asleep beyond the eastern mountains, down the valley of the River Alphaiós*, beyond the ruins at the base of the steep rise.

The two donkeys just had made it to the top. It was all dirt paths and scurrying cats in the night, olive trees, and much too much

* Pronounced: al-fay-OS; last syllable rhymes with *gross*.

dust. To the right was an old house, with an elevated porch. The house and porch were covered with flowers. Surprisingly—at this ungodly hour—a pair of little naked children were poking their heads above the railing, to see what was disrupting the calm of their domain. Spying in the moonlight, at the crazy foreigner still wearing the wreath made of olive boughs, they began to giggle and to point, then to yell to their mama to come look. Roused from bed, she did come but, on seeing the pair on the asses, she crossed herself three times, hustled the kids inside, and slammed the door.

As the donkeys veered a sudden left, Hefferon stole a quick look at the rest of the so-called "village". It seemed made of an equal distribution of abandoned shells of buildings and of those still in use, all of the same yellow stone, and none more than two storeys tall. Were there a dozen houses in all? To their immediate right they were passing one of the shells. Bushes were growing inside.

Then, the burros were halting. The leader began to bray. Ivor looked back at the old geezer. He was propt on a stick of an arm, as if keeping his cheese-coloured head from tumbling right off. With his free hand the old fellow was motioning towards the ground.

There was nothing to do but jump. Owls were making a racket in the trees of the yard. At least two of the trees had flowers. One of them looked like a fig. Ivor jumped. Once more he gazed to the person behind. Was he dozing? Ivor undid his baggage anyways.

With the greatest effort the old man revived, and pulled a key from his tatty shirt pocket. He gave it a heave, but it landed far from its mark, right in a plate of goat-dung. Hefferon felt like flinging the bastard in after it, but sadly restrained himself. At least the dropping was dry.

The old man said nothing, just pointed to the porch at the end of the stone building up ahead. He made a turning motion with his hand, as if opening the door, but then crossed his opened palms before each other twice, meaning that the foreigner should lock himself inside and go to bed. He then departed with his asses, as the bell bonged the whole of the way.

So, Ivor nipped into the abode and drew the latch, never more thankful that just inside the door was an electrical switch on the wall. A bare bulb hissed, then fizzed on above his head. The first room was the kitchen. He went to the refrigerator, that couldn't have been older, yet its contents were poorer than Mother Hubbard's Cupboard. Nobody had left him even a drop of local plonk. "Blimey—would some *scrumpy* hit the spot right now!" he said aloud.

The place was virtually uninhabitable. It was dry, and smelt like a manor's garret. Of four bedrooms, but one had a bed with a mattress. Someone had lately put on sheets. A sole woolen blanket was folded on the foot. There was a pillow with a pillowcase beside it. Ivor put on the pillowcase, so exhausted that he almost fell asleep on his feet.

"No—one last thing." Professor Rembetikós had told him to

367

promise to hide his papers, from the UK Embassy for diplomatic immunity. Until he did that, he must not sleep.

Thus, as he searched the abandoned house, which was certainly larger than it looked from the outside, he kept hearing the IOC Member's other warning. Rembetikós had made him vow to go along with all that Thýella might inflict on him: "Just count the days till Saturday—when the whole plot—at last—will be exposed. That should sustain you. Come Saturday, you'll have the sweetest revenge known to Man. Against Thýella, and the General, and Major Movóros, and the whole infernal dynasty of maniacs, you'll disclaim their scheme, as the whole world is watching." Indeed, that would be worth a few days of no matter what discomfort.

At least this house did not appear infested with scorpions, Ivor prayed, as he continued looking about the crumbling plaster walls and dry wooden floors. Sticking his papers beneath the floorboards would be too obvious. The pantry's and kitchen's shelves were a giveaway. How about the loo...*was* there one? Yes—next to the pantry. Grotty old toilet. Newspapers on the floor. "Is *that* what they use...to wipe their shitty bums?"

He glanced up. A shelf. Newspapers up *there*, too. Perfect. He stood on the bog and balanced himself, as he shoved the papers between pages of the bottom-most newspaper. It was now 3.03 AM.

Back to the bedroom with the mattress on the springs, Ivor slowly crawled. The bare bulb in that lonesome room looked as if it pre-dated Edison. He shut it off by pulling a chain, then chucked his clothing onto one of the posters of the bed. Until his tired frame went to sleep, hooting owls kept serenading.

23rd April – Easter Sunday – 6.10 PM

When I got back to our small cabin of stone, on the edge of the ravine, there was a note on my sleeping bag, from Ada. I picked it up, dreading to read it. Her sleeping bag and pack were gone. I sat on the edge of the upraised platform of our bed and unfolded the single sheet of paper. It read:

Belovèd Ivor,

Uncle Kóstas telephoned shortly after you went to work for Leftéris. Aunt Georgia is dead. She died this Easter afternoon, after attending church. Must return to the village. Please understand. Her funeral will be Wednesday morning. Leaving with the muletrain right away. Stay here—climb the Sacred Mountain. You must do it—without me. God has intervened. Shall be waiting for you in Litóchoron. Ivor—do not rush things—take as much time up here as you need. You've gone through a lot— you owe it to yourself to think things out. Don't worry about me.

A lovely Swiss couple named Hartmund arrived at the Hut after I'd heard the news. They've been to the top many times. Go with them to Skála peak. But go to Mýtikas with Leftéris. I'll be praying for you. You know I love you—with all my Heart and Soul,

Your fiancée,
Ada

This news pulled the rug from beneath me. I had been deriving such intense joy, from having Ada by my side, twenty-four hours a day. I stood from the platform and went to the concrete balcony.

It was getting dark. That was no consolation, either. Poor girl, I said to myself, she revered the matriarch of her family so much. A great link with The Past now has gone.

I wanted to crawl into the sleeping bag and doze the bad news away. But it was dinner time, so I shut the cabin door behind me. As I mounted the dozen steps to the walkway that led back to the main Refuge Hut, it hit me that Kitty likely had come to fetch me in order to soften the news. So I went to seek her out first, to thank her for the consideration. I went the back way, continuing straight upwards from the steps, instead of turning right, to arrive at the kitchen quicker. Leftéris saw me first and said: "Have you seen Ada's note?"

"Yes."

"I'm terribly sorry, Ivor. We'll *all* Miss Aunt Georgia. The whole village of Litóchoron is mourning her. You understand, of course, that Ada *had* to go."

"Yes—of course," I said. "Is Kitty here?"

"In the clubroom, peeling potatoes," he answered. "Wait here—drink a glass of this."

"What is it?" I wondered, but accepted a shot of something from a glass decanter. "Cheers, Guv."

"Pure malt liquor," he offered.

"You're a jolly good man."

"By the way, the Hartmunds are eager to meet you. They're inside."

I hoisted my glass to the kind chap and descended the five steps to the warmth of the clubroom. At the far end were Kitty and two elderly strangers. "Come on over and be sociable," Kitty hollered. She was busy carving the spuds. "I want ya to meet two of the nicest people, Mister and Missus Hartmund, from Bern."

I stept past a dozen others, some of whom I recognised, then approached the couple from Switzerland. The gentleman was as solid as an oak, and rose upon being introduced. He was taller than I, and wearing lederhosen and green knee-stockings. His wife was demure, with pretty white hair, and at least two feet shorter than the man. They both looked to be at least seventy.

"I think these two can take yar mind off things," Kitty said

369

matter of factly. "He's a Doctor and she's helped run a clinic in Darkest Africa. We've been gossipin' about ya for hours."

"She's joking about the gossip," Hartmund corrected politely and suggested, "please feel free to call me Otto. And this is my wife, Sieglinde."

"They climbed Olympos—what—six times?" Kitty tried to recall.

"Four," Frau Hartmund defined.

"Well—this will be yar fifth," Kitty stated and finished her chore. She rose, "Now, Olympic Gold Medallist, I'm off to bake ya a cake ya'll never forget all the days of yar life."

"I'd prefer some tart," I joked.

"I'll tart ya," she razzed, and departed to the kitchen, swerving her delicious behind.

So I was left with the couple that evening. The hours were passed pleasantly enough. I kept trying not to worry about Ada, but of course never could get my fiancée out of my mind.

22nd March – Wednesday – 10.00 AM

Crows in the trees had been cawwing and waking the exhausted traveler all through the night, and into the morning, too. Then, at ten, there was a fearful banging on the front door, followed by an automobile's horn sounding. Ivor Hefferon thought he was dreaming, and refused to rouse from bed. Presently, the door was opening and footsteps were coming up the hall, then an ominous figure was striding into the bedroom unannounced. The Runner was startled to see that it was the Orthodox Priest, Psychopompós. "Long time no see," he said and chuckled to himself.

"What're you doing here?" Ivor wondered as he rubbed the sleep from his eyes.

"Going to snooze all day?" the illegitimate son of Thýella and Theódoros said snidely.

Ivor had just been dreaming about Ada, and had an erection, and certainly wasn't about to uncover himself while being stared at by this Priest, whom everyone said was gay. "If you don't mind, I'd prefer dressing...in peace?"

"I'll be waiting outside," the Holy-Man intoned and turned to leave. At the doorway he spun round and said loudly: "Wear your three-piece suit."

"The grey one?"

"That will be presentable enough—yes. We shall have to introduce you to a few local dignitaries. This's a day of work."

"Of course."

"We shall have breakfast in the village."

"I thought this was the village," Ivor said dubiously.

The Greek laughed. "You British have such a wry sense of

humour. This is Throúva, the *former* village. It was here before the Germans began excavating the ruins in the previous century. This house was the residence of the chief German archaeologist. You haven't seen *modern* Olympia yet?"

"Would I be talking like this if I *had?*"

"Well—take off that silly wreath, or I shan't be showing you a single thing," the disagreeable man said, snapt his tongue, then left.

The fellow removed the olive wreath, then laughed aloud: "God —was I sleeping with *this* bloody thing?" He got out of bed and put on the trousers to the suit, then staggered through the hall to the dry kitchen.

Psychopompós was standing guard on the porch, shouting anathemas at a flock of crows.

"Now look," the Athlete demanded, "I'm going to shave. Is there *no* running water?"

"We thought you'd enjoy conditions similar to Evtychía's," he replied.

"Funny."

"I do think the water's connected. Try the kitchen sink."

"You'll have to provide me with a mirror."

"Wasn't one left behind the dresser in your room?"

"Righty ho. That's the *first* place that popped into my head to look!"

The Runner took his grand old time shaving, as the Priest began to pace the so-called grounds. He went round the bramble-infested property to the back of the house, in order to gaze at the view. From the hilltop, all the Alphaiós Valley could be seen, including Mount Krónos to the left and, to the right of that, the ruins of the temple-city for Olympian Zeus.

When Psychopompós returned to the porch, Ivor was leaning against the man's black Peugeot, looking as impatient as possible. His briefcase was in hand. "Where've you *been?*" Ivor asked crassly.

Shooting him an evil glance, the bearded one muttered: "We'll just be a minute getting downhill." The two got into the car. The estimate was precise.

Modern Olympia was just a high-street with a couple of side-streets, and a few parallels. From the way that the Man-Of-The-Cloth was sailing up and down every single road, Olympia wasn't making much of an impression on Ivor, anyway.

He was now barreling down the parallel lane called Apóstolou Kosmópoulou.

"Museum Of The Olympice Games," Psychopompós said as the Peugeot dashed past a modern one-storey cement edifice painted blazing white, at the top of a wide flight of white marble stairs. "It's a *private* museum, not owned by the Government, who do own the two Archaeological Museums, as well as the ruins. *This* Museum," he said

371

as he was burning rubber turning right, "contains exhibits of the *Modern* Games. You may find it fascinating."

We were now in Avgerinoú Street. "It means Morning Star. We're eating here, in The Sheep Shed, which in local dialect is called Stroúka." The Peugeot came to a screeching halt. This Priest's driving was *not* divinely ordained. The owner of The Sheep Shed came rushing out in his apron, still holding a glass he was wiping. Ivor was hastily introduced and the two proceeded inside.

Hefferon's mind still was reeling from the rapid transit, as well as from what he had been able to see, the utter modernity and rampant commerciality of the endless queue of tourist shops in the high-street, as opposed to the pastel blocks of flats, all with balconies, set against a backdrop of horses, donkeys, mules, roosters, and gaggles of chickens in side-streets. And there was a plethora of widows, of course, dressed in (need one say) black.

"The Sheep Shed is a modern building that's never known a sheep," the Priest tried to joke with Ivor, who smiled mock-politely. It was a pastry-shop and milk-bar combined. "Its best feature is this delightful little terrace," he continued and led the Athlete leftwards between little round tables to a sliding glass panel. "One can see the clothing-shop next door and this open courtyard with the wooden balcony. There's always some old woman up there, knitting something." Indeed, the woman *was* up there, taking it all in, like a buzzard, and she was certainly knitting furiously.

Two breakfasts were brought. "This one's on me," Psychopompós said and beamed.

Ivor noticed something that was posing as butter on a tiny metal plate. Honey, in a great gooey dollop, was spreading beside it. There were a couple of rolls to compliment this. The supposèd butter looked like lard. "Is this butter from...goats?" Hefferon asked.

"It's good for you," the Priest replied.

"Send it back," Ivor answered. "I only indulge in *cow*-butter."

"Big Olympian—you're not a sissy?" responded Thýella's son.

"Look, Arsehole, send the *fucking* butter *back*—or you're going to be *wearing* this shit in that grease-ball beard!"

The Priest gulped, and yelled for the waiter to change the butter. He soon returned, with something yellow. "Now," the Priest began, evidently quite in earnest to say something serious, "my father and I have had a long talk."

Hefferon almost made the *faux pas* of saying that he didn't think that Psychopompós's father was still alive, but decided to reply humorously: "Oh—are you only *now* learning about the birds and the bees?"

The Priest did not bat an eye. "Affedikó said for me to remind you...that you're now The Keeper Of The Olympian Ideal."

"I'm charmed," Ivor answered.

"Therefore, this Saturday, you'll be expected to participate in the Deed Ceremony in the Ancient Stadium...in that capacity."

"Needless to say."

"I knew you'd see sense...sooner or later," he said, mightily pleased with the thought that the Athlete at last had sold out. "Of course—you never should have been so reticent, on the eleventh, when I made you that most *generous* offer. Had you concurred, back then, we never would have needed to resort to Dora Cain's skill as an amateur photographer."

"Where *is* our dildo-wielding friend now?" Ivor wondered.

The Priest frowned. "I can't be certain—Dodóna perhaps?" He coughed. "Of course, you do realise that Thýella was *not* amused when you refused our first offer to you."

"She said nothing to me."

"She wouldn't. She's too well-bred."

That's a laugh, Hefferon thought.

"Nevertheless, it's our responsibility, this week, to concern ourselves with the proper *organization* anent the flawless staging of Saturday's Deed Ceremony. *Your* help will be most appreciated."

"Is that so?"

"Attending to Protocol, of course."

"Nothing more?"

"Well—I myself have been mulling over the most diplomatic way that you might win back the Chief of Protocol's esteem."

"That would please me very much," Ivor lied.

"I'm so very grateful to hear you say that," said the Priest. "Given that you refused to pose as an Olympic Runner...by means of photography...I now can't think of a better way to incorporate your services...than by means of utilising you as an Olympic Runner...in the flesh..."

All but sickened by it all, Ivor knew that he had no choice but to go along with this nasty new twist. He quickly realised, above and beyond everything, that by agreeing to do this he would be guaranteeing himself a place inside the Arena, and therefore he would be in perfect position to do exactly what he and Aristídis Rembetikós had agreed.

"What is your answer?" pressured the Orthodox Priest.

"Sorry," Ivor responded, "I just was imagining how good it will be to have the chance to run once again...before an Olympic assembly."

"Just as wonderfully as you did...before the whole world...at Lake Placid?"

"Better..." stated Hefferon, hatching a newer, bolder plan in his virile mind.

The son of the Cretan rebel responded: "Now, let's leave this Sheep Shed, as I've got somebody who's most eager to make your acquaintance."

The Athlete was taken to Tourist Police headquarters, situated

373

directly in the centre of the high-street, and on the left-hand side of the road as one would head for the ruins on the outskirts of town. One entered the precincts through a door in a side-street that contained the best bakery. Given that the Tourist Police were on the first floor, one had to ascend a steep L-shaped flight of stairs. When the two arrived there, it was 11.20 AM.

Three to four rooms were in use. The Priest led to the leftmost one and poked in his head, then gestured to Ivor. The Officer in charge was a young slim one, quite dashing in fact. Not one crease of his grey uniform was not perfectly pressed. He looked as if he had just come from inspecting some formal dress parade. He stood tall, upon seeing the Orthodox Religious enter. The Officer was erect and formal. The two greeted each other like unfriendly brothers.

"Míkis," the Priest said to the Athlete, in introduction. "He was an Evzone, under my brother."

"Ah yes," Hefferon noted, "I did have the pleasure of attending a party at the house of Major Movóros."

"This is Ivor Hefferon," Psychopompós said.

The young Officer shot the Runner a glance that sized him up in an instant. "Sit please," he commanded.

"This man is an Olympic Gold Medallist," the Priest affirmed.

The Officer was not impressed, but was playing with a pencil. His desk was good defence against all these tourists.

"The last Games," the bearded-one continued. "He won the Men's 1500 Metres. He's English."

"I like Americans," the Officer announced. His humour was dry as a bone.

"Of course, my father *approves* of him," Psychopompós said, solely for the shock-effect.

The Officer did not smile.

"Affediko has created a special position in the Organizing Committee just for Mister Hefferon."

"And what title does Mister Hefferon have?" the Officer wondered, still playing with his pencil, this time running it carefully through his well-tended curly-black close-cropt hair.

"Mister Hefferon The Keeper Of The Olympian Ideal."

On hearing that, the Tourist Policeman all but smiled. But he just could not quite do it. He had the look on his handsome face that he had no idea at all how to deal with somebody with such an appendage. It was too Byzantine, too far back in Greek History to comprehend. He began tapping his pencil. "He's...the what?"

"You heard me." Psychopompós said unpleasantly. He seemed to be relishing this duty, as Director of Communications for the MOON.

"Does that mean...he's a VIP?" Míkis asked. At least, if the new arrival were a VIP, he could be justly dealt with.

"*Very* VIP," the Priest admitted, without cracking a smile.

374

The Officer swallowed. "Well...what are we supposed to *do?*"

"The usual," Thýella's son responded.

"The tour?"

"The tour," answered Psychopompós. "Plus—it's *your* responsibility to be Mister Hefferon's *bodyguard.* We want nothing untoward to happen to him, before Saturday. I shall see to having an extra bed installed in the Throúva house." The Priest rose. His grin was lewd as a child molester at a Boy Scout pow-wow.

The young Officer did not rise with him, nor did he smile.

"Now, I must beg your leave," said the Man of God. "I have to check the venues, in order to make sure that the communications network we're installing will be ready by Saturday—since we have to broadcast this Deed Ceremony to the entire damned world."

24ᵗʰ April – Monday – 7.45 PM

I was too depressed in the evening to socialise. Leftéris was in a grumpy mood, angry at Kitty for something, so I didn't think it was the proper time to continue the discussion we'd started on Thursday. Plus, now that Ada was gone, my heart wasn't into chit-chat. Of course, I cared about knowing how the world was reacting to the revelations of the Olympics plot—but without Ada to discuss these weighty matters, I just couldn't force myself to ask about them. One could discuss such things on lower ground.

Another rotten day had enveloped the heights in abysmal fog, and there was absolutely nothing to do but wait it out. All day I had been pining over Ada, and felt as if I were in a daze. Our separation now was only a bit longer than twenty-four hours, but it felt like a prison term of years.

Stranded up here, I began to have nagging doubts about our relationship. Foolish of me, I know, when down below she was likely having a bloody rough time of it as well, coping with countless relatives who must be converging on Litóchoron. Maybe her *parents* would be coming from further north? Maybe I might get to meet them? Maybe I should ask her father formally for her hand?

The climb to the top, to Mýtikas, was now secondary in my mind. If only Ada had been able to stay at the Hut, at least, and not have gone so very far away.

Since breakfast I had been staying in the Refuge, by the fire, with the others, sitting alone, reading some American paperback some hiker had left last year. I finished the whole thick thing, and didn't even recollect a single word. It was all about whores in Hollywood, a typical US fairy tale, minus the tale, but with plenty of emphasis on *fairies!* Frau Hartmund had asked me, as I was leaving the clubroom, how I enjoyed the book, and what it was about? I think I said: "Movies!" But all I could keep thinking about was whether Ada would phone...

I returned to our little cabin and made myself a fire. If I couldn't have her with me, I might as well be alone. Once, during the day, I remember now, some character in that book had a brother who was a bohemian painter in San Francisco. As a child I used to paint. I really quite enjoyed it. Alexander's grandmother, the Dowager Duchess of Brendon, had once "sat" to me, and I had done her "portrait". It was ghastly, of course, but she had praised it to the whole family. I was so ashamed that I touched no brush again, although she constantly suggested I do so.

My fire was getting low. I rose from my cross-legged position of dejection on the floor, and put one more log on the coals. Something within me was stirring. Whatever it was...it was even more unnerving than not having Ada present. I wanted to get something inside...*out*. I almost wanted to draw something...out of my very Blood. But what? What *was* it? I kept telling myself I didn't dare. There was no *talent* within me for that!

I sat again...more frustrated than before...and put my head in my hands. I began praying to God, to give me some direction, for my totally unmistakably mucked-about life.

22ⁿᵈ March – Wednesday – Noon

Officer Míkis was driving his patrol car on the road that led to the ruins of Olympia. Ivor Hefferon was sitting in the front seat. The automobile was crossing a small concrete bridge, when the Tourist Policeman said: "The River Kladéos. It's just a small stream. Where it joins the River Alphaiós, a couple thousand metres distant, the right angle creates the natural boundaries for the Ancient Games site, which is just over there."

Without admitting that he had come out of those very ruins last night, Ivor was quite startled that instead of turning right Míkis was bearing left, into a dusty field doubling as a parking lot with about thirty vehicles. The humpy pine-covered hill called Krónion, named after Krónos, father of Zeus, was just to the right. Thousands of ravens were making a racket in its treetops.

"Tourists, always more tourists," the Officer snapt as he dodged a coachload of people from Northern Europe. "I *hate* tourists!" He continued so deeply into the field-cum-parking-lot that the Runner thought he might be trying to blaze a new trail. At last, he was parking the car and saying: "Hurry."

The Policeman and Hefferon hastened along a dirt path amid a grove of olive trees. Off to the left was some old stone farm house. A nondescript modern building was up ahead.

"Where're we going?" Hefferon asked.

"The *New* Archaeological Museum."

"It couldn't be further away."

The Sun was sizzling hot. No shade fell from an olive tree.

"Where's the *Old* Archaeological Museum?"

No answer. The building was drab, some recent architect's futile attempt to be functional, minimal, and classical, all at one time. It looked like a pre-fabricated Japanese computer factory, done in a veneer of marble. It even had an enclosed "Zen" garden of sorts, off to the left. Míkis didn't even bother explaining to the two tired guards at the desk by the portal that he and the foreigner were on their way to meet the Director. The guards seemed to know in advance.

The two turned right, into an enclosed and very tacky version of a "cloister", then turned right again. The Officer began rapping his knuckles on a wooden door. A woman's voice answered. The two walked in.

"Doctor Selináki," Míkis said. "This's Ivor Hefferon, Deputy Chief of Protocol for the MOON. He's just arrived in the village...to help co-ordinate Saturday's Deed Ceremony."

"I see," the lady said and extended her hand to the Athlete, then gestured for the two to sit. "I am Evanthía Selináki, Director of the Archaeological Site of Olympia."

The woman's voice was as succulent as orange-blossom honey. It was as sexy as anything the Runner had ever heard. In fact, it was *two* voices, one on top of the other, like a couple, making love, and simultaneously moaning. The sound on top was low and strong, and that on the bottom was high and excited. Hefferon was hoping that he would be able to hear it for hours. The voices carried on, in sensual abandon.

"This Museum, as well as the Old Museum, and of course the ruins, are under *my* jurisdiction, as are, technically, all the archaeological sites and digs of the Western Pelopónnesos."

"That's a lot of ground to cover, I mean *uncover*," Ivor said, and was surprised that the lady laughed. She appeared most charming, and could be in her late thirties. Her hair was light brown, and was pulled back to drape behind her ears. She was wearing a simple butterscotch cotton suit. She had thick large-framed blue glasses.

"The lay of the land hasn't bothered me half as much as *this* coming Saturday. Are you recently hired...by Madame Ouranoú?"

"Yes."

"Well, this Deed Ceremony, as it's called, happened so quickly that we've all been praying it occurs without a hitch."

"Such as?"

"My ruins! Do you MOON people realise that we're *not* running a *sideshow* here? We are *trying*, with *limited* means, to preserve a very *delicate* archaic environment...from destruction!" She paused to catch her breath, as if shocked at her own vituperation. "*Every* single tourist, who tramps through the Sacred Compound, called the Áltis, has the potential to *desecrate*. *Your* Ceremony, this Saturday, not only is going

377

to *fill* the site of our Ancient Stadium, but also the whole event is going to be televised and broadcast by satellite worldwide!"

The Director was loosing her cool, and grabbed for a cigarette. Her voices sounded even more sexy in their aroused state. Míkis rose and handed her one of his own. Evanthía could see that he already had a raging hardon, and that pre-cum was staining right through his undershorts and clear through his trousers. He didn't even bat an eye, and just stood there, with his great big cock bulging out. The two began smoking, profusely, as if sucking on their cigarettes in exchange for sucking on each other's bodies. Taking his royal time, the big sexy Cop slowly sat down and re-adjusted his swollen penis, all the while staring the entranced woman in the eyes.

"By Áltis you mean..." I began, as I, too, started getting a goddamned big erection and was starting to sweat like a pig.

"I mean the whole of the Holy Enclosure. The Ancient Games Site *wasn't* just some two-bit sports stadium, like the Roman Colosseum. It was a whole *religious* compound, a virtual *temple-city* in its own right. The enormous acreage of it was protected by a wall. And what was within that wall was called the Áltis."

"And you're worried about..." Ivor tried again.

"I'm scared stiff that some *cock*-eyed Reporter, or rabid Sports Official, is going to get carried away trying to get the event on tape, and that some *priceless* piece of our heritage will be destroyed, forever, all in the name of that Omnipotent Modern God, Video!"

"But you're...."

"I *am* responsible, yes, if any piece of any column falls off, or is knocked off, or is chipt off, by any means whatsoever, this Saturday. *I* am the one the Government will blame, since *I* am a Government employee. And let me warn you, the Government's nasty *brain* knows every single stone in those ruins!"

"It must be difficult..."

"Difficult's being kind—it's Hell! Whenever you Olympics people, either in Athens or in Lausanne, dream up some sort of a latter-day ceremony, to take place in *my* ruins, it becomes an absolute *nightmare* for me. Can you conceive of the clean-up job alone? The damned tourists slop the place up badly enough. If it were up to *me*, I wouldn't allow *anybody* inside my territory, especially not you Olympics people!"

"But —the Olympic Games were *born* here..."

"And they just might well *die* here, Saturday, too! Now," she said and stood, "I'm sure that the Officer has *plenty* of other Dignitaries on his agenda to whom to introduce you—but—I hope you don't mind that I can honestly say that I'm going *crazy* with my *own* pile of work. You realise, of course, that my Museum is being turned into a *hotel?*"

"Yes," Hefferon admitted and rose, adjusting his own dick so that it wouldn't be so damned noticeable, hard. Again, Míkis didn't even bother adjusting his. The cum-spot on his uniform was now large as the palm of his hand. It was plain to all three that the Officer had just ejaculated.

"Thanks to your MOON crew, Friday and Saturday will see the Head of State of Greece lodged here. That means...I've got to close *everything* to the public, starting to-night, in order to tend to the urgent needs of Executive Security," the Museum Director said, as she opened her office door, while gawking at the waistlines of both of the sexually excited men.

"I'm sure that the Head of State will appreciate your every effort," Ivor said, for diplomacy's sake, then added slowly: "Speaking of urgent needs, I was wondering if yours is the correct office for answering this query..."

"Which query?" Evanthía Selináki said impatiently.

"You're likely aware that I'm a Runner."

"We do keep somewhat abreast of the news here, Mister Hefferon."

"Then, would you be averse to allowing me a little permit...to be able to run in the Ancient Stadium...at night? I can't perform...my duties...if my body...isn't in the best of shape. And I don't think General Ouranós would appreciate it...if I *weren't* in shape."

The Director released the door and returned to her desk. She was not amused, not with the rampant locker-room atmosphere of semen that had suddenly filled her whole office with a ruttish musk, nor with the fact that she was extremely sexually aroused by *both* of these handsome young men. She took her vaginal frustration out on a slip of paper, scratching a note on it with emphatic female heat, then stamped it brutally with her seal. She handed the permit begrudgingly and said: "I shall notify my guards. You are allowed to run in the Ancient Stadium —at night—and *nowhere* else."

"Thank you," Ivor said but then pretended to remember another thing. "Oh—I almost forgot. This is my *bodyguard*," and the Olympic Gold Medallist pointed right at Míkis's cock, which the Policeman was caressing back down into a hanging position, then he was actually rubbing his thumb and forefinger together to feel the stickiness of his own sperm that had worked its way out the cloth. "Míkis must remain with me...at all times. He'll be needing...a little permit, too."

The Director looked as if she were about to blow a gasket. But she took her anger out on the slip of paper, which her handwriting all but hacked through. She stamped her seal down onto it so hard that she hurt her hand.

"Thank you," Ivor said and smiled sweetly. Then the pair of horny men stept out the door.

Míkis muttered something intranslatable in guttural Greek, then walked, crotch-bound, through the whole ersatz-cloister with Ivor before saying: "She's been under pressure. She's a very dedicated woman, but she's petrified that something's going to happen to some of her artifacts. Her Museums' collections are some of the most magnificent in all the world. But—if she's afraid that anybody's going to so much as *touch* the tiniest thing this week, then she has *much* to learn about the Greek military. This place's going to be *crawling* with soldiers, starting to-night. You'll see. She has *nothing* to fear. All she has to do…is go along with everything we say, then, *everything* will be fine." The Officer then pinched some more cum that was oozing through his trousers, and licked it off his fingers, staring Ivor in the eyes. Then he laughed, and Hefferon couldn't help laughing along with him. "I'll *fuck* that woman before this event's over," the Cop boasted. "You just watch. I'll have her licking this spunk right *through* my pants—and she'll love every goddamned drop!"

"I don't think she's your type," the Runner said, just to piss the Policeman off. "She's too intellectual!"

"She watches things too closely!"

"I'm sure that General Ouranós has taken care of guarding whatever he can," Hefferon remarked, as they were opening the doors of the patrol car. "Where next?"

"The midday meal," Míkis said. "I'm starving."

"Don't you want to change your clothes?" Ivor queried lewdly. "Or are you going to walk around all day with that great big cum-spot on your trousers showing through?"

"I love the *stink* of it. It makes me hot!" The cop-car crossed the little bridge, then swerved right. Míkis announced: "The Old Museum's up there."

Ivor barely caught the neoclassical orange stucco edifice from the last century, upon a little rise, surrounded not only by the obligatory pines but also by beautiful cypress trees. The automobile was quickly bearing left then swerving right again, as the road became the high-street, but Hefferon was daydreaming of the just-completed appointment, and kept hearing the voices of Evanthía coupling in his mind.

Directly across from Tourist Police Headquarters, and directly beside the Bookshop, was the taverna that Míkis and most of the locals preferred.

"What's this joint called?" Ivor asked, as he followed the Officer to a table on the upper level. They were now seated beneath a roof.

"The Áltis."

"Awl Teess Awl Teess—God, if I hear that bloody word one more time to-day, I'm going to puke!"

"My feelings exactly," responded the Cop.

"They had to call it something," the Athlete said and glanced round. Faces of half-starved hitchhikers glared at him from the lower level, as they stuffed themselves with Greek salad and moussaká.

"Used to be a vacant lot. They put a floor *down* and a roof *up*," Míkis declaimed. His erudition was as improbable as it was imponderable.

Exterior walls of the Bookstore had been whitewashed. Black squiggly designs from the Minoan Culture had been affixed to offset the glare.

"Tourists eat down there," the Officer said and brushed away the whole street-level section of the taverna. He began cleaning his manicured fingernails with a pocket-knife, being careful to sniff and suck them every now and then, to get the taste and aroma of sperm. The day's "special", served for the locals, which differed from the tourist menu, was finally brought by a waitress. "All the local boys in the taverna, those who own or work in tourist shops, eat here, because it's the cheapest," Míkis said in his dead-pan voice.

"Looks convivial," Ivor added, not agreeing with his own banality at all. Not one Greek in the taverna was speaking. The whole lot were quiet as clams.

Feeling as if they were being ostracised for having let loose a plague, the Briton and the Greek began to hit the bottle. The way that Míkis drank soon convinced the Athlete that ostracism was the Policeman's wont. But the pinky-golden musky retsina, the same that Movóros had served in Athens, was addicting, and Ivor was soon forgetting more than just a few pressing cares.

"So...what are your plans?" the Officer asked, in an almost friendly manner.

"In the bedroom?" the Runner replied and laughed.

All the Greeks in the taverna now were staring, openly, and whispering and pointing and snickering and generally talking about the Deputy Chief of Protocol and the Officer behind their backs.

The Policeman affirmed: "Here. Saturday."

All ears in The Áltis now swivelled their way. Saturday was certainly the password. Everybody in the gossipy community had no lack of opinions about Saturday. It had been *the* topic since the Mount Olympos Olympic Nation Organizing Committee had publicly announced that the Head of State of Greece, the President of the Republic, would be handing over, at Olympia, a deed of land on the twenty-fifth of March, Greece's National Day. Everybody was dying for the latest scoop. But nobody but the Officer was asking any questions, of course. Nobody wanted to admit being interested.

"Here? Saturday?" Ivor repeated, loudly, just to milk the audience a little bit. "Well—I think you *do* realise that, in my position as Deputy Chief of Protocol, I can only tell you that certain things have to be kept *classified*. But—I *can* tell you that neither the Ambassador nor the Member of the International Olympic Committee will be coming."

Míkis insisted on knowing: "From which goddamned country?"

Ivor cleared his throat in order to pronounce the name properly, then declaimed: "From...Turkey!"

Forks dropt in all directions, but all the boys caught them before they hit the plates. Greeks have quick reflexes. They kept on eating as if nothing had been heard at all. Then, to heighten the drama, Ivor crooked his index finger, so that he could whisper something in the Policeman's ear.

Everyone watched, although pretended to look the other way, drink wine, or watch some pretty tourist wiggling past the taverna. But nobody missed a trick. Ivor had his hand cupped over the Officer's ear for a full two minutes. *That* certainly set tongues a-wagging. Everyone was dying of curiosity. Everyone wondered if the Deputy Chief of Protocol and the Policeman were *queer*.

Midway in the whispering, Míkis came up for air and said... "No!"... as if he had just heard something terribly shocking. His mouth was opening wide, then he was covering it with surprise. His hand was on his dick, where it usually was, where *most* Greek men usually keep their hands! "You're *not!*"

Whisper whisper—then it ended, at long last—by Míkis's saying loudly: "You haven't got the balls!"

Every fork in the restaurant dropt this time, since all the local salesmen could speak English, and not one single fork was caught before it hit the plate. Then, The Áltis became silent as the grave, as everybody strained to hear a juicy secret.

But Tourist Police are shrewd, and Míkis had not risen in the ranks by his sullen good looks alone. He said, for the whole taverna: "I think...we should continue this conversation another time...like now...when we take our siesta...at *your* place..."

Ivor burst out laughing at *that* lewd line. Míkis wasn't all brawn after all. The taverna, meanwhile, was gossiping up a storm. Everyone was scandalised. Everyone was convinced that the two big men were having a sexual affair.

Just as the two were standing from their table, and for old time's sake, Hefferon couldn't help feeding the gossip mill just a little bit more, by saying: "By the way, Mike Old Chap, I was just wondering why it is that you haven't yet taken me to visit the International Olympic *Academy*? Isn't *that* where I'm supposed to be working?"

The Officer's sole response was: "Nobody's there." Then he winked, and they both departed.

25th April – Tuesday – 8.05 AM

Rosy was howling again. Even though she was outside, the dog often did that when the telephone rang. Kitty finally went to answer it, in Leftéris's cluttered office, behind the Hut's kitchen. "Ivor—for you—it's Ada!"

I bolted from the private plank table used by the Manager and invited guests and dashed to speak to her: "Ada! Oh my Darling—how are you? Yes? You sure? Are your parents there? They are? Oh I'm so glad for you. No—yesterday was horrid. It hailed. How about you?

Sunshine? I'm so happy. The funeral—is it to-morrow? How're you holding up? Well? I *knew* you'd be the strength of the whole family. Have you told your parents yet—about us? What? You're joking! The Press are saying what? We've *eloped*? Go on—no—not the London papers, too? Silly buggers. Oh God—how I *miss* you! It's Heaven hearing your voice again. I can't *tell* you how deeply I've missed you. What do you mean—of course I can't be my old self. It's *Hell* not having you here! When? They're saying we left Greece for Lausanne? Last week? Who spotted us? That's crazy! *Gold Medallist Kidnaps Torch Woman?* Is *that* what Fleet Street's calling you? What a hoot! *Anything* to sell a story. Did I hear what? Course not—I haven't heard a sodding *thing* up here. Leftéris and I've been meaning to continue a discussion we started *Thursday!* What? No! You're pulling my leg! Stop this! He did? He honestly did? Because of *us*? No—I'm *never* going to say it was only because of *me!* If *you* hadn't been there, I never would have had the guts. Good Lord—wait till I tell Leftéris! Dear—I *miss* you so. Yes— *please* say a prayer for me. I'm *trying*—I really am—to come to some decisions up here—but it's so damned difficult—*without* you. I love you. I love you with *all* my heart. Good-bye."

Tears were streaming down my cheeks. I choked back the ones in my eyes, and stood by the telephone, feeling utterly strange. After wiping my face and trying to look normal, I stept back to the kitchen table. Kitty was fussing at the stove, pretending she had nothing better to do. Both she and her boss were waiting for me to speak.

I let out a chestful of air: "Ada just informed me...that the Director of the CIA *resigned* in Washington late yesterday. The Director wouldn't admit that the Agency, as a unit, had been sponsoring the MOON plot, but he *did* say that certain individuals in the Agency's employ were directly involved."

Kitty said nothing, but adjusted her bra and refilled my cup with the golden herbal tea. Then she put the metal canister atop the table and opened the lid to see how much longer the tea would last. There were just two shafts of the fattish bushy flower that looked something like a dry asparagus. They were yellow, but all I could notice were Kitty's magnificent tits. Her big nipples kept rubbing against the tabletop like scrub-brushes.

Leftéris was pondering the CIA situation gravely. He was a very serious man, one who brooded everything, especially Kitty. He had one of his strong hands upon his brow, then at last he started to laugh softly. "Well, Olympian," he finally said, "I think it's safe to presume that you won't be needing to hear the news from *me* to-day!" Then he stood and slapt me on the back so hard that it felt as if I were being attacked by a Kodiak bear. "How about a day's honest work...to celebrate?"

"Anything," I responded and stood. We shook hands. His gilt tooth flashed. "A little bit of labour will take your mind off monsters and other ghastly things," he said and opened the door and stept outside.

"Vasanákis?" the Manager yelled.

The worker, tough as the Mystic Mountain itself, poked his bald head out a door of the incompleted new wing. His face was smeared in dust.

"What're you doing?" the boss barked.

"Pounding through the stone wall to the old part of the Hut."

"Do you have much rubble?"

"Plenty."

"Well, let Hefferon cart it out for you. He needs to get some exercise, since he's not having much luck *running* up here."

Leftéris turned and left. I looked into the room. It was more like a mine, with a heap of chipped rock on the floor, enough to fill a lorry. Vasanákis carried on with his chisel and hammer. The wall was a good two-foot thick.

So, for hours I carted away stone, uphill to a pile by the sand. Sometime that morning Kitty came bounding to my rescue with hot tea. By then the rocks had worn my fingers down to such a degree that the heat from the thick cup scorched me.

Lugging limestone was good therapy, in theory. Against my will, I began to wax philosophic. It seemed that the only way to learn a foreign language, and better yet the land where the language is spoken, is to go right *to* that land and turn oneself over to a foreign labourer. Let him work you over. It'll *never* do a damned bit of good studying things in books or institutions. Just go. Work. Listen to orders. Ask questions. Make mistakes. But *don't* speak the mother-tongue. If you're told to pick up *that stone*—with a boss laughing or screaming if you fuck up when you hand him *this broom*—then the bloody language *will* be learnt rapidly, simply because *no* one likes being laughed at or screamed at!

Vasanákis, every so often, asked me to give him a hand, an offer I didn't refuse, as it meant a respite from rocks. "Here—hold this up like this," he ordered, standing atop the rubble in the doorframe, balancing a wood maquette just hammered together.

As I was holding the lumber, I recollected a funny passage from that pulp fiction I'd read the other day. That San Francisco painter, now back in Santa Monica, was trying to seduce some wealthy Silent Era actress who only wanted her portrait done. As I kept holding the wood, it struck me that such labour, on Olympos, would itself make a comical drawing—like something by Goya. Then my mind led me even further back in time, to the Archaic Period of Greece, when the Olympics were their purest. Those who competed then had had such exceptional educations. Limber nude youths were trained in Poetry, Music, and Dance, as well as in Athletics. They thought nothing of Inspiration, since it was a fact of everyday existence. They didn't have to worry about *creating* something from within them. If the urge came...they just did it, they just recited an original poem, played a tune invented on their favourite instrument, or danced until sated. But that archaic spontaneity...long ago had *died*. What *had* killed it? What *had* made the natural flow, like water, turn to ice?

By lunch-time at one o'clock, I was ready to be shipped downslope in a rough pine box. "Sodding rocks," I cursed aloud. "Lifting and pushing rubble, upslope, to the dump-pile, shovelling the small stuff, carrying hernia-inducing boulders to another spot, all *uphill*...is *this* why I came to Mount Olympos?"

I had dreamt about climbing this very mountain for years. I guess I had to admit that I had all but done it now. But *what* a way to do it...moving bits of the mountain hither and yon. I couldn't help feeling that it was some hilarious example of divine retribution, for some nasty thing I likely said or did someplace! Perhaps it *was* ironic imprisonment, for being so idiotic at Oxford?

"Bugger!" I said aloud and followed Vasanákis to the Hut's kitchen. "Oxford's the *last* sodding thing I need to have plaguing me today!"

22ⁿᵈ March – Wednesday – 5.50 PM

Officer Míkis rose from the extra bed that had been placed in a spare room of the Throúva house. He yawned and sat up. He'd been masturbating, the whole time since lunch, and threw on his bikini briefs to go wash his hands in the kitchen, then ambled to the Deputy Chief of Protocol's room with half an erection. "Time we get back to work," he ordered. "I'll be in the sitting-room. Bring that sealed dossier Madame gave you in Athens. You have it?"

"In my briefcase," Hefferon said and stretched, naked beneath the single sheet. He, too, had been wanking like a monkey, straight since lunch.

"And put that MOON-OC Accreditation round your neck—you'll need it—starting to-night." The Tourist Policeman turned to leave.

Slipping into his undershorts, Ivor dragged his carcass into the kitchen to rinse the cum off his hands and to splash cold water on his face. It certainly was *hot* inside this house, though it was getting dark outside. He decided to dress later. The Cop was only wearing his undershorts, anyhow.

Briefcase in tow, but with his Accreditation not about his neck, Hefferon stept into the largest room of the archaeologist's old house. In the stark chamber two wooden chairs and a table had been arranged. One bare bulb provided light. The near-naked Officer was seated. He was smoking. He offererd one to the Athlete.

"Never smoke. Who brought the furniture?" Ivor wondered.

"Soldiers," was the response. "In exactly one minute, every single hotel in the village is to be cleared."

"For VIPs and officials?"

"And Press. It's now six o'clock. You may unseal the dossier."

The Runner performed the combination to unlock his briefcase, then extracted the documents in question. As Míkis blew smoke-rings and fondled himself as usual, Ivor cracked the sealing wax imprinted with Thýella's signet of the vampire, Lamía.

"At eight we'll return to The Áltis, to eat. Till then, I recommend you study that material."

For the next two hours, Ivor carefully looked over the classified information pertaining to every single phase of activity slated for Olympia between this evening and Saturday afternoon. Scheduling had been co-ordinated by the Executive Committee of the MOON-OC, meaning by the General and his wife, by their son Major Movóros, and by Thýella's bastard son, the Priest.

For an overall idea of what was occurring day to day, the Deputy saw that Army convoys were en route at this very moment from various locations in Greece, and that their job was to implement security, communications, and supply installations throughout the night. Later this evening, a security check would be made at the three principal hotels designated for use by Dignitaries and World Press.

To-morrow morning the Ancient Stadium would be transformed, so that seating could be arranged and the television network installed. Ivor would be going to the International Olympic Academy later in the morning, whilst a ticket-distribution system would be set up in the village, for the local people's attendance at the Deed Ceremony. Security arrangements would be under Major Movóros's command, who was arriving midday.

At six o'clock to-morrow evening, the whole region would be cordoned off by the Army, exactly as the Lake Placid Olympic Organizing Committee did for the XIII Olympic Winter Games. Here, at Olympia, the situation was uncannily similar, given that so few roads fed into the area. Access to the Olympic Region was *not* to be free.

The day after to-morrow would see the arrival of the General and his wife. Accreditation of all VIPs and Press would be under Thýella's control. The Army would be preparing the Old Museum for the Session of the International Olympic Committee, to be declared open later that evening. The Session was under Ouranós's personal jurisdiction. Friday morning also would see the start of the arrival of VIPs. There would be a Security Rehearsal in the Ancient Stadium as well. Press would be accredited in the afternoon, and before the evening meal their seating arrangements would be rehearsed, then followed by a Cocktail Party and Press Conference. There would be a VIP Banquet Friday evening, then the IOC Session would be declared open by the Head of State of Greece. It looked to be a day to give any security official an embolism.

But all of this was a mere fly in the ointment compared to Saturday, the National Day of Greece. All throughout Friday night, testing of the international satellite-link would be conducted. From dawn of Saturday, the minute by minute scheduling of events, of truly Cecil B. DeMille proportions, would be organised and assisted by the Army, in absolutely faultless military precision. It *had* to be that way, given that the IOC contain so many prestigious individuals, not to mention Heads of State in their own right.

Just going over Saturday morning's schedule was a laborious read. It did demand all of Ivor's concentration. Seeing the timetable reminded him of Placid, of how complex an organism was an Olympic event of this magnitude.

"This's as complicated as the Opening Ceremonies for the Games I competed in four summers ago," the astounded Athlete said to the Greek. "No wonder they take four years to organize."

"That's why Organizing Committees exist," added the Officer, who was sniffing, licking, and cleaning his nails again. He was fully hard, and once again had come, just from cupping his big penis with the whole of his hand for the last half hour. "Keep on with your reading. It's getting late." He rose, with the gooey glans of his manhood stuck right out above the top of his bikini-briefs, and went into the kitchen to rinse himself off.

Hefferon did as told, wondering what in Hell he ever did to get imprisoned with such a sex-maniac for a captor. And he also wondered what in The Devil's Name was in the very *air* of Greece, that made everybody so goddamned horny all the time. All you had to do was breathe it in, and you got all hot to trot. No wonder so many of their ancient myths had to do with sex, he said to himself. "Listen to this," he announced. "10.35 AM. Director of Archaeological Site of Olympia turns Ceremony over to Chief of Protocol of MOON-OC; 10.36 AM. Chief of Protocol of MOON-OC introduces Senior Member in Greece of the IOC; 10.37 AM. Senior Member in Greece of the IOC, 9-minute maximum speech, introduces IOC President..."

"Ok ok," Míkis snapt, now back in room, as he gestured impatiently with his pocket-knife, "that's *your* job. I got enough of my *own* shit to worry about...just guarding *your* raunchy ass!" He pronounced *ass* just like an American.

"Yeah," snorted Hefferon, "I *see* how you guard *me*, what with your hands on your balls the whole time."

The two laughed. They felt like brothers by now. What a pair.

As for Ivor's own responsibilities at the Deed Ceremony, everybody was certainly in for a big surprise. Officially, he had been forced to accept a public rôle in events, as Keeper Of The Olympian Ideal, representative of all Olympic Athletes. Obviously, with all the hooplah over Heads of State and VIPs, no big nod would be given to mere *Athletes*, without whom of course there could *be* no Olympics *or* Ceremonies. Ivor would be running, through the ruins, and into the filled Stadium, and he was required to recite a short prepared speech.

But woe to the MOON-OC. Ivor Hefferon had absolutely *no* intention of saying *anything* in favour of such maniacs. He now was contemplating just what exactly he *would* dare to say.

26th April – Wednesday – 6.00 AM

It was as clear a morning as ever appeared on Olympos. Leftéris was huddling over a large map of the upper peaks of the mountain. Huddling as well were the Hartmunds and myself. Just to remind the couple from Bern, the Manager of the Hut wanted to make sure that both of them knew exactly which route to take.

"And remember, Olympian," he said to me, "*you* are going to the very top with yours truly. To-day you're to go to Skála peak, with the Hartmunds, but no higher. I have to oversee Vasanákis to-day. But this climb will be good exercise for you. Anyhow—Ada's going to be in mourning to-day, as they're burying Aunt Georgia four hours from now."

"You sure you still want to climb?" Herr Hartmund asked.

"Maybe he'd rather be going up with his fiancée," Frau Hartmund said kindly.

"Oh no," I objected. "I think the climb will do me a world of good."

"I think the atmosphere up there will clear your fuzzy head, at the very least," Leftéris said and his golden tooth sparkled.

"Ya guys wanna bit more coffee?" Kitty asked. She refilled all the cups without waiting for an answer. To-day her eyeshadow was black and her wig the canary-yellow.

"That's my girl," the Manager said and pinched her behind.

"Now look, ya Animal, I told ya *never* to do that again!" she retorted but cracked a cheeky grin. "Hey Athlete—been meanin' to ask ya somethin'."

"You *fancy* something?"

"Are ya close with them *IOC* people?"

"I know a few, yes."

"How close?"

"Fairly. Why?"

"Because—well—I don't know—seems to me they could be done away with—ya know?"

"No—I *don't* know."

"Well what *good* are they? They're all pushin' ninety!'

"Watch your tongue," Leftéris joked.

"*I'm* pushing ninety, as you say," Herr Hartmund responded, "and look at me...I'm still fit as a fiddle."

"Youth is a state of mind," Frau Hartmund added.

"Precisely," the Manager concurred.

"Well—I don't think it's right—that these old geezers—what're there only about *eighty* of 'em in the whole wide world?—got the right to have so *much* control over the Planet Earth's sports activities. Who gave these guys the say-so, huh?"

"You can't say that they *control* Planet Earth," I objected.

"Of course I can. I just did. Anyways—I think it *stinks* of royalty and all that crap—the *oldest* men in the world—and a *closed* club at that!"

"Nobody ever pretended that the IOC was democratic," I stated.

"Well it got founded in an age when much of the world was still ruled by *kings*," Kitty announced. "But things have changed!"

"How?" Leftéris wondered, with a mouthful of fresh preserves. "The IOC should be *abolished*! God—are ya for real! *Everybody* knows they got a strangle-hold on the Olympics!"

"Kitty—they were what *revived* the Olympics in the first place," I countered.

"Look—I know who Baron Koo Bare Poon Tang was—don't think I don't! I ain't just another dumb blonde, Hot Feet."

Leftéris was highly amused. He loved arguments, especially with his temperamental cook. "Tell us, Kitty, all about 'Baron Koo Bare Poon Tang'. Come on."

"He was a French *aristocrat*—don't *that* say it all?"

"That says nothing," the Manager put in.

"And if *you* were living in Paris, under Robespierre," Frau Hartmund retorted, "you'd have chopped off the Baron's *head*, just because he was *titled*?"

"Aren't these Americans *silly*?" Leftéris said, just to get Kitty riled.

"*Silly*?" Kitty screamed with her hands on her hips and her breasts pointed out like cannons: "Lemme tell ya somethin'—I know what I'm talkin' 'bout—and all I'm sayin' is that the IOC is the most goddamned *unfair* organization this side of The Kremlin!"

"Oh come on," I said.

"Grow up," Leftéris added.

"It is! It's the most élite club in the world. Its Members vote themselves *in*, then appoint their own successors. And ya gotta be filthy-rich to belong. It ain't for just a nobody like me!"

"That says it all!" Leftéris announced.

We all roared.

The Manager said lustily: "Poor Kitty—your name is *so* appropriate."

"Why's that?" she said, hurt for being laughed at.

"Because—you always think you're *playing*, but you always manage to *scratch*!"

22nd March – Wednesday – 8.00 PM

We were dining again in The Áltis, at the same table as before. Again, all

389

suspicions about what was happening to the tiny village were glancing our way. It made for quite the uncomfortable meal.

We had hardly had a moment to sit for our first glass of retsina, when the high-street, that had been cleared of all parked vehicles and now was closed to all traffic except for the to-ing and fro-ing of officials, suddenly became the focus of everybody's attention.

Míkis said: "Watch."

The first Army convoy began passing. It was led by a half dozen motorcycles driven by Military Police, following a Tourist Police car whose siren was blaring. The convoy came from the left and passed on the right.

"They're en route to the Xénia Hotel," the Officer surmised, as he watched a dozen troop transport vehicles filing by.

The Áltis was silent until the twelfth vehicle had vanished, when the taverna exploded in gossip. Everybody was quite honestly impressed.

"This's nothing," Míkis announced.

Soon after our dinner had been served, a second convoy emerged from the outskirts of town. This one, though, was headed by the same black Peugeot of Psychopompós.

"Your Director of Communications," the Tourist Policeman said, "is leading the way to the Stadium."

This convoy was endless. It was the bulk of the security forces, every soldier armed, and was aiming towards the ruins at the eastern end of town. Jeeps bearing Commanding Officers alone took ten minutes to pass.

"They're setting up camp in the huge parking lot we were in to-day."

"That field? It did look large enough for the whole Greek Army," Hefferon agreed.

"These men'll pitch tent there, then begin installations for the Stadium. They'll be working through the night," the Officer said.

By now, local people in the taverna, whose curiosity could not be deterred, were coming up and asking Míkis all sorts of questions.

Ivor was introduced to the group, in his position of Deputy Chief of Protocol for the MOON Organizing Committee. To the local people, Thýella had specifically ordered her Deputy to say only that everything was classified, should anybody ask. This reduced conversation to a minimum. Míkis, however, rose to the occasion by admitting: "Just keep your eyes peeled. You'll see as much as anyone else is going to see."

"Will the President be here?" many Greeks were wondering.

"Yes, that I am allowed to tell you. The President *will* be here—late Friday," said the Officer, who then ordered: "Now—please let us continue our meal."

Satisfied that their Head of State was arriving in two evenings' time, the crowd returned to their tables and began to consume inordinate amounts of retsina, ouzo, Metaxas, and then putty-thick coffee *métrio* to counteract all that booze.

"We have to leave here soon ourselves," Míkis announced.

"For security checks?" Ivor asked.

"The initial one, yes, at the three hotels," the Officer replied. "Isn't that Movóros's responsibility?"

"It's Protocol's problem as well. Think of how you'd feel if a major international incident were caused because of some slip-up at any of the venues?"

"Thýella would roast me alive!"

"Anyhow—Movóros isn't expected until to-morrow. The Priest will be busy at the Stadium. So it's *your* responsibility to make sure things are under control, at least until your Superior Officers arrive."

Towards nine, the village was roughly returning to normal, when a *third* convoy's siren and motorcycle escort arrived. This one was exactly like the first, with the same amount of vehicles and manpower, except for a deployment of two howitzer guns pulling up the rear. Seeing those, the whole of Olympia took note and became as silent as a tomb.

"People must think it's a goddamned invasion," Hefferon said, looking at all the shocked faces.

"It is," the Tourist Policeman concurred. "It's for everybody's good. Guns will be deployed to the blockade being set up just beyond the roadway that leads to the International Olympic Academy."

"Isn't that for six o'clock to-morrow?"

"Correct. Guns will be ready."

Needless to say, it was as exciting as it was frightening. Everybody present was feeling emotions not frequently felt in peace-time. The awesome presence of the Army, in so short a time, for something that would be over and done with in days, was alarming.

"Besides," Míkis added, "there've been threats of insurgent reaction against Saturday's Deed Ceremony. Many agitators have protested the awarding of the Deed to the MOON, and the military hierarchy fear that there might be mass demonstrations this weekend."

"But this town's so *small*," the Deputy challenged. "Protestors would have to be *brought in*—from outside."

"Exactly. That's why the Army's own television cameras will be rolling, starting to-morrow, to broadcast to the country that everything here is totally under control. When the cameras point towards the howitzers, and when the Army reporters tell the viewing audience that *nobody* not invited will be allowed inside, then we hope that everybody will get the picture, and will watch events more safely...at home."

On that note, Míkis polished off his drink and rose. This time he didn't have a hardon. "Let's get back to work."

There was silence in the taverna, as the two men were departing. Then, boisterous gossip erupted, from everyone who had

391

been avidly eavesdropping, as the pair hopped in the police car and drove towards the west.

They first went past the edge of town, in the direction that Ivor had never been, over the railroad tracks that connected the village with Pátras.

"This is the Hotel Amalía," the officer announced and pulled into the parking lot of a sparkling white edifice only recently constructed. A convoy of twelve Army vehicles already had arrived. Two howitzers were waiting for deployment here as well. "It's the largest place of accommodation we have. It's also the furthest away—which's why we're putting the *Press* here."

"So they can't bother the VIPs in town with nosy questions."

"So *we* can keep them under surveillance."

The two entered the low-ceilinged lobby of the sparkling modern hotel. At the door two armed soldiers with submachine guns flanked the prim short Hotel Manager, who recognised Míkis, of course. Given that Ivor was wearing Accreditation, he was allowed through, once both soldiers scrutinised it.

"The Deputy Chief of Protocol," the Officer stated to the Hotel Manager and soldiers.

The Manager of the Amalía then led the way. He headed to the left wing of the large L-shaped edifice, and the men walked along the hall. It was spotlessly clean, way different from The Club in Lake Placid, Hefferon said to himself. He remembered how some of the so-called VIP Suites in The Club had wallpaper peeling off the plaster and water dripping through the ceiling. *This* Manager, however, seemed very proud and eager for events to get under way.

Soldiers were everywhere. Attack-dogs passed by. "One is trained to sniff for bombs, the other for drugs," boasted the Manager. "I'm sure *neither* will be found in *my* hotel!"

He opened a door, and scared a busy maid. She was scrubbing the floor on hands and knees. She rose and curtsied.

"Never mind, Anna, continue with your work," her boss stated. "The men are just looking at the room. This is a representative bedroom. Of course, it has all the modern conveniences—telephone, television, room-service, et cetera. When the Press are allowed into the village, beginning Friday morning, I assure you, Mister Hefferon, everything will be awaiting them in perfect order."

"How many have you made arrangements for?" Míkis wondered.

"One thousand exactly," bragged the Manager. "It will be our pleasure to make everything here as convenient for them, as if they were at home."

"They'll all be gone by Saturday evening anyhow," stated the Deputy.

"We *are* looking forward to them. Our hotel has never had the privilege of attending to so many distinguished Reporters and Photographers from all over the world. Needless to say, this will do wonders for our publicity."

He shut the door and retraced his steps to the lobby, then led them to the convention hall. Soldiers were scurrying everywhere, with cables, computers, typewriters, photocopiers, telephones and all the technical apparati required by a major international press headquarters. The place was a beehive of activity. Commanding Officers were shouting to have things done properly.

"This is your Priest's brain-child," admitted the Amalía's Manager. "He's been here all day."

"We saw him just leading the contingent towards the Stadium," Hefferon replied.

"One thing must be made absolutely clear to early arrivals," stated Míkis, "is that the Press will *not* be allowed beyond this point, starting to-morrow at six in the evening. Friday afternoon, at half past one, till five o'clock, the Press will be allowed to travel through the village to the Academy, in a special transport system provided by the military. This is the *sole* time they may be accredited. Only those on the Chief of Protocol's Master List are eligible for residency here. At the Academy, they must present their hotel bills and invitations to the Accreditation Staff, plus proper ID, on Friday, to be allowed to observe events this weekend. Given that the Press have all been told to come to this Hotel first, via this one road of access only, soldiers will be forced to turn away any Press if they try to arrive from the opposite end of the village. This will ensure maximum protection and privacy for the VIPs, especially for Members of the IOC, who do *not* like to be badgered by troubleshooting reporters. In fact, we have been told that the IOC are not to be talked to *at all*."

"Psychopompós told us that the VIPs won't be arriving via this direction anyhow," remarked the Manager. "They'll be coming from the direction of the Academy."

"Correct," the Tourist Police Officer concurred.

"All this space-age technology..." the Amalía's boss remarked with awe, "...this ancient community never has seen the likes of..."

The Tourist Policeman looked at his watch. "We have to go to the Xénia now. Thank you very much."

"It's been my pleasure to meet you, Mister Hefferon. I watched you on television from Lake Placid, lighting the Sacred Cauldron, and I also saw your Gold Medal victory at the last Summer Games. I must say...indeed it's an *honour* to meet a *true* Olympic Athlete!"

The Amalía's Manager shook Ivor Hefferon's hand with honest respect verging on awe, then escorted the men to the door. The soldiers snapt to attention as the two departed.

Driving back into town, Míkis put on the siren and rushed at top speed. Ivor sat back and enjoyed watching pedestrians scattering from the trafficless road. They passed The Áltis eatery and the siren wailed right up to the Hotel Xénia's door.

Again, it was much the same in this three-storey building just a few hundred feet from the Old Museum. Soldiers, soldiers everywhere were making sure that Presidents and Secretary Generals of the National Olympic Committees who would be attending, along with these people's Special Guests, would be receiving the absolute best accommodations. In almost all cases, the VIPs were men, and they would be coming to Olympia with wives. Some of course brought girlfriends, or boyfriends, or relatives. As well, the Xénia would be housing Presidents and Secretary Generals of the International Sporting Federations, who likewise were free to bring one Guest apiece.

The Manager of the Xénia, taller, older, and much stouter than the Amalía's, showed the two the obligatory bedroom, then proceeded to the dining hall. "Insofar as this room will witness Friday evening's VIP Banquet," the man declaimed, "we are requested by Madame Ouranoú to festoon it in the local manner."

"How charming," Hefferon agreed.

"That's why the local women of the village are bringing in their rugs and best weavings, to decorate the walls to-morrow, then Friday morning they're returning with floral displays."

"It should be most appropriate," the Athlete said, honestly pleased.

The Xénia's pompous Manager began to natter on and on about this and about that, detailing to the two every single spice that would go into the aforesaid Banquet, so exhaustingly, that the Tourist Policeman had to call it quits. He looked at his watch. "Eleven o'clock. We've *got* to move on."

With some difficulty, the Xénia's Manager agreed to let them leave, and escorted them to the door. Again, they were saluted by guards.

As it was late, and given that they were on the edge of the village anyway, Míkis did not sound the siren this time but simply drove downslope towards the ruins.

"To-morrow, you're scheduled to go to the Academy," Míkis announced, so we need not visit there to-night."

"I want to run," Ivor said.

"I could use a bit of exercise myself," the Officer challenged. He had never run against, or with, an Olympic Gold Medallist before, and was stirred by the idea. He pulled into the smaller parking lot on the right side of the road, that was directly opposite the huge parking lot buzzing with military activity. They got out of the squad-car. Two soldiers from nowhere rushed up, but when they saw that the Policeman and Deputy were official, they retreated towards their camp.

"I believe there are two thousand troops here," Míkis said matter of factly.

Astounded by the number, Hefferon simply said: "Quite."

"They're scheduled to relax till midnight, then the big-push into the ruins begins. They'll march along the road here, past the foot of the Hill of Krónos, then into the Ancient Stadium from the locked gate at the eastern end."

"Then let's hurry."

"There'll be guards at this end, of course."

"I didn't see any when I arrived by helicopter."

"But they saw *you*. They were told you were *British*, that you were *eccentric*, and that you were to be left *alone*, no matter how weird you'd might act!"

"Eccentric?"

"Aren't *all* you Englishmen?"

"And what do you call jerking off in public, like *you* did, right in front of Evanthía this afternoon? I'd say that was downright *funky!*"

"That was what Greeks call...a nocturnal emission. My hands didn't have anything to do *with* it! The woman's double-voices just *willed* me to come!" the Cop said with a laugh.

Míkis proceeded to the locked gate just past the little forest-green Kiosk, where tickets to the ruins were sold to tourists. Indeed, a blue-uniformed Archaeological Guard, under the employ of Miss Selináki, was there to greet the two.

"Passes?" he asked, although the Director of the Olympia Ruins had forewarned the fellow of their arrival. The visitors both held up the properly stamped permits that were legible by the guard's torch. He unlocked the gate and allowed the two into the Sacred Compound.

It was still the Full Moon. Visibility was even better than it was last night. There was less mist in the air. Fireflies were radiating everywhere. The landscape was absolutely enchanting. "Listen to the owls," Míkis said, as they approached the ancient Gymnasium, off to the right.

"Not to mention crickets," Ivor added. "Now remember...what we were whispering about at lunch."

"Go on! You think I'm *crazy!*"

"Míkis—I *know* you're completely nuts—just from the way I couldn't help seeing you constantly playing with your *dick* all day! So don't tell me a big boy like you will be chickening *out* now, *are* you?"

"Who? Me?"

"I don't think you've got it *in* you."

"Get off it!"

"*None* of you Greeks have the *balls* to go *totally* against convention. You're all still just a bunch of conformists. You don't *dare* be individualists! You're *scared!*"

"What to fuck're you talking about, Hefferon?"

"About our *race*—you *have* chickened out, haven't you?"

"Who says?"

"*I* say!"

They were now past the Hera Temple, heading towards the ruined vaulted entrance to the Stadium. It was still standing in its primitive potency, with nary a weed disturbed. Ivor dreaded seeing it tomorrow, even though the seats would only be temporary.

"*What* did you say?" Míkis insisted.

"I *say*—you don't have the guts to run *naked*—like your goddamned Greek *ancestors* did here! You *don't* have the guts—let alone the *balls*! All you know how to do is beat your meat!"

"You're talking garbage!"

"Rubbish—Man—*rubbish* is the word! If you're going to speak *English*—speak it *properly*!"

"You British think you're so damned *smart*. You still think the whole world's *yours* for the taking!"

"Come on, Míkis, put your big fat mouth where your bragging is! Take off your clothes! Every sodding stitch!"

Ivor Hefferon then put down his briefcase, removed his laminated Accreditation, and began taking off the three-piece suit of the businessman. By so doing, he felt as if he were liberating his very Soul.

"Come on—Officer! *Strip!* Show me that you know how to do something other than *play* with yourself!"

Míkis was dumbfounded. His macho reluctance to be shown up was battling visibly with his whole life's inculcation by Orthodox Church values, ported over the Mediterranean from puritan Palestine, that said: Nudity is *sinful*! Nudity is *sinful*! Nudity is *sinful*!

"But—they'll *arrest* us! This is verboten! *Nobody's* supposed to be allowed to do such a sacrilegious thing!"

"*Who'll* arrest us? You? *You're* the Officer here—aren't you? Well—goddamn it—take charge! Are you going to arrest yourself? Don't be a fool, Míkis! *Strip!*"

"But we've been taught..."

"You've been taught *rubbish*, Míkis, and you goddamned well *know* it in your Soul—in that *Greek* Soul of yours—if you do have even a *drop* of that old Greek spunk left *inside* you!"

"What're you getting at?"

"Ho—maybe all you so-called Greeks *aren't* even connected to the Ancient Greeks at all—maybe all the *Greek* in you was *bred* out—centuries ago—by *Turkish* sperm!"

"Why you lousy son of a bitch!"

"Then *prove* to me you're Greek! I bet *I've* got more goddamned Pure Greek Blood in me than *you've* got! *Mine* goes back millenia—how far does *yours* go back—huh, Míkis! *Prove* to me now—in this very Stadium1—where your Greek Olympics were sired by *real* men—prove to me *right* now, Míkis, that you *do* have the courage to shed your outmoded Orthodox imported *un*-Greek morals—prove to me, in the name of your late Greek *ancestors*, prove to *them* you're a *Greek* man—

prove to *them* that you do have a cock and two balls between those *tough* legs of yours, and not just some dithering *slit*—prove to *them*, now, Míkis! Bare your Greek *manhood*—to the moonlight!"

The Policeman stood, frozen on the spot. A war was raging within him. He could not even speak.

"Well—come *on!*" Ivor commanded, now completely naked. "Are you *going* to be a man—or are you going to give in—like some scared little schoolgirl—just standing there—fearing that The Big Bad Church's going to spank your *tight* little arse—if you so much as misbehave! Come *on*—Chicken Shit! *Strip!*"

That did it. Nobody ever had called the Officer such a name. He'd now show this goddamned British *bastard* that he *was* a Greek, and unafraid.

"*Strip!*" yelled Hefferon. "*Strip!*"

The Officer was tearing off his clothes.

"*Strip!* Nobody's looking! And if they are—*sod* the lot! That's right—strip!"

"All right—Mother *Fucker*—I'm naked!" the young Greek growled.

The two were glaring at each other in utter hatred, all fired up to beat the other in the race.

Stars above were twinkling mightily bright, as both these physically fit male creatures hastily shook hands, at last, in the moonlight. How long had it been...since two *naked* men...exactly as so many Athletes...so many centuries before...had stood on this very spot...on these very starting stones...to race? The Ancient Greeks had *not* run with clothing...so why should *we*...to-day?

The feeling was indescribable, as the two went to their mark. The Briton had told the Greek that the Greek could begin the race. And then...

Two agile men were off, and the Briton, of course, took the lead. He was over the finish line before he hardly had a chance to breathe. But the Greek had put up a jolly good fight. He was no Olympian, by any means. But now, breathing hard, and laughing uproariously, the two men had a truly unforgettable bond. They shook each other's hand, this time with brotherhood in their hearts, with mutual admiration in their eyes.

26th April – Wednesday – Dawn

The climb began. At long last, after days of delays, after years of imagining and waiting, I began the ascent to the uppermost reaches of Mount Olympos.

It was a moment not unlike that just seconds before my Olympic race. I was nervous, albeit frightened. This was something that was happening for the very first time in my life. The next time...if there be a next time...sensations would be different.

I looked myself over. Green wide-wale corduroy trousers, two pairs of woolen socks, mountaineering boots that cost me just a few quid, undershirt, an overshirt, a thick jersey, and a winter down-lined jacket of blue nylon that Leftéris let me borrow, leather fleece-lined mittens, and a woolen ski cap. It was cold!

On my back was a light nylon pack, with biscuits, a sandwich, and of all things to carry...a sketch-book. Kitty had produced one that some climber left behind a couple weeks ago, just after the Hut re-opened from winter. "Well—it could still very well *be* winter, up there," she said, before our departure from the Refuge.

"Then again," Leftéris added, "one never knows what conditions on the top *will* be like, hour to hour. It may snow...then brilliant sunshine might bake the treeless landscape so fervently that flowers blossom right before your very eyes."

"That's why I want to bring the sketch-book," I laughed as Kitty said: "God—he tells the tallest tales!"

In case anything might catch my woolly imagination, if I might be inclined to draw a few squiggles on paper, I took the sketch-book anyhow. It would be a few hours' wait, alone, at Skála peak, whilst the Hartmunds made their way to Mýtikas and back, so I might do a bit of drawing then.

So we were now setting out. In deference to the Swiss couple's age, they preceded and set the climb's pace. Both of them had their own sticks, with which they aided their steps. At first this seemed a bit too stodgy for someone as young as I. But, by watching the pair for a few minutes, using a third arm or leg seemed to prove beneficial.

Shortly after we pierced the forest above the Hut, I requested that my comrades halt a bit and I dashed about till I found a fallen limb to serve the purpose of a walking stick. Seeing the three of us, slowly mounting upwards at a snail's pace, anyone would assume us father, mother, and son.

But snail's pace was imprecise. These two were veterans. The native Swiss have corpuscles of iron in their veins. Raised with mountains much higher than Olympos, they take to the heights as dear friends. They know their cantankerous ways. They know how moody a mate they can be. They also realise, far better than most, that *no* mountain is meant to be scaled on a run!

The pace of mountaineering, even to the elevation of the Refuge Hut with Ada, had been a painful revelation to me. The body has a tremendously difficult time, with readjustment to superior heights. It must not be hurried. Blood takes time to adjust to each advanced elevation's larger want of oxygen. This the two Swiss knew. They were in no rush at all. They saved my life!

And here we were...yet in the forest. Dawn was just breaking from the distant Aegean Sea. Crimson light was beginning to warm the packs on our backs, and to caress the hams of our legs...that is, when light *could* reach us through shade. My breath, already, was strained. It was already like long-distance running, which never was my specialty. I began to pray to have the strength to continue.

The elderly couple stept along the worn path in silence. All of their concentration was in their feet. Their presence in the environment was one of Perfect Peace. They were at home. I felt like an alien from a troubled distant galaxy.

23rd March – Thursday – 9.45 AM

From midnight, right past the dawn, troops worked and transformed the Ancient Stadium of Olympia into an instant sports venue, with all of the latest features. In fact, the whole of the sacred temple-city of Zeus achieved a startling metamorphosis, a virtual rebirth. A triumphal lane, flanked by the famed five-ringed flag of the International Olympic Committee, was roped off from the Kiosk for ticket sales at the western end of the ruins, all the way to the Stadium itself. This would be where Dignitaries would promenade.

Five separate video-units were positioned along the processional route. Ivor was inspecting the last of them with the Tourist Police Officer. Both men were standing atop the ramparts of the western end of the barrel-vaulted lane. Atop this ridge ran a line of flagpoles with the IOC pennant flapping in the breeze. From this vantage point could be seen the ruins behind them, and the busy Stadium before them. A parallel line of flagpoles extended atop both summits of temporary grandstands that had been set up that night, along the lengths of the Running Track.

"I can hardly believe my eyes," Míkis said in astonishment. "The Army's done wonders."

Ivor's reaction was coloured with a bit more education. "It appears that the set designer had a recent nightmare of the Circus Maximus...during Caligula's reign."

"Everything's been accomplished most diligently," peremptorily stated a young Army Captain with a patch over one eye. He was over-seeing progress. "The ruins are being given *prime* consideration. My men *know* they'll be demoted...should *one* single ancient stone be moved from its spot in History."

"What about the stones the *Germans* moved!" Míkis asked, "when *they* were excavating?"

The men laughed.

"That's the Lady Director's concern," answered the one-eyed Captain. "By the way...Germans are *still* excavating."

"Where's Madame Selináki?" asked Hefferon.

"*Everywhere!* She's been running round here, driving us all absolutely crazy," retorted the Army Officer, "but we all crave it...as we love to hear her talk! I believe she's down *there*." The Captain pointed to the far end of the Stadium. Beyond the finish line rose a gigantic platform on scaffolding. "The stage will support the Fanfare Trumpets, the Orchestra, and the Chorus," said the Captain.

"Too bad we didn't have all that accompaniment *last* night!" Ivor said for Míkis's benefit. The two broke up in laughter.

The Captain thought they were making fun of the Museum Director, and said: "Yes—Selináki most certainly is a pain. But listening to her when she gets mad—which is fairly often—is a man's version of Carnal Paradise! God—what a sexy broad!"

"She does serve a necessary deterrent to vandalism," Ivor said in her defence. "I'm quite on her side. It's almost *blasphemy* to see this peaceful site being turned into this cauldron of activity."

"Excuse me, Captain," said an Army video technician who'd been standing by the huge camera positioned on its platform nearby, "but may we get a bit of footage of the three of you? We're shooting for National News to-night."

"Roll it," barked the Captain.

An Army reporter with a microphone appeared beside the three, and requested that the men state name and rank for the camera. When this was done, the reporter asked Ivor: "As one of the world's most famous Athletes and Runners, and as Deputy Chief of Protocol, will *you* be taking part in Saturday's Deed Ceremony?"

"In some capacity, yes," the Olympian responded.

"Are you free to tell the nation *how*?"

"The MOON-OC are planning events for this Saturday. The Ceremony will be televised nationally, and broadcast internationally by satellite. We're all looking forward to the presence, in this magnificent Shrine To Sport, of the International Olympic Committee, and of the Representatives from the National Olympic Committees from all over the globe. Saturday's Ceremony will be unique, a turning point in organized sporting history. We shall be pleased to know that *this* country, as well as the whole world, will be following events closely." Ivor sighed with relief. He hadn't given anything away.

"Cut," shouted the technician. "Thank you, Mister Hefferon." Then he saluted the two other men.

Having retraced their steps along the flag-embellished processional route, through the ruins of the Áltis, Míkis and Ivor got into the patrol car by the Kiosk. The Army camp across the road was sending smoke signals, delicious odours of the midday meal for one o'clock. Fumes from the kitchen tent were wafting lazily in a spiral, laterally, towards the Hill of Krónos, then snaking through the upper branches of pines. An unusually brash flock of rooks, in the thousands, kept hooping upwards in the sky, from one slope of the mound to

400

another. Cicalas were adding *their* two bits, as well, vibrating strenuously on branches.

The Krónion, now behind the patrol car, was getting smaller by the second. Míkis and Ivor were glad to leave the cacophony behind. The driver laughed at a thought and said: "Zeus pitched a thunderbolt, so the myth goes, from Mount Olympos one day. And it struck Olympia—which is why he claimed it."

"But—it already was sacred to Krónos, his father," Ivor corrected. "He probably was aiming at the old man—you know how he was."

"See if you know *this* then. Why do they say that *Hercules* was one of the original patrons of the Games?"

The blue signposts to the Coubertin Memorial and the Olympic Academy now were behind them. The Army blockade had not yet been erected, so the soldiers flagged the car further east.

"Isn't it Herakles—in the Greek?" Hefferon asked, just to be irksome.

"Pronounced: EE-rah-kleez."

The two had become quite good friends since last night's run. Even though the Athlete couldn't trust the Policeman, he respected him nonetheless.

To their right were the fertile flat fields of the wide valley of the River Alphaiós, one of the most prominent of Greece. The land, blest by water and exceptionally rich soil, supported a bounty of crops, foremost of which were grapes.

"Did Herakles's being patron not have to do with his Twelve Labours?" the Deputy wondered.

To their right, beyond the vineyards and the farmers and the river rose a lengthy green ridge of many mounds, a true mountain, a beauty but a couple miles from the opposite shore.

"Which Labour?"

"The Sixth?"

Everywhere, everywhere, the ground was carpeted by flowers. Spring had now taken all of Greece for her glorious, if all too short, ride. Ivor had never dreamt of living anywhere that spring was so passionately felt.

"The Fifth," corrected Míkis, at last able to better his rival. "Herakles had to clean the filthy rotten stables of Augeías, not far away from here in fact, at Ílis."

"That's right. Didn't he use that very river right over there?"

"After he diverted the Alphaiós, in order to wash the stables clean, that's when Herakles began the Ancient Games," the Greek said. He pulled the car over to turn around, in a small dirt road leading to the freshly verdant vines.

"*You'd* celebrate too, if you'd been successful in removing all that horse-shit!" Ivor said and they both roared with laughter.

"Now—you *are* starting to sound just like a goddamned Greek!" Míkis kidded, then punched his new buddy in the shoulder affectionately.

It wasn't long after passing the soldiers again that Míkis was turning right, down a gravel lane of pedestrian access only. It was a road from a fairy-tale, lined with tall dark-green cypresses, that led straight to a round piazza at the end. Directly ahead, centred at the end of the trees, and standing before a wall of cypresses ringing the modest circle, was the white marble memorial to Pierre Frédy, the Baron de Coubertin.

Halfway along the road, the Tourist Police Officer parked the car. The two got out and slowly began to walk. Nobody was there but cicalas. A few ravens had taken flight at the entrance of the lane.

"Tourists, it seems, either are ignorant of this place or, if they do know about it, they feel that it's too far from the village to be seen," Míkis said.

At the edge of the circular piazza, just made of gravel coloured beige, the Olympic Gold Medallist paused, and looked from left to right. To the left, placed at a right angle to the road, were three white flagpoles. No banners were flying. Before these, on a square inset in the circle, was a block of white marble no more than one metre tall. A votive altar, it was precisely identical to the ancient one unearthed from the ruins of Delphi, the one on which no other embellishment was carved save for the now world-famous Five Enjoined Rings. The design on the Delphic altar, of course, History knows, was what had inspired de Coubertin to choose it as the symbol for the Modern Olympic Games. How very fitting that such an altar now should be here.

Straight ahead was the stela that contained the noble Baron's heart. A good ten foot tall, and maybe only two foot wide at the base, the four-sided shaft was carved with classical precision. Executed in two pieces, the rectilinear base, a metre tall, supported the taller segment that slightly and gracefully angled inwards and upwards, like an obelisk. A bas-relief of the Baron's bearded head, in profile, was inset within an olive wreath, and faced the east, eternally faced the Olympic ruins themselves...

Ninety degrees rightwards, a gravel path led up a small rise. Beige stones, spread two yards wide, gradually climbed over rustic risers, made of logs instead of formalised stairs. Cypresses were standing at attention alongside.

Glancing back to the central stela, and feeling awed by the serenity of the modest site, Ivor noticed what at first looked like a fancy wreath, that had been placed on the marble ledge atop the rectilinear segment. He slowly approached the Baron's memorial.

Upon arriving before the white marble shaft, the wreath turned out to be mere cuts of wildflowers, branches of cypress, and fern. No ribbon held them together. They balanced on the ledge beneath the pylon and the profile.

There was something so poignant in this silent and humble tribute, something far more eloquent than any formal ceremony or expensive floral spray, that it brought tears to the Olympian's eyes. To think that someone had been so thoughtful...as to place a few blossoms here...when the Olympic Games themselves, revived by the very man whose heart was encased inside, were about to be maligned...less than a mile away...where they blossomed...once...upon ...a time...

What a great, great man had been the dreamer de Coubertin! What Tragedy...misunderstood dreams...could wean...

26th April – Wednesday – 7.00 AM

We were on the ice sheet now. "This's where I had to dig that hole—three metres deep," I explained to Herr and Frau Hartmund, as we were midway along the snow.

"What on Earth for?" the elderly lady wondered.

"So that the water-main to the Refuge Hut could breathe," I answered, then told them all about the scare by the jet.

"I almost was killed by an avalanche," Herr Hartmund admitted.

"Oh Otto, *don't* tell that one," his wife objected.

The old man proceeded to tell the whole story anyway. It carried us across the rest of the snow. We all sighed with relief when the story was over, and when our boots once again were on firm ground.

We were entering a forest, quite unlike that on the other side. The trees weren't as large, and the path more rocky than before.

"Do you want to sit, Sieglinde?" Herr Hartmund asked.

"If only a few minutes."

We paused for the first time, on some rocks. Fog was approaching from downslope. The Sun had vanished behind grey clouds.

"I hope it doesn't storm," I said.

"That would *not* be pleasant," Frau Hartmund said, as she dug in her pack for some biscuits. "Ivor?"

"Ta."

"Only a few days ago we were on the southern shore of Crete, with medical friends of ours," Herr Hartmund acknowledged.

"Oh Ivor, it was simply enchanting. They have the most beautiful villa in the world. He's a brain surgeon in Athens, and spends the month of April by the sea. The place is a Garden of Eden," recalled the lady.

"Hot as Hades," her husband objected. "We mustn't over-do ourselves, Dear. This change of climate hasn't been easy."

403

"We thought that, by climbing Olympos again, we would better prepare ourselves for Bern," the wife said.

"I admire your fortitude very much," I said in all honesty.

"He means he can't believe how two old fogeys like us are up here!" Herr Hartmund laughed. "Well Son—you come and stay with us in Switzerland—we'll introduce you to people old enough to be *our* parents, who still climb."

I didn't know what to say to that one, so just grinned at the adventurous twosome.

"Anyhow—you're an Olympian, Ivor, and if anything happens to *us* to-day, you'll carry us back, for sure," joked the big man, whom I couldn't imagine carrying anywhere.

"Did I hear you say yesterday that you both have a clinic in Africa?"

Frau Hartmund answered: "We assist with one...in The Camerouns."

"How very admirable."

"'Tis most satisfying indeed," concurred the man.

"Did you know Albert Schweitzer?"

"We did," replied the lady. She then looked down the mountain-side, thinking about her memories. The man at her side did likewise.

They were not an easy couple with whom to talk, given that their bond of a lifetime together, and intricacy of their lives dedicated to service, seemed too complete, as if almost to preclude penetration from outside. However, I felt as if they did enjoy my company, but I still was uncomfortable besides. I wanted to ask them questions, but felt that mine would only seem naïve. After the tension increased with silence, save for rustling in the trees, I asked: "How many mountains *have* you climbed, Sir?"

He gave it a thought, for a moment, then responded: "Almost three hundred. Why?"

I felt so green when I had to say: "Because...this is my very first *one*..."

23rd March – Thursday – 11.00 AM

As the Olympic Gold Medallist was silently praying for the future of the Olympic Movement, and for Divine Guidance for what he would have to do on Saturday, before the memorial that contained the heart of the human being who caused that Movement, in 1896, to *be*, not a hint of a breeze was rustling in the trees.

But then, a loud roaring suddenly arrived at the end of the beige gravel lane, and quickly usurped the calm, all along the way between the cypresses that now began swaying with horrid disruption.

Iconoclastic as any barbarian, a brash Army Jeep swerved right inside the little piazza, jerked to a screeching halt, and sent dust billowing everywhere. Two figures jumped out, a man, lean and tall, in uniform, and a woman, wide shoulders and small hips, in civilian dress. Major Movóros and Dora Cain approached the Baron's memorial, together, abreast. The contrast between the immaculately groomed Major, with his cherished gold worry-beads, and the cheap lavender nylon outfit of the mistress was disturbing. The chauffeur, a new recruit, handsome as Romeo, waited in the seat. At the Major's approach, Míkis came to attention, stiff as his customary hardon.

"At ease, " ordered Movóros.

"I thought you were coming alone?" the Tourist Policeman asked.

"I did," the Major joked. "You see anyone else?" The tallest member of the Ouranós clan stood beside the memorial, flicking his worry-beads dextrously with one hand. All could feel he was bound to become a General, with his stripes, his medals, his shiny buttons.

"Lipón," he began, as he always did, as he ran a manicured middle finger down the length of his facial scar, as he licked it. Now Hefferon knew where Míkis got his finger-licking routine. The Major tilted his broad-brimmed cap closer towards his eyes, ever so slowly. If these were his troops, they would have known what the gesture meant. "I have more than enough to cope with to-day," he began as if speaking to children, "so I don't have time to mince words. You, Dora, have already received instructions. Míkis, I'll be with you in a moment. So these words are meant for our Olympic Gold Medallist."

Míkis smiled towards the stela and Ivor, who smiled towards the American spy returning from the altar.

"Lipón," the Major continued, "you, Athlete, as Keeper Of The Olympian Ideal, should never forget this spot."

"I shan't," Ivor promised.

"Lipón...as Keeper, you have certain noble responsibilities, of which, I'm sure, you're aware. Therefore, it is my responsibility, as Director of Sports for the Mount Olympos Olympic Nation, to remind you that it is your duty to be bold in defence of the Olympian Ideal, to be fearless, to be a fighter for right and even, when need be, to take things into your own hands. You will know when that moment arrives."

The Major stared right into the Deputy Chief of Protocol's eyes. Neither man flinched. What in Hell was the soldier getting at?

"Lipón," Movóros said in conclusion, "I have said enough here. Come with me now, I'll show you some things you should know." He turned on his polished heels and marched to the Jeep. Ivor, Míkis, and Dora followed, in that order.

"Míkis, take yourself to The Áltis taverna," ordered the Major, then pointed into his Jeep. "That red box—it contains five thousand passes for the public. Set up a distribution centre. Give only two per person. Tell the locals that they're to be admitted Saturday to the

405

Ancient Stadium only between 0730 and 0900. No sooner, no later. Is that clear?"

"Yes, Sir."

"Then carry out your orders."

"Yes, Sir," Míkis stated, saluted, then turned on his heels for his car. He soon was speeding away.

Ivor, Dora, and the Major got inside the Jeep. At the end of the lane, they sped leftwards in the opposite direction, only a few metres down the road, when they turned left again, next to the two waiting howitzers, onto the property of the International Olympic Academy. A group of soldiers, viewing the Superior Officer in charge of the whole operation, snapt to attention. Movóros merely glanced at them sternly, as he squeezed one of Dora's legs high up her thigh. She smiled to see that this road was lined with great bushes of flowering oleander.

"Jean Ketseas and Carl Diem, two great Olympians, succeeded in having this built," Movóros said proudly, as Ivor noticed that they seemed to be aiming for what looked like a Caribbean country club. "It's only been open some years."

The International Olympic Academy, superbly designed to be invisible from the road, dazzled Ivor's eyes. It was built in a wide natural amphitheatre of a low hill that faced the River Alphaiós, perhaps only half a mile from the Ancient Stadium.

"It's gorgeous...like Eden," Dora said, as the Major's hand slid upwards on her leg.

The beauty was pronounced most visibly by a low one-storey curve of interconnected bungalows of lovely tan stucco. Tan tiles connected the bungalows' three sets of roofs, which wiggled like lazy snakes in the sunshine and which conformed to the landscape in the shape of a C. Gracefully making the bungalows flow across the hillside, from left to right, were a series of separate doorways, wide Roman-arches with burnt-sienna paint.

"But look at these palms!" Dora exclaimed, never having seen so many before. "It's Paradise."

"Date palms," Movóros replied.

Ivor suddenly thought of the statue of Evrynomía in the garden of MOON-OC Headquarters in Athens, and how Thýella had said that its breasts were really dates.

As the chauffeur drove slowly up the avenue, with palms and bungalows to the left, Dora delighted in the fact that the tropical trees were chattering, that their spiky metallic fan-tailed fronds kept clacking against each other in the breeze. But, in her state of arousal, being brought on by the Major's right middle finger, that had found the woman's clitoris beneath her tacky skirt, what were palm trees? There was one palm for every third doorway, but Dora lost count of the doorways...

"The Track," Movóros said. The chauffeur crawled at a snail's pace.

Ivor had just turned backwards when the Major had just spoken. Dora was just about crying in heat. Her lover was getting an erection, and she was gripping it beneath the cloth between his legs. All this the Athlete caught with his eyes. The Major just winked at the Deputy, and thrust his finger all the way inside. It was somewhat difficult for Hefferon to concentrate on the oval Running Track to his right, on the next level immediately below the palms.

"And courts for tennis...and basketball," the Major said coolly. "And a swimming pool..."

"Paradise..." Dora whimpered again.

The chauffeur accelerated to the end of the bungalows, then swung leftwards up to the level of the Administration Buildings. There were three of them, all interconnected as well, and of the same design as the structures below, only these were larger.

"The first is for Seminars and Lectures, the second a Cafeteria, and last is Headquarters itself," the man in the rear said, still stroking the unashamed girl.

Out of the middle building a short middle-aged man came running. He was deeply tanned and wearing a most decorative shirt. It looked Hawaiian. On seeing him, Movóros at last pulled his finger out of the woman's vagina, slowly. Ivor couldn't help seeing *that* as well, since the approaching man was in his line of sight.

"The Administrator," said the Major without moving from his seat, "Pános Mavrolóngos." To the Administrator he said: "Ivor Hefferon —my mother's Deputy."

Everybody got out of the Jeep, except the chap at the wheel. Movóros adjusted his erect penis upwards, to full attention and, just like Míkis, did not even try to hide the bulging thing. Dora looked as if she were about to faint.

It was plain by the Administrator's eyes that he was up on all the gossip. "Deeply honoured," he said and bowed to the Athlete. They shook hands. Then to the Major he said: "And how is...Alcibiades?"

"Horny as ever," Movóros replied without cracking a smile.

The Administrator pretended he did not hear this. "Please stay for a bit of coffee."

Dora was trembling and picking at some lint dangling from her skirt.

"If we can sit outside," the Major responded. His conditional sentence was as good as a command. Three workers, hovering within earshot, within moments produced an umbrella-covered table, four chairs, coffee, iced water, and little citrus-cakes.

Having seated, and having let the Greek morning caress them with its silence, the Major juggled his worry-beads of gold, then ran his same well-manicured finger down the length of his facial scar, until the end of it rested alongside his lips. His tongue then sucked the knob slowly. He took a deep breath, in order to smell the juice of the woman, then said: *"Lipón."*

The Administrator smiled, and sipped his coffee.

"Lipón," Movóros said again, like a broken record, "my mother has designated Hefferon as Keeper Of The Olympian Ideal."

"The purpose of this Academy is to foster the goals of Olympism," the Administrator was most careful to say, without stepping on anybody's toes, "in this idyllic setting," he added, meaning that the Keeper was welcome within it.

Movóros seemed amused. "Saturday being National Day...it pleases us to see that the august Members of the International Olympic Committee will be accommodated here. Is everything ready?"

"No problem at all," the Administrator admitted. He was a hearty fellow, who looked both Coach and Athlete, one who would say "no problem" to anything. Ivor liked his confidence.

"This Academy will be ringed with soldiers, starting at 1800 this evening...when the region will be cordoned off from the rest of the country. I have arranged for one thousand troops to man these hills."

"I shall fear nothing," Mavrolóngos replied.

"You never do," Movóros answered. "Is the Protocol Centre set up inside?"

"Yes."

"Fine. Thirty soldiers will be stationed here, starting Friday morning. You'll need them, Ivor, to assist Accreditation. By 0800, when my parents arrive from Athens, everything will start rolling. VIP Accreditation is from 0800 till 1300. If VIPs can't meet that deadline, too bad for VIPs. Press Accreditation is between 1330 and 1700. You, Ivor, will be here all day. Is that clear?"

"Absolutely."

"Any questions?"

"Yes—my bodyguard—when will he be finished with ticket distribution?"

"He will fetch you at 2000 to-night. You are to remain here, with the Administrator, getting to know the Academy, until then. Miss Cain is to remain with you, as your Executive Secretary."

The woman, having resumed her composure, merely smiled.

"Dora—you know what to do," her lover said.

"I have one more question," Hefferon interjected. "My dossier stated that I shall be delivering a short prepared speech. It wasn't with my papers."

"My mother is composing it to-day. She'll bring it to-morrow, from the capital."

The Administrator slit an orange-cake with a very sharp blade. "What contingency plans are to be put into effect, at the Academy

408

specifically, if the threatened protest demonstrations occur as people fear?"

"I am sorry, Mavrolóngos, but that's classified," answered the Major, who rose. "*Lipón*...things, though, are under control. Whoever is out to *get* us...on Saturday...has another thing coming. *Nobody* monkeys with Greeks. You can cut off our arms, but we'll get you with *daggers* in our teeth."

26ᵗʰ April – Wednesday 8.00 AM

"The first mountain...you've ever climbed?" repeated Herr Hartmund after we three had been silent quite awhile.

I was so ashamed that I did not even answer. The question had said it all. We resumed our silence again. Fog kept rolling in and out of the ever-thinning forest, as if it alone were gobbling and dissolving the few remaining trees. We were entering a realm completely out of my ken, one where Imagination played the most uncanny tricks.

"We'll soon be at the end of the timber line," Frau Hartmund ventured and turned back to look me in the eye. The gesture was strange. She seemed to be checking to see if I still were there.

In fact, we *all* looked strange now. Nippy weather had forced us, at our biscuit break, to don the hoods of our coats. Only a few thousand metres below, Greece was experiencing the tail-end of spring. Athens already was parched from heat. Summer had already clamped down its lid on most of the country, putting the land on bake until many months ahead. But up here...three of us...only visible as fleshly beings by our quickly reddening faces...were stepping backwards in time...into winter.

"Not many trees at all now," the medical doctor said.

What passed as trunks now were more like leaping brown snakes. Altitude and wind and omnipresence of harshness harangued the few pines that *had* taken root, and haunted their every inch of growth. Tons of liquified atmosphere, three out of every four seasons, snarled branches even more. The brief respite of sleet and hail, whilst summer reigned on high, never was long enough for poor plants to stand tall.

These were the scariest trees that I ever had seen. In fog they would suddenly appear, out of nowhere, and look as if they were trying, with all their photosynthetic might, to push themselves *up* from rocky soil, yet fog would dance about their palsied limbs and press them down again. They then would vanish. I wondered what Herr Hartmund's first mountain had been like. He had probably been so young that he hadn't even been aware of where he was.

I almost felt glad inside...that it had taken *this* long for me to get here. Each step was Novelty. Each shape Revelation. Each step Forced Breath, laboured and almost tasting of blood. Each shape No Relief.

My whole Being was tingling. More was going on inside Body

409

and Mind...much much more in fact...than I ever had felt when I was closer to the seaside...when I was running...

This mountain-climbing business...it was all an *inside* thing. Conversation was getting to be a strain. What could one possibly *say*...

The timber line?

It certainly deserved comment...but how? Trees below, no trees above? Patches of snow? April must have melted acres of it? Do birds *roost* up here?

Birds?

Light was grey?

Nobody else up here?

I started recollecting people from my childhood...whom I thought I had long ago forgotten.

Father O'Hanrahan had me on his bony knee. He had just told me that my mother had passed away. I had a plate of pudding in my hands—and threw it across the room—it smashed—I screamed...

When I was twenty-four...I took the boat from Holyhead to Dublin. Father O'Hanrahan was dying. He was at his sister's, in a poor brick row-house, near Saint Patrick's Cathedral. I was there...holding his hand...when his Spirit left...fled his devout frame. I wanted to fly away with it...wherever that might be. I pledged to his Soul, right there, that I would try to live my life...as honourably as I could. Then, as his sister's family prepared the body, I walked to the Cathedral, feeling utterly lost inside. A rainy Sunday afternoon it was...in Eire. I needed to pray...to be in protection of The Lord...but doors to the Cathedral were closed. And it was *Sunday*! And this was *Ireland*! And my dead mother...had *come* from Northern Ireland! And the Cathedral of the Patron Saint of Ireland...was locked up drum tight...of a Sunday afternoon! Oh how I *beat* on those doors...of that building of God...that day! I screamed! I *cursed* so much that someone had to call the police! I was sobbing...on the porch of that Cathedral...for the one man who had cared for me...who now was cold...was dead! I only wanted to light *one* single candle...for my friend...for the Priest...for the Deceased! But the Cathedral of Saint Patrick was *shut*...of a Sunday...

On this lonely mountain slope...I couldn't help but wonder...if The Dead *do* watch The Quick? If they do...how *can* they? Must we *be* where they're interred...or can their Spirits come to *us*...no matter where we wander?

"I think that this...is the very last tree," Herr Hartmund said, up ahead.

23rd March – Thursday 12.15 PM

Motorcycles arrived. Psychopompós's black Peugeot was leading a convoy just come from Athens. The Orthodox Priest, assigned a soldier boy as chauffeur, was not now at the wheel, but was in the back,

410

studying a dossier on communications installations for the Academy. The chauffeur opened his door and the berobed Greek stept out. Pános Mavrolóngos had already excused himself from table. Ivor and Dora were left temporarily alone. Neither spoke. Both were watching the convoy. "Now, Pános," the Priest said without further greeting, "I'm again required at the Stadium, but you know this dossier as well as I. Telephone equipment in the first three lorries has been assigned to your Seminar Building, to be installed immediately by troops. This is for use by Members of the IOC. They are always on the telephone—to somebody or other—abroad. All their office equipment will be placed in the Seminar Building as well. Multilingual secretaries will be arriving from Athens to-night."

Just then an Army Lieutenant wearing glasses came from a military Jeep and said to the Priest: "As soon as you're ready, we shall begin."

"Has the Seminar Building been cleared?" Psychopompós inquired.

"Everything's ready," responded Mavrolóngos proudly.

"Then tell your men to begin," the Man Of God ordered. He shouted for Ivor and Dora to come to his side.

The Lieutenant turned and shouted a list of commands to his troops who were standing at attention alongside the military vehicles. Then a flurry of activity began.

Psychopompós turned again to the Academy's Administrator, without acknowledging the presence of the Athlete or Spy. "Once men are through in the Seminar Building, they'll bring the rest of the equipment into Administration Headquarters...telex machines and coded telephones that the IOC have been designated for receiving messages from abroad. That's what Hefferon and Cain will be watching, once they've been installed. A military guard, posted in the Library where we're putting the equipment, will function twenty-four hours a day. As calls come in, a transfer system, to be implemented later this afternoon, manned by Army personnel, will connect this Reception Centre with seven other venues in the region."

"These venues are?" the Administrator asked.

"One, IOC Member Bungalows. Two, Pavilion Tent for IOC Luncheon Saturday, to be erected down there, in the midst of your Running Track. Three, Stadium of course. Four, Temple of Zeus, where the IOC must wait before their entrance into the Stadium. Five, Kiosk Gate to the ruins. Six, Old Museum, where the IOC Session will occur. Seven, Hotel Xénia, where the IOC Banquet will take place to-morrow evening."

"What about incoming calls for National Olympic Committees and heads of International Sporting Federations?" asked Dora.

"What about them?" responded the Priest. "They're *not* important. They'll get and receive their *own* messages—by staff at their *own* hotel. We've installed office facilities in the Xénia for their use, should such services be required."

"The Athenian chefs...when are *they* coming for my kitchens?" wondered the Administrator.

"This evening."

"Well I certainly hope that *their* quarters, as well as tents for the multilingual secretaries, will be in order, since the troops seem to have their hands full."

"Soldiers are in control, Mavrolóngos. Don't be *nervous*! They will have ample time to attend to everything. Even converting part of your Cafeteria into a dormitory for a dozen chefs is *not* beyond their means."

"When's the Pavilion Tent going to be put up?" Mavrolóngos wanted to know.

"Before sunset," the Priest replied, getting annoyed with all these questions. "Everything's scheduled—to be in place by sunset! The village will be shut off—from the world—at six o'clock this evening."

"Well what about *power*?" the Administrator insisted, just to be irksome, as he could see that he was *getting* to the Orthodox Pastor.

"What *about* power?" the Priest flared. "*I* control it—*you* receive it!"

"Not *that* kind of power—*electrical* power!" answered Pános, who could give as good as he could receive.

"Oh—that—well—yes—haven't you been informed?"

"No I have not! This operation has been cloaked in secrecy—for weeks. I hope you realise that this tiny village hasn't the means to *sustain* such electrical voltage."

The Orthodox Priest frowned, in a particularly un-Christian demeanour, looking downright vituperative. "Listen, Mavrolóngos. Nobody's said that your position here is indispensable. Just because you secured this post *without* my father's backing does *not* mean you cannot be *removed*."

"Just answer my question about *power!*"

"Power...is fully under *our* control...what else do you *think*? We shall be installing transportable electrical generators here...and at every other Olympic venue. Yours will go *right* beside your Seminar Building. It's awaiting deployment, at this very moment, inside the last vehicle, at the end of this convoy. Is that clear?"

"Thank you so much for volunteering to share information with me," Mavrolóngos said and smiled.

The Priest was looking furiously cross, but only said: "I must return now to the Ancient Stadium." He turned on his heels and strode towards his black Peugeot. His chauffeur drove him off.

Until half past one, the Administrator took the Deputy Chief of Protocol, and his newly appointed Executive Secretary, on a walking tour of the International Olympic Academy. They viewed the accommo-

412

dations provided for Members of the IOC, as well as progress of installations in the Seminar Building.

"When one stops to consider the amount of activity just within this valley," Ivor remarked, as the three were returning to the umbrella-covered table, "then one can begin to comprehend the extraordinary amount of planning it takes to organize an Olympic Games."

"This, compared to that, is like a snowflake in a blizzard," Mavrolóngos replied. "And you, who survived Lake Placid, ought to know all *about* blizzards!" He chuckled as he held the chair for Dora Cain. Table had already been set. Instantly, three workers seen earlier were bringing a delicious makarónia served with sautéed veal, a rarity in Greece. Aubergine spread was presented for freshly baked bread. A great carafe of local retsina appeared.

"*Bon appétit,*" Pános stated. He poured the wine. Ivor had already been told by him, inside the Seminar Building, whilst Dora was speaking with the Lieutenant, that Ivor was to drink lightly and that Mavrolóngos would proceed to get the American woman drunk. He had no time to explain more. Hefferon, therefore, had been tipped off that the Academy's Administrator might be on his side.

"Is this the largest type of event that the Academy has had to date?" asked the Athlete.

"By all means," responded the host. "This whole *thing* is complicated—by anybody's standards. The Protocol alone must be a nightmare."

"Tricky mess!" Ivor agreed. "The Greek Government are giving a Deed, not directly to the IOC, but to an Olympic Organizing Committee recognised by the IOC. Final Deed of Transfer, for the Olympic Nation on Olympos, won't be given by the MOON-OC to the IOC until all construction's complete. General Ouranós is presently trying to negotiate with the IOC in Lausanne about eventual transfer of the IOC to Olympos, once the Olympic Nation's built."

"When do MOON Execs foresee *that* occurring?" Pános inquired.

"Not for at least six years."

"Then—the next set of Games will be located abroad, as has been customary, but those afterwards may take place within the walls of the Olympic Nation?"

"Yes—if construction goes as planned."

"Well, it will certainly save on costs—having the Games come to rest in one final spot," Dora said at last. She had been silent until now. Her remark reminded Hefferon of the first discussion that they had had. He wondered if Pános had been brought up to date about her.

The Administrator turned his attention to the spy. "Dora...*Cain* is it?"

"That's right."

"Dora is a Greek name. You have *Greek* blood in you?"

The Athlete almost laughed. Boy—did she *ever* have Greek blood in her! With conniving *Thýella* for a mother, Dora's blood simultaneously couldn't have been *Greeker* or more Evil!

"Not that I know of," Dora lied. "Why?"

"Because—if you had—you wouldn't have to undergo this initiation rite."

"What initiation rite?" she asked, wide-eyed.

"Oh," the Administrator said dramatically, "*all* foreign girls who come to Olympia have to test their strength. It's an ancient ritual—from days of the first Games."

"How do you mean?"

"You know of the Goddess Hera?"

"Of course she does—she's an Archaeologist—with the American School in Athens," Ivor admitted.

The Administrator reacted most surprised: "Well then you'll appreciate this all the more. It's just for women. All visiting women to the shrine of Hera, in the ruins not far from here, were obliged to be tested by the Great Goddess, before any woman might be granted a single divine favour."

"*How* were they tested?"

"By this same local wine...which we still drink to-day."

"A cinch! I can drink *buckets* of this kid's stuff!" she bragged and guzzled down a big swallow. "Ain't I from Texas, Ivor?"

"That she is," the Athlete complied.

"Women were *not* allowed to cut their wine with water, as the men were," Pános continued and poured iced water into his and Hefferon's glasses.

"Big deal! I don't like mine doctored, anyhow! That's for *sissies*. How much's the limit?"

"The limit wasn't the problem. Women had to drink their wine *neat*, at midday, in sunshine. Four glasses were usually the limit."

"They didn't *have* glasses! I'm an Archaeologist, remember. They had *bowls*." So, rising to the occasion, Dora moved her chair into the full heat of day. "Sunshine never bothers me. I spend hours at a clip...bent over...pawing in the dirt beneath it. Plus—I'll do *five* glasses. We Texans can out-drink *any*body...*any*time! I'll show you sons of bitches who's tough and who ain't!"

So, throughout the delicious luncheon, Dora Cain drank herself senseless. By two o'clock, she was pissed as a newt, and violently arguing with anybody who so much as looked at her sideways. She was not a "happy drunk", convinced she was sober and too willing to prove it.

Pános Mavrolóngos ignored her and said to the Athlete: "So many things are better left to the IOC."

"Screw them!" the girl muttered, sloshed as a parson.

"Look at this beautiful countryside. It's still virgin land," the

414

Administrator continued and swept a hand in a demonstrative gesture towards all the region's lush vegetation.

"*I'm* still a...virgin, too," Dora boasted, teetering on total incapacity. But she managed, as well, to flail both of her arms in a mimicking gesture, as if shooing away all *men* in sight. She then yawned.

Pános shook his head. "No," he said sadly, "if the much-discussed Olympic Nation were built in *this* ancient valley—God forbid—it would ruin this gorgeous site irreparably. The Games are just too big now—even for the *three* proposed sites on the Mediterranean seacoast nearby."

"Screw *them*, too!" Dora spat and waved her hands like a monkey. "Bomb 'em—to smithereens!"

"What sites are they?" Ivor asked, barely able to keep a straight face.

"Peloponnesian sites, favoured by many in the IOC and in the Government of Greece, are at Kylíni, Katákolo, and Kaïphá...but, in my opinion, *none* of the Three-Ks is appropriate, as *none* of the three could cope with the building or the change."

"Fuck 'em...fuck 'em all!" Dora cursed then promptly put her throbbing head in her hands upon the table.

The Administrator nudged the Deputy then asked: "Ms. Cain, are you all right?"

No response.

"You've passed the test in flying colours, Ms. Cain. Now we have to fulfil the Goddess's wish, and allow you sleep. Hera will come to you in a beautiful dream, when she will give you your just desserts."

Dora revived, partially, and said: "Tell Hera to go suck! Screw her *yicky* desserts, too!"

"Come," Pános said, "we'll take you to a cabin so you can sleep."

Hefferon and Mavrolóngos hoisted the besotted woman by the armpits and carried her down the wide run of stairs. The number of steps seemed endless, even to Ivor, who was feeling tipsy himself for the little amount of this god-awful strong retsina he'd imbibed. There must have been over three dozen steps.

They turned a sharp right and entered the door of the first bungalow. Two beds were along two of the walls. The room was comfy, cool, and spotlessly clean. They placed the woman on a bed and the Administrator said: "Dream sweet dreams...of the Great Goddess."

"Tell 'er...to drop dead..." Dora muttered, then passed out in an alcoholic stupour.

The two men retraced their steps upslope, then entered the left-most building. Pános and Ivor passed through the blue-grey lobby, with murals of Herakles, Pindar, and Zeus on the walls. Seeing Pindar, Ivor couldn't help chuckling to himself and thinking about Lucille, wondering what pranks she was up to now. The last she'd told him, in a phone call to Athens, she was off to Bangkok, with some new escort she'd found. The two men entered the Library and the Administrator locked the door.

"I'm a confidant of Aristídis Rembetikós," the man admitted hastily. He kept looking about for eavesdroppers. Nobody was in sight. "He was my Professor, years ago, and due to him I secured this job. I'm utterly opposed to what the MOON-OC are doing, and am at your service..." The Administrator then gave the Deputy the secret telephone number used by Rembetikós, and produced a letter from his wallet in a trouser pocket. "He knew we'd be meeting here, and didn't want to pre-occupy you with any worries other than those absolutely necessary."

"I'm used to his sneaky tactics by now. I rather *like* them."

"He's in total control of this whole epic," Pános said assuredly. "He, and the IOC, have staged this whole thing as conscientiously as if they were Olympian Deities, but in this war, Zeus, who's the General, is *not* going to win after all. Ouranós thinks he's got it all in his grip, and to visible considerations he's right. But, come Saturday, the tide will turn against him. Just watch."

"Such drama's not unknown to the Greeks," Ivor responded.

"Drama is *the* guiding force of our lives," Pános agreed. "We Greeks invented it!"

"And Saturday...your *kátharsis* must come," the Athlete answered.

"I have no doubts."

The two men looked at each other, with a bond of collusion.

"It's now half past two," Mavrolóngos observed. "All five thousand tickets for the locals were distributed thirty minutes ago. The people should enjoy this Ceremony. By the way, your bodyguard Míkis is a *plant*, for Major Movóros."

"I presumed as much from the start."

"He's not a Tourist Police Officer at all."

"No?"

"He's a Captain of Movóros's Evzónes."

"How nice."

"He's the Major's favourite. They're lovers."

"Fancy that."

"Has Míkis tried to *screw* you yet?"

"No."

"Keep your arse to the wall. He might. He raped a local boy."

"Charming."

"As for Museum Director Selináki, she's on our side, too."

"You're joking. She seemed like *ice* to me yesterday."

"Evanthía's a courageous woman. Besides being the top lady Archaeologist of Greece, she's also a superlative actress. She was famous in her university days, for her stage rôles. Greeks are born actors, but Evi's *paramount* at knowing how to wear a mask, at dealing

416

with government incompetency every day. She's also got the sexiest voice this side of Cypriot Aphrodite."

"*That* I've already enjoyed. In fact, when Míkis and I called on her, he actually *came*, right in his goddamned underwear, a big bold cum-stain showing right through his cop-uniform, just from listening to that woman talk. I almost shit my pants!"

"Yeah—that Míkis is one helluva weirdo, as the Americans would say! I've heard, besides drilling boys and women, he also likes fucking horses! He's from near Sparta, and it shows! He's a Thoroughbred Throwback! Evanthía, on the other hand, she's a Pure Soul. One of the few left. She said she fell in love with you. Of course, we briefed her on your arrival, at Rembetikós's orders."

"Has she studied under him as well?"

"Of course. *All* intellectual Greece has! Rembetikós is one of the country's top scholars. Evanthía's been trying to avoid Míkis since the Major sent him here on reconnaissance, about a month ago. He's been mooning about her farm house, the old one in that big field where the troops are based, on the way to the New Museum. To be perfectly honest, I really think she wants to have sex with him, just to get it out of his and her systems. She knows, once she lets him have her, he'll go back to fucking boys, then won't be bothering her anymore. So don't think her vitriol was aimed at *you*—it was aimed at *him*! She was pleased, in fact, that you wished to run in the Ancient Stadium, an Athlete of Olympic calibre."

"Thank you."

"Now—lastly we've got to deal with Dora."

"You seem to have dealt with her already."

"We Greeks are very convincing in our cunning. We've never forgotten the Trojan War. Thýella's daughter, meanwhile, is to be given a taste of her *own* medicine."

"How do you mean?"

"Dora's a classic nymphomaniac...right?"

"The Professor told you *that*, too?"

"Of course—it's her dominant personality trait. And...the way Greek men deal with nymphomaniacs...is to *fuck* them till they're dead. That way...the women stay happy...and the men are never frustrated. So...it's my recommendation that you take your siesta in her bungalow down there. I'll take mine here. Remove your clothes and lie facing her, naked. Whenever she comes out of her torpid state, there you'll be. As long as she's having it *off*, the longer she's staying *out* of harm's way."

"What about Movorós?"

"God—he's happy just to be in Míkis's big arms to-day. They can't suck enough of each other. So the Major won't mind if another man gets a piece of his female action. He's a man. He's a *Greek* man. He understands that *any* normal man is going to pump that bitch as soon as look at her. As long as the Major's getting *his* dick in her too, every

417

now and then, when he tires of Míkis and all the *other* Evzónes he's manhandling, then he doesn't mind *what* that hot little Tex-Mex Spy does on *her* side."

"That's what I thought. Did you just say...Tex-Mex?"

"Dora's father, Clinton, is the bastard son of some Chihuahua cleaning lady, so the Professor says. *Ask* him about it sometime. Anyways—the Major already knows all about you and his mistress. If you don't knock her off a couple times, for *auld lang syne*, he'll suspect something's up."

"You Greeks are amazing!"

"Yeah—we're a real work of Art, aren't we!"

Both men laughed.

"Well—I better get to it," Hefferon said with a leer.

"Such hard labour," Pános retorted, "emphasis on *hard!*"

26th April – Wednesday – 8.30 AM

There were no more trees in sight. There were no more scrub pines, either. What plants there were looked tawdry, indeed. Raggedy bushes, at most a single foot high, crept along the nasty soil and held on for dear life. Some of them would have made marvellous bonsais. If one were tiny, say, a gnome, one could easily hide in their scraggly branches, and peek out at the bundled passerby.

There was no fog up ahead. There was just the winding path, that zig-zagged along this part of the mountainslope. In fact, I didn't even feel that we were climbing a mountain at all. The land wasn't flat, but the slope was interminably angled at the gentlest degree.

We were only on a hike, it seemed. I was getting annoyed, at everything. I had already gone through the emotions of Wonder, Fear, and Sadness, and now was stuck in the gutter of Anger. The old Swiss up ahead were just crawling. I felt that we should all be waffling on about something indecent. Didn't these people know any dirty jokes?

Noise of walking sticks going tick-tick tick-tick on the gravelly path was *irksome*. No cicalas, no birds, no traffic, no babbling brooks, no giggling girls, no radios...no *thing* to listen to but the horrid little tick-tick tick-tick on crumbling rock.

Where in Hell were we going?

Tick-tick.

"Guess it's tundra up ahead," I said, simply to be able to hear something said.

"Isn't tundra a word for the Arctic?" Frau Hartmund responded.

A voice!

"Think it can be used for *any* alpine elevation, between timber line and barren waste," Herr Hartmund turned and stated. He was so good at definitive responses. One never doubted the big man's word.

I still felt angry, so took it out on something. "I can't *bear* this

418

goddamned path!" I swore just for the melodramatic effect. Nobody noticed—or, if one did, one said nothing. So I persisted: "This crumbling rock's driving me completely *batty!*"

"'Tis no fun," Frau Hartmund agreed.

Good. She was miserable, too.

"Hope it's worth it—once we get higher," I shouted to the man at the lead. I took a swing at a nasty bush on the pathside, just for fun, tearing it up by the roots.

"I think Leftéris told me once...mules made this path," Herr Hartmund recollected.

"They did a *horrid* job," I remarked. "*I* could've done better ...with a seeing-eye dog!" I had to laugh with myself for that one.

"Animals know how to climb mountains...naturally," Frau Hartmund observed.

"Why?" I wondered.

"Haven't you ever watched *goats?*" the lady asked.

"Only in porn-films," I replied, for the shock-value. "How long *does* one have to watch them?"

"Hours," Herr Hartmund inserted and laughed.

No one laughed with him.

"Animals zig-zag naturally," the woman persisted. "First they go left, then they go right, then they go left again...it keeps their muscles from getting tired."

Was this old woman putting me on?

"By so doing, the body shifts its bulk naturally," the Medical Doctor explained. "If one goes *upslope*, directly forwards, all strain is on the balls of the feet. If one goes laterally, like the animals, but only towards the right, then all weight is on the *downslope* part of *both* feet. But if one *zig-zags*, then the weight keeps shifting, because downslope, when one is angling left, the same part of the foot doesn't take the pressure as when the foot's angling right."

"Bravo, Otto," Frau Hartmund said, perhaps sarcastically. "Bravo."

All snow up here was gone. Occasionally, we would stop to look at a flower. To date I had not seen a single *edelweiss*, much to my continued annoyance. I became *obsessed* with the thought of edelweiss. Never in my life had I given the plant more than passing notice. In fact, I *hated* that goddamned song...named after the albino thing. But... wouldn't you guess it—of course—the bleeding little ditty now was stuck inside my brain, slowly working to drive me completely insane. Hearing it, over and over, in this egregious want of oxygen, and not knowing a single word of its lyrics other than *"edelweiss...edelweiss"*...I had to do something to exorcise it!

"Do you people have *edelweiss* in Switzerland?" I asked, knowing how idiotic I was sounding. I couldn't imagine how bright I *soon* would sound, on *top* of the damned mountain!

419

"Of course," Frau Hartmund said, "Swiss pick it."

"Does it bring good luck? I heard it does."

"When?" Herr Hartmund demanded to know. He halted himself completely.

God! What *nerve* had I just touched?

"Isn't it for...lucky charms?" I heard myself saying. Where *were* these wet-in-the-head words *coming* from?

"Maybe in Hannibal's day," he retorted and turned his back.

Caww...getting grumpy, aren't we?

"*I* like to think of edelweiss...as an endangered species..." his wife interjected. "*I* wouldn't pick it...if I were *paid*. I think it's sacrilegious!"

"Oh stop lying!" her husband retorted. "You pick the damned stuff all the time at home!"

Instead of unjustly invoking further wrath and indignation, I just shut up, whilst the ghastly melody kept pestering me. I concentrated on the landscape, or lack of it, and tried to "forget" the music away.

"Tundra!" I heard the old man up ahead muttering aloud. "Tundra!"

23ʳᵈ March – Thursday – 5.00 PM

Dora Cain was waking up. "Oh..." she groaned and gripped her head like a vise. "Oh..." She hadn't yet opened her bloodshot eyes. The Athlete was naked, lying on his side. His eager plonker was ready for action.

"Oh...do I need an Excedrin!" she moaned and suddenly her eyes opened wide. "Oh gimme a break—get your mitts off your Purple Passion, Buster, and hand me my purse." She pointed somewhere on the floor.

"Have sweet dreams?" Ivor said, not moving an inch.

"You got wax in your ears? I *said*—my *pocketbook*! Oh my head's *killing* me!"

"Did the Great Goddess come...visit you?"

"Yeah—Shitface—she's on your bed! And Honey—does she have hairy legs!" She propt herself up on one elbow and whined: "*Please* find my bag!"

The fellow stopt playing with himself and walked towards her bed. He had placed her purse beneath it. Of bright blue patent leather, the ugly thing did not match her tasteless lavender outfit.

"Gimme that!"

He sat on her bed, then she shoved him and barked for some water. The little green bottle was already opened and she had three tablets in her hand.

"Water! There's *gotta* be water in this clip-joint. Oh my head..."

Hefferon stood and went into the bathroom and drew cold water from the tap. When he returned with it she remarked: "Your prick's going limp."

"Not for long!" the man replied, and lay down beside her.

"What makes you think my head can take *that*?" and she grabbed his manhood. "Hell's Bells—if Excedrin didn't exist—I'd have to invent it. It's the *only* thing on the market that ever works for me! I *never* go anywhere without it. Someday—I'm gonna do the most *convincing* commercial for them in the whole world!"

"Like this?" Ivor asked.

She still had ahold of his dork. It was getting hard again.

"Come on, Baby. You know it's the best cure on Earth for what ails you!" The fellow grabbed her head and shoved it down towards his crotch. She began licking his bollocks. "That's it, Luv. That's the way to do it. That's it, Luv."

"Oh Ivor," she moaned. "I missed your cock so much!"

"I know. You *know* how to make it feel good. That's it, Luv."

"I'm sorry they *made* me do it, Ivor! I really *am* sorry!"

"Do what? You're doing beautifully. Don't stop. That's it—suck it—suck it!"

She took the shaft in her hand and massaged it with spit. "They *forced* me, Ivor, to take those dirty pictures. I know you and that guy aren't *queer*! Movóros put a gun to my head. A real *gun*—Ivor—a *real* one! They tied me to his bed—when Thýella was there. It was awful. It was a dinner party. Some dinner! It was *me* they served to eat! The General and Thýella and Sultana and Movóros—the *four* of them—*forced* me to go to Theatrínos's house. They *pistol*-whipt me, Ivor, don't you *believe* me? You *do* believe me, *don't* you?"

"Just suck me. Don't stop."

"I'll *prove* it to you, damn it! They *beat* me—don't you *hear* what I'm saying? It all started because I'm *cock*-crazy! Okay—I admit it—I *am*. I am! But I *wasn't* trying to get involved in all this—I honestly wasn't. I really do crave being left alone by them—to continue my *studies*—to pursue my *career*—as an Archaeologist! That's the *real* me! It's just that my *whole* life, right from earliest childhood, way back in Galveston, has been a constant case of *abuse*—*sexual* abuse—so I just don't *know* left from right from centre anymore! All I *did* know—was that it was *Evil*—the General and his wife—the *pair* of them—they're in league with *The Devil*—Ivor, with *Satan Himself*—do you *hear* me?"

"Yes—I hear you—keep stroking—*more*—come on, Luv, suck it some *more*!"

She did, then she began unbuttoning her tacky outfit. She wasn't wearing any knickers anyhow, and just had to remove a brassière. "Now—do you *believe* me? Now—can you *see* it—with your own two eyes!"

"Good God! You're *covered* by bruises!"

421

"Fuck them! Fuck them *all*, Ivor! I'm now Webster's *definition* of black-and-blue!"

The man clutched her and turned her over on her back, and began to suck on her tits. "Just relax, Dora, just relax."

"Oh Ivor—I *love* you! Take me *with* you! Get me *out* of this Living Hell! *Please!* Help me! I *beg* of you!"

The Athlete let her say anything that she wished. He felt truly sorry for her but, nevertheless, she simply could *not* be trusted. She was in another world, the devious-pathetic woman. She was so far gone, beyond the other side of goodness, that she might have even believed her own lies.

"*You're* the man I want now, Ivor. Oh—that feels so great! Don't stop! Oh you *Beast*—ram it *up* me! Ram it! Don't stop! Ivor! Go at it! Go for it! Go for *Gold!*"

She passed out into animal moaning and had more orgasms than any stud ever could count.

They were standing atop the great flight of steps, before the Olympic Academy's Cafeteria. It now was six o'clock. If Dora's head had been aching at five, she appeared calm and collected now, after six whole Excedrin, and at least six comings. Pános must have been right. Greek men certainly do know how to control their women.

After they had had sex, again Dora apologised for the blackmail. Even though Ivor did not believe a single word, he nodded and accepted every one of her rotten falsehoods. What else did he have to lose? Truth would out in two days' time.

Her pleading with him, in fact, was one of her best scenes to date. It even outdid her battle with the dancing bear. She had begun to cry. She had said that, when she met Movóros, she had been picked up by the Major one afternoon in the Café Ellenikón, in Kolonáki Square. He had taken her to a deserted road atop Mount Imitós, overlooking the whole of Athens, then had repeatedly raped her in the open air. He had *forced* her into sodomy, which she said she loathed. He had *forced* her to become his lover.

"Why did you *stay* his mistress, then?" Ivor had asked, wondering what excuse *this* would engender.

"He threatened to have me deported—after my career as an Archaeologist would have been smeared. Then—he paid me off. I have a vault filled with Lalaoúnis jewels he's bought me," she had admitted. Whether or not there was a grain of truth to it, Ivor could not know. He just had smiled and had said: "You're lucky he hasn't done worse."

"Ivor—you've *got* to help met You've *got* to get me out of this *nightmare!*" she had begged.

"I can only do what I'm instructed to do," he said softly.

"They're all *envious* of you—you know that?"

"Why?" he had asked.

"Your damned Olympic *Ideal*! I *told* you—right from the very beginning—that they were up to no good. I was trying to *warn* you. This so-called *Ideal* of yours—it's like some crappy *inkblot* on their dirty record. That's why they're now using *you*—just like they're using *me!*"

Perhaps...there was some semblance of veracity to her alibi. Perhaps...Dora Cain, as Thýella's daughter, had never wanted to be so closely allied with the woman who wished to conquer all of Greece. Perhaps...Dora Cain, for all of her complicity, *was* being used against her will... but had become so brainwashed, by the omnipresence of Evil in the Ouranós clan, that she had succumbed, awhile back, to its malicious sting. Perhaps...

The Athlete had held this woman, whatever she was, and had whispered in her ear that they had duties above. So they had ceased their discussion, if that's what it could be called. She had halted the delivery of somebody else's lines, and he had halted his *own* hypocrisy. They had mounted those three dozen steps together, side by side.

With Pános Mavrolóngos in the middle, they were standing atop the steps and watching the so-called view. It was as if they were witnessing an invasion. One thousand soldiers were marching in file, up the main road, being drilled by a deep-voiced Sergeant. The men were answering back, with the beat of their steps, with boots stomping the packed macadam. The whole thing was macabre. The soldiers now began singing. What in God's Name had happened to *Sport*?

At the head of the troops was a slowly moving Jeep, proceeding past the clacking palm fronds, at the same velocity as the marching feet.

"What's this—the 1936 Hitler Olympics?" Pános remarked to himself, with tears in his eyes. "Where's Leni Riefenstahl now?"

"It's necessary," Dora inserted, "to prevent another Munich."

"But the Athletes aren't even *staying* here! There *aren't* even any Athletes in the damned Ceremony—except for Ivor!" Mavrolóngos retorted. "This Academy was *built* for Olympic Athletes—*not* for the IOC!"

"*Somebody* has to protect the IOC!" she answered. "They have Heads of State."

"That's their biggest problem," Pános responded. He shook his head. "It's six o'clock. The whole Olympia region's now a military camp. No one who's not wanted may now enter. No one—without an urgent legitimate excuse—is even allowed to *leave*! What is this—*democracy?*"

"It's all for the good of Sport," Dora answered.

"And they *dare* say there's no politics in the Olympics!" Pános stated and spat. "If *this's* how they're running this *first* Ceremony for this new Olympic Nation—God forbid how they'll be running the Nation itself. All the Athletes will be *goosestepping* into the arena—shouting 'Sieg Heil—Sieg Heil—Sieg Heil!'"

Ivor felt that anything he'd say—if his true feeling of revulsion would come out now—would negate all the work done so far. So he said

423

nothing—let the two of them go at it for awhile—and just thought ahead to Saturday.

"Come," Pános ordered and turned away from the advancing male voices.

"No—wait," Dora said and grabbed the Administrator's arm. "It's the Major. He'll probably want to speak with us."

The Jeep went into high-gear and hastened to the base of the steps. The Major ran his middle finger down the length of his facial scar and then looked up to the three at the top.

"Begin to man the IOC Reception Centre in the Library," Movóros shouted. "Soldiers who'll handle calls will be with you promptly. If any telexes arrive, set them in the IOC pigeon-holes. The receptionists will be instructed to take all messages and say that the IOC are arriving to-morrow morning."

The Administrator shouted: "The chefs are in the kitchens. When are the multilingual secretaries arriving?"

"At 2000 hours," the Major replied.

"Their tents are up."

"I told you so. I see the Pavilion's erected in the Racing Track."

"It went up at four o'clock."

"Then all's well."

"It seems that way," Pános responded.

"I'll now oversee positioning of the troops about the Academy perimeter. I'll be checking back when the secretaries arrive."

The Jeep pulled away slowly, once again at the head of the phalanx of soldiers proceeding up the access drive, who continued marching rightward round the Seminar Building and the electrical generator provided by the Greek Army's Corps of Engineers. They headed further upslope into the hill, then split ranks, five hundred going left, five hundred going right.

The last of the column broke from the mass. Two dozen men marched to the top of the flight of stairs, and presented themselves at attention to Mavrolóngos. A young recruit began speaking: "Sir—twelve of us will be posted outside your three Administration Buildings. Four by each structure. One at each corner. Twelve of us will be posted inside your three edifices. Four per building. The four in the Administrative Library will man all incoming communications—Sir."

"Then do your duty," requested the Administrator.

The recruit shouted orders. Men took their positions. Four soldiers followed the three into the Library. Equipment was switched on and everyone sat back to relax. The four soldiers each went to the bookshelves and found themselves something to read. They had been instructed not to tamper with the Executive Secretary. Dora Cain was in her element, obviously, having four good-looking boys to gawk at. And did she gawk.

Soon enough, within minutes, the first telex arrived, an urgent message for the Senior Member of the International Olympic Committee in the United States of America. The receptionist handed the note to Miss Cain, who handed it to the Deputy. He read it—it made not one iota of sense—and put it in its proper pigeon-hole.

Then—telephones started ringing. Olympic Events were starting to roll, of their own athletic momentum. Nobody now could stop them, even if one controlled all the Gold Medals issued since 1896.

26ᵗʰ April – Wednesday – 9.00 AM

"Edelweiss" at last had gone away. Thank God! With it went all signs of Life, too. Nothing now was growing, save microscopic zoospore and lichens. It certainly was unfit real estate.

Weather was getting balmy. We now had our heads from our hoods. That made for a more cogent sense of reality. I think that being able to *hear*, wind on rocks and not thoughts on the rocks of my head, was preferable.

Silence had gript us again. That was allowed. In fact, I was quietly chuckling to myself, over everything, bringing up the rear of the queue. It was High Comedy...as in *serious elevation*. Here we were, three weirdos, walking where human beings feared to tread, lost in thoughts, giddy for lack of oxygen. One long stretch was up ahead.

I began to doubt the existence of Mount Olympos. That one made me laugh aloud. My legs were aching, but that was humorous, too. They were tingling. Every step felt funny. Who said the flaming *Gods* kept house up here? Where *were* their flipping Temples in the sky? Show me ruins of Palaces crafted from gold! Point out foundations of cut cyclopean stone! Where *was*...The Past? Hiding? Vanished! Where *was*... one Myth? Rotted! Where *was*...all that glory once glimpsed by great Homer? Where *was*...the Blind Bard now...looking down from On High? Where *was*...one bit of meaning...at all...to three mortal specks...on the great mountainside?

One single snowball...shoved by Zeus...could bury us...at any time. I shook inside. My spinal cord jerked. Who *did* that? Who set the nerves a-twitching? Who made *nerves*...in the first place?

Time passed so slowly here. Nothing to look at...but stones...and more stones. They weren't even *nice* ones to peer at. Boring old waste, really. Looked like it'd been slaked for lime. Dregs. Just dregs.

So the mountain was limestone, they say. One colossal hunk of rock. Think how big the poor *clam* was...that had to be squashed...to form *this*?

I remember, as a boy, hunting for fossils. Out in the West Country...with my mate Alexander. How we'd hold up the finds...how we'd wonder about all the Time it took to make one clam turn to rock...

If felt myself reverting back to childhood. You know...how boys just spend hours and hours wandering everywhere...noses to the ground...looking and looking and looking for something that only *they* can find? So now—I too let my gaze drop down, and began to get the purest puerile pleasure out of examining every square inch of path, looking for something, looking for something, looking for what? Certainly not...Life...

23ʳᵈ March – Thursday – 8.00 PM

The Administrator of the International Olympic Academy was telephoned in the Library at quarter to eight, by soldiers on the eastern road, to warn him that the limousines were arriving. Soldiers were left to man Reception, whilst Mavrolóngos, Hefferon, and Cain stept outside to wait for the arrival. Guards were still at parade-rest on corners of the three Administration Buildings.

After a fifteen minute wait (exactly on time) the people atop the cement stairs heard the roaring of motorycles of the Police escort, then saw the palm trees illuminated by diamond-bright lights. As the procession commenced to swing by the fronts of bungalows, Ivor counted two motorcycles at the head, a Police patrol-car, then eight black automobiles behind. The first three cars were flanked by motorcycles as well. At the tail followed another patrol-car, then two more motorcycles.

No one said a word as the limousines passed by the base of the steps and then swerved upwards to where the three were standing. In the first patrol car was Míkis, still in his uniform of Tourist Police Officer. He pulled his vehicle to the kerb before Administration Headquarters and got out. Next, in a black Mercedes-Benz came Major Movóros, in full parade uniform this time. Behind, in the black Peugeot was his half-brother, the Orthodox Priest. Behind him was a black Fiat, from which a big bear of a black-suited man, whom Ivor had never seen, was stepping. From the five black Chevrolet sedans then exited five gorgeous girls apiece. Each dressed alike. Behind followed an Army transport vehicle laden with two pieces of identical luggage per girl.

"Multilingual secretaries," Pános explained. He was now wearing a dark suit.

Mikis, Movóros, Psychopompós, and the unknown man were advancing towards the three.

"I believe everybody knows everybody?" the Administrator said.

"*We* haven't been introduced," boomed the biggest of the men, who pointed at the Athlete. "I'm Sitherás!"

"Director of Construction for the Organizing Committee. This's Ivor Hefferon."

"At last we meet!" the brother bellowed and gript the Runner's hand. He was maybe just an inch shy of Movóros's height, but easily twice his weight. The bulk was solid muscle. He was bearded, and brown-haired. He had a cleft chin and dimpled cheeks.

"Sitherás's our *nickname* for him," Psychopompós explained.

"Means Iron Man," the Major said and laughed.

"Ma's been telling me about you," Sitherás grinned. He was ruggedly handsome, like a miner.

Movóros and Psychopompós smirked at each other. The Priest said: "He's been on Olympos...taking soundings of the Games Site."

"It's going to be one Hell of a difficult engineering job. Especially spanning that goddamned gorge with that plexiglass pedestrian tube. Nothing like it's ever been attempted outside the United States. I'm going to be off to America soon, to consult with the best American engineers, including meeting with the Chief of the Army Corps of Engineers at The Pentagon." The brawny chap winked at Dora Cain, then pinched her.

"First things first," interrupted the Priest. "We have twenty-five talented girls ready to be shown things. We might as well attend to *them.*"

"Yeah, *I'll* tend to them," Sitherás joked. "All twenty-five. All at once!*"

Hefferon could tell that this chunky bruiser was certainly cut from the same randy piece of cloth as his horny brothers! The party moved towards the Seminar Building. The dark blue designer-suited ladies were looking as eager as flight stewardesses.

"Aren't they lovely?" the Major asked Hefferon.

"When do we divide them up?" he responded. The loose Ouranós way of sexuality was rubbing off on the Briton.

"You men will do *nothing* of the kind," the Man Of God upbraided, then turned his attention on the girls. "Good evening. My— how charming you all look. May I introduce the Administrator of the Academy, Pános Mavrolóngos. And these are my brothers, the Major being Director of Sports for the MOON-OC, and the civilian of the family being Director of Construction. And this's the Deputy Chief of Protocol and his Executive Secretary."

The girls all looked properly impressed. "Let's now go where you'll be working," he announced as everybody followed. Once inside the Seminar Building he said that they could leave their luggage and coats in the corner, then everybody was served the evening meal, prepared by the newly arrived chefs, a simple repast of coldcuts of beef, tomato and cucumber salad, chipped potatoes, wine, feta cheese, and fruit. The Priest picked at his food like a bird, after having blest the meal. Midway through it he rose and banged on his plate with his knife. The din ceased abruptly.

"Now—let me officially welcome your participation in this prestige event for our country. I wish to thank the Government in Athens for allowing you to be with us for these few days. As you know, your duties here will principally be those of multilingual secretaries. Officially, you are to be addressed as Olympic Hostesses. To-night is your night to get to know the facilities of this Academy, and the Administrator will be taking you on a tour as soon as we're through with the meal. But I should say now that your foremost obligation is to keep the International Olympic Committee satisfied. By that, I mean that the IOC, who are arriving to-morrow morning, are Members of the most élite club in the world, and they are used to privilege. Things *happen* for them. Do you understand?"

Twenty-five gorgeous girls replied: "Yes, Father!"

"You have been studying your Hostess Handbook?" Satisfied with their answer, the Priest continued: "To-night, before bed, study it one more time. One never knows what the IOC might want done. Some of you may be posted to-morrow evening in the Hotel Xénia during the VIP Banquet. One Member of the IOC might lose his contact lenses and need new ones instantly. You girls are the ones to whom they'll turn. Girls all over the world have served the IOC for many years. It is a very great honour. You will meet some of the most interesting people on the face of this Earth. Do not, I repeat, do *not* bother them. By no means are you to ask the IOC questions! They wish to remain undisturbed. If you are told something, in confidence, *keep* it that way. Is that clear? Remember—you've all signed declarations of perpetual secrecy!"

"Yes, Father," they all responded again.

"We are content you'll be as courteous as possible. Remember— it is *you* with whom the IOC will be speaking. You are Greece's Ambassadresses, from to-night until the end of Saturday. Enjoy yourselves. To-morrow, the Chief of Protocol is to arrive. You will be directly responsible to Madame Ouranoú. She will meet you here at eight o'clock. Thank you." The Priest sat.

The meal concluded and Mavrolóngos took the Hostesses on a tour of the Academy, as the rest of the party returned to the Library.

"I want to run a test of equipment. Have there been any telexes?" Psychopompós inquired of one of the soldiers.

"Yes, quite a few."

"Hostesses know, Ivor, they're to check with you, about pigeon-holing messages. Girls will be working in shifts."

"Run a test of the transfer equipment," ordered Movóros.

"Aye aye, Sir," said a recruit who placed on headphones. He switched on a video screen, and asked: "Which IOC Member?"

"Oh—try India," Sitherás suggested, causing Ivor to think of his friend Alexander, en route there.

"Room Twenty-Nine," said the recruit who pushed System-1, then extension 29. The screen stayed blank. "Now—should the Member be there—or anybody else answer—the person would be seen on the screen when he responds."

"Okay," muttered the Priest. "Try the Pavilion."

System-2 was pushed and a recruit came onscreen. "Pavilion. I read you," answered the boy.

"Just testing," replied Reception.

All five other venues answered as well.

"Marvellous," said Sitherás.

"It's new Bell equipment from America," bragged the Orthodox Priest.

"Shut it off—I have an important thing to say," the Major ordered.

Just then the telephone rang. "It's Madame Ouranoú, from Athens," the recruit announced.

"I'll take it," Movóros stated and grabbed the receiver. "Yes, Mother, we're all here. Everything's fine. Don't worry. Yes—I was just going to tell them. Of course it's serious. Who's *running* this military operation—you or me? All right! Look—if the little henna-haired whore *dares* charge the light brigade...then we'll toss his pimpled arse into solitary confinement. Yes—he's here. See you and Father to-morrow. Ivor—your boss!"

The telephone was passed to Hefferon. "Yes, Madame. Yes—it's functioning beautifully. Yes—I'm enjoying it immensely. It reminds me of Lake Placid *and* the last Summer Games. What? On *national* news? Yes—I gave a very short interview in the Stadium this morning. You liked it? Great! I knew you wouldn't want me to ruin suspense. Thank you. I'm glad it looked well when broadcast. Where *are* you? At the British Embassy? The Ambassador said it made him proud? Oh good. I'm so glad. I'm proud to be participating. Yes—see you in the morning. Good-bye."

"I take it she saw to-night's national news?" asked Psychopompós. "So did I." He did not look amused.

"I shall try once more to tell you what I was beginning to say before Mother interrupted," cut in Movóros. It was humorous seeing the brothers together, vying for control. The Major then ran his middle finger down the length of his facial scar, and put it to his lips. Dora began to fidget, seeing this.

"Well, hurry up, Mo! We haven't got all night!" roared Sitherás, who slapt him on the back.

One could tell how the Major loathed such treatment, especially before new recruits. He cleared his voice. "I was saying...that the Press are already arriving at the Amalía. They are furious because we're not allowing them access to the village, until after Accreditation. They've already begun complaining bitterly about the fact that we're driving them to the Academy at 1330."

"They are *my* responsibility," snapt the Priest.

"Well then...humour them!" returned his half-brother the Major. "But do it to-night!"

The Orthodox Priest grinned. "Don't worry. I'll have a press conference. I'll bring *Ivor* with me."

429

"Press are the *least* of my worries," Movóros continued. "And ...Ivor stays here!"

"Why?" challenged the Priest.

"Because—I said so. His job's *Protocol*. Protocol's based *here*. You do your *own* work—is that clear?" The Major stared the Priest down, easily. Their sibling rivalry was not very subtle. "Now—I was saying—trouble's brewing. Protest demonstrations are being planned—in all the country's major cities—to send people to Olympia—by the thousands—come Saturday. It's the biggest rebelliousness—by the people of Greece—since the Junta."

That certainly shut everybody up.

"In Pátras, in Kórinthos, in Athens, in Lárissa, in Thessaloníki—*everywhere*—they're sending people to mass outside checkpoints to the village—in order to protest the awarding of the Deed to the MOON-OC."

"Is that *punk* behind this too!" Sitherás blared.

"What do *you* think!" snapt Psychopompós.

"Of course Theatrínos is in on it! But it's grown bigger and bigger all week. All sorts of peaceniks and environmentalists and even sports addicts and sporting celebrities—footballers—our own soccer players—are rebelling! Nobody knows *how* many protesters will show up!"

"Call in more troops!" Sitherás blared.

"Don't you think I think of anything!" the Major returned. "I already cleared it with Father—an hour ago."

"Good!" said Sitherás, satisfied.

"How many?" asked Psychopmpós.

"Fifteen thousand more soldiers," boasted Movóros.

"Fifteen thousand?" responded the whole Library.

"Has Papa lost his head?" Sitherás exploded. "That's cracked! Where in Hell will we *put* them all?"

Hefferon had gone white. Even Dora Cain didn't know what to think.

"Oh you *Pussies!*" growled the Major. "Spread in a ring—round this whole Olympic Region—from here through fields and over hills and along the River Alphaiós—all the way to the Amalía—it's *easy!* Fifteen thousand will *vanish*—just like that. And who—in The Name Of Satan—will ever *know?*"

Nobody answered.

"That's right—*nobody* in this town will ever guess—because *nobody's* to be told! Do you all *get* this—loud and clear? And you—Psychopompós—do *you* hear that? *Nobody's* to know...a *thing!* You're *looking* at all those—right in this room—who *need* to know!"

"Of course," the Orthodox Priest avowed.

"That's the way it *has* to be!" the Major continued. "This *is* a large-scale *military* operation—being conducted *quietly*. In fact, as I look at my watch, it's now 2200 hours. Most of the troops are already moving into place—stealthily—as we're discussing these very manoeuvres. The soldiers will sleep in pup-tents, pitched along the ring enclosing the Olympic Region. Of course—come to-morrow evening—we shall mass fair amounts at the Amalía and at the entrance to this Academy—the two gateways to this area. When demonstrators show up—certain soldiers will be visible. Most will not. Those visible to the public will be those most adept at crowd control—but they won't exercise force unless provoked. We are hoping for peaceful demonstrations. Soldiers are being instructed *not* to open fire...that is, not unless they're fired *upon*."

26th April – Wednesday – 10.00 AM

The long stretch was an incessant sequence of splinters of rock. Suddenly—a red piece caught my eye. Why I bent and picked it up, I'll never know. It wasn't ruby red. It wasn't garnet red. It wasn't even rust red. It was a duller red than all three. Nevertheless, its hue was different enough, against the blanket of grey, to warrant inspection. The two Swiss carried on.

I picked up the fragment. It was as wide as the palm of my hand. It was not terracotta. It was not made by man. It was natural. In thickness the chunk was three-quarters of an inch at most.

Frau Hartmund turned round, thirty foot ahead. I held up the piece, then brought my arm down. She kept on going. I flipped the oval-shaped disk, and gasped aloud. "Good God—it's petrified coral!"

The lady and gentleman both stopt. They looked backwards.

"What did you just say?" the man asked.

"Look—it's coral! It really is!" I ran with my find and showed them, feeling exhilarated as a schoolboy finding treasure on an outing when all the other boys find naught. "See!"

The rock was displayed, but I held onto it. I didn't even want to part with it, for a second.

"My Lord—you're right," agreed Herr Hartmund, as if he were relieved to have anything to talk about.

We were all quite tired. For the past thirty minutes I had been convinced that the old couple were completely lost. They hadn't a clue, I was sure, where we were heading.

"Isn't it lovely?" asked the man's wife.

I decided to release the object and let the woman examine it first. Of course, her husband, like any man, snatched it from her, in order to show off his knowledge. She snatched it right back.

Suddenly—a tiny bit of the enormous mountain—comparable to planet Earth seen against our galaxy—was absorbing our total concentration. We three were hovering over this creation from Nature, as if it held the very key to Nature herself.

In fact, the back of the piece, which had been facing the soil for who knows how long, was more than just a key to some lost secret of the mountain, it was literal proof itself. "Do you *realise* what this means?" I interrogated them both, wide-eyed with awe.

They both shook their heads yes.

"It is proof—living proof—that Mount Olympos once *was* beneath the sea," Herr Hartmund said, reverentially.

"I have never seen such a thing, in all my years, at such an altitude," Frau Hartmund answered.

"Nor have I," agreed her husband. "And I have climbed too many peaks to recount."

I took the petrified coral back. The tiny ossified granules, that once were polyps breathing beneath the infant Aegean Sea, now were white cystals standing out from the field of dull red. In all likelihood, the red had once been sand. I blew on the little white towers and began to uncover how truly beautiful the object could be. Dirt from æons flew off in space, and landed where wind might plant the specks someplace else for æons to come. Tunnels and passage ways, arches and nooks were revealing themselves to the naked eye.

Removing my gloves...human hands for the very first time began to warm the magical stone. We resumed our progress, ever upwards, but now I truly was happy. I had a memorable souvenir of this day, and something no money could purchase. No man nor woman ever could replicate what I was holding. I felt as content as I ever could recall. The feeling was primitive, and pulled my Psyche enormously far backwards in time...

Before refinement of hypocrisies, that we label Civilisation, and before Gods themselves made war and staked claim to these very peaks, and, perhaps before one dinosaur had been born, let alone had died, it defies imagination to envision this Olympos completely covered by some prehistoric ocean. Yet, on these windswept slopes, where nothing now would grow, once swam eel and shark and squid, or maybe even *they* did not yet exist. Maybe such a temporal metamorphosis happened right here...maybe only primal saline life, coral and anenome and worm, squirmed slowly cross *this* vast face where snow now freely flurried.

The topsy-turvy evolution of this megalithic mound made cogitation intense at the very least. But now, my imagination (provoked sense-wise by the coral's message radiating right through my fingertips and into my hæmoglobic circulation, hence upwards to my brain) could see ghosts of trilobytes, infrared tracings of starfish, and flashing phosphorescent fish that always were blind, always were grovelling in briny seafloor slime, always hunting plankton to eat. This barren clime, so devoid of all signs of life, now began to pulsate before my very eyes, wonderfully, as the creative vigour of biology breathed animation into every shard of limestone within sight.

24th March – Friday – 8.00 AM

Thýella arrived. Winds of adversity instantly gusted with flame. Nobody at Olympia ever remembered such a hot morning. By eight, the heat was as stifling as noontime in the month of August. The white helicopter of the MOON-OC was lifting away. Dust was spreading like plague in all directions. The Chief of Protocol of the Organizing Committee, on the arm of her uniformed husband, was standing coolly impervious to the drama that her appearance was causing, as if she were a mediæval queen on the arm of the court's biggest jester. The General might have the manpower, but the General's wife had his manhood by the balls.

The official receiving line for the nasty woman was at the far end of the Running Track of the International Olympia Academy. Twenty-five Olympic Hostesses were in a queue, like silly cheerleaders for some horrid ball game. All were coughing from the grotty dirt. Some were rubbing their eyes. One girl proceeded to faint. None of the others dared touch her.

"It's hot," General Ouranós said to his wife.

"So are *we*—big deal! We've too much to worry about trifles like *weather*! Honestly!" Thýella was dressed in a bright green print dress made of Chinese silk. It was long-sleeved, but flared enough about the arms to permit a flow of air. The soft material was gathered at the neck, in a loose long-tailed bow. A sparkling emerald set in silver could be seen reflecting verdant light every time she turned. She had matching accessories of forest-green Florentine leather. She was not wearing gloves, but carrying them. She looked mean enough to slap the first face that glanced crossways. She was wearing a wide-brimmed milk-green hat. She seemed to think that everybody should drop to their knees.

A small military band struck up a bellicose tune. The woman was not amused. All soldiers on either side of the band, and all Officers commanding manoeuvres at Olympia, who were ordered to attend, were at attention. Both the General and his wife surveyed the troops, passing them like Heads of State, then stopt at the end of the phalanx.

There were Local Dignitaries, from the village, and there were the Academy's Administrator and his wife, rarely seen anywhere outside the house, and there were Thýella's family. She nodded to Major Movóros, Sitherás, and Psychopompós, all at once, then said: "Let's get inside. This heat could stoke the fires of Hades."

"I'm sorry, Madame, but the Hostesses..." interrupted Mavrolóngos.

"What about them? They see us...we see them. We shall address them up above."

"I think you'll have to walk," sighed the General, who was glancing beyond the Pavilion Tent to the line of bungalows and tall flight of steps.

433

The Chief of Protocol frowned at Greece's Junior Member of the IOC, and released his arm. The band continued playing martial airs, as Thýella shouted: "Ivor—take our arm."

Her Deputy stept forward to escort her.

"Now Dear," she said to the General, "you brief your Officers with Movóros, while we attend to little things, like Accreditation. Oh how we're dreading that, Ivor—you're going to have to relieve us most of the day."

The Major stept forward and shouted an order that could have been heard in Athens, Georgia, let alone in Athens, Greece. All the Officers began marching towards the Pavilion Tent. The Chief of Protocol and her Deputy led the way beyond the Tent, towards the terribly tall flight of steps. Sitherás and Psychopompós proceeded to their own limousines and departed for the Stadium. Pános Mavrolóngos commanded the Hostesses to bring up the rear. Two of them had at last picked up the girl who collapsed.

The climb up the stairs was a nightmare. Everybody was sweating like a brood-sow. The whole length of the way, Madame Ouranoú diverted herself by asking the Olympic Athlete all sorts of questions. He answered them to the best of his ability. They passed a black Rolls-Royce, to be used for Madame's service, then they strutted straight into the first building ahead.

"This damned Cafeteria *better* be air-conditioned," she griped and aimed straight for the lady's lavatory. The thirty soldiers assigned to Accreditation jumped to attention along a wall.

Whilst she freshened herself, all who had been following filed inside. The Hostesses stood at attention with the soldiers, awaiting her appearance. She took her royal time. Finally, ten minutes later, she made her grand entrance. She looked more pleasant, but her disposition had not changed.

"We're behind schedule!" she barked. She then stomped to the Hostesses and scrutinised every single girl. Some she accused of sluttishness. She didn't like others' make-up. Some she told to press their suits. To others she said: "Wash your hair!" The girls looked traumatised. "Never mind," Thýella said at last, "you'll *have* to do." The soldiers were choking back laughter. She obviously preferred men. She looked at the girls once more, then ordered: "Man your battle stations; The IOC are arriving at any time." She laughed at the off-colour joke, as twenty-five antagonised young Greek females scattered. "Get us a pitcher of iced water," she then commanded the Administrator. Soldiers then went across the room to the Protocol Centre, where they would be working. Thýella strode through the Cafeteria to a dining table, as far away as possible, and sat in a chair. "Hefferon," she shouted, "sit here. Now—your job is to oversee Accreditation. Make sure everyone on our Master List is sent through. Any left out, please make note. All VIPs, of course, are to be dealt with discreetly. Make sure the soldiers are considerate. These recruits look like bumpkins, so we'll have to *groom* these boys. While we're off looking at the venues to-day, it's *your* duty to stay here...and *groom*." She then shouted to the doorway: "Dora!"

The young American left the Administrator and walked the distance to the head table. "Cain—your job's to man Reception—in the Library. Log in all incoming telexes and telephone calls. Photostat all telexes and file them. Make sure the Hostesses report to you hourly to deliver messages to Members of the IOC. Keep in half-hourly touch with Protocol, to see what IOC Members have arrived, and who's gone through Accreditation. The IOC are remaining here at the Academy, where they're safe from the Press, until seven this evening, whence they're being chauffeured to the Xénia for the Banquet. They'll be meeting with each other here, in private, all day long. Is that clear?"

"Absolutely."

"Now go."

Dora went. She left the cafeteria and proceeded next door to Administration Headquarters.

"Ivor—now before we forget—you as our Deputy are responsible for greeting the IOC as they arrive at this building. Do this most conscientiously, at the door, with Mavrolóngos. To-night, at the Xénia, Local Dignitaries will be able to meet the IOC, with select Officers of our Army who'll be present besides. It should prove very grand."

"I'm looking forward to it, indeed."

"Simultaneously arriving this morning, don't forget, are all the Presidents and Secretary Generals, and their Guests, of the National Olympic Committees, along with same for the Sporting Federations. Both groups are instructed to proceed here, first, get accredited and refreshed, then their limousines are to take them to the Xénia, where they're staying. Be just as courteous to the NOCs and IFs as we know you'll be to the IOC. Of course, we shall be making short appearances, back here, throughout the day, as will the General, to be sure. We do hope that everyone arrives as scheduled. Sir Cecil said, last night, that every single limousine in Athens has been reserved for weeks. Each VIP was sent the proper window badge so that security can clear them easily at checkpoints. The Devil only knows if there's not going to be a huge traffic jam, but Movóros's plans for that have been precise."

"He seems most capable of large-scale operations," Ivor remarked.

"We're glad you appreciate his genius," his mother replied. "By the way, how do you like our emerald?" She held up the gigantic gemstone pinned beneath her chin upon the bow.

"It's stunning. Is that Herakles with the club?"

"Of course. He began the Games, you know."

"Rumour has it."

On that note, the Chief and Deputy then stood and walked to the Administrator by the door.

"Any sign of VIPs?" Thýella asked.

"Not yet."

"Good. Hefferon—stay with Mavrolóngos—while we attend to scrutinising these new recruits. On their break, we'll have them all go shave!" She went and said just that, and more. They were made to understand that authority flowed from above, from their General, to her, to her Deputy, in that order. They were to take orders from Mister Hefferon in her absence. Like the Hostesses, the soldiers hoped Thýella Ouranoú would be frequently absent.

"Madame!" Pános Mavrolóngos suddenly shouted. "I think the first limousine's arriving!" In his hand he had a telephone, especially installed for the purpose of being notified of arrivals on the compound. It was connected to the Academy checkpoint along the motorway. "It's the IOC Member of Canada."

"Which one?" she retorted. "Where's your list? Many countries have *two*—or hasn't anybody informed you? If a country's had an Olympics, then it may have *two* Members maximum. We have two Members, here in Greece, because we *invented* the Olympics. By the way, now that we're talking IOC Protocol, one must *never* say that IOC Members are Members *of* their countries, because that's absolutely *not* the case. The IOC are extraterritorial, meaning that the IOC exist as a club wherewith they have Members *in* various countries, but never *of* various countries. So—it's not the IOC member *of* Canada, but the IOC member *in* Canada. Don't you *dare* let us hear that you're messing up the prepositions ever again!"

God—hearing the nasty bitch go on about the IOC prepositions reminded Ivor, unpleasantly, of all the many harangues he had to suffer through in Lake Placid, with the cantankerous Barleys, whom God had spared him to think about for days. His spine shook with involuntary nerves, just recollecting Heidi and Butch.

On that note of warning from the MOON's Chief of Protocol, the first arrival did appear in a few minutes' time. Thýella, relishing her boss-rôle, met the Junior Member of the IOC in Canada, and watched as the black Cadillac's chauffeur took his bags to his bungalow. The man was accompanied by his very elegant wife. Madame Ouranoú greeted them, showed them to the Protocol Centre, then excused herself by saying: "What a frightfully busy morning this is! We're late for an appointment already—in the Old Museum with its Director—to see to arrangements for to-night's Opening of the IOC. Then we have to rush to the New Museum to inspect the Pediments of Zeus Gallery being converted for overnight use by our country's Head of State. Oh—it's going to give us a *migraine* before noon!" She shook the IOC Member's hand one more time, then hastily departed the Academy in her Rolls.

Thus it started, and continued throughout the day. Food and refreshing drinks were on hand in the Cafeteria Building continually, whilst the

VIPs kept arriving. From nine o'clock onwards, there was a non-stop flow of stately automobiles, of Princes and Princesses, of Generals and their wives, of Dukes, of Counts, of great Olympic Athletes of former days, of Professors, of the Wealthy and the Aristocratic from the four corners of this world.

Their faces were likely some of the most distinguished miens that one could ever see. Their bearing and carriage were indicative of decades of *noblesse oblige*. These were the Stellar Beings who *owned* the Olympic Games. These were the Sacrosanct Few, who had inestimable power in their hands and who could say: "All right, Los Angeles, *you* have the Games." These were the people to whom the Organizing Committees of any Olympics turned over the keys, once the Twelve Labours were done, once all Organizing was complete, once the Cauldron was lit by the Sacred Flame.

As the Olympic Gold Medallist stood greeting them and as he was being presented to their illustrious Guests, he couldn't help but be strengthened by his belief that, in twenty-four hours' time, he would be doing them all one of the biggest favours that they likely would ever receive. He was doubly strengthened when Professor Rembetikós finally appeared. By then, there was quite a party atmosphere in the edifice, as Members, who had not seen each other for months, were exchanging *bons mots* and even more rarified gossip, the very gossip that made nations rise and fall.

Rembetikós arrived before any other Member of the IOC's Sub-Committee which had been established to investigate the possibility that Greece be returned the Games. He quickly brought Mavrolóngos and Hefferon together and said: "All in our Sub-Committee stand unanimously behind you, as does the President of the IOC. Just act as your conscience directs you, Ivor. Not even the Greek Army will dare intervene. With almost every Ambassador from the capital arriving tomorrow, and with the support of the Head of State of Greece, with whom I dined last night, in fact, after he had received General Ouranós in private audience, the Evil Few cannot but be entrapped. The jaws of steel are gaping wide. The culprits are marching towards their very own doom, as if Wagner's *Götterdämmerung* were premiering in the next few hours."

"You know, then, that the General ordered deployment of fifteen thousand more troops?" Ivor asked.

"The Head of State told me last night, that he had allowed this. There is nothing to fear. The majority of Officers posted here are on *our* side. Of course, the troops themselves are ignorant of the war being waged between the forces of Good and Evil. They, though, have the President of Greece's explicit orders *not* to fire unless grievously provoked. All of this will end peacefully, I assure you. Now, I must not linger here, as many eyes are watching."

"By the way—you came without a Guest?" the Administrator asked, intrigued. "Your sister usually accompanies you. Is she not well?"

"The Head of State told Anna to prepare for transfer to New York, to be Greece's new Ambassador to the United Nations. She's home with a pile of briefing papers a mile high," he said then took his leave.

Shortly thereafter, the Senior Member of the International Olympic Committee in Great Britain arrived, in a sparkling night-blue Bentley. Lord Dalbeattie, a tall nobleman with a handsome head of white hair parted on the side, threw back his famously wide shoulders. He beamed and watched the absolute joy on Ivor's face as his young protégé recognised that His Lordship's Guest was none other than Alexander's grandmother, the Dowager Duchess of Brendon. She looked as majestic as ever, a true English Duchess if ever there was one. Her still-blonde hair was crimped in the 1930s-style and her favourite topaz pendants hung gracefully from her ears. For a hat, due to the hot climate, all she was wearing was a Déco-era creation of two pieces of black fabric over a light metal frame that was somewhat in the shape of a slice of cantaloupe. The cloth was oversewn with bits of jet. A short piece of veil came to her eyebrows as a net. It was very chic, very *rétro*. It was by Coco Chanel, who had personally made it for the Duchess decades ago. To compliment the *cloche*, she was wearing a black serge suit with a lemon chiffon blouse.

In an instant the Athlete was embracing the neck of the lady who had cared for him, just like her son, since he was eight. He then kissed both her cheeks and held her elderly shoulders and said ecstatically: "Your Grace!"

26th April – Wednesday – 10.30 AM

There was a battle brewing between Biology and Physics. Atop Olympos, forces one never feels by the seashore were surging upwards from unknown crevasses, and were creeping like phantoms for some fated prey.

"I feel strange," Frau Hartmund announced to us two.

Her husband looked alarmed, but tried to deflect her mind, because his was head in the very same direction.

"Should we turn back?" I asked.

"No!" blurted Herr Hartmund.

We three stood transfixed on the barren rise, as two squadrons of clouds were approaching. From upslope, straight for us, belligerently advanced a tumbling cavalry-charge of the densest clouds, the hue of ebony wood. There was a mesmeric rumbling within their maw, as if the very rock above us was being devoured and chewed like a cud. This was coming from due west to due east. But due north to due south, across the whole eastern façade of the highest mountain peaks, simultaneously

438

was churning a column of clouds of the purest colour white. And both were aiming straight towards us.

"Oh dear God—help us!" Frau Hartmund began to whine. She started to pray in German.

"It'll pass!" Herr Hartmund said with authority, if not with conviction. "Everybody sit—in a circle together."

The two of them sat. I could not sit—too curious to see these two phenomena with my very own eyes.

"Ivor—sit!" Herr Hartmund bellowed.

"I'm watching."

"Let the boy be!" the woman attacked her husband.

"The white clouds are beating the black ones," I announced.

"We'll see!" the old man retorted.

Just then, a tremendous pull of winds began assaulting us, as the powers at strife reached our location before the clouds themselves. First, we were hit from the north, then we were hit from the west.

"Dearest Lord Jesus—save us!" Frau Hartmund began to cry. Her husband put his big arms about her, rocking her, whispering to her, consoling her.

Then we were engulfed by white fog. So thick was it that I could not even see the old couple.

"Ivor?" Herr Hartmund yelled.

"Don't move, Boy!" his wife shouted. "Where *are* you?"

"Here—right *beside* you. I'm sitting *down*."

"Good," they both answered at once.

"Don't go anywhere!" Frau Hartmund cajoled.

"This will pass, Sieglinde," the old man muttered. "I have climbed too many mountains to count—and I know how queer are their ways. Olympos is no different—just because it's Olympos!"

"Huh—so *you* say!" screeched the wife. "Who're you—Zeus?"

"I say—this will *pass*! The northern clouds are whizzing by us— at this very moment."

"Whizzing *through* us, you mean!" she responded and shivered.

Temperature was dropping by the second. We were putting up our hoods and huddling in foetus position. Our backs were to the north, against the horrid winds. Then, to make matters worse, as we were buffeted every so often on the right side of our faces by wet blasts from the west, the white clouds shrouding us began to belch forth fat flakes of snow.

"Oh Otto, I'm scared."

"Don't be, Sieglinde. Don't be. There's nothing wrong. In Switzerland—a little snowstorm never bothered you."

"But we were just in Crete. We're not as young as we once were."

Just as leagues beneath the ocean the salt currents have their own time-tested routes, even in the grip of tidal waves, so too, on high, currents of æthereal air swim and know whither they are going. So now, at some juncture not far above us, these two colossal streams of wind were linking together, were blending their powers, into one almighty river, flowing free, heading by the potent force of gravity, ever downwards, over the barren wastes of Mount Olympos, over the tundra land, sparse with spiky vegetation, against the passive resistance of the poor bedraggled pines.

"They're mating," the old man smiled and squeezed his agèd wife.

24ᵗʰ March – Friday – 11.00 AM

Thýella was returning from her tour of the venues, and was stepping from her shiny Rolls-Royce. One could say that it was "rush hour", since the access road into the Academy precincts was jammed with limousines, bumper to bumper, slowly making their way past the bungalows. Soldiers were directing traffic, in order to facilitate passage of the IOC, NOCs, and IFs.

"Never before has this Academy coped with such activity," the Administrator remarked to the Deputy Chief of Protocol, just as the Chief of Protocol was approaching. The phrase was certainly double-bladed.

"How *are* we doing?" asked the General's wife. She looked onto Ivor's G-List.

"So far...fifty-eight Members of the IOC have arrived," Hefferon noted.

Mavrolóngos was continually answering the telephone, to hear what VIPs were arriving next.

"And NOCs? The Presidents and Secretary Generals are instructed to arrive together, with their Guests."

"Let's see...yes, in fact...of the one hundred and nine National Olympic Committees sending delegations, already eighty-eight have passed this way."

"IFs?"

"All the Federations have been cleared."

"Splendid, Ivor. Keep up the good work. We shall be making the rounds inside. All the IOC Members have to be made aware that they must be in the Pavilion Tent at one o'clock sharp, for the midday meal. The Press are being ferried into the compound starting at half past one—and of course we want to keep the IOC well out of line of fire. Soldiers won't let the Press down to the Track anyways. Let's see—we need to see how the Protocol Centre's doing and the Hostesses—and if anybody rings us from the Stadium, have a Hostess find us immediately. We'll station a girl here, by your side. We *may* have to rush to the Stadium—as they're beginning the Security Rehearsal in five minutes' time. We do hope those vicious dogs that sniff for bombs know what in

Hell they're doing! Oh—yes—we first must check on the chefs. Carry on!"

Thýella strode into the building and was lost in the sea of elegant people. She was in a state of near hysteria. How anybody could have allowed such a woman, in the first place, to become Chief of Protocol, for the Olympic Nation no less, was beyond most human beings' imaginations. Ivor and Pános simply shook their heads and shuddered, as she disappeared. A blue-suited Hostess was soon standing at their side. She introduced herself as Katína. She was ravishingly beautiful, with huge brown eyes.

"My. This *is* exciting," she admitted to Ivor.

"Yes—it certainly is," the Athlete replied.

"It beats working in an office in Athens," she said. "I'm a Secretary for Parliament."

"Isn't that exciting as well?"

"Some days things get active...when we have visits by Heads of State...but I never get to see dignitaries face to face. These people look so ... rich!"

"They are! Shhh!" Ivor cautioned, as more people were approaching from limousines.

"The Senior IOC Member in Italy," whispered the Administrator.

"Oh—and just look at that gorgeous lady at his side!" cooed Katína, obviously transported into her own Seventh Heaven.

As they were being greeted by the Deputy, Pános's telephone rang. It was the Stadium. "The Chief of Protocol's wanted there *immediately*," the Administrator reported to the Hostess. "Please find her—and tell Madame Ouranoú it's her husband's order!"

Katína vanished. It took her some time to find the General's wife. Whilst she was searching, the Dowager Duchess of Brendon finished a friendly chat with an Oriental Princess whom she knew, and came out of doors to speak with her favourite Athlete.

"Dear dear," Her Grace announced and produced a black lace fan from her purse, "this heat..."

"Are you all right?" Ivor asked, deeply concerned.

"Well Ivor, if I shan't survive this climate, then this retsina will likely polish me off," she laughed.

"I can't tell you how wonderful a surprise it is to see you here!"

"I shouldn't have missed it for the world."

"Alexander didn't breathe a word about your being here."

"My Dear—that peripatetic grandson of mine isn't privy to my *every* movement."

"Let me, please, extend to you now...my most heartfelt sympathy for the recent loss of your son."

"Alexander's uncle was not his usual self...for some time," the Duchess responded. "It hit me very hard, but as you know, from your childhood with us, Egbert was not the most convivial person. He had

441

many enemies, all of his own making. And, as you *well* know, he did not treat *me* with the kindness that *other* blood-relatives have shown me. Months would go by...and he wouldn't even say hello to me...his own mother...and he lived there right on our *own* estate! But then, I'm not telling you anything new. You...*know* the whole family. You...are *part* of the whole family. And, Ivor my Child, *you*...have always treated *me* with *more* loving concern than, sad to say, my own late son. Life with him...indeed was a constant trial...and especially since he refused to live in the big house and took to self-imposed social-exile in that farmer's thatched cottage. A Duke...choosing to live like a hermit! That Brendon bloodline's *peppered* with true eccentrics...almost as many as are in the Cavendish-Bentinck line. Yet, you know that my son's paternal grand-mother *was* a Cavendish-Bentinck of the Dukes of Portland, so that likely explains where my son's stranger traits derived."

"So your sister-in-law, Lady Dalbeattie, wasn't well enough to leave England?"

"Clarice has claimed bad health for years. But she'll outlive us all. She's more Cavendish-Bentinck than the whole lot of them! It takes a silver bullet to polish *them* off! No—she's actually gone to some villa—in Morocco—to dry out her joints, as she puts it. So I've been left to fend for myself these past weeks. Lord Dalbeattie's been my strength, through all this. Only last week, he sat down with both Alexander and me, at Shrove Tor, and told us both that what we need now, more than anything, is *travel*. I scoffed at the suggestion, as I was in mourning. Clarice was smart—she left for Africa right after we buried Egbert. Then Alexander, being a bit more sensible about things of psychology and the like, took her suggestion...and he, too, left me...off for a jaunt to India. We've many friends there, you know. You know how fanatic he is about *ancestors*, well, he's lately become simply *potty* about tracking down the goings-on of that rake of a forefather of his, that Marquis Wellesley, from whom he, and The Queen, descend on that crazy Cavendish-Bentinck side of their clan..."

Ivor answered: "I guess he didn't have a chance to tell you he passed through Athens en route to the Subcontinent? I just saw him briefly...a few hours...it was so painful...but that's when he informed me of Egbert's demise." The Athlete sighed. "So...His Lordship had to twist your arm into coming here?"

"Dalby convinced me to come only the day before yesterday. It's been years since I've been to Greece. This remarkable land holds many a cherished memory for me. It's hard to believe that, in such an historic setting, *any* Evil at all could be on the prowl."

"Good *will* triumph."

"With your involvement, my Dear." The Duchess paused and looked over the landscape. She had tears in her eyes. "The late Duke and I...once visited Olympia."

"I didn't know that."

"Early in the 1950s, shortly after the Greek Civil War. My husband was a Colonel, you know." She thought back in time, then returned to The Present. The Duchess began speaking very softly. "The presence of the military doesn't scare me in the least. A soldier can be as virtuous as the next man. It's just that the enemy are far too frequently mistaken. Honour of intention too often masquerades above crime."

The young Athlete exhaled deeply, then whispered: "Just knowing that you're here, Your Grace, has given me untold resolution. I now know that what I have to do to-morrow I shall perform in complete faith of success."

"God be with you," said the Dowager Duchess, who then placed a kiss upon the man's cheek.

"God be with whom?" suddenly asked a voice behind them. It was Thýella. "And who, may we ask, are you?" She couched her rude phrase in a saccharine tone of voice.

The Duchess was not amused. She looked the woman up and down, then said to the emerald brooch: "*We*...are Katharine Brendon."

"Her Grace, the Dowager Duchess," Ivor explained. "Lord Dalbeattie's Guest."

"We're aware," Thýella responded, suddenly as sweet as *marron glacé*. "What an honour...to make Your Grace's acquaintance."

"Madame Ouranoú, the Chief of Protocol," her Deputy replied.

The Duchess extended an arm. The two ladies touched fingertips, ever so briefly.

"We hope you'll excuse us, please, but General Ouranós just telephoned from the Stadium and requested we get there soon as possible."

The Duchess did not smile nor say farewell. She waited, whilst the lady's Rolls-Royce departed with her. "Scum," was all that Her Grace would deign to utter. Then, she returned to seek her brother-in-law, the Senior Member of the International Olympic Committee in Great Britain.

26th April – Wednesday – 10.50 AM

It snowed for twenty minutes, then the flurries suddenly stopt. Straggler gusts, at the rear of the wind, punctuated the finale of the storm, with a tirade of staccato notes, that stung our faces and chilled our backs, then they, too, dashed down the mountainslope.

We three stood. The old man brushed the snow off his wife, then she knocked if off my back.

"Lucky, aren't we?" I asked.

"I think we'll have no problem with the path," asserted Herr Hartmund.

"What path?" his wife inquired.

443

"Oh don't be a spoil-sport, Sieglinde," huffed Otto, "you can see as well as I that this path is as plain as a trench."

That it was. The thousands of climbers had furrowed a width big enough to drive a car through. Almost.

"There'll be no problem," I agreed.

"So—are you ready?" inquired the fellow, of his wife.

"Yes."

"Are you sure?"

"Yes. And if you don't get moving soon—I'm certainly *going* to freeze."

"Now now," Herr Hartmund consoled. "I promise you it's going to get warmer, soon."

So upwards we trekked. For about five minutes the trail was as before, now a downy white, but with snags of limestone ever more rapidly poking their points through snow.

"I told you so. It's melting," bragged the old man. "Oh look we're almost there."

"Where?" I wondered.

"This is the snow-ridge that rims the last stretch that leading up to Skála peak. You're almost at the height where Leftéris told you to stop."

"Maybe I'll *come* with you," I added, just to be pugilistic.

"No—you *must* climb to Mýtikas later."

We were now on a field of snow. It was all at a cock-eyed angle, falling downhill but drooped on its side, higher on the right than on the left. We were stepping ever closer to the very edge of the mountain.

Suddenly—the old Doctor let out a whoop. "Here—look here!"

"Magnificent," said Frau Hartmund.

The view had taken my breath away. Here, on the top row of the stage-left side of the balcony seats of what Ada had called the Olympian Amphitheatre of Comedy, much as where one says one sits in London "up in the gods" at Covent Garden, we now stood, surveying the whole of the house below.

If an opera were to be set here, try to imagine its complexity, its leitmotifs, its arias, duets, blocking, costumes, acting, technical engineering, drama, power. If this great natural bowl, on the eastern flank of the Olympian summits, was said to be less inspiring than that on the western flank, then some truly *awesome* sight was awaiting.

But we were now on the very edge of the mythical realm of ether, described by Homer and by those great poets of the previous age. Towering high above so many clouds, that clung like cotton puffs to some of the lower seats of the house, as if their padding had sprung loose from frayed material, we ourselves were no longer merely ourselves, but players, now in the celestial Comedy itself.

Nobody was there to direct us.

Nobody was there to prompt.

Nobody was there to understudy.

This was it. The curtain was up. It was do...or die. Thus, we three, like a troupe in humble exile, were beginning to move towards the end of the act. And oh how this was real. One slip now...could be the end...and there certainly would be *no* applause.

Slowly...in the lead, Herr Hartmund began advancing along the edge of the ridge, staying about a yard from the precipice. Slowly...Frau Hartmund used her stick and put her boots in her husband's steps. Slowly...I too did the same.

The fears I felt now were those of peril. This wasn't rope-climbing, to be sure. If this was something that could be done by a woman who was seventy years of age, then it could not rightfully be called perilous. Nevertheless, there *was* great danger involved, call it what you will. For the very first time, I knew that the *hike* had ended...the *mountain-climbing* had commenced.

Strange—heights had never bothered me. I decided, conscious-ly, that they would *not* do so now. Since the decision was conscious, at this elevation of over nine thousand feet, it provoked more and more thought, like that song "Edelweiss" had done. Sometimes, I would look to the view to my right and say—no it's not really there—it's not *that* far down—we're not really *above* the clouds. Sometimes, I would not look at the view at all, but glance to my left and watch as a little swirl of the ever-present breeze would form a miniature tornado of snowflakes, and leap about the snowbank like a prima ballerina. But most of the times, concentration had to be firmly in control, with no furtive glances right or left. One had to deal with the path, keeping on it, moving upwards, and not falling into the snow.

There was an eerie primæval force at work, over the edge of the ridge. It was called Death. It was *always* there now, in all likelihood, *laughing*. Here, on this top row of this Amphitheatre of Comedy, stage-left, Death *must* be laughing. Over *there*, on the top row of the Amphitheatre of Tragedy, who knows...perchance Death was *singing*... as they say your *ancestors* do...when their Ghosts come *calling* for you... to take you away permanently to the Spirit World...*singing* something so seductively surreal as to make the hearer walk right over the edge...in order to try to kiss the illicit harmony?

"We're almost there," Herr Hartmund announced. "Not many metres ahead."

"Thank God," sighed Sieglinde, who was getting very tired.

"This *is* exhausting," I agreed.

"Now you see why—for your very first mountain—*this* far is enough to-day?" the old man queried. "You see—*you* may return to these heights soon—*we*, though, may not."

Did he mean...*ever*...in their lifetimes?

On these summits, all utterances took on added meaning. It took so much energy, and oxygen, to give voice to one single phrase, and wasted brainpower to boot, that no one said more than one had to. We trod onwards, upwards, yet higher, then suddenly the fellow was turning a sharp right. "We're here! We're here! This is Skála!" The old woman let out such a long deep sigh of relief that I feared all her oxygen would be lost forever. She was removing her pack hastily, then sitting. Fog was back again, flimsy clouds like lace, that swished about the rocks, as if spectres from the grave.

"What is this—some sort of plâteau?" I asked as I removed my pack. We had entered something like an enclosure between a double-stoned gate.

"It's flat here—we can rest," Frau Hartmund yawned with a tremendous lessening of suspense. "We *must* eat."

"I'll make tea," her husband offered.

"Tea?" I asked, incredulous. "How?"

"We've little burners—tins of heat," replied the lady, now sitting.

Tea...made my thoughts go flying off in all directions of the compass. My head felt like it had just exploded with carnival fireworks. I had to sit, too. I felt as exhilarated as a puppy at feeding time. "Bloody Hell—*tea*—up here!" I also felt as if I might tumble off the mountain top, in all the excitement, so grabbed ahold of a rock to keep myself anchored. I honestly didn't know *what* to think first.

As tea was brewed, then poured into plastic cups, and as biscuits were passed round, I sat in silence, feeling transported right into *Alice In Wonderland*, but feeling as close to the old couple as I ever had felt with anyone. I knew, now, that they would *always* be a part of me, inside, deep within the heart.

Fog was *not* letting up, just kept hovering about the rocks, like peeping-toms, then occasionally shimmying into sight for a brief little tango, then vanishing round the bend.

My head was beginning to spin, sipping hot brewed tea. "Which way are you facing—I'm confused," I said to Herr Hartmund.

He took out his compass. "I'm facing due south. Sieglinde's facing north-east. You're facing the west."

"Which way will *you two* be going?" I wondered.

"Roughly due north," was the reply. "If you'd like to continue, along the ridge from here, Skála to Skólio Peak, down there," and the man pointed straight ahead of himself, "then you'll be going south."

"But please—don't go far. Stay well off the edge of the cliff, Ivor," Frau Hartmund warned. "It's a solid three thousand foot drop."

"I'm glad it's foggy!" I admitted. "So I don't have to see down."

"Fog will pass." said the old man. "I predict."

But it didn't, after ten more minutes, so the Swiss couple stood anyhow. They put on their packs.

"Now remember, Son," Frau Hartmund reminded, "even if you *do* go to Skólio, go slowly, stay far from the edge, and be *back* here by three o'clock sharp." She looked at me as if I were eight years old, and that's exactly how I felt.

"There's absolutely *no* way you can get lost," Herr Hartmund remarked. "By going south, to Skólio, along the ridge, you're basically staying at this same elevation. It's a gentle plain, that connects these two peaks, unlike *our* route, north to Mýtikas, which is as stickle-backed and as treacherous as a poisonous tropical fish."

"Well—if we're *going* to do it, Otto, *let's* do it," the lady ordered.

"The boss says we've got to move," Herr Hartmund smiled and patted my shoulder. "Take care now—and remember—*be* back here—by three. The descent will be *much* quicker, back to the Hut."

"I'll be here," I promised. "Don't worry about a thing."

"We shan't," Frau Hartmund said.

They moved to the edge of this little plâteau, at the summit of Skála Peak, then they slowly lowered themselves down the face of the rock, cautiously, as if they were going deep-sea diving. Fog was coursing, in ghostly white wisps, upwards from the stalls of the Amphitheatre of Comedy, miles below. The bottom of the great Olympian Vale was nowhere in sight, buried beneath a coverlet of clouds. The old couple kept descending, one step at a time, slowly, slowly, getting further away, getting smaller, getting fuzzier, getting *dissolved* into nothingness by vapours.

24th March – Friday – 1.00 PM

With her typical Gestapo tactics, the Chief of Protocol got on the public address system, that had been installed in the Academy's Library. It reached all the Academy's buildings, as well as inside each bungalow. "Members of the International Olympic Committee and Honoured Guests. This is the Chief of Protocol for the Mount Olympos Olympic Nation Organizing Committee. It is now one o'clock. We're glad to welcome you here, and are pleased that everyone has been accredited exactly on schedule. Would the IOC and Guests immediately proceed to the air-conditioned Pavilion Tent erected within the oval of the Running Track. An informal luncheon will be served promptly. It is imperative that you proceed as quickly as possible. The Press, numbering one thousand, will be arriving here by Army convoy, from the Hotel Amalía, at precisely half past one, for Accreditation. Press have been told that, under no circumstances, will they be allowed to wander from Administrative Buildings of the Academy. They realise that the IOC bungalows, and all other parts of Academy grounds, are off limits. Soldiers will be making sure that *no* Reporters or Photographers get anywhere *near* the Pavilion during the Luncheon. Should IOC and Guests wish to remain in the Pavilion, for private meetings, during the afternoon, staff will be there at your disposal. For those who prefer siesta, it is not far to return to the bungalows. At this time, limousines for Representatives of National Olympic Committees and International Federations are arriving, to transport you to the Hotel Xénia. Luncheon is being prepared there, to begin at half past one. This evening, at seven o'clock, all of us will meet again at the Hotel Xénia, for the VIP Banquet. At nine o'clock, the IOC Session will begin. This afternoon, after your respective luncheons, if anyone would like to attend the MOON-OC Press Conference and Cocktails, in the Ancient Stadium, which is scheduled for six o'clock, please sign up, so that limousine service can be co-ordinated. Thank you very much."

"Well done," Thýella's Deputy lied.

"You know how we *love* telling people where to go," she responded. "Now listen—you and Cain are to sit at *our* table during the Luncheon. Everyone on the MOON-OC staff will be there. None of us are to be available to the Press until six o'clock. Let them chomp at the bit a little while longer. What do *we* care if they get mad as hornets? Anyhow don't bees *die*...once they sting?"

"I'm not a biologist," Hefferon replied.

"Come this way. We've work to do," Thýella ordered and led the two out of the Library, through the frescoed lobby, and into the sunshine. She fanned herself with a hand and shielded her eyes from the glare. She was not getting much shade from her ghastly milk-green hat.

"They're leaving," Dora noticed.

"Of course—*everybody* jumps when we say *leap!*" she snapt. "This heat's enough to make people scurry anyways!"

Limousines in a queue a mile long were backed up to transport VIPs to the Hotel Xénia. "Thanks to the Army," Madame Ouranoú observed, "nothing has yet gone wrong. Imagine organizing all this...with *civilian* volunteers? Spare us!"

The Chief of Protocol strode before the Cafeteria Building. Members of the IOC and Guests were saying farewell to NOC and IF friends, then slowly descending the treacherous steps that led to the Pavilion Tent. Thýella ignored every Distinguished Visitor and halted atop the stairs. "Well—troops are in place. Don't they look lovely?"

"Handsome as The Devil," replied Dora.

Indeed, it was rather impressive seeing the whole road that swang past the bungalows chock-a-block with armed soldiers. No Reporter nor Photographer in his right mind would dare try piercing *these* ranks.

Thýella, trooper that she was, forced Hefferon and Cain to stand atop the steps until the very last limousine drove away, and until the very last Member of the IOC vanished inside the Pavilion Tent. Then, she marched into the Cafeteria Building, right past the Administrator who was looking exhausted, but to whom Ivor winked, and halted before her Protocol crew. "Now listen—this has to be quick. The Army convoy of the Press will be arriving at any moment. Under *no* circumstances are you to answer *any* of their questions. Only answer matters dealing with

Accreditation—their *sole* reason for being on Academy grounds. Is that clear? Whenever a Reporter asks you something, tell him or her politely that the Press Conference is scheduled for six o'clock. Remind them that they are to be in the Ancient Stadium by five fifteen—at the latest—that we'll be conducting the Press Rehearsal for seating then. Is that clear?"

All thirty soldier-assistants responded: "Yes, Madame."

Thýella beamed. "You boys are wonderful. Keep your peckers up." She retraced her steps with Dora and Ivor, outside, to the top of the steps. Again, the Deputy winked at the Administrator as they were passing.

"Ahah," the Chief of Protocol cooed, "look what's arriving. The convoy. It's time we make our move."

Slowly, as the bright lights of the transport lorries bearing the Press were calmly advancing alongside the clacking palm fronds, Thýella Ouranoú, Dora Cain, and Ivor Hefferon were descending the hazardous steps. Just as they were reaching the bottom, the first of the vehicles was arriving.

"Tell them to stop," ordered the vile woman.

A young Officer directing traffic stept into the road and halted the whole convoy. Thýella, pretending she were Sheba or somebody truly grand, pushed back her shoulders, puffed out her emerald-studded chest, and advanced across the lane without as much as deigning to look at the long queue of vehicles she was impeding.

Of course, she and her two sidekicks had not got to the Pavilion Tent before the vehicles began to move, so plenty of Photographers got zoom-shots of their backs. In fact, the Press weren't missing a trick. They were obliged, for the time being, to play by *her* rules, but nobody in his right mind would have dreamt that rules would be so rigidly defined, not to mention so obviously militaristic. Just the photographs being taken of the things that the Press *could* see were enough, in their own right, to give the audience back home more than just an idea about what was going on behind the scenes. And pictures *do* tell a thousand words.

What fools the conspirators had been, to have imagined that they ever could have got away with all of this. But some of the grandest capers in all of history have been pulled off by the world's biggest idiots. It takes total commitment to one's own insanity to transcend all decency with disregard. There are so many monsters, a-walk on this globe, who pose as humankind. They are possessed by satanic dreams, that to them are absolute bliss, but, to the Earth, are nothing but night-mares...gone amiss...

Truth will out. It has been said before, and must be said again. Thank God for Investigative Journalists, Nosy Photographers, and Embarrassing Questions. And to-day, air was rife with all three. Things *were* being stirred up, of which the MOON-OC were totally unaware. Reporters had already been finding out little bits, here and there, at the

Hotel Amalía. Staff of the hotel were composed of many local people totally opposed to the Government's granting of the Deed to the MOON-OC. Everybody in town, from shopkeeper to hotel manager, had been aware that Míkis was no Tourist Police Officer, but an Evzone. The local Tourist Policemen themselves resented his intrusion into their domain. They had discussed it amongst themselves, and with Local Dignitaries secretly against the Organizing Committee, namely with Evanthía Selináki and with Pános Mavrolóngos. And Professor Rembetikós had met with the local resistance two weeks ago, inside the New Museum. Everyone had been counselled to exercise *silent* restraint. Everyone was made to realise that the IOC would be seen to be going along with the MOON-OC arrangements for the Deed Ceremony, but come Saturday, Olympia would be in for a big surprise.

Of none of this the Press were knowledgeable. They only could sense that some great Greek drama was in dress rehearsal. It was apparent on everybody's face. The air was as tense as it was hot and dry.

What registered most, as the Press continued to be accredited all afternoon, was *Suspicion...* that kept radiating from the soldiers everywhere. From the back of a lorry, every so often, a famous Reporter from one of the world's great newspapers, magazines, or television networks would recognise one of the Members of the IOC, as the Member would be leaving the Pavilion Tent and strolling towards the avenue of palms. Everyone *was* in costume, indeed, and soon enough the grand-drape would be elevating, and the audience, at last, would be able to witness scenes taking place on the stage.

26ᵗʰ April – Wednesday – 11.40 AM

As if some mechanical wizard were hovering in the sky, afloat atop some lonesome aerial cloud, someone seemed to be pulling some celestial string, and causing fog on the Peak of Skála to rise. All of the vapours simply began to elevate, from stones whereabout their gossamer arms did cling, as if they were leaping outwards, bound for Infinity.

Warm breezes from the south were then hastening the filaments away, and they were twisting and meshing in a cord that kept revolving and curving northwards in the sky, like some wan and ichor-filled umbilical chord on the look-out for some unborn Deity.

I rose from my seat, some grey stone, and went to the ledge where I had last seen my two Swiss friends. But they were gone, perhaps round the bend. I began to sweat, nervous for them both, but equally warming because of the wind.

Leftéris had said that it had been one of the hottest springs on the Mystic Mountain that he had ever seen. If that were true, this tepid blowing was the first *I'd* experienced of this so-called gracious weather. My watch said it was quarter to noon. Just three hours to kill. What could I *do* in the meantime? Then...I noticed it...off to the left. I could not believe my eyes!

Feeling something akin to panic...my knees all but gave out from under me. There, off the edge, just a few yards away, to the left, was the Amphitheatre of Tragedy...in all its gory glory! I felt as if I might faint, but inched closer to its edge. The awesome sight was pulling me, as if down into its gaping yap. I had *never* been so scared—*truly* terrified—in the whole of my life.

This was no joke! This was...*high!*

I tried looking down.

No—don't do it.

I said: Sit and get *used* to it.

I sat.

I sat and faced the west.

I sat and faced the west as close to the edge as I dared.

There were only two metres between my feet and the edge. A little bit longer than my legs. My legs were shaking, right up on the inside of the thighs, as if they were having separate fits.

Oh—*why* did I ever come here?

What ever propelled me to mountain-climb?

I grabbed my thighs. No—I took off my gloves, then grabbed my thighs again. This was *Fright!*

It was no fun.

It was something *physical*...I just had to get used to?

Why'd they leave me *alone* here?

Stuck way up on some pinnacle...impaled?

Ada—I thought of Ada! Why in Hell couldn't *she* have been here?

The funeral—I know—she had family obligations—to ministrate unto Death.

Death.

Here...it resided.

This...was Death's Home...if anywhere...

Death lived!

Death lived, right here, on the fine line, on the utmost seat, of the very last row, the same seat, the same row, that was the sole link between Comedy and Tragedy. *Here* Death sat, ready to step, left or step right, ready to go down, down or go up, ready to head east, east or head west. *Ready*...for anything...at all...

Well—if Death could sit, so could I.

I wasn't about to be budged!

Uh uh.

Not me.

No.

My thighs still were shaking.

Not so much?

Oh no?

Calming down—what?

Why?

The feeling was sensational!

It was going away?

Should I chase it?

I might on all fours!

That's it. Crawl. Crawl.

Towards the edge...I crawled.

Curiosity...had catnipt me.

Isn't that just like a *man*?

Couldn't resist a sneak peek.

What *was* over the edge?

Couldn't be all that bad.

Little bit of a drop-off?

Just a mile or so.

Straight down?

I was *not* prepared to look.

Would *you* be?

I was not willing to stick out my neck.

How many *would* be?

I *was* sticking my fool neck out.

What could the *matter* be?

I was pulling my bloody neck back *in*.

Even turtles have phobias?

Ah stick the bleeder out *one* more time.

Just for good measure?

Go on—stick it out—be a man.

Stick it?

I stuck it—and held it out there.

Fascination was alive, like pus. Here was nothing I had ever seen before. Here was a whole world—devoid of Life. Here was a whole canyon—without one single tree. Here was The Abyss...and it was coloured *grey*.

It scared the *shit* out of me!

Head back in safety—my mind was reeling—trying to forget what it had just seen. The arc of the bowl, that faced due west, was the largest geologic creation I had ever imagined existed. The drop, over the edge, was about a mile in depth, and went straight down, to an inevitable crash upon a bank of stones and boulders, that had been dropping off the edge for too many millenia to count. And the bowl was converging inwards, as the grandest peaks of Olympos were ringing it, like the cusp of a squeezing semicircle. And all, within the static motion, was *grey*.

My nerves never had been so foolishly skittish. Sunshine suddenly hit my face. I flinched, and my heart started racing.

24ᵗʰ March – Friday – 5.50 PM

Bomb-sniffing Army dogs were growling their way around the scaffolding of grandstands. Twenty dogs were being deployed, just as Press were being allowed their first visit into the ruins of Olympia. Given that so many had been accredited at the Academy within the first hour, and given that so many had been getting angrier and angrier by the minute, because of the overbearing security measures, Major Movóros had agreed, reluctantly, that all Press should have free run of the village of Olympia, until they were required to rehearse their seating arrangements in the Stadium. Venues for the evening, of course, were off-limits, these being the Hotel Xénia, the Old Museum, and the New Museum.

The colourful shops along the high-street had diverted most Reporters and Photographers, as did the vociferous locals, eager for sales, and just as eager for ears into which they could spread their own pent-up gossip. Many of the local people were horrified by the large concentration of troops ringing the area, not to mention by the fact that *they* could not leave their own village. Nor could their friends or relatives come in.

"Just like civil war," screeched the citizens, to anyone who would listen. Reporters were told of the locals' knowledge that *many* more recruits had arrived in the night, just yesterday. Plus, people were afraid of all the Demonstrators, who had been threatening to come, and who, at this very moment, already *were* arriving.

The President of the Republic had allowed that Demonstrators be stopt twenty kilometres away, only until three this afternoon. Since that time, a few thousand, waiting along both eastern and western routes, had been allowed to go only as far as the two checkpoints. There, soldiers from the night before had come out of hiding and now were massing to prevent further trouble. So far, nothing was developing. Demonstrators were leaving their cars, coaches, and vans along sides of the road, and from the air it was beginning to look like a Balkan Woodstock.

Three helicopters now were crisscrossing the region, to assist in crowd control. Everybody's excitement-level was reaching peak-form by three, when Heat began bearing down strongest, when Demonstrators began pressing forwards, when Press began invading the village.

Given that some Demonstrators had begun camping outside the Hotel Amalía checkpoint, many Reporters had stayed there, to cover that story. But the majority had gone back to the village, by Army convoy, and were left to their own means to get to the ruins by five fifteen.

With three hot-spots that afternoon to cover (Demonstrators, Village, Stadium), it was little wonder that everybody was getting tired. Ruins provided shady diversion, and rugged contrast against the latest video equipment, special lighting, and cables running everywhere. It was looking like some giant backlot Hollywood movie-set. Plenty of photographs of the IOC flags lining the Processional Route past the temples and the columns were taken, and plenty more of the soldiers guarding them, too.

Into the Stadium all the thousand bodies of the Press began filing at five o'clock sharp. By quarter past, everything was set. The Master of Ceremonies chosen for the Press Rehearsal for Seating was the same young Army Captain with the patch over his eye. He was standing with the Director of the Olympia Archaeological Site, Evanthía Selináki. She had her eagle-eye on everything. They were both on a flatbed Army lorry, stationed exactly in the centre of the Stadium.

It was a lovely sight, that made many of the Press gasp with delight, as they entered the Arena where the Olympic Games were born, many now seeing the Stadium for the very first time. No matter *what* their politics, or pre-conceived notions, all seemed moved, each in his or her own way, to realise that something *alive* was soon to be happening on this desiccated museum site. Electricity was pulsing in the air.

"Please—please hurry up," the Captain said as calmly as he knew how. A microphone was in his hand.

All of the Press were milling at the starting-block end of the Stadium, the end closest to the ruined temples.

"Please come this way, so we can seat you."

The crowd soon was encircling the two.

"Please pay attention. Press are to be seated in the centre of the *north* flank of the Stadium," and he pointed north. "You'll have direct view, across the Arena, to seats for the IOC. We'll seat you in ten rows of one hundred seats each. In the centre of the first row are your Video Units for hand-held cameras. Of course, most countries from which you've come are receiving this emission via direct-broadcast satellite. Flanking Video Crews, and immediately behind them, are Photographers, then Journalists."

The Captain took a deep breath and glanced at Madame Selináki. She was gazing towards her ruins. The patch-eyed Captain carried on: "Now—will all Video Crews please go to the front row, of the section behind you, marked 10."

Everybody turned and looked.

"The north flank contains six thousand seats, two long sectors, one on top of the other, and each holds three thousand seats. 13, 14, and 15, at the top, seat three thousand Locals. 11, left bottom, is for Locals, one thousand seats. 10, centre bottom, for Press. 12, right bottom, for Locals, again one thousand seats. You in 10 will be protected by soldiers, who will ring your section in the aisles beside and above you."

Thus, Seating progressed. Twenty minutes later all Press had been attended to, and were calmly relaxing on bleachers. They had been

454

mollified by knowledge that they too would be having armed protection, like the VIPs whom they were to be facing.

"As you notice," continued the Captain, "VIP Seating, across the way, is different. Their numbers are smaller. To your far left, in B-1, will be half the National Olympic Committees. To the right, in D, will be Dignitaries of the Government of Greece, who arrive to-morrow morning, not to-night. In the centre, in A, are the IOC. To the right, in E, are the Ambassadors, arriving to-morrow, from Athens. And on the far right, in B-2, are the remaining half of the NOCs. The IFs, in C-1 and C-2, will be above the Government of Greece and the Ambassadors, respectively. Above the IOC, in F, will be the Members of the Greek Olympic Committee, arriving to-morrow as well. Above the GOC will sit the MOON-OC, in the last two rows, in F."

The Captain then handed the microphone to the lady. "Good afternoon. I am Evanthía Selináki, Director of the Olympia Archaeological Museums."

The Press, almost asleep from exhaustion and heat, suddenly perked up like a plant given water. The beauty and sensuality of the woman's double-tiered voice began to caress them, to make them squirm in their seats.

"These ruins, and this whole Sacred Site, are *my* responsibility. *Please* make an extra effort, from this moment until you leave to-morrow, to treat this place as you would *any* religious shrine. This Áltis, as the ancients called it, was a place where our ancestors worshipped their Gods. This was a place that they came to...for prayer." She took a breath, and courage as well. She was shaking, but said her mind anyways. "This...was *never*...a place...for *war*. This...always was an enclave...for Peace."

She now was staring directly at the young Captain, who turned away.

"Olympia...is *more*...than just the birthplace of the Olympic Games. Olympia...is a message...to *all* Mankind. People weren't *allowed* here...carrying weapons. Arms...in fact...were *sacrificed*. Soldiers... when they came here...many travelling great distances...on foot...openly offered up their *best* fighting tools...in order to propitiate...the Gods. And...must I remind you...during that time...every four years...when the Olympiad grandly was fêted...by athletic contests of classic renown and undying fame...that *all* war...in the Greek world...*ceased!*"

Not surprisingly, the whole of the Press Corps suddenly began cheering. Men and the women, whose lives are dedicated to capturing, if only ever so briefly, the Evanescence of Earthly Truth, were rising to their feet, were giving the lady a standing ovation. They were cheering her courage, and they were letting their *own* worries and repressed outrage, at all the overlay of militarism at Olympia, burst unashamedly forth. Evanthía Selináki, who had held all Athens in the palm of her hand, as an Actress in her student days, had never known a rôle as demanding as this, and the lady was totally taken aback by the fervent reaction that her words were engendering. She now had tears in her eyes.

"I...am *no* public-speaker...I gave Oration up when my theatre-days at University came to a close," she stressed and wiped away her tears, "but...I do know what my *heart* feels. I am...a *Greek*! I cannot ever be anything...*but* a Greek! I'm not *used* to keeping my feelings inside me. I *love* what my country has contributed to the world. I am *proud* inside...of what my ancestors have left for me...and for my people...and for this whole troubled planet named Earth. If I...a mere woman...could put into *words*...how I feel right now...standing here before you...on this Mystic Site...with the *Army* everywhere in sight...then I would be somebody...with the command of my language...somebody as great as *Sophokles*. But...I am only...Evanthía Selináki...no more...no less...and I *beg* of you...from *this* moment on...until you *leave* here to-morrow...*honour* this land...and its heritage...with whatever Truth you do possess!"

The Press cheered her wildly.

"Remember...much *Blood*...already has been shed...on this Peninsula...called The Balkans. *Much* Blood...already *has* been shed...so that my country...can call herself a *nation* once again. Let the Fates...on Mount Olympos...pass judgement now...on what is scheduled to transpire here. If there be *Goodness*...bless it. If there be *Evil*...cleanse it...by Fire...of the Sacred Olympic Flame!"

A thousand *bravas* rose towards the sky. Evanthía had commenced the Drama, and had not left one single eye dry. But, she did leave the young Captain, standing alone, as Flashbulbs and Reporters charged her way. She descended the steps from the lorry, then silently stalked across the whole length of the Arena. Even though Reporters galore followed her through the tunnel of the Crypt, then past the ruins of the Temple of Hera, the Director of the Ruins would say not one single word more.

"*Bitch!*" snapt Thýella, in a furious rage. "Conniving *viperess*—we'll get her *fired* for that escapade!" She now was in a day-suit of vermilion weave. Her hat was deckt with plumage. She was wearing "costume jewelry", as she called it, a "cheap" necklace of uncut rose quartz crystals strung between a few golden beads. On the beads were bas-reliefs, of Perseus as an infant, with his mother, Danaë. Both were in a box, and both had been cast to sea, by Danaë's own father, Akrísios, who was prophesied to die by the hand of his grandson.

The Chief of Protocol and her Deputy, accompanied now by Míkis, who was still posing in the uniform of the Tourist Police, had arrived at the ruins just after the Press had taken their seats.

"Please—resume your places again—please!" shouted the Captain. He was looking towards Camera-3, atop the mound by the Crypt where he had met Ivor Hefferon yesterday. He was gesturing to

456

the Chief of Protocol to restore order. "The Press Conference is soon to begin. Afterwards will be the Cocktails."

"*Bitch*—do you *believe* what she just said!" Madame Ouranoú was still ranting, yelling in her Deputy's ear.

"Well it was nothing really *wrong*," the Athlete replied.

"Nothing *wrong*? What? She's just jealous! She wishes *she* could command such muscle over this damned site!"

"I think we'd better get down. The Press Conference should be beginning soon," said Ivor.

"Oh—what *shall* we say to them now?"

"By the way...speaking of *saying* something...when are you going to be giving me my speech for to-morrow?"

"To-night. We forgot it. We did bring it from Athens—but it's in our room at the Academy. Remind us after this Press Conference."

"Mother? Aren't you coming?" shouted someone behind them, from below. It was Major Movóros, with the General, Psychopompós, and Sitherás.

"You've *got* to go through with it," cajoled the Orthodox Priest.

"Of course—what do you think we are—*stupid*?" she retorted and took her Deputy's arm, to descend the makeshift wooden stairs. Míkis remained where he was.

The General shouted upwards to the radio man, to give the young Captain the cue.

"The Organizing Committee are ready," the radio man said into his walkie-talkie.

"The Mount Olympos Olympic Nation Organizing Committee," announced the young Captain from the lorry.

It was now pushing six o'clock. Air was cooling and people were beginning to relish this play. They were enjoying the spectacle, albeit in miniature, of seeing themselves seated in an historic setting, of resting content with the knowledge that they were in for something equally historic. They were enjoying watching the principal players, now crossing the sand, strutting towards a khaki-green Army vehicle. They were enjoying wondering what was going on inside the minds of these six individuals, these five Greeks and this one Briton. They were enjoying wondering what bound them, what passions they contained, what hatreds co-existed within their apparent unity. They were enjoying just looking at the lady at the lead, the blonde woman on the far side of middle age, notorious as a tigress, known all over the world for her wardrobe and her jewels, who was dressed to kill to-day.

In the orange light of the waning Grecian Sun, that superlatively beautiful final hour before dusk, Thýella Ouranoú's vermilion weave was almost the hue of the sunset itself. The long plumes of her hat were fluttering in the dulcet breeze. She was like a full-masted schooner, sailing, sailing, sailing, quietly into port, bearing a hold that harboured a child...with cholera.

457

Behind her was the battleship, her husband. The General was a magnificently handsome man. His beard was as stunning as his physique. He was holding his wide-brimmed cap in his hand, in order to accentuate his manly face. He was wearing every single medal he'd ever won, which was every single medal known in Greece. He tinkled like a Turkish dancer in the Sultan's wanton harem. It was a delicious meal, just watching him sauntering along. He was enjoying the fact that he had deferred to a woman, and that he should have been in the lead.

His six-foot-four-inch son, whom all the girls loved, was as sleek as a military fighter-bomber. You could just about feel his rockets hitting you, fired from his virile mind. He did not so much as *move* along the sand, he *glided*, as if on a jet-propelled air-stream. No sound at all was stirred by *his* feet. He was literally...walking away with the show. Cameras were clicking like crazy. The lady Reporters were fantasising... nothing good about him at all. His body was a pulsing erection.

Next came the Orthodox Priest. He was stirring up dust as he shuffled along. He was so goddamned clumsy that the people at first thought that he had brought his censer, in order to purify the lorry like an altar. He was swinging only one arm, his left one, which added to the smoky confusion. He was deckt out in his finest silken robes, as if he were competing in the Miss Universe Pageant. He walked like a constipated nun. He was clutching with his right hand a massive mediæval cross of gold, with gobby semi-precious shined-but-uncut stones, that looked like American Jelly Beans. His cross was hanging round his neck. His head was covered by a black flat-topped hat, that looked like something Fred Astaire sat upon when he had had to move his bowels.

The brawn-brother was bringing up the family's rear. Sitherás was every inch a gorilla, out of some B-grade Mafia Spoof. The Press adored him. He didn't just walk, he ambled out, onto the floor of the Ancient Stadium, as if he were the Sheriff and everyone else was under arrest. Where did he come from? Everybody wondered. People poked each other and began to giggle. He came from the General and his wife? Probably was *just* what they both deserved, everybody whispered. This man looked as if steroids were invented just for him. Did he pump iron—or was he *hatched* like that—from the egg that beat Godzilla?

Then there was this crazy British Olympic Athlete. How in Hell did *he* fit in? He wasn't *Greek*? He wasn't *Family*? He was *really* in collusion? He'd *finally* sold his Olympic Gold? He was ten times more famous than the other five arseholes ever would be in a billion years. He was a real, honest to goodness, dedicated, proven, *amateur* Athlete, probably the only one left on the whole face of this Earth, whom *the whole wide world* had seen win that much-publicised race at the last Summer Games. Most of the Press, here gathered, knew him by first name alone. Rumours galore, ever since he'd been broadcast all over the planet, in February, when he lit the Sacred Cauldron at Lake Placid, had been running rife about him, and certainly were doing so here in

Olympia, especially in the Hotel Amalía, since the Press began to arrive. Nobody really believed for a moment that Ivor Hefferon himself was part of this screwball cock-a-mamey bunch of bonafide thieves. But there Ivor was now—making *his* grand entrance—*with* them! Everybody almost died.

You know how excited Journalists and Photographers get—when they smell a real honest-to-goodness *scandal* in the breeze. *This* one was too good to be true. Fotogs couldn't *wait* to get back to their chemical baths to develop *these* rolls of film. Headlines would be selling rags like hotcakes to-morrow morning: OLYMPIC GOLD SELLS CHEAP!

Unbeknownst to everyone, a *new* group was watching, too. Quite a sizeable contingent of the IOC and their Guests wouldn't have missed this variety-act for all the world. Curiosity did not even have a single thing to do with it. Their whole international reputation was at stake. One of their *own*...had broken the hallowèd vow. The Olympian Ideal was now up for grabs. And by a Greek!

The IOC were watching now, atop the same ridge, by Camera-3, where Thýella and Ivor just had been. And amongst them were all five Members of the IOC Sub-Committee that had been debating the issue of returning the Games to Greece. There stood Professor Rembetikós and Lord Dalbeattie. There stood the President of the IOC himself. There stood many others, Members and Guests alike. Everybody was watching.

The MOON-OC did not even glance to the ridge to their left. The MOON-OC were too busy getting steeled to defend themselves, as they would momentarily be trying to save their very lives.

Flashbulbs followed the sextet all the way up the makeshift stairs that put the group atop the Army lorry. The young patch-eyed Captain smiled, then said: "It gives me the greatest pleasure...to introduce to you...from my left...the Executive Arm...of the Organizing Committee...of the future home for the Olympic Games."

What *was* this—the *Oscars?*

Reporters were scribbling like mystics in a fit of automatic writing.

"The Chief of Protocol, the President of the MOON-OC, the Director of Sports, the Director of Communications, the Director of Construction, and the Keeper Of The Olympian Ideal."

Ivor felt that he would die for shame.

"The what?" everybody shouted.

"Tell them—Deputy Chief of Protocol," Thýella whispered.

"The Deputy Chief of Protocol," announced the Captain, which was something that the Press could understand. "Now—if you would please ask your questions from the ten microphone stands placed for your disposal in the aisles."

459

FIRST REPORTER

This is for the President. Given that you're Greece's Junior IOC Member, don't you feel that it's presumptuous of you to be heading the new Olympic Nation?

MOON-OC PRESIDENT

Given that the three proposed alternate sites for the Olympic Nation, which are nearby here on the coast, are too isolated from the main population axis of Greece, that is, Athens-Thessaloníki, my proposal, to locate the Nation between these two strategic points, won out. And because my idea was favoured, I was elected President.

SECOND REPORTER

Rumour has it, Mister President, that you seized control by exercising your own political and military contacts in Athens. Is there any truth to these allegations?

MOON-OC PRESIDENT

My election into the IOC occurred before my involvement with the MOON-OC, as everyone is aware. Had the IOC not seen me fit for Olympic involvement, the IOC never would have approved my election into their august Membership.

THIRD REPORTER

For the Chief of Protocol: Intense speculation amongst the world's sporting community has loudly disapproved of the fact that the Chief of Protocol for the MOON-OC is the Junior IOC Member in Greece's *wife*. Do you care to comment?

MOON-OC CHIEF OF PROTOCOL

No. But since you brought it up—we should like to put this issue to rest. Wasn't the Chief of Protocol for the Lake Placid Olympics the wife of the Director of the whole Protocol Division? Nepotism, as it's called, is no new thing. Needless to say, we could cite recent examples of it, for good and for bad, in each of the countries from which you all come. Like anything in life, *families* can be sweet or sour. Ours just happens to be *sweet*. We've been blest by intelligence, diligence, and confidence. As you're probably aware, the Ancient Games, on this very site, were governed by *clans*, whose duties passed down from generation to generation. We have no intention of founding an Olympic *dynasty*, but, we do have the intention of founding the Olympic Nation. In Greece, things are far easier accomplished with the involvement of the whole *family*. Greeks are a *very* jealous people, especially amongst themselves. If one is left *out*, all Hell breaks loose, but if all are *included*, then the totality can create a little Heaven on this Earth. *That*, in sum, has always been *our* noble intent.

FOURTH REPORTER
For the Chief of Protocol: Are these young men your sons?

MOON-OC CHIEF OF PROTOCOL
Everyone but my Deputy.

FIFTH REPORTER
Are they the *General's* sons?

MOON-OC CHIEF OF PROTOCOL
You had better let the General answer that himself.

MOON-OC PRESIDENT
Everyone but Mister Hefferon.

SIXTH REPORTER
Once the Deed has been turned over to the MOON-OC, will you turn it
over to the IOC, after construction is completed?

MOON-OC PRESIDENT
Absolutely. This should be after a period of seven years maximum.

SEVENTH REPORTER
For the Director of Construction: How is construction being *financed?*

MOON-OC DIRECTOR OF CONSTRUCTION
Initial costs are being defrayed by a fund established in co-ordination
with all of the world's National Olympic Committees. Given that there
are roughly one hundred and thirty NOCs, each NOC is contributing
half a million US-Dollars apiece. Multiply that, and you get a fund of
sixty-five million US-Dollars, which is sufficient for construction to
begin.

EIGHTH REPORTER
And consecutive funding? How will that be managed?

MOON-OC DIRECTOR OF CONSTRUCTION
Simultaneously—we're asking for half a million US-Dollars apiece from
the world's International Sporting Federations, who are accredited as
being Olympic. Secondly, the United Nations is to provide a substantial
grant. A not-for-profit Foundation also is being established, based in
New York, for private contributions to be made. American corporations,
in particular, are looking forward to this as a worthy tax deduction.
Similar arrangements, where feasible, and where legal, will be
implemented in other countries.

NINTH REPORTER
Management costs—how will these be borne?

MOON-OC DIRECTOR OF CONSTRUCTION
Once the Deed is turned over to the IOC—this question will be *their* responsibility. On our side, we shall be attempting the latest technology and engineering, with subterranean ducts linking all venues, for the maximum in efficiency, to lower cost of maintenance. This is the secret to Disney World, in Florida, for example.

TENTH REPORTER
What style of architecture will it be—futuristic?

MOON-OC DIRECTOR OF CONSTRUCTION
Classical Greek. Doric, in fact, will dominate. It will be structured in steel, on gigantic springs, to withstand earthquakes, but will be faced in white Grecian marble. To-night, in the front hall of the Old Museum, an architectural model will be on display.

ELEVENTH REPORTER
Will the Army be as omnipresent in the Olympic Nation as it is here to-day? For the Director of Sports.

MOON-OC DIRECTOR OF SPORTS
The Olympic Nation is to be completely autonomous. It will be as free a State as The Vatican and The United Nations. As a gift from Greece to the world, it will be assisted into being by the Greek Army's Corps of Engineers. You may be aware that Litóchoron Army Base is at the foot of Mount Olympos. But—once the Deed is turned over to the IOC, there will be no more need for any manifestation of Greek Army presence ever again. The Olympic Nation will be so constructed, within its own towering walls, as to negate any necessity for armed troops. Public Sectors, for both Winter and Summer Sites, will be below those of the Administrative Offices and Residences, and below those of the Olympic Village for the Athletes as well. The IOC may choose to initiate their own Security Force, to be sure, for patrol of Public Sectors, but by no means will this be manned by any Greek troops.

TWELFTH REPORTER
For the Director of Communications: As an Orthodox Priest, with responsibilities in the Archdiocesan Headquarters of Athens, near the National Cathedral, aren't you in a position of spiritual compromise by attending to such lay matters as the Olympic Games?

MOON-OC DIRECTOR OF COMMUNICATIONS
I have special dispensation from the Metropolitan of Athens, to attend to such duties as the MOON-OC see fit.

THIRTEENTH REPORTER
Will Press be kept up to date as Olympic Nation construction proceeds?

MOON-OC DIRECTOR OF COMMUNICATIONS
Every six months—every April and October—the Press are to be invited to the construction site of the Nation, on the two foothills of Olympos, in order to inspect all progress. To-night, in the lobby of the Old Museum, before the Solemn Opening of the IOC Session, you may each pick up a detailed *Catalogue Of Construction-Plans* for the Nation, that we have prepared for you. Now—we only have time for one more question.

FOURTEENTH REPORTER
For the Deputy Chief of Protocol: It has been widely published that you remarked to the Press, upon your arrival in Greece last month, that you had come to fight against bastardisation of the Olympian Ideal. Do you feel that, by participating in the MOON-OC, your fight is being successful?

MOON-OC DEPUTY CHIEF OF PROTOCOL
Only Time may tell.

There was pandemonium from the Press, as all thousand began shouting at once for one last photograph, one last question. But it was time for other things. The MOON-OC stood and the Chief of Protocol announced: "If you will please stay for Cocktails, staff are ready and eager to serve you, to your left. Thank you all very much for your patience."

The sound-system was shut off. Special lighting on the lorry became dim, then went out completely. But at the other end of the Stadium, the far end by the Academy suddenly was being illuminated by theatrical light. This was the colossal raked stage, that had been erected on scaffolding. To-morrow it would support the Athens Symphony Orchestra and Chorus, and Fanfare Trumpets for the Grand Procession. As a backdrop, Army technicians had erected the largest video screen ever seen in this part of the world. Directly before it was a huge bouzouki band, now beginning a warm-up tune. Dancers were coming out of the wings, in gay peasant costumes from various isles and inland locales of Hellas. Video images were being projected onto the screen, from footage that had been made all over the country. It was breathtaking to witness, as the Sun was just finishing to set behind the giant screen. A horizon-

463

to-horizon wash of scarlet provided a fabulous velvet background for the imagery.

But to the Press, parched with thirst and hungry as vultures, the main attraction was the hundred-foot bar at the base of the stage scaffolding. It was loaded with every hors-d'oeuvre known to the Balkans, from little bite-sized sandwiches, to spreads, to cheeses, to meat balls, to mouth-watering dry and moist sweets. Everyone was going crazy, and wine of every sort of vintage, from every island in the Ionian and Aegean Seas, was flowing like tropical rain.

Satisfied by sight, sound, taste, touch, and smell, the Press hardly noticed the MOON-OC getaway. Those *paparazzi* types of Reporters and Photographers, very few admitted to the precincts to-day, did chase the six to the vaulted tunnel exit from the Stadium, but not one of the six would speak. Then these bothersome fellows retraced their steps, prevented by soldiers from further pursuit, and rushed to stuff themselves on stuffed grape leaves.

The Organizing Committee Members, meanwhile, were escorted by Míkis, and rushed by limousines from the Kiosk Gate of the ruins back to the Academy to change, where the cars wasted fuel, waiting to transport the six back to the edge of the latter-day village. It was fast approaching seven o'clock. The VIP Banquet soon would begin.

An Honour Guard of Evzónes, in their decorative folk uniforms, such as worn on duty before Parliament, was marching up the village high-street towards the Xénia. This was being staged for the local people's benefit. But the whole village, anyways, was crowding towards the large Hotel, in order to be able to get as close as possible to the entrance way. Everyone wanted to see the elegant automobiles that were arriving from the Academy and the Stadium.

Vendors had been doing a booming business in little flags. Those of Greece and the IOC were being sold together. To the people, regardless of the controversy, it was a cause of celebration, and legitimate excuse for the most ebullient national pride. The distance between the Hotel Xénia and the Old Museum, on its mound not far away, was thronging with men, women, and children, and the air was festive indeed.

The VIPs would be walking from Hotel to Museum, and the cameras and flags were ready. The Fanfare Trumpeters were ready, as well, standing at attention atop platforms outside the entrance to both edifices. The Military Band was ready, outside Museum portals, to play the National Anthem for the country's Head of State.

Limousines were arriving now by the score. The people had never seen anything like it in their lives. A Major-Domo from the military had been assigned to the Xénia's doorway, in order to announce to the public who was stepping inside. All automobiles had been instructed to carry on through town, to fill every side-street, so that the convoy returning Reporters to the Amalía later that eve would not be blocked.

The Press Cocktails and Show were continuing till eight. This had been ingeniously planned, so that no Press would be at the entrance to the Xénia whilst the Dignitaries were arriving to dine.

People behind barriers and behind soldiers, who were as overwhelmed by it all as were their rural compatriots, kept ooh-ing and aah-ing at every single limousine that arrived. Countless rolls of film were being used to preserve the memory of the débonnaire gentlemen in formal evening wear and the extravagant ladies in precious gowns and glittering jewels. To many, visions of castles and unfulfilled dreams were passing right before their very eyes. Rustic women were seen drying their cheeks. Poor farmer children were staring, as if it were something out of fairy tales, as if it were all make-believe. Old men who had travelled a bit were recalling *les boulévards de Paris*, the fancy squares of London, the canyon-sized avenues of Midtown Manhattan. Things that one just read about, or heard about, now were right here, within arm's length. But always...the arm was too short. This would be the closest that many in the crowd ever would get to the class that ruled the world.

26th April – Wednesday – 12.15 PM

It was fun. Teetering on the edge, of the Amphitheatre of Tragedy, no big deal was *it*. Once one began to *do* it, it was a lark.

Sunshine was being turned up full blast. Whoever ruled the skies kept adjusting the flipping knob, hotter, hotter, hotter, hotter, hotter.

Skála Peak and our little tea party and the spooky fog were behind. I felt great, glad to be alone, way upon Olympos, taking my good ole time. I had pulled off my winter jacket, had rolled up my flannel sleeves. Whew—was it getting balmy!

I almost dropt my pack and coat, but decided the weather might suddenly change. What a bore, dragging around excess weight. I felt like skipping about...a mountain goat...taking off all of my clothes...running balls-to-the-wind...nude...like a lunatic...over warming stone. I decided I'd damn well *do* it, too. This country had got to me—infected my mind!

But not quite yet. It was still getting hotter.

Maybe I'd just yank everything off—and wank. The heat was making me horny. There wasn't a whore for miles and miles and miles.

In full sunlight, the Amphitheatre of Tragedy, ever off to my right, was no less ponderous for its leaden brilliance. Tragedy was no more friendly, minus fog, than a cobra coiled, asleep. Tragedy was something to appreciate, even approach, quietly, but it was nothing to poke with a stick.

In my own odd way I began to feel that I was becoming Tragedy's Friend, balanced, on its lip, like a cat, on a fence, *part* of it now, no longer an alien intruder. There was not one hint of wind, just heat, and still more heat. Mounds of snow, in shadows, here and there, crossed my path occasionally. I now was aiming across an upward-sloping plain, still along the canyon's edge, but angling lightly higher, to the summit known as Skólio.

Here was a yellow butterfly. It danced around my sweating brow, then leapt into The Abyss.

This was living! *This* truly was what any red-blooded man *dreamt* of doing...one time in his life. All alone, on a mountain top, in magnificent sunshine. Beneath wisps of cirrus clouds. Taking the shirt off. Stripping to bare essentials. Then...leaping...to The Abyss?

Not yet. Wait a little longer.

I began to run!

Even with impedimenta, coat and shirt and pack, I now couldn't stop Feet Heart Soul Spirit...running...like I never have run in my life...

Freedom?

I was...high on Mount Olympos...

I was...all alone...

I was...running...after...my *Destiny*?

It's been said that the ancients had their altar up here. On this gentle mound named Skólio, slang for School or Treacherous, take your pick, some people think that the old Greeks thought that the high-point of Olympos was *here*. A few crud-encrusted coins have been found in the ground, and a couple shards of pottery, but it's certainly no great archaeological find. Nothing for a Schliemann to write home about.

I put my pack on the soil, and removed boots, trousers, knickers, socks. I still was panting from the uphill run. Looking three hundred and sixty degrees, there wasn't a creature for miles, only butterflies, in a Terpsichorean horde. It was so good...standing here... naked...

The edge of the summit was calling, ever so gently now. I stept right to it, and sat on a saucer-shaped boulder. My bollocks drooped down to the stone 'neath my rump, and kept touching the rock then rolling back up. Testicles move with the force of the tide.

The vector from this point, across The Abyss, to the three summits that dominated the view, veered with the arc of the immense Tragic Bowl beneath my smelly feet. Closest was Skála, from which I'd just run, nothing more than a nondescript hump. In the middle was Mýtikas, a veritable Wizard's Retreat, because of its hundreds of pinnacles sticking skywards, reptile fangs. But drawing all attention was the loveliest of the peaks, appropriately named Throne Of Zeus. It was ten times wider than the absolute top of Olympos, which was Mýtikas. A wondrous work of geologic sculpture, Throne Of Zeus surged straight from the bottom of the lifeless canyon, in one unbroken piece. It looked like a primordial megalith, some inhuman monument to commemorate the levitation of Olympos from the sea. As if it were made of slate, its face was polished and rose erect, without hardly curving inwards in the least. Its crown was flat and gently rolled back. In many ways, it looked like one of a man's two top front teeth.

I stood from the rock and pissed off the edge. What a joy...not to have to hold my stupid prick...just letting the waste water spray where it wanted to hit. Quietly satisfying it was...seeing urine vanish into nothingness. This primitive pleasure made me feel more at one with the environment than anything I had done on Olympos to date. I felt like a happy animal, no better no worse than the flitting butterflies that suddenly were everywhere..

Why did the little creatures come *here*? There wasn't a single happy animal, no better no worse than the butterflies flitting through flower, no pollen to eat. Juicy blossoms far below...did abundance *bore* them? Did butterflies...*think*? Did they like to go *exploring*...as much as a human being? Did they *have* a home...where they returned by dusk each day? Did they roam about...*aimlessly*...letting the breeze carry them where it may? I remembered Ada, in the Vale, saying: "I never once killed a single one."

Butterflies were probably the most beautiful animals ever to grace this Earth. If ever a beast were free, the example would be the butterfly. I decided to *follow* one!

Just to see how long I could, I chose one heading *away* from the edge of Tragedy—thank you. It was just a typical one, totally white, a creature I chose at random. This was something I'd always wanted to do, ever since I was the smallest boy. Of course, in England, I never had such a vast expanse of barren land on which to play, so never had the opportunity to pursue the elusive things beyond the nearest hedge.

Then—my tiny new friend was flipping in the air—a dozen times—as if saying to me: Chase me, if you *dare*! Then it was off—heading downslope, towards the foothills and the beckoning Aegean Sea.

24th March – Friday – 8.45 PM

Trumpets began the Fanfare. Outside the Hotel Xénia, all the locals had waited throughout the VIP Banquet, wondering what the dinner might be like. They were content to hear that it was the grandest meal ever prepared in this part of Greece since ancient days. Anything less would have been too far-fetched for their rampant imaginations. In fact, throughout the Banquet, nothing more unusual than always occurs on such formal occasions, in any cosmopolitan capital of the world, did transpire. The rich and the famous and the powerful sat, ate well, and drank even better. There were no speeches. Those were coming next. The VIPs did not wish to ruin their digestion.

But the Trumpet Fanfare was beginning. All the locals had been as silent as the grave, for over an hour, even when the Press had begun

467

returning from the Stadium, a bit more tipsy than before the Seating Rehearsal. But suddenly—everything was erupting. A great big cheer was arising from the throng, especially from the children who had never heard a trumpet in their life.

The Fanfare was in duplicate, in fact. Trumpets posted outside the Xénia were being echoed by trumpets atop the Old Museum's hill. It was splendid, and was sending shivers down the spine and bringing tears to the dullest eye.

Helicopters now began hovering over the route. There was a Sergeant barking orders to his Evzónes. All soldiers lining the Processional Route were presenting arms. The throng began surging behind barriers and squeezing like sardines in a tin. Nobody wanted to miss a single thing.

At the far end of town, by the Hotel Amalía, security was bolstering its might. The President of Greece's helicopter, and a fleet of others, soon would be arriving in the night. There were now three thousand Demonstrators outside the checkpoint, dancing with placards and banners in the floodlight. A Television Crew was recording their resistance to events. Limousines for the party of the Head of State were turning over their engines, readying for the ride through the village streets.

The Fanfare was continuing, and the echoing did not cease. Now the throng was going wild. VIPs were coming out of the Hotel. They were proceeding between the barriers past the crowd. A military band, outside the entrance, was playing a medley of tunes, from all over the world. Flags galore were waving in the warm air of night. Even though the way was lit, the Moon had been Full, just two nights before, so everyone could see perfectly clearly. And the big attraction, of course, was the jewels. Nobody had ever seen so many *diamonds*!

Many people tried to follow the last of the VIPs, who strolled up the Processional Route. It only took each Glamorous Visitor five minutes, at most, to walk the short route. But for the Locals, the Procession was endless. There were about one hundred and sixty Members of the IOC including Guests, about four hundred Members of NOCs including Guests, and about one hundred and twenty Members of IFs including Guests, almost seven hundred VIPs in all. That made for roughly three hundred and fifty elegant ladies to gawk at, to criticise, and to gawk at again.

There were just too many Locals in the high-street at the end of town for anybody to move. The last of the VIPs was ascending the Museum's hill, was being treated to another military band at its portals, and was being given programmes and escorted by Olympic Hostesses to seats within the Great Hall of the Old Museum.

The Press had already taken every last *Catalogue Of Construction-Plans* published by the MOON-OC and had photographed innumerable times the scale model of the proposed Olympic Nation to be built on Mount Olympos. The Press, now with those from the community, were massed outside the Old Museum's doors. Only select Reporters and Photographers, who long ago had pledged allegiance to the IOC, and who customarily covered their events, were admitted past the guards. The remaining majority had to do their best outside.

All was eerily still. The air wasn't moving an inch. The extreme opposite end of town, though, was exploding in manic action. The helicopters from Athens were descending, onto the blacktop of the Hotel Amalía, and troops were restraining the mass of Demonstrators, who were singing a patriotic song by Míkis Theodorákis. The Head of State was just being greeted by the Mayor and by other Local Officials from the Western Pelopónnesos, then everyone was jumping into black limousines.

Engines were revving as sirens began wailing. Anybody within miles could hear them. It sounded as if there had been a tremendous disaster, as if ambulances were rushing to the scene. One dozen motorcycles began leading the way.

The President's car was last. Before his Lincoln Continental were those of Ministers of the Cabinet, and other high-ranking Athenian Dignitaries. Motorcycles were flanking the whole fleet. Armed soldiers in open Jeeps were holding machine-guns on their laps, and were looking menacingly effective, directly before and directly after the limousine of the President of the Republic of Greece. Flags were flying from the four corners of his car. He was alone, in the back seat. Bullet-proof see-through windows were allowing him to be visible to the public.

Demonstrators behind checkpoints were going crazy now, jumping up and down like puppets on a string. They knew that they were absolutely ineffective, that there wasn't a rat's chance in Hell that their leader would deign to speak to them. And he did not, he only waved, as the President's entourage passed the people by.

Everyone in the village now was tingling head to toe. It might be one thing to see *diamonds* walking by, but to see your *own* President, of your *own* country, arriving in your *own* town, at night, was quite another.

The people could hear him coming, as the death-defying squealing of the horrid sirens kept getting closer and closer and closer. The President's party now was reaching the first open-air café on the edge of Olympia, then was slowing, so that as many people as possible could get a look at the leader of the Hellenes. Even though the Prime Minister was more often in the news, the President, who was above him, was always more belovèd.

There was euphoria, all along the way, as soldiers were standing at attention, as Officers were saluting, as children were screaming with delight, as old men were tipping their hats, as old women were crossing themselves, for their country, rapidly three times. Everybody would be talking about this one night until he or she would die...the night that the President of the Republic arrived with his motorcycles and his limousines...

The President's car was now passing the headquarters of the Tourist Police, as the first pair of motorcycles was arriving by the Hotel Xénia. People were in rhapsody. There was total pandemonium. The limousines now were passing. Motorcycles and armed guards were continuing round the hill of the Old Museum and down the road towards the ruins. Only the limousines carried on up the swerving road that led to the Old Museum's portals. There was very little space for excess traffic, especially with the contagious glee of the populace, that had spread to the guards, indubitably.

Then, as the people below the hill began repeating what they just had seen, and as waves of hysteria kept pulsing throughout their numbers, the Military Band outside the Old Museum struck up the National Anthem of Greece. Even those safely inside and waiting now were turning in their seats.

The President now was stepping from his automobile. All of the Ministers and Dignitaries were standing proudly to the side. The President's Chief of Protocol, a dapper man in black tie, was introducing to the Head of State the Director of the Museum, Evanthía Selináki, who bowed and graciously was welcoming him to the Olympia Archaeological Site, then who was requesting that he kindly enter the neo-classical building.

The Chief of Protocol of Greece stood at the portals and stated loudly and clearly: "The President of the Republic of Greece!"

All of those gathered within the Great Hall did rise. Everybody began applauding, as the Presidential Party began proceeding down the central aisle, and all continued applauding the whole time that the Party was taking their places before the front row of seats.

The Executive Committee of the IOC, directly facing the arrivals, were loudly applauding as well, as they now were watching with greatest interest the entrance of the President of the Hellenes. Alternating flags of Greece and the IOC were ringing the assembly.

The President was striding forwards and the applause was trebling. Excitement was at fever pitch, even amongst those who were quite at home with international protocol. This was no inconsequential event. This was History In The Making. The President was arriving, at the dais before the elevated table being used by the IOC Executive Committee. He was bowing slightly, in recognition of the IOC, then was turning to face the emotional group of Visiting Dignitaries. Applause was continuing for a couple of minutes more, then the President was taking his seat.

The Head of State of Greece was surveying the multitude, from the superior vantage point of his raised platform. Even though his chair was lower than those of the Executive Committee of the IOC, highest of which being their President's, all eyes were directed *his* way. It was no slight to his office, that the President of the IOC's chair was at a higher elevation, because all the world's leaders recognise the fact that the IOC is a supra-national organization, transcending political boundaries, and that their President is accorded top status. It is as if the President of the IOC is the acknowledged Head of State of the whole World of Sport, and his realm is wherever he happens to be.

Now that the President of the IOC happened to be in this very Hall, so resplendently decorated with flags and invaluable original sculptures from the ruins of Olympia's Áltis, *this* was his realm, and even the President of the Hellenes was bowing to it. The IOC's power, when convened, is awe-inspiring. Everyone present to-night felt it.

The President of the International Olympic Committee now was rising, slowly. He was glancing about the enormous room, then was saying: "In the name of the International Olympic Committee, it gives us the greatest pleasure that to-night we are being honoured by the presence of the Head of State of this noble country that gave birth to the Olympic Games. Please welcome the President of the Republic of Greece, who will declare open this Session of the International Olympic Committee."

The President of the IOC sat, as applause, now in official response, once again was welcoming the President of the Hellenes, who was rising. Then, the Greek Head of State let the din die down. Of course, he had been briefed, up to the very last minute, of developments with respect to the plot to wreck the Games being conspired by the MOON-OC, who were seated in a special section off to the Greek leader's right, beyond the end of the IOC Executive Table and at a right angle to the majority in the Great Hall. His eyes made a quick survey of the evil group, then he began his carefully worded speech:

"Members of the august International Olympic Committee, Representatives of the National Olympic Committees and International Sporting Federations, Officers of the Mount Olympos Olympic Nation Organizing Committee, and Distinguished Guests, it is a great honour to be invited to participate in events of the next two days. My Government are deeply committed, as you all know, to eternal fostering of the Olympian Ideal. That goes without question. For years, Greece has prayed that the Olympic Games, born but a few steps from this very edifice, would once more return home, permanently. That prayer has not been one without controversy. Many Hellenes, who are allied in theory, have balked, for decades, at the idea that the Games finally return to their homeland. The many difficulties that the IOC and the Olympics have faced, since the revival of the Games in 1896, in this country's capital, Athens, have prevented many people, here and abroad, from being able to look at the *benefits* that would, and will, accrue by bringing the Games back home. As a political leader, I personally understand such anxiety, more than most would like to think. Pros and cons, of decisions that involve external affairs, are always the hardest for any governor to make. There always will be one person who argues against any proposed course of action, no matter how evidently wise that course be. For many decades, the IOC have diligently applied their efforts towards fostering a worldwide community of Athletes, who come together every four years, in order to compete, as much as to promulgate Fair Competition as to accelerate World Peace. As President of this ancient country, I have absolutely no doubts whatsoever about the IOC's intentional nobility. However, in any aggregation of Youth, and Officials, and people from different countries, tensions, that the world can't hide, are bound to surface, even in the midst of Olympic Games. We are all aware of international disputes, involving decisions about athletic victories, and we are all aware of Olympic Games, where historical intrusion has bared a violent remedy. Never, though, has Greece abandoned *her* belief in the Games. Never has Greece abandoned *her* belief...in the Olympian Ideal!"

The Hall erupted in intense applause. The President was staring at the Members of the Executive Committee of the MOON-OC, then he was raising his hand, in order to carry on.

"It is *not* the request of the International Olympic Committee that the President of the Republic of Greece harangue you until to-night's wee hours...but...that one get on...with business at hand. To-morrow, need one say, will see us all gathered together again, inside the Ancient Stadium, where the Olympic Games were born. To-morrow...is the time for speeches. To-morrow...is the much awaited Deed Ceremony, when the Government of Greece, scheduled to present the Deed of Transfer of Land to the Mount Olympos Olympic Nation Organizing Committee, will demonstrate, to the whole world, her aforementioned belief in the Olympian Ideal."

Everyone applauded again.

"But to-night...we are gathered here for the Solemn Opening of this Session of the International Olympic Committee. Therefore, with all due respect to the much esteemed International Olympic Committee, I herewith declare this Session...*open!*"

Thýella, never more imposing, fidgeted as if she needed to go to the lavatory. She was wearing royal-purple velvet. A diamond tiara was gracing her blonde hair, which a famous hairdresser from Athens had done in a matter of minutes, during her quick-change-act at the Academy earlier in the evening. A magnificent ensemble of amethysts surrounded by extravagantly radiant diamonds embellished her ears, her neck, her arms. She was wearing just one ring, an amethyst cameo of Leda and the Swan.

But the Chief of Protocol of the MOON-OC was having an anxiety attack. During applause for the President of Greece, she started hiccuping.

"Now what's wrong!" snapt General Ouranós.

She hiccuped: "He knows!"

472

"Who knows?" asked the General, playing dumb.

"Damn you—the President *knows*—we just *know* he knows," she hiccuped again.

"You're being *ridiculous!*" be ordered, meaning for his wife to shut up, given that the President again was seated and applause just had stopt.

But Thýella was in an altered state. She was thinking the vilest thoughts of her life, as she kept trying to control the awful hiccups. It was getting embarrassing. People would think she were drunk. She hadn't even had a drop of the expensive champagne. She had been too wound up.

People now were staring. Members of the IOC and Cabinet Ministers from Athens, all of whom she knew, were noticing. Everybody hated her, and thought she deserved every noisy burp. She was dying to rise and run outside, but had to fight the idea down, as she was trying to do with the hiccuping. The General, beside her, was ready to put her out of her damned misery. She had been a problem *all* his life. *Why* hadn't he just plugged her with lead...*years* ago!

The President of the IOC was now speaking. He, too, was saying nothing against the MOON-OC. Thýella had kept praying that the Head of State would denigrate the Organizing Committee, in some subtle way, but the fish wouldn't rise to the bait. She hated him, for that, because she had feared that he would play politics in Olympia, as delftly as he always played politics in Athens. She hiccuped again. It was getting out of control.

All her political life, from the early 1950s, Thýella had known this character, who had risen, ever so slowly, into her country's highest position. She had had *more* fights with him than she had even had with her own husband. This President had not been amused when the Junta had made it possible for Ouranós to be elected to the IOC. This President had not been amused, right from the start, with the idea that Ouranós wanted the future Olympic Nation to be built, not in the Pelopónnesos, but in Thessaly. But—this President had turned around when—a year ago? Yes—he had suddenly called the General into his office and had announced, privately, that he had changed his mind. *Why?* Why had the Head of State *changed?* This had always vexed Thýella. The hiccups were continuing,

She didn't hear a word that the President of the IOC was saying. Who was *he*—anyhow? Just some bit-player in this Drama. The *biggest* cheese had just spoken, at least according to her. It was all up to this President of Greece—her so-called Head of State—who held the prize— the *Deed*. *Would* he give it—Thýella wondered? *Would* he honour his word? He'd gone *back* on his word...so many times. He *was* a politician...after all. She wouldn't respect him...if he'd *never* gone back on his word. Only *pussies* kept their word...one hundred percent of the time! *She* broke her word—*all* the time. Anybody with an ounce of *sense* did. Anybody with *balls* did. She hiccuped. What *was* the IOC saying? Ah—never mind! Twaddle—and just more twaddle! Look at them all—that Executive Committee up there—like Kings. *Who* do they think they are? Why *is* everyone here, Thýella asked herself loudly.

Was she having a *breakdown*—right here—right inside this Old Museum? Why were these goddamned statues the Germans dug up *looking* at her so intently? Why *were* these eyeless white faces *staring* so? She hiccuped.

The wife of a Minister, a woman whose eyes she'd gladly scratch out with her own two paws, was handing Thýella a cough drop. The Chief of Protocol snatched it and began sucking, sucking, furiously sucking, like a baby going after its first drop of milk.

Why were these people *clapping*? What were they—*mad*? The IOC President was sitting—*already*? What in Hell had he said? Why was everybody now looking at *us*—Thýella asked?

General Ouranós was standing. Where in Hell was *he* going? Straight ahead? Should we follow? Thýella sucked even harder. She sucked and she sucked...till the hiccups were going away. She was wiping her chin with her white opera glove. She had been slobbering.

Something snapt. Had somebody *hit* her? Thýella was coming back—back to reality—back to her own sick, demented, perverse plane of so-called Existence, whereon her Evil Self resided. She stopt hiccuping. She sat up, to hear her husband speaking.

"...and honoured guests," Ouranós said and looked at his wife, who was now beaming. She turned and made the diamonds on her rotten head throw off flames like rainbows. "As the Junior Member of the IOC in Greece, it is a rare courtesy to be allowed to address this Session in the capacity of President of the Olympic Nation's Organizing Committee. To-morrow is to be the most noteworthy day in the history of the revival of the Olympic Games, since Opening Ceremonies of the celebration of the First Olympiad in 1896. It is a great tribute, to far more than the MOON-OC, that the Deed Ceremony is going to be conducted. Thousands of individuals, worldwide, have been working towards this very goal...for decades. To-night, before this IOC Session, I wish to pledge, to you, my unfailing dedication to the successful establishment of the proposed Olympic Nation. I wish that from henceforth you consider me a servant of the peoples of the world. To *this* effect, I now have an important announcement to make. In particular, I am addressing this to my Head of State, whom I, as a soldier, and as a General, am sworn to obey. After the Deed Ceremony, should the President of the Republic of Greece warrant that my duties, as Member of the IOC and as President of the MOON-OC, place me in a position of compromise, with respect to my avowèd duties in the military, then let me say, before you all, to-night, that I shall be willing to *abrogate* my duties as General and *retire* from the Armed Services of Greece."

Pandemonium all but broke out among this staid crowd.

Everybody was shocked, not least of whom was the General's wife, who heard herself saying: "What—is he *crazy?*" She promptly commenced hiccuping again.

The public uproar, albeit restrained in a societal way, was loud. People could not refrain from whispering, from gossiping. The Press, in particular, seated exactly opposite Thýella and the MOON-OC, way on the other side of the Hall, were aghast. What was the crafty General *up* to? The President of the Republic remained aloof. Inside he was exultant. The General would not need to worry...about *after* any Ceremony...

General Ouranós, basking in the furor he was causing, was returning to his seat. The President of the IOC was standing and was shouting. "Order—may we please come to order. Thank you. Now—as you see from your programmes..."

Thýella hiccuped: "What in Hell are you *doing!*"

The General growled: "Shut your stupid *trap!*"

The IOC President proceeded to tell the Distinguished Guests and NOCs and IFs that the true purpose of the evening was about to commence. "This Session will convene in exactly half an hour's time. Only Members of the IOC are allowed to participate. All limousines are ready. After those for the Head of State of Greece and the Government depart, those for Guests of the IOC will be leaving for the Academy. Thank you all so very much for attending this Solemn Opening. We shall look forward to your Distinguished Presence again, to-morrow morning."

Outside, the Fanfare Trumpeters atop Museum Hill sounded first, then echoed before the Hotel Xénia. The people at least would be seeing the NOCs, IFs, and Guests one more time, if not the President of Greece. The Military Band began playing Greece's National Anthem, as the Head of State, then his Ministers, were the first to leave. Applause followed him all along the aisle, and it was *not* just the more astute who noted that he looked highly amused. Applause trebled as he stept from the Hall and stood on the Museum's portico, for the Press. All the reporters were screaming: "*Are* you going to strip the General of command?"

Soldiers were snapping to attention. The Lincoln Continental was waiting. From the hillslope, as the motorcycles and machine-gun escort began proceeding from the controversial event, great bursts of fireworks started shooting through the pines and exploding high above the stately cypresses. The sirens and the wailing then were fading in the darkening sky. Clouds were just commencing to roll before the Moon. The President of the Hellenes was being whisked down the road, towards the ruins, towards the Hill of Krónos, towards the New Museum, where he was scheduled to spend the night.

475

26th April – Wednesday – 1.00 PM

Chasing a butterfly...thus is Life. Nothing less...nothing more. Gossamer scintillation in the air...pulls us towards it...as it flits away...with our heart...leaving us...often...in despair. We move even quicker...it's always a few steps beyond our fingertips. It pauses for breath, on a rock up ahead, and we're certain that this time we'll catch it. We creep, like a cat, on the balls of our feet, stalking the thing, as we don't even breathe. The butterfly turns its tiny back, cleans its face with delicate paws: we're one step behind it, with open claws. But like all Life...the creature *perceives*. We leap...but it's faster than we'll ever be!

Sometime, as a child, I used to imagine that clouds weren't really made of water, but were flocks of butterflies, alive in the sky, migrating to secret kingdoms, where no human being could chase them. But then came soldiers, on the prowl, thunderheads boasting of weapons, charging like madmen after the flocks, unleashing electric destruction.

In a horrid world...where soldiers do kill butterflies...should one just sit on a rock, and weep? Should one, naked, just lie back, fingertips extended, waiting for wingèd beings to land?

On my hand was the one I was chasing. A rash move easily could crush it. What would it matter—one less? Who would ever know? Where this one came from...always were dozens more? Would it be a loss...to kill it? Do butterflies weep...over gore?

The beautiful little creature...walking along my hand...up my arm...was tasting the sun-bleached hairs...licking the salt...feeling the warmth...exploring another animal...with Life! It knew I wanted to be friends...that I never would hurt it for all of the world. It paused... midway...up my forearm...and just *stared*.

"What *is* this world like...in the eyes of such a one? Is it any better...or worse...for *you*? *Are* your colours less harsh? *Are* your rocks less rough? *Are* your distances not even so great? *What* are you seeking, Butterfly? You're off now? Don't go! Tumbling in the air...showing me how accomplished an *Acrobat* you are—how consummate an *Athlete* you can be! Let me say: 'Will you...*share* with me...where you're going...with your Life? Will you...live much longer? Will you...survive...to-night?'"

There I lay, taking the Sun, talking out loud, in a landscape that looked like Mars. The sole sound was the occasional fly. Not one single plant, of any sort, was nearby. Heatwaves kept rippling upwards, from a vista totally of shades of grey. Already, it had been a bizarre day.

Nobody had ever bothered to give a name to this pyramidal mound, midway along this plain, between the Peaks of Skólio and Ághios Antónios.

I had been pursuing the elusive butterfly, and now I was supine *here*. I had been heading east for Saint Anthony Peak, as something to do before having to return to Skála and hence to Reality. Awhile before, with the two Swiss, I had been peering at their map of the mountain, but where I was now sprawling was nameless.

Lying here, without any clothes, and soaking up the heat-rays, which might vanish at any second, I simply decided, all on my own, to call this rise: "Sokrates". Gods willing, they wouldn't mind. My butterfly had vanished from sight.

Facing south, all that could be seen was a gently curving bowl, a vale, some few hundred metres below, filled with snow. Two rounded peaks, with nary a bump nor a ridge, were hemming the bowl in. Graceful roadways of glistening snow were falling down sides of both hills. Perfect for skiing: Also...just nice *to see.*

Further southwards, another chain of peaks, snow-patched ramparts for tremendous squads of cumulus clouds, slowly were crawling towards the city of Athena.

Wondering where the butterfly had gone, for some reason I was suddenly possessed by the urge to draw. I would try capturing this landscape. Somehow...I'd take it home with me...wherever that might someday be...I hadn't a clue any longer. I just began to draw. But my pencil could only trace gossamer wings...

Miles from home? Maybe I *was*...sleeping? Overhead the sky was just going from pinks and orangey blues to sable black. The Sun had set, dramatically so, behind Olympos. Air now was crisp, vibrantly charged from rain. I was with General Ouranós, on a foothill of the mountain, on Gólna. Neither of us was clothed, though it was now the dead of night.

The Olympic Nation *was* being constructed. Evil *had* had its omnipotent way. The Organizing Committee had *not* been defeated. Machines *were* boring into Stávros. The silo for death and destruction *was* being carved from living rock. Neutron bombs *were* being built within the domicile of the Olympian Gods.

The naked General had me in his Stadium, in his own white marble Colosseum. He was nodding, to the seats, like an Emperor, as if they were crammed full of people. Not one single Soul was to be seen...though in truth the Stadium was packed...standing room only...filled with Shades...filled with Shades of The Dead And The Gone Olympic Athletes Of All Time...filled with *their* Shades...(Gods, rest them one and all!)...and not one single Soul was *clothed*...and not one single Soul was *visible!*

Dead Olympians...were making me think...about the day I triumphed...when I won my Olympic Gold. Dead Olympians...were making me imagine...the Stadium packed with so many thousands ...four joyous summers ago. Dead Olympians...were making me remember...all those Fans...cheering wildly...as that last lap was being made...

With his penchant for hypocrisy, the General was happy to ruin my thought and was saying: "Such a feeling of *Goodness* is in a Sports

Fan...watching the strain and vigour of competition. Something does reach out...from Athlete straight to Fan. Something *is* there...that the Fan truly can feel. It's the stamina proven...the pride of an honest win. The Fan knows...in the heart...that the Athlete's race is different...from *devious* success...from gain by politics. Hear how the Fan reacts...with thrill in the guts...to the Victor's triumph...no matter who the Victor be. The Olympics *are* very special. There *is* something gained...just by *competing*...just by being *present*...at an Olympic Games. Good sportsmanship merits applause...not only for the Victor...but also for the one whom the Victor must beat..."

At that moment, Dead Olympians, the unseen Ghosts in this giant sports edifice, were beginning a group-howl, like a starved pack of wolves, and I noticed the appearance of Light, at the end of the tunnel, which was leading from the north side of the General's eerie Stadium. At the far end of this passageway, this vomitorium, something bright was moving. Ouranós was turning to me and saying: "Surprise..."

A Runner...was bearing the Sacred Olympic Flame. And the howling, of Dead Olympic Athletes, now was turning into one sustained note, one five-tiered single note, one "C", stretching from bass to soprano, four full octaves of sound.

At that moment, in my mind, recollections of Winter Games and Summer Games were commencing to wrestle. Bittersweet tumbled with jubilant, and I felt everything tightening inside. Memories were jostling ...Dead Olympians were singing...and I could stop neither...if required to save my life! I just shook...as teardrops kept falling...

"You *will* climb Olympos," the General was saying.

Across the Athletic Track the Runner now was aiming, holding the Torch aloft. It was borne by a girl. Naked...

"On Olympos...you will fall...you will crash...you will live."

It seemed to be taking forever...for the Torch Runner to reach us...

"Go to the heights, Young Man. Forget about plots down below..."

At last, there she was standing. Chorusing Dead Olympians now were silent. The Torch-Bearer almost looked familiar. She almost appeared to resemble my belovèd Ada. Whoever she was...she saw me weeping...

"*Take* the Fire," the General commanded. "*Run* with the Fire, all the way to the top, to the Cauldron. *Take* and *run* with the Fire! *Light* the Olympic Flame. You'll be the *first* to do so in this new Arena. We must see if the Cauldron...*works*. We must *test* it...before the next Games."

I felt my legs begin moving. There I was, running, as if Satan himself were after me, in the General's bastard Stadium, for his bastard Olympic Games. Metre after metre, stride after stride, the legs felt good, and the Torch was burning bright. And visible, above the very last row, a ponderous Full Moon was rising in the night, was ordering an indigo aureole to becircle its obstinate orb with eldritch light.

Inside this wan Olympic Arena...bearing this Sacred Flame...once again I was hearing the thousands...the thousands of Olympic Athletes From The Grave...and I now was bearing their Pain...unable to see them but able to hear them...cheering for all their worth...as I kept on running...fiercely...fighting to stay the first. And, as that last lap raced nearer...that huge empty Stadium...that capacity crowd of Invisible Ghosts...was going berserk...as some Spectre now beside me was holding second place...as the Shade was falling behind me...was giving way to the speeding third. And what did I hear in my mind then...*singing*? Fans Dead? Athletes Demised? My own inner mind? Racing. Faster. Lungs burnt alive. And the animalistic roar of Mankind. Everyone standing! Everyone jumping! Everyone waving! Closer! Closer...

I felt myself racing upwards, and every row of seats I passed was now materialising a full array of Spirits, becoming visible now, row by row, who were urging me higher, higher, higher, to continue my running, running upwards, row after row, Dead Olympians now visible, row after row, Dead Olympians now visible, row after row after row. Dead Olympians now visible...a whole Stadium's worth of Shades!

It was not easy...running past them! I wanted to shout out, to embrace every one! But there was nothing to touch...as I kept reaching out...with my free left hand...nothing to hold onto...on the hands of The Dead...

And the Torch kept pulling me...kept pulling me up...up...up by a power all its own...

Then there, in the black of the night, and feeling like a Ghost myself, at the base of the white marble tower for the Light, I was stopping to face the Arena. And again I was turning, then running once more, up one final flight...

Thrice behind the tower I was vanishing, as the steps made three complete revolutions, on the way to the top. Then, there I stood, moonlight on my face, at the summit, looking so small, as glimmering bronze Light kept reflecting off the burnished Cauldron's base. And below me, were thousands of Dead Olympians, one smile, one hope, one embrace...

For thirty seconds I dared not move...then...slowly...began mounting the final dozen steps...that barely were perceptible from below...and the Torch *ever* was aloft. Then...towards the mouth of the Tripod...I began to bring the Flame. The Fire leapt! The Cauldron blazed!

I awoke. Quick as cavalry a huge posse of fog was making a sudden battle-charge straight towards me, over the ridge, off to the right. The wind was freezing; my skin ice-cold.

479

As I scrambled into clothing, fog kept tumbling downslope, filling the bowl with bleachèd vapour. Fine time to be on the rocks balls-arse naked!

Just as I was zipping my trousers, right up to my boots advanced belligerent clouds. "Damn," I shouted as I jammed my blank sketchbook into my pack, "the only thing predictable here is that sunshine never lasts!"

25ᵗʰ March – National Day – 5.45 AM

Lights were on in the Ancient Stadium of Olympia all throughout the night. Constant adjustment of equipment, testing of cameras, quick rehearsals of the Deed Ceremony, using soldiers as VIPs, occurred right until the dawn.

Driving through the night, as well, were the young bastard son of General Ouranós and the woman whose duty it was to ignite the Sacred Flame for all Olympic Games. Theatrínos and Ada, both wearing black leather cycling suits and helmets, were speeding across the Peloponnesian Peninsula on the Harley-Davidson.

Meanwhile, the Security Corps, who attended the Head of State of Greece, who travelled with him everywhere, were awakening early to discuss the soldiers under General Ouranós's command and their plans for coping with possible crowd reactions. These men were inside the New Museum. The President still was asleep. He had stayed up rather late, discussing many things with the Director of the Museum and with the President of the IOC.

The chamber that contained the most priceless treasures from excavations at Olympia, sculptures from the two pediments of the Temple of Zeus, had been converted into a bedroom for the Head of State. The President had found it hard to fall asleep, with massive Olympian Deities glaring at his bed. He kept wondering if his course of action was right.

Suddenly—the Security Corps were telephoned. The man who was answering was being notified of a disturbance. Protesters, outside the Hotel Amalía checkpoint, were getting unruly. The Harley-Davidson had just arrived. The Pop Singer now was on a makeshift podium, delivering some speech. Troops were getting restless. There could be violence.

"Under no conditions must Theatrínos be harmed," was the executive order of the Presidential Bodyguard who had been informed of the Singer's work with Professor Rembetikós. "And Ada's participating in the Ceremony, as Chief Priestess of Hera, so let her *through!*"

Outside the checkpoint, the leather-clad Entertainer was waving his helmet in the air. Demonstrators, now four thousand strong, were cheering him. He was shaking his henna-dyed hair and gesturing for them to be quiet. "But we can't be fooled—can we? We *know* that this collusion between the Army and the Olympics is pulling wool over *nobody's* eyes! We know *better* than that!"

Another great cheer went up. The crowd started chanting the now-famous verse from his much-discussed performance at the opening of The Bitchy Bacchante:

> *Our Olympics are a farce...the Soul's no longer in it;*
> *Is the Medal worth it all...what's the sense to win it?*

Over and over and over the group kept chanting and chanting, until they were getting hoarse. But this was just what invigorated somebody like Theatrínos. He now was clapping along to the beat, assuming leadership over them all, making the whole mass of human beings rock back and forth as one. It was scary. It was verging on wholesale hysteria.

Recruits were getting nervous. If this mob, so quiet all night, now decided to push, they easily could trample the barriers down and stampede right into town. Attack-dogs were now straining on their leads, barking ferociously. Suddenly, from the village came a rushing wail of sirens, which egged on the throng even more.

Theatrínos was doing his best to whip the lot into frenzy, one of his easiest tasks, because the four thousand knew him as a Celebrity, one who always brought out their most primitive emotions. His mere presence here, like some mad reincarnation of Jim Morrison or a dozen other Dead Pop Deities, made the horde heave and holler all the more. He still was clapping to the beat of his verse when he began shouting out more lyrics, with all the thespian drama at his command:

> *And somewhere in this landscape a true Revival waits—*
> *Many don't believe it—most prefer their hates.*
> *But it will come, will come at last, if the Land just lets it::*
> *Then once again Greece will be great, and no one will regret it.*
> *But this True Spirit won't return...till the Games return to Greece:*
> *Then the Spirit...at last restored...will justly work for Peace!*

Standing like a statue, as sirens were charging to the fray, Theatrínos remained absolutely motionless, balanced on his right leg, with his head turned towards the left. He did not move till sirens ceased and enemy were jumping from vehicles. Then, he roused into fury with a new war-chant:

> *Olympos—no!*
> *Olympics—yes!*
> *Olympos—no!*
> *Olympics—yes!*
> *Olympos—no!*
> *Olympics—yes!*

Soldiers, in riot gear, began advancing, attack-dogs to the fore. But Theatrínos, calm as a babe asleep, was not showing any fear. Ada, though, was petrified. She was tugging at Theatrínos to get down from the makeshift stage. She was begging. She was shouting: "Please—they just might *shoot* you!"

"Stay under control—People! Do *nothing* to provoke them. Stay out of their way. Move back! Move back!" shouted the Singer at the crowd, that was retreating back along the motorway, away from the shields, the riot helmets, the clubs, the dogs, and the soldiers threatening to throw tear-gas.

"*Keep* moving back!" Theatrínos kept hollering.

"Come with them!" Ada kept begging. She'd never dealt with a crowd like this. It had never been her fortune to be confronted with advancing troops. She was terrified. "They'll *arrest* us for inciting a riot! Hurry!"

Theatrínos wouldn't budge. He had recognised someone at the lead of the nearing forces: "My *sibling*! And I'm going to *tell* him that— to-day!"

Major Movóros was approaching. He was wearing a great big smile. To him, this was a joy. He'd been *hoping* to see the famous Singer …on National Day. Just twenty foot away, he ordered his men to halt. He stept forward. He was as neat as a prima donna. He wasn't bearing arms, just his trusty golden worry-beads.

As the two young men glared at each other, silently, the crowd in the rear hushed, too. Even the miserable dogs sat and whined, then shut their lethal mugs. The Major let a full minute go by. Theatrínos watched him, most critically, as if both were auditioning for the same play, to win the coveted rôle of the teenage tough. Theatrínos watched with interest, one might call it, as the Major prepared to speak, as the Major began running his right middle finger down the length of his facial scar, as the Major let the knob of the finger linger against his lips, as the Major licked it ever so lightly.

Then—not to be upstaged—Theatrínos began *his* number—he started to applaud. Ada almost died, but she said nothing. She saw herself and Theatrínos, locked in some dank cell, as the Junta had done to dissenters, both of them tortured and tried without jury. Theatrínos shouted out: "*Bravo!*" Then he looked smugly at the man and said: "But, watch this. *I* can do it better!" Then the youth ran *his* middle finger down the length of an imaginary facial scar, painfully slowly, then finally the digit reached the crease of his lips, whence, after deliberation, he then moistened the tip of it, then thrust the whole finger inside his mouth and began to run his tongue round and round it as if it were his own cock. Then, he slowly extracted the lubricated finger, with a great big *pop* as it finally exited his mouth, and then he sniffed it, a good long time.

The tension amongst the amazed soldiers was so high that the attack-dogs started to growl and to lunge towards the Performer. Movóros simply said: "Thank you—for the gratuitous sex." He was now only ten foot away. "Now Ada—if you would be so kind—I have come here to escort you to the Stadium. For to-day's appearance, as Chief Priestess of Hera, I think you'd better change."

The irony of it all was disconcerting. Ada almost began to weep for the strain. She did not want to leave. She looked up at Theatrínos for help. The Singer said: "Do as he requests. You have a more important matter to attend to...in the Stadium."

"That's right, Ada. You have a more important matter to attend to...in the Stadium," echoed Movóros cruelly.

The mob began to shout back: "Don't go! Don't go! Don't go!"

"I can't," she pled with the Singer. "Not with *you* staying here!"

"Go!" ordered Theatrínos.

"Don't go! Don't go!" the throng now was screaming.

"Go!" shouted the one clad in black.

"No! Don't go!" yelled the people.

"I've *got* to!" she yelled back at them, and grabbed her carrying case that had her costume and make-up for the Ceremony.

"Don't go! Don't go!" they kept shouting, as she began advancing towards the wall of shields of the troops.

"Part," ordered the Major.

"Don't go!" the people hollered.

"*I have to!*" Ada now screamed back, as the soldiers parted, then engulfed her.

"Traitor! Traitor! Traitor!" the mob began chanting.

But now Theatrínos was the sole focus. The Major played with his worry-beads a bit more, as the crowd began yelling advice to the Singer. He suddenly spun round on his makeshift stage and waved his arms at the people: "Sssshhhh! I have an *interesting* bit of news...to announce. Listen!"

With some strain, the crowd became quiet. Theatrínos waited for the right moment, then began: "We are all brothers and sisters—am I not right?"

The mob behind shouted: "We are!"

"But—some of us are *more* than just brothers and sisters—some of us are *blood*-brothers and *blood*-sisters!"

What *is* he getting at, Movóros wondered?

"Some of us, indeed, have the good fortune, or the bad fortune, of having the same *mother*...or...the same *father*."

The crowd was enjoying this. The Major was not. It was a waste of his time.

"Indeed—some of us are *blest*—by knowing who our father *and* our mother are! Some of us know *both* of them. Some of us are very *lucky* people...indeed!"

Finally—Movóros couldn't stand this display any longer and shouted: "What in *Hell* are you ranting on about?"

"Why—Movóros—don't be so *hard* on your brother!"

"That'll be the saddest day—when I call a punk like you *brother!*"

Theatrínos then exploded into the Performing Dæmon of whom he'd so often been accused. He jumped off the stage, and into the road, then strutted across the blacktop to the mob and screamed: "*Look* at me! *Look* at this beautiful face! *Look* at these locks! *Look* at this hand!" Then he snapt apart the studs on his cycling suit and bared the whole of his muscular chest, right down to his coal-black pubic hairs, then yanked the sleeves off his arms, so he now was nude from the groin up, and shouted: "Look at *this*! See this *body*! See it!" Then he strode the thirty feet back to where Movóros was standing amazed.

"What in Hell're you doing—going completely *crazy*!" screamed the Major. He was now getting paranoid. Hundreds of Reporters and Photographers had been rushing out of the Hotel Amalía, just yards away, to document the goings-on.

Theatrínos, of course, had noticed the Press arriving, too. He now was marching about a foot in front of the shielded troops, and was banging on their riot shields, with his left fist, making racket all down the line. "Look at me!" he kept shouting. "Take a goddamned *good* long look!"

"Knock it *off*!" growled Movóros, as attack-dogs began snarling. Then Theatrínos strode belligerently right up beside Movóros and stood, first smiling at the troops and at the Reporters, then smiling at the wildly excited people. Nobody had *any* idea what was going on. Then, he let loose with his bombshell. "Come *on*—don't you people notice—the *resemblance*?"

He was pausing, melodramatically, letting everybody have a good long look; he realised that Movóros had never been told. The Major, for once, was at a total loss for words.

"That's right," Theatrínos screamed, "*his* father, the man who sired the Major, is no one else but General Ouranós. But guess what? *My* father is Ouranós, too! I—a good for nothing *punk*, as my brother here and our father say—*I'm* the son of the man who, at this very minute, is plotting to *wreck* the Olympic Games! *Now,*" he shouted to the people, "do you all *finally* understand why I've been so *against* this *evil* man, this General?"

Movóros, publicly shamed before his very own troops, could have murdered the little bastard right then and there. He was so angry inside that he was boiling, yet was trying to clear his brain by thinking of *slower* ways of exacting fit punishment. As calmly, therefore, as the Major knew how, and it now was bloody difficult, he simply said: "Arrest him."

The mob went berserk, as Theatrínos fought to keep the people calm: "Don't *fight* them! That's what they *want*! *Don't* fight them! I'll *go*! *I* don't have any fear! Don't fight them *physically*—sit—down in the road—use *passive* resistance—remember Gandhi!"

So the troops advanced. Attack-dogs kept the mob at bay, as the famous Performer was handcuffed, was led away. People were beginning to sit in the road, screaming every invective in the book, as canines were starting to foam at the mouth. Chaos was reigning as the Singer was put in a Jeep and driven off, to an unknown destination. It was now six fifteen.

The Security Corps were just receiving another call, being informed of the latest development. "Damn that man," snapt the Presidential Bodyguard. "Wait till the Head of State hears that it was the *Major* who authorised arrest!"

For some reason Ada had not been driven directly to the ruins. The Jeep she was in had turned beside the Hotel Xénia, and had climbed the large hill above the village to the hamlet of Throúva. Officer Míkis, on Thýella's instructions, had moved his bed into Ivor's room. He had woken Hefferon at quarter to six, in order to interrogate and intimidate him. Míkis, now nude, was throwing off the covers from the Deputy's bed. He was standing with a gun in his hand.

"Well well well." Míkis noticed that Hefferon had been sleeping with an erection. "What do we have *here*?"

The Athlete turned away and covered himself. "What in *Hell* are you doing? What's with the gun?"

"Lie full length," Míkis ordered. "I want to take a good long look at you."

"What are you—cracked?"

"Shut up! Lie full length! That's it. Now *play* with yourself. *Milk* that thing! Get your hand on that *big* tool—or I'm going to shoot the *fucker* off!" Míkis now was masturbating. "I've been *longing* for this chance—to get *back* at you—for those *filthy* things you said to me— inside that Stadium Wednesday night!"

"What's *wrong* with you?" Hefferon was fighting to keep under control, not to give anything away. It was hard—with a firearm at his head.

"Now I want *you* to tell *me*! Hefferon, what's going *on* between you and the MOON-OC?"

"What do you mean?"

"Thýella suspects you're a rat. She hasn't got any proof. But *I* think you *have* to be, too!"

"Don't be crazy—what does she suspect?"

"I can *kill* you right now. It would be far *easier* to deal with. You're up to no good—*aren't* you!"

"Of course not!"

"You liar!"

"I'm *not* a liar!"

"Then *prove* you're not a liar! Suck my *dick*—if you're not a liar!"

"Are you out of your mind?"

"I said: *Suck* me!"

Míkis had the gun pointed straight for Ivor's brain. But suddenly a Jeep was arriving outside. Then banging on the door was heard.

"*Jesus!*" the Officer snapt then commanded: "Get yourself covered up!" In a flash he was throwing on undershorts and uniform trousers. He kept the gun in his hand. At the door he saw it was someone he knew. He unlocked the door and said: "What do you want?"

"Major Movóros, Sir, orders you report instantly to the Hotel Amalía. I'm to relieve you of your post, Sir!"

"What's going on?" Míkis insisted on knowing and stept onto the porch. He saw a woman in a black leather cycling suit. "Who's *she?*"

"You are to report to Major Movóros—on the double, Sir."

"We shall *see* about this!" Míkis said and pulled his keys from his pocket, but changed his mind. "Get the Amalía command on the phone!"

Following the Corporal, Míkis walked barefooted and bare-chested towards the Jeep. The Corporal got ahold of the Amalía on his walkie-talkie and reported in: "Yes. I'm at the Throúva house. You're asking...is *Ivor Hefferon* here?"

"Yes—I'm here," announced the Olympic Athlete, now in his trousers and standing on the porch. He was coming towards the Jeep.

"Give me that thing," snapt Míkis. "Captain Sostópoulos reporting, Sir. Yes—she's here. They're both here. Tell her what? The Amalía has just told me to tell you," he said to Ada, "that your comrade, Singer Theatrínos, has been placed under arrest."

Ada remained expressionless. She did not dare look at Ivor. She did not want to give a thing away.

"Any comment?" Míkis asked.

"None," Ada responded.

The Captain who had been posing as the Tourist Police Officer said: "Yessir. I do have the things in my possession. Of course, Sir, I'll give them to him immediately, and report to you as soon as I can. Aye aye, Sir." He handed the walkie-talkie back to the soldier, then ordered Hefferon: "Follow me inside!" Míkis was silent until they got to the bedroom, then spun round and said: "You're one *lucky* mother-fucker *this* time!"

"Look—rest assured I'm bound to do my duty at the Ceremony," Ivor answered.

From beneath his bed, Sostópoulos was pulling a small red sportsbag. "Here!"" he said and tossed it onto Hefferon's bed. "It's your Olympic skin-flick outfit. You should enjoy *exhibiting* yourself...this morning...practically *nude!*"

486

"You should enjoy *watching*," Ivor responded, "You can finish tossing yourself off!"

"Don't worry—I'm going to be having even *more* fun."

"How?

"Interrogating Theatrínos...about certain photographs...that someone took of you both."

"I only met him that once!"

"Well—you didn't waste any time getting down and dirty!"

"It was a joke...we both were playing...on Dora Cain!"

"That's what *all* the queer-boys say! But when I get *my* hands on that jumped-up Pop Star...we'll see what that *cocksucker* sings for lyrics! By the way—your *speech* is in that bag—the one Madame wrote *just* for you. *Study* it! She expects to hear it—*verbatim!*"

Then the Captain finished getting dressed and left. Little did he know that the Head of State had already been awoken. And when the President heard that Theatrínos had been arrested, he said to his Security Corps: "Tell Major Movóros, this minute, that Theatrínos is to be brought directly to *me!* Convince him that I'm concerned, but on the Major's side. I don't want Movóros's *goons* interrogating that boy. God knows what they'd try to do to him. Keep that Singer inside this Museum—under constant surveillance and protection. When he arrives here, have him brought *directly* to me!"

26th April – Wednesday – 1.45 PM

I knew I shouldn't have, but did it anyways. With the foggy mound of Sokrates behind, I began to aim even further east. Somehow I knew I wouldn't get back to Skála in time for the Swiss, but never mind, I was feeling free, and didn't want to be bothered with them anyhow.

At least Saint Anthony still was bathed in sunshine. Ághios Antónios, the nearest summit, maybe twenty minutes east, was about 8,500 feet above sea level. It had a long low slope leading up to it, on its right flank, running upwards northerly. The slope looked like a wedge of cheese, so I decided to take a deep breath and advance towards it. But I knew all along that I shouldn't have done so.

It took about twenty-five minutes to get up the wedge. Whew—it was the most morbid hill. Situated, like Sokrates, in the desert-like plâteau of the southern rim of the Amphitheatre of Comedy, due south of the great Olympian Vale, this bump sat all by itself, forlorn, woebegone.

At its top...I couldn't believe how ugly it was! Way up here somebody had stuck a meteorological station of stone. It was boarded up, plates of corrugated metal where windows must have been. Dotting the yard about the building were cement foundations for iron-framed wind-towers, long collapsed to the ground. Everything had been abandoned. All junk was still in place. L-beams, two inches wide and perforated all along their length by quarter-inch holes, were sticking straight towards the sky, then flopping over like wilted vines. A hilltop destroyed. But it, too, seemed to have its place, atop Olympos. I decided to sit, to try to draw it. It wasn't easy. The rusted litter was nothing if not depressing. My bloody hands were getting too damned cold even to hold a flipping pencil.

Why couldn't they have carted this rubbish away? I shoved the sketchbook back in the pack and began to pace. I wasn't getting anywhere...up here! I wasn't solving a sodding question ...about my life! If this wasn't the *perfect* place to end up!

There never would be a meaning...to why the site had not been cleared. Wind certainly wasn't about to give away the answer.

The rock shack was locked tight. A plaque fixed above its metal door coldly said that it once had been a weather station. What was the point? *Olympian Weather*...I already knew! All predictions could only forecast *change*!

The place reeked of celestial redundancy. It seemed to speak for garbage in the skies. It set the scene for all the crap being left upon the craters of the Moon. The place was so sickening it was pushing me away. I just wanted to go...

Where?

Not where I *should* be going?

Doing something strange?

Looking for what was taboo?

Olympos held some tawny secret someplace, on this height.

I hadn't seen it yet, though.

I hadn't smelt its aura of The Truth.

But I'd be damned if I was going to give up now.

I'd find it! I'd find it! I'd *find* that something...to-day!

Instead of backtracking towards Skólio, instead of rushing to the rendezvous at Skála, instead of letting the Swiss know anything at all...I turned the cheek...and went the other way!

I began to race down a slight slope, northwards, directly for the Comedy Bowl. The snow was looking inviting, and I was beginning to slide. It was like skiing. I was happy inside. Let them *all* worry! Let them all *wonder*...if I'm dead...or if...I'm alive! But deep within my heart...I knew that the choice I was making...was the *wrong* choice. The *unknown* way...was the *stupid* man's way. Or...*was* it? Had any True Knowledge been gleaned...ever...by those walking *charted* ground? Onwards I plodded...*knowing* full well I was getting *lost*!

25th March – National Day – 6.25 AM

"We don't have much time. Can you shave and wash as quickly as possible, Mister Hefferon? Then we'll have a few minutes for breakfast before you have to be delivered to the Stadium," said the young recruit by the Jeep, who seemed quite a decent chap. He was smiling, then whistling some bouzouki tune.

"May I look?" Ada asked him. "It's been ages since I've been inside this house. It's too bad they've let it go to seed."

"Please hurry. I'll be waiting in the Jeep."

Ada followed Ivor inside. He was starting to lather his face with a bar of soap, using the mirror that had been in the bedroom. It was the first time she'd seen him for six long days.

"Since Carnevale Sunday," she began, entranced at viewing him nude to the waist and shaving, "I've been thinking about you... continually..."

Ivor wiped his soapy mouth to be able to speak: "And I you. I've really missed you. I've been thinking about you constantly. You've been the only pleasant thought I've been having lately."

"Has it been that bad for you?"

"That Captain you just saw—he just was pointing his pistol at my head when you two arrived."

"Oh Ivor!" She ran to him and clutched the Athlete from behind and kissed his bare back.

"It's over. I think I'm safe now."

"But Theatrínos isn't."

"That has me terribly worried."

"Ivor—they might *torture* him! I'm petrified! Do you know what he told Major Movóros?"

"I can't imagine."

"In front of all his troops that crazy kid had the guts to tell the Major that *both* of them were the sons of *Ouranós!*"

"*You* were there—and he said *that?*"

"No—I mean—the Corporal outside was just told that—on his walkie-talkie. It was Movóros himself. I was being taken to the Stadium. But because Theatrínos was so stupid to make up such a lie..."

"Lie? Ada—don't you *know?*"

"Know? What're you saying?"

"The chap *is* the General's son! He told Rembetikós and me at Piraeus. I thought you knew."

"I didn't know...my God! No wonder...Movóros got so upset."

"Movóros didn't know, either, as far as I can gather. Theatrínos is *certain* the Major knew nothing."

"Then they'll torture him for *sure* now! Oh God..."

"Ada listen!"

"This whole thing is a double-cross."

"But we *have* to participate."

"No—I refuse. This is a set-up, don't you see? You don't *know* the Greeks. They'll get us *all*—before noon."

"Ada—I've got to do *something*—to save the Games!"

"What *can* you possibly do now?" Ada said as loudly as she could, without raising her voice above a resonant whisper.

"Hurry up, you two!" shouted the Corporal.

"We're coming," Ada replied.

"Look, Ada," Ivor continued in a soft voice, "if you *don't* go along with the Ceremony, then they *will* know something's up. Even though they do suspect something—as that Captain admitted to me just a few minutes ago—they've *no* hard evidence to prove a thing."

"What about those photographs taken by Dora Cain?"

"I told him that the one with Theatrínos on my lap was just a joke he and I were playing on Cain. I said it was the first time we'd met."

"And the Captain believed *that*? Oh this's going to explode, Ivor, this's going to explode! They *will* get it out of Theatrínos, Ivor, I *know* they will. Just you watch!"

"Please hurry!" shouted the person outside.

"Coming," Ada yelled and stept to the porch.

A minute later Ivor was in the back seat of the Jeep. His small sportsbag, with his running gear and speech he was to read in the Ceremony, was beside him. He unzipped the bag and found the single piece of paper on top of the clothing.

"Corporal Drómos?" a voice asked over the walkie-talkie.

"Corporal Drómos, I read you, Sir."

"State your position."

"En route to the Stroúka, Sir."

"Just pick up the food, then proceed straight to the Stadium."

"Aye aye, Sir."

Ivor began looking over the dreadful speech that Thýella had composed. It read:

> I am an Athlete. I have competed as an Amateur in organized sporting competitions, in many places around the world. It always was my greatest dream to compete in an Olympic Games. I did that, and the event in which I competed I won. I never cheated. I never took drugs. I never did anything against the Olympic Charter. I always competed fairly. And I'm proud to say that my record is clean.
> *(pause)*
> Recently I heard about the good work being done by the Mount Olympos Olympic Nation Organizing Committee. I decided to meet these people for myself, so I came to Athens, in February, after having been employed by the Lake Placid Olympic Organizing Committee in America. I found the Olympos Organizing Committee to be composed of forthright individuals, whose dedication to Olympism cannot be denied. I was very impressed by their noble intentions—and offered them my services. The Organizing Committee made me a Member of the team, and now I'm proud to have been named their Keeper Of The Olympian Ideal.
> *(pause)*

So—I'm working with them, and have been enjoying the experience immensely. For an Olympic Gold Medallist to work on the inside, with the group who are creating the new Olympic Nation, is indeed a big responsibility. But I shall serve the MOON-OC with all of the Idealism with which I have competed for the Olympic Gold—because I believe in what they are doing!

The Jeep came to a halt before The Sheep Shed. Ivor felt that he was going to puke. The Corporal entered the milkbar and as he did so Hefferon handed Ada the speech. "Read it and weep," he said.

Presently, the Corporal returned to the wheel, with three cappuccino-style coffees to take away, and a sack filled with luscious pastries. Ivor held the food as the woman read the horrid speech. As the Jeep was being flagged past the Hotel Xénia, and was dashing down the road towards the ruins, Ada was handing the typed words back. She didn't know what to say. The whole thing was just a nightmare.

26th April – Wednesday – 2.35 PM

Fog was rolling in. As I was trying to aim due north, to hit the path that must invariably lead down to the Refuge Hut, fog was starting to roll in. I felt myself beginning to panic. No—I mustn't let that happen. It's my own fault—I must try to keep my cool. In no way was I going to allow myself to panic—or—to turn back? There still was time? No!

This was the course you've charted, I said! There is no turning back.

But you're getting lost—and it's getting late!

The two Swiss—think how *they'll* feel. Maybe it will worry them so much they might even have heart-attacks?

It would never happen.

They'd *have* to realise I'd already left. They'd *have* to!

I was in the right direction—I know I was. Skála was east—no west—of the Hut. I had gone to Saint Anthony. Anthony was at a right angle to Skála. Therefore Anthony was due *south* of the Hut. So...if I just headed due *north*...

Tautology.

If the Sun was heading west...and I was going *this* way...yes... *this* was north. It *had* to be...

The axiom of the theorem...and it's solved! Skála, Skólio, Sokrates, Anthony...oh they were all just *names*...

The formula?

Where's the bloody path...I heard some little voice asking?

Antónios wasn't *that* far south...or...was it?

Never fear...the path will be just around the very next corner.

There were no corners. It was all planes of curves. All was liquid algebra—and I'd always hated maths. All was trigonometry—which I long ago forgot from school.

491

Each step deeper, down the Vale, supposedly was leading to the warmth of the Hut, now my Home Sweet Home? Each step was one more exercise in calculus. But my equation was utterly refusing to check.

"Cursèd arithmetic!" I shouted aloud.

The human brain...usually...can have a sense of direction?

I stood. I breathed wearily. I just stood. Let's not go anywhere... hastily. Here we were...at the edge of another Abyss...approaching the timber line at least. Things again were starting to look *green*?

"How could I be so far *off*?" I sighed.

Fear was working its way *outside*.

I stood. *Let* it work outside.

I was talking out loud.

"It's...frightening. If fog rolls really heavily...I can be gobbled up...with no means of rescue till full sunshine...whenever *that* might be."

I clenched my lips. "Leave it to The Gods to place obstruction! Those who seek too much too soon...have to expect impediments in the pathway?"

What theosophical nonsense!

I pulled out the poem Theatrínos had given me in Athens. Why did I want to see *that*...of all damned things right now?

And towards the Stars
Upwards from the brine,
Olympos—slowly woke and left
Its womb within the Deep,
For greater things, for purposes divine...

Well—show me Divinity now! Where *were* those goddamned Gods—off on some windswept perch—tittering?

There—ahead—look—my voice inside was saying.

Ahead—there—as the fog had broken an instant—straight ahead—no—a bit off to the left—reared Mýtikas, Olympos's highest peak. Aim straight for it. Go on! The path was certainly over *there*!

No?

Why was I...succumbing to this fatal urge?

Why was I...giving in?

Why was I...letting myself...get lost?

No!

"That's not true—that's not true!" I was shouting. "It's only just *happening*...somehow!"

The Abyss...before my eyes...though tinged...with forest green....Hue Of Life...was so steep a drop...as to beckon but a fool...

Race onwards, it challenged?

Onwards I raced!

25th March – National Day – 7.00 AM

Trumpets were sounding. The show was beginning. The ruins were jumping to life. The Áltis of Olympia was resurrecting, right before everyone's eyes.

The Chief Priestess of the Goddess Hera had successfully ignited the Sacred Flame, from the rays of the Sun, which had reflected off the concave metal bowl that was placed near the Doric ruins, of the Temple of the Queen Of The Gods. The Priestess, and her five Female Attendants, had just completed their procession, from Temple to their Tent. The Flame now was patiently waiting, safely encased in its Votive Urn. Soon, it would be doing its duty, and would be igniting the Olympic Torch.

Three sets of Fanfare Trumpets had been placed at various locations. The first four Trumpeters were by the Kiosk Gate. These were echoed, through the pines, by four other instruments, alongside the Temple of Hera, above the foundation of the Great Goddess's shrine, and where Votive Treasuries used to stand. The last set of Trumpets echoed from a high platform especially constructed, at the far end of the Stadium on the colossal stage.

And just now, the first Trumpeters were beginning to sound, and the two echoes were resounding with notes, a whole-tone higher each time, sending nervous rooks leaping from stalwart evergreens.

It was exactly seven o'clock. The Press now were piling out of Army transport lorries that had just brought the thousand from the Hotel Amalía. To Reporters and Photographers, the incident with the Demonstrators had been like a potent cup of coffee, nothing out of the usual for them, just a good way to wake them up, a morning greeting. They'd been talking of nothing else all the way through the village, but now that they were entering the Sacred Olympian Precincts, their thoughts were quickly transferring to the Deed Ceremony ahead. Whatever Theatrínos had done was now behind them, filed away in copious notes and properly recorded on costly film.

It had been a busy night for the Communications Centre in the Amalía. Of course, the big story was that the General, who had conceived the idea for the Olympic Nation for Mount Olympos, had told the President of his country that he would quit the military if the President willed it. This was the morning's "wake-up", for Athens especially.

But the Drama was only beginning. Fanfares were making sure that everybody's adrenalin was flowing. Nobody now seemed to care *what* had happened to the Pop Singer. Only Major Movóros was concerned. Still at the Amalía, he I was cursing his lover, Captain Míkis Sostópoulos, because Theatrínos had been summoned personally by the Head of State. Reciprocating his Major's anxiety over the fear that perhaps the President of Greece *did* know, after all, more than he

493

should know about the real reasons behind the MOON-OC and to-day's Deed Ceremony, the Major's belovèd Captain was not about to tell Movóros that he had just been masturbating while holding a gun to *anybody's* head! There were enough problems already. Each of them simply glowered at the other, relishing the private thrill that their torrid sex-life was just temporarily placed on hold. Movóros then turned his attention to the closed circuit televisions, that were monitoring events from the ruins. The Major yelled to a Technician: "Give me Camera-3."

Camera-3 was showing the whole length of the temple-city, along the flag-draped Grand Procession route, from the ridge over-looking the Ancient Stadium. Streams of Reporters and Photographers were being joined now, at the Philippeíon, by people looking like penguins.

"Musicians," snarled the Major.

"Symphony and Chorus of Athens, Sir," said the Technician, who had been watching them coming in. "They passed the Academy checkpoint fifteen minutes ago."

The Major stared morosely, as scores of Singers and professional Musicians were carrying instruments and sheet-music beneath the pines. "That damned Conductor—he *insisted* we have a concert grand piano—a Steinway—ready and tuned! Imagine—a goddamned concert grand piano—so he could show off his skinny little tinkly hands!"

It was a long walk for four Bass Viols and two Tympanists especially, but everybody was helping one another and nobody seemed to mind.

"Give me Camera-5."

"Temple of Zeus, Sir. Nobody's there yet."

"Have the doves arrived?"

"Yessir, last night, Sir. They're in place."

"I want to see. Camera-1."

Camera-1, atop the Communications Control Tower, at the back of the stage, was directly behind the huge video screen. The lens was pointed at the once-vaulted Crypt that was admitting the throng to the Stadium.

"Tell them to show me those goddamned birds!" growled the Major.

The Technician buzzed the Tower: "Amalía HQ here, at the Major's request. Do you read me?"

"Hurry up!" snapt Movóros.

"Pronto! Do you read me?"

"Yessir! What does the Major *want*, Sir?"

"Show the *doves* onscreen!"

"Aye aye, Sir!"

The video image went fuzzy as Camera-1 swivelled and changed lens for a close-up of the catwalk directly behind the huge video screen,

It soon came into focus and showed ten soldiers each seated behind a cage that contained one hundred white doves apiece.

"Are the men absolutely ready?" Movóros asked.

"Are the men absolutely ready, Sir?" asked the Technician. Camera-1 queried the commander of the doves and the response was affirmative. "They don't have to free them until eleven o'clock, Sir," stated the Technician in reply to Camera-1's reminder.

"Good," the Major smiled. "Just as long as those *goddamned* doves do their job, we're in business."

"Sorry, Sir?" the Technician asked.

"Nothing," the Major replied. "Try the *other* Cameras."

"Camera-2, behind the Press, functioning, Sir. Camera-4, behind the MOON-OC, functioning, Sir. Camera-6, the Philippeíon, functioning, Sir. Camera-7, the Gymnasium, functioning, Sir."

"Hold that there—get them on the wire."

"Yessir, Camera-7, do you read me, Sir?"

"I read you," was the answer.

"Ask if the Deputy and Priestess have arrived."

"Are the Deputy and Priestess ready, Sir?"

"Affirmative. They're in their Tents, Sir."

"Camera-8," ordered the Major.

"Camera-8, Kiosk Gate, functioning, Sir."

"Camera-9."

"Camera-9, Checkpoint Amalía, functioning, Sir."

"Hold. Looks as if they're quieting down."

"Yessir. Demonstrators are lying in the motorway."

"Good thing that the Ambassadors and Members of the Greek Olympic Committee are entering from the other way...or else the Perpetrators would have been run over by friendly-fire! Camera-10."

"Camera-10, Checkpoint Academy, functioning, Sir."

"Give me those earphones!" The Major yanked them from the Technician and spoke into the mouthpiece. "Camera-10, do you read me? It's the Major!"

"Yessir—loud and clear."

"Get the Captain to phone me as soon as he can!"

"He's standing right here, Sir."

"Put him on,"

"Captain Benákis, answering, Sir."

"Listen—Benákis—keep that mob *back*. And for The Devil's Sake don't breathe a word to them about anything. *Nothing* to those people about the incident outside the Amalía this morning! *Nothing* about who's arriving! *Nothing* about the Ceremony!" he paused, then carried on. *"Nothing at all! Is that perfectly clear?"*

"Yessir."

"If I hear one *peep* out of that ragged mob—you're court-martialled."

"Yessir."

"Put Camera-10 back on." The Major handed his Technician the headphones, as the Captain did the same. "Now put Camera-8 back on and keep it on."

"Yessir," the Technician replied.

The Major was silent for a minute, watching the last of the Reporters and Photographers getting down from the transport vehicles. Camera-8 followed them to the Kiosk Gate itself, then through the Weapon Detectors.

"Damn that man, damn him!"

"Sir?" the Technician asked.

"*Your* Head of State—*not* mine!"

"Excuse me, Sir?"

"Idiot—don't you have *eyes?*"

"Yessir."

"Then look what he's done! The President's forbidden *anybody* to go inside the Áltis carrying arms."

"I'm aware, Sir."

"And what do you think?"

"It's not my place to think, Sir."

"Well—I'll think *for* you! Your Head of State has forbidden *any* weapons inside the Áltis, or anywhere *near* the Deed Ceremony, because that's ancient Olympic tradition! What do you think of *that?*"

"Sir—that *is* ancient tradition."

"And he's enforcing it—to the letter! The bastard wouldn't even agree to this Ceremony to-day, if a single person, civilian or military, were armed."

"I know, Sir."

"Well—we were *only* trying to protect him!"

"I know, Sir."

"He's had his Security Corps inside the Stadium, since five o'clock, going round every single pipe of scaffolding with bomb-dogs."

"I imagine he has, Sir."

"And his *own* Security Corps are going to be guarding him!"

"I imagine they are, Sir."

"You imagine too much, Boy. I *like* you. You're sharp!" the Major said in a friendly tone, and slung his arm over the Technician's shoulders.

Míkis, who had been standing by silently all the while, flushed hot with sudden jealousy. But the Major turned and stared at his best Captain, deeply in the eyes, and smiled lewdly, causing Míkis to lick his lips, which were knife-dry.

It was half past seven, and local people were beginning to be admitted into the Áltis. Everybody was being searched, then told to pass through Weapon Detectors exactly as one sees at airports. The public were

496

thrilled that their entrance into the Sacred Precincts was being greeted by Fanfares in three different places.

Inside the walled enclosure of the Gymnasium, where the best Olympic Athletes of the ancient world used to train for competition, two Tents, khaki green, had been erected, one for men, one for women. Before the Tent For Men were standing seven of Olympia's handsomest boys, all in late teens. They were dressed in white linen ancient costumes, high kilt-type wraps about their loins and a drape over their right shoulders. About their heads were olive wreaths; sandals were on their feet. They could not be seen by the crowd. Nor, could the five lovely girls before the other Tent, the most beautiful the village could boast. Their flowing gowns went down to their feet, over both shoulders, and were sleeveless. They were high-waisted, in classical style. All girls were wearing their hair up, decorated with olive wreaths. The dozen young people represented suppliants for the Twelve Principal Ancient Olympian Deities. Then out of the Tent For Men stept Ivor Hefferon. Boys gasped and girls stared incredulously.

The Olympic Gold Medallist was wearing just a skimpy loincloth of woven gold cloth. His sandals were golden, as well as the straps that wrapt up his legs to the knees. Around his head a band was tied, likewise of woven gold. Against his blond hair it looked stunning. In his hand was the cursèd speech. He stood alone, looking at it, oblivious to all the tender eyes directed at his groin.

Within moments, out of the Tent For Women stept Ada, and the sight took Ivor's breath away. All of her attendants clapped. "Brava," her girls began cheering. The young people had worked with her before, just a few weeks ago, for kindling of the Sacred Flame for the Lake Placid Winter Games, and had not forgotten how impressive the Athenian Actress always appeared.

This morning, though, Ada emerged from her Tent looking sombre indeed, as if she were about to dramatise Medea, or even the wicked Elektra. Her girls began whispering, and even her boys were startled. She was wearing her hair *down*.

Ivor went up to her, concerned. She wouldn't let him touch her. She was now in character for her rôle. "Your eyes..." he said, "...your make-up..."

She said nothing, just stared at him comprehendingly. Then, she took his hand and kissed it, and brought it to her breast. Her heart was racing, Ivor could hardly believe the transformation. By skilful application of make-up, this indeed was the Chief Priestess of Hera, reborn, but for a blood-fest, not for a mere Deed Ceremony. "All you Girls—into my Tent this minute—hurry—blacken your eyes and lips!" The girls did as told, in order to obey their Priestess, whose eyeshadow and lipstick were dark as Egyptian kohl. She opened the flap of her Tent, and ordered: "Let down your hair: You're in mourning!"

Suddenly, between the two Tents strode Thýella, looking

inordinately menacing. She was alone, and carrying a small velvet jewelry case. Dripping in gold inset with lapis-lazuli, mimicking some oriental archaeological find, the nasty woman had her hiccups under control. She could have stood up against all the terrors of Hades—one could tell just by a single glance. Wearing a see-through peacock-blue chiffon dress, lightly patterned with an antique key-motif in shimmering gold-dust, she could have been some wicked færy trying to swindle her way into an innocent princess's heart. Staring for an instant, at all the crotches of the teenage boys, she then turned her ire upon her Deputy. Licking her lips, she slowly advanced for the prey. Standing a foot away from his body, she slowly reached out her hand and caressed his bulging codpiece, right in front of everybody. At that instant, Ada opened her Tent flap, but swiftly closed it again. Ivor didn't move a single inch. He just stared into the bitch's eyes.

"We...like what you've got...to show the people," Thýella began. "It's apparent why Míkis found you...such a delight...to protect." Finally, she took her hand off the Athlete's balls, then said: "How do you like our beaten gold? It's the Rape of Europa."

"How appropriate," Ivor remarked.

"We thought you would concur," she replied. The jewelry was large and quite gaudy. The lapis-lazuli was inlaid, as if the bull and the woman being carried away were mosaics on the floor of some ancient bordello. Then she frowned and said: "Where's the Priestess?"

"Still inside."

"Call her out."

Ivor went to the flap and said: "Madame would have a word with you."

"Tell her that *we* shall be seen inside *here!*" Ada shouted, mocking the woman's incessant use of the Royal We, in a voice that the Athlete had never heard before. He recoiled.

Thýella did not need to hear *that* twice. She strode into the Tent unannounced, then gasped: "What in The Name Of Hell are you *doing?*"

The conversation could be heard outside by one and all. The young men listened attentively.

"Get that *slop* off your faces this instant!"

"Leave every drop *on*, Girls! Don't you *dare* budge!"

"We say: *Remove* it! "

"Who's the Chief Priestess—you—or I?"

"You have *no* right to parade into that Stadium—looking as if you're fit for burying Agamemnon! You'll *ruin* our Deed Ceremony! Put that hair back *up*—this very *instant!*"

"Get *out* of this Tent, Thýella, before I scratch your horrid *eyes* out! *I* am the Priestess—chosen so and signed by *writ*—from Professor Rembetikós—to *remain* so, until my time *expires*—and neither you nor *anybody* can dictate a single thing to me! Is that absolutely *clear?*"

"No!"

498

Then Ada pounced. Like a lioness, with one quick movement of her long-nailed paw, she clawed the woman's neck. Blood started spurting onto her expensive dress! "Now get your rotten carcass *out* of here—before I tear that sickening meat right off your measly bones and *toss* them to the mangiest dogs of Greece! Out!" she snapt and lunged for the woman one last time. The Chief of Protocol began uncontrollable hiccuping, worse than the night before. She began screaming: "Don't you *dare* try entering that Stadium with that Torch!" and Thýella pointed to a table that displayed both the Votive Urn holding the just-lit Sacred Flame and the 18-karat gold Torch used for the previous Summer Games, the very competitions in which Ivor won his Gold Medal for the Men's 1500 Metre Race.

"You can't *stop* me!"

"Oh no?"

"You wouldn't *dare*!"

"Oh—*wouldn't* we?" then she grabbed the Torch in an instant and held it by one hand like a club. "One step nearer, Ada, and this *Torch* of yours will split your pretty little head."

The Five girls were in total shock—looking to their Priestess for direction. Bolstered by her office, Ada stept backwards but said with true pride: "*Take* the Torch. Go ahead. I wasn't planning on lighting it anyhow. But if I had...I would have set fire to *you*...by igniting your ugly blonde wig!"

Thýella burst out, in vicious humour, holding her gashed neck, trying to staunch blood. Ada, inside, was laughing horribly. In the foul protagonist's left hand were the velvet box and Olympic Torch. She took her spite out on Ivor: "What in Hell have *you* got?"

"My speech you wrote," he replied.

"Give us that!" she snatched the speech and used it to suck up blood. Her hiccuping was ghastly. "There's another at the Podium— where you're to speak—use that." She hiccuped. "And tell that *feline*, who's escorting our Head of State..."

"Tell this feline *what*?" hollered Ada, now showing herself menacingly, like some monster, talons curved and upraised on arms held way above her head, ready to strike again. "Good for you! *Bleed!* And I hope you hiccup yourself to *death!*"

"You're going to have *your* moment of suffering...and you're going to have it *soon!*" Thýella screamed at Ada in warning, then vented her wrath on her aide: "Hefferon—*take* this goddamned thing," and she handed Ivor the velvet box. "It's your Golden Wreath. Carry it aloft into the Stadium, as you're running." Then, as hiccuping and coagulating blood began making her feel as if she might faint, she pulled her dæmonic Self together, and rushed away with the Torch to scrounge some Medical aid.

26th April – Wednesday – 3.00 PM

Where was Skála? Miles away? I now was feel horribly guilty for not honouring my pledge to be where I should have been. And where I was presently...the strain was becoming too much. Already, down in the tundra land, or lower, there now were sharp herbal bushes everywhere, springing from living rock, like leafy fountains of joy, spiked with needle-sharp thorns that drew blood at the merest touch. This was a landscape from a psychotic's dream. If Darker Deities of pre-Christian days ever ran amok, this was the spot they must have called home. I now was on top of their faultiest towers, glancing downwards, telling myself: In no way am I ever going to make it down *that*!

This was no geologic formation. Only some super-powered cognisant arm could have stacked such cut stone to this gruesome height. What it was, in fact, was a monstrous *wall*, constructed of hundred-ton blocks of rock. The wall was probably assembled on the alluvial plain, beside the sea, then squashed together and carried, by a Titan, in one piece, like children haul a queue of dominoes, up the Vale, then slammed against the mountainslope, as some toy for mammoth giantlings.

Everything was razor-edged, right-angled, dropped-down, what looked like more than a mile. If I had any sense, I never would have been in this No Man's Land in the first place. But then...I *didn't* have any sense...

I pulled out that damned poem again, as if it were some holy relic, or at least some prayer card. I looked at it for some tiny rune, some clue, some hidden message, some abracadabra that would allow me to rub its lines and produce a genie *to get me out of here*! I was ready to piss my pants, I was so fucking scared.

And there it sat, mute, one piece of rock...
Until its limestone bulk was stirred to be,
Whence, Time itself roused the saline stone,

"Help me!" I shouted to no one, to the atmosphere. Fog again had gone into hiding, at least for the time being.

"Down...just get *down* this," I commanded, aloud.

Down...each foot began to search for a ledge, on which to balance. Hands were scraping rock, root, clump, as legs were bumping, down this heinous wall.

"Yes—*wall*!" I yelled at the maniacal cyclopean line of defence, running upslope eighty degrees...

Eighty degrees!

"Eighty degrees..."

I murmured. But I continued going downslope, one foot at a time, my stomach doing flip-flops, my nerves shattering like breaking glass goblets dropping onto polished marble floors. I was feeling like an escapee from a lunatic asylum, hurling my ingrate body down, headlong into the Law's certain paws.

25ᵗʰ March – National Day – 8.00 AM

Theatrínos was being admitted into the presence of the President of the Republic of Greece. The guard departed and left the two alone, in the magnificence of sculptures from the pediments of the ancient Temple of Zeus. The young Singer was approaching, yet looking quite embarrassed. He was still in his black leather cycling suit. "Excuse my appearance, Sir, but I just arrived on my Harley and..."

"No need to apologise. Won't you please sit?"

The two men sat round a small breakfast table already set. A telephone was next to a dish with croissants. A television was on a stand not far away. "Are you hungry?" the Head of State asked, in order to help the youth relax.

"I think so. I'm more nervous than anything," the Singer admitted. "Those attack-dogs have given me an ulcer."

"You're one brave young man."

"Thank you."

"Pour yourself some coffee."

"Am I in deep trouble, Sir?"

"Not at all."

"But..."

"This whole drama is in the Head of State's hands."

"Movóros arrested me."

"You're a free man. For your own sake, Son, we request you remain inside this room, with The Gods' protection," and the President gestured to the heroic-sized statues watching their every move, "until the dénouement has occurred."

"Dénouement?"

"You recall your meeting this past Monday?"

"At the British Embassy?"

"Correct. Professor Rembetikós, your good friend as well as mine, mentioned that certain investigations were taking place. My Chief of Staff was able to find out a few interesting facts indeed—about what's supposed to be taking place in Athens this very day."

"Excuse me, Sir. I don't quite follow you."

"At three o'clock this morning I ordered the arrest of five of General Ouranós's friends. Three of them are Generals, and two of them Colonels. As you're aware, I was in exile during the Junta, because of my stand Left of Centre, so it's only natural that certain Rightists try to dissuade me from office."

"You mean..."

"Yes," the President said in such a way as to preclude any more queries. "I am not at liberty to discuss this further at this moment. My Prime Minister and Chief of Staff are expected to be telephoning me shortly."

"Should I leave, Sir?"

"Under no circumstances. Now relax—it's all under control. When I make my public statement, around eleven o'clock, you'll watch it on this television. So—tell me about yourself. I'd enjoy hearing your story. It'll shake some lack of sleep from my wearied mind."

Thýella, meanwhile, was having her wound dressed. She was given a sedative for nerves and some morphine for a torrid migraine headache that had developed. With drugs combining potency with what aggressive humours normally coursed betwixt her vituperative veins, the Chief of Protocol was almost feeling gay. The thought that things were developing well, both in Olympia and in Athens, eased her anxieties aroused by the horrid Priestess of Hera, whom she was plotting to murder in some fiendish way.

As the Chief of Protocol was sitting inside the Red Cross Tent, fanning herself and awaiting the right moment to make her next appearance, in walked her husband, looking upset. Seeing that nobody was being treated except his wife, he ordered the Tent cleared of Medics.

"Out—return in ten minutes—and don't you dare let me catch a single one of you hovering outside this Tent!" Then he turned on his wife. "What in Hell are you up to now? One of your *hypochondria* stunts again?"

"But Darling—we had another *hiccup* attack and then," she decided to lie, what she did best, "then...we were calling on the Priestess when we were...we were *stung*...by some horrid wasp...here...look...on our neck! It was awful. We were so mortified. We have to go into the Stadium wearing this bandage."

"You must have been *provoking* the damned wasp!"

"Don't start!" She gripped her head. "And please leave us be! You *mustn't* upset us anymore than we've already been. Do you *want* us to hiccup...inside the Stadium?"

"I don't care if you shit in your own *ear*! You embarrassed me for a lifetime...last night!"

"What about *you*? Did you *once* breathe a word of your lousy little plot to abrogate your Army responsibilities...to *us*? Don't you appreciate all we've been *doing* for you—these past two miserable years? Don't you understand what this damned Olympic Nation idea of yours has been *putting* us through? Don't you have *any* feelings for *our* sacrifice at all?"

"None whatsoever."

"You're *cruel*."

"You're not?"

"We've been doing every single *rotten* thing you've *wanted*—up

502

till now! But listen to us—you're *not* going to be in complete control—when you become Prime Minister! *We* are!"

"Give me a break!"

"Did *we* tell our son that *your* bastard child—scum of this Earth they call Theatrínos—was the brother of Movóros and Sitherás? No—we kept our fat mouth shut on *that* one—just like *you* wanted us to do. Then to-day—all Hell breaks loose—that little punk blurts it out himself—right in Movóros's face. So what're *you* doing, Affedikó, blaming *us*, for *that* one? *Are* you?"

"If you'll quit your *rancour* for just one single second, I have some *urgent* news to tell you."

"What?"

"I suspect the plot's going *badly* in Athens."

"How can it? It can't possibly fail—are you crazy? It's fool-proof!"

"I have my doubts."

"You ball-less nitwit—if the bollocks of this family weren't between *our* legs, you'd be wearing them on your curly-locked head, and calling them your dunce-cap!"

"*Listen* to me!"

"*You* listen. We've got a scheme so well set up that even Zeus himself, if he were to rise from these ruins this very minute, couldn't defeat it! Look—all Greece's glued to televisions at this moment. The rest of the lackies are lined up in front of Parliament! The most important man in Athens is stuck out here with *us*. What *can* he do—to prevent a little change or two in the capital? And when it's all *over*—the people themselves won't even know what in Hell's *hit* them! We'll get rid of the Government *here*, in one fell swoop, and nobody will *ever* know the difference. We'll return to Athens victorious. Then we'll *really* start...to *rule!*"

"I telephoned The Five," Ouranós admitted, "just this morning, before I came here."

"So?"

"I spoke with Barbándis, Boukálas, Peripóthytos, Zonáris, and Andrikákis."

"We *know* their damned names! *So?*"

"They sounded strange."

"So do *you*—right now! By the way—what *did* The Five think of your half-arsed idea to quit the military, should the President think it wise?"

"As good politicians, *all* of them thought that it was a brilliant diversionary tactic."

"So you *did* get through to them?"

"Yes."

"Well—then? What's your *problem?*"

"I don't know. Something's wrong, Thýella!"

"No shit! It's *your* mind. Don't you have the *guts* to carry this out?"

"Of course."

"Don't you look *forward* to being Prime Minister? Isn't that what you've always wanted?"

"Of course."

"Then—live *up* to that virtuous dream! You know damned well that this country's no good, that the path she's been following *sucks!* You know damned well that the Junta *has* to return!"

"Of course. But...just in case...you *know* what we've agreed to do...if this thing fails."

"*You* agreed. *We* never did."

"Just be prepared."

"Anything more...you'd like to say?"

"I also spoke with Theotókis."

"And?"

"The Chief of Staff said everything's ready—everybody's going to be at the National Day Parade, as planned, ready for the *coup.*"

"Grand!"

"But..."

"But what, Bone Head, what? If the man who's going to be our President gives you his assurance, that all is well in Athens, then damn you, you'd better learn *quick* how to shape up...you'd better learn *quick* about pecking order...you'd better learn *quick* about flow of responsibility and acceptance of same...because...if you *don't*, then *he'll* soon be doing away with *you!*"

The pair of conspirators stared at each other, morbidly, then a vile smile stretched the skin of their faces. The woman took the man's cheeks in her hands, pinched his whiskers, then set her red lips upon his brown ones, with a vigorous bæstial kiss.

26th April – Wednesday – 3.30 PM

Here was the first true feat of outright danger. I closed my eyes, and prayed. I saw Ada's face, illuminated by candlelight, before her ikon of the Archangel Michael. "I *must* cross this snow-run," I said, then crossed myself three times, Greek fashion.

The wall had produced a dead-end. It hadn't gone away. In fact, the building blocks of the colossal child were even more gigantic than before. I was trapt now, and knew it in my bones. Directly to my right, a rectangular solid of limestone jigged up so flat and so high, that even with suction cups for hands I never would have been able to scale it in my life. And this was going *downslope!* It didn't make any sense. At right angles to this, was my only way out...crossing one of those glacier-like slicks which dove down so precipitously for some unseen valley floor.

504

I felt faint. The deathly smell of snow was making me nauseous. I leant up against the limestone to my right, and shut my eyes. All I could see were nightmare visions of my body falling...crashing. Opening my eyes...I realised that there was no alternative. Either I lean against this limestone, and die, or cross this eighty degree slope of snow and...maybe live?

"I must—there's no other way," I sighed. "Carry on. That's the boy."

The snow's width was fifty foot or more...fifty *more* foot of experience in doing such a thing as ever I had.

"Nothing to back me up..."

How *could* one get across it...angled as lethally as it was?"

"One slip...that's it?"

Wonder if snow could give way, in the middle? Maybe it would hold, till the very end?

I breathed in deeply.

"Well—take your heart in your mit and *do* it!"

One first step...then...push shove shove shove into snow. Make your own little shelf.

Balance.

Careful.

Clutch the upslope deeply...by digging right into the ice with bare left hand. That's it. Move slowly. Don't throw the weight on your back. Watch the pack. Don't let it swing.

Gradually...

Gradually...

Move the next foot.

That's good.

Stamp down again again again...there...you're doing it. Just a few more.

Don't look down.

Only across.

There're rocks and grass across. You'll *get* there.

You'll get *there*.

You must!

Fucking nightmare!

Hail Mary, full of Grace...The Lord is with thee...

"I'm going to weep..."

It took forever, but snow was crossed. I did weep. Once I crossed that horrid drop, my insides felt like jelly. "Dear God...the snow's crossed!" my voice inside rejoiced. But there was no stopping now, There was *more*. There *was* more. *And* there was more. And more *again*. Ever downwards. Ever downwards...without stop.

"Where can I just rest?"

I kept searching, praying there'd be a path somewhere. *More* snows were crossed. *More* walls kept getting in the way. I lost count of how many deadly slicks I crossed—five?

"One's too many for mortals!" I screamed. "Anybody who's sane..."

Bits and snatches of Theatrínos's poem now began haunting me. I'd even have settled for "Edelweiss" again. It wasn't to be. It was just:

> And towards the Stars,
> Upwards from the brine...

There I stood, blocked again. So far down in the dale now, at the timber line, were trees that loomed too large for man to see! And what was this ahead...another glacier?

"I can't...I just can't do it...I don't have the strength anymore!"

It was getting late.

Half past lifetime?

"Where am I?"

Sit, the voice commanded. Just sit. Think it over. Is it worth it? Get your wind.

"You've done it...five? You'll do it...six..."

No!

"You've got to!"

No!

"What're you *going* to do...sit here till you *rot*?"

25ᵗʰ March – National Day – 9.15 AM

By nine o'clock the last of the public had been admitted to the Sacred Enclosure of Olympia's ruins. As soon as the final person had passed through the Weapon Detectors, the Chief of Protocol gathered her wits, frowned in the mirror at the unsightly bandage on her neck, then left the Red Cross Tent. All of the Medics had been so intimidated by her that none dared utter a word.

Slowly, the General's wife was puffing up her slashed pride, and was advancing towards the Kiosk Gate. Her husband was milling about, speaking with no one. As a matter of habit, she assumed a position beside him, but remained mute. It was very difficult for her, appearing acquiescent. But in public, she could pull off anything, given the proper motivation.

Only cicalas and crows were talking. Across the road, a bit to the right, the Mound of Father Time was bustling with black-feathered beings. It was as if every raven for miles had booked a branch. A few were fighting for seats, of course, but mainly the mob was waiting patiently, cawwing to egg on the show.

506

"Those fowl have *got* to go!" Thýella snapt, just to say something pleasant.

"Never *mind*," Ouranós retorted.

"When *are* the VIPs going to get here?" his wife replied, with no hiding of exasperation.

"When the limousines *are* ready to arrive," retorted the man, mocking her inflection.

"Don't get smart with us!"

"You'd better *man* your post—now!"

Thýella did. The female was glad to leave the male standing there, alone. The General decided to wander through the ruins. He looked like a boy who'd lost his favourite toy. Something noisome was pestering his mind. If he were a monk, one could presume that his thoughts were turning to God. Needless to say, his were not. His never did. His turned to Hades, if he pondered Divinity at all. The General was trying to convince himself that all was faring well, that everyone would do as he had been told, that Athens would soon be in *Ouranós* control. Of course, being Prime Minister was *not* being Head of State. But it was as high a position as he could bargain for. He had to juggle with the Chief of Staff anyways. Greece's highest ranking General was no pushover. Theotókis had *older* scores to settle than did Ouranós. Theotókis had always been slippery—since childhood—that's how the character rose to be Chief of Staff in the first place, an eel that incessantly wriggled quicker than any school of fish. Theotókis had gone along, though, and that was all that mattered. To-day, he'd be pretending to be ill all morning. He'd be complaining about stomach cramps. Recalling their conversation this morning, Ouranós took heart. Of course, The Five sounded nervous, but all of them were quiet gamblers, unlike Theotókis and Ouranós himself, who were reckless. It was only natural that the other conspirators' voices sounded high, that they were under stress. But had the Chief of Staff sounded nervous? No. He was a man. He was a man's man. He knew how to lead. He would make Greece *crawl*...on bended knee. He would be a true delight to serve beneath. Thýella would make *sure*...Theotókis would stay in his place!

As General Ouranós proceeded around the colossal barrels from the Doric pillars of the Temple of Zeus, lying like fallen sequoia logs on the ground, he quickly went through the Athenian scenario in his mind. The Prime Minister and Chief of Staff were officiating at the National Day Parade. On the dais with them would be The Five. The Parade would be starting at half past nine. The mob of Athens would be lining the route, oohing and aahing at the weaponry passing by. Meanwhile, The Five would each have a venue to take. The two Colonels would handle the residences of Prime Minister and President of the Republic. The three Generals would handle Parliament. The Parade would be allowed to pass quietly. The masses would suspect nothing. By the time that the last

507

contingent of troops passed by, the Residences and Parliament would be secure, even as the Parade was passing Parliament. The Prime Minister and Chief of Staff would be watching the televised broadcast from Olympia, on a small screen invisible to the public. The television would be behind the barrier of the dais. Towards eleven o'clock at Olympia, one thousand doves would be released. This was the cue. The Chief of Staff would be complaining that he had to leave the viewing stand, he was going to vomit. Nobody *ever* stood in the way of a man who had to *puke!* Then the Chief would quietly slip into Parliament. And that would be that.

The General laughed to himself, and mounted the ramp to the portico of the Temple of Zeus. Like great Gothic Cathedrals, Temples too had been built to face the east, to catch the first light of day. Atop a barrel from a column the man sat, with his back to the way he just came. He began rolling over in his mind the steps that were to be followed here at Olympia, for removal of the Head of State. Ouranós slipt into a monstrous dream...

"Are you all right?" the Member of the IOC in the Union of Soviet Socialist Republics asked General Ouranós. The man and his wife were the first of the IOC to arrive at the Temple, where all Members were to gather for their entrance into the Stadium.

"You look pale," said the Member's stout wife. She looked like a shotputter.

"It's this heat," volunteered the General, who managed to stand.

"One should think that one could get accustomed," replied the wife.

More Members were ascending the ramp that led to the floor of the ruined shrine to the King of the Gods.

"Is this not *imperial?*" the Muscovite wife asked her husband, who seemed impressed.

"Just think," the Communist replied, "one of the Seven Wonders of the Ancient World was right beneath our very feet."

"Excuse me, please," stated Ouranós, who wanted to speak to an IOC member from Equatorial Africa.

When the General had gone, the Russian wife whispered to her mate: "It won't be long...till we shan't have to deal with *him!*"

"The fool," replied the Communist. "To think that everybody knows but himself."

The Áltis was Fanfare Heaven. It was now nine fifteen. The Symphony Orchestra of Athens began playing Beethoven's *Ninth Symphony*, to be sung by Soloists and Chorus in Greek, and to be co-ordinated perfectly so that the finale would coincide with the entrance of the last Ambassador into the Stadium, who was supposed to be seated by ten eighteen. Their Excellencies now were jamming the motorway beyond the Academy, en route to the Áltis, as were Members of the Greek Olympic Committee.

At the Kiosk Gate, as the welcoming of VIPs was proceeding beautifully, Thýella suddenly took on a glow, heretofore not seen all morning. "Ah—Beethoven," she said sweetly to the IOC Member in the Democratic Republic of Germany. "That was our *personal* choice," she boasted and thought how appropriate, for her schemes, to have everybody listening to *"Alle Menschen werden Brüdern"*, in Greek, just before the International Olympic Committee would be marching into the Stadium to the music of their own "Olympic Hymn".

Exactly at the moment that the Symphony Orchestra commenced the first note of the First Movement, *allegro ma non troppo,* soldiers standing at attention beside every flagpole that ringed the Stadium like a forest of leafless trees suddenly began raising the hundreds of flags of the IOC. The public began cheering wildly, seeing white flags, everywhere, in three hundred and sixty degrees, slowly mounting flagpoles, in time to the music, in perfect sync. But Thýella suddenly froze, with an evil premonition. Her heart actually stopt for a couple seconds, as she realised that, inside the Red Cross Tent, she had left the priceless Torch of gold.

For fifteen minutes more, tension was allowed to build, as the power of the genius of Beethoven began sweeping soldiers and media and public away, until the first of the VIPs began entering the passageway that once had been the vaulted tunnel of stone.

An Announcer, with a deeply resonant voice, began announcing in three languages whom the public would be seeing, in French, English, and Greek, respectively. Thýella had insisted that all be done according to IOC Protocol, and for the Grand Procession especially, everything had to be absolutely precise.

It was nine twenty-nine. The Second Movement of the *Ninth Symphony* began to be played, *molto vivace.* First to enter were the Local Dignitaries, ecclesiastic and lay. Behind the Mayor and local Priest was Pános Mavrolóngos, Administrator of the Academy. Evanthía Selináki, Director of the Museums, also was among this group, and she got a great big hand, both from Press and from Officials. Everybody was finding oneself constantly looking from colossal video screen, for close-ups, to the real thing happening on the field.

At nine thirty-one, Members of the Organizing Committee of the Mount Olympos Olympic Nation were announced, and began the long walk across the Arena. The Chief of Protocol headed this group. Quite a few people began to boo. She paid the hecklers no mind, and strutted with her neck held high, rather proud in fact of her most recent battle scar. Following her were the Directors of Sports, Communications, and Construction, the first and the last with wives. Also in the MOON-OC contingent were various and sundry kin of the Ouranós clan whom most of Greece never got the chance to see, including the General's two elder

509

brothers, mythical monied figures of the Greek marketplace. None of these individuals was publicly announced, but lumped together as "members of the family". It was like seeing the Mafia springing to life. Those of the Press from Greece quickly spread word through the ten rows of Reporters and Photographers that the bald old man was commonly referred to as Kokkálas, meaning Bones, and that he handled the family's *landed* interests, and that the portly gentleman with white beard was nicknamed Captain Fourtoúnas, because he handled the family's *marine* interests. Both men had a gaggle of grown children and wives and all were being photographed intently. Dora Cain was nowhere to be seen. The MOON-OC filled the final three rows behind the place reserved for the Greek Olympic Committee, that is, behind the IOC, but before the final two rows reserved for Local Dignitaries.

Between nine thirty-four and nine thirty-seven Members of the Greek Olympic Committee and their spouses came in, to the great delight of the throng in the grandstands.

At nine thirty-seven, Representatives of the International Sporting Federations and their Guests were announced, and continued until the Second Movement of the Symphony concluded.

Simultaneously, an extra contingent of Security Corps were arriving from Athens by helicopters, landing in the parking lot of the Hotel Amalía. Thýella forbade that the announcer mention anybody by name from here on out, insofar as too much time would be taken and that the IFs, NOCs, Greek Government officials, Ambassadors, and IOC wished anonymity.

At nine forty-two, the largest group of Dignitaries began filing into the Stadium, those representing the world's National Olympic Committees. NOC Members, all four hundred of them, had the whole of the majestic Third Movement of the *Ninth Symphony* for their accompaniment. Given that the Chorus had not yet begun to sing, many considered this Movement the most lovely so far. It was evoking a true feeling of Peace and Intellect combined, as if Beethoven could have written the notes upon this very site, so well did they blend with the bucolic landscape. Many of the farmers listening, who had never witnessed a Symphony Orchestra performing in their lives, had tears in their eyes, especially when the Third Movement was concluding with those plaintive and melancholy chords that tug so at one's heart strings.

The NOCs had been instructed to sit alphabetically, by the proper IOC Protocol used for abbreviating their NOC initials. For example, the NOC of Japan was always abbreviated JPN. Italy was ITA, The Netherlands HOL, Iraq IRQ, Libya LBA, Malaysia MAL, and Malawi MAW. Seeing initials in threes made it all so much simpler to handle. All the first half of the alphabet sat closest to the stage, and the rest furthest from the stage, on either side of the IOC.

Up in her seat, scrutinising everything, Thýella started to whisper to her son: "Do you know what, Movóros?"

"No—what?"

"We lost our *Olympic Directory*. Last week."

"You what?" retorted the Major, who recoiled in horror.

"Imagine...nobody *ever* loses a *Directory!*"

"Nobody dares! Do you think it was stolen?"

"Of course. It's precious...all those classified addresses and telephone numbers."

The Major did not know how to deal with this, so said: "But... how on Earth did you ever co-ordinate this seating plan?"

"Now you see why we have a migraine?"

It was now nine fifty-six. Greek Government Officials were entering the Stadium, during the five minutes and thirty seconds of orchestration of the Final Movement of the Symphony before the Chorus began singing. At the Kiosk Gate, the Head of State had just arrived from the New Museum. He had decided to risk his life, and walk. He knew that nothing at all could occur without his participation. He knew that he held the so-called Deed. He had a smile on his wily face. A platoon of bodyguards surrounded him.

Five minutes and thirty seconds later, the Announcer proceeded to tell the public that the Ambassadors from Athens were entering. This caused a stir. Most of the public had never seen a single one, let alone the whole Ambassadorial Corps put together. Dressed in morning suits, Their Excellencies began walking majestically, as the stirring choral music of Ludwig van Beethoven began, and as a hush washed over the gathered throng. The Ambassadresses were particularly commanding. Their entrances had been staggered, to the second, so that they and their illustrious husbands would take twenty-four minutes and thirty seconds to pass across the Arena and be seated. It was amazing to see, because the people being watched seemed to be giving colour and deeper meaning to the music, and not vice versa. All of them sat to the left of the IOC, and to the right of the last half of the NOC alphabet. The Olympic Hostesses evidently were paying strict attention to handing Their Excellencies their programmes, and in seating them. After the Chorus had been singing *allegro*, with the Soloists joining in, the Tenor began a rousing interpretation of the passage being played *alla marcia*. As soon as the people began hearing that the Orchestra was now performing a stirring march, all of the thousands began clapping along to the strutting beat. Then they resumed listening, as the Chorus was still for the *andante maestoso*. But everybody resumed clapping along with the *allegro energico, sempre ben marcato*. Then, the whole assembly was transported away till the finale, especially by the upper register of the female choristers, who sounded just like angels. As the last Ambassador was being escorted to his chair, the rousing finale of Beethoven's *Ninth Symphony* was exhorting the Grecian air. The crowd was now jumping to its feet, spontaneously. Many people were wiping tears from their cheeks.

511

Even the greatest of classical music connoisseurs find it impossible not to be deeply moved by the time that the Fourth Movement of Beethoven's *Ninth Symphony* is reaching its stupendous climax. Listening to the *chef d'oeuvre* takes a lot out of one, but it grants one even more in return. Even the *resisting* listener cannot but be totally absorbed by the work, which ingests one into its ecstatic message—that Peace *can* reign—that all men *can* be brothers!

The people now were thinking dreamy thoughts. This would be the closest that most of them would ever come to attending an Olympic Games. Then, as the last note of the emotional music was being played, an earthy cheer was leaping forth from everybody's frame. The shout, likely one of the greatest to be heard inside this Stadium, since ancient days, must have made the many ghosts of the shrine stir from their musty hiding place.

Then, as the whole Stadium was trying to recover, the Announcer said solemnly: "Please stand—for the entrance of Members of the International Olympic Committee."

Whilst the whole congregation was standing, the Symphony Orchestra began playing the beautiful melody of the "Olympic Hymn". This Greek musical creation was composed in 1896 for the Games of the First Olympiad, by Spíros Samára, with lyrics by Kóstas Palamás. The Chorus, having sung the Beethoven to perfection, now were in better form than ever, and their voices were raising in exultation.

From ten twenty-four until the next ten minutes were through, Members of the IOC and their Guests began crossing the dusty Arena, towards the reserved seating in the middle of the south flank of the Stadium, directly opposite the Press. The people were watching spellbound, as the privileged Committee that *owned* the Olympics were taking their special places. Again, Thýella had chosen that they adhere to alphabetical Protocol, even though she had the option to request that they enter according to seniority, as they were listed in the *Directory*. But it was easier to deal with the alphabet than with age. Some Members might not like to be recognised as *new*, and others might not like to be recognised as *old*.

The IOC Executive Committee entered next, and then the last to proceed was the President of the IOC, who received much applause as he was crossing the Arena. Everybody was watching this man's every motion. Given that he did not yet sit, neither did the others. The "Olympic Hymn" was just concluding. For a second, the President of the International Olympic Committee glanced sideways, both to the left and to the right. He was hoping that the Head of State's Security Corps were in place.

Then, a hush fell over the multitude. The Announcer said: "Would you please remain standing...for the Procession of the President of the Republic of Greece."

512

All of the thousands now were staring towards the once-covered Crypt. It was precisely ten thirty-four. There was not a single noise to be heard. Then...a chill rippled through the large crowd. The first person to be seen entering the Arena was the Chief Priestess of the Great Goddess. She, whom all the locals knew, and whom everyone had expected to be holding either Torch or Urn, now was holding only one small thing that was gleaming brightly...as her arms were upraised and were pleading for some intervention from the sky. She had streaked her lovely white classical gown with black and crimson paint. Her hair was down in mourning. Her eyes and lips were black. And she only made five short steps into the Stadium, where she halted.

Thýella paled when she noticed that the small object being held aloft was nothing other than the crown of olive leaves, of pure gold, that Ivor Hefferon was supposed to be carrying. Something...was *wrong!*

The Priestess, like a prisoner being taken to the stake, slowly began lowering her gesturing arms and hands and fingertips, as blinding glints from the diadem ricochéd in hundreds of directions. Then, she slowly began lowering her eyes, that were staring straight towards the sky. When her eyes were finally able to be seen...all who were staring were stupefied. She was weeping.

The Priestess did not say one single word...yet. She did not need to. She now was jerking her head upwards and clicking her tongue...the ancient Greek gesture for *no*. Then, she commenced shaking her tresses, left to right...and the long black fibres began swaying.

She started to chant, more like a moan, deep within her throat, as she kept on swaying...then, just when she felt that those watching would have to begin to shout back, the Priestess spun backwards and looked at the five beautiful maidens, who likewise had ruined their gowns with red and black paint.

As if they were hearing music, the Priestess and girls began a foot-pounding dance, outwards into the Arena, at which they constantly were moaning their primitive dirge. To watch them, it was apparent that The Past indeed was alive, because even when the first of the seven paint-stained young men was appearing as escort for the Head of State, not one single person in the throng was daring to clap, or even to raise a cheer. The President, too, was gesturing, but directly to the crowd, to remain absolutely silent.

As the dust-stomping maidens were reaching the centre of the oval, there the Chief Priestess paused, beside a single square block of Parian marble, that had been brought to Olympia especially for this Deed Ceremony. The seven youths, two to each side and one to the fore and two to the aft, were encircling their country's leader. Then, all fourteen beings halted.

They were facing the people, with their backs to the VIPs. All of the youths began to take off their olive wreaths, then all of the maidens were doing the same. The Priestess was stepping before them, and was holding aloft the golden wreath. Then the twelve young people were following suit. The dozen then were turning around, after the Priestess had faced the VIPs. Then the dozen were taking as many steps backwards as need be, so that all thirteen now were in a straight queue, shoulder to shoulder, with right arms raised high. The Priestess, in the middle, now was bowing and was tossing her wreath before the Head of State. Then one youth was doing the same, and one maiden was following suit, until there were twelve olive wreaths and one wreath of gold lying at the feet of the President of Greece.

This eloquent gesture was being interpreted a thousand different ways. As the multitude watching began leaping from their seats and cheering wildly, people in the stands began throwing flowers, coins, worry-beads, scarves, little things that were saying: We are *united* with you.

The Priestess now began kneeling, upon one bended knee, as did her suppliants, in all the innocent beauty of their radiant youth. The Greek National Anthem commenced to be played by the Athens Symphony Orchestra. It was exactly ten forty in the morning. As the President of the Hellenes began to be escorted by the Priestess to his honoured seat, beside the President of the IOC, a fly-past of fifty jets, in perfect formation of the Five Olympic Rings, soared directly overhead. They were arriving especially from Athens, where they just had astonished those viewing the National Day Parade.

As the tumult from the public and the fighter-jet engines slowly began simmering down, the Head of State was shaking hands with various Members of the IOC Executive Committee and their Guests. Then, the President of the Republic was taking his seat. The time was forty-one minutes past ten.

26th April – Wednesday – 4.10 PM

There I stood, blocked again. So far down in the dale now, at the timber line, were trees that loomed too large for Man to see! And what was this ahead... *another* glacier?

"I can't...I just can't do it...I don't have the strength anymore..."
Sit the voice had commanded.
I sat.
I sat and thought it over.
"Is it worth it?"
Get your wind.
"You've done it...six?"
No!
"You've got to?"
No!
"What're you going to do...sit here till you *rot*?"

514

No? Maybe?

"Not one human being's within sight."

That's right stand—stand and look.

"Go on—look—damn you!"

Where?

"What's *that?*"

High—up there—look—look behind you!

Up—high up—a silhouette—of black—was standing—standing out—before a mandorla mad burst of the Sun. The Sun was directly behind something—way up there—something above. The Sun was way up there balanced—and there *was* something—before it—like some sprite—something alive—with four little legs—on four little hooves—on a penny-sized peak. The Sun was *up* there—way up there balanced— stuck atop a pinnacle of stone—atop some natural obelisk—atop something Nelson would stand upon—upon some sodding natural column—of split rock. Divine Sign? Dæmon?

"Staring down—*laughing* likely!"

Something up there was a silhouette—and staring before the Sun—and that *something* up there was *black!*

"Bleeding Beast...Sheep Goat Chamois?"

The silhouette was moving—it had to be alive!

"Why can't *I* leap about like *that*—like *it?*"

The pillar—whatever it was—was part of some Demigod's Fortress, miles above. With the Sun behind it—it was a phantom—with a body-sized halo.

I could barely see what it was—and was squinting—and it was making me awfully mad—awfully scared—scared shitless—though I was squinting. I *kept* squinting—was it *moving?*

"Turrets and towers—all of stone—where in Hell *was* I?"

It moved. What *was* it?

"And The Beast...balanced...and it's deranging me!"

Down—just get *down*—the voice was trying to order.

"Down *where?*"

Oh no—I'm not going down there!

"*Down* there..."

Even if—no—there was some *island* down there. And I was standing at the top of some place, some glacier, and there was no where to go but *down* there. Away from that Thing—*up* there! There was *no* other choice. You couldn't go left. You couldn't go right. You couldn't go back up—to that Beast—on that pole made of stone. Forget it—don't even *look* back there.

Just *down* there...

That *isle* down there...far far down...what? Hundred metres midmost in the flaming wide glacier's an *island?* With gorgeous winded pines...like some Japanese tea site...some jaded Emperor's *garden?*

"Yes—*that's* where I'll rest. In that garden..."

It'll be a *good* slide down, the voice was saying.
"Even the voice has given up trying to stop you."
I know, I replied, I know.
"Won't it be a *good* slide down?"

Back in Athens were two women I made love to. One was a real case; the other just may be my salvation? Dora Cain...and Ada...
Dora really knew how to hook a man—with those fat green eyes but she had horsy hands and feet, an itsy-bitsy nose, and wads of freckles. But Ada...now there was one *gorgeous* woman!

"Won't it be a *good* slide down?"
No answer.
"Well—take a deep breath. Step onto the flow."
What? Can't stand? Too steep?
"Remind yourself," I said, "before you *do* this now—before you begin this slide—down this glacier or whatever the flaming Hell it's called—this gigantic pile of snow angling down the hillside at sixty or more degrees—remind yourself—you're *mortal*!"

And there it sat, mute, one piece of rock...

"Do it! You have no more options. You're stuck here. The Sun's going to set. You can't go back—uphill. Get going. You're lost."
I'm not!
"You *are*!"

Until its limestone bulk was stirred to be.

"Jesus—we're *already* sliding—like a dunce down a runaway roller coaster's tallest bend—oh Heaven Hell *save* me!"

Whence, Time itself roused the saline stone,

"I'm on my arse. It's sopping. My ungloved hands. Down sliding. To Death?"
Can't break...
"Can't brake..."
Can't stop...

And towards the Stars,

"Oh Hail Mary!"
I'm going to crash!
"That little island in the snow!"
Rushing!

Upwards from the brine,

"Please save me!"

Olympos—slowly woke and left

"Jesus!"

Its womb within the Deep,

"I'm crashing!"

For greater things, for purposes divine...

Three crashes...and they all were soporific. I felt as if I were apt to die... justly dead...deserved to...
Strange thoughts in dire needs...
I was flying through the air like a kite...
The leg that crashed was blue with pain...
"Breaking somewhat?"
My *legs*!
My life's sole asset!
My *legs*!
My lamenting Lord!
My *legs*!
I was landing...having crashed...three times?
"What's the problem?" I was actually asking aloud, delirious from the impact. "Body on the rocks. Certainly no island..."
Then...
I blacked out!

25th March – National Day – 10.41 AM

The crowd filling the Ancient Stadium of Olympia was expectant. People still were whispering about the dramatic entrance of the President. Many eyes were jumping from the thirteen olive wreaths, now lying in the dust, to the central section of VIPs.

The Announcer was giving everybody only a few seconds to breathe, then was beginning the proceedings formally: "On behalf of Olympia, would you please welcome the Director of Archaeology for the Western Pelopónnesos, Doctor Evanthía Selináki."

The Museum Director rose from her place in the front row, and stept to the Podium. In fact, there were two rostra from which to speak, one to be used by Ada, as translator for the Greeks, because the two recognised languages of the IOC were French first then English. But given that Evanthía Selináki was a well educated woman, she did not

517

require translation and spoke in both French and in Greek. Her rôle in the programme was brief.

"It is the greatest honour to welcome the President of the Republic, the Ministers, the Ambassadors, and the many dedicated individuals of the worldwide Olympic Family...back home." Doctor Selináki paused, and let her last two words sink in. "As Custodian of this Sacred Stadium, it is very moving indeed...to see everybody here gathered." Again, she paused. "Now...would you please welcome...the Chief of Protocol of the Mount Olympos Olympic Nation, Madame Ouranoú."

It was impossible not to detect the irony expressed. Evanthía and Thýella had been at each other's throats for months. Many of those gathered were aware of this. The Archaeologist was highly amused to see the Chief of Protocol's neck bandaged. Everybody had been speculating on how she got the wound—vampirism was the biggest joke—until Ada had arrived and had begun to tell the VIPs the truth, which caused the news to spread through their ranks like wildfire.

Madame Ouranoú was now descending the steps from her top-row position above the Members of the Greek Olympic Committee. For all purposes, she should have been sitting in the very front row, as she was to speak. But she had organized this Ceremony, and she could damned well sit where she pleased. Where she pleased was with the MOON-OC, to demonstrate, so that nobody would miss it, that she was not trying to steal the limelight. Of course, by having to traipse the whole length of the stairs, she was stealing absolutely everything. As she was arriving at the level of the Arena, nobody missed the particularly venomous look she gave the Chief Priestess. But nobody missed, either, the fact that Ada was holding her right hand beside her breasts, with fingers open and ready to claw her again. Thýella looked away. She hoped that she would not begin hiccuping.

Not to be outdone by Selináki, the Chief of Protocol displayed equal linguistic hippodromics, by speaking both English and Greek. There was no way that she was going to share the stage with the woman who drew her blood.

"To-day is a momentous occasion...for all of us," she began. "It has been a very long time in coming. The path has now been cleared... for resumption of the *true* Olympic Spirit...as once we witnessed here. But—there is one amongst us, whose eloquence embodies the Olympic Games, and whose common-sense is ready to amaze us. May we present...the Senior Member of the International Olympic Committee in Greece, the Professor of Philosophy at the University of Athens, Aristídis Rembetikós."

Thýella turned and smiled, nastily, at both her Head of State and at the Professor, then retraced her steps up the long flight. Rembetikós, meanwhile, was radiating a *joie de vivre*. He stood and nodded to a very sullen Chief Priestess, who rose and took his hand.

The two of them walked the few feet to the left and right Podia. They certainly were a pair. The Professor was looking like a jovial grandfather, with his bushy moustache twitching and with the gleam in his dark eyes. And, of course, Ada was looking anything but....

It was now ten forty-three. The IOC Member had decided to address his constituency in French, whilst Ada would translate into the Greek.

Up in the section of the MOON-OC, Thýella just was resuming her seat beside General Ouranós. He, too, had acquiesced to his wife's insistence that he sit with her and not with the more prestigious IOC, even though he had refused to march in with her. He at least wanted to be seen entering as a Member of the International Olympic Committee.

Thýella whispered: "So far so good."

"I agree," replied Ouranós. "As long as those goddamned doves are released, we've nothing to fear."

"We don't mean that," she snapt. "*Protocol*—we mean."

"What about your damned Protocol?" The General had grown to loathe that word, even though it had come to the world from the Greek.

"All is well—as long as this Ceremony *follows* it!" retorted his nasty wife. "We're *both* in the clear, if they adhere to our dictates. It's: IOC President, Head of State, Deed turned over to you, Hefferon's run...then we have *Athens*, too!"

"And if not..." Ouranós asked strangely. "Are you prepared?"

"Listen to Rembetikós," Thýella hissed, and the subject was dropt.

The Professor, a slow and deliberate speaker, whose accent was as perfectly punctuated as a classical actor of Euripides, was just completing his thanks on behalf of the Greek Olympic Committee, of which he was Past President.

"...Fellow Countrymen, and kindred Souls For Peace. There rarely comes a time, in the life of any nation, when all events of that country's Past, and all prayers for her Future, adjoin. There rarely comes a time, when what the land and people want *unite*, on one single site. There rarely comes a time, nowadays, when any nation that purports to be civilised can pause and proudly stand, with all the power of the Present Moment linking hands with what that country believes herself to be. But, my Friends, that *rare* time, indeed, has come...to Greece."

The old Professor, whose wisdom and love for his nation were spreading out to everyone's heart, by means of his words, then smiled. "To us, to Greeks, we need not have some grey old man point out our gifts to all Mankind. We need not tolerate such pomposity. We need... simply...to look around. Look...around...you now! This is *your* land, your *own* inheritance. This is *Hellas*! And right beneath your very feet...is soil so very sacred...that it makes me weep to think what great human beings have *walked* where we now merely *be*."

519

The old man took a very deep breath and sighed.

"This morning...we are gathered for a Deed Ceremony. After much debate, and after even *more* introspection, it has been decided that it *is* this country's bounden duty...to restore to the Olympic Games ...that purity of Spirit...which has gone away. By so saying this, as a long-time Member of the IOC, I am no more blaming the IOC than I am condoning each and every decision that the IOC ever made. All organizations, no matter how revered, can stray. And what may appear correct behaviour yesterday, now may be seen as incorrect by clearer eyes today."

The Professor paused, to take a drink of water.

"For past decades, since resumption of the Olympics in our era, the world has gone from a planet with barely one light bulb to a gridwork of computerised mega-technology. The philosophy of Pierre Frédy, Baron de Coubertin, was apt, in its time, and by that I mean the idea that the *best* way to foster Olympism was to take the Games *to* the people, in various parts of the world. But, my Friends, phase has now been completed. There is hardly one human being alive, on the whole of this globe, who hasn't now heard of the Olympic Games...and...who hasn't now heard of the Olympian Ideal...however much our globe would see *both* Games *and* Ideal shamed. It never ceases to amaze me, no matter how remote the region wherein I travel, to note that youth, the world over, no matter how poor, *want* to compete in the Olympics. And many do. And those who cannot...send their best Athletes away while many good hearts remain home...nurturing their Olympic dreams. Those who *stay* home...perhaps *they* are fated, often, to be *more* idealistic than those who *do* get to compete. Those who stay home ...know what they *expect*...from the Games...and they are not afraid to speak out. *My* words...now...are *their* words!"

The people now, deeply moved, were applauding.

"Everybody now realises that the Olympic Games are at the end of the Baron's phase. Were he alive, and were his heart not encased but a few metres from this very site, I am absolutely certain that Pierre de Coubertin would wish, now, that the Olympic Games *return*, permanently, to Greece!"

The people now rose to their feet, cheering wildly.

"We must not fear. Of all the world's great institutions, the IOC are known for dauntless *courage*. But now is the time to demonstrate *common-sense!*"

The multitude appreciated this sentiment.

"Now—it is the greatest honour to introduce to you the President of the International Olympic Committee."

Whilst applause rocked the grandstands, the Professor was shaking hands, first with Ada and then with the President of the IOC, who had come to the Podium.

Thýella, up above, simply said: "So far—Protocol is being

observed. She looked at the General's watch. It was ten fifty-one. She wanted him to say something, but he would not. He did not appear well, so all that she said was: "Aren't they delivering *carefully* worded speeches?" She was reading between every line, like a secret agent whose forté was cracking codes.

As the din abated, the IOC Leader nodded to the Chief Priestess of Hera, then he commenced to speak. "On behalf of the International Olympic Committee, thank you all very much for extending to us the invitation to attend this Deed Ceremony. It is no little privilege, to be able to stand inside this Ancient Stadium, as President of the IOC. Our Committee, as Professor Rembetikós so appropriately said, have been following a course, since 1896, that we might call 'experimental'. When the Olympics were held here—right here—the Games did *not* need to move, in order to embrace the world. But...the world, for the Ancient Games, was that of *Greece*, and of her colonies. Only *Greek* citizens were allowed to compete. The Baron de Coubertin, of course, knew this very well. It was his life's vision, to see established a worldwide movement of brotherhood through sport. That vision did become reality, as now we know. And true...when the noble Baron was alive, the Olympic Games, and their message, were still awaiting the communications break-through that we, presently, have seen become an accepted fact of life. Times *have* changed, incalculably, since 1896. And the IOC are *not* about to deny this!"

Polite applause came from the other side of the Arena.

"Our planet Earth is now called the Global Village. We can get to Tokyo from here as easily as Tokyo can get to New York. Satellites in the sky, at this very instant, are beaming these words I speak to the furthest reaches of the globe. It is a *very* exciting time...in which to be alive. This world *is* one. Its problems of pollution...are *universal*. Its problems of energy...are *universal*. Its problems of interconnection of economies...are *universal*. What happens in Nairobi has a synergic reaction of entropy in Rio de Janeiro. The world is *one*—and *all* of us have *responsibility*—to make this planet safe, sound, and inhabitable."

Greater applause was welling. The people indeed were listening.

"No one of us has all the answers. But the IOC are composed of individuals who do try to think globally. We meant only well by bringing Olympism to such varied places as Sapporo, Rome, Los Angeles, Mexico City, Grenoble, Innsbruck, and Lake Placid. By so doing, many people who might not ever have been able to get to a distant clime were able to work for, or to observe, an Olympic Games. And those who have done so...*never* are able to forget it."

The IOC President paused for a drink of water, and looked to the Priestess at his side.

"In 1948...the world was just crawling from beneath the rubble of the Second World War. Many of you seated on the opposite side...were there...and to remember those days may be too painful. In spite of despair, at this very site, which in fact was in the midst of its own Civil War, a moment of Peace was allowed to transpire, and yes...I see that many of you recall now...how the Olympic Flame was ignited... here...back in 1948..."

Ada's voice now was breaking. She was finding it too emotional to translate this from English into the Greek.

"The IOC had to rise...from the flame of battle...as did the world. Thus, we decided to award the first Olympic Games, since Hitler's time, to the decimated city...of London. In 1948...London was no pretty sight."

Again, he paused to wet his lips, as Ada wiped tears from her cheeks.

"At Olympia...we were told that we *shouldn't* do it, that the IOC were *wrong* to light the Sacred Flame again, at Olympia, because brother was fighting father, and daughter was fighting son. But, we did *not* give in. We felt that the Flame *had* to be lit. And so we *did* it—right here. And let me tell you—when the British battleship, that was entrusted with the Flame's care, landed at Bari, in Italy, the *whole* of that city...was there...at the harbour...to greet it! And *why?*"

Never in her life had Ada required such a reserve of strength, even as an actress, as she was needing now...just to translate this speech. Even many Members of the IOC now were wiping their faces with handkerchiefs.

"*Why* did the Olympic Torch draw them that day? *Why* did all of Italy, it seems, wait through the night, all along the route, throughout the whole length of the country, to see a bit of Fire pass by? *Why?* Tell me!"

Then Ada heard herself saying aloud the word *freedom*, both in English and in Greek.

"That...is...right," the President of the International Olympic Committee agreed. "*All* of war-scarred Europe...watched that little Light ...as it ran past the bombed buildings...as it saluted the sorrowing people...in the day...in the night. So now—inspired by this noble memory—it gives me the profoundest joy to introduce to you now a man who has embodied the Olympian Ideal, the Gold Medal Winner of the Men's 1500 Metre Race for the last Summer Olympic Games, Ivor Hefferon!"

Thýella almost stood, but the General had her wrist gript like a vise. "He's altered Protocol!" she snapt. "Something's *up*! Ouranós! Something's *up*!"

People were turning and looking. Beside her, Major Movóros was gripping her other wrist, saying: "Mother—just shut up and watch!"

"We're *through*—we tell you—we're *through*!"

The General was turning a very strange colour. His legs were beginning to shake. But he did not move from his seat.

"The Head of *State's* supposed to be speaking next," the Chief of Protocol moaned. "Can't they read the Programme?"

Ouranós just shook his head, closed his eyes, and began to gnash his teeth.

From where he was waiting, inside the circular foundation of the Philippeíon, which had been tented over by canvas, but which was open above to the sky, Ivor Hefferon was now absolutely naked. The Olympian heard the Announcer's voice speaking through the walkie-talkie held by a young Recruit. This Soldier was an Athlete, from Alexandrópolis near Istanbul, and the two of them had been talking about running.

On a table were the loincloth, sandals, and headband that Thýella had wanted Ivor to wear. But the Briton had decided, in only the last few minutes, to wear *nothing*, to run into the Ancient Stadium exactly as had the *original* Olympic Athletes, in no more than the graceful human form that The Gods themselves had bequeathed him.

In Ivor's hand was the velvet box that Thýella had given him, and from which he had handed Ada the diadem that she had tossed to the feet of the President of Greece. Beside the Soldier was the Medic who had rushed from the Red Cross Tent, where Thýella had been nursed, the fellow who had hastened to Ivor with the priceless pure-gold Olympic Torch.

The Soldier, who had been instructed by Ada to carry to Ivor the Votive Urn that was holding the Sacred Flame, now was uncovering the lid of the Votive Urn, which had a hole drilled into its centre, so that the Sacred Flame could breathe, so that it could not suffocate.

The Medic was now igniting the Torch, by dipping it into the Urn, then was handing the Torch to the Olympic Gold Medallist, who was giving the velvet box to the Medic in exchange. The time was three minutes to eleven.

The Recruit shook the Athlete's free left hand and said sincerely: "It's been a True Inspiration...talking to you. Good luck with your life...whatever you choose to do."

The Olympic Runner squeezed tight the rod of the Torch. He now knew that his whole life had been leading up to this very action which soon would be visible to all.

Made by Lalaoúnis of Athens, the Torch was of solid gold, and was worth no small fortune. As Soldier and Medic now were staring at it, both of them simultaneously whistled aloud. It had so many small diamond-shaped embossed surfaces that it didn't even need to be turned to reflect a brilliant amount of bright yellow light.

Just then, Ivor had an eldritch image appear in his mind, which made him feel faint. It was something that he had never seen before, something like a creature from a mythical time, something half human, a mammal of sorts, high high above him, way up on the very top of some natural spire of rock, in some mountainous setting, some wilderness. The creature was golden, was radiating some disturbing lustrous light, as if on fire, as if burning alive, as if sacrosanct in flames shaped like a mandorla. A silhouette of black was standing out before a mandorla—mad burst of the Sun. The Sun was directly behind something—way up there—something high above. What *was* this thing before it—like a sprite—some thing alive —with four little legs—with four little hooves—on some penny-sized peak. Some Divine Sign? Some Dæmon?

Ivor's body shook spasmodically, involuntarily, and his skin shivered. The awful image vanished. The Medic and the Soldier thought that he just was experiencing "stage fright".

The Runner now was steadying himself, by holding the Torch up to the sunlight that was streaming down through the evergreens. A shaft was catching the golden object and sending eye-blinding glitters onto all of the trees and all of the dark grey base-stones of the small temple completed by Alexander the Great.

"Twist it," said the Recruit.

Ivor did, and reflections burst apart in all directions, flying like bullets off the sparkling pine needles. Then, the Athlete took a deep breath, and held the object aloft in his right hand.

Through the walkie-talkie the Announcer was asking: "Where *is* he?"

"Coming, Sir," answered the Recruit. "Go—please!"

Hefferon went—commencing what would forever be remembered as the most memorable run of his whole career. He knew it—knew it in his inmost Soul—that this run, without any doubt whatsoever, would far transcend even that of his race for the Men's 1500 Metres at the last Summer Games. Timing was timing—and it was now the penultimate moment of his very life. It was now ten fifty-nine in the morning. Those in the Stadium were beginning to stamp their feet, in unison.

Slowly, holding the precious Torch high, the Olympic Gold Medallist began running, towards the Temple of Hera, as the Greek Army along the route began cheering him on, even as their mouths all were dropping to their knees. As Ivor continued running, he was feeling deeply moved, privileged, to be doing this inside such a sacrosanct setting. He was not even conscious of his nudity; it seemed meet and right; his body just was flowing, naturally, as it was *meant* to do, in this incomparable site.

He was continuing, slowly, past the ruined Nymphæum and Metroön, then past the row of votive Treasuries built by the ancient city-states, at which point a large crowd of Security Corps in the Portico of Echo cheered him with all their might, though utterly astonished at seeing the man unclothed. There was something that gripped at everyone's emotions, seeing an Olympic Runner, naked, in this locale.

Above the ruins of the Portico, atop the flag-bedecked ridge that formed the western end of the Stadium, friends of the Athlete, but totally unbeknownst by him, as a surprise, had flown over from the

United States especially for this Ceremony. They were an invited Delegation representing the Lake Placid Olympic Organizing Committee. And all of them, seeing Ivor, coming proudly through the grove as a living embodiment of the Olympic Ideal that had been born here two thousands years ago, were weeping. The contingent was comprised of the Reverend Arnold Courtney, Judge Ronson, Rebecca Harper, Ambassador and Mrs Levitt, and Lucille McSorley, who had paid the party's fares. Professor Rembetikós had been the one who had contacted the LPOOC's President, just a week ago. Would Ivor be amazed to see them, after this event concluded!

Atop the same ridge with the group from Lake Placid were two Members of the Security Corps, who were standing alongside Theatrínos who, after all, had been allowed to attend the Ceremony. They were next to Camera-3. The boy had been told to wear an Army uniform, and to put all of his hair beneath a helmet, for his own safety, so that he would not be recognised. The Security Corps were guarding him. The Athlete did not even notice the sextet from the Adirondacks, nor anyone atop the ridge.

Hefferon had imagined, as he was waiting in the Philippeíon, that people would *laugh* as he was running by. But the beauty of the nearly nude body seemed appropriate to these ruins that he was passing. It was an image out of some classical dream. And all eyes were mesmerised, by the sparkling of the burnished Torch itself.

Then, the Olympian was taking a deep breath, and was entering the high narrow walls of what was once called the Crypt. It was no more than ten seconds before he was at the other end. The Athlete was just now penetrating the Stadium. Not one Soul was stirring from his or her place. The time was one minute past eleven.

But such a cheer, as Ivor had not heard since the previous Summer Games...since he ran for the Medal that day...was greeting him this time. The animalistic roar of mankind...

This lake of humanity and their applause were filling the whole Alphaiós Valley. Ivor couldn't help it...he had to close his eyes. He was coming to a halt, beside the cube of Parian marble, in the very centre of the Arena, where the dozen wreaths made of the olive tree, in a circle about the golden one, were bronzing in the heat. All the while, as he kept standing there, for one full minute with his eyes closed tight, quietly praying for guidance, he kept twisting his hand, so that rays of yellow Light kept dancing upon the faces of the crowd. Then, he noticed that the white cube of stone had been hollowed out, in a cylindrical core, and he recalled that the rod of the Torch was supposed to be placed into this shaft, so that the Torch could stand erect and burn naturally until it went out.

As the multitude kept gazing on in stupefaction, the naked Olympian was placing the Torch where it was meant to be, then was kneeling on one knee to pay it reverence. Ivor then was standing,

525

straight, as if at attention, and was turning and looking towards the throng of Dignitaries, whom he commenced to approach ever so slowly. The whole Arena was gazing at him with a mixture of awe and shock. Ada, no less astounded than all the others, suddenly made a loud rip of her garment, at the hem by her feet, and tore off a piece of fabric to offer to the Athlete for cover. Since it was coming from the Arch Priestess, Hefferon accepted the cloth and girded his loins, as best he could, then proceeded towards the second Podium, next to Ada's. He took a deep breath, then began to speak. It was four past eleven in the morning.

"This Torch, of solid gold, was supposed to have been given, by the Chief Priestess of Hera, to Madame Ouranoú, who intended to give it to her husband, the General, the Junior Member of the IOC in Greece. But, once this assembly hear my story, I am certain that Ouranós will no longer be connected either with the IOC or with his country's military."

There was absolute silence everywhere—especially from those seated directly behind the Athlete's now minimally covered body—high above—in the reserved seating for the MOON-OC. It was beginning to dawn on them that they were trapt, that it was all over for them. The General was sweating like a pig. Thýella was going a shade of green. The Major's tough heart was racing. They all were watching the Torch, midway in the Arena, smoking and burning. They all looked hypnotised.

"I am instructed by the Head of State of Greece, as well as by the President of the International Olympic Committee, to inform you, now, that General Ouranós, and his wife, have been conspiring to *wreck* the Olympic Games!"

Pandemonium erupted in the whole Arena. The lid was off. And everybody began shouting at once. The emotions unleashed were horrifying. It took Ivor a full three minutes to calm the crowd down. It was now eight past eleven.

"Madame Ouranoú wanted to give this Torch to General Ouranós, but since he does not deserve it, and your country's President will soon tell you what he does deserve, I am requested by your Head of State to offer this Torch of gold to the President of the International Olympic Committee. But...the Sacred Flame first...must burn out..."

People clapped, but only as a way to release tension and confusion. The President of the IOC rose, strode to Ivor, shook his hand on behalf of the Committee, then sat. Nobody else moved an inch. Nobody dared approach the Torch...which still was burning...

"First, I am instructed to tell you all *not* to fear. Please stay seated, no matter what you may be hearing in the next few minutes. Everything *is* under control. There will be no harm from the military. The troops in the Áltis are *not* armed. The troops, under the General's command, remain loyal to their Head of State. There is no possible means of escape, for Members of the MOON-OC, so everyone is to remain in his or her seat."

The Athlete let his words sink in, then continued: "Two years ago, General Ouranós conceived of the Mount Olympos Olympic Nation. It never was a *noble* goal...on his part. It always was just a *scheme*. My presence, here in Greece, this past month, has been to infiltrate the Organizing Committee headquarters for the MOON, which I have done. The idea that Greece would see the Olympic Games returned, permanently, is one which I am behind. But General Ouranós consistently *bastardised* this noble idea, by espousing it under a pretext. The General's only reason, for wanting an Olympic Nation built, in Thessaly, at the foot of Mount Olympos, by the Army town Litóchoron, was to bore inside the mountain, while construction was going on above, and while construction was providing a protective smokescreen. What General Ouranós was screening was his *real* reason to want to build at Litóchoron. Ouranós was intending that the cavern carved out of living rock, out of the foothill named Stávros, would become a secret missile base for NATO, wherein nuclear warheads would be stockpiled, and wherein neutron bombs would be designed and made!"

The Press were now going crazy. It was eleven minutes past eleven. They were shoving to cross the Arena, but troops were locking arm in arm in order to restrain them. People all over the civilian sections of the grandstands were jumping up, raising their fists, denouncing the General, demanding his hide.

Above Hefferon's back, Thýella was trying to bolt upright, but her husband and son were gripping her wrists, which she almost broke in her fury. "Slander!" she kept screaming. "Slander! Hefferon—you'll *die* for this—you'll *die*!"

"Lies!" Movóros began shouting. "Lies!"

The General was speechless. He was taking everything out on his wife's black and blue wrist.

"Slander!" Thýella screamed again, as the President's Security Corps, numbering about a hundred men, who were specially trained in martial arts and whose hands and feet were lethal weapons, even though they were not armed, began advancing into the Arena through the vaulted Crypt. Seeing them, the Chief of Protocol broke away from both her son and husband, and began running in the aisle, towards the eastern end of the Stadium. Nobody wanted to touch her. She seemed to be exuding atomic radiation.

Madame kept heading in the direction of the huge video screen. Suddenly, she noticed that she was being followed by Camera-1. Her head, now looking as mad as Medusa, filled the whole enormous width of the closed-circuit screen. She began staring at herself—horrified— then was halting where she was and began letting out a manly scream.

Soldiers began advancing up all the aisles towards her. She

kept looking backwards, towards her son and husband, and kept screaming: "Well—aren't you *Cowards* going to *do* anything!"

"Yes," her husband was suddenly standing and shouting back at her across a hundred feet. The time was now eleven thirteen.

There was now a split-screen, showing Thýella on the left and Ouranós on the right.

"Well—*what* can you possibly do!" she yelled.

"This!" the General hollered and reached into his dress-coat pocket of his majestic uniform, and extracted a little tablet. He held it up—for all to see.

"Oh—you don't have the *balls!*" she screeched. "Cyanide? You *don't* have the balls!"

"Father—don't!" yelled Movóros. Then Sitherás kept up an unearthly screaming, chorused by the Orthodox Priest.

Other family Members were too mortified or too terrified to speak, especially when they realised that their relatives were being viewed at this very instant all over the world by satellite.

"Father—stop! Let yourself live! Don't *do* this! *Don't* do this!" Movóros kept begging.

"Father—*don't* do this!" Thýella kept echoing, eerily. Then suddenly, her whole visage was changing. She was beginning to advance towards her husband now, getting to within twenty feet of him. Soldiers were at the tops of all the stairs, holding onto the railings of the aisle where Thýella was standing. She was looking horrendous, and kept bellowing: "Well—*kill* yourself—go ahead! Kill yourself—for *them!*" and she swept her right arm in an arc and meant the whole Stadium, giving the assembly an obscene gesture with her hand. "What *do* you have to lose now? You...are...at...your...wits'...*end!*"

"Mother—shut *up!*" Movóros kept hollering. "Father—*please* don't! Don't *listen* to her! She's *Evil!*"

Sultana, wife of the Major, was immobile with fright. She was hunched over like an ailing leper, looking about at all the monsters of this her wedded family. She kept whimpering, then crying: "Don't!" She kept sobbing aloud: "Help!"

The Security Corps were advancing. They had their hands ready to attack.

"*Take* it—damn you—*take* it!" yelled Thýella. "See if it'll make a *goddamned* difference!"

Then, as everybody in the whole section of the Stadium began moaning, the General hastily put the tablet in his mouth, and right there, in front of everybody, committed suicide.

He stood, half alive, for some seconds longer, but the poison was acting fast. His knees were buckling. He was collapsing. And the whole world was watching. The time was eleven fifteen.

Thýella kept letting out an ungodly shriek, that was freezing everybody's heart. Then she was beginning a ghastly clucking, that would not stop, as if she were hiccuping whilst some unseen club kept belting her repeatedly across the back. "There's *no* difference," she kept shouting. "There's *no* difference at all! Dead or alive—what's the goddamned *difference!*"

Movóros now was panicking. The Security Corps were closing in. His wife was huddled, in foetal position, shrinking away from the dead body at her feet. The General's head was on her left shoe. Her shoe had come off...when he had fallen on her.

"I'm *going,*" the Major kept saying as he kept shaking his wife roughly by the shoulders. "I'm *going*—do *you* even care?"

Sultana was saying absolutely nothing. Her tongue was traumatised. People everywhere were babbling. The whole place was a nightmare, and it was all being televised.

"*Don't* you care?" he was shaking her again, more rudely this time. "*Answer* me!"

Thýella kept howling: "*Care?* Of course the silly *Bitch* doesn't care! Go join your *father*—but see if *anybody* cares! Death's the *same* as Life...Son...Death's the *same* as Life! And it *all* takes place...in *Hell!*"

"You *killed* him! *You* killed him! Aaaaahhhhh!" the son was beginning to rave. "Well I'll show *you*—you can't keep *me* under your *clutches* any longer!"

"*Kill* yourself! Go *ahead!*"

"I'm *going*...to!" he kept responding, now hoarse, as he started reaching into his pocket for his pill. "I'm *going*...to!" His hand was shaking. "I'm *going*...to!" Women all around were wailing. "I'm *not* going...to be tortured...any longer...by *you!* I'm not *going*...to give them any...*secret* that I...know!"

"Tell yourself *another* lie! Satan will make you *squirm!*"

"Tell them...Mother! Tell them...*everything* you...know! But let this...*cyanide*...now silence...*me!*" And the young Officer, her favourite son, was beginning to put the tablet to his lips, then was opening his mouth wide. "Father—*wait* for me!" he was shouting then swallowing the pill. He kept standing just a bit longer. Then atop his father's body, the Major was collapsing. The time was eleven seventeen.

Thýella now was gripping both of her ears, then ripping off her expensive blonde wig. A gasp was swooping up from everybody. The rotten lady was absolutely bald. She was now throwing her hairpiece in the aisle, and was beginning to stomp upon it, in some gruesome Pagan Dance. Then, she was taking both fists, as she kept letting out horrific screams, and was ripping apart her Rape of Europa necklace of lapis-lazuli and gold, and flinging the bits to the wind. All around her people were ducking. The woman was going completely *mad!*

"Don't—don't *shoot* her!" the brawny son, Sitherás, kept blubbering like a baby.

The Orthodox Priest kept weeping—atop the dead bodies.

"Don't...*shoot* her!" Sitherás continued to scream and was rushing to shield his horrid mother.

"Don't...*shoot* her!" she kept repeating, in an insane mimicking.

"What...does it *matter*...anymore?"

"Mother—come along now!" Sitherás now was begging—with out-stretched hands. He was shaking with fright. His teeth were chattering. Two huge soldiers were grabbing his mother's arms from behind. Four huge soldiers were grabbing *him*.

"Don't *fight* them," the son was insisting, going limp in the captors' arms.

But, Madame had slipt, into the Nether World of Delirium, never again to return to this side of Mortal Existence. The time was eleven nineteen.

Thýella Ouranoú was as good as dead. Although Madame still could walk on two feet, she could not now even talk. Her eyes were rolling in her head. Madame was beginning to drool. Madame was beginning to chuckle...as soldiers now were leading her along the aisle, as soldiers were proceeding with her, down the steps, past the horrified contingent of the Greek Olympic Committee, then past the traumatised IOC, who never would forget this vision of this bald-headed female monster, with these great gobby earrings of lapis-lazuli and beaten gold.

Many people were crossing themselves, as the dæmonic woman was passing. People had been praying, all over the Stadium, for minutes now, anyway. The Security Corps were continuing to lead off every single person from the section reserved for the MOON-OC. Two Red Cross stretchers were now being carried across the Arena, up to the deceased.

Everywhere...people were in shock but...as well...everywhere...there was *kátharsis*...there was relief...

PART
III

Non enim palma in stadio proposita,
sed recta corporis exercitatio
potior æstimanda est.

—Pope John XXIII

(words of His Holiness, delivered to a special audience
of Athletes and Officials attending the Games of the XVII Olympiad,
Rome, 24th August 1960)

26th April – Wednesday – 4.15 PM

I woke up. I thought I had died. Was I on another Plane of Spiritual Existence? My eyes would not open. Where *was* I?
"Have I been out long?"
Only five minutes.
"Am I alive?"
Who was that asking?
"What time was it?"
Was it much later? Than what?
"It still was light out."
Where?
"Maybe just a minute?"
Was that singing?
"Voices? A Chorus?"
Am I dead?
"I did go unconscious..."
Blood?
"Bonsai..."
What was that you said?

I woke up? *Had* I died? Wasn't I on another Plane at all? My eyes widened. I was really opening up my eyes! Then shutting them again...

"Fall. You had a wicked fall. You almost were killed."
Who was saying these things? I opened my eyes again...slowly. I couldn't focus...yet. Beside my nose...a bonsai tree...I could smell the pine pitch. At least *that* was a start!
"You were almost killed! Maybe you're *dying*...right now?"
That made me focus!

A stunted baby pine tree was right beside my nostrils...on this island of sorts...in the middle of the ice-slick. The snow...as well as the islet...both were angled sixty degrees. I closed my eyes. But then opened them again. Then...I felt the *pain*!
Oh how I felt the *pain*!
Somebody was branding my leg!
My right leg!
Maybe...it was paralysed!
Maybe...it was shattered!
Maybe...it was cut and bleeding!
Maybe...I'd never *run*...again...
Oh God—I felt like I *was* about to die!

Stabbing jabs of incessant pain now were breaking through my consciousness. I was in bad shape. I'd have to get help. As yet...I couldn't even move. I saw my watch. It still was ticking. The sodding thing was ticking so bloody loud, beside my face, upon my arm...

"I'd been out five minutes?"

You were only blacked out five minutes!

"Can't believe it! Seems like a million years."

You were only out five bleeding minutes!

"All right!"

But what you *thought*...in those five minutes...

"What *did* I think? I think I was thinking about...Lake Placid ...about Athens...about Olympia...about Olympos..."

You were. You remembered them *all*.

"Just like a drowning man?"

Just like a drowning man. They *all* came back.

"My love for Ada? Oh God—will I ever get to see *her* again? Am I going to *die*? Here on this lonely mountain? All alone? *Am* I? Tell me! *Tell* me!"

The voice was going. There was just wind through nearby pines. Beside my nose the little bonsai was shaking. I could smell The Universe...in that one tiny tree...

I closed my eyes...and began to pray.

"Help me!" I screamed, stuck by a knifepoint of pain. At that instant, when I began to call out, I remembered precisely what I had last been seeing...as I lay unconscious. It was the Deed Ceremony...after the General's suicide...

25th March – National Day – 11.22 AM

Theatrínos, and the Dignitaries from Lake Placid, atop the mound that was above the Portico of Echo, and alongside the barrel-vaulted Crypt, could see everything perfectly. The famous Greek Performer hadn't spoken to the foreigners, and the foreigners hadn't said a word to him. They didn't know each other. It was not the type of event that gave a moment's pause for introductions between strangers. As the Americans were getting more and more nauseous by it all, as the women were vomiting onto the desiccated grass, the Singer was timing it all, like a Judge for Olympic competition. At 11.01 Hefferon had entered the Stadium. 11.04 Hefferon had begun to speak. 11.15 the General committed suicide. 11.17 the Major committed suicide. 11.19 Thýella became demented. 11.21 Thýella was led away. It was now 11.22.

Two bodies now were coming out of the end of the tunnel. Four Red Cross Volunteers were carrying off the dead. They were heading towards the Temple of Hera, the Philippeíon, the Red Cross Tent.

As Theatrínos kept watching the sheet-covered corpses heading away, only then did the nineteen-year-old boy start crying. That man, however mad, however star-crossed, was his very own *father!* He had never really had a chance to get to know the man. The man had cut him off from an early age. He had grown up lonely, fatherless, and had been forced to strike out on his own, to go the *lonesome* way. He had wanted, in his heart, to break through *to* the man, somehow, but the opportunity never arose. There hadn't been time. And it certainly was too late now. And his half-brother...dead now too...a kinsman whom he never would have the chance to know...

Theatrínos was turning away from the melancholy pines and the sombre ruins. The man nearest him, with a clerical collar, was Lake Placid's Reverend Courtney, who had been watching the boy for the past few minutes, sensing that he, in some sad way, was very much connected with this dire family saga. "Father!" the boy started screaming over and over, then was collapsing and weeping on the shoulders of this total stranger beside him, this kindly American man who was radiating a sensitivity that was beckoning. "I understand, I understand!" the Reverend kept saying, as tears, too, began falling from his eyes, as he held the quivering lad tightly to his breast, as the Security Corpsmen who had been guarding the lad, men likewise old enough to be the Singer's father, were breaking down and crying. The whole of Olympia now was mourning...recollecting the demise of fathers...recalling the painful passage of sons...

Inside the Stadium, a gloomy hand was pressed upon the multitude's heart. Professor Rembetikós had just spoken from the Podium by telephone, to the Ceremony's Announcer, and had urged him to tell the Conductor to begin playing something appropriate, as soon as was humanly possible. The Head of State needed some more time to collect his wits, in order to deliver an appropriate explanation of the altered circumstances of the Tragedy. He was consoling Ivor Hefferon, who kept blaming himself for what had happened, for the deaths.

The Announcer was attempting to speak, with great difficulty: "Will...everybody please...will everyone...resume his place? The President...of the Hellenic Republic will...will try...will address...this gathering...presently. As soon as...everybody...gets back in his seat...the Conductor of the...Symphony Orchestra of...Athens, Mándis Loulákis ...he will play the...*Nocturne in F Sharp Minor*...Opus 48...Number 2... by Frédéric Chopin..."

At the age of thirty-three, Loulákis was still the unchallenged Greek *wunderkind* of classical music. Since he was fifteen, when he appeared out of the blue and won second place in the Warsaw Chopin Competition, performing this very Nocturne, the fellow had never ceased to astound the European musical community. He had been conducting since he was twenty-one. Two years later, he saw the world première of his *First Piano Concerto*, which he performed in the Odíon during that year's Festival of Athens. As a composer, his works had been gaining steady popularity, via recordings, even among his compatriots who usually preferred the bouzoukia. For the last two years he had been Resident Composer and Conductor with the Athens Symphony

Orchestra. To-day, the world première of his newest composition, his First Symphony for Full Chorus and Soloists, was to have concluded the Programme. Due to such accomplishments, the Press had long ago labelled him "Mándis" Loulákis, meaning "Wizard". His given name was Manólis.

All of the thousands were tremendously relieved that something ...anything...now was happening. The Conductor was going to the beautiful concert grand that was atop the huge stage, and was receiving a warm ovation. Everybody was cheering his rescuing the situation, far more than his command of the keyboard. But, as soon as the handsome young Maestro from Corfu began to interpret the complexities of the hauntingly lovely Nocturne, the people and their witnessing of the Tragedy began to be transported away, and healing began to be brought about, by the dulcet notes and by the sensitive playing.

If anything, Music is one of God's greatest gifts to Man. That a pleasant melody can cure the mind's worst worry is undeniable. How many of us...when times get rough...have our own special tune...that has the potency...to restore us?

So now, the rhythms of this Nocturne, likely the most beautiful of all of those that Chopin ever was gifted enough to compose, commenced to soothe the people's Souls. And for those five enchanted minutes, when the sound of falling autumn leaves was removing the sweltering heat of summer from the heart, the people were at Peace.

Then, as the *Nocturne in F Sharp Minor* was concluding, all ten thousand, from Technician to Farmer to august Member of the International Olympic Committee to the President of Greece, were getting off their chairs...to give the young Maestro a standing ovation. And that ovation was as much for applauding *Life*...as it was for God's Gift...of *Music*!

26th April – Wednesday – 4.20 PM

There must be *blood*, I said, quickly regaining composure. The pain was just as bad, but I was fully conscious now, and had just managed to prop myself up on my left elbow.

"God—this island is vertical!"

I looked to my right leg. The left was not really smarting. The right was still there—all of it. There *was* blood...

I figured there'd be blood. I could smell it.

My trouser leg was ripped. Two places. At the hip-bone, and at the knee. For the first time...I began to reach out with my right hand...to see if anything was broken. Pain in my hip shot a shout out of me: "Jesus!" I must have moved something.

Thank the Lord my arms, hands, ribs, spine, and skull were all right!

How nothing cracked I'll never know.

I took a deep breath...and put my fingertips on my hip. There was nothing sharp sticking through the skin.

"Oh God!" The pain was Hell.

I had to touch it, though.

"Nothing's split!"

I couldn't get over it.

"Lift the knee. That'll be the final test."

Knowing it would hurt like The Devil, I began to hoist up the whole right leg.

"Thank God!" I said aloud, as I grimaced with pain. "It's *not* broken! It's not *broken!* Then *can* I walk?"

I was bleeding at the right knee. I had to see how badly. The three impacts of the crash had gashed a large hole in the heavy corduroy trousers. Through the hole, I could feel that the cut wasn't deep.

"Thank God—both legs can *move!*"

I felt a rush of euphoria suffusing my whole Being. I had been *incredibly* lucky—perhaps even *blest*. Not one bone was broken somehow...

"How in God's name is it possible?" I kept muttering over and over. Then, overcome by the experience, I began to weep.

25ᵗʰ March – National Day – 11.27 AM

As applause for the Conductor was abating, those in the Stadium assumed their seats. Everyone indeed, was feeling a little better. The Programme, though irreparably altered, began to proceed.

The President of International Olympic Committee once again was standing, and taking the Chief Priestess's hand. "On behalf of all of us," he was stating, "I should like to offer everybody our deepest understanding, whether you be at home and viewing this event by television, or whether you be with us now, in this very Stadium."

He paused, and exhaled, wondering how to carry on.

"I think...that we all are still under...a *lot* of shock. This has been the most heinous day, for the IOC, since 1972, when the eleven Israeli Athletes were brutally murdered by Palestinian terrorists, during the Games of the XX Olympiad. As President of the Committee that had approved General Ouranós's Membership, it is my responsibility now to tell you a few things. And then, the President of this Republic will be good enough to speak."

He took a long drink of water.

"The IOC...were aware...of the plot conceived by the late General Ouranós. We were likewise aware...of the dissent...within Greece...that had been debating...,for the last few years...the idea that this country again be Permanent Home to the Olympic Games. We wanted the invitation, by Greece, to us, to have been made with the people's *wholehearted* consent. We did not ever intend to *force* this issue upon

541

this country, lest we exacerbate matters here unduly. Two Januarys ago, it was brought to my attention, personally, by two Members of the IOC Sub-Committee who had been studying the possibility that Greece be returned the Games, by Lord Dalbeattie of Britain and by Professor Rembetikós of this country, that General Ouranós was publicly boosting Greece only as a means to secure his own political advancement. He had gone ahead, behind his own leaders' backs, here and abroad, to secure endorsement for his scheme, that beneath the Olympic Nation he would see built a nuclear arsenal, and a research and development facility, such as never before was known in this whole region. At first, my own personal notion was to *blackball* the man, to throw him out of the IOC! But two Januarys ago, Lord Dalbeattie reassured me and said: 'Let the fool move ahead with his monstrous schemes—*then* we shall lay him bare, when the moment is ripe.' Well to-day—that moment arrived. I, personally, am extremely sorry that the General felt it necessary to take his own life, and even moreso that his son, a fine Officer and former Athlete, had been subverted by his own father's schemes. If there be need to point a finger of responsibility, for what we have just seen, then that responsibility does not lie with the International Olympic Committee, but with General and Madame Ouranós. They had this planned, for two solid years, and the consequences are entirely *their* fault. *We* chartered the MOON-OC, yes, but we did so with the sole understanding that, before too long, we would have the opportunity to watch them prepare their own downfall."

The President of the IOC paused, and looked to the Priestess, who was trying to grasp it all.

"Thus...those who have schemed...*have* fallen. Let this be an example—to the world—that Evil accrues its own reward. I should just like to say one thing in closing, before I bow to the President of Greece. We, of the International Olympic Committee, as I said over half an hour ago, now *know* that the Olympic Games have completed the first phase of their Modern Era. To-day has been a veritable *rite de passage* for all of us, but especially so for the IOC. We knew, in advance, that this day would *not* be easy. We knew, in advance, that this day would likely involve *pain*. We were not even sure if there might be a ritual sacrifice...and alas...there did happen to be. But the Olympic Games will endure—even this! They *will* live on, albeit strengthened. It is a measure of the Games' potency, and relevancy, that this Deed Ceremony has been considered worthy enough to be broadcast all over the world. This event, to-day, certainly befits the name that it has been given. But in the next few days, and weeks, and months, we must all take time to ponder...what was the ultimate purpose...of this *Deed* done to-day?"

The President of the IOC looked straight ahead, as the television cameras took the intended stare to the furthest reaches of the Earth. People watching, everywhere, felt that he was speaking directly to *them*.

"People of the world, I ask you now. What do *you* want...for the

542

future of the Olympic Games? The decision is now up to *you*. Tell us, write to us, send us your ideas, please, we beg of you. Contact us, about your thoughts. Just write: IOC, Lausanne, Switzerland. All letters, thus addressed, will reach us. But tell us *now*. Do you, People Of The World, now wish the Olympics to *continue* on, as they have been, in perpetual motion, since 1896, or do you wish that they be *restored*, to the land that gave them birth? *Tell* us: Should the Olympic Games return, permanently...to Greece?"

The people now were cheering. They were slowly rising, up from their seats, as if they were rising from the grave. So shocked had they been...by events of this morning...that they never imagined that the President of the International Olympic Committee would be asking a single thing of *them*. Now, the people began shouting, in a chant that was unleashing all of the agony that they had been containing inside:

> *Give the Games*
> *Back to Greece!*
> *Give the Games*
> *Back to Greece!*
> *Give the Games*
> *Back to Greece!*

The IOC President sat, and the Head of State of Greece was standing. The latter was looking upon the chanting thousands, and hoping in his heart that the IOC would finally act to answer the people's prayers. Then, after two more minutes, when it was eleven thirty-four, he raised his arms for silence. "Let us pray," he began, "that our country's dream may soon come true."

The people again began cheering.

"Now—you must listen. After I am through speaking, what you have come to witness will be put in perspective. You must bear with me, and accept, for the time being, while repercussions of to-day's events are still being felt, that I am not at liberty to divulge all the classified information pertaining to this conspiracy. I say this only because we now have certain matters to discuss with our NATO allies, in particular with the United States. Between now and Holy Week, a thorough investigation is going to be made. On Maundy Thursday, that is on the twentieth of April, I shall publish the results of this investigation, and this will coincide with a Press Conference at eleven o'clock that morning. Properly accredited Journalists and Photographers, who are present here to-day, shall be invited. The Press Conference will be held in the Zappeíon of Athens. Some of you may know that building already. It was built as the Athletes' Residence for the Games of the First Olympiad. Now—let me begin to describe what I can to-day. Shortly after the President of the IOC was informed of what General Ouranós was really up to—that his boosting Greece for the Games was only a cover-up for a more dæmonic scheme—I too was informed. I have been pursuing this now for just under fifteen months. I, too, agreed that the best way to put a stop to such tampering with the Olympics, by politics, was to allow politics to develop until to-day, and this has now been done. As the General was being allowed to think that he really was going to see an Olympic Nation, of his own devising, built above the Army base at Litóchoron, I was following all of his activities. It so happened that the Olympic Gold Medallist, Ivor Hefferon, was free to come to Athens, on the twenty-ninth of February. Mister Hefferon had been informed, of certain facts of the situation, but I, as well as Mister Hefferon's advisers, Lord Dalbeattie and Professor Rembetikós, and the President of the IOC, felt that the Olympic Athlete should not be swamped with too much information, especially as much of it was hinting at being more aimed to damage our *own* Government than to thwart the Olympics or the IOC."

The President cleared his throat, then carried on.

"On Sunday, the twelfth of this month, Ivor Hefferon was successful in getting ahold of certain documents. These he handed over to Professor Rembetikós, who immediately turned them over to me. I then summoned my Chief of Staff, General Pétros Theotókis, and confronted him with the documents. The documents described, in great detail, the nuclear arms silo that Ouranós was planning to construct beneath the Olympic Nation. My Chief of Staff and I then had a very serious talk."

The Head of State looked over all of the Stadium. He took another drink of water.

"General Ouranós was planning a *coup d'état*. To-day, in Athens, on National Day, he was scheming to oust me as your President, and to replace me by General Pétros Theotókis!"

The President's voice was shaking now, and he was pounding his fist on the Podium.

"Now—you my people—you *know* my past. You know that, when the Junta was mis-governing this country, I was living in exile. My life was in danger. I was able to survive, by being granted asylum, in Paris, where many of our countrymen went. That you all know, I do not often discuss this publicly now. But to-day...has called for it!"

For the first time since he took the stand, the people found reason to applaud him. Everybody was on the edge of his or her seat. The whole gathering was getting nervous. The applause was short. People were curious to hear more of the inside story.

"Need you guess...I had many old scores to settle with my Chief of Staff. He was a good soldier. He was a tough man. He had been a powerful person during the Junta. I had been personally requested to leave Greece, when the Colonels took over, by General Pétros Theotókis. But...our correspondence is even older than this. He and I fought together, in the Civil War, and his sister married my cousin. I felt...when I became President...that I *must* bury the ax. So—I *tried* to bury the ax—and allowed myself to pardon Theotókis."

The people applauded again, but even shorter this time.

"Two Mondays ago, I was ready to relieve the Chief of Staff of his command. But I confronted him directly, by saying: 'How could you possibly have let General Ouranós proceed this far with his monstrous schemes?' To stand here and admit to you all that Theotókis's reply to my query shocked me...would be to belie the expressive eloquence of the great Greek language! My Chief of Staff proceeded to detail to me the *real* reason behind General Ouranós's burning desire to stage a Deed Ceremony, here, on National Day. Ouranós's motive was to *oust* me, and to oust the whole of the elected Government of Athens, while everyone was out of town, in order to return the dictatorship! General Theotókis confessed this to me...and I use the word *confess* deliberately...because, until the thirteenth of this month, Theotókis himself was part of this conspiracy. Theotókis had struck a deal with General Ouranós, to become your new President, with the understanding that Ouranós become your new Prime Minister. Everybody knows that the two of them have been like father and son. I just wonder what the Chief of Staff is now thinking...as he watches this broadcast from Olympia. In exchange for his agreeing to tell me all that he knew, I agreed to keep him on as Chief of Staff, but only for the duration of my investigation of these matters, until Maundy Thursday, when I shall be appointing a new man. On the twentieth of April, General Pétros Theotókis will retire to his family home, on the island of Zákynthos. Theotókis will not be court-martialled."

The President of the Republic took a long drink of water, as the crowd remained absolutely still.

"I am able, now, to inform you of the names of the five men in the Army, who have been placed under arrest, as of three o'clock this morning. They are Generals Barbándis, Peripóthytos, and Andrikákis, along with Colonels Boukálas and Zonáris. All five men are presently being detained, and all five men have been given *dishonourable* discharges. They have been stripped of all rank, privilege, and benefits."

The people applauded now, but wanted to hear the conclusion.

The President now burst into pure anger: "Imagine—a *coup d'état* was going to happen *this* morning! I was supposed to have given Ouranós the Deed, which I never had any intention of giving, and he was supposed to have *killed* me, after this Ceremony! But I gave instructions to General Theotókis to inform Ouranós that there was nothing to fear, that everything was ready. Thus perpetuate madmen ...they'll believe anything at all...if it fits their futile plans. And the most ironic thing is...that their *coup d'état* was to have occurred when one thousand white *doves* were being released from this Ancient Stadium! Imagine...using the symbol of *Peace*...for declaring their own personal *War*!"

Contemplating these words...one could have heard a pin drop in the Stadium. The multitude was mute.

People were looking afraid to move their heads side to side. Even furtive glances now were absolutely useless.

"Well—I am *not* going to let those doves of Peace sit in cages of Dictatorship! I am *not* going to keep them there—until their feathers rot! I am *not* going to leave this Ancient Stadium...I am *not* going to leave Olympia...until every single dove is flying *free*...in the warmth of our Grecian air! Soldiers—I command you—in the name of the President of the Republic of Greece—in the name of the *Free People* of Greece!—*release* those doves! Release those doves this instant! Release those doves—from their prisons—and let those doves fly *free!*"

Suddenly—from behind the huge video screen that towered above the Symphony Orchestra—the first of the doves was seen...then others...then dozens of others...then hundreds...then all of the thousand were swooping up into the atmosphere as one.

"Fly—My Beauties—fly—fly—fly! Fly—My Beauties—high as your bodies dare soar, dare reach! Fly—My Beauties—fly high as you can—for Peace!"

The Head of State now was shouting, and could be seen by three cameras upon the large screen. His right arm was raised aloft, as the birds, now high in the air, were turning ninety degrees. The white doves now were sailing, in a great oval in the sky, directly above the multitude's thousands of astonished heads.

"Fly—My Beauties—to Athens—white doves—fly to our nation's Heartland—to the tragic city of Pallas—fly there—with your message of Peace!"

The central screen of three images now was showing the soaring doves, who suddenly were turning one hundred and eighty degrees. They were coursing back across the Arena, to the awed amazement of the whole Stadium. Everybody now was standing...cheering...but mainly...crying...

"Fly—My Beauties—my Cherished Ones—take your kind message across *all* of Hellas—across *all* of this war-ravaged Balkan Peninsula—over *all* of Europe—over *all* of this Earth—sail high—with the clouds—on your glorious wings—for *Peace!*"

The President of the Republic was now openly weeping. The stunned throng kept watching, tearfully, emotionally, as the great mass of doves now began heading due east, up the Alphaiós Valley, towards the capital of Greece. The white ball, in motion, kept getting smaller, and smaller, and smaller. Many of the people, as they kept on watching, continually were praying to God for their safety.

The President was now wiping his eyes and was barely able to say softly: "Let us *now* begin to heal to-day's wounds. I...am a man who *can* forgive. I...would *never* have returned to my homeland...had this *not* been true. I...do *not* hate those people who were plotting to put me away. I...pity them, and above all, feel compassion for whatever ignominy may befall their poor families. *To* them, I extend my deepest sympathy. *From* them...I ask compassion and forgiveness...as well...for their loved ones...for this our whole country..."

The Head of State paused, to clear his voice.

"As this Deed Ceremony is concluding...let us take this time now to contemplate what we *all* have just gone through. A *bad* part of us *has* just died, so that a *better* part of us may now *thrive!*"

26th April – Wednesday – 4.25 PM

I was recalling the liberation of the doves, as I lay upon some forsaken hillslope of Olympos, when the answer came. For weeks...I had been torturing myself, trying to force some response from my brain, that would deduce my reason for Being, in order to aid my future days. But the answer was...that I had *already* been living...exactly as I should. My small contribution to the Olympic Movement, on Greece's National Day, was the evidence. What more proof did I need?

Until this epiphany, as I lay in such pain, my whole Being had *not* been able to accept the contribution that it had made. Everything had happened so fast. The events were of epical proportions. Due to the words that I had spoken that Saturday...two human beings had ended their lives...as I had looked on...helplessly...horrified.

Perhaps the guilt, over that, had required some superhuman force, such as this fall and recovery, to knock some sense into my head? Realising this, I suddenly began feeling Spiritual Peace transfusing my every limb.

I now knew I *could* make it—no matter what I would choose to do—with the rest of my life. If it were painting, I'd do it and enjoy it. What was the requirement for public acclaim? If that would come...then it could be accepted it...and one would proceed again.

Suddenly—I was truly feeling happy!

I wanted to dance for joy!

I wanted to get up and shout!

And by God—my body *was* getting up!

So I began shouting, for the whole mountain to hear: "Thank you! Thank you! Thank you!"

The Olympian Ideal is *mens sana in corpore sano*, as the Latin language put it so well. And the Greeks, before the Romans, expressed it in *their* language, too.

In all my sporting life, I had believed it.

But not until *this* very moment—had I *felt* it—within my innermost tissue!

Even though my body outwardly was exhibiting hurt, the realisation, within, that was radiating, outwards, in all directions, was the most jubilant feeling that I ever have known...before...during...or

547

after...my Olympic win. This was something that was coming from that same source that energised The Very First Nebula, that created Gravity, that made The First Amœba.

On my back was my pack—and in it I couldn't help searching for the fossil that I had found earlier in the day. Yes—what I was feeling was what caused this very fossil to *be*. As I now was holding this crystallised coral, and shutting tight my eyes, even Time itself seemed no longer a Mystery, but The Very Energy Of Energies, without which The Universe would have remained formless, without which even *God* never could have been!

25th March – National Day – 11.45 AM

The Announcer was waiting until the thousand doves could no longer be seen by anyone. Then he began saying: "Would everybody please rise. This Deed Ceremony now is concluded. The Symphony Orchestra of Athens, under the baton of Maestro Mándis Loulákis, now will perform portions of the last composition of Amadeus Mozart, the *Requiem Mass in D Minor*, for Full Chorus and Soprano Soloist. This work, which was left incomplete when Mozart died at age thirty-five, has been personally chosen by the Conductor. As you will notice from the Programme, the *First Piano Concerto* of Frédéric Chopin had been scheduled. The Athens Symphony Orchestra and Chorus performed Mozart's *Requiem* only last Sunday, in tribute to our country's late Nobel Prize winning Poet, who died in February. As the music is beginning, will everybody please remain standing until the President of the Republic has left the Ancient Stadium with his party. We shall then instruct you, by groups, to proceed in an orderly fashion through the ruins, to the Kiosk Gate. Please leave only when it is your turn, as the single road will be filled with traffic that has been timed to flow by the second. Your limousines will be waiting. Do follow instructions—please."

As soon as the Announcer ceased talking, the Conductor was raising his baton. In the Maestro's mind, as the mournful cadence of the last work ever composed by Mozart began to be played by his Orchestra, the thirty-three-year-old man could not help but feel the true tragedy of Mozart's early demise. Loulákis, as he was becoming one with the sonorous beauty of the haunting melody, felt very much saddened that Mozart *knew* that he was dying as he was writing the *Requiem*, and in many respects wrote it as his own epitaph. The Mass had been commissioned anonymously, by someone unknown to the genius. When Mozart was passing away, that final night, he gave the incomplete work to his pupil Franz Süssmeyer, who added the Sanctus, the Benedictus,. and the Agnus Dei. When the *Requiem* was turned over to the anonymous stranger, this man gave it to his employer, Count Franz von Walsegg of Ruppach, who then plagiarised the dead composer's last work. The vicious Count copied the whole

Mass, by his own hand, then had it performed as his very own work. But, Truth eventually did out...

The orchestral introduction was making everybody sad. It had been quite a day already. Weight of events was now bearing down on one and all. But that was as it should be.

At the head of the President's Procession was the Chief Priestess of Hera, walking mournfully to the beat of the music. Her five maidens were following, and behind them were the Head of State, looking very sombre indeed, and the Director of the Ruins, Evanthía Selináki. Beside them were the young men, three to the right, three to the left, dressed as in ancient times. Behind Doctor Selináki followed the last of the seven youths, and then Ivor Hefferon pursued.

Behind the Olympic Gold Medallist were all of the Ministers and their wives, officials of the Government, and the Security Corps. Everybody now was taking a deep breath, as the Chorus were just beginning to raise their voices high. The time was eleven forty-six.

INTROIT

CHORUS
Requiem æternam dona eis, Domine:
Et lux perpetua luceat eis.

SOPRANO
Te decet hymnus, Deus, in Sion:
Et tibi reddetur votum in Jerusalem.

The President and his party now were entering the tunnel of the Crypt. The multitude were sitting down, and beginning to listen more and more to the moving *Requiem.*

CHORUS
Exaudi orationem meam:
Ad te omnis caro veniet.

As the Presidential party had come to the other side of the tunnel, the Head of State was gesturing to the young lad Theatrínos, who was once again standing between the two fellows of the Security Corps. Remaining motionless, to their right, was the Delegation from Northern New York State. The Singer had removed his helmet, as the President began approaching, and now was easily recognised. The grieving boy gladly descended the mound to join the Procession with the others, then was walking beneath the pines and out of the Áltis. The time was eleven fifty-one.

Waiting limousines quickly began filling with Dignitaries, then were speeding through the deserted village towards the Hotel Amalía. No sirens were being allowed to blare this time. The President of the

549

Republic would soon be on his way back to Athens, by helicopter, which was beginning to start its engines. Inside the Stadium, the Chorus had just begun singing the Kýrie Eléison of the *Requiem*. Members of the International Olympic Committee and their Guests were already entering the Crypt to leave the Stadium behind. When the Kýrie was wringing the last tears out of the seated Greek populace, with the incandescent brilliance of the funereal music, the President of the Hellenes was just getting into his Helicopter Of State and soaring away. It was eleven fifty-three.

The Kýrie was now finishing, and the IOC limousines, that had been waiting in the side-streets of the village until the President's entourage had passed, now started picking up their dignified passengers, four to the car, and were rushing them as quickly as possible back to Academy precincts.

DIES IRAE

CHORUS
Confutatis maledictis:
Flammis acribus addictis.

"Ambassadors may now proceed through the Áltis, to their limousines," the Announcer was stating, and their march across the dusty Arena was commencing. It was now eleven fifty-five.

CHORUS
Voca me cum benedictis:
Oro supplex et acclinis.
Cor contritum quasi cinis:
Gere curam mei finis.

Four minutes after they had left their seats, the first of the Ambassadors was on his way from the site. And at twelve noon exactly, the Announcer was saying: "Would all Members of the world's National Olympic Committees and their Guests, as well as those Representatives of the world's International Sporting Federations and their Guests, please proceed through the Áltis. You are requested to stroll the short distance past the Old Museum to the Hotel Xénia. Thank you."

CHORUS
Lacrimosa dies illa:
Qua resurget ex favilla.
Judicandus homo reus:
Huic ergo parce, Deus.
Pie Jesu Domine:
Dona eis requiem.

550

As the final portion of the *Requiem Mass in D Minor* was concluding, the last Member of the International Olympic Committee was being driven away. The Announcer then told those who were still waiting: "It is a great honour to announce the world première of the *First Symphony* of Mándis Loulákis, which he has entitled *The Transmigration Of The Soul*. It is a work for Full Chorus, Soloists, and Orchestra, and is inspired by the 'Myth Of Er' from *The Republic* of Plato."

Just then, the lowest notes possible of the bass viols began to sound, lugubriously, as the men of the Chorus began chanting in Homeric Greek. This kept building and building, until a deep-throated gong caused a flute and a bassoon to join in a tender duet. A Soprano began accompanying the instruments.

Throughout the First Movement of the Symphony, the large contingent of the NOCs and IFs proceeded to the Kiosk Gate, as the stirring new music was being broadcast amongst the evergreens. The VIPs did not even seem to mind that they had been told to walk, due to the traffic congestion. It was refreshing and, by the time that they had left the Sacred Olympian Compound, many had found themselves smiling and laughing again. This great throng continued upwards and round the three bends in the road. By twenty minutes, almost all of them were inside the Xénia, and everybody was aiming for the dining-room.

At twelve ten the Announcer was saying: "Would all Members of the Greek Olympic Association and Guests please proceed through the Áltis. Twenty-five limousines are waiting in the Army camp across the road to return you as quickly as possible to Athens."

Five minutes later, the Press were allowed to leave. "Please proceed directly to the Army convoy now waiting just outside the Kiosk Gate." And at twelve twenty the convoy began loading in all the Journalists and Photographers. When the all-clear signal was sent from the Xénia, that the last of the NOCs and IFs were safely inside the hotel, the Army convoy started to proceed uphill past the Xénia into the village. Then it wasn't long before all of them were unloading at the Hotel Amalía. The Press had until six o'clock to file their reports and use the darkrooms and communications facilities. With all that had happened, the place became a maelstrom of frenetic activity.

But presently, with all of the VIPs and the Press having vacated the Stadium, *The Transmigration Of The Soul* was gaining momentum and was shifting mood dramatically. The Chorus, now full-throated, along with the four Bass Soloists, were singing in contrapuntal harmony. The five thousand local people sitting motionless, entranced. The Announcer plainly could see how intently the people were listening, so he decided to forego the rest of the schedule entirely. The Announcer was Greek. The people were Greek. And the young Maestro conducting his world première performance was Greek. It would have been a crime to have the people *leave* now—a crime to have *nobody* cheer. This

551

Ancient Stadium, of the Olympic Games, this morning, had witnessed *twin deaths*. The least this Holy Shrine could do now would be to hear a *single birth*, something harmonic, inspirational, *alive*.

Thus, for the next half hour, Technicians, Soldiers, and Locals of Olympia listened...as *The Transmigration Of The Soul* moved them even more than anything they had seen or heard this fatal day.

26ᵗʰ April — Wednesday – 4.35 PM

I had just crossed the ice-sheet, that spanned the sloping island of my fall and the towering pines of the forest. Having vaunted Death, I now was limping badly, but attempting to envalue my Life.

If that rocky patch of land where I had crashed was an isle, in an icy sea, then this forest I now was entering was its mainland. And *somewhere* on this mainland was the Refuge Hut, await with warmth, food, drink.

Every step of the way massaged the pain in my right leg. It had to get exercise. Walking wasn't easy. It was more like stumbling. Zig-zagging like a sheep with anthrax, I now was immersed in a realm of green, of titanic trees, of lush bushy ferns, of vines and white brazen flowers.

Lavish primæval beauty, virgin pure...it was inconceivable that one human footstep ever had been here. Tingling with wonder at the natural splendour, as if I were walking through a cathedral built for Gods and not for meagre human beings, some massive tree trunks were upright, some struck by lightning bolts and felled, æons back, and some just too tough to rotten.

I was making paths where no paths ever existed, and none will ever again. My breathing now was heavier than it ever had been in all of the races I had won. Air here sank like stones—onto the gonads. My very Soul felt chilled—yet eerily alive.

"I'm exceptionally lucky just to be breathing!" I shouted out loud and limped along. "I *know* I'll get back to the Hut. I *know* it! The Gods are *with* me!"

I wasn't killed! "Even if there's no escape from this alpine *terre sauvage*...I know I'm lucky!"

But was I deceiving myself? Had my good luck, at long last, truly taken flight? Perhaps my fall was but a foretaste of greater disaster?

Beware snakes! Serpents surely scaled these untouched climes? Without a doubt vipers called *this* land, of prehistoric myth untrammeled, *home*!

Down dale. Up hill. Down dale. Up hill. Exhaustion. Lost. Fear.

Three whole more ridges had to be scaled, then descaled, like fish. Each one, I prayed, would be the last.

Faith? Was it gone already? Fast to flee!

At the top of each ridge I prayed with my last ounce of strength that the view would be of the mountain's central Vale, whence I could be gazing downslope to the Hut. But...each ridge...was just another let-down...

Night was coming...and with it descending fog. Clouds were creeping slowly down from high above, and with them no chance of survival? Rescue? Lost—I kept plodding on.

Up up...zig...zag. "Just one more ridge..." Getting near dusk... By direction of the Sun...west...I had to be going...north? Then one last push...and oh my God I was up it! This was it—this was it!

There—below—was the tremendous Olympian Amphitheatre of Comedy, its seats filled to capacity with beeches and pines. Wind was rustling all their billions of needles and leaves. All the two-hued green things were giggling...politely.

But suddenly, out of the green, the most beautiful sound I ever could hear came softly rising upwards from below.

Bells! Bells from afar! Bells! Of mules—bells—filtering—through the green—upwards—down there—from somewhere—from something alive—and with Mankind!

25ᵗʰ March – National Day – 1.30 PM

The weather had taken a turn for the worse. As if Zeus had been angered by contravention of the Sanctity of his Shrine, thunderheads had started rolling southwards, from the Gulf of Korinth, and a storm was quickly approaching the Valley Alphaiós.

The International Olympic Committee and Guests were meeting one last time, at an informal luncheon, before the limousines would retrace their route to Athens. Everyone was gathered inside the Pavilion Tent erected within the Running Track of the International Olympic Academy.

At one of the tables were seated Professor Rembetikós, Lord Dalbeattie, the Dowager Duchess of Brendon, Ada, Ivor, Pános Mavrolóngos, Theatrínos, and Evanthía Selináki.

"Wasn't that new Symphony simply brilliant?" the Academy's Administrator asked.

"Oh it was wonderful!" Ada responded.

"Ada and I went back into the Stadium, with Theatrínos, after changing, so that we could hear it."

"It was magnificent," Theatrínos agreed.

"You know," Professor Rembetikós said proudly, "Loulákis is a friend of mine...and I recall his saying to me once...that he likes your poetry."

"Really? *My* little scribbles?" the young Singer queried.

Then to the Duchess the Director of the Museums explained: "Don't listen to him—he's pretending to be modest—which he isn't at all!

553

Theatrínos is only our country's most popular Singer and Lyricist—with a huge following of fans—including *me!*"

"Me, too!" Pános added and patted the boy's back.

The Duchess raised her glass of wine and said: "Then to your continued success, young Man."

Everyone responded to the toast.

"By the way," the Professor said to Theatrínos, "when things calm down, say next week or so, I shall have you and Loulákis over to my house, for dinner."

"That's very kind," replied the youth.

"Not at all—it's my duty," and the Professor winked at Lord Dalbeattie. "I think you two should collaborate. How about a grand modern *opera?* Your poetry would be perfectly suited—for such a venture. In fact—I'll announce right now—that *I* am going to commission it!"

"Hear hear," Lord Dalbeattie responded heartily and raised his glass. "To the new opera!"

Everybody clinked Theatrínos's glass.

"Well—this, indeed, has been a most exciting day," the Duchess announced. "One shouldn't know what to do for amusement...back in London."

"You're *not* leaving Hellas, Your Grace," Professor Rembetikós stated jovially. "In fact—both His Lordship and your good self are now my willing captives. I've already made plans for us all to sail to Páros, for a rest at my country villa."

"How wonderful!" Doctor Selináki sighed. "But I simply can't... my Museums!"

"Oh you'll love it there," Pános added. "It'll do you *and* your Museums good to break away...for a few days! Remember—what was it—*five* years ago, Professor?"

"We had the whole *island* dancing!" Rembetikós recalled.

"You Greeks are the most *amazing* people!" the Dowager Duchess said honestly. "One minute—you're up to your necks in some insurmountable Tragedy—and the very next, you're out in the sunshine celebrating The Dance Of Life Itself!"

"How on Earth do you do it?" Ivor asked.

Theatrínos admitted for all: "Genetics!"

"True," the Administrator agreed.

"That's why we of the IOC jump at the slimmest chance to come here. You know—the sooner Greece gets the Games back—and the sooner the IOC *do* move from Switzerland—the better," Lord Dalbeattie confessed.

"What was that I just heard you say?" inquired the President of the IOC, at the next table. He was laughing.

"Now—you know damned well my feelings on the subject," retorted Dalbeattie to his organization's leader.

"Yes," the IOC President responded. "And you know what?"

"No," answered His Lordship.

"I'm beginning to agree!" the IOC President concluded.

"Well, it's about time," Lord Dalbeattie replied, and the two dignified gentlemen clinked glasses.

"By the way," Ivor asked the Administrator, "what ever happened to Dora Cain? Was she allowed to attend the Ceremony?"

"No," Pános said. "I believe that the late Major was worried that his Italian wife would scratch the American girl's eyes out."

"Of whom are we speaking?" inquired the Duchess.

"Dora Cain, Ma'am," the Olympic Athlete answered. "Thýella's bastard-daughter, and her son's (the late Major's) mistress. A spy. Working with the MOON-OC, from the States."

"I see," Her Grace nodded.

Mavrolóngos added: "I was informed by the military, on my return here after the Ceremony, that Dora Cain, whom Movóros had stationed in the Academy Library, had been watching events on the closed-circuit television. When matters increasingly pointed to the downfall of the MOON-OC, Dora Cain fled the Academy and headed due north, over the ridge of this hill. She was apprehended, trying to escape, by troops encircling the compound. Presently she's aboard the Presidential Flight back to Athens, where she'll be held for questioning, then deported."

"Did you notice that the Head of State tactfully refrained from mentioning her rôle?" Lord Dalbeattie asked.

"Did you notice that the Head of State steered clear of all the international fur that's presently flying, all over the world, because of this?" Professor Rembetikós replied. "As for myself, I never had to deliver a more circumspect speech in my life!"

"How do you think poor *Ivor* feels?" the Duchess said tenderly and placed her hand over that of the Athlete.

"Nasty that," Dalbeattie agreed, "poor Ivor's having to let the cat out of the bag..."

"*Somebody* had to do it," Theatrínos said.

"Agreed," Evanthía replied.

"Well—I'm bloody well glad I did it!" Ivor now said proudly. "At first—when it was all happening—it was as if my worst nightmare had suddenly sprung to life."

"I know," Her Grace said sincerely. "But you did a noble service to the Olympics."

"And one for which we all are humbly grateful," stated Lord Dalbeattie.

The President of the International Olympic Committee, eavesdropping again, unashamedly, decided that now was the appropriate moment to stand. He rose slowly, cleared his throat, then said: "Friends—to-day, when all the dust may clear—we shall look back upon these momentous events with a clean conscience. Our Committee have taken a great step forward, albeit one not without pain. Compared to the longevity of the Ancient Games, our lifetime, in this Modern Era, still must be acknowledged as being in infancy., But, infants do grow, and God knows, infants do learn, by their own mistakes. We have *walked* ..but now the time has come for us to start to *speak*."

There was silence in the Pavilion Tent. On the northern ridge of the Academy's grounds distant thunder could be heard approaching.

"Just as the President of the Republic of Greece will be publishing the report of his investigation, this forthcoming Maundy Thursday, so too should the IOC Sub-Committee, who have been studying the feasibility that the Games return permanently to Greece, publish their conclusion."

"But, Sir," Lord Dalbeattie replied, "the conclusion has not yet been reached."

The President of the IOC took a deep breath, then he said: "This Session of the International Olympic Committee is still convened. I propose, here and now, as President of this organization, that this Session go down in history. Enough of rhetoric...enough of stalling ...enough of worrying about superpower opinion! Events of *this* day have ineradicably changed us all. To deny this is folly—and does our Committee great disservice. Therefore, I am hereby bringing our debate, that Greece be returned the Games permanently, to an end. I am calling now for a vote. All in favour say aye."

"Aye!" shouted the assembly, with such vigour, that everyone present was clearly startled.

"All opposed..."

Not one single voice arose in opposition. Just then, lightning flashed and a terrifyingly large clap of thunder sounded behind the Academy's hillslope. The awestruck President of the IOC, who practically jumped out of his skin, laughed nervously and announced: "Olympian Zeus approves! The motion is carried! The Games of the Olympiad immediately succeeding those next scheduled are to be given *back* to the land that sired them, and given back *unto perpetuity!*"

United by a truly major moment in modern history, everyone in the Pavilion Tent felt him or herself rising. All in the august assembly were deeply, deeply moved. Professor Rembetikós was bursting into tears, and Pános Mavrolóngos was sobbing; their belief in the Games so innate.

Looking with intense relief, at all of the movèd Members of the IOC, their President lifted high his glass, and said, as his voice was shaking: "*Citius—Altius—Fortius!* To the powers of The Past, that have never left this site, we hereby lift our glasses. And thus, by the Eternal Inspiration that *is* Greece...our long-awaited decision, to return the Olympic Games where they belong, has triumphed. It now is our most fervent prayer...that the Olympic Ideal...that we have ever attempted to foster...will now loudly proclaim itself...for the noble aim...of Peace!"

26th April – Wednesday – 5.50 PM

Bells continued. Where were they coming from? Where were the mules? I couldn't see a thing. I went west a bit higher, in order to be able to see better. "Maybe the Hut's *westward*? Maybe I'm *way* off mark? Maybe I'll still have to climb—back *uphill!*" Oh God...
But it's got to be somewhere nearby! Where were those bloody mule-bells coming from? Somewhere...here? But...
No! Fog down below—and to the left—was suddenly clearing—elevating mysteriously—in a great big bunch—horizontally—like a tablecloth hoisted by two wives.
"There! Straight down—below there—*below* there!"
I began shouting, whooping for joy! Right below I now could see red tiles. Red-orange tiles. Roofs. Buildings. Smoke. Safety. Warmth. Food. Rest! I was dancing—elated—hurt leg or not!
Ow! It kept smarting so with pain. I kept clenching my teeth, as down a rough path I kept descending, quickly as my bum-thigh would move. Downwards I shot for those bells! Limping all the way!

The path was C-shaped. I was in a daze. I was so eager to get back to the Refuge that I don't really recall much of anything. That same ice-sheet where Leftéris had me dig for the water pipe...I do remember that...and how I crossed it in a flash. And then the downward trek along the path that led invariably to the Hut...
There it was...bastion against avalanches!
"*Help!*" I kept shouting and limping even quicker. "*It's me!*" I was so excited I was even happy to see the *rockpile* where Leftéris had me sweating. Nobody was within sight. It soon would be dark.
"*Help!*" I screamed.
Out rushed Leftéris—from the kitchen. "My God—you're *alive!*" he was shouting and running to catch me. I was collapsing, feeling like I was going to faint. His strong arms were catching my body, then lifting it up from the ground.

They had me stretched out on the bench, along one of the clubroom's walls. Kitty was in a chair beside me—putting a spoon of brandy to my lips. "That's all right—don't talk!" she commanded.
"I have to..."
"No! Leftéris's orders! He'll *kill* ya!"
"Where'd he go?"
"In the kitchen with the Hartmunds. They've almost been having seizures over ya! Ya certainly owe everybody a great big apology!" She was angry.

I tried pushing up from the bench.

"Stay put!" Kitty bellowed and forced me to acquiesce.

Someone had already cleansed my wounded leg. I think it was Leftéris. But it might have been Doctor Hartmund.

"Don't ya dare move! I'm gonna go fetch ya some soup!" Kitty then vanished.

My back was to the door. Mountain climbers were behind me whispering. I felt such a stupid fool. Footsteps approached. A man's boots. "So—you're alive!" boomed the voice of the Manager. "You gave us all heart-attacks!"

"I'm terribly, terribly sorry..."

"Don't you *ever* do a crazy thing like that again—not on *my* goddamned mountain!" Leftéris hollered.

I shook with chills: "I'm so sorry..." I started to cry.

He took my right hand between both of his. "God, how you scared us," he said tenderly, like a sorrowing father to his lost son. He kissed my forehead. There were tears in his eyes. "We've all grown to *love* you so...up here...we couldn't believe you had...perished."

"I...didn't..."

"The Gods were testing you—you *know* that?"

"I know..."

"And you *survived* the test."

"I guess so..."

The kindly face of Frau Hartmund now was looking down upon me. She was wiping a tear from her face. She was taking my hand, as Leftéris was releasing it, and saying: "I...prayed so hard...you'd be all right..."

"Thank you..." I said and turned my head to the wood of the bench. "I feel so ashamed..."

"Don't, Boy, please," she responded tenderly. "Something... supramundane...was out there...calling you..."

"It *scared* me so! I *saw* something! I *really* did! I *saw* something ...glowing...way atop a spire of rock...like some Gothic gargoyle...on some great cathedral...suddenly coming *alive*...pulsing...with *Light*..."

Nobody knew what to say. I couldn't go on.

Leftéris sighed. "There *is* something up there...something none of us *ever* will be able to describe...something no man...for all of Time... will be able to classify."

I just shook my head yes.

"Each time I go to the top...I feel its presence."

"I have felt it, too," Frau Hartmund agreed, "just to-day."

"And I, too," said a man's low voice. It was Herr Hartmund, suddenly behind his wife. "It's why we keep coming back here..."

"Of all the many mountains we have climbed..." stated his wife tenderly, "*this* one...has a *Presence*...as none other..."

There was silence.

"The Ineluctable Presence...atop this Mystic Mountain..."
Leftéris declared slowly, "never reveals Itself, in Its various manifestations, but to those whom It seeks. No one who goes chasing after It...can expect to see but Its Shadow, which stirs the Breeze. And...always will It appear...when the one on the Path is least prepared for its Evidencing." He paused, to choose his words carefully. "And...to the best of my Knowledge...from too many years upon this Sacred Mount...I am only certain that always It appears when the mountaineer ...has strayed..."

"The key to understanding It..." Frau and Herr Hartmund said together, "...is to traverse the landscape of your Heart..."

Fire in the hearth crackled with its own energy. I suddenly felt a great rush of love for the three, and smiled at each of them. Leftéris smiled back paternally, and said: "I just was speaking on the telephone...with Ada."

"You were? God...was...was to-day the funeral?"
"It was."
"Million years ago...since this morning...it seems..."
"For us...as well," Herr Hartmund agreed.
I asked: "How is she? How's Ada?"
"She'll be here to-morrow," Leftéris announced.
"Here? She's really coming back?"
"She is."
"Did...did you tell her...about my fall?"
"I had to."
Just as I was on the verge of slipping into some dream, along came Kitty, laden with a bowl of hearty soup.

Gladly was I being banished to bed, for the whole of the next day. It was about eight o'clock of the evening. Kitty had my right arm slung over her well-endowed shoulders and Leftéris had my left. They were walking me rightwards in the circuit round the Hut. We just had arrived at the Eastern Overlook, when I paused, to have a quick look. The Half Moon was visible above the violet-shaded Amphitheatre of Comedy.

Leftéris, always one to augur omens from the sky, said: "I knew you had The Fates inside your pocket."

I smiled, as both he and Kitty kissed me on the lips, delicately. Then, I looked with tears in my eyes to the heavens on high. Indigo were the skies above, and diamond brights were pulsing through to grant a little Light.

1st April – Saturday – High Noon

Thunderheads kept hovering above the Olympian region for six and a half solid days. Rain, from the heavens, cleansed, and kept cleansing,

559

what the Deed Ceremony had done, as well as what the Deed Ceremony had left behind.

The heavy presence of the Army was gone by the next morning after General Ouranós's suicide. Ordered to disperse as quickly as possible, by General Pétros Theotókis, the military establishment was undergoing its *own* ritual cleansing, during the week, as many more Officers than publicly announced were given dishonourable discharges. The Press, as well, had been made to understand that it was to no avail to remain in tiny Olympia. The investigation was now being conducted in Athens. The Press had one last flurry of activity, at the Hotel Amalía, when the President of the International Olympic Committee had paid them a surprise visit, with the official communiqué that announced the IOC Session's endorsement of the Games being returned permanently to Greece. *That*, indeed, had even transcended the attempted *coup d'état* as world news. So the Press, after filing their stories, had left Olympia happy, even though it was pouring down with rain.

In order to give Ivor and Ada a respite from the Press, who had hounded the IOC Chief as to their whereabouts, all that he had stated was: "They've returned to Athens, on the President's Flight." Given that the Media were not allowed to follow the Head of State's exit, they presumed that these words were true.

"Oh—I'm so glad, Ivor, that we've had this week to be together," Ada was stating this first weekend after the Deed Ceremony. "Finally—the Sun's begun poking through!"

Only since eleven this morning had the rains finally let up. She and Ivor just were walking from the Academy, past the ruins, to the huge parking lot where the troops had been encamped. They were on their way to the New Museum, through the olive grove, when a shout was rushing their way. It was from the old farmhouse, of brown tufa stone, off to the left. A window was being thrown open, and Evanthía Selináki was appearing: "Hey—where're you Two going—stay and have lunch with me!"

"All right!" Ada was yelling. As they were approaching the modest home, the Archaeologist stept onto her porch that was on the left side of the poor-man's domicile. Its dozen steps were invisible, as they fell down from the platform atop of which Evanthía was standing, but in the opposite direction from their approach. "I love this old house," she was saying passionately.

"I love hearing you speak!" Ivor admitted just as passionately, and Ada agreed.

"You should be an actress..." Ada said and laughed: "...*again!*"

"Don't worry—I have to be!" the Director laughed and the three sat down at her white lawn-table ten yards from the porch. The women didn't sit long, and soon were bustling to set the table and bring food.

"Hasn't this weather been incredible?" Evanthía asked. She looked lovely to-day, very relaxed in a black skirt and pretty pink blouse. "I adore it here when it rains. Only then do the delicious aromas of the soil blossom forth—like perfumes from India. I also love it because none of my staff *mind* being cooped up indoors! We always get ten times more work done when it rains."

Her laughter was as delicious as the odiferous air. They all were immensely enjoying the simple repast. Only retsina, three types of olives, fresh bread, feta cheese, and tomato-cucumber salad with olive oil and fresh-cut lemons were present.

"Everything tastes wonderful!" Ada said in raptures.

"I think we're all just a bit crazy...to be out of doors," Ivor said.

"Tell me, what have you two been *doing* all week, or should I use my imagination?" Evanthía wondered. It was a revelation, this sensual side of her personality.

"Well—as soon as you gave us permission—last weekend—to use the Stadium..." Ivor began.

"Then it's all set? You're going ahead with your Rededication Rite? Marvellous!" the Director said approvingly. "I'm all in favour of it!"

"It's for the evening of the New Moon, this Wednesday," Ada announced.

"Splendid," Evanthía said.

"And there won't be a single soldier present," Ada added.

"Thank The Gods for that!" the Director sighed with relief. "My nerves couldn't suffer *another* day like last week!"

"And guess what?" Ada asked.

"What?" replied Evanthía.

"The Government are sending us a helicopter, after the Rite, and flying us to Mount Olympos!" Ada bragged.

"Do you believe that?" Ivor queried incredulously.

"Look—after what you two've done for Greece—that's the very least they can do!" the Director retorted. "I hope you both get some peace of mind up north. By the way—don't forget to watch the news this evening."

"That's right," Ivor said.

"I forgot all about it," Ada added.

"I did, too, but my brightest young Archaeologist reminded me about the big pro-Peloponnesian Games Site rally in Athens to-day," Evanthía stated.

"Theatrínos is doing the organizing—in the Panathenian Stadium, isn't he?" queried Ada.

"Yes," Ivor responded, "with the Professor and the President of the IOC giving speeches. I wish we were there."

"I know," Evanthía concurred. "One gets to feel somewhat isolated out here."

"Listen to her." Ada joked. "She just took part in History—and will inevitably continue doing so—yet she has the nerve to say she's isolated!"

"Women!" Ivor laughed.

"We'll *never* be satisfied!" laughed Evanthía. "Now—if you'll excuse me, I have to rush back to my office. I've a ton of correspondence to catch up on. We've received thousands of letters—just this week!"

"See? One appearance on world-TV, and she's already getting fan-mail!" Ada laughed wickedly.

"And still I'm isolated, I know," Evanthía said, rose, and winked. "Now, just sit and enjoy yourselves. We'll have dinner out of town tonight. I've discovered a great little taverna, only ten kilometres from here."

Ivor replied: "Super—we'll go gladly!"

"Oh—Evanthía?" asked Ada.

"Yes."

"One quick favour. For the three nights previous to the Rededication Rite, Ivor and I shall need to sleep inside the Áltis. Is it all right?"

"Wait till you do!" the Director of the Ruins said devilishly. "I have. And I certainly *didn't* sleep there alone."

"In fact—you didn't even get to sleep at all!" Ada laughed hilariously. "Thanks, Evanthía. You're a living doll."

Just as Zeus had not been amused by the suicides in his Stadium, so too the cicalas of Olympia had not been amused by the Thunderer's perpetual storms. By far outnumbering the omnipresent ravens of the region, this disgruntled and wingèd insect community was no little force to be reckoned with.

Ivor and Ada both seemed to notice the buzzing at once. Suddenly—the grating sound of cicalas was coming from absolutely everywhere, but mostly from the Hill of Krónos, not far through the olive grove.

It was three hundred and sixty degrees of stereo cicalas. They had stored up their scratchy racket inside them somewhere, for shy of one solid week, and now they were itching themselves all over.

Ivor laughed to himself, then said: "They all must have fleas!"

"They are rather loud," Ada retorted. Then she looked at her lover longingly. The look was saying: Make love to me.

The Athlete felt a blood-rush in his loins.

"You never climbed Krónion?" the young Greek woman asked.

Ivor shook his head no.

"Let's hurry up. It's good exercise...for Olympos," she said.

The two left the yard and entered the dirt lane, arm in arm. Puddles were everywhere. All the spring plants looked fresher than fresh, greener than green.

"I love you so much, Ada," Ivor said and kissed her passionately on the mouth. The smell of the air was intoxicating, and different every few steps of the way. The pair were soon turning off the road, leftwards into a donkey path.

Closer and closer they got to Krónion and its pines, louder and louder got the cicalas, and deeper and deeper drove the arrows of Eros into their arteries and veins. Soon as the couple began trudging up the zig-zags of the Hill of Father Time, an enormous flock of crows, that had been sitting in the boughs unseen, rose up, bunched together, and squawked like Harpies who had just provoked something obscene. They flew off towards the ruins. The cicalas trebled in intensity.

"Why is it...this land makes people so *randy?*" the Athlete asked as he kept watching his woman's buttocks from behind. She was wearing very short shorts. He was getting an erection.

"Sounds like a million maracas," she answered cryptically.

"What an image!" the lad announced, but shook his head in agreement.

"That's why Latin Americans love to come here," Ada said.

"Are you joking?"

"No—they don't give a damn about the temples."

"They have their own!"

"Right—but we have *music* in our pines!"

"In this heat—with the noisy beat of these fiendish bugs—playing their sambas—this climb's more difficult than it looks!" Ivor panted. "Didn't I ever tell you I'm used to *horizontal* exercise!"

"*I'll* give you some horizontal!"

"You better!"

"We're not climbing this for nothing!"

They stopt more than once on the ascent, to make each other even hotter than before, with kisses they found impossible to stop.

"If this's what Olympos is going to be like..."

Ada concluded: "Then...this's just a pimple on its butt."

They persisted, soon nearing the summit. A toppled pine, split by the storm, of course was blocking the path. But with a few more vigorous strides, grunts, and flexed muscles the pair were quickly round it. Then, they were on the top. So many pines there were that one couldn't even *see* the ruins.

Who in Hell was interested in ruins, anyway? Right now, all the female and the male were after was The Here and The Now! The male was grabbing the female hard and he kept rubbing himself, fully erect, against her, as he kept burying his tongue in her mouth. The female kept coming up for wind and egging him on by saying: "These *malákas*, I mean, these *maracas* are driving me crazy!"

The word was Greek for *wankers*, the most commonly used invective in the country.

"Don't worry about the *malákas*," the male was responding and the two were tumbling onto the moistened soil. "Oh I want you so bad!" the male kept grunting as he kept squeezing the female and pressing his dick into her pelvis and kissing her again and again: "Loving you...makes all my worries vanish!"

The *maracas* weren't about to vanish. They doubled. What a weird mountain, the male was thinking as both he and the female now were tearing off their clothes. Not even a mountain...just a hill. An earthy reddish bump...hovering between Now and Then...like this horny pair just were!

The male's big hardon just was entering the female's moist slit, nice and slow, all the way up. The female was squatting down onto it, facing the male, who was seated upon the ground, with his penis pointing straight up. The female was impaling herself...slowly...upon his blood-filled spike. What a strange place the odd Ancient Greeks chose for Father Time! The male and the female movements were putting them both right out of this harried world.

The female was sighing: "Whenever I come here..."

"Don't come yet..." the male was groaning.

"I always leave here feeling purged..."

"You've made love up here before?"

"No—never."

"Good."

"I always wanted to."

"Now you are."

"Oh this feels so good!"

"I love you! I love you, Ada, so very much!"

"Being here...it's as if...whatever sins I've committed till to-day...oh God, this feels wonderful...they're...carried away...oh you do it so...well...aloft...to the very heart...of The Universe..."

Then, the moaning female said nothing more. Midday heat, and bodies' own, were increasing by the second. On this summit, with this beautiful young couple making love, the air was as dry as if no drop of rain ever had fallen on the mount in the whole of its temporal career. Yet the male and the female, going at it like the piston of an engine, were sopping wet, from their organs' lubrication, and now they both were gasping aloud, animals, gulping for breath!

30th April – Sunday – Night

If there is anything that can cure the anxious heart, then it is Love. Ada returned to the Refuge Hut, late in the afternoon of the twenty-seventh, whilst I was still asleep. And when I awoke...there she was, sleeping beside me. She, too, had gone through a lot and needed her rest.

But when we both had woken, and were staring in each other's eyes, we felt our energies flowing, in and out of each other's body, and we both felt at Home, at Peace. We began making love, slowly, and our passion increased, for three solid days.

Not once during that period did I stir from the small stone cabin, on the edge of the icy ravine. Ada wouldn't let me. She went to the Hut for food, and carried it to me. And she kissed my sore leg innumerable times, until the pain had gone away. We exercised together inside the cabin. The strength of the muscles and tendons came back with amazing speed. At last, this Sunday evening, when Ada was preparing to bring us our dinner, I said: "No—I'll come with you—and see Leftéris."

It was good to get back out again. Of course, it was impossible to avoid "fresh air", even in the cabin, at this alpine height. But being in the elements again indeed was invigorating.

As we both were turning round the northeast corner of the Refuge Hut, we bumped into the Manager playing with Rosy. She left her master and danced about us both, barking.

"Good girl," Lefteris challenged and boxed her tenderly. "*Good Rosy!*" He loved that dog as much as he loved Olympos. "So," he stated and put an arm about my shoulder. "My *old* Olympian returns."

I laughed.

Ada kissed my cheek. "He's feeling fine."

"Any man lucky enough to have *you* nurse him...*would* revive!" Leftéris complimented her cavalierly.

"She's a remarkable woman," I agreed.

"Are you hungry?" the Manager asked.

"Starving."

"Well let's go in and eat. Come on, Rosy."

We stayed for two hours in the kitchen, away from the four climbers from Sweden who had gone to the summit to-day.

"Been quiet these last few days," the Manager said. "Just as well. Gives me less to worry about..."

"Will you ever forgive me? I'm so very sorry..."

"Of course, Ivor. It's just I worry constantly. Running an enterprise like this...I have to be Mother Hen."

Kitty, sitting opposite us, piped up: "And lemme tell ya, he ain't no *Bantam Banger* about it, either!"

Leftéris squeezed her shoulders: "Now—if you really hated it so, would you have stayed this long?"

Kitty winked at Ada: "*Somebody's* gotta teach this Hen...how to *Goose* out an egg now and then!"

"And does she ever know how to scramble them...just the way I like them," Leftéris joked and fondled his big balls playfully. "Now, my Golden Boy, are you ready?"

"Not for what *you've* got in your hands. But I'll take a stiff *drink*, though."

"Not a bad idea. Kitty—where's my brandy?"

"Right where ya left it last—beside yar pillow!"

"Would you please bring it in here?"

"Purtty please," she insisted.

"Yanks! Okay—*purtty* please?"

"Ain't he sweet-tempered?" Kitty asked sarcastically, but went to the back to fetch the beverage.

"You still haven't answered my question: Are you *ready?*"

I must have looked puzzled, but then I saw the silly grin on the rugged man's face. His golden tooth was gleaming. "Oh—you don't mean—already—the final climb—to Mýtikas?"

"Mytikas."

"But...when?" I asked.

The Manager exhaled deeply. "To-morrow morning. You, too, Ada. It's time you went up again."

I put my arm about Ada's beautiful neck and queried: "Are *you* of the mind...to *climb* this...Sacred Mountain?"

She stared for a moment, at all of us, then responded: "If *you* are—yes."

I kissed her cheek. "Then—we agree."

"To-morrow morning then. Six o'clock. Be here, with your sleeping bags. We'll have breakfast."

"Sleeping bags?" Ada wondered.

Leftéris had a sheepish grin on his face, then his tooth flashed golden light: "We're going to be spending the night...up there..."

"On the very top?" I gasped. "But—wonder if we fall off?"

"Don't worry—The Gods, as always, will watch over you," he responded, then laughed. "You don't sleep-walk, I hope."

"Here's the booze, Guys!" Kitty announced and slammed the plonk atop the plank table. "Get yar own cups!"

"Oh come on, Kitty! This's a celebration—at least give them glasses," Leftéris bellowed.

She puckered her lips and blew him a kiss, and had no intention of making us serve ourselves in cups. She put out glasses, and poured.

"To a new beginning, to-morrow," the Manager toasted.

"And..." I said and paused dramatically, "to *this* announce-ment."

"What announcement?" Kitty asked slyly.

"That...as soon as we can arrange it, Ada and I will be *married*... down on the plains below."

"Oh—isn't that wonderful?" Kitty bubbled over with the greatest excitement. "Oh Ada Honey—I'm so *happy* for ya!" she said and reached across the table to hug and kiss us both. As she was doing so, her enormous breasts that were hanging so prominently were being fondled by the Manager. "Oh—he's such a pig!" she said mockingly when she

566

realised what he was doing. "Where will the service be—in Litóchoron?"

"My parents said they'll wait for us both in the village."

"Well—we'll telephone to-night. You can tell them to meet you at Prióni, where they brought you Thursday afternoon. Tell them you'll be there by noontime, two days from now," Leftéris said.

"When will that be—I've completely lost all track of time," I admitted.

"To-morrow's May Day," Kitty volunteered. "Oh—I'm so excited for ya both! If ya get married in Litóchoron—will ya invite me?"

"Of course," Ada said. "You can be a Bridesmaid!"

"Me—a Bridesmaid?"

Everybody laughed.

"And you, too, Leftéris," Ada added.

"I'd make some *hairy* Bridesmaid!"

"You can be my Best Man!" Hefferon offered, and the two men shook hands.

"Yes—in fact there's lots I need to do down there, before I sequester myself up here for the summer," the Manager stated jovially, with a toothy grin. "But you be sure you let us know, Ada. Your mother might want to see you married in Macedonia."

"If so—you're invited to Macedonia!" Ada said.

"Oh Honey—don't tell *me* twice—I'll get *my* ass there even if I have to *hitchhike!*" Kitty said and giggled. The two girls kissed again.

Ada said: "We'll discuss it with the folks. They won't mind my marrying a Brit—because of what Ivor's done for the Olympics. My family's now convinced his Soul's as *Greek* as these hills!"

Leftéris added: *"Greeker!"*

They all laughed at the word.

"Well—to Love!" Kitty toasted, and everybody raised a glass, then clinked.

"Now, Lovebirds, you two must get your beauty rest. Remember, six o'clock comes early. And to-night—don't waste all your energy...in each other's embrace," Leftéris joked. "Save a couple BTUs for the hike!"

"BTUs!" Kitty hit him: "Ya should talk!"

3rd April – Monday – First Light

In order to prepare themselves for Wednesday evening's Rededication of the Ancient Stadium, Ada and Ivor had slept for the past two nights in the ruins of the enclave to Zeus. They had not made love since midday of April first. Both of them had slept in separate sleeping bags, the woman on the floor of the Temple of Hera, the man within the round perimeter of the Philippeíon. Ada had counseled Ivor against sleeping on the floor of the ancient Temple of Zeus. Both now were readying to cleanse themselves, to participate in a Purification Rite.

After the Deed Ceremony, the Torch that Thýella had snatched

567

from Ada had been reclaimed by the Hera Priestess. It had burnt throughout the Loulákis Symphony, then had extinguished of its own free volition. Ada herself had gone back for it, as nobody else dared touch it. She had it safely in a box beneath her chair, at the final IOC luncheon at the Academy.

During the week of the rains, the woman had made sure that she checked the Votive Urn for fuel. It was usually stored in the Museum For The Modern Olympic Games, but since the Deed Ceremony it had not left Ada's care.

Preparations, therefore, had been readied for dawn of April the third. Ada was the first to waken. Crows in treetops were announcing the approach of the Sun, as if they were barnyard roosters. Having slept well, the woman stretched and came out from within her sleeping bag. She was nude, and hastily put on her now-washed gown of the Chief Priestess. The guards of the ruins had been informed *not* to be anywhere around. They had already opened one of the back gates, nearest the River Alphaiós.

It was bound to be a hot day. Very little mist was hovering over the archaic stones. The woman stood, looking radiantly lovely, and pinned her hair on top of her head. Then she left the Temple foundation and walked towards the Philippeíon.

The Athlete still was dozing when the Priestess gently roused him. She put her finger to her mouth, to prevent his speaking, then waited as he put on the loincloth, headband, and sandals of thread of gold, that Thýella had thought so fetching. Together, they walked in stillness back to the Great Goddess's Shrine.

Directly facing the east, the main entrance to the Temple now was looking at their backs. The woman was just arranging the concave mirrored bowl. It was no more than a foot and a half in diameter. She was pointing it at the Sun, just coming up over the far end of the Ancient Stadium, and angling it slightly upwards. The Votive Urn was to its left, and the Torch was to its right, the former upon the dewy soil, the latter standing erect with the help of the Parian marble cube.

To the left of the Urn, the woman knelt to pray, and to the right of the Torch prayed the man. Then, they both rose from their knees. The woman reached for the Torch. Then slowly, she raised it to the level in the air where a little white spot showed upon the head of the Torch, which was being reflected from the centre of the mirrored bowl. She held it there.

The Sun, Apollo, son of Zeus, was rising in the sky, slowly. His rays continued to be reflected from the mirror of the bowl, and ever continued to increase in intensity, as they kept being beamed through the air to the Torch. Woman and man watched expectantly. They both were holding their breath.

Then...the flash-point seemed to be arriving, as a tiny puff of smoke began to ascend. Then a dot of black on the Torch was suddenly illuminating red, whence the whole of the Torch was bursting into the Sacred Flame. Thus it is...with all Olympic Games!

The woman now smiled a primitive smile at the man, then handed him the Torch. He held it, with awe, as she bent down to pick up the Sacred Urn. This had two large handles, about an iron vase that was covered by a lid with a hole in it. The woman removed the lid, whilst gazing at the man in the eyes, then he dipped the head of the burning Torch down into the Urn. The fuel ignited, and was covered by the lid. It now was safe, from wind.

From the Temple of Hera, past the Portico of Echo, past the mighty ruins of the Temple of Zeus, the woman led the way with the Sacred Urn, as the man slowly followed with the Torch.

Past the Studio of the great Sculptor, Phidias, past the new archaeological digs, woman and man kept aiming, majestically, towards the River Alphaiós. In the first light of day, Guards who witnessed them passing reverently bowed their heads.

At the southwest corner of the ruins, the gate had already been opened. Woman and man then proceeded from the Holy Áltis and down a ten-foot bank of clay, below boughs of olive trees. Soon, they were walking along the shallow stream Kladéos, at most only ten-foot wide. Gorgeous flowers of every hue, and butterflies, were awakening to the new day. The six-inch bed of the brook was rounded pebbles, and alongside followed cypress and willow and pine, and tall wavy grass, like papyrus.

Only wind and cicalas in trees could be heard. Woman and man were now nearing the juncture with the River Alphaiós. A disagreeable odour could be smelt blowing their way. Black smoke ahead warned that something was burning. The pair carried on.

Soon it was impossible not to notice that, at a right angle, where the Kladéos joined the Alphaiós, a refuse dump, of one whole acre, had been placed. In pre-Christian days, these two streams had been sacrosanct. Now, it appeared that people could care less. In the centre of this rubble, amidst plastic and glass and metal, a pile of used tyres was burning. Nobody was around to watch the fire. A lone yellow bulldozer was parked off to the left. One could tell that it was used to plow the rounded stones of the banks of the Alphaiós onto the rubbish, once burning was done. What a sad, sad sight. Smell from the dump was revolting.

Woman kept going, and man kept following, past bulldozer, onto rounded stones, ever more to the left, upstream. The river was now twenty yards to the right. The end was just up ahead. The woman glanced over her shoulder at the man, and came to a halt beside a stand of bushy trees along the river. She placed the Sacred Urn securely on a bed of sand, then reached to hold the Torch. The man released it.

The rushing flow of water was a beautiful light green. It was perhaps fifty foot across. The man reached down to feel of it. The liquid was freezing. Almost in the river was a huge brown stump. It might have once been a proud stately oak. It was just lying there. The Gods alone knew how it got there.

At least with the stand of trees, the dump was not so visible. The breeze was blowing the rotten smoke downriver, towards the Mediterranean Sea.

Across the Alphaiós was a second sight *not* for sore eyes. Somebody had started a quarry. Plentiful river pebbles, so good for construction, obviously had gone the way of construction. The landscape was strange enough anyhow, even without the I-beamed "sculpture" of sorts at the quarry, that must have been used for washing or crushing or loading stone. But, still the narrow river was beautiful, agile, virile.

Finally, the woman said: "Take off your clothes."

The man did as he was told, then the woman handed him the Torch and removed her sandals and gown. He gave her back the Torch. She held it aloft, like a battle spear.

"Come with me...into the river," she commanded. "Wade slowly. Hold the Torch with me. Wade slowly."

The current was fiendishly strong. Not used to the cold and the force, the two took their time going atop the slippery round stones. At last, they stood midstream. Water was above their loins. Ada started chanting:

I...who light the Sacred Flame,
From the rays of the Sun:
I...who give this Torch
To those who run:
I...your Priestess...
Now call upon...
The Ancient Gods...
Every one!
Powers, see us here:
An Athlete...who competed
In your Games...
Now but one Individual...
Trying to uphold your Aims;
And a Greek...
Who yearns for better days...
That The Present now defames...
An Actress whose Fate
Is to spark your Sacred Flames:
Give us now The Spirit
To overcome this ill...
That has tried to obliterate
What the Olympics would instil,

And which, given
Half a chance, will!

Then the woman looked steadily at the Flame, and said:

With this water
Wash yourself of wrong
That's done before.
Cleanse yourself
For newer, purer endeavour.

Then to the man she said:

With this Fire,
That we have carried
Past this modern waste,
Let us now pledge
The Ideal to defend
That this sad site once graced,
And for which the Ancient Ones raced.

Then the woman lifted her eyes to the sky and prayed:

I give this Flame
Back to you now!
Carry its Spark
To the Sea,
As only you know how!
And purify all
The lands of this world...
With this my Sacred Vow!

With those words, the Priestess surprised the Athlete by suddenly dipping the Torch into the stream and extinguishing the Sacred Flame. Then, she pushed the man's hand away, and flung the object back upon the river bank. It landed with a thud upon rocks, but did not break.

The whole time, she kept her eyes upon the water, following the spot where the Flame had kissed its surface en route to the sea.

Then, the woman began to sing. She began a sad song, for Torch, for Flame, for Future of the Olympic Games. The words that she sang were of Pindar.

May Day – Tuesday – 11.10 AM

We had been climbing for four solid hours, Leftéris and Ada and Rosy and I. The route had been the same, as five days previously, but the circumstances had been akin as Day is to Night. We had *talked*, the whole way up Olympos. And now we were nearing our tea break.

571

We trod onwards, upwards, yet higher. Then suddenly, our guide was turning sharp right. "We're here!" Leftéris was shouting. "We're here! Welcome to Skála Peak!"

Ada let out such a long deep sigh of relief that I feared that all of her oxygen would be released forever. She hadn't had as much time to acclimate to the change from the lowlands as had I. She was removing her pack and sleeping bag hastily, then sitting. Fog was back again, flimsy clouds like lace, that swished about the rocks, as if spectres from the grave.

"What is this—some sort of plâteau?" I asked as I removed my pack.

We had entered something like an enclosure between a double-stoned gate.

"It's flat here—we can rest," Leftéris yawned with a tremendous lessening of suspense. "We must eat. I'll make tea."

"Tea?" Ada asked, incredulous. "How?"

"We've little burners—tins of heat," replied the Greek, now sitting.

My thoughts were flying off in all directions of the compass. I had to sit, too, though I felt as exhilarated as a puppy at feeding time. My hands grabbed a rock—to keep myself anchored.

"I just was thinking of the May Day wreath," responded Ada when I asked: "Penny for your thoughts?"

Ada had brought a beautiful floral wreath from Litóchoron. Her uncle had given her one from the funeral. Being superstitious, Ada had refused to bring a wreath associated with Death to celebrate the rejuvenation of the land, the meaning of May Day, so she had made her own wreath, from roses from Aunt Georgia's house. It is a Greek custom to hang a wreath on the house, then to burn it on May Day. One must jump over the flames, to ensure good luck. Ada laughed: "I can still see you and Leftéris jumping over that wreath...at seven o'clock!"

"This tea's smashing," I said, glad for anything warm inside. Rosy, snuggled against my side, was glad to be offered a biscuit. "Does this dog *always* climb with you?"

"On a *natural* climb—yes—but she balks at rope climbs," her master answered.

"Suppose she's a bit slow using a pick," I replied.

"No—she's bloody quick! She's just sorry to-day's sky's so muggy," Leftéris said, patting her rump.

"It's colder this morning than last Wednesday," I answered. "Are seasons here in reverse?"

"Most of the time," the man laughed. "I always like to think of clouds as voyeurs."

Ada laughed: "You would."

"Aw—go on," I said for the man's benefit. "I'm certain Leftéris has a poet's mind. One would have to...wanting to play house up *here*."

"When I come up here...I feel it frees my very Soul," he responded.

The three sat in silence awhile, till Rosy whined.

"In such a deistic setting," Leftéris pronounced, "the most simple musing turns upon its own axis...and spins into poetry." Then he added softly, as if it were a prayer: "The summit does it...pulls each thought up to its own height...then flings it off into Space...in order to send it with a kiss up to Time...which is peacefully at home beyond the altitude of clouds...beyond the Moon...beyond the Sun...beyond Beyond...where The Voicings Of Voices originate...beside The True God Of True Gods..."

"Amen," sang Ada, in her voice as Priestess.

"Homer lived...and learnt to hear the humblest and hardest Heart," Leftéris whispered. "Here, Homer said, The Gods had their palaces, walled from mortal sight by The Clouds. The gate to their abode was kept by The Hours, and The Nine Muses kept The Deities entertained. Even I, a mere taverner, can't but turn to The Bard... Spiritual Father Of Greece...for calm...amidst the dearth of Inspiration to-day...when I am lucky enough to come up here..."

"I'm suddenly thinking of Achilles," I said, "allowing Patroklos to go fight in his stead...a battle that brought about the other's death."

"The Hero warred...for God knows what...to secure a seat in Mankind's mind," Leftéris said but added: "The Poet watched...and smelt the gore...then swore to wash, with Truth's Conviction, The Fields Of Fight."

There was silence. Then the man asked: "Did Homer never *see* these heights...whereon his conscience abided? Could words so great... trust *others'* eyes...The Facts Of Life to state? Did he go *blind*...in having seen...The Very Ultimate Vision...like Saint Francis...as many think...whom neither Dark nor Satan ever could pry? *What*...did Homer's blindness...*signify?*"

Of a sudden I recollected one of the most beautiful passages of Alexander Pope's translation of *The Iliad*, when Thétis, mother of Achilles, hastened to this very mountain to intervene for her fated son:

> *Twelve days were past, and now the dawning light*
> *The Gods had summon'd to th' Olympian height:*
> *Jove first ascending, from the wat'ry bow'rs,*
> *Leads the long order of æthereal pow'rs,*
> *When like the morning mist in early day,*
> *Rose from the flood the daughter of the sea;*
> *And to the feats divine her flight addressed.*
> *There, far apart, and high above the rest,*
> *The Thund'rer sat; where old Olympos shrouds*
> *His hundred heads in heav'n, and props the clouds.*
> *Suppliant the Goddess stood: one hand she placed*
> *Beneath his beard, and one his knees embrac'd.*

Lefteris and Ada listened to the lines with the greatest concentration. Then, the man asked: "Can you *believe*...that Homer *never* was here?" I shook my head no.

The man replied: "To capture with the Word...exactly what He feels...no honour more to Man...our God reveals."

5th April – Wednesday – Midnight

Between National Day and the fifth of April, word had slowly spread throughout the Valley Alphaiós that the Chief Priestess and the Olympic Gold Medallist were going to appear at midnight, inside the Ancient Stadium, for a Rededication Rite. None of the Press had been invited, and only a handful of people in Athens even knew that the Rite would take place. One of those was Theatrínos, who had brought along the young Maestro, Mándis Loulákis, on his Harley-Davidson. Professor Rembetikós indeed had introduced them, and already they were planning an epical operatic collaboration.

Nobody was allowed into the Áltis until eleven at night. Pots of burning kerosene had been set along the path for light. The route from the Kiosk Gate, down towards the Gymnasium, then left at the Philippeíon to the Temple of Hera, was so magnificently illuminated that many of the local people swore they had never seen it look so beautiful.

It was a night of a New Moon. Pitch black was the sky, and owls were hooting in evergreens. Everybody who was entering, and there had been a few thousand making a slow stroll from the village's tavernas and cafés, was given a tall white candle. Everyone was instructed not to light it along the way, but to wait for the proper moment in the Rite.

Out of sight completely were Priestess, her Twelve, and Olympic Athlete. They were waiting, silently, in a circle, inside the walls of the workshop of the great Sculptor, Phidias. On the floor of the old edifice, that had been built for the Artist's work on the superlative statue of Zeus, was the Sacred Urn, by the Priestess's feet.

That ghastly day of the Deed Ceremony, not one single person in the Stadium had dared touch the thirteen olive wreaths. An Army Private had finally put them in a box and had presented them to the Priestess afterwards, including the one made of gold. The box was now beside the Urn. And on the other side of the box was the Torch, dried, cleaned, functional, albeit dented.

At ten to twelve, the Kiosk Gate was locked. Local people, estimated at close to three thousand, were spreading out on both long grassy flanks of the Stadium. They were sitting on small woven rugs and quilts, and were silent. Many small children were present. Everybody was sitting in darkness, watching the shadows dance in tall pine trees of the Áltis, as wind made lamplight flicker. Then, at precisely midnight, the Compound's Guards had been instructed to extinguish the lamps, one by one, from Kiosk to Crypt, and this they began doing, as the people's excitement kept mounting, whilst the sable pall of night was enveloping them all.

The Priestess was rising from workshop floor, and so were all the others. She delicately was reaching into the box and handing each of the Twelve a desiccated wreath. Five, Maidens, and Seven, Youths, were placing the dried boughs carefully on their heads. Then, upon the Runner's head, she was placing the one of gold. Next, she was handing him the Torch. She herself was picking up the Urn. The procession was beginning.

Ever so quietly, through darkness, in ruins, past leering of Shades Of The Dead, Fourteen did wend, where once was masonic brilliance. Now diminishèd, the Altis, not unlike the bottom of a murky pond, was but a reflection of the glorious likes of Narcissus, recalled by no more than a minnow.

Something weird was in the air this Pagan Mid Night. Everyone's nerves jittered. Fourteen kept having feelings that they never had had before, and probably never would have again. They were passing the toppled giant...remnants of the Temple of Zeus...

Silently stepping on pine needles, the group continued, beneath evergreens that had ceased to sway in the night. The very air was pausing...to observe this progress towards the Portico of Echo. When had something like this...*last* happened on this site?

At the end of the ruins of the Portico, beside the entrance to the once-tunneled Crypt, the Chief Priestess was halting. Intently, she kept listening. The Stadium was silent. She was content. She was proceeding.

Slowly, as if literally being born again, through the amniotic sac of Time Itself, the Priestess kept feeling each step, and how the pressure kept mounting. Midway into the vault she began lifting the Sacred Urn, delftly, above her waist and higher. By the time that she was at the mouth of the tunnel, at the entrance to the Stadium, the Urn was beneath her chin.

People now could see her face, starkly illuminated by the Sacred Flame. Instinctively...they were rising from their places...to their feet. The Priestess was leading. In single file behind her followed Five, lovely Maidens, then Seven, handsome Youths. The Olympic Gold Medallist was last to enter the Stadium.

The Priestess now was lifting the Urn, above her head, to as high as her arms could reach. She was turning sharp right, and proceeding along the starting-stones from which the Ancient Runners used to race. Midway along the stones she was stopping, where the Official who called the races used to stand. Beside her, to her right as she was facing the crowd, continued Three, Maidens, each making sure that she halted with one starting stone between. The remaining Two, Maidens, were halting to the Priestess's left, one stone between her and nearest Maiden. Then, Youths took their places, Three to right and Four to left of the Priestess.

Waiting by the Crypt was the Olympic Athlete. After pausing, once the others were on the starting-blocks, he was taking a deep breath then slowly running with his unlit Torch aloft, to the waiting Priestess. Once he was standing before her, she was lowering the Sacred Urn and bowing to him. He was dropping to right knee, extending the Torch towards lid of the Urn, and like magic, the Sacred Flame was leaping from container and igniting, with a Spark coloured orange. Then, a great yellow radiance was illuminating the young couple's faces. They were smiling at each other, deepest tenderness.

Those now watching were bursting into applause. The Athlete rose and faced them, presenting the Sacred Flame to right and to left. Then, to the delight of all watching, the Olympian began running...with the Torch...in a circuit through the Stygian darkness of the whole Ancient Stadium...towards the right...along the edge of the mound with the people...to the end...past the finishing blocks...then down the other side...as the people kept cheering for the Light...

As he was finishing the course, he was slowing now to a trot and proceeding to stop, for a split-second only, before the Priestess, then was advancing, Torch aloft, up the very centre of the Arena, as Thirteen, behind, were now following suit. Midmost in the Stadium, where the olive wreaths had been tossed, the Torch Runner now was stopping.

The Priestess then was addressing both sides of the gathering individually: "People—Friends. We are here this night for a Rededication Rite...to cleanse this Stadium of what took place on National Day. So that every one of you may hear, we now ask you to come closer and join us. And just as The Twelve encircle the Athlete and me, please allow your youngest children to encircle us first, then older children, then young women, then mothers, then young men, then fathers. And everyone is to join, hand in hand, in a great circle ever widening about us."

The Twelve then enclosed their group. A Youth was on either side of a Maiden. Then young children were approaching the Sacred Flame, and afterwards all others were, too, exactly as the Priestess had directed. And as soon as all of the throng were holding hands, about the Torch, the Rite began.

"*Nekromandeion,*" the Priestess said.
"*Ora,*" a youth responded.
"*Mandeion,*" a maiden replied.

The Chief Priestess was raising the Urn high:

Oracles of The Past,
As well as of The Dead,
Of The Present,
And of The Future,

Inspire us now,
For what must needs be said:
Let this Sacred Flame
Enkindle Love, to cleanse
The Evil hovering...away...
By Almighty Omnipotence
Above, back to the Nether Sphere,
Enchained, forever, to stay,
That Good may chanticleer!

The Athlete then reached with the Flame across the shoulders of The Twelve. The first person to have a candle lit was a tiny girl, who looked enormously proud. The Athlete lit just four, in cardinal directions of the compass, but the people understood that Light must radiate outwards. So, from the hands of the wee ones, progressively through childhood to all the adults, Light began spreading, and the people truly began to be happy.

Then, the beautiful Priestess, centred splendidly in all this Candlepower, in this Night, said loudly: *"The Counsel Of The Gods!"*

One, a Maiden, stood, said her name, and chanted her verse. Thus did all the others, in order of birth, from youngest to eldest, according to the Olympic Pantheon:

APHRODITE
Your time in Greece has been very well spent here—
But Time, alone, is toil...if not subdued by Love:
So don't forget us who...have worked to bring you cheer!

ATHENA
This maxim, too, recall: As below...so above:
The arcane lore of ages past that guides one's flight
Imperils those who harm, not honour, Wisdom's Dove!

ARTEMIS
If e'er you scare and wonder why it's dark at Night,
The Moon will take your fears into her white embrace:
Impatience never knows this...can't wait each Month's Light.

APOLLO
Not one day comes no lesson to instil. So chase
Those Dreams that seem too mute to speak: Before too long
A Voice, an Answering, the honest quest must grace.

HERMES
A Soul hears many lusty lays and Sirens' songs:
Indulgence can be Bliss...but only if one's search
Continues: Perseverance rights unhealthy wrongs.

577

HEPHAISTOS
Yet as one climbs up to a lofty mortal perch,
Each higher step seems *but to start one's hike again.*
So...sacrifice. Nobleness's sacred as a Church.

ARES
But be prepared to fight...as well to suffer pain:
The purer men are always *sought by Jealousy!*
Dishonesty can't wait...to see all Goodness slain!

HERA
How schemes, threats, plots, lies love *a sweet Conspiracy—*
Adore to watch Man's Weakness overcome his Mind:
Alert do be! Evade the base...the Truth you'll see!

ZEUS
Crude Thunder is but sound...and Lightning oft is kind
And shooes the Storm. The portents in the Sky will point
The pathway out, when Rain does dry. Then Peace you'll find.

POSEIDON
The ship that sails through savage Seas, that snap the joint
And crack the jib, is free *at last! No mut'nous wave*
More mauls the helm. The Captain can his hull annoint!

HADES
And then the weary seek their rest...within the grave.
A Life is hard...*but Virtue has its due: Respect*
Cannot but go to whom exists etern'ly brave.

DEMETER
Elysium...can be on Earth! This Globe so deckt
For mortal use must tended be with much *more Care:*
Immortal gifts are Irony...those easiest wreckt!

Silence was the people's heartfelt response. The Chief Priestess turned in a complete circle, to view their staring eyes. Then she commanded The Twelve to turn and face her. She stated, loudly and clearly, for all to hear:

As I point to each of you in turn,
The Sacred Flame your olive bough must burn:
Let Fire now cleanse the Victor's Wreath;
Let Smoke to Peace this Shrine bequeath.
Protect the Games from Strife, from War;
And justly guide them...evermore!

Each of The Twelve let the Flame consume his and her olive wreath. The Olympic Athlete then removed the golden diadem, and handed it to the tiny girl, whose candle had been the first lit. She accepted it, with wildly wide eyes. Then, the Chief Priestess said: "This Rite is over. Go your way ...in Peace!"

In silence...all of those gathered began parting, as the young Athlete commenced their departure by walking, slowly, out of the Ancient Stadium, holding the tiny girl's hand, while continuing to bear the Flame aloft. The multitude followed, quietly, behind The Twelve and their silent Priestess. Past ruins, beneath pines, the candle-lit procession did wind.

May Day – Tuesday – Late Afternoon

We three proceeded past boulders, beneath clouds, while wind, fierce and constant, was now blowing. But *nothing* now could keep Leftéris and Ada and I from moving. Again, Rosy led the way.

"We'll be going along the thin ridge," Leftéris said, "right between the vast stages of Comedy and Tragedy. I can only tell you: Do *not* look down! Here...at Skála Peak...the world still looks mortal." Then—the guide took a breath and dropt over the edge, like a man going deep-sea diving. To get to Mýtikas, due north, we had to follow him, so into the fog we both vanished.

Instantly—the world took a turn. Scenery—now absolutely dangerous—was straight down. One could fall to a horrible death. Now—*hike* had ended. Now—*scaling* began. Now—*each* footstep must be taken—as if it were one's *last*.

Following the old pro, we both felt inconsequential. "For God's Sakes—don't slip—don't!" he said then became silent.

I tried to imagine how many times he had done this—but couldn't. Every ounce of training, concentration, instinct now was bent on one single thing: Survival!

"Don't slip—don't!" kept echoing in my head.

Watch your footing. Hold on with each hand. Go slowly. Don't hasten. Look! Look as each foot goes to each outcropping of grey rock. Watch out for wetness. Watch out for loose stone. Go easy. Easy. Easy...

We descended, ascended, descended, ascended, en route, in the fog, to Mýtikas.

"I'm scared," I heard my voice saying, "so much that I can't speak."

Who was that talking?

"I'm jealous...even of Rosy...bounding...rock to rock...shelf to shelf...like some flipping frog...lily pad to lily pad."

Was she *really* just a dog? What luck...having *four* legs!

"This Universe up here," I heard my mind saying, "with its

579

blanchèd-liquid speedway-dashing clouds, dancing about our feet, with its eerie-incessant wind slamming against our hooded faces, with its knocking of great dollops of mucous from our running noses, *isn't* at all of our *lower* world!"

Perhaps my sensations, terrified by my recent fall, and exacerbated by too many years of study and imagining, now were too acute? Were *years* precluding true estimation of constantly shifting vistas before me?

"With fog—nothing is as it seems."

But this up-down up-down so-called progress...to the very height of Greece...somehow was producing endless insights into forms and feelings divine...

All three of us were on the edge, holding on for dear life, never letting up, ever pressing onwards. We halted only briefly, intermittently, then again began another upward push.

"Excelsior!"

We suddenly were traversing an exotic land of lichen, of the rarest appearance of a grasping tuft of grass. Flowers, junipers, pines... all the most gorgeous plants of this Earth...were far...far...beneath us now. All that we were seeing...in essence...were the forms...forms of grey...grey forms made of limestone...piled high...limestone striated and always angled...angled at thirty degrees.

Not one single thing was horizontal!

The path we were taking often was a series of stairs. Grey rock leading up to Heaven, I wondered? They couldn't be less...

Crooked stairs were everywhere, at angles of thirty degrees. *Our* steps, up these *immortal* steps, often came dead against sculpture ...the wildest most modern of shapes...the very shapes the best contemporary artists only can see in their dreams...in their sleep...in their night. The Sun would set soon, anyways.

Atop these exceptional pieces of Art...some looming high as a Norman castle tower...it wasn't at all difficult for us to see Deities... staring fixedly at our own puny progress...smirking at the slowness and mere physicality of Man...quietly laughing at this wan wasteful character, of bone, of muscle...whose frame was so fastened to Fate...

"We're close now," Leftéris suddenly said. The Gods alone knew where Rosy was. "This is the last big drop," the man warned. "And I do mean *drop*! Just cross it—without looking down either side. Watch only the bridge at your feet."

"Bridge" was being polite, I thought. The whole goddamned mountain was split right down the middle.

Leftéris crossed the sodding "bridge".

Ada crossed it, too.

I could not. I had to think about it—no—don't! All there was, between Life and Death, was a grey sliver of rock. *This* side of Olympos

...was over *here*. *That* side of Olympos...was over *there*! And the whole thing was shooting upwards, and sideways! The flaming chip of rock was a whole yard long. And just a foot wide. And nothing, absolutely nothing, was below. It just was balancing there. Between hither...and yon...

I crossed it! Leftéris grabbed me on the other side and flung me past him. Ada caught me.

Without any doubt, this would remain the most dangerous and most dramatic sight of my life. That one split-second, doing that tightrope walk. The whole of lopsided Mount Olympos had been slit in two, with such a sharp cleaver that it appeared to have been cut this very noon.

Only as my fear was beginning to abate, on the other side, did it hit me that the Sun now was getting ready to set. But due west was nowhere to be seen. All we could detect was limestone. We were on the eastern face of Mýtikas. But fog, now stranger than ever in the dusk, only whirled and sparkled like vapour of melted opals.

"We're within sight of the top!" Leftéris shouted at last. Rosy, already up there, began to bark. The dog's voice, above and unseen, gave us shivers. Suddenly, we could see her. There was the damned acrobatic dog, best climber of us all! I shouted out loud to her: "Sod you—we can't help it if we're *human*!"

Ada laughed, as Leftéris was hoisting her up between him and his ambidextrous pet. I still had a ways to go. Yes, right up there the two humans and the shepherd dog sat, staring down at me, as if saying: "God—are you slow!"

Yes...

Up...

Up...

Up...

Up...

Those last vital moments...

I kept climbing...now with tears welling in my eyes...tears of exultation, of exhaustion...tears of pain, of imagination...tears of expectation, of ecstasy...at the realisation that *this* was my very first mountain...to be ascended in the whole of my life...and it was none other than fabled Mount Olympos!

And my body kept pushing...

And pushing...

Higher...

Those last...

Those last...

Those very last...

Few steps...

And...

"There!" I shouted, as Leftéris and Ada were embracing and kissing me. "I've done it! I've done it! I'm *here!"*

And Rosy barked and barked. Then I crouched and embraced her, too. The dog's kisses on my face were the sweetest that I ever shall remember.

"Here—relax," Leftéris commanded, and handed me my sleeping bag. "I'll wake you up before midnight."

"Promise?" was all that I asked. Then I blacked out—and snoozed like a baby.

But Olympos had different ideas. And likewise had the Night. And the two conspired and the winds suddenly ceased. The mountaintop became hauntingly silent. I twitched in the grip of strange dreams...

Slowly, from the east, a new breeze began stirring. It was warm, and was coming straight from the sea, straight through the Gateway, many miles below, straight up the vast Vale of Olympos itself, straight up the façade of Mýtikas, like a gracefully flying dove.

The freezing grey rock at first refused to respond, and clutched all the more the wet clouds that were chasing about. But the eastern breeze did not stop blowing. Slowly, it continued, like the constant caress of somebody who knows how to love. And after an hour or so...such tenderness began to convince the unrelenting rock...and the clouds took flight to the west.

One last cloud suddenly swooped up the peak's high face, then vanished behind us, to the west. And there, beneath indigo skies that soon would be the hue of violet, the whole of Olympos reclined, a marvel to behold. Every star on high began to throb with the full revelation.

The dog was watching this all. She continued to stare around. Suddenly...from down the mountain's flank...the dog sensed the approach of something. She did not bark. She just kept twisting her curious head, wiggling her ears, sniffing at the wind. Her eyes were diamond bright. If only she could speak...our language...and we hers...

It now was midnight.

Leftéris was rousing Ada and me.

We were standing again.

The dog stood before us.

We were facing east.

The view was indescribable...

The nocturnal opulence of Nature...

From such a stupendous height...

Suddenly, from a hundred feet beneath us, stept two forms. Something dark. Something light. From behind grey rock.

Did the dog understand that she must not bark?

I rubbed my eyes to convince myself that I was seeing right. Hadn't there just been two *people?* Moving like shadows creep?

I looked to Ada for the answer. She and Leftéris refused to explain. Fifty feet below us now...was it a *miracle*...they weren't making any noise? Whoever they were...they certainly seemed to know where they were going.

"Isn't it...a woman and child?" I queried. Leftéris hushed me with a glance. I said nothing more. With greater and greater apprehension, I watched the ascent of the pair.

Closer now, it was apparent that the two *were* a woman and child. They seemed borne by some alien force. Their arms were as rigid as their legs. They were directly below us now. Only a metre below, stood an ancient lady, all in black, and a tiny boy, all in white.

Too dumbfounded to do anything, some vague ancestral memory told me that I must *know* them somehow. Another vague memory said that, even if I did, I must keep silent. I shut my eyes.

The dog began to howl, to bay at the Music of the Spheres. Snout pointed starwards, she began howling for all she was worth.

I opened my eyes. The old woman and boy were gone.

Just then, miles and miles down the length of the Vale of Olympos, just beyond the Gateway to the Mystic Mountain, fireworks began bursting apart red, then in multi-coloured light.

"May Day!" Ada exclaimed, and her hands clapt together with glee. She was acting just like a little girl. "They're celebrating! Fireworks in the village!"

The dog's howling continued...as if she were attempting to communicate...some urgent message to some distant galaxy.

Now—the series of explosions was so spectacular—yellow flowers with diamond white bombs, red trailers, blue stars, then golden comets going off in hundreds of directions—that it wasn't impossible to imagine the ill-fated Olympic Nation atop the two tall foothills way below. One could just picture its edifices, built of marble, sparkling white. One could also picture its missiles encased beneath the site. One could see the idiots working on neutron bombs. One could see the fools thinking they were doing *Good* for Mankind. One could watch the cretins being radiated into cancer by their very own playthings of annihilation. And, one could see it all a-flash, in the night, of an evening as lovely as this. One could see it all a-glow, like fireworks in the sky, but fireworks that were making people cry! One could see the mushroom clouds, clawing their way, like monsters, magnificent in might, but lacking in all intelligence, freed from all fear or foresight. Yes—from Olympos—Seat Of The Gods—one could see—for *lightyears*! But...about *Man*...did one single thing make one iota of sense?

The dog...she just kept on howling...

EPILOGUE

A Few Months Later

Ada and I were in the West Country of England, now man and wife. We were staying as guests of the Dowager Duchess of Brendon, at her country estate, Shrove Tor, in Somerset. One morning, in the post came a letter from Theatrínos. He said that his collaboration with Loulákis was going well. He wanted to send us this poem:

Ode To The Modern Olympics

In Pindar's day the Games' Awards
Went to Athletes, who were Lords—
Noble sons of Ancient Blood,
Whose glory flowed from Heroes
From Before, from Myth, from Might, from Gods.

In Pindar's day the Games had lasted longer
Than ours now...and thousands stronger
Tramped across dry roads, in heat,
In Greece's savage summer, each four years,
Not just come for Sport, but likewise come for Worship.

Twelve Olympian Deities dignified the Vale:
Pilgrim and Contestant...neither one could fail
To purify the Body with the Mind,
In such a Shrine, bowed especially before Zeus
The Thunderer, who meted Fame (whose Victory was blind).

To Ancient Man...Olympia was more Olympiakós—
Where Humans tried to be Divine, where most
Stayed put on planes of mere mortality—
Where some *transcended up to heights sublime—*
Where some up to Olympos...*even escaped* Time!

Yet we...to-day...have none of this.
We have Muscle...we have Bliss
Of Brain and Flesh inseparably linked
And fighting for Nation and Id and Ink
Of Print...Publicity...perhaps Something More...

And we have Countries, allied against War
At least (they profess). And we have Athletes...who abhor
Violence...and vivify our lives a little while...
By incomparably elegant corporal style...
Who make us all wish that we were so very blest...

Yes—as we scan the televised events,
Which show the Medals, Torches, Tears, and Dents
Into the Consciousness of Man (since these Games
Are for real!), the Commentator maybe lets us know
That Greece gave birth to our Games...long ago...

And we may muse of Columns and of Urns,
Of Marble white, so white it seems to burn
A Flame Eternal through our very inmost Soul!
Yet, as we try to conjure up this distant Past,
The Flame goes cold...our Games do end...at last...

And we all wonder...was it worth the cost?
We all gained something...but wasn't one thing lost?
The Sport's the same...the Spirit, though, has changed.
The Victor triumphs...still our World's a shame:
The Winner's tempted to be sold...before he even makes it home.

But monetary forces fooled the Ancients too:
By such disease the Games of Eld were eaten through and through,
As Hucksters hawked within the Sacred Groves,
As Agents hustled Athletes quick as Light
Away from Zeus...towards Professional Fight.

Thus the Greek Games died! Pillars relaxed,
The Stadium snored in silt, barbarians axed
Off Deities' heads, and pines polluted the site...
As lizards smirked on mounds once artful delight,
As Archaeology waited, with picks, within its Black Hole of Night!

Perhaps it's time now*...to think* this *one through:*
Why don't we give the Games back to
Greece? Let two *sites, forever, be now set aside,*
One Winter, one Summer, before our pride
(To out-do each previous venue) wrecks *the Games—*

Before some New *Site, and Politics, obliterates the aims*
Of the Olympian Ideal! Time is now*...*
To halt this! Time is now*...to vow*
We can—and will*—halt this! Time is*
Now...and Greece's not a stupid choice for this!

Summer Contests are natural *to Greece—*
Maybe some long-dormant God of Peace
Might stir and stop our fiendish fickle frays—
At least for a period before, during, and after the days
When Fitness pauses to struggle, as in the centuries ago.

And Hellas has northern *mountains, don't forget!*
A Permanent Winter Complex for Sport yet
Can be built up there...it can even be built
On Olympos! Care *can build anything* anywhere*!*
Think*...before the Games vanish...back to History's thin air!*

END OF THE NOVEL

Written in Athens and Olympia, at Olympos Beach along the Aegean, in
Litóchoron, and upon Mount Olympos itself, of Greece; in Lake Placid
and Watertown, New York, and in Winder, Georgia, of the United States
of America. 1979-1996.

Glossary

For assisting the Reader in correct pronunciation of Greek words and names in this text, this Glossary has been included. The first thing that the Reader will note is the presence of accent marks. These have been placed above the proper vowel of the syllable that should be stressed harder than those without the marks. In Greek, most of the syllables of even the longest words are spoken with the same amount of pressure and/or inflection as is every other syllable, *except for the accented syllable*. This syllable just should be pronounced a bit stronger than all the others. The others are pronounced as if to a metrical beat, which is regular and flowing, but the accented one is more vigorous, such as in this beat: tum-tum-TAH-tum, for the name: Theatrínos: thay-ah-TREE-knows.

Other Greek words in this text look as if they should have accent marks, but in fact (for English transliteration, in this text) they do not, only because the first vowel, which begins the word, is accented, and in this case the accented first vowel is printed in upper-case. Such words are: Aegina and Agora. Many proper Greek names beginning with A or O are stressed on that A or O. In fact, for absolutely correct pronunciation of the name of the Sacred Mountain so prominent in this novel's storyline, one should say: OH-limb-bose. Note, that the "mp" of Olympos, in Modern Greek, is not pronounced as "mp" but as "mb". The same goes for Olympia, in Contemporary Greek, which is pronounced "mb" and not "mp". With the word Olympia, though, one should not stress the first syllable, but should pronounce it thus: oh-limb-BEE-yah.

For the Reader's ease, here is a partial list of those Greek words found in this text which one is free to pronounce exactly as he or she likes. In other words, for the sake of the Reader, it was decided not to encumber this novel with accent marks on the following old standbys: Metamorphosis, Names of the Gods, Phidias, Parthenon, and Piraeus, etc. Do note that use of the Greek letter "Kappa", i.e., "K", is this book's preferred letter for rendering Greek names in this book which usually, in English, have traditionally been published with the letter "C" (which only came into our language via transliteration from the Latin): e.g., Akropolis, Herakles, Sokrates, Sophokles, et cetera.

Some usages in this text do retain the improper Latin spellings, given that dogged tradition of their usage in the English language has obviated stubborn continuance, despite their evident impropriety, in such names as: Alcibiades, Cerberus, Corfu, Hecate, and Macedonia.

Another difficulty in transliterating Greek spellings into the English is demonstrated by the word: Litóchoron. The "ch" of this place-name actually is the Greek letter *X* which has traditionally been spelt "ch" throughout Modern English linguistic history. Another word exemplifying this is *Christ*. In Greek, the "Ch" of His Name is spelt with the Greek letter *X*.

Lastly, there is the big problem of how to pronounce Greek diphthongs, a few of which are rendered, as best as is possible, below:

AE, as in Aegina, like the English word "pet": EGG-ee-nah
AI, as in Alphaiós, like the English word "pay": al-fay-OSE
EI, as in Mandeíon, like the English word "Greece": mahn-DEE-own
IA, as in Iamídas, like the English word "yacht": yah-MEE-thas
OU, as in Mousikí, like the English word "shoe": moo-zee-KEY

If anybody has any more questions about pronunciation of Greek, the best advice is to hop on a plane, go to Hellas, find yourself a partner, and start listening to the beautiful poetry pouring into your ear...then you'll learn quickly, and the *right* way...by speaking the language in the living landscape that gave it birth.

How This Book Was Written

Édition von Rapp would like to posit the belief that nobody can talk about a book like the Author. Therefore, it is going to be a policy of this House to let the Author have his or her soapbox, so that we can get the inside scoop, so that Readers and Salespeople can be better informed. Everybody loves a good story, and all books, no matter how good or how bad, have tales about how they were written. This Coda Chapter may strike many in the Trade as radical, putting a Non-Fiction Finale to a Fiction Publication, but too bad for the die-hards and traditionalists. Putting a Coda Chapter called "How This Book Was Written", at the end of every book we publish, is exactly what Édition von Rapp is going to do. So, take it away, Lawrence David Moon, and speak out: Tell us, how did this novel come to be?

WinterGames/SummerGames, by its very size and depth, has had a genesis of over twenty years, and it certainly did not come into existence by spontaneous generation. Just by considering all the research involved, the Reader should now be able to comprehend why nobody, to date, has ever written a novel that is set inside the top echelon of the Olympic Games. For one, access to such an echelon is not a wide-open door. For two, most who amble there are not novelists to start with. Most are sports officials, dedicated to their careers, with hardly time for *reading* a book, let alone *writing* one.

With respect to my own gravitation, all my life, to Greek culture, which provides the bedrock for this whole novel, since the Olympics are and always have been a Greek phenomenon, I am convinced that it is innately owed to bloodlines of my mother, née Edith Mildred Green, which came to her from her own mother, née Esther Lillian von Rapp, both of whose parents had Royal Descent. Esther's father, Louis Norris von Rapp (1872-1942) and mother, Etta Delano Whitney (1860-1940) provided Esther, and Edith, and myself, the genetic lineage from at least fifteen Emperors of the East, otherwise more familiarly known as Emperors of Byzantium, and just for the purpose of documentation, I am going to cite those rulers in order of approximate chronology: Basil I, Leo VI, Konstantínos VII Porphyrogénnetos, Romános I Lekapénos, Romános II Porphyrogénnetos, Konstantínos IX Monomáchos, Konstantínos X Doúkas, Eudokía Makrembolítissa (Empress 1067-1071), Michael VII Doúkas, Aléxios I Komninós, Ioánnes II Komninós, Andrónikos I Komninós, Isáakos II Ángelos, Aléxios III Ángelos, and Theódoros I Láskaris. To my knowledge, we also descend from three Latin Rulers of Byzantium: Baudouin XI, Count of Flanders (aka Baudouin VI de Hainaut, aka Baudouin I of Byzantium); Yolande de Flandres, sister to Baudouin; and Pierre de Courtenay, husband to Yolande. From my years of extensive research into mediæval bloodlines, it is no mystery to scholars that a great amount of Armenian blood flowed in the veins of the Imperial Families of Byzance, but it also is recognised that the Monomáchos Family did hail from mainland Greece. Early in childhood, my own preoccupations were often on Egypt, Greece, and Rome, and that is another big formative influence on the shaping of this book.

In New York City, in late March of 1974, I moved to a flat in the Upper East Side, in what then was hardly a fashionable section, north of Elaine's famed eatery, and I think it was East 92nd Street, between 2nd and 1st Avenues, way over by 1st and on the north side of the block. My Journal for Sunday 31 March 1974 records what likely was a fated encounter: "Went to the Greek diner, corner of 2nd Avenue and 91st Street. Fell into a discussion with the young men, who talked freely about their country. Met Ernie, Spiro, and Angelo, the latter a poet." It was Ernie's coffee shop, I believe; all the Greeks in the neighbourhood hung out there. If addresses in my 1976 Journal are correct, then Ernie may have been the nickname for Athenásios Raftópoulos, whose correct address was Three Decker Food Shop, 1746 2nd Avenue, New York City.

I need to backtrack to the previous year, when I removed myself back down to New York from a period of less than a year Upstate in Watertown, New York. In summer of 1973 I was working privately for the legendary doyenne of New York's literary scene, Miss Frances Steloff, foundress of The Gotham Book Mart. I worked for her in her own apartment above the Gallery where the store still is located. I helped the great lady with her vast archives. Frances and I got on remarkably well, and she always took time to ask about my mother and grandmother, since she was fascinated by Upstate New York. That summer of '73 I was beginning the first draft of my first play, *Sokrates*, which of course dealt with the most famous philosopher of Ancient Greece, although I set the play in contemporary New York. Later, in Lake Placid in 1979, I rectified that stupid error, and reset the drama in Greece. It now is my intent to use the work as the libretto for my next (third) grand-opera. But for purposes of documentation, I want it on the record that as early as summer of 1973, Greece was highly on my mind, and this encouragement was indeed due to the urging of Miss Steloff herself, with whom I discussed all aspects of the *Sokrates* script. So, by March 1974, after months of living with the *Sokrates* project, I was already primed for this fated encounter in the Greek diner at 91st and 2nd.

My Tuesday 2 April 1974 Journal entry shows: "Ernie told me to call Rýta at the Greek radio station, that she might be able to tell me where Theodorákis is. Called her, she said: Hotel Navarro. Called there, not expecting anything—but there was the great composer himself, very soft voiced, almost inaudible. I almost lost control when he said to call him in a couple weeks, that he might consider reading *Sokrates*."

Never one to let moss grow on rocks, I rang again on Sunday 7 April 1974, which my Journal records: "Called Theodorákis again, and because he couldn't speak good English he put me on with a Roúli Tatáki, who said she read my letter to Míkis [Theodorákis] and they had liked it: I felt so happy, so humble! She said I could give her the script for him and meet him at The Paradise, where he's rehearsing for next Monday's concert before he goes back to Paris."

In 1974, many prominent Greeks, whose lives were in danger from the Colonels' Junta then ruling their country, had to live in exile. Among them were composer, Míkis Theodorákis, and the legendary actress, Melina Mercouri, both of whom were then in Manhattan, where many of the more brilliant exiles were based. This hotbed of Greeks, who were valiantly holding onto the belief that the Junta was destined to fall, was the milieu in which I suddenly found myself. I am now convinced that my meeting these people was one of those fated encounters in one's life, to which one is led when ready. Even the youths at The Three Decker café were a part of this crowd, though not such stellar personalities. All of them, to the man and woman, provided direct Inspiration to the making of this book, which of course does have a plotline involving the Junta.

Tuesday 9 April 1974: "Tried the Navarro again for Miss Mercouri, and this time a woman answered. It was like her maid, or Lady-In-Waiting. She said: Of course Miss Mercouri would read the script, bring it up. Called later, affirmed this for 6.00 PM. Left work early and went to Central Park South. Put on the phone, and Miss Mercouri answers, very deep voice. She said she was in bed, but I could bring the manuscript up. I did and two ladies met me at the door, and said to call back in a month, after she returns from California. Melina was on the phone. I heard her voice."

Wednesday 10 April 1974: "7.30 PM. Paradise [in Astoria, New York]: Theodorákis! Went with Angelo Polimenéas, to the upstairs banquet hall, much like any social club in the Midwest. But what excitement in the air. 30 or so young Greeks were gathered for the Chorus of Theodorákis's coming concert. There *he* was, in the flesh. Went up and introduced myself and he called over Roúli Tatáki, whom I'd spoken with on the phone. She spoke better English and she would read the play first. Elated. Listened to the Chorus sing, watched him conduct. Very moved."

[Roman Calendar] Good Friday 12 April 1974: "Good's hardly the word. Went to Stonehill Books to drop off my novel-in-progress [*SoHoHo*, a novel of New York's Art World, I later destroyed], then to Gotham Book Mart to chat with Frances Steloff, who said she'd keep her fingers crossed about my play. Then to the studio where I thought Theodorákis was doing sound for a new film. Miss Tatáki brought me inside. Everyone was hushed. I wondered what in Hell could be going on at 512 West 19th Street, over with the warehouses? As soon as she led me in, we made a sharp left and in front of my eyes, stretching a hundred yards, was a movie studio, shooting in progress for Jules Dassin's new film about the November 1973 student unrest at Athens University (when the régime came in with tanks). The room was filled with people, some guests, others helping the film. All were *volunteers!*

594

Roúli sat, and I stood against a movable scaffold. Then the scene broke, and I went to her and asked if Melina Mercouri were there. I felt she was, and was correct. I took a gulp, and feasted my eyes. She came and sat, and I went up to her, introduced myself. She was so kind, putting her arm around me and saying she wrote me yesterday. I was like putty. People were staring, wondering who I was. I was wondering who I was. She told me to tell [Kermit] Bloomgarden [her Broadway producer of *Ilya, Darling*] to call her, she'd consider the rôle [of Death] for the stage." I recall that, during this first actual meeting with Melina, she was seated in her chair and I was crouched down at her side, squatting. She ran her fingers through my long blond hair and said to me, with a great sensual smile: "My—but how *young* you are!" Needless to say, one does not remain "young" forever; but to have a Great Actress say this to one, when one is only 24 years old, would make *any* young man's head spin!

Monday 15 April 1974: "Theodorákis concert in Astoria. Was wonderful. I felt so at home with the audience, due to my growing acquaintance with many Greek friends. It was so good to see Angelo happy. There were moments when he had to clap too hard, to keep from crying. The music brought back so many memories." Angelo had himself been imprisoned, as my Journal entry for 7 April 1974 records, in the notorious Averrof Prison, mentioned in Theodorákis's book, *Journal Of Resistance*.

Wednesday 17 April 1974: "Reading Melina's book, *I Was Born Greek*. Intensely moving."

Thursday 18 April 1974: "Learned from Melina's book that the 18th is always an omen-filled day. I left a copy of [my poem] 'The Rule Of Night' for her at her hotel. There was quite an 'interview' with her in to-day's *Post*, in which they criticised her as hating Americans. I thought the poem might cheer her up, for when I called a few days ago she was pissed that Bloomgarden hadn't called her."

Saturday 20 April 1974: "Went to the studio about 12.15 PM and was soon pulled in as an extra. Gulp. In a group scene, Dassin pulled me from the back and told me to go to the front of an advancing line of Athenians marching to the Polytechnic, to show their support for the students. The University gate was straight ahead, with the students locked behind it. We marched up, singing a song by Theodorákis (my first lesson in Greek) and tossed apples, oranges, and bread to the students. It was very emotional. One student, Dimítri, kept grabbing for my hand to shake. At first, I felt clumsy and almost reluctant, but soon felt myself joining in full solidarity. The times I had marched many miles through the New York streets, as a student at New York University, up to the time of Kent State, all came back. Marching in Washington. Seeing the White House completely surrounded by buses. Yet here we were, in a studio on 19th Street, with arc lights, ADs, and asbestos walls. The time dragged on. People got headaches, under the glare of the lights. Thank God lunch came: delicious hot moussaká, peas, and bread. Much better fare than an orange tossed to a hungry student. But who thought of that? The next scene was on. Children, this time, came up to the gates to offer the students flowers. Roúli told me to-day, that during the demonstrations, children as little as 5½ were killed. For flowers! Cause enough to make such a film, for sure! As the children passed the flowers through the gates, Dimítri, again, grabbed one of the boys to kiss him for such a kind gesture. The scene had to be shot over and over, for the boy didn't seem to want to be kissed. It was hard for the child to imagine that he was really doing this in Athens."

Sunday 21 April 1974: "To the studio at 9 AM. Took [painter] Phil DiGiacomo [to whom I sat; who rendered me in oils] along. Filmed the prison visitation scene, in which we extras had been standing for hours to visit our kin inside, and the guards repeatedly kept saying: There are no prisoners here! Finally, after 1½ hours of standing, another scene (same action) was marked, and Phil got in. Then Melina came. She mentioned she starts *Once Is Not Enough* to-morrow." [Melina actually paid for production of *The Rehearsal*, which this drama about the 1973 student rebellion in Greece came to be called, with money she was grossing from starring in the Jackie Susann movie.]

Thursday 25 April 1974: "To studio. Just sat and watched Melina do a fantastically moving reading of a Law Professor's letter that had been smuggled out of his prison cell. She read with such vigour. I didn't speak to her, not wanting to bother her, but once, during a cut in the reading, she stared at me long and friendly." This scene, with Melina, must certainly go down as the most moving dramatic portrayal that I have ever had the awed pleasure to be so close to in the flesh. Melina was crying. We all were crying. She was not "acting", in the flippant conception of taking on some rôle; she *was* Tragedy, in its purest, most Greek essence. I feel immensely privileged to have been there, so close to her, to have witnessed this remarkable event. It profoundly influenced me. I shall never ever forget it.

Thus, with experiences such as these, was I introduced to the highest levels of contemporary Greek culture. If anyone wants to doubt that I had an entrée, or that I made all the things "up" in *WinterGames/-SummerGames*, which deal with Greeks, then he or she is free to think whatever he or she would be able to conjure. This is the first appearance of these Journal citings; my Journals are *filled* with such juicy things.

In 1975-1976, I left New York and worked for a year in London, as commissioning editor for W. H. Allen & Co. publishers, Mayfair, who just so happened to have been publishers for my great-great-great-great-great-grandfather, Richard Marquess Wellesley, in the first half of the 19th century. For my hard work involved in editing the English language edition of the *mémoires* of Kaiser Wilhelm II's only daughter, H.R.H. Viktoria Luise, who became Duchess of Lüneburg upon marriage to the head of the House of Hannover, I was enabled, by the Princess's

German publisher, Leonhard Schlüter, of Göttinger Verlagsanstalt, to make my first pilgrimage, long overdue, to Greece. It should be said that Viktoria Luise was the mother to Queen Friederike of Greece, so there was another bit of Fate a-work in this assignment in London as the editor for the Greek Queen's mother's autobiography, which Allen's published as *The Kaiser's Daughter* in 1976. I was the editor who bought and who worked on the minutiae of that book.

Getting to Greece by coach was quite the experience! We left Kings Cross, London, at 7.30 AM, Saturday 3 April 1976, and rode that day to Paris. The coach continued between 4 and 5 April through Switzerland to Mont Blanc, then into Milano, then down the Adriatic side of Italy to Brindisi, where we boarded a big vessel and set sail for Greece at 11.30 PM of 5 April 1976. I shall continue with a few Journal citings for this trip, which was very formative in the genesis of this present novel, *WinterGames/SummerGames*:

Tuesday 6 April 1976: "Awoke 5.30 [AM] to go to deck for the sunrise, as the vessel sailed along the Albanian coast, past idyllic isles. [I recall being delighted at seeing flying fish jumping out of the sea.] Had breakfast with new friend, Kóstas Vasiléos, onboard at Kékira City. Sailed to mainland, then past Ithaca, and on to Pátras. Touched foot on Greek soil. Coach into Athens!"

Friday 9 April 1976: "Roúli Tatáki, Fokilidoú Street, for lunch after going atop Lykavitós. [I had met her father, with her, the noted scholar, Professor Tatákis, of Epeírou Street, two days before.] She told me to call Melina (who lives also in Kolonáki), so I did (later that day, from Piraeus). Jules [Dassin, Melina's American husband] got on the phone and recalled me and my script *Sokrates*, and said to call him next week at the Hotel Mediterraneo, Thessaloníki."

That very weekend, Saturday 10 April 1976, I made my spiritual pilgrimage to Delphi, which so greatly influenced my artistic life. It was there, at Delphi, on Mount Parnassos, that the idea germinated to write a work set there, where the Oracle of Apollo was located. This I sketched out, in spring of 1977, conceiving (in London) the plot for this work, an opera libretto, which I later wrote in full during four days of intense Inspiration, in April of 1979, when I again returned to Delphi a second time. This libretto came to be called *Court Masque*; in 1987 I myself expanded it into music, by composing it as a grand-opera, which was my compositional Opus 1 of my music career. Thus, Greece has had the profoundest impact upon me as a Composer, not just as a Poet, Playwright, and Novelist. My whole Being, as an Artist, has been enormously influenced by Greece.

The first time I spent in Athens, which can be regarded as the "Inferno" in the structure of *WinterGames/SummerGames* as a contemporary *Commœdia Divina*, was between Tuesday 6 April and Saturday 10 April 1976. I was fortunate to be the houseguest of the Athenian journalist, Christopher Elíou, who wrote for the London

597

newspaper, *The Daily Mail*. Therefore, my very first "residence" in Athens was a fabulous location, atop Mount Lykavitós, in Daphnomíli Street, with a tremendous view of the whole Vale of Attika lit up at night. I left Delphi, the first time, on Wednesday 14 April 1976. My Journal entry for that day states: "Travelled 5-11 AM Delphi to Levadía; 12-6 PM to Thessaloníki, with train past Mount Olympos." I did speak with Jules Dassin by phone, at the Hotel Mediterraneo, on Thursday 15 April 1976, the same day I took a daytrip out to Pella, capital of Ancient Macedonia and city of Alexander the Great. Alexander, of course, is a big factor in the Inspiration of my quintet-in-progress in which *this* book fits. My character, Alexander Pella, Earl of Luxborough, for whom *The Luxborough Quintet* is named, appears in this book as Duke of Brendon; much of his characterisation derives from the Macedon King, just as James Joyce culled material from Hellas's Past for *Ulysses*.

That 14th of April '76, the Mount Olympos segment for this book began by chance. I was on the Orient Express, en route to Munich. As the train kept rushing northwards, along the beach of the Aegean Sea, in Thessaly, I was startled to realise that out the window, to our left, the most fabled mountain of European Civilisation suddenly was coming into view. Greece was then at its most delightful, in the month of April. As the train kept speeding towards Macedonia, I could not help imagining what it must be like to climb such a majestic peak.

It was impossible for me to take my gaze away from the lofty heights, shrouded in clouds, just as Homer had said they would be. Passengers on the train seemed oblivious to the alpine beauty. Everyone seemed more concerned with the view to the right, the shimmering Aegean. But I could only stare inland.

Then, suddenly, as if a great fist of Zeus were punching a hole in the clouds, in order to admit the penetration of sunlight, a colossal shaft of rays fell through the sky, and illuminated the whole of the mountain's upper peaks. My mouth must have dropt down to my knees. It was the most awe-inspiring sight that I had ever seen. I never forgot it. I never shall. It was the epiphanic moment that united sperm with egg, which started this book, till then mere cosmic pulsings, to gestate. That eerie moment *communicated* something to me. I cannot explain it. I know the Sacred Mountain was *calling* to me. I would *have* to go there, and climb it, *some* day! This did happen, but not until three years later.

Fate enabled my return to Greece, shortly after New Year's of 1979. I got to Athens at 7.00 AM, Wednesday 17 January. For the first five months, I resided in Athens and documented the various sets of the capital that appear in this novel. At that time, I was doing various tutoring jobs, for Greek girls who wanted private lessons in English. I also was hired as an English teacher at Phrontistírion Tsekléni, in the northern suburb of Maroússi, which I really liked, especially because my boss, Iró Tsekléni, was such a gorgeous woman, and some of my kids were a joy, too, especially the older ones, who were about 16.

During this Athenian phase, I got deeply into the intellectual circles of the capital, and mingled with what one would call VIPs. One of the most prominent of the city was the Director of the Akropolis, whom I got to know from a family connection from Paris, Dr George Dontás. Given that the Parthenon scene in *WinterGames/SummerGames* likely will remain in the Reader's mind as unforgettable, allow me to reproduce the following Journal entry for the eve Dr Dontas granted me the rare honour, one of my life's most cherished, of going onto the Akropolis and into the Parthenon, alone, at night, in order to write poetry:

Saturday 31 March 1979: "This day was...well, what does one expect a day to be, what with having the Akropolis all to oneself as part of it? Usual? It started unusual—in my breakfast café someone heard me talking so invited me to his/her table, he being English, a musician, who'd had a lot of money stolen here, so who'd turned to crime—stealing jewelry, one ring which he showed me, then gave me, a silver one with the curly horned ram of Alexander the Great [this ring looked just like one I'd been eyeing, for weeks, in a local shop window!]. I suppose it was fitting [knowing my quintet of novels was directly inspired by said Alexander]—to be given this, even *if* stolen! [I kept this ring for years, but somehow it got lost, I think in the mid-1980s, back to Stealers Void from which it came!] Then I wrote another chapter, in order to pass time till going to the Parthenon. All day I'd avoided thinking of it—almost feeling glib about it—but as I walked along the rim of streets and made my way to the Shrine, I began to feel almost faint and tightened inside. It was unnerving. More unnerving was *waiting* at the locked-tight gate for admittance—standing there, wondering maybe I *wouldn't* be admitted. At last, 20 minutes late, a Guard came, and one who seemed to know *nothing* of my *being* admitted. But on hearing the Director's name, he relented and took me round to the side Police Cabin, over the theatre, where I waited 10 minutes more for the Head Guard, Mr Kapoiánnis, to descend from the Museum Office. They hassled over the phone whether or not I would try to take photos—the *last* thing on my mind—but were reassured I was a mere Poet with no commercial interests other than to sit in the Shrine and write verse. But the Cop and Guard and then Head Guard were extremely kind and gave me consideration as the event was at the Director's discretion. It was strange—as the Head held wide the gate—to know I was entering the site *alone*. Kapoiánnis held back and urged me go alone—I hesitated but then went—up the marble stairs—very nervous. And then, there it was—the Parthenon—with not one person in sight. The Sun had all but vanished—yet even though the day had been grey and dour, the beauty of the Temple, so *still* against the blackening sky, was so awesome that tears came into my eyes. I looked way back—and there was Kapoiánnis, waving me onwards, to make me enter the Parthenon itself, from his frame in the Propýlaea. And so I went, like a child, with fear and with joy, and climbed up the very steep foundation and entered the marble

Hall. Almost immediately, I went to the centre and then off to the side and began writing. Within 45 minutes, 'Inside The Parthenon' was completed—a poem which gave me so much of both agony and ecstasy to write that I felt I'd never accomplish the deed, as I kept changing positions, vantage points, within the great ruin, to keep the juices flowing, to let the vast place not overwhelm me. The Head Guard was there the whole time—but not being in uniform he stood against a marble wall more as a fellow *human* being to whom I could relate than to react against—and his presence was reassuring. He watched me as I wrote, and I believe was moved. We'd occasionally falter a few words between us, in English-Greek, then off I'd go again to write. Soon after I'd just sat down the first time, I gasped as experimental rose-coloured lights suddenly illumined the whole edifice—this being the *first* evening they were being tried for the spring's *son-et-lumière*. Wouldn't you *know* I'd be *in* the Temple, just as this took place? As soon as my poem was finished, I couldn't take it anymore—the Beauty!—but I *had* been so at home in Athena's grand house that it *didn't* overwhelm me. Only when I stepped off it, onto the Akropolis's rock itself, and gazed back at where I'd just *been*—at the shafts so alive and glowing in the rosiness of the light—*did* it overwhelm me! The size of it was human, once in it—but beside it, I paled. Each step further away, it seemed to *grow in size*! The sensation was so eerie—the Parthenon's magnitude and perfection so dizzying. I retreated to the scaffolded Erectheíon, gazed up at the polluted rot-faced Karyatídes to get my bearings. At least these urban sisters, standing there for their very *last* time, to come down soon and go peacefully to their death in a museum, were human. But the Parthenon was an Act *Divine* Itself! Kapoiánnis and I walked back together, down the slippery stones, an old man with a young man, as the modern-ancient city glimmered and flashed *everywhere* in the valley below. At the Propýlaea, we stopped—he urging me to go look at the tiny Nike shrine suspended like garlic from the beam of the sky, swinging in the breeze above Athens. Then over to the other side we went into the Pinakotéka—and I gazed about—then we descended. At the side gate above the theatre, I gave the Head Guard 250 Drachmas—but how *could* I ever *pay* for the experience? As I staggered away in the night, I felt drunk—pummeled—sated! The hour truly had *drained* me..."

Draft-1, therefore, of this book was commenced in Athens, and took place solely in Athens and on Mount Olympos. This was penned prior to my involvement with the Olympics, or with any aspect of Olympism. After much kindness by Athenians, I was enabled to proceed to the mountain itself, in June of 1979, principally due to kind help from the Hellenic Alpine Club and its boss, Ath.-Nássos A. Tzártzanos. My first day on Mount Olympos is recorded thus:

Friday 1 June 1979: "Mounted Mount Olympos, or almost, as I arrived in one piece at 2100 metres at the Refuge 'A', Spílios Agápitos, where Kóstas Zolótas is Manager. The trip up is well cited in the novel, as likely *every* experience of import for this next month will be—so I'll only document the outlines, not details, herefrom: (1) up 6 AM; (2) met two workers at Litóchoron Police Station at 7 AM; (3) went via cab with them up 6 kilometres to the first Hut 'Stávros', and there joined by Konstanzerin 'Sonja', and walked 6 kilometres as she and a worker brought mules up with packs. The scenery kept getting more stunning, I reveling in the fact of at last being *on* Olympos! 12 kilometres up, went via mule train—as there were now 12 mules, the other worker having got 9 more. At Prióni, 6 more kilometres where the road ends, and the 2 stayed with mules to load sand/tiles, and Sonja and I walked up—the path getting increasingly worse as the scenery got better. I thought I'd get a heart attack—so exhausted I was. The bloody mule train at last humiliated us by passing us just before the Hut. At Hut met Kóstas—a true gent—and I liked him instantly. He took to me, too, so I feel the month'll be good. Said he'd help me find work when I must back down the slopes."

On the fifth of the month I did climb to the very summit of Olympos, to Mýikas, thus witnessing another dream come true. As opposed to this novel's plot, I myself did *not* have my own fall down a sideslope of the mountain until the day *after* the actual climb to the top. Ivor, in this book, has his fall first, then his climb. With me, it was the reverse. My climb to Mýtikas occurred on 5 June, and my fall and near-death on 6 June 1979. My Journal records:

Tuesday 5 June 1979: "Left Hut at 7.15 AM and reached top of Skála Peak at 9.45. Ascended with Zolótas and two elderly Swiss [Professor Franz Escher and his wife Marie-Louise]. Slowly. All in fog and wind. From Skála to Mýtikas in 45 minutes—arrive at peak highest of Olympos at 10.30. Very emotional moment in my life—see book. Atop Mýtikas wrote—in the book there for signing in—the three lines of Hephaistos from 'Counsel Of The Gods' (about mountain-climbing) and put signature. Thereon wrote the first section of chapter '5th June – Quarter To Ten'. Saw 'Gipfel Maus'—the peak's wild pet [meaning, from the German, Mountaintop Mouse], looking for crumbs!" [Rosy The Dog did, indeed, climb Olympos with us that day!]

Wednesday 6 June 1979 [The day I was almost killed, and which provides the whole of the novel, *WinterGames/SummerGames*, with its temporality with regard to the complete plot of the book, which takes place as a set of intertwined flashbacks in the Olympic Gold Medallist's mind, as he is lying unconscious after his fall down this very mountain]: "8.00 AM to Skála, then to Skólio. [I believe I went back up the mountain alone, this day, since I now felt that I knew the route, from the climb of the day before.] View along walk was like a peer down into Grand Canyon—from backside of Mýtikas. Terrifyingly deep. Good thing it was foggy yesterday—so I couldn't *see* it! Went from Skólio with German girl to pyramid hill 'tween it and Ághios Antónios and sat a long while, eating and sunning self nude (when she left) and writing '5th June

- Half Past Ten' and '6th June – Five Before Two'. After that, I scaled Antónios then descended and proceeded to get lost, *and* traumatised. Read the book. Return to Hut at 6.00 PM—badly shaken. Kóstas says I'll be better working 'down below'—I agree!"

Thursday 7 June 1979: "After being forced to ascend/descend the roof with tiles, me with my bum legs, I gave out at noon and refused any more. I've got my limits. After lunch I hardly could walk. Sleep last night was agony—as I only could use my left side. Wrote about yesterday's nightmare fall: '6th June – 3 PM Plus' and '6th June – Sixish'—the return."

Friday 8 June 1979: "Was woken at 6.00 by Zolótas saying tersely: 'You can go down now'—meaning off Olympos to Litóchoron. He said I was wanted for my next job—on the sea. I was quite shocked—as he'd said but yesterday he's use me through the weekend with all the Greeks. To cut my stay was rather rude—I felt he was angry because I was limping yesterday. So—I had to *walk* to Prióni—6 kilometres with a bum leg and it was *no* fun. How odd—I'd written at the *top* of Mount Olympos the 3 lines from 'Counsel' delivered by Hephaistos, the *Lame God*, and just 3 days later I, too, am limping *down* the slope! Only 20 days ago I was caught in the Temple of Hephaistos, Athens, during a storm. It was the *last* Temple of Athens I stood in. Strange. When I reached Prióni, Irmgild Zolótas was there to fetch me, and she did not even know I'd had a bad fall—and was shocked. She said Kóstas wasn't angry—but my job was waiting, so she thought it best I go down. When in Litóchoron, I truly was *glad* to be down and on flat land. The whole experience, up above, was such a strain. In the VW coming down, a wasp flew in and stung my sore leg—and even Irmgild mentioned that she thought that The Gods wanted me down!"

Since I climbed Olympos, my whole life changed. On 12 August 1979 I journeyed back to America, after recovering from Greece for most of the month of July 1979 with the family of Alfred Philipp in Castle Eggmühl south of Regensburg near the Danube, and when I got back Stateside I travelled back to Upstate New York with the notion that I would somehow end up working for the XIII Olympic Winter Games then gearing up in Lake Placid. After climbing Zeus's Mountain, it just seemed natural to seek a job for the Games which worship of Zeus inspired. That dream came true, like so many others in my life, where Reality has so effectively blended with Inspiration.

I got my job for the Lake Placid Olympic Organizing Committee due to nepotism. How *else* does anyone *ever* end up working for the Olympics? Certainly not on good looks or being well hung alone! Due to intervention by my mother's father's brother's wife, my great-aunt, née Blanche Brown, a stalwart Northern New York Democrat who campaigned tirelessly for Ambassador Roger Tubby of Saranac Lake when Roger was running against Daniel Patrick Moynihan for the Senate seat which Moynihan won, Aunt Blanche put me in her car and shuttled me from Jefferson County to Placid, convinced that Roger wouldn't let her down, that he would come to her rescue and help her nephew, fresh from Europe. Roger indeed did not let her down. In fact, just for fun, the very day before Aunt Blanche carted me to the Adirondacks, she had me meet Moynihan, Tubby's rival, at a Democratic do on the Saint Lawrence River, a scenic boattrip, Sunday 26 August 1979. My Journal reads: "Dropt off at Howard Johnson's [Watertown, New York]. Claude [Williams, of Rodman, New York, where Aunt Blanche was Postmistress] and his wife and a Mrs Fish and daughter Donna picked me up and we drove to Alexandria Bay for the Senatorial boatride. Note the *omens*: on the Saint Lawrence [River], my Name Saint, and from a town whose name came from the most famous city founded by Alexander the Great. We saw a balloon ascend from the Edgewood [Resort] then went to the pier and Claude introduced me to some people. The Senator Moynihan looked very Upper East Side. Knickerbocker. Seersucker suit, hair long and white and fastidiously unkempt, and white leather shoes. As I boarded he shook and said: 'Ah—a man in a three-piece suit.'"

On Monday 27 August 1979, Aunt Blanche, her husband Uncle Kenneth Greene, brother of my mother's father, and their daughter Eloise drove me to Lake Placid. I got a place to live, and with my kin saw some local sights. I was armed, for the next day's trip to the actual LPOOC offices inside Town Hall, with an introduction to Roger Tubby from my Aunt, as well as a letter of introduction from New York State's Tug Hill Plateau Commission boss, Benjamin Coe, of Watertown, New York, because Aunt Blanche was a charter Board Member of the Commission, a Governor Rockefeller appointee no less, which wasn't doing badly, given Blanche was no Rockefeller GOP fan but an FDR New Dealer!

Tuesday 28 August 1979: "Morn: Went to Lake Placid Olympic Organizing Committee HQ and introduced self to Roger Tubby, former Ambassador, working there for liaison with Government of New York State. He liked my CV and fact of Jefferson County's Democratic Chairman's sponsoring me for a diplomatic job [which was why I ended up on that bloody boatride with Moynihan; I asked Moynihan for an application form for whatever Civil Service test was required to get into the diplomatic corps, and he said he would have one sent to me; no form ever was sent to me by Senator Moynihan nor by any of his handlers!] and Roger had received the letter (urged by Aunt Blanche) written to him by Ben Coe, head of the Tug Hill Commission."

Next day, 29 August 1979, due to Roger, I met the appropriate people in the Protocol Division, at the LPOOC, and the rest is history. I got offered the job of Deputy Chief of Protocol on 30 August 1979.

31 August 1979 [my first full day on the job]: "Had short meeting in morn, listening in on a discussion with the Attaché to the Games from Andorra, who needed more accommodation for Officials. All housing is scarce, and he'll have difficulty. Returned at 2.00, briefed on the LPOOC's organizational structure. I still can't believe I'm the 'man

603

relied on' in Protocol now. To Tubby my boss said he was bombarding me with info prior to Tuesday (1000 pages of material to plow through)—but they all seem confident of my abilities. The Olympic Season actually begins in 3 short weeks—that the site-testing of the new Arena occurs as a pre-Games Figure Skating meet. All the top skaters in contention will be here in advance. From there on out it's: Hard Work. Moved 3 houses upstreet (even closer to the job than ever) to 333 Main Street. It's a charming old farmhouse with a white picket fence and old verandah with wicker chairs. Terribly charming, and totally 'Upstate NY'. My room I arranged to my liking and for the first time since 28 May's leaving Athens I feel I can relax and it was so good to unpack."

Shit started hitting the fan, from certain Protocol stuffies over my head, when they found out that I was trying to organize a gala fundraiser for the Placid Games to be held at Carnegie Hall. See the novel, about that. For real-life, here's a snippet from my Journal:

Tuesday 25 October 1979: "Began organizing for a New York City Poetry extravaganza at Carnegie Hall, to be sponsored by the non-profit organization, the 'New York State Waterways Project, of Ten Penny Players, Inc.' [whether or not said group still exists, in 1996, I haven't the foggiest!]. The name Penny is applicable—strangely so—in that the T-shirt my mother posted had on it stamped a blowup of a photograph of my dearly beloved dog of my childhood, who was named Penny. When I received the shirt I was *very* moved. The Poetry Gala really came as a placation to me, a press release sent to me by the Arts Department (under our Division of Protocol), since I had suggested to them that there be something in the Olympics Arts Festival for Poetry, and had also volunteered my services, but no money was left in their budget. As per the Carnegie Gala, I got the support of ex-Broadway showman, Cliff Ammon in our Ceremonies Department, and the Waterways people (both poet Richard Spiegel and Barbara Fisher) and the NYC promo agency, Janice Burenga Inc., and the Carnegie Booking Office—so it'll *be*, somehow!" [Well—just as in Fiction, so in Reality—and the so-called Carnegie Gala never did transpire —due to stick-in-the-muds higher up in the LPOOC organization!]

My Journal entry for Thursday, All Souls Day, the day after my Gala Nostalgia Costume Ball of Halloween 1979, records the rancour my Balls, concocted by me to instil Olympic Spirit into the moribund Olympic Committee, engendered, and shows how they royally pissed many boneheads off, namely my immediate Protocol superiors: "Needless to say, was coming down from high adrenalin level of the Ball, all day. Everyone kept coming and saying what fun they had, what a success it was. On the other hand, the Attachés Conference began to-day and I wasn't even invited to one meeting or informed of a thing. I think my boss, who didn't even show at the Ball, is trying to tell me something. Returned PA system to Arena (Lussi Rink) used by our six-foot-five-inch Black Major Domo at the door to announce Guests last night. Worked all day on keeping the Carnegie project alive."

Things came to a head with all this backstage bull, about the "do" at Carnegie Hall, on Thursday 8 November 1979, whose Journal entry for that day just about sums up how frenetic my life had become in a few short weeks in Lake Placid: "Spoke with Julian Roosevelt [by telephone; the then Junior Member of the International Olympic Committee in the United States] who sounds so honourable and his advice was to speak with William Simon, former Secretary of the Treasury, so I rang his office—but before morn was out decided to stop the project entirely and quit bothering people for money—it had all just got to be too much! Plus—I felt if I carry on it would never allow my work on my *Sokrates* drama to be realised—an act of hybris? I did feel badly—but had also heard from the Gotham Book Mart that the Waterways poetry people were sort of sneered at by the New York literary scene and that the reason John Ashberry declined was because yesterday he just decided that the Waterways were 'for the birds'. So bitchy. I just wanted *out* of it—for the Olympics' sake!"

Well, as days advanced ever closer to Opening Ceremonies, things got bitchier, all over the whole Olympic Primary Region. Not one single LPOOC department was spared the pressure, which just mounted and mounted. It became a real loony bin, real quick. Olympic employees got to the point where they coped as best they could, what with all the fur constantly flying from bosses. I just tried to weather each new daily storm, coasting on as even a keel as I could. Needless to say, my own personal even keels are most *other* people's stegasaurus spines!

A Journal entry near Christmas pins the tail on the donkey's asshole, and gives Readers a glimpse at how I came up with the characters I call the Dong Brothers. Wednesday 19 December 1979: "Met 2 Attachés from the People's Republic Of China at the USSR vs CSSR hockey game, as I was 'ushering' in the VIP Section, and sat with them and joked about how the crowd hated the Russians and how the *Czechs* hated the Russians. Suggested that Peking buy TV Rights so their people, for the first time in history, could watch the Olympics. *That* thought seemed to amuse them. I said everyone was very pleased China was participating, and said Peking should bid for the Summer Games 'since I'm sure you could stage a better show than they will in Moscow'. They enjoyed my humour and frankness. I asked them about travel in China, and especially about Hangchow and Lhasa (Tibet), and they said Tibet was now 'open to foreigners'. They said I could teach...as I mentioned having done so in Athens."

More bitchery, from my notes, Friday 21 December 1979: "Office party [which is an oxymoron, if there ever was one!]—at which point of my leaving with my coat on at 5.30 my boss asks me—'Oh—where're *you* going?'—meaning, away for Christmas. I felt like saying: 'Not to *your* house!' as it was the first 'friendly' Xmas cheer she'd sent my way. I *didn't* give her an invite to my New Year's Party, after all, ha ha."

On Sunday 23 December 1979 I was taken by a lady-admirer to Lake Ampersand, the multi-millionaire family's retreat, recapped in Fiction in this novel. That's all I'll say on *that* subject, for the time being.

I spent Christmas Day (Tuesday) 1979 with the Tubby family, in Saranac Lake, and see that on that day: "Came home with Roger's Jeep and I began writing my 'Ode To The Modern Olympics'—which is when I got the mad idea that the Olympics *should* be returned once and for all to Greece! Spent morning getting my manuscript for *Olympian Souls* ready for the printer."

Wednesday 26 December 1979: "Completed writing 'Ode To The Modern Olympics'—can't wait to see what a furor *it* will cause!"

The rest of the month was spent getting The Whiteface Inn preparations done for my New Year's Eve Ball, fictionalised in this novel.

Tuesday 1 January 1980 [was *anybody* sober, this first day of the Exultational Eighties?] [Did anybody have a *good* time, the night before?]: "Reeled under the reality of the party—but steeled self that I must fight it. The group of performers breached the contract—as they did not come onstage till one hour late from their scheduled time, 10.20 PM. Went at 10 AM this morn to Convention Hall to police up, and retrieved a very valuable piece of legal weaponry, the letter forced by the New York agency on me, near midnight, which I refused to sign and tore up. It said I had to pay $855 within 10 days and mentioned my position with The Committee, both of which rankled me. Left the 20 kegs intact, and 2 cold-taps, and 2 carbon-dioxide cylinders all together in the Hall's Lobby behind screens for morning pickup."

Wednesday 2 January 1980: "2 kegs and cold-tap stolen—value $235. Told I was 'terminated'—given 2 weeks' notice. Judge Wolff said I should do an in-house transfer. Suggested working with Dan McCormick. Went with Trooper Kubasiak to Whiteface Inn to interrogate employees. Told agent of the musicians from New York City to 'ring me Monday', when I'd give him my lawyer's number. Rang lawyer and told him of breach of contract and the threats of intimidation."

Thursday 3 January 1980: "Rallied and worked on my 'defence'. Rang two lawyers (one NYC, one local) about my rights as a worker to contest 'termination'. The local Lake Placid lawyer said get my contract with the LPOOC and have bosses state 'facts in writing', and my New York lawyer said to find a transfer or he'd defend me if they pressed to fire me. Dan McCormick offered me a Directorship of his new soon-to-open Relief Service Centre, a better position but lower pay. I accepted! I phoned Commissioner Testo of the New York State Labour Office in Albany, and told him of the threat to fire me, and he said he'd defend me as I was a legal New York State resident and the contention was against a German alien (my immediate superior)! I loved it! I then told the German alien that she and her husband better not pressure me any more, or I'd contest *them* against the Labour Department, and pointed at her saying: 'It would make *you* look pretty *bad!*' *That* scared the wits out of *her*. I also made it known 'that my lawyer requests I get a copy of my contract'! So she and Personnel got the hint that I wasn't taking their shit. Another turn of luck was that the Troopers rang and said my one keg and the cold-tap were 'found' on Whiteface Inn property! So I drove out in eve and found the keg by the roadside behind Convention Hall and the tap in an abandoned cabana room poolside. Very sinister."

Friday 4 January 1980: "Issued termination cheque, in spite of all the 'agreements' of yesterday. Felt horridly double-crossed, but vowed not to show it. Got LPOOC's Legal Department to ok that all employees get the right to see and to copy all of their employment records. When I was looking through them, I saw that 16 Gs had been budgeted for my job, but I'd only been offered 13, in September, since the boss of the Protocol Division knew I'd 'accept anything' [since I arrived in Placid penniless]. Rang my New York lawyer and discussed it all with him. Decided definitely to take this to court if my offer for the Director of the Crisis Centre falls through, and said so to the New York State Labour Commissioner, Testo. This whole thing's a scandal. Dan McCormick, my new boss, came to the house after work and said he wants to give me a chance, and 'that there is *no* Spirit left in the Olympic Movement at all'! Reverend Fell, President of the LPOOC, said he'd sign my new hiring papers."

Tuesday 8 January 1980: "Posted originals of Witness Statements to New York lawyer. Was phoned by Marcy Hotel saying they'd issue a summons for my arrest (how nice) if I only would not pay the musicians' hotel bill. I said that their contract was breached, but even then I was only liable for *one* night by law/contract anyhow, and that I would pay one night should that make them happy. It was upsetting, as I only had enough in my account, plus $20 cash, to pay this, but agreed to. So I walked to the bank, withdrew my $97, and paid them. David Heim from work phoned Marcy for my behalf and had talked Manager Paul Trippi into my paying only one night, so that was very kind, and on seeing the contract he agreed to write a receipt saying the total bill of $192 was 'paid in full'—so I was saved! I walked away feeling a Sitwellian disdain for the whole sordid affair (I'm reading Roger Tubby's Sitwell family biography now) [a few years later, in the early 1990s, while conducting my Cavendish family research of descent from the Dukes of Devonshire and Dukes of Portland, it struck me that we, *are* Plantagenet cousins of the Sitwells, so it's no wonder I always felt an affinity with them]. Of course, the Sitwells are a very *bad* influence. Roger [Tubby] gave me $200 on loan to-day to help my debt. A cheque. LPOOC Personnel had me see them, and to-day on top of a gaol threat I was told I should 'get out'—in other words, LPOOC's Personnel Department doublecrossed our agreement of last Friday, which was made between Personnel, Protocol, and myself, that I could stay upstairs [in Protocol] till my new job came through. So—it suddenly hit me that this was my 'last day'. How entertaining. So I went back to my office and couldn't contain myself from giving my boss precisely my true opinion of her. I said she showed not *one* ounce of human gratitude for all the work I'd done, that I felt she was worse than a snake in the grass, and that she was a *monster*! I repeated the word *monster* to her again, as she fled out to my desk area by the coffee machine, and she snuck away shaking, to run to Saranac Airport, to pick up H.R.H. Don Alfonso de Borbón, Duke of Cadiz, visiting from Spain. If I'd bump into *him* later, I was going to say I published his Queen's grandmother's memoirs, *The Kaiser's Daughter*, which I did, of course [Queen Sophia of Spain being Queen Friederike of Greece's daughter, and Friederike being the aforementioned daughter of Princess Viktoria Luise, the Kaiser's girl]. I didn't see the Don about, though. So—my stint as Deputy Chief of Protocol ended on a blah note. I thought, well I'll make a few calls, so rang New York City a few times, and then my best call was to Lindsay Anderson [the director, in London] who sounded *very* pleased indeed to hear from me and that I was almost done with [my revision of] *Sokrates*. For evening meal, my two 'buddies' at The Committee, Maura Domoracki and Lorna Stio, took me to dinner at the Belvedere in Saranac. There, while eating spaghetti and meatballs, was hatched my conviction to write a novel NOW about Lake Placid, to be an instant-book—given I know so much about the organization and its characters. I'd already thought up a mad title—*WinterGames*—weeks ago—so decided on that. Also thought up title for chapter 1: 'Genesis Of A Dæmon'. I'm just reproducing what I know. I might as well—as no one *else* could! Plus, it's my best way to posit my beliefs about the Olympian Ideal and how it's lost all its Spirit! So I rang Ann Lynch [publisher of my poetry volume, *Olympian Souls*] and she agreed to loan me her electric typewriter, and so Maura had me pick it up, then right there on the machine I began completing in a short time the first two chapters."

Wednesday 9 January 1980: "What a literary day—one not unlike those I gave up by leaving Greece! Wrote: 'On Stage On Ice', 'Backstage', 'Mister Protocol, Mister Protocol', 'No Peace For The Wicked', 'Palpo Island', 'Petunias', and 'The Birch Burns Quick As The Pine'."

Thursday 10 January 1980: "Carried on with *WinterGames*; also did paste-up (7½ hours solid work) for the design of *Olympian Souls*. It looks smashing—truly a gorgeous book! Saw Dan [McCormick] and he assured me I'd be hired next week again, on the 18th, to work with him."

Friday 11 January 1980: "*WinterGames* growing so quick I'll have ½ done this weekend!"

Saturday 12 January 1980: "Wrote and wrote all day, through chapter 22 now, and plotted out chapter names for rest of book. To be roughly 42 chapters. Proofread my paste-up of *Olympian Souls*."

Sunday 13 January 1980: "Picked up at 10.30 AM by Ann Lynch and driven to her Clinton Press, Plattsburgh. On way read first 5 chapters of *WinterGames*. Returned home late to write 2 chapters of novel, 'Zig-Zag Wipe-Out' and 'A Childe Is Born'."

Monday 14 January 1980: "Wrote only 1 long chapter, 'Chinese Hockey'." [Featuring the Dongs!]

Tuesday 15 January 1980: "Did the impossible and wrote 7 chapters as I'd scheduled self to do, for *WinterGames*—up through chapter 32. It could be a scream...on film."

Wednesday 16 January 1980: "Wrote 7 more chapters to-day— therefore through chapter 39. Now only need to write 5 more and it'll be done, thank God! Spoke with Mrs Tubby, who's lucky enough to be going to Olympia for the Torch Lighting."

Thursday 17 January 1980: "Finished *WinterGames* in 10 days! Wrote 4 chapters and finished the book. Decided not to do 'It All Happens Somehow'." Told by my new boss-man, whom I don't know if I like after all, that I can't retain my Infinity Clearance for accreditation, and thus for the whole Olympics I'm stuck inside the American Legion building! Why has Fate been so cruel?"

Friday 18 January 1980: "First 'official' day back at the LPOOC. Worked all day getting our Human Services Centre shaped up—2 floors of office space above the American Legion building."

Tuesday 22 January 1980: "Was at Ray Brook Environmental Conservation HQ for a day-long seminar on crisis control (drug abuse, alcohol, and mental illness) [which sounded just like LPOOC *Protocol*, to me!]—so it was quite the education. The most interesting speaker, from NYC, emphasised the problems of PCP—a drug I'd never heard of, invented as an anesthetic but now used as an LSD/cocaine spray for grass, causing extreme toxic states, fear, loss of motor control, and irrationality [sounded even *more* like LPOOC Protocol, to me!]. The Cops fear a large amount of it during the Games. Ate lunch gratis at the Security Centre for the whole of the Games, at Camp Adirondack—filled with Soldiers, Air Force, Troopers, etc. etc., from all manners of Olympic personnel. So many uniforms in a 'mess hall' reminded me of a 1940s musical."

Saturday 26 January 1980: "Spent all day in bed, reading. It was glorious! I went into total retreat, recharging my batteries. First, finished John Pearson's *The Sitwells*, then read in entirety Christine Crawford's *Mommie Dearest* [which, for a place as insane as Lake Placid in January 1980, should have been required reading!]."

Sunday 27 January 1980: "Am feeling *very* bored with Lake Placid...and the Olympics all but seem over for me...I couldn't care less."

Monday 28 January 1980: "Spent a while with Peter Gelles on his driving shift—we took an 'official business' run to the new Whiteface Mountain Ski Lodge, as I'd not yet seen it *ever* since I got here in September! I was nicely impressed with it. Also—got a Press Pass for access into the Press Centre (the High School), and saw on the computer screen at the Accreditation Centre that I get access to *all* venues now, and not just what I thought. Pinkerton Guards now are at all Olympic buildings 'protecting' us."

Tuesday 29 January 1980: "I cut cardboard to-day, to cover windows of our Crisis Centre's romper room, a good utilisation of my talents."

Friday 1 February 1980: "Tom Franjola, owner/editor of *The Lake Placid Reporter*, one of my favourite locals, agreed to publish 'Ode To The Modern Olympics' in its entirety next week (Friday) as a guest editorial."

Saturday 2 February 1980: "Worked 1-6 with Chief Chaplain, Matti Terho from Finland (now Montréal) and the Father Superior, Monsignor Riani, of Wadhams Seminary, Ogdensburg, New York, helping both to set up accommodations in the Pius X Centre's house in Saranac, to be used as Chief Residence for Olympic Chaplains. After, we went to the Olympic Village, most exciting. The Religious Affairs Office is in the Entertainment Building!—between the Milk Bar of the Disco and the Game Room with all the kinky vending machines. The Peking Athletes in particular loved the machines. From 7-9.30 I stayed and watched *Superman*, from row 1 of the Ciné, and got sick. It was too close—what with all the flying missiles and San Andreas Faults and loud *noise!* While talking with the Chinese Attaché after the flic, a girl (Hostess Charmain Porteous) introduced herself saying: 'Didn't we meet at a Christmas party in Florence?' Sure enough [1977], we did, in Patrick Hamilton's studio! God—on *that* note I took a Tylenol. Stayed at Olympic Village till 11."

Sunday 3 February 1980: "Slept at Pius X Centre then came back to Olympic Village with Terho and Riani to help set up for the first Ecumenical Services then first Catholic Masses ever sanctioned officially by the rather atheistic IOC. I even took part in the historic occasion—reading, for both, the First Lesson, of *Jeremiah*. The services were in the cinema. Only 6 came for the first, at 9 AM, but about 20 for the Mass, including the Mayor of the Olympic Village and wife, Harry Fregoe. I stayed and bought lunch for $2, eating in the Cafeteria, then at 1 PM went to see *The Wizard Of Oz* on full screen. I'd only seen it on TV, which is *not* the same! I couldn't believe the beauty of the colourful sets. Such a bit of escapism was *just* what I needed. The Chinese Athletes went ga-ga over this!"

Monday 4 February 1980: "The Chief Press Writer said that into the *Olympic News* only went hard-cold facts about Sports—not Poetry! So— my book [*Olympian Souls*] won't get cited. I think it's scandalous—after they promised me for months it *could* get mentioned! Pissed me *right* off!"

Wednesday 6 February 1980: "I'm getting on better with Dan [McCormick] each day, as he sees I'm a good worker and who else does he have?"

Friday 8 February 1980: "This evening, not long after the Sacred Flame arrived in Lake Placid after its long journey from Olympia, so too my book *Olympian Souls* arrived, delivered from the printer and likewise having been inspired by Ancient Greece. I was very very moved by both events —need one say. The first I watched closely from the Press Railing overlooking the Speed Skating Oval. The latter was first seen inside Ann Lynch's house in Hillcrest Avenue—the hill crest, Mount Olympos, indeed had sustained me since leaving the Mystic Mountain at the end of June. Also to-day, saw 'Ode To The Modern Olympics' published with no errors in *The Lake Placid Reporter* as guest editorial, the February 7-12 issue."

Monday 11 February 1980: "The Crisis Centre opened to the accompaniment of a fiasco called the Official Transport System, which only yesterday (we had heard, at the briefing by Kulascz of the Transport Department) had only 350 coaches assigned to cover maybe 50,000 people per day. Also, he said that 21,000 had been accredited, instead of 5,000 that had been forecast. I think that the excess is Security People and that there are far too many Soldiers protecting us now than they'll ever admit. Got my 2 tickets to Opening Ceremonies. I didn't think Personnel would give them—since they might say I've only been working since 18 January, but they didn't try that stunt, having been talked to by Dan."

Tuesday 12 February 1980: "Another long day. My duties have quickly defined themselves—as a liaison person between the LPOOC and the volunteers and the ongoing events here in town. Things to-day seemed very 'carnival'—but almost in suspension—waiting for the Opening of to-morrow. I was interviewed for 20 minutes by Lisa Morey of the *Plattsburgh Press-Republican* and photographed for an article about me and my book. I took the opportunity to inject a remedy for the IOC—saying that each participating nation in the Olympic Movement should contribute ½ million dollars for a sink-fund of $65 million and then get further sources from the UN and private philanthropies [to build a Permanent Games Site]. The Summer Games could be in Athens, the Winter in Salonika—both in Greece."

Wednesday 13 February 1980: "Everything built up to the Opening Ceremonies at 2.30 PM—months and months built up! As I sat in the bleachers, having walked to Horse Grounds with Barbara [J. Jones] from our house, it was such a carnival atmosphere, but not as jubilant as what I'd seen last year this time in Athens. The Ceremonies themselves were colossal, on a D. W. Griffiths scale, and I loved every minute of it. For once, the LPOOC didn't slip up too badly—but the PA system wasn't in sync with the orchestra, since the music blared too loudly in parts and overrode the Master of Ceremonies, T. Walker, whose voice I detest. But all in all the cast of thousands was fabulously well co-ordinated and the colours of the Athletes' uniforms of particular beauty. The pageantry was on a grandiose enough level to please even a Pharaoh, and I adored it. The Programmes were well done, too. The event kept coming at one in great rushes of emotion. I could hardly believe that there *I* was...and even though I've worked for the Olympics for six months it all seemed so surreal. It was as if all the pain I'd gone through...vanished. But, strange, I still didn't feel a part of it all. What was happening...was that it all had suddenly transcended far above all the heads of the LPOOC's workers...like the inflated balloons which coasted way above...like the US Army Parachute Team, the Golden Knights, dropping out of the sky with birdlike grace and bearing in correct order the flags of Greece, the IOC, and the USA, and landing perfectly into the wildly cheering Arena. I'd *heard* of many of these theatricalities—but to *see* them...put it all in the realm of

Hollywood or something. A most touching tribute, though, was the release of the doves—a very beautiful gesture but which rather appalled me, also, since the poor birds seemed quite terrified flying over 25,000 people and one poor dove, in particular, seemed injured and flapped from the middle of the Arena, atop the snow, as if it had been shot, and most eerily it flopped directly, in an abysmally wavering line, *directly* to the feet of the *Russian* Athletes, who bent down to pick the sad omen up [remember—the Moscow Games were only five months away!]. It was very cold —and every one in my section looked at each other, aghast, as we realised, together, that this *was* an omen Then soon thereafter, the Torch Runner came in—the moment I'd waited a lifetime to see. Ever since I'd been a boy I'd prayed, one day, to watch that Sacred Cauldron being lit ...at an Olympic Games...then...after years of hoping...there I was...in a seat ...watching that very dream. I was deeply, deeply moved. The Torch Runner stood there...a little too proudly...perhaps he could have knelt before igniting the Flame. But as soon as he did so—as the Great Cauldron exploded into orange shimmering Light—it began its slow rise, up, up, above all the problems of Mankind below, up to its place of prophetic burning, in the large bowl of honour, towering so loftily, and so emphatically, like a Tripod sizeable enough for the Olympian Deities Themselves."

On Friday eve, 23 May 1980, I flew back to London, this time officially recognised as a novelist, having had luck from my former boss, Jeffrey Simmons, then my literary agent. While I was in Lake Placid, Jeffrey had placed with a New York publisher *God's Fool*, Book 1 of this quintet-in-progress and which Édition von Rapp will re-release, so I felt on top of the world, not with the New York publisher, but with being back in Europe. My first venture to the offices of the British Olympic Association, then just off Oxford Circus, 1-2 John Prince's Street, was on Tuesday 27 May 1980: "...where I researched about running. Read *Official Report* of 1936 Games and Roger Bannister's *First Four Minutes* (written shortly after he was at Oxford), and the Ekthodikí Athenón book on the history of the Olympics." This was propitious, since I've quoted a short passage from Sir Roger's book in this one, and while living in Athens in 1979 one of the other places I worked for was the Greek publishing house, Ekthodikí Athenón, thanks to my friend, Roúli Tatáki.

Thursday 29 May 1980: "Walked to BOA offices and at last met with General Secretary Richard Palmer. We talked, seriously a bit, but soon were gossiping about Lake Placid, which he called 'a right cock-up'. His forthrightness I liked and he liked mine. He told me that my bosses at Placid only got into the Olympic Movement because the man had been scheduling flights to Placid back in '69 for Air Canada, for whom he was a booking agent in Brussels. Palmer said 'he weasled in'. Hmm. After overhearing a phone call when he said the British would march behind the Olympic Flag and not the Union Jack, I volunteered my services till the Moscow Games. He was gladdened and called in his assistant, Mike Blake, to meet me. They realised my initiation at Placid was valuable."

My deeper involvement with the BOA began on Tuesday 3 June 1980: "Got to Olympic office about 4 and had session with Palmer. He had me help with ID forms for F-Accreditation (Athletes), so I stuffed the proper amount of forms in envelopes for each sport-group going (e.g. canoeing), then corrected his addition of number of Athletes/Officials to be in the Olympic Village day by day at Moscow. He offered to let me write an article for the BOA about the reaction pro/con to Carter's Boycott."

Wednesday 4 June 1980: "Began with notes on clippings. I'm just going through the lot, chronologically, from January 20th, Carter's day he announced Olympic Boycott, and working to to-day. Bloody difficult—it takes hours to read them all and digest them."

Friday 6 June 1980: "Spent all day over clippings, getting through April, and then posing quite a few questions to Dick Palmer, who surprised me by saying that I could keep all profits from an article I could write and then he let me have his own personal files on the Boycott issue. He handed 3 great folders over the desk to me. He said I should contact the BOA Education Director, Donald Anthony.

Monday 9 June 1980: "Spent much of afternoon going over with Mike [Blake] at BOA the timing of certain events in the Boycott debate. Mike told me some quite startling things about Maggie Thatcher's pressuring for a Boycott."

Tuesday 10 June 1980: "Had prepared questions for Sir Denis Follows, Chairman of BOA, but after I rushed and got there by 9.45 AM his General Secretary said he [Sir Denis] didn't have time to see me, that I should ask him [Dick]. Spent 1 hour with Dick, thus, from 11.30 to 12.30, and got his clearance to say I have 'access to BOA files' and that I can contact the Marquess of Exeter and Lord Luke (two UK IOC men). My investigative work helped Dick to note certain dates he'd forgot. Met BOA Education Director, Don Anthony, who said I should meet Lord Noel-Baker, 1959 Nobel Peace Prize Winner and 1920 Silver Medallist in the 1500 Metre Run at Antwerp, so I rang the 92-year-old Life Peer in Belgravia, and made appointment for to-morrow. Dick Palmer also ok'd I contact the Shadow Minister of Sports, Denis Howell, so I rang and he arranged I meet with his aide in Parliament to-morrow, Patrick Cheney."

Wednesday 11 June 1980: "Rushed to Parliament, stopping in St Margaret's, and before Cheney came to Central Lobby I met (a good omen) a young Hostess from Lake Placid Games, a young girl from Lake Placid, in fact, who'd stood beside Brenda Tubby at Opening Ceremonies. Patrick Cheney came and whisked me straight back and down stairs and corridors (left) to the Commons Café, where he bought me tea and I grilled him on many questions. He gave me scoops galore of Tory and US meddling of Olympic affairs. I gave him and his boss, Denis Howell (twice Sports Minister under Labour) 2 copies of *Olympian Souls*. And later on phone Pat said he enjoyed the Parthenon ode best! Rushed to [Westminster] Abbey and caught Dean Carpenter giving the lunch service, and had short word with him, then rushed to Belgravia via

Chester Square to South Eaton Place. At Noel-Baker's, I was in my element, and needless to say I was quite awed to be in the presence of a man who had won a Nobel Prize for Peace. We met in his tiny study, facing the back garden. I wanted to weep—the man was so old (90+) and tottered in in his bathrobe and slippers, but said I must excuse the fact that he soon must ready himself to attend the House of Lords! His eyes looked almost blind, but I felt he saw everything I said. God—I was honoured just to be in the same room with him—not to mention his own room—he so wise and experienced, I so young and naïve. I asked him only four questions, which I pulled from letters sent to the BOA by the public. He answered so slowly and deliberately, letting me copy as quickly as I could, that I felt to be listening to a true prophet. I didn't want to leave him. I felt my Soul was gaining Goodness just by being near him. God—such men are so few and far between. He brought tears to my eyes, telling me of how thousands of people lined the roads of Europe, in 1948, before I was born, just to be able to watch the Olympic Flame pass by. Sandy Duncan later told me, in the BOA offices, that it was he, Sandy, who co-ordinated that Torch Run from Bari to Dover, and how so many people saw the Flame as a symbol of the end of World War II, and how they wanted to reach out and touch the Sacred Fire! Oh God, at the moment of hearing this from Lord Noel-Baker, I so wished that the poor oppressed folk of Russia could be able to be so inspired to Peace, on seeing the Flame in their motherland this summer! So many thoughts were going on in my mind, as I sat quietly speaking with, and drawing in the Wisdom of, Lord Noel-Baker. I gave him a copy of my poetry volume—but felt it a paltry gift in comparison to what he gave me. Later, at BOA, Mr Duncan arranged that I get a free pass to sit with him for the UK National Athletics Meet on Sunday at The Crystal Palace."

Thursday 12 June 1980: "Spent all afternoon and evening reading Hansards [meetings of Parliament] and flagging questions to ask about facts/dates."

Friday 13 June 1980: "I did not expect to go to Parliament to-day—but only to ring MP Tam Dalyell, head of Labour's Foreign Affairs Committee, for his views and confirmation of facts/dates, since he seemed so lucid in my reading of the Commons Boycott debate of 17 March. But he urged me come see him immediately, though he was leading an Adjournment this afternoon on nuclear weapons. So I took a taxi to Commons and requested a green slip and sent to trace him in the Chamber. Presently he came and gave me 22 April's Hansard and some clippings to read and sent me down to the Terrace. I wasn't allowed onto it by the Police, as I'm not an MP (yet), so went again as on Wednesday into the Café and flagged more queries. I waited an hour then went back to Lobby and was told Tam was looking all over for me. So I sent another apologetic green slip and out he came. To me the hour was necessary to get my questions prepared. So he took me to lunch through the Members' Café out to the Terrace, in sunshine, where we sat discussing the future of the

Olympic Movement and world politics! I was really quite overwhelmed by it all and kept wondering how in Hell I got into such a position?"

Sunday 15 June 1980: "Viewed festivities of UK National Athletics Championships and enjoyed company of old Olympian, Mr Duncan. Saw my 'boss', Dick Palmer, briefly. It was very chilly sitting in the stand. The seats, 5th row, were good. Saw Seb Coe doing a practice run for the 400 Metres, coming in last. Obviously, he didn't want to upstage the others who were striving for Olympic placement—as he's already assured."

Monday 16 June 1980: "Organized all my documents in chronological order. Have now about 9 pages done [on my Report for the BOA]."

Tuesday 17 June 1980: "Did lots of work on Report, now have 18 pages. Am up to the point when Olympic Flame gets to Lake Placid. It's quite a document, what I'm doing."

Wednesday 18 June 1980 [at 11.00 AM I was received by the Marchioness and Marquess of Exeter, he being the UK's Senior Member of the IOC, and Olympic Gold Medallist, Britain's most powerful man in the sporting world, at their London residence in Thurloe Place]: "Her Ladyship sat in the small sitting-room the *whole* time I questioned her husband about IOC policy. I think he enjoyed my queries, though was vague on many responses. He didn't admit to being nearly as informed as I'd imagined, perhaps he was just being shrewd. He spoke of his illustrious ancestors [who also are *mine*, as I am a Cecil descendant from The Virgin Queen's Baron Burghley, just as he is]—the Cecils— notably the great man of Elizabeth I. I hadn't realised his Cecil connection [nor did I, then, in 1980 realise my own, since my investigations into our Cavendish lineage from Dukes of Devonshire and of Portland didn't begin till 1983], but he gave me a nice edition of the booklet of their home, Burghley, and said to ring if I'm in the area. He also gave me a sherry—which seemed a compliment. I could've stayed and chatted all day—but, of course, had to beg leave to the BOA."

Said secret Report that I did for the BOA has never been seen in public. I am not publishing all of it here, just a few excerpts. I want it for the record that I was its researcher, compiler, and author. Having had access to letters written from Number 10 Downing Street and signed personally by Margaret Thatcher, then Prime Minister, was no little thrill, especially for an American citizen. Given that the former Prime Minister is still living, and a Life Peer, I'm not going to reproduce her own words of her Downing Street letters to the BOA, because a writer owns copyright, and I am not about to beg her for permission to quote from those letters, since permission, for *this* book, would hardly be granted, given that *this* book does not look kindly upon Margaret Thatcher nor Jimmy Carter nor their absurd Olympics Boycott of 1980, which was a travesty!

That said, my hush-hush Report was titled by me: *Politics And Sport: An Analysis Of The Debate In The United Kingdom To Boycott The Games Of The XXII Olympiad 1980, To Be Held In Moscow, With Emphasis On The Pressures Put Upon The Olympic Movement By The*

Party In Power. The original typescript, which I personally typed with my own two hands, at BOA headquarters, near Oxford Circus, is now in the Archives of the BOA, presently located, coincidentally, in Wandsworth, just a few blocks from where I myself resided in the mid-1970s. My signature on the original is dated by me 15 July 1980, when I completed the final typescript. If anybody wants to reproduce it, they have to get permission both from me, in writing, and from the British Olympic Association, in writing. I personally retain the right to edit, and approve, all final copy, and if anybody wants it, they'll have to *pay!*

My Introduction states: "This analysis is not intended to be a sensationalisation of events, nor is it an exposé of some 'governmental plot to do away with the Olympic Movement'. But, need we belabour the point that the Olympic Movement has been under more threat, during the first six months of 1980, than it ever has since the rebirth of the Modern Games in 1896. Those who have kept attacking the Olympic Movement these past months simply do not comprehend the good which the Movement does provide. It does not, though, take much intelligence to realise that *Sport* provides far more millions of people with enjoyment than *Politics* ever could provide. And that is the heart of the matter. As if over night, Politics, which wishes to have a monopoly on anything dealing with international intercourse, has suddenly woken up to the fact that Sport cuts across international bounds and really does not give a damn about Politics. And Politics, ever jealous of its international interests and aspirations, simply can't bear the fact that Sport is not something which Politics can control. Therefore, as you read this analysis, be ever mindful of the jealousy shown to Sport by Politicians, whose attempt to woo this fit, this youthful Free Spirit have constantly been rejected."

My typescript page 6B contains some interesting lines, all penned by me: "Labour believes that Downing Street had not been telling Hector Monro, Parliamentary Under-Secretary of State for the Environment, Minister for Sport, about these Conservative Party plans for Sport, although Sport of course was his balliwick. Therefore, the decision by Downing Street to turn decisions of Sport over to the Foreign Office is believed to have been made in agreement with the U.S. State Department shortly after, if not before, President Carter's public announcement on American television the morning of 20th January. [viz. page 4A, which states in my words: 'Sunday, the 20th of January, was when President Carter was interviewed lived in NBC studios, in Washington, D.C., on the television programme *Meet The Press.* He announced then that he had sent a letter that day to the United States Olympic Committee, located in Colorado Springs, Colorado, and that he had urged the USOC to help with the President's plea that the Summer Games be changed from Moscow to another site outside of the USSR, and that if this weren't possible that the athletes of the world should boycott the Moscow Games in condemnation of the Soviet invasion of Afghanistan.'] It is Labour's belief that Downing Street composed the

22nd of January letter to the BOA, and afterwards a secretary telephoned Mr Monro and read it to him. Sport was thus out of Sport's hands. It was at this time that Mrs Thatcher began putting the screws on her Parliamentary Private Secretary, Ian Gow, so that he might rally in-party support for her Boycott campaign. Messrs Edward Heath and Enoch Powell, early on, had decided to give private support for the preservation of the Games as planned, and Conservative MP and Chairman of the Conservative Sports Committee and dedicated athlete, Terrance Higgins (Worthing), soon came out publicly to support this. Meanwhile, the two IOC Members in Britain, the Marquess of Exeter and the Lord Luke, were in close consultation with the BOA due to these matters. This letter from Downing Street [of 22 January 1980] would be the first of four to the BOA. The Prime Minister signed letters on the 22nd of January, the 19th of February, the 19th of March, and most recently the 20th of May. Never before in the history of the Kingdom had so much official governmental interest been showered upon Sport, let alone upon the British Olympic Association. But this is just the tip of the iceberg. The Central Council of Physical Recreation found itself involved on Thursday the 24th of January, much to Mrs Thatcher's chagrin. On that day, representatives of 54 Governing Bodies of Sports, 18 of which were planning to compete in the Moscow Games, met in the London office of the CCPR and issued a press statement which said that the meeting '...regrets the current dramatic intrusion of political considerations into the management of International Sport, the long-term effect of which can only prove detrimental to British sportsmen and women. Furthermore, it is essential that the Government understand that the decision to stage the Olympic Games in Moscow is the responsibility of the International Olympic Committee and not of the British Olympic Association. Any eleventh hour exhortation to change the venue for the 1980 Games should be addressed to the IOC. The meeting stresses that in the final analysis, in a truly democratic society, as opposed to a totalitarian one, it must be the responsibility of the individuals concerned and the British Olympic Association to determine whether to participate in the Moscow Olympics.' Viewing this as renegade, Mrs Thatcher would set an inquisition to work, and the CCPR as well as the Sports Council and of course the BOA would be summonsed to testify before the Foreign Affairs Committee during the Winter Games in Lake Placid."

This is just a précis of the scandal caused by Margaret Thatcher and her Tory intruders who dove head-first into the world of Britain's sporting community, expecting to do a jackknife but who merely did a risible belly-flop. However, the mess she caused, along with Jimmy Carter's muddying the waters over in America, had even more *far*-reaching repercussions than those that upset a whole host of Olympic Athletes and Officials, since the mess she caused impinged upon the very Throne that the Iron Lady was supposed to be standing behind. Very little of *this* story is known, outside of the UK. So here it goes:

Given that Her Majesty Queen Elizabeth The Queen Mother is my blood-cousin, via our common Cavendish-Bentinck family lineage that only goes back to the previous century, I feel that it is my duty to speak out on behalf of The Royal Family and to support them now, when everybody worldwide keeps impugning them left, right, and centre. They've suffered enough. Let's let them regain their Royal Dignity. Ok— there *are* errant Royals and always will be some, and there *are* those who've tried to *be* Royal and who've failed. However, in 1980, when Margaret Thatcher got lathered up over her Boycott issue, her interference upset a lot of people higher up than she, and by that I mean Queen Elizabeth II, the Duke of Edinburgh, and H.R.H. The Princess Anne, now known as The Princess Royal. At that time, Anne had been spending a great amount of time preparing to compete in the Moscow Olympics as an Equestrian. She was a great horsewoman, of Olympic calibre. Nobody doubted that. But—did the Prime Minister give a single thought to how devastated would be *Princess Anne* by all of this? Did Margaret Thatcher give a single thought to how let down the Princess's *mother* would be...who was La Thatcher's Head of State, no less, and to whom La Thatcher was in fact acting as First Minister...when all of this Boycott nonsense got to be such a sticky wicket for The Royal Family...when the mess made by Mrs Thatcher precluded Princess Anne's further involvement with Olympic competition and thus, for all intensive purposes, *wrecked* the Princess's sporting career? No—Margaret Thatcher carried on oblivious to the feelings of The Royal Family, who were truly placed in a political bind. If Princess Anne were to compete in the very Olympics that Mrs Thatcher was fighting against—Moscow—then that would be seen by many as a slap in the face of Mrs Thatcher by none other than The Queen herself! But it goes further than this, the Sporting Federations of Britain were put in a quandary, especially the Equestrian, which had to decline from competing in Moscow to save face for Princess Anne, so that it wouldn't look as if the Princess herself was lobbying to showjump. And the ermine-fur didn't stop flying here, either, since this whole sordid episode dragged The Queen's husband into the thick of it, too. At that time, Prince Philip was President of the International Equestrian Federation itself, and of course should have attended the Moscow Games by virtue of his office. Because of what Mrs Thatcher kept stirring up, The Queen's Consort was not able to go to the competitions. If he had, all Hell would have broken loose, and even a crisis on the level of a showdown between Queen and Prime Minister could have evolved. I, personally, wish that I could have been able to have heard dialogue between Elizabeth Windsor and her Conservative Lady Minister during this fray. God—picture it—touchy Tuesday evenings at The Palace! I never could see how those two tough women got along together in the *first* place!

Page 28 of my Report states: "Wednesday the 27th of February is another big day in the Boycott debate. His Royal Highness The Prince Philip, Duke of Edinburgh, who is President of the International Equestrian Federation, had been placed in the most discomforting position since the Prime Minister had begun the debate in this country. We shall only say that on the 27th of February he showed once more how astute is his wit by a remark made at a luncheon which had been organized by the Recreation Managers' Association in London. Prince Philip said, in brief: 'A popular fallacy is that International Sport inevitably creates goodwill...' (*Daily Mirror*, 28 February 1980)."

Prince Philip, who can't even go to the lavatory in Britain without somebody finding it an affront to Magna Carta, has and always has had a rough row to hoe. He is charged with "meddling" in matters of State every time he opens up his mouth. At that time, besides being highly involved with Equestrianism, he also was President of the Central Council of Physical Recreation. A lot of internal debate had been going on for weeks until a decision by Britain's horse-set was arrived at, regarding going to Moscow to compete. My Report's pages 64-65 go into this:

"The papers of Tuesday the 8th of April [1980] devoted quite a lot of space to the previous day's decision by the British Equestrian Federation not to send a team to Moscow. Hardly so much space would have been devoted had members of The Royal Family (as is their tradition) not been quite interested in Equestrianism. In particular, H.R.H. The Princess Anne and her husband, Captain Mark Phillips, aroused intense curiosity, due to this Federation's decision, because both are Olympic equestrian competitors. The *Daily Mail* used this opportunity to declare in a leading article (8 April 1980) entitled 'A Clear Round For Freedom' that: 'Britain's horse riders are among the best in the world. They have won medals at every Olympiad held since the last war. Had riders of the calibre of Lucinda Prior-Palmer and Mark Phillips competed at the Moscow Games, hopes for gold must have been high. But they have chosen not to go.' But as the *Guardian* noted (8 April 1980): 'The withdrawal of Britain's riders along with those from other Western countries could force the abandonment of equestrian events in Moscow. It may also save Prince Philip, President of the International Equestrian Federation, the embarrassment of having to attend the Games.' In a sense, the papers found it more fascinating that H.R.H. The Princess Anne's father was H.R.H. The Prince Philip. It seems that the Press really wanted to ask the father how he felt about the daughter's now not being able to compete in Moscow, but of course Prince Philip's other sporting connections could not be forgotten. The leading article of the *Daily Express* (8 April 1980) put it thus: 'He is President of the International Equestrian Federation. To put it mildly, it would look rather odd if he attended the Games at which the British team was not present.' But, as the *Daily Star* (8 April 1980) reported: 'A Buckingham Palace spokesman said yesterday: The Prince has not yet made a decision.'"

Later that month, things got even stickier for the Duke of Edinburgh. My Report's page 74 relates: "The Prince Philip, it seemed to Lausanne [IOC Headquarters], was the inevitable 'fall-guy' for the Press. His position being delicate to say the least, one could hardly presume that he *could* call in on the IOC Headquarters in Switzerland without the Press going crazy over anything he might say. As it happened, the Duke of Edinburgh was present on the evening of the 22nd of April, Tuesday, for a meeting of the governing bodies of the international summer sports, in his capacity as President of the International Equestrian Federation. Wednesday's newspapers thus had a field-day, in describing the night before, as exemplified in three huge headlines on the front pages of daily newspapers: 'Forked Tongue Philip!' (*The Sun*, 23 April 1980), 'Philip Raps Games Ban' (*Daily Express*, 23 April 1980), and 'Philip In Games Ban Riddle' (*Daily Mail*, 23 April 1980). Given that *The Sun* seemed to word this the strongest, let us quote what they said: 'First, he followed *The Sun*'s repeated advice by declaring there was no way he would go to the Games. But then, he dropped a bombshell by defiantly putting the finishing touches to a scathing resolution condemning Premier Margaret Thatcher's bid to stop British athletes competing in Russia. *Last night, critics accused him of speaking about the Games with a forked tongue.* And they wanted to know what right he had to meddle in Government affairs.' (The italics were as published in *The Sun*.) Prince Philip, though, was not meddling in Government affairs, insofar as he was only doing a duty with respect to his rightful position within the International Equestrian Federation. Government, it would seem, was what would meddle in Sport's affairs. John Rodda was consistent with his past of reporting clearly what was being debated. As for the 'resolution' mentioned in *The Sun*, Mr Rodda in the *Guardian* (23 April 1980) reported: 'There was, apparently, much re-writing of their intention but finally Prince Philip and Nigel Hacking, the Secretary of the International Yacht Racing Union, were brought in to achieve the final draft.' Mr Rodda then cited the official Press Release entitled 'Meeting of the International Olympic Federations in Lausanne' which supported the IOC's declaration of Lake Placid, and which emphasised that 'a boycott of a sporting event is an improper method to use in trying to obtain a political end and that the real victims of any such action are the sportsmen and sportswomen of the world. The International Olympic Federations are deeply concerned by such measures which they believe could have disastrous consequences for the future of world Sport and (recognising that it is the duty of their affiliated National Federations to take all legitimate actions in their power within their National Olympic Committees to see that the competitors whom they represent should have the opportunity to compete—according to their ability—in this forthcoming and in future Olympic Games) confirm that all the International Olympic Federations, with their Sport on the programme, will be present at the 1980 Olympic Games in order to ensure the best possible technical arrangements for the competitors.'"

On that note, with the IOC having spoken sanely, let me just conclude this book by saying that after having worked as an employee for the Lake Placid Olympic Organizing Committee, and after having witnessed the build-up and progress of the XIII Olympic Winter Games, and after having become so deeply involved in the sporting world of London during the Boycott period prior to the Moscow Olympics, I realised that, in my own Art, with my own abilities as a Novelist, I *had* to write about the Olympic experience from the viewpoint of Fiction, which often presents Reality in a format more pronounced than Reality itself. I felt that this was my Destiny. I also knew that, to do so, it was obligatory to return to Greece, to live for a period of time at Olympia, birthplace of the Games. This dream, too, did come true, in 1980, due to understanding of many empathetic people. Dick Palmer wrote a kind letter of introduction for me to the Senior Member of the International Olympic Committee in Greece, Professor Nikoláos Nissiótis, and I was provided access to all that Olympia had to offer by the good Professor. Life there, in many respects, was very much as it is described in the *SummerGames* segment of this novel, minus the Deed Ceremony which, of course, is totally fictitious. At Olympia, I actually resided right inside the Museum Of The Modern Olympic Games, and had carte blanche use of the International Olympic Academy and free access to all the ruins. Having completed my Olympia notes and draft, I then crossed the Mediterranean by ship and sailed to Africa, to Alexandria, later that year. My Olympics experiences continued in Egypt, where the Egyptian Olympic Committee befriended me and so too did Ahmed Touny, the IOC Member in Egypt. Accompanying Touny, my life was truly like something out of *1001 Arabian Nights*. I'll end this by letting you savour two citings from October 1980, the first excerpt from Wednesday the 1st:

"My taxi to Heliopolis was quite unnerving. We passed too many strange sights. I was happy to get to Touny's. He was very kind and rang Adel Tahir, Under-Secretary for Tourism, and arranged I see him Thursday. We were driven [by armoured-car] to Nasser Stadium, and Touny showed me its VIP Lounge and his own Olympic collection [his own Museum, built inside the biggest Stadium of Egypt, filled with marvellous Olympic memorabilia]. Then were driven to Heliopolis Sporting Club [where I never saw such bowing and scraping outside of a Hollywood movie of the Pharaohs: So awesome a personality was Mr Touny, to the Egyptians, that just walking with him, beside and pool and beneath the palm trees, was like being transported into a completely different realm of existence]." Mr Touny then sent me up the Nile to his family estate at Mallawy, where I was taken one night (Friday 10 October 1980): "To Omar's plantation and to a grand country villa of another Touny cousin. Learnt that the Touny are one branch of four, of a larger family of Pasha rank, with surname er-Ridy. The villa was owned by a cousin of Omar (whose mother was a Touny er-Ridy). The owner took me into two State Rooms, 100 years old, in old faded velvet, first in olive green, the other in crimson..."

621

Acknowledgments

Editor's Note: Édition von Rapp shall require all of its Authors to provide, for the Reading Public, and for the reciprocal appreciation of those to whom a bow of thanks is due, an Acknowledgments section at the back of its books, so that people can know the human routes by which Inspiration came to the Author and so that these vital people, in the bookmaking process, can be properly recognised.

For the Greek genetics and love of culture and reading that made this book possible, I owe lifelong thanks to my mother, née Edith Mildred Green, and to her late mother, née Esther Lillian von Rapp (1906-1991).

New York City (1974): Frances Steloff of The Gotham Book Mart; "Ernie" aka Athenásios Raftópoulos of The Three Decker Food Shop; Angelo Polimenéas; Rýta of the Greek radio station; Roúli Tatáki; Míkis Theodorákis; Jules Dassin & his late wife, magnificent Melina Mercouri.

London (1975-1976): Patrick Janson-Smith, of Corgi Books; Marc Goulden, Jeffrey Simmons, and Yvette Morgan-Griffiths, of W. H. Allen & Co. Ltd, publishers; Robert Vacha; and Rudolf H. Seedorff.

Germany (1976): H.R.H. Viktoria Luise, Duchess of Brunswick and Lüneburg, of Braunschweig; Leonhard Schlüter, of Hannover; and my beloved family of Alfred and Emma Philipp, then of Schloß Eggmühl, Niederbayern.

Athens (1976): Christopher Elíou.

Athens (1979): Ath.-Nássos A. Tzártzanos, of the Hellenic Alpine Club and Member of the Hellenic Olympic Committee; Professor Giorgio Márcou; Iphigénia Anastassiádou, of the Benáki Museum; Professor Álkis Karávelas; poetess, Élli Nezeríti; Iró Tsekléni, my employer at Phrontistírion Tsekléni, in Maroússi; my student of English, Natásia Mitropoúlou, of the bookstore family of Viktoria Square; Father Pirounákis; my dear friend, Commodore Tássos Kórfis of the Greek Navy, the publisher who, under *nom de plume* of Tássos Robótis, published fabulous translations into the Greek of many of the West's best poets, and his wife Eléna; Eléni Vláchou, the renowned publisher of the influential daily newspaper, *I Kathimeriní*; Sophía Christodoúlou; Margaríta Gregoriádes, my marvellous landlady at 12 Mniskléos Street; Sophía Demitriádou, Margaríta's daughter, and her husband, Pános Kókkinos; Signora Antonietta Dosi, of the Istituto Italiano, where I used to go to write, to be at peace from the Athenian crowds; Dómna Dontá, of UNESCO; Dr George Dontás, Director of the Akropolis, who granted me access to the Parthenon, alone, at night, in order to write poetry; former Minister of Culture, Kóstas Tripánis, and the Academy of Athens; and Tólis Lizárthos, whom I immortalised by name, from the scene in Tólis's Cafë, in Hadrian Street.

Mount Olympos and Litóchoron (1979): The Hellenic Alpine Club; Kóstas Zolótas, Chief Mountain Guide and Refuge Hut Manager, and his kind wife, Irmgild, and Rosy the miraculous immortal mountain-climbing shepherd dog; Professor Franz Escher and his gentle wife, Marie Louise, of Bern, Switzerland; Ludwig and Ingeborg Griesshammer, of München, Germany.

Watertown, New York (1979): My dearly beloved late great-aunt, Blanche Brown Greene, who provided my entrée to the Lake Placid Olympic Organizing Committee; Blanche's two daughters, Beverly Greene Bibbins and the late Eloise Greene Malady; Benjamin P. Coe, first Executive Director of the Tug Hill Plateau Commission; the late, superb man, my Episcopal parish priest at Trinity Church, the Reverend Michael Metcalf and certain kind friends; and the late Irene Kellogg, a great patroness of the Old School.

Lake Placid, New York (1979-1980): Ambassador Roger Tubby and Ann, his wife, and Brenda, their daughter; Ursula Trudeau; Judge Phil Wolff and his wife, Elsie; the late Reverend Bernard J. Fell, President of the Lake Placid Olympic Organizing Committee, God bless his magnanimous Soul; Barbara J. Jones, and her incomparable puppy, Buffy; Dan McCormick; Doctor Virginia ("Ginger") Weeks, who helped maintain my sanity and my health; my LPOOC buddies, David Brimlow, David Bergan-Heim, Maura Domoracki, Lorna Stio, Maureen Fitzpatrick; my Whitney cousin, Heather Hosford; Peter Gelles, and our numerous good times, and his dad, Henry; Jo Glotzer, who really did sing "Embraceable You" atop a piano at my Halloween Ball of 1979; Ruth Hart; George "Chris" Ortloff and his wife Ruth Mary Hart Ortloff; Raymond Pratt; Jutta Wiesenthal; Ann Lynch, on whose typewriter the *WinterGames* first-draft was created; and Denise Wilson, a vivacious lady, who taught me all I ever needed to know, and then some, about Olympic Protocol!

New York (1970s-1980s): Steven S. Harvis, Esq., and Cynthia Allen, whose guidance and friendship ever will be cherished.

London (1980): The British Olympic Association; BOA General Secretary, Dick Palmer, and its Assistant, Mike Blake; BOA Chairman, Sir Denis Follows; BOA Education Director, Donald Anthony; BOA Legal Counsel, David Dixon; BOA Member, Sandy Duncan, who gave me a BOA tie and an Achilles Club tie for Oxford and Cambridge Universities combined; my bosom pals, the Reverend V. A. ("Tony") Davies, Elaine Baly, aka Vivienne Browning, and Lesley Guthrie; great theatre and film director, Lindsay Anderson; the Dean of Westminster Abbey, the Most Reverend C. W. Carpenter; Nobel Peace Price Winner and Olympic Silver Medallist, the Lord Philip Noel-Baker; Member of Parliament, Tam Dalyell; my Cecil blood-cousin, the late Marquess of Exeter, then Senior Member in the UK of the International Olympic Committee; Jeffrey Simmons, then my literary agent; John Lovesey, of *The Times;* the then Shadow Sports Minister, Denis Howell, and his aide, Patrick Cheney.

Olympia (1980): Professor Nikoláos Nissiótis, Senior Member of the International Olympic Committee in Greece, and Kýria Christodoúli; Aléxandros Andýpas, Administrator, International Olympic Academy, and Sophía Doná; Kýria Triánti, Director of the Olympia Archaeological Sites and Museums; Archaeologist Kostantínos Záhos.

Cairo (1980): Ahmed Touny, Member of the International Olympic Committee in Egypt; and the Egyptian Olympic Committee. Georgia, U.S.A. (1982): My father's sister, my dearly beloved aunt, Louise Moon Whitley, of Winder, Georgia; and the Reverend Franklin C. Ferguson, Emmanuel Episcopal Church, Athens, Georgia.

Upstate New York (1996): Jane Bowman Jenkins, Jefferson County Treasurer and dear friend; former Watertown Mayor T. Urling Walker and his wife, Mabel; Jeremy T. Graves, for computer guidance at the firm's start-up phase; my incomparable bankers, Theodore P. Ward, Vice President and Manager, Community Bank, Watertown, New York, and Shanie L. Strife, his Platform Assistant, and the Branch Manager at Black River, New York, Elizabeth J. Strife, all of whom have been and continue to be godsends; especial thanks to schoolchum & Upstate Attorney, Lawrence D. Hasseler, Esq., & Carthage NY aides, Nancy Plopper & Susan M. O'Dell, & the whole staff of the law firm of Conboy, McKay, Bachman & Kendall; WinterGames/SummerGames Cover-Design Illustrator and Art Director, and Advertising Artist and all around excellent Graphic Artist, Charles "Chuck" Costantino, and Typographer, Jan Larrow; Thomas J. Lawrence for computer assistance during many stages of this book's 1996 development, and for his expertise in enabling the Édition von Rapp World Wide Web Page become a reality; the whole staff of Minuteman Press, Watertown, New York, under the proprietorship of Charles and Vita Adams; AMF Printing of Watertown, New York, under the proprietorship of Richard and Jean Bonci, and their computer wiz, Brenda Young, for help with the halftones for this book, and a special thanks to George Neher; costume assistance and excellent tailoring for publicity goes to Kathy Carreira of Watertown, New York; silkscreening of the novel's cover for PR at the ABA Convention 1996 in Chicago, compliments of Gary Hopps, KTI Prince, Carthage, New York, who worked as a New York State Trooper at the Lake Placid Games; Rent-A-Wreck, of Watertown, New York, under proprietorship of Jim Widrick; and Sister Mary Grace & all the Sisters, Monastery of the Precious Blood, Watertown, New York.

New York City (1996): For encouragement and impeccable professional counsel in all aspects of planning and promoting the launch of WinterGames/SummerGames, a voicing of gratitude goes to Rob Wardlaw of Publishers Weekly magazine, and to his co-worker, Cathy Hoey of Library Journal.; and for computer guidance at the start-up phase of Édition von Rapp's existence, thanks to Fernando Duque.

San Jose, California (1996): Acer Computers John Kirkpatrick, Earl Weber, & Eugene Alfaro, who fielded questions at all hours.

Louiseville, Québec (1996): Our printers at Imprimerie Gagné–Best Book Manufacturers, with thanks to the whole staff, and with profoundest gratitude to Isabelle Gagné.

LDM: March 1979, at the Café Kéa, Pan Street, in the Monastiráki quarter of Athens, writing the first draft of the Athenian segment of this novel. This outdoor café is the setting for the "dancing bear" chapter. LDM resided just a few blocks away. Photographer unknown.

LDM: 5 June 1979, on Mount Olympos, a ridge between Skála and Skólio Peaks, with the highest summit, Mýtikas, looming to the left. This photograph was taken by Professor Franz Escher, of Bern, Switzerland, who climbed Olympos that day with his wife, Marie-Louise.

LDM: 6 June 1979, on Mount Olympos, at what is called in this novel "Sokrates" Peak. Caught in the act of writing the Olympos sequence of this book. Shortly after this was taken, by Ludwig Griesshammer, of Münchberg, Germany, LDM got lost and almost died in a fall down the mountainslope, details of which this book regales.

LDM: 27 June 1979, dusk. On the edge of the Aegean, with Mount Olympos inland, its highest ridges just above LDM's right shoulder. On this beach, in this novel's storyline, is set Ada's modest cottage, near Litóchoron. Photograph by Élisabeth Belhomme, of Paris.

LDM: 31 October 1979, as Host of the "Gala Nostalgia Costume Ball".
Halloween at Holiday Harbor, Lake Placid, New York, an event now of
legendary repute. Due to being a "party animal", LDM incurred
the wrath of his Lake Placid Olympic Organizing Committee Protocol
bosses, who thought that having fun was "improper behaviour" for a
Deputy Chief of Protocol, which LDM then was. Photographer unknown.

LDM & the Reverend Bernard J. Fell, President, Lake Placid Olympic
Organizing Committee, 4 November 1979, at Horse Grounds, Lake
Placid. First rehearsal for Opening Ceremonies of the XIII Olympic
Winter Games, LDM in the rôle of Lord Killanin, President of the
International Olympic Committee. Photographer unknown.

LDM: December 1979, inside Town Hall, Lake Placid, Headquarters for the Lake Placid Olympic Organizing Committee. Feeling up Buffy, one of the two bitches in this novel immortalised by real name (the other is Rosy, of Mount Olympos). Bæstiality, too, was frowned upon by the LPOOC Protocol bosses, but LDM found time to sneak in a little on the side. Photograph by Protocol co-worker, Maureen Fitzpatrick.

LDM: 1 March 1980, outside the Adirondack Community Church, Lake Placid, where LDM staged a performance of his writings, for all the Torch Runners of the Lake Placid Olympics, on 18 February 1980 during the middle of the Winter Games, to thank them for helping to bring the Sacred Flame from Greece. Photograph by LDM's mother's cousin, the late Eloise Greene Malady, of Watertown, New York.